THE
SOVEREIGN

By C. L. Clark

MAGIC OF THE LOST

The Unbroken
The Faithless
The Sovereign

ARCANE: LEAGUE OF LEGENDS

Ambessa: Chosen of the Wolf

Fate's Bane

"You can't leave me here!" Taurvide sputtered.
"Do you know who I am?"

Touraine turned her back on him and faced the crowd of blackcoats. Everyone who wasn't on duty had come to watch. Some expressions knowing, some shuttered and angry. A few even looked relieved.

"Soldiers. Officers. I'm General Touraine El-Qazāli, soon to be Prince-General Touraine El-Qazāli. Queen Luca has tasked me with the preparation of her armies as we face down the threat of the Withering and the rise of banditry on the roads. Some of you might have certain attitudes about Shālans and about Qazāli in particular. You might have heard rumors about me. You might agree with the good colonel here."

She paused to give them a chance to take in the good colonel and see if that was still how they sided themselves. He tried to stifle his frustrated whimpers of pain, but the yard was so quiet. Everyone could hear.

"Whether you wish or no, your lives are in my hands now, and so is the rest of Balladaire. There's no time for you to act like spoiled children. You'll be dealt with just as swiftly. If you have any questions, you'll take it up with my—" Shit. She needed an aide. "Take it up with my aide. Dismissed."

Stunned silence hung in the air as the soldiers trickled back to their tasks and drills.

"Are you sure that was wise?" Camille de Moyenne murmured when they were alone in the field.

"It needed doing."

For the rest of the afternoon, soldiers who passed through the whipping field pretended to ignore their colonel strung up like a deer carcass, but almost all of them at least glanced from the corners of their eyes. It was having the effect Touraine wanted.

She would claim her power the way Balladaire always did. The way Cantic had wooed her as a child.

Whips and honey.

Praise for

C. L. CLARK

"C. L. Clark gives us an unflinching story of colonialism and revolution and the people caught between. *The Unbroken* grabs you by the collar, breaks your heart over its knee, and mends it. An astonishing debut."
—Andrea Stewart, author of *The Bone Shard Daughter*

"Rife with political, familial, and romantic tension, *The Unbroken* is a riveting epic fantasy about a city on the knife's edge of rebellion, a tangle of alliances, and a desperate search for magic and hope."
—K. A. Doore, author of *The Perfect Assassin*

"Get ready to fall in love with Touraine and Luca in one of the best fantasy debuts I have ever read!"
—Matt Wallace, Hugo Award winner and author of the Savage Rebellion series

"A bold and exciting work that helps steer the evolution of the genre into the next decade."
—Marshall Ryan Maresca, author of the Maradaine novels

"*The Unbroken* grabs you by the throat and doesn't let go. A perfect military fantasy: brutal, complex, human, and impossible to put down."
—Tasha Suri, author of *The Jasmine Throne*

"With its incisive look at the irreconcilable conflicts that colonialism wedges between desire, duty, individuality, and community, C. L. Clark's *The Unbroken* is a compelling and persuasive reimagining of both heroism and heroics as something inseparable from identity, perspective, and history. It's a deeply needed look at the myths we make, the stories we tell, and the bitterly binding ties of both blood and bondage."
   —Evan Winter, author of *The Rage of Dragons*

"*The Unbroken* is a thrilling examination of love and loyalty under the crushing weight of empire. It's high adventure on a human scale—don't miss it."
   —Alix E. Harrow, author of *The Ten Thousand Doors of January*

"C. L. Clark's epic fantasy debut reveals all the ugly, painful, deeply personal complexities of revolution against empire, captured in shimmering pointillist detail. I'm in awe!"
   —Shelley Parker-Chan, author of *She Who Became the Sun*

"It doesn't take long to realize *The Unbroken* is something special. I'm going to need the second book ASAP."
   —David Dalglish, author of the Shadowdance series

"This strong debut is filled with exciting action and worldbulding, intriguing characters dealing with themes of colonization, military conscription and indoctrination, and an explosion of feelings. Readers will be clamoring for more of Touraine and Luca before they finish."
   —*Library Journal* (starred review)

"Clark's debut introduces a remarkable LGBTQ+ culture amid a story of colonial conquest, exploitation, prejudice, and brewing revolt in a land with a lost history of mystical powers.... Fans of epic military fantasy will eagerly await more from Clark."
   —*Booklist*

"Clark conjures an elaborate fantasy world inspired by Northern Africa and delves into an international political conflict that draws on real histories of colonialism and conquest in their excellent debut...."

Clark's precise, thorough worldbuilding allows this remarkable novel to dive deep into the intricate workings of colonialism, exposing how power structures are maintained through social conditioning and exploring the emotional toll of political conflict. The result is a captivating story that works both as high fantasy and skillful cultural commentary."   —*Publishers Weekly* (starred review)

"Clark's worldbuilding [continues] to grow.... The sequel to *The Unbroken* extends the deliberate journey towards independence from an empire and the past, and the love in two women's hearts."
                                —*Library Journal* (starred review)

"Clark's worldbuilding in *The Faithless* is just as stellar as in *The Unbroken*.... Where the novel and series shine brightest is in their gritty reckoning with power and humanity and their delivery of an uncompromising worldview in which there are few good choices."   —*Locus*

"It's impressive to watch [Clark] meet—and surpass—reader expectations in the sequel *The Faithless*.... The series feels like layers of sedimentary rock, striated with colors and sheens that show the eras in which they were both born and compressed.... Whether the scene is a dance or a battle or a simple conversation, that feeling of depth and history is present on every page."   —*Paste*

THE
SOVEREIGN

MAGIC OF THE LOST: BOOK THREE

C. L. CLARK

orbitbooks.net

Copyright © 2025 by Cherae Clark

Cover design by Lauren Panepinto
Cover illustration by Tommy Arnold
Cover copyright © 2025 by Hachette Book Group, Inc.
Map by Tim Paul
Author photograph by Meg White

Orbit
Hachette Book Group
1290 Avenue of the Americas
New York, NY 10104
orbitbooks.net

First Edition: September 2025
Simultaneously published in Great Britain by Orbit

Orbit is an imprint of Hachette Book Group.
The Orbit name and logo are registered trademarks of Little, Brown Book Group Limited.

The publisher is not responsible for websites (or their content) that are not owned by the publisher.

The Hachette Speakers Bureau provides a wide range of authors for speaking events. To find out more, go to hachettespeakersbureau.com or email HachetteSpeakers@hbgusa.com.

Orbit books may be purchased in bulk for business, educational, or promotional use. For information, please contact your local bookseller or the Hachette Book Group Special Markets Department at special.markets@hbgusa.com.

Library of Congress Cataloging-in-Publication Data
Names: Clark, C. L. (Cherae L.), author.
Title: The sovereign / C.L. Clark.
Description: First edition. | New York, NY : Orbit, 2025. | Series: Magic of the Lost ; book 3
Identifiers: LCCN 2024060279 | ISBN 9780316542883 (trade paperback) | ISBN 9780316542869 (ebook)
Subjects: LCGFT: Fantasy fiction. | Novels.
Classification: LCC PS3603.L356626 S68 2025 | DDC 813/.6—dc23/eng/20241223
LC record available at https://lccn.loc.gov/2024060279

ISBNs: 9780316542883 (trade paperback), 9780316542869 (ebook)

Printed in the United States of America

LSC-C

Printing 1, 2025

Free Palestine.

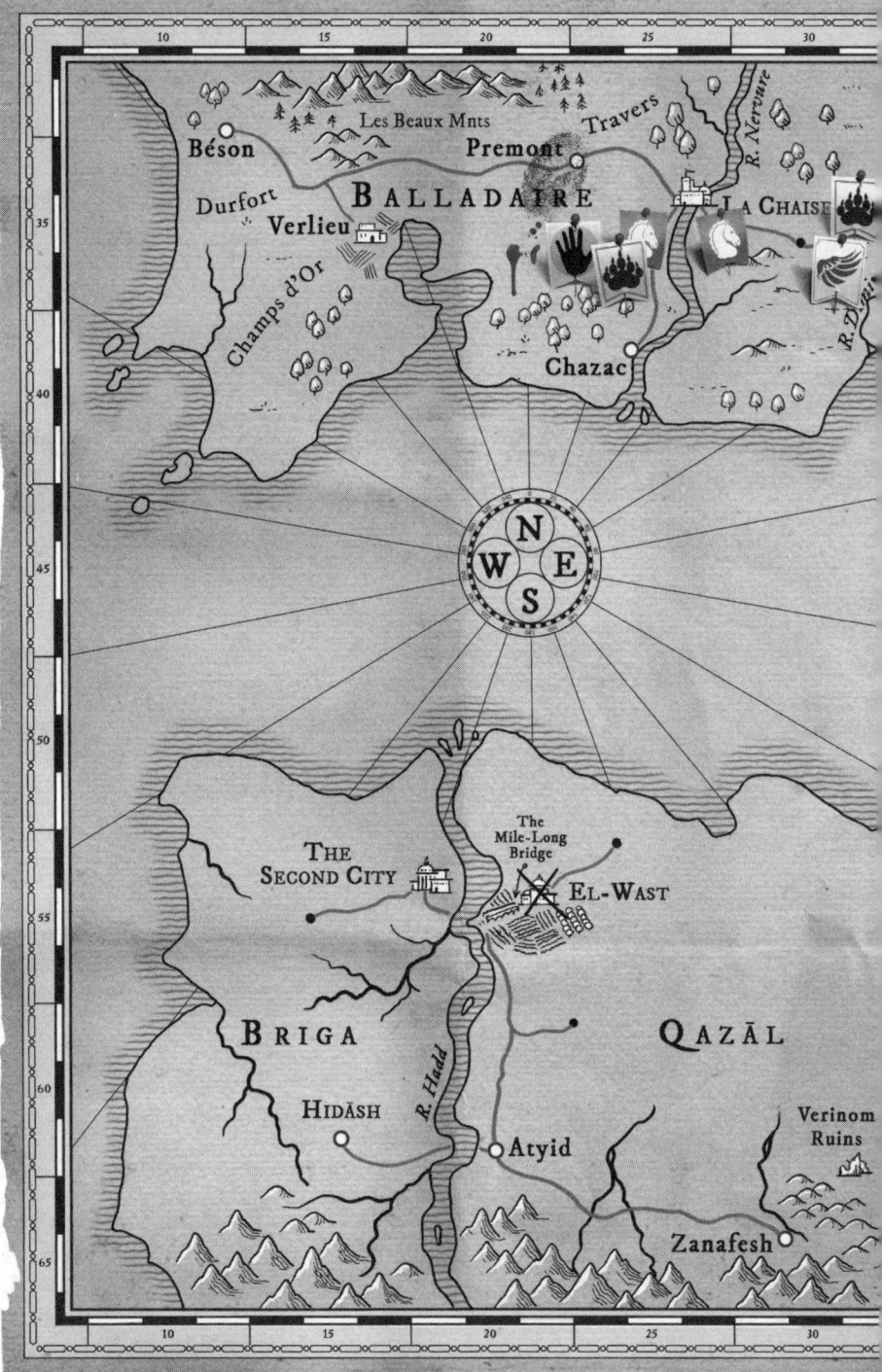

40   45   50   55   35

Moyenne

TAARGEN

Bay El-Aqabrir

LUNAB

Triaume Sea

40

45

RA's EL-BAHR

50

Samrà'

MASRIDĀN

55

The Middle Desert

The Empire of
BALLADAIRE

60

By Her Majesty's Cartographer Albert Jaillot.
Dedicated to Queen Luca.

65

40   45   50   55

Map by Tim Paul

PART 1
BY PLAGUE

CHAPTER 1

GLASS

Touraine and Sabine stood behind the queen of Balladaire as she knelt on the half-frozen earth before the Royal Oak. Her cane lay on the ground at her side. She held a small gold casket between trembling gloved hands, and poured some of the dark grains of ash directly into a hole in the earth.

Thick banks of snow were heaped against the rose hedges to clear the paths. The air felt just as thick, sound muffled so even the wind in the bare branches overhead was muted.

Touraine shivered. They had been standing there for a long time.

Luca lowered the casket with the rest of Gil's ashes into the grave. Her breath caught and she stopped with her hand above the pile of dirt and snow that would have covered all Luca had left of the man she'd loved most. Luca didn't move but for the jerking hitch of her shoulders.

Touraine shared a look with Sabine. The marquise's eyes were red. Touraine scrubbed her own tears from her cheek and knelt at Luca's side. She felt Sabine drop to Luca's other, and together, they held her.

Their touch sapped the last wall holding Luca together. She collapsed into them, burying her face in Touraine's coat.

Around them, the guards kept their silent vigil, ensuring no one would interrupt the queen's mourning.

They let Luca stay there until her shudders became shivers and her teeth chattered, less grief than cold. Then they helped Luca scoop the earth down onto the little gleaming casket. The metal was cold and beautiful, etched in the curling oak leaves decorating so much of the palace. Words marked the sides, but Touraine couldn't make them out before Luca buried it completely.

Slowly, Touraine and Sabine helped Luca to her feet.

"Thank you." Luca dabbed at her face with the back of one gloved hand and turned toward the palace.

They followed her in silence until Touraine asked, "Are your mother and father buried there, too?"

Luca shook her head, a single sharp twist, her mouth tight. "It was thought unwise to keep the ashes of the plague dead."

A few moments later, though, softer, she added: "He would have liked that, though. To be buried with them. I wish—" Her voice broke. "I wish he could have been. That they'd all—" Luca huffed. She didn't speak again.

At the door to Luca's chambers, they stood awkwardly together.

"If you'd like, we could play a game of échecs?" Sabine ventured a wry smile, though her eyes were still red. "Trouncing me might cheer you up. Or tarot?"

Touraine smiled. For days, Sabine had been trying to get them to play a version of tarot that involved taking off their clothes. She hadn't succeeded yet. Luca only ever nodded, said all right, and then—

"There's too much work to be done. I have to write to the lords on the southern coast about ships, and then make sure the Beau-Sang seneschal has the estate under control until Aliez de Beau-Sang returns from Qazāl. If she ever returns. And then—"

"I understand," Sabine cut in softly, but heavy with disappointment.

"I'm sorry I cannot entertain you." Luca's tart voice was ragged at the edges. She raked her hand through her hair and closed her eyes. Her lids were puffy with weeping and shadowed blue with exhaustion. She looked like Touraine felt.

Sabine flinched, then looked at Touraine for help, but Touraine didn't know what she was meant to do. She shrugged apologetically. "Luca's right."

Touraine couldn't relax, either. Not with fear riding her shoulder. Since Luca had told her about the Withering two days ago, Touraine couldn't stop herself from imagining the disease stealing through the city and into her body, sucking her strength away. The havoc it would wreak just as Luca was settling into her rule. Not to mention the questions Luca had asked her.

Will you be my general? Will you be my wife?

One question Touraine had answered. One she had not.

Pruett's letter still burned in the back of Touraine's mind, also unanswered.

"Then I'll go." Sabine dipped a curt version of her flourishing bow. "I'm sure I would only be a distraction."

"Sabine—"

"Don't go—"

Sabine waved her hand dismissively and clicked her tongue. "No, no. I'll leave you to it. But the world won't fall if you spend a single day to care for your own happiness. Good day, Your Majesty. Your Excellency."

Luca sighed and entered her rooms. She sat at the small table where she and Touraine ate together or played échecs. Right now, it was strewn with papers. Missives, requests, accountings. She buried her head in her hands, letting her hair curtain over her face.

"She doesn't understand."

Touraine let her shoulders sag and her head fall back. On the ceiling, more fine swirls of oak leaves, curled in plaster along the borders of it, weaving in and out of carved vines. She pressed her palms to her eyes to stave off her headache. "Maybe she's right."

For the last two days, Touraine and Luca had locked themselves here, in bed or at the desk, hashing out worst-cases and best-cases for the country. They'd seen only what sun came through the window, and most of the time they kept it closed against the midwinter cold. Breakfast plates would remain on the table hours later because Luca had asked not to be disturbed. Today, though, they'd taken a respite, if only for sorrow.

On cue, Touraine's stomach growled so loudly that Luca startled. She blinked owlishly at Touraine. The smallest hint of a smile tugged at her mouth. Then Luca's own stomach growled even louder.

"All right." Luca pinched the bridge of her nose. "All right. Our baser natures have spoken."

"Shall I ask for food to be brought up?" Touraine walked to the bell pull to call the lunch service back in. Or—early dinner, more like.

It wasn't hard to get used to someone else delivering her meals; she'd rarely cooked as a Sand. What differed was the choice. The flavor. Having it brought directly to her and served at her leisure until she was satisfied. Even with fears of poison at the back of her mind, Touraine had filled out these past months, regaining muscle and softening her sharpest edges. Luxury.

The last few days, though, she'd barely tasted it at all, if she even had an appetite.

She knew what Pruett would say, if she could see the rich food, the fine wool clothing lined in silk, the eiderdown bed stuffing and goose feather pillows.

Luca didn't seem to be listening. She stared, unfocused, over the table.

"She is right. At least a little. I'm sorry that you're here now. While I'm like this, I mean." She met Touraine's eyes. "There are so many things I'd like to show you. The art in the palace, all the sculptures, the theater— Have you ever been to a play? An opera?"

Touraine shook her head, an eyebrow raised. "You know I haven't."

"I wish I could take you, or even hire performers." Luca's face fell. "It's just that..."

"You're afraid."

Luca's face went pink.

"I understand," Touraine said quickly. "It's not wise." To make themselves a target in the Queen's Box at the Théâtre Royal, or to invite strangers into the palace. Fili Guérin, who Luca called "the Rose," was still at large, along with the rest of the Fingers. A little fun wasn't worth the risk, no matter what Sabine said.

Luca chewed on her bottom lip.

Touraine narrowed her eyes. "What?"

By now, she knew this expression, the moment of a conflict Luca hadn't quite worked out—usually when she knew what she *wanted*, but knew it wasn't the right answer.

"We could go out anylight."

"No. Absolutely not."

It was the wrong thing to say. Luca seized the idea like a terrier and dug her heels in. The fervor ate up her grief. "We can. Not obviously, of course. But it's winter. We'll be so covered up no one will recognize us."

"Covered up in... these?" Touraine held up the edge of her cloak on her shoulders, showing off the fine embroidery, the rabbit-fur lining. Luca ducked her head from side to side. "Adile can find us something to help us blend in."

There was a determined light in Luca's eyes, and Touraine wasn't sure it was excitement alone. There was something manic about the way she began stacking all her papers together. Occasionally, she even glanced back toward the door, as if looking for Sabine. Luca wanted to prove something.

She always wanted to prove something.

Touraine sputtered a wordless protest, and Luca stopped striding around the room. She curled an arm around Touraine's waist and slipped behind her, resting her head on Touraine's shoulder and kissing her once on the neck.

"Come with me," she whispered.

Touraine took a shaky breath. "This is a bad idea."

"All the best ones are."

"You sound like Sabine. We could stay here, instead. I'll make it worth it." She tightened Luca's arm about her, dug her nails in.

She felt the minute shake of Luca's head against her cheek. "We'll be careful."

There was no changing Luca's mind now. Touraine sighed and sank into Luca's embrace. The warmth of it. The ease. A brave person might even call it happiness.

It couldn't last.

This wouldn't last.

The warmth of Touraine's hand in hers. The wonderment in Touraine's eyes as she watched the street performers act out a tale from the Chevaliers des Fruits for the first time, while snowflakes caught upon her long lashes.

Even the laughter of her people as they enjoyed the show. Soon, they would know what she knew, and it would all crumble around them.

Luca shouldn't have let Sabine's words prick her like she did, but she was glad they had come out. She didn't want to spend the day locked up with the ache in her heart. Still, she kept her plain scarf pulled high on her cheeks, and her coat was simple enough to belong to a merchant. Touraine stood out a little more, as a Qazāli with golden eyes, but—as Touraine tilted her head back and crinkled those eyes in laughter, Luca couldn't quite bring herself to care. The risk was worth it.

They slipped away at the end of the show, and Luca saw Deniaud and Mareau, also in plain clothes, peel away from their posts and follow along at a discreet distance. Luca didn't have her cane with its sword today; instead, she used a crutch. It would help to differentiate herself from the queen with her cane, but, and she hated to admit it to herself, she was relying on the aids more than she used to. The crutch was more supportive.

They stopped at a stand for piping-hot crêpes filled with preserves and cream. It wasn't the kind of thing the palace kitchen served. Luca moaned as she ate it and caught Touraine's mischievous look. Luca couldn't help it: she laughed. Holding the rest of the crêpe in front of her face and trying to keep her food in her mouth, she laughed. Touraine laughed, too, and they might have been nothing more and nothing less than two women in love in the days before the world ended.

Because this would not last.

But Luca could try to make it last as long as possible. She was queen. She could do that much.

Touraine shivered pleasantly with cold as she and Luca left the stables. There'd been no incident while they were in the city, though her neck had prickled and she'd tried not to glance over her shoulder too often. She had her own pair of guards now, to shadow her around like Deniaud and Mareau. She trusted them well enough, but she didn't trust anyone over her own senses and instincts.

Whenever this ended, whatever it was, she didn't want it to be because of a knife in the back.

Still, Touraine had enjoyed the street show, and the crêpe after, and even the small cup of drinking chocolate, though it was still too sweet for her taste. It made her think of Ghadin with a sharp twist of guilt. She would visit the girl tomorrow, maybe. She had a lot to explain to her, including the upcoming marriage—

Icy wet thudded into Touraine's back. She ducked, rolling out of position and onto her knees, reaching for the knife hidden in her boot.

Several paces behind her, Luca hiked her arm back to throw a ball of snow, while Deniaud prepared another with her usual devoted concentration.

Touraine shouted in outrage and scooped up her own handful. The snow trickled in her bare hands, but it was sticky and easy to press into shape. She launched it and grinned; it would hit true—then Mareau jumped in front of Luca, taking the blow in the chest.

"That's cheating!" Touraine looked to her own guards, fanned out behind her. One of them raised a dubious eyebrow. His name was Aubrille. "Cover me."

Aubrille's mouth fell open as if he were going to protest, but Baudriel grinned. She was younger, and eager. "Yes, Your Excellency."

Touraine ran for Luca and her tiny army, ducking under a wild throw from Luca, dodging a more precise one from Deniaud. Before Deniaud loosed her second volley, she was hit by one of Touraine's guards and fell to the ground in surrender. Luca backed away, holding her empty hand in front of her, bent over with laughter.

Touraine almost skidded to a stop at the sight. The queen of Balladaire, giggling. The split grin on that usually condescending mouth, the haughty glare now flushed with exertion and the bite of the wind. It made Touraine's chest too full to take a proper breath.

She didn't stop, though. She crashed into Luca, scooping her up and barreling her into the pile of snow the groundskeepers had shoveled aside. Luca squealed—Queen Luca Ancier fucking squealed—while Touraine peppered kisses all over her face.

Then they sobered and the real world threatened to smother them, held off only by the thick snow and the cold. The heat between them made it easy to ignore a little longer. Luca pored over Touraine, her mouth parted with their heavy breathing, a cloud of mist. Touraine kissed her slowly, pressing her deeper into the snowbank.

Luca smiled against Touraine's mouth. "You know, we have a bed. And a fire."

And so they went inside the palace, to bed and fire and all the other warmth between them.

Luca dreamed of it ending. She dreamed of it ending often these days. She dreamed of Touraine in Le Fontinard, arrested by Luca's own soldiers. She dreamed of burning Touraine on the plague fires, as she'd burned her parents. She dreamed of holding a knife to Touraine's throat until a deep-red line split the skin while Touraine begged her, *please don't*. In the dream, Luca tried to pull back, but her arms were leaden.

Luca jerked awake. She sensed the emptiness of the bed immediately, but reached with grasping fingers regardless. The other side of the bed was still warm.

"Touraine?"

"I'm here." Touraine's voice came from the window, quick and soothing.

Luca rolled over in the bed to watch her. Her strong profile was shadowed against the light of the moon reflecting on the snow. Luca admired the sleek play of the Shālan robe against Touraine's broad back and the curve of her backside, at odds with the twisting agony of her dreams. Touraine was here, alive. This was real. Her sigh of relief was loud in the silent night.

"Bad dreams?"

"Yes." Luca went to Touraine, digging her toes into the soft rug, avoiding the bare patches of stone. The fire had died down to its coals, but the room still had enough of its heat that Luca didn't flinch—too much—at the air on her naked body. "You?"

Touraine chuckled darkly and turned, sweeping Luca in close. Luca buried her nose in Touraine's neck and inhaled. She smelled so good. Of sex and sweat and the last lingering of a smoky cologne.

"Aye. What this time?"

The truth caught in Luca's throat. How did you tell the woman you were sleeping with that you dreamed of killing her? With a history like theirs, with a possible future like theirs—it was better to keep some secrets.

"Him," Luca lied. Which him she meant, it was hard to say. Gil. Nicolas. Her father. Sky above, poor Tiro, even, or Bastien. It wasn't much of a lie. They all haunted her nights. Just not every night. Just not tonight.

"I'm sorry," Touraine murmured into Luca's hair.

"Don't apologize." Luca squeezed Touraine's hip. More honestly, she said, "Every morning I wake up and think, this is only the beginning. There will be more pyres soon, and it's my job to fix it." She felt herself winding up again and dispelled the building pressure with a sigh and a shake of her head. "What woke you?"

Touraine turned back to the window, her chest rising against Luca with each deep breath. The night outside was dark, but the spillage of light from La Chaise made the horizon glow as if it were sunrise. Luca wished she could set her life to this steady rhythm.

"I dreamed about my soldiers. The war—the Taargen War. The rebellion." She sounded as if it were nothing, but Luca felt the tension Touraine held between her shoulder blades.

She rubbed the spot until it relaxed. When Touraine regarded Luca, though, her dark brows were knit with worry.

"We should tell Aranen and the High Court tomorrow. I'll send word to Qazāl. We just have to decide when."

Luca hesitated. "It will be winter festival soon. People are always looking for omens winter will end soon—not that they would admit it aloud."

Touraine snorted. "Uncivilized."

"Mm. We could be that good omen. A reason to celebrate before..."

"It's fine." Not dismissive, quite, but unbothered.

"And the other matter?" Luca pushed.

"General of Balladaire's armies." Touraine's voice was husky and low. "You want to make another Cantic out of me."

"Not a Blood General."

"Is there any other kind?"

The question caught Luca off guard, her mouth hanging open. She grew serious. "Everything and everyone is threatening my throne. I need you to help me keep it." She searched Touraine's face steadily, grave as an oathtaking.

Touraine sat with that gravity a moment, then smiled sadly. "It's what I always wanted."

Luca pulled back. "It's not funny."

"I'm not joking."

Instead of elaborating, Touraine swept her hands up Luca's waist and to her breasts as she pulled her into a kiss, deep and hungry for answers. For certainty. As if she'd find it in Luca, when Luca was lost in a fog herself.

They were rulers. They couldn't afford uncertainty.

Luca hiked Touraine's robe up to her hips and backed her against the windowsill. Touraine gasped beneath her touch.

Touraine dreamed of it ending.

She'd lied to Luca.

She hadn't dreamed of soldiers. She'd dreamed of a scaffold in Qazāl, a warm breeze across the back of her neck. Dry dust from the east swirling with the damp river air from the west. Grit beneath her boots and the raucous sound of voices cheering.

Pruett was at the lever, as she had been when Beau-Sang was executed, as she had been when they killed the rebels that first day in Qazāl. Only, it was Luca's neck that Touraine tightened the noose around. Pruett smiled. And then, in the fucked-up way of dreams, it was Touraine's hand on the lever, pulling it, at the same time as she watched Luca drop right in front of her, her neck snapping.

Naked and still breathless with pleasure, Touraine fought sleep. Tried to remember this feeling, right here.

Instead, she thumbed her grief rings and thought guiltily of Pruett while Luca breathed peacefully, curled into Touraine's side.

Touraine and Pruett hadn't always been lovers. They hadn't even always been friends. The first time they'd fucked had been right before they marched off to fight the Taargens. Fear of the fighting to come, frustrated helplessness that they had no control over their lives, and all the pent-up sexual tension of their forced proximity, bursting like a blister.

Touraine hadn't told Luca everything in Pruett's letter. Pruett wanted Touraine to join her. To help her lead Masridān. A place of their own, for the Sands, where no one would look down on them.

She didn't need to tell Luca that because she wasn't going to leave Balladaire, not after the promises she'd made to Luca and the Qazāli.

Moonlight spilled lovingly over Luca's skin, subtle light, blurred light. Touraine stroked the short hairs curling around Luca's ears. Luca's mouth, usually pinched and condescending, was slack. She was soft now, like this. All her rigidity gone for this one secret moment.

It was so fragile, this thing between them.

Fragile and beautiful and stained with blood.

How could it possibly last?

CHAPTER 2

THE WARLORD

The sun shone bright into the Conqueror's Square, onto the heads of the remaining soldiers of the King's Own. Out of a hundred men and women, twenty-four remained. They'd fought like dogs to the bitter end, Pruett could say that much for them. Among them were the Masridāni blackcoats who'd remained loyal to Balladaire. *Also like dogs to the bitter end.* They stood in their ranks, bound hand and foot before the statue of General Rosen Cantic in the center of Samra'. A breeze ruffled Pruett's coat. A red coat, slashed in black.

"A day for justice," Pruett muttered to herself.

From her right side, Noé gave her an unreadable look. "Are you sure?"

She wished he wouldn't ask her that.

"It's what Cantic would do. It's what she *did* do. That's why there's a giant fucking statue of her right in front of us."

Both of the Sands gazed up at the general. Her stone tricorne, that implacable frown. The fucking woman had shaped everything Pruett had ever done even down to this moment.

"I'm with you, Qā'id." Kiras was a steadying presence at Pruett's left side, hushing the second and third thoughts threatening to swallow Pruett up.

Many of the Samra'een watched from windows and rooftops above, from their carts and their stalls. Some huddled together in fear and suspicion, some cheered and shouted victoriously, some even pelted rubbish at the once-conquerors. A marked turn from a city that had gone belly-up for the Balladairans to start with, but maybe that was the way of it here—allegiances molting for the newest season. Opposite the ranks of prisoners stood the Masridāni blackcoats who'd sworn that allegiance to her. Red paint daubed on their coats or red patches sewn into the sleeves.

How quickly things changed.

How dull that they were still so much the same.

Pruett raised her hand, and the blackcoats—*her* blackcoats—raised their muskets to their shoulders.

"Please, Qā'id! Mercy, please!" A sobbing voice erupted from the front row of the prisoners. Governor-General Yoroub dropped to his knees, dragging down the prisoners tied to him. The Balladairan soldiers sneered down at him in disgust. All his sucking up to them, and they still didn't think he was worth a rank shit.

Granted, neither did Pruett.

"Please, Qā'id! I can help you, I know this city better than anyone else, please—"

"Hold." Pruett lowered her hand.

She met his dark eyes. He was pitiful. His robes were stained with weeks' worth of prison grime; his once carefully shaven face and strong chin were covered with a thick growth of matted beard. His luxurious curls were knotted now. Even begging, he didn't drop his Balladairan cadence. Maybe he couldn't. Maybe the accent was as ingrained in him as it was in her.

Silence so deep that the click of her boots on the stone pavers echoed through the square. Even the myriad growls and chirps and hisses in the back of her head went quiet. Pruett went to a knee in front of him. Her lip curled into that fishhook smile.

"I asked you for help once," she said. How stupid she'd been, hoping for something like welcome. "You called us savages."

"I didn't know—"

"You sent soldiers in the night to ambush us."

Yoroub only sobbed. He'd earned this for himself. Now he'd die as he lived—leashed to Balladairan heels.

Pruett stood and looked for one other prisoner. General Marquis de Moyenne was held between two Sands, apart from those about to be executed, and bound in irons instead of ropes. He was too valuable to throw away, as much as Pruett wanted to get rid of him.

In a murmur for nearby ears only, she asked him, "Have you considered my terms? You could spare your men and be well on your way to Balladaire in the bargain."

"A Moyenne does not surrender." Moyenne tried to spit at her, but he was so dehydrated no moisture came out. Say that for the noble, he had a bigger pair on him than Yoroub. "And only the duke regent can cede territory to an invading army."

Pruett's fishhook smile grew more vicious. "You and I both know that's not true."

The rights of the Balladairan military hierarchy had been drilled into her deeper than her own desires. As an active field general and a member of the High Court besides, Moyenne outranked all the Balladairans at the other garrisons in Masridān. Pruett needed to secure Samra', and Masridān as a whole, but without Moyenne's cooperation, she was looking at one bloody battle after another, and the other cities wouldn't fall as easily as Samra'.

Well, she thought. *Let the blood begin.*

She spun on her heel to the blackcoat lieutenant waiting for her signal.

She raised her hand. She let it fall.

As the Conqueror's Square filled with blood once more, Pruett raised her eyes to Cantic's immortal stone gaze.

Congratulations, you old bitch.

The next day, Pruett was in the Governor's Hall, where she'd made her base, when a young Masridāni messenger knocked on her door. He saluted eagerly when she opened it. Kiras kept between them. He was young, a recent recruit—not a blackcoat under Balladaire, but an eager malcontent who'd been waiting for a chance to overthrow those bastards, if only anyone in Samra' had had half a spine like the qā'id.

"What?" Pruett snapped.

"Captain Noé is at the Old Hospital. He told me to fetch you, sir." He spoke in Shālan. The Masridāni dialect slithered away from Pruett and took a few extra seconds to parse. When she did, her heart plummeted to her stomach.

"Is he hurt?" Pruett didn't give the young man a chance to answer, her long strides forcing him to chase her. As ever, Kiras followed.

"It's not him, Qā'id," he said, trotting at her side. "Just some people. They've gone...funny."

"Funny?"

The kid ducked his head into his shoulders. "Ill, I mean."

Pruett's palms itched with that Balladairan-bred fear of disease. Anyone else, it would have been called superstition, but civilized people didn't have those.

They wound through tight roads of high buildings, a mix of gray stone and the famous red-clay brick. Pruett pulled out a rolled cigarette from the gold case she'd commandeered from one of Moyenne's men. The burn in her lungs gave her something to focus on that wasn't the dread in her belly or the fear-scraped faces staring out at her from every corner.

It also dulled the consistent throb in the back of her skull.

"What's your name, soldier?" Pruett exhaled a plume of smoke into the winter day. Warmer than it would be in Balladaire this time of year, but still cool enough for her jacket.

"Saqr."

"Is that what you called yourself with the Balladairans, or after I came?"

"It's my name." He straightened his shoulders.

"As you like." Not her business either way, whether he'd named himself for a hawk or his parents had. She remembered her old name. She didn't wonder if her parents had named her imagining a happier child. A happier life. That girl was dead. Sold and long, long gone. No sense trying to puppet her corpse around.

Even some of the newer buildings they passed, the ones made of paler clay, had been painted red to imitate the older ones. Stone, too. Pruett had asked about it after they arrived. Fitting, in a way, for a city soaked in as much blood as Samra'. From her own takeover to Cantic's, and probably all the way back to Emperor Djaya and beyond. It was why she'd chosen the color of her coat. The color of the flag if they ever made one.

The hospital was one of the original red-clay buildings, old and big. It looked like original Shālan work, with the great keyhole doors and ornate stone tiling. The motifs were different from the ones in Qazāl—Pruett swore the shapes in the Masridāni tiles swirled into animals—but you could tell there was a shared history between the two countries. In the small courtyard at the center, water bubbled from the stump of two sandaled stone feet, and around it, people were tended on pallets.

Saqr led her past this courtyard and to a side room. Noé stood in the corner, speaking to a concerned pair, their gazes drifting to a figure lying on the ground.

"What's going on?" Pruett asked.

Noé nodded down to the handful of people in the room. Some darker skinned, some pale, some richly dressed, some not, in Balladairan style or Shālan. The one thing they had in common was the blank stare they leveled at no one. They registered neither her arrival nor her words.

Pruett jerked back in revulsion. "Fuck me."

It was exactly like the Sands who'd been taken prisoner in the Taargen War. When Pruett recovered them, they'd been like this. If they were conscious, they stared, unseeing, not reacting. Better at least, when they slept, if you could call it sleeping.

Suddenly, she felt cold. Like it was that sky-falling awful winter all over again.

A spike of pain lanced through Pruett's skull, bringing with it the sickly-sweet scent of dung and the taste of hay. She pressed the heels of her palms against her temples and growled.

When the pain passed, Pruett bent down to better look into one young man's face. She snapped her fingers in front of him. Nothing. He didn't even twitch his eyelids.

"Oy!" she yelled. Nothing. She backed away. "Put them out of their misery."

The order was met with silence.

"I said—"

Kiras stepped close to her, her hawkish nose brushing Pruett's cheek as she whispered, "Look."

She flicked her head to the side and Pruett followed. The man and woman Noé had been speaking to held each other, mooning at her with weepy eyes and snotty noses. She looked between them and the young man on the pallet.

Pruett grunted. "He yours, then?"

"Our brother," the man said in Balladairan, and the woman said, "Mercy, please."

Pruett walked over to them, gave them a long look up and down. Noé's tender disapproval followed her. She needed another smoke.

"When?"

"We found him like this three days ago." The woman glanced uncertainly at her brother. "We thought he'd hit his head working—a fall, from a building—but when he didn't get better, we brought him here."

"You know what's wrong with him?"

"No, my lord." The man's voice quavered only a little.

"You know how to fix him?"

"No, my lord."

"Then I've got bad news for you. This is it for him. Something in him is gone. He'll never answer to his name again, never recognize you, never speak—" Pruett's voice cracked and she cleared her throat. "He'll never speak to you again. Never smile. You want that for him? You want that for you? Death *is* a mercy."

That's what the Balladairan officers had said, before shooting the Sands Pruett had risked her life to rescue. Something had been gone in them, too, broken by whatever the Taargen priests had done. The other Sands hadn't even been given the choice to take care of them. It was either kill them quick or leave them to starve to death, alone in the no-man's-land between Balladaire and Taargen.

"We'll take care of him as best we can." The man lifted his chin and looked down his nose at her. There was love there. Loyalty. Devotion.

Made her feel like shit.

Pruett sucked her teeth. "Good. Then you'll take care of them all. These and any more that come up. Samra' thanks you."

Pruett didn't bask in their shock. She stomped out of the hospital, Kiras falling in beside her.

Outside again, in the clean air, she could breathe again. The noise of the animals grew louder in the back of her head, but it was better than facing her past in those blank stares.

"You seen anything like that before?" Pruett asked quietly.

"No," Kiras said. A thoughtful line appeared between her thick eyebrows. "Head injuries, yes. People born...different, yes. But awake and not awake at the same time?" She shook her head.

"I have. One time. One cause."

Kiras looked sideways at her as they walked, eyebrow cocked, waiting. She wore a gold ring in it now. It was handsome. The gold suited her brown skin. Gold bangles on her wrists, too, in the Masridāni custom. Pruett dodged around a donkey. Touching an animal accidentally was a sure way to call down a migraine, if it didn't knock her unconscious.

"When we fought in the war—"

"You and the other dāyiein?"

Pruett snorted. They'd been lost, all right. "Aye. When we fought the Taargens, if they captured a Sand, they didn't kill us. They...used us. In some fucked-up ritual that let them turn into bears or wolves. It left the prisoners—" She shuddered and jerked her head back toward the hospital. "Like that."

The line between Kiras's brows didn't deepen, didn't relax. She took it in stride. Pruett laughed bitterly. Of course Kiras wasn't fazed. She was an Eater.

"Everything that made them who they were, they took it, gone." Pruett snapped her fingers.

And now it was *here*, in *her city*.

Kiras said something solemnly in Shālan that Pruett didn't understand.

"What?" They were approaching the marble steps of the Governor's Hall.

"*Rouh*," Kiras repeated slowly. Her accent was thick when she spoke

Balladairan. "What makes you *you* and me *me*. Like a breath, the difference between a corpse and a person. The Taargens take that from
people, for their magic?"

"Oh. The soul. That's what the theorists in Balladaire call it. What
separates man from the animal and allows us to be civilized. Always
thought it was a load of bearshit."

Now Kiras's frown did deepen. "Why would a soul be bearshit?"

"Well, for one, the Droitists didn't think Shālans had souls. We
couldn't be civilized naturally, so they had to beat it into us like dogs."

Kiras's lip curled, showing off one sharpened canine. "I'll slit whoever told you you don't have a soul from cunt to crop."

Her vehemence surprised Pruett.

"And now?" Kiras tilted her head back toward the hospital. "That
changed your mind?"

"No. This did." Pruett tapped her temple. "Now I know they were
full of shit. Animals are loads more civilized than we are."

She waited for Kiras to probe deeper, to pick and pick at her, but all
Kiras did was rake her hand through the messy side sweep of her curls
and say, "I'm sorry."

"Aye. But what's more fucked," Pruett said, lowering her voice, "is
that a Taargen priest is here. Or was. Spies or worse. I'm not giving up
this city, Kiras. Not to them or anyone else."

Kiras's golden eyes bored into Pruett's. There was a flicker of something in there, but Pruett couldn't read it for the life of her. It was what
she liked most about Kiras. That inscrutableness. The steadiness. Slow
and careful, unlike someone else Pruett could name.

Speaking of animals. Pruett felt Sevroush in her head before his
winged shadow swooped above her. She held out her arm with the
bracer and the vulture settled comfortably. He waited, head tilted, for
her to give him a piece of fresh meat, but all she had was the dried meat
in her pouch. He couldn't frown, and yet his disapproval was clear. He
snapped the meat up anylight, then stuck out his leg.

Pruett took the scroll to see what news Sev had brought from
Touraine.

She read through it once and her stomach dropped, but there was
no reason to be upset. A final peace treaty signed between Balladaire

and Qazāl. The princess was now the queen. And then the last lines—not saying, "Yes, I'll come" or "No, I won't come" but "I have business here for Qazāl."

It was Touraine, all buttoned up in duty and obedience, and it wasn't Touraine. It was a stranger, and she was hiding something.

"It's good?" Kiras asked in a low, careful voice.

"Yes," Pruett said tightly. "It's good. Everything is good."

CHAPTER 3

OF DEBT AND DUTY

Thus convenes the first meeting of the Courts Noble under Her Majesty Queen Luca Ancier, may her reign be bright!"

The nobles of the High and Middle Courts stood along the benches as Luca entered the Chambre des Graines; they curtsied and bowed as she passed, murmuring, "Your Majesty." Even Ghislaine Bel-Jadot des Champs d'Or, who remained in La Chaise only under threat of Le Fontinard, dipped a graceful curtsy in her crimson dress. The room was warm, lit by candles along the walls, and servants served hot tea and coffee and chocolate as each courtier desired.

If it was a little cramped, Luca decided to consider it cozy instead. And if moments before, she had entered to the undercurrent of gossip speculating on her role in the death of Duke Nicolas's young heir and her very obvious motivations to cognaticide, she chose to ignore it. No one, not even Ghislaine, could use it to question her legitimacy; she was still the rightful heir.

Luca smiled her court smile, but the swell of hope in her chest was genuine. Or perhaps that was simply the remaining happiness from her day with Touraine. Touraine was away right now, taking charge of the barracks east of La Chaise, apprising them of what Luca was about to announce to the court.

She could *do* this. With Touraine's help, with Sabine's, and Minister Beaufoi's, she could save Balladaire. She could *rule* it. Even the artwork on the ceiling that gave the room its name seemed to carry that hope with it: rolling fields of grain in every shade of yellow and brown framed by fecund orchards.

She sat on her chair that was not quite a throne, resting her elbows on the carved wooden arms. All other seats faced hers, row upon row with her at the center. The four lords of the High Court sat nearest her, arrayed on handsomely carved—but noticeably smaller—chairs. At her right shoulder stood the financial minister, Beaufoi. They radiated a competent confidence, which was good, because Luca was relying on their figures to smooth out her other announcement.

Luca took a deep breath and began.

"My lords. My ladies. As you know by now, the Withering has been reported in the outskirts of Champs d'Or and Durfort in the west, in the villages along Le Dent Sec." She didn't mention that the reports were dated weeks before Tiro's death and her inadvertent coup. "We must prepare La Chaise and the neighboring cities—"

Ghislaine rose. "What about *our* cities? In Champs d'Or and Durfort?"

Luca fixed a calm gaze on the comtesse. "Every citizen of Balladaire is mine. Every loss is mine. I intend to keep that to as few as possible, which means we need to safeguard the places still untouched, as well as aid those already impacted. Do not worry." Luca nodded to Minister Beaufoi, who readied themselves. "However—"

"My people will want to see their leader offering hope, which I cannot do from here. And I have no daughter to sit at my place in Verlieu." Ghislaine's look was acid. Her daughter, Marie Bel-Jadot, had died at the end of the occupation of El-Wast—of the Qazāli illness that swept through the Balladairans or on one of the ships burned for quarantine.

Before Luca could order Ghislaine to be seated, Evrard Castide de Travers stood and said smoothly, "You are correct, of course, Your Majesty." The comte stroked his mustaches, his elderly face the picture of grave concern. "We should lock down the nearest cities. Halt travel along the main roads, set guards upon them and around the contaminated cities."

Camille LaVasse de Moyenne bristled. She rose to attention, her pale brown brows knit close. "Do you mean to punish those who would seek refuge?"

Stiff and proper, Camille wore a coat in Moyenne blue, striped in silver, echoing the cut of an officer's uniform. Like Luca, her hair was pulled back in an elaborate braid, the style of the old nobility. It wasn't the same bright red as her brother's, but she was just as pale and freckled.

"Punish, no, deter, yes," said Evrard, accompanied by the agreement of several among the Middle Court.

Some among the amassed were already wearing scarves about their faces, not to fend off the chill, but to protect from the spread of disease. Luca suspected the peculiar and pungent odors occasionally wafting toward her were some unguent that a "doctor" had promised would grant them immunity. Luca could not help glancing down at her own hands, but they remained strong and supple.

She reached for the reins of this beast that was hers to master.

"I will not let Balladairan soldiers kill Balladairan citizens."

There was enough unrest in that quarter already. Unconsciously, Luca pressed a hand against her ribs, where Fili had stabbed her. She forced it back to the arm of her chair, gripping the stylized lion claws (which, Luca was certain, had been carved by someone who had never seen a lion nor its claws).

"With attention to Balladaire's security and the needs of her borders, I have an important announcement to make." Luca stared pointedly at Ghislaine and Evrard, who were still standing. Evrard sat graciously, but Ghislaine waited an extra second longer than necessary. "Balladaire needs a new commander of her armies."

"Allow me, Your Majesty." Sabine stood and bowed with only a touch of her usual flourish, her charm restrained. Despite her exhortation for Luca and Touraine to have a care for their own happiness, Sabine had also grown more serious since the coup against Nicolas. Her rakish charm had been replaced by a weary dignity that sat well on her handsome brow. "I'm still fit, Your Majesty."

"Lord Durfort," Luca admonished gently.

A tic pulled Sabine's mouth into a twitching rictus. She turned away as she sat, hiding her face in the shadow of one spasming hand. This, too, was new.

"Touraine El-Qazāli will be the new grand general of the armies." Luca swallowed and stared into the middle of the chamber. "I will also take her as my royal consort."

Sabine jerked her head up immediately, her face still twitching even as she fought to control it. Her lips parted but she said nothing. Evrard's eyes narrowed; with his long nose and small mouth, it gave him a pinched expression. Camille pressed her mouth together thoughtfully. Though she was only recently come to La Chaise, there had been time enough for her to have heard the rumors. Ghislaine looked almost bored. Murmuring spread among the Middle Court, but none were bold enough to speak until the High Court did.

"Wedding Touraine El-Qazāli is the best next step to ensure mutual benefit and cooperation. With good will between us, we can heal the wounds we've caused and build a lasting peace."

"How lovely," Ghislaine said, before muttering something else under her breath.

"What about the Taargens, Your Majesty?" Camille asked. "Should we not look to them for an alliance first? We haven't had marital ties with them in generations, and I can tell you from my recent time in Moyenne, the peace is fragile."

Misgiving shot through Luca. "The Qazāli have not had ties with us even longer still. They need assurances from us that we intend to hold true."

Evrard slowly lifted a hand to call attention back to him. When the room quieted, he stood using the arms of his chair for support. "Young Lady Moyenne is quite correct. Perhaps Your Majesty's personal feelings cloud your judgment in this area. The ramifications of such ties…" Though he spoke to Luca, he held an open arm out to the nobles of the Middle Court, inviting them to agree with him. "The mood of the people. The public feelings toward the Qazāli. You risk their displeasure when we need trust and compliance the most."

Even Minister Beaufoi shifted uncomfortably at Luca's elbow.

The doubt grew. But, no. For once, what was right for Balladaire happened to be something she wanted for herself. It was one choice of many on the playing board. She kept herself from looking to Sabine for reassurance; she would get none from that hurt expression.

"Lord Travers," Luca started. If possible, the room went even more quiet, the better to hear her speak. "If people do not understand the Qazāli are our allies, they will learn by my example and by all of yours.

Anything that speaks to the contrary will be punished under our laws and, if necessary, Qazāl's."

"Your Majesty," Evrard said, "there remain the Taargens to contend with. As the young Lady Moyenne says."

"I am not so young you need mention it repeatedly, old Lord Travers." Camille cut a sidelong glance at Evrard. Nervous tittering broke out.

Luca curled one side of her mouth. "The Taargens are fine, my lord." Again that spike of fear. Nothing in the letters she'd found on her uncle's desk indicated reopened hostilities with their eastern neighbors. She pushed that fear away. She had enemies enough before her.

"They will feel this as a snub."

"They have no suitable candidates."

"Your Majesty," he pressed—*oh, how he kept pressing!* "We will need help if the Withering spreads out of hand. Have you given any thought—"

"Enough, Lord Travers. It is done." Luca's nostrils flared, the sole admission to her temper she allowed. As if she had given anything but thought to all the singular ways Balladaire might be fucked in the coming months! "There are other things to be gained by marriage that were not part of our treaty, things that may aid us in the dark times to come."

She tried to summon the hope she'd felt when she first sat down.

"Uncivilized magic." Ghislaine's quiet words rang through the hush of the small room.

Suddenly, the chamber felt claustrophobic, the braziers no longer comfortable but stifling. Luca longed for the airy Oak Hall, but it still smelled of smoke and mildew, like all the rooms on that side of the palace.

When she could speak without her voice trembling with anger, Luca said, "If I were you, I would consider myself lucky the Qazāli have agreed to unite our countries with a marriage alone. As for the Taargens—do they not also keep a god? Are they less 'uncivilized' than the Qazāli?" She glared around the room, but this time, no one spoke. She repeated again, louder and just as coldly: "It is done."

After a long moment, Evrard bowed deeply. "Your Majesty. My apologies." He sat and said no more.

"When?" The word rasped from Sabine's throat. She met Luca's eyes and, ah, there was the pain Luca had expected.

"Winter festival. We'll need a reason to celebrate. Something to remember when things do get hard." She knew that wasn't what Sabine was truly asking.

Sabine pressed her lips together and gave a knowing nod.

"Now we have that settled." Luca gestured for Minister Beaufoi to step forward. They bowed, hands clutched together as if they didn't know what to do without their papers in hand.

Luca had dismissed as much of Nicolas's previous staff as it was prudent to, but there was sense in maintaining continuity. Most importantly, Minister Beaufoi didn't seem attached to any politicking themselves: they were quietly competent and so far down in the succession of such a minor house in the Travers region that Luca wasn't overworried.

Minister Beaufoi presented the new tiers of taxation over the years to come, as well as outlined the need for immediate loans from the banks to prepare for the Withering, and how, with the court's vote, the banks would have more faith in the loan, and thus, this was the best course of action not just for the crown but for all of Balladaire.

"And so you see, I have made provisions for everyone," Luca added when Beaufoi finished with the figures. "In addition, we will also create a true Low Court. One that represents everyone, from the merchants to the laborers."

Luca sat back, taking in the expressions of the nobles before her, some patiently thoughtful, some carefully neutral, some obviously confused, and some—

"*This* is what you call provisions?" Ghislaine erupted yet again from her seat, a geyser of red silk. "This will be a ruination not only of all our houses, but the empire as well."

The poor financial minister's hands trembled.

"I encourage you, Comtesse, to consider the proposition carefully over the next several days. Minister Beaufoi will provide copies of the figures necessary to all who wish it, and then after the wedding, we'll reconvene for voting—"

"I will not vote for the destruction of my own house! To give up my power to the very farmers *I* provide for?" Ghislaine gathered her skirts and strode to the aisle that bisected the Chambre des Graines. "I refuse, and any member of this court with sense will, too."

Luca caught the subtle movement of Ghislaine's guards, uncertain if they should restrain her or not. Luca flicked her fingers to stay them. She let Ghislaine storm out. A moment later, several of the Middle Court followed suit, and Luca marked them well.

Those who remained were stunned into silence. She heard the click of Evrard's nails on the wooden arms of his chair and then the delicate clearing of Sabine's throat.

"I think this plan is exactly what the empire needs," Sabine said, standing. "We are a great nation because of our fields, and those who work those fields ought to have a say in how we govern them. Durfort will consider this proposal carefully, Your Majesty."

Evrard and Camille didn't commit themselves in either direction.

"Thank you, Marquise." To the rest of the chamber, Luca said, "That concludes our business. Thank you."

The Middle Court left in clumps, then Minister Beaufoi, perhaps slightly traumatized by the reaction to their proposition, and Camille, courteous but reserved. Luca looked between Evrard and Sabine.

"Was there something else, my lord?"

Evrard inhaled as if he did have more to say—but he shook his head. "No, Your Majesty. If you would only remember—some of us are not your enemies, and we have more political experience than the Qazāli girl. You will need it." He bowed deeply and left Luca alone with Sabine.

"That went…worse than I hoped." Luca sighed and stood, stretching out the ache in her hip.

"Why didn't you tell me you were marrying her?" Sabine said flatly.

Luca drew up short. Sabine slouched in her chair. Luca went to her. Sabine smelled of autumn, apples and woodsmoke, warm spices. Her cologne was as familiar as the rose soap Luca washed her own hair in. Luca placed her hand on Sabine's shoulder.

"We only decided last night. I'm sorry," Luca said. "And after the last time we…I thought you would tell me not to."

"I wouldn't have. Not anymore." Sabine turned her face away from

Luca's, but she couldn't hide the tension in her jaw and the wet shine of her eyes. "I'm sorry I wasn't always fair about you two, but I'm not—I won't—I deserved to know sooner. Not to be blindsided in front of Evrard and Ghislaine, for the sky's sake." Her voice cracked and she cleared her throat roughly. She bunched her fists on her lap. "You can trust me, Luca. You both can."

Luca stroked up the back of Sabine's neck, past the little mole behind her ear. "I know I can trust you, Sabine. I apologize. You do deserve better than that."

Sabine raised her eyes to Luca's. "How long have I known you, Luca?"

"I don't— Twenty years? More."

"A long time. All the better to know this was coming. Since the day she saved you in the throne room, I knew if you lived..." Sabine smiled, wan and crooked. "I'm glad you have each other. Sky above, that woman needs to smile more, and I can never make her. Wait— can *you?*"

"Not nearly as much as I would like." Luca made to shove Sabine away in jest, then hesitated; she seemed so much more fragile now.

Sabine misread the withdrawal. She sobered and sat up straight, the corners of her eyes tightening. "Shall I keep my distance from now on?"

"What? No." Luca cupped the back of Sabine's neck again. "You will always have a place with me. My father never gave up Gil for my mother."

"That's different," Sabine said, turning away.

"It is not."

"It is. You're—she's—you never would have married me. I'm not the right kind of person. Your father had a warrior in one arm, a queen in the other. I'm just...the court fop."

"You are no more a court fop than Touraine is an obedient soldier. Don't insult me like that." Luca tugged Sabine back to her by the chin. "I need you, Sabine. I need you as much as I need Touraine. As much as my father needed my mother. If Touraine is my warrior, then you are my courtier. She connects me to the Qazāli, but she doesn't know the court like you and she never will. I need *you* to bind the nobles to me."

"And this?" Sabine turned her mouth into Luca's palm, meeting her gaze once more. "If she says no?"

"I haven't spoken to her yet," Luca answered honestly. "About how it might work. The three of us. But she knows what you are to me."

Sabine sighed and took Luca's hand from her face to press it between her own. Her large hands were warm around Luca's, but instead of reassuring her, the gesture filled Luca with dread.

"Perhaps I should go. Give you two time to figure things out together. Give myself time to..." Sabine trailed off.

"Go where?"

"Home. To Durfort."

Luca's stomach twisted sharply. "You can't leave."

"Are you saying that as my friend or my queen?"

"Must I make it an order?" Luca took her hand from Sabine's and held it tight at her side. "All because I'm marrying her? Sabine—"

"Luca." Sabine looked to the ceiling, to the fields of painted hope. "I'm the marquise de Durfort, and my marquisate is facing the worst tragedy since the last Withering. Ghislaine is right about one thing: I should be there."

"You'll put yourself right in the Withering's path." Luca spoke as calmly as she could, hiding her fear and the shiver of future grief. "We know it's already in Premont."

Sabine inhaled sharp with surprise. "*My people* are in the Withering's path. If they suffer, I should suffer with them. Isn't that how the chevalier tales go? Hearten them with my august presence, rally them around my courage, salve their pain by mourning with them?" Her crooked smile didn't meet her dark, somber eyes.

"You're trying to prove you're still useful. You're more than a fop, you don't need to prove—"

"I'll *be* more than a fop by managing my responsibilities. I—" Sabine worked her jaw angrily. When she spoke again, her voice was quieter, but no less fierce. "This isn't because of today. I've been thinking a lot about who I've been. What I would regret if I were poisoned yet again. I have no heir, I have no siblings. I have a duty, Luca. As you do."

A lump thickened in Luca's throat against her will. Her desires were selfish. It didn't make her want them any less. She wanted Sabine close. She wanted Sabine safe. Sabine dropped her gaze from Luca's, tapping her short nails on the arms of her chair in sporadic rhythm. Her eyelashes stood out, long and dark over her pale cheeks.

"Before you leave, I need you to sign witness to the marriage contract."

Sabine puffed her cheeks out. "Of course. Show it to me before I go and you'll have it." She stood and bowed. "Your Majesty."

CHAPTER 4

THE COLONEL

How many years had it been since Touraine last saw her old compound?

How many years since she left for the Taargen War? Five years? Six? She couldn't say; the war years were a blur of seasons—of blood and death and desperate companionship. Familiarity shivered up her ramrod spine as she rode Cendre up to the small gray fortress. Memories of the Balladairan compound in Qazāl further blurred the past. Here, dark stone, thick arches at the north and south. The walls weren't as high here—or maybe they were just bigger in her memory.

Camille de Moyenne rode beside Touraine on a more appropriate warhorse, along with several blackcoats Commander Perrot had vouched for. Terse silence tethered them together.

Earlier on the journey, the acting marquise had turned to Touraine and asked her frankly, "Are you ready for a responsibility of this magnitude?"

Touraine had bristled, but she was used to this line of questioning from Balladairan officers. "Just because I'm Qazāli—"

"No. I don't care where you come from. The queen could pick a general from the other side of the world and I wouldn't care so long as their loyalty was assured and they'd been tested in battle and proven sound of strategy." Moyenne gave Touraine a sidelong glance, taking in her new general's coat and her placid horse.

Heat rose in Touraine's cheeks. "I'm beyond loyal to the queen, and

I've been trained for war since I was five under General Cantic herself. While you nobles were busy picking out silk stockings for your sixteenth birthdays, I was fighting the Taargens for mine."

"That is not how we do things in Moyenne," Moyenne said tartly. "I rode in the last war as a messenger, even in winter."

"Infantry. On the front lines. Through the winter."

Moyenne regarded Touraine with grudging appraisal. After a time, she asked, "What was it like working with her?"

"Who?"

"General Cantic. I wanted to train with her while she was at the La Chaise barracks, but Papa considered me too young. Then Brice left to ride cavalry in the King's Own and I had to learn to run the estate."

Camille de Moyenne didn't seem like she could be of an age with Touraine. Wear-lines creased the corners of her eyes, and her skin was admittedly more leathery than most nobles' in La Chaise.

"It was complicated." Hard enough to understand the mix of her own feelings as she rode back to the place where it all began, let alone to bare it all to someone while trying not to say the wrong things. Touraine evaded instead. "Are you all soldiers, the scions Moyenne?"

"All of us have served in some capacity or another. So that we understand the duty of our house. What it costs to hold the border." With a sniff, the marquise added, "The grand general has come from Moyenne for the last hundred years."

"I'm sorry you feel I've taken your place," Touraine said stiffly.

"Don't be sorry," Moyenne said, as if she couldn't hear the sarcasm. "Only earn it. They will say the queen places you here only because you warm her bed. Prove it isn't true."

Touraine rode the rest of the way as if she had a burr in her saddle.

A pair of on-duty soldiers hailed them at the northern arch.

"Halt. State your business." A young Balladairan woman tilted her head up to look at Touraine from below the rim of her field cap. Her eyes widened slightly. Then she saw Moyenne and they widened further.

A volley of rifle fire cracked through the air, and Touraine's hands spasmed around her reins. The horse shied beneath her. Moyenne tracked the tension with a sharp eye. Touraine tried to wipe the shakiness from her voice.

"I'm General El-Qazāli. Take me to your commander."

"Sir. Yes, sir. I'll find him, sir? If you'll wait here, sir?" The blackcoat shared a nervous glance with her compatriot, then hoisted her rifle and ran deeper into the compound.

It took Touraine aback. She should have been permitted to ride through. Moyenne's pale brows furrowed in disapproval. She waited anylight, observing what she could of the camp. A track ran along the inside of the wall, a deeper line of dirt worn by thousands of steps, hundreds of thousands of clomping boots. There were the barracks, more dilapidated than she would have expected after this much time.

The horses grew restless, their tack jangling as the soldiers she'd brought from the palace were surely speaking wordlessly behind her back. No officer should be made to wait like this, especially not the grand general.

Touraine couldn't hide from this, though. She'd told Luca as much. She needed to break resistance down immediately, no hesitation.

She nudged her horse into the compound, following the main road. Odd, to be on horseback instead of her own two feet, but everything was as she'd left it.

There, the pole jutting out of the ground with its metal holds for tying up ropes, was where Touraine had been whipped. Where Mallorie had been executed for deserting. The training field where Touraine had learned to fight and glory in her newfound strength. There, behind barrack two, was where Captain Rogan had almost raped her. She'd kissed Pruett for the first time behind barrack four, and Aimée and a few others besides. She'd met Cantic here, Cantic, who had explained their monthly courses while they sat cross-legged in the mess hall. She'd said goodbye to Cantic for the first time, and then years later, a different instructor explained the surgeries that would render those monthly courses irrelevant.

At the training yard, Touraine slid off her horse. Soldiers lined up facing hay-stuffed targets, rifles loaded. She tipped her tricorne to block the glare of the setting sun. Forced herself to stand still as they fired. Then the next line, and then the first line again. She watched them, her heart stuttering each time gunpowder flared, until she could at least keep her flinching to the inner grasp of her gut.

A few of them noticed her. Stared. She noticed some of them, too, especially the few with especially sharp eyes, whose targets lost a lot of stuffing from the head.

Touraine's stomach growled, not for the delicacies of the palace but for the rich, hearty stews and crusty loaves of bread common when she'd last been a soldier—food cooked in bulk and ready to feed an army. She half imagined she could smell it beneath all the sulfur.

"And who are you?" barked a voice behind Touraine.

Inured for the moment to the explosions of the guns in front of her, Touraine managed not to jump at the colonel's booming voice. She spun on her heel to face him. Though she was shorter than him by a head, she'd been watching Luca Ancier stare down the world for months. Her nose wasn't quite as sharp, and she couldn't twist her mouth into quite the same level of condescension—Luca was a master—but Touraine did her best.

"Colonel Taurvide. I remember you."

Taurvide had blustered over her in the court-martial when Captain Rogan tried to have her executed.

He blinked at her, close-set eyes dark and large like a bull. The flare of his nostrils didn't help the impression. Then recognition broke over him like an unpleasant splash of water.

"You're the Sand."

"I'm General Touraine El-Qazāli." Touraine took the folded letter from her pocket with Luca's golden seal and handed it to him. "I bear a letter of the command change from the queen herself. I'm sure that will be sufficient."

She almost laughed, hearing herself. Even now, with all the power in the world, second only to Luca, it was them she imitated. *The imitation is what gives you that power*, sneered a voice in her mind.

Here in her barracks, though, another truth was unlocked, the truth she'd been hiding from herself whenever she looked at Luca. *It's not imitation if it is who you were raised to be.*

Taurvide blew his breath out heavy like a bull, too, laughing in her face as he closed the letter again. She leaned away from the stench of meat and mouth rot.

"I'm not surrendering control of the compound to the princess's whore of a Sand."

"The queen," Touraine said coldly. "And no, in fact, you are not. You're simply being informed of the new chain of command and your new commanding officer. Who will be the prince consort."

"Phaw." Colonel Taurvide turned away, waving the back of his hand at her dismissively. "I'll write to the *queen* myself. Tell her to see sense. I know these soldiers. The next thing you'll want is to invite more Shālans into the ranks. This is preposterous. I won't be ordered about by uncivilized little desert rats."

As he walked away, Moyenne widened her eyes at her. She hissed, "You can't—"

Touraine held up her hand to silence her. She locked eyes with the platoon that had followed her from La Chaise, then said, "Colonel, I gave you an order."

The Chaisien soldiers blocked Taurvide's path.

Taurvide about-faced, barging into Touraine's space. He raked her up and down with contempt. "How old were you during the last Taargen War, hein?"

Touraine curled her lip and held her silence.

"Because I was a colonel then," he continued. "Fucking Her Royal Majesty won't prepare you for a command. Not like my years of experience."

"Experience?" Touraine picked open the raw wound she'd already scraped for Moyenne's sake. "I was a child. Is that what you want me to say? I was a child and you sent me to war. You sent me to war because you were too cowardly, and I came back. I fought the Taargens face-to-fucking-face and came back. Now will you obey or are you refusing the queen's order?"

Taurvide held himself back from her outburst. "I don't take orders from sand fleas."

"Very well." To her Chaisien blackcoats, she said, "Arrest the good colonel. Field punishment number three. The whipping pole will do nicely."

While others blocked the path with their horses, three of Touraine's burlier soldiers dismounted and approached the colonel.

"You will not!" His face reddened with anger. He shoved the men away, but the struggle was short-lived. He'd spent too much time enjoying the fruits of his rank without any of its hardships.

"You." Touraine pointed to an unranked Balladairan blackcoat, young enough that she was still spotty with acne. "Fetch some rope."

"Sir?" She looked between Touraine and Taurvide, uncertain.

Touraine held her rank arm up, indicating the solid-gold sleeve. Then she pointed to Taurvide's colonel's sleeve, which was only striped gold. "I said, 'Fetch. Some. Rope.' Thank you, soldier."

"Yes, sir!" The young woman saluted and sprinted off.

By the time she returned, they'd marched Taurvide to the whipping pole and he was seething, panting in their grip.

"You'll pay for this, El-Qazāli," he said, spittle spraying as they tied each of his hands to the iron loops screwed into the pole so his hands hung above his head. There were several loops—some for tall disobedient troops and some for shorter ones. Touraine had been tied to the loops in the middle.

When she was younger, she'd been tied to the loops at the bottom.

The weight of Taurvide's body smashed his face into the pillar, and Touraine could feel the splinters digging into his face as if it were her own pressed against the rough wood again.

This will never be you again.

"You can't leave me here!" Taurvide sputtered. "Do you know who I am?"

Touraine turned her back on him and faced the crowd of blackcoats. Everyone who wasn't on duty had come to watch. Some expressions knowing, some shuttered and angry. A few even looked relieved.

"Soldiers. Officers. I'm General Touraine El-Qazāli, soon to be Prince-General Touraine El-Qazāli. Queen Luca has tasked me with the preparation of her armies as we face down the threat of the Withering and the rise of banditry on the roads. Some of you might have certain attitudes about Shālans and about Qazāli in particular. You might have heard rumors about me. You might agree with the good colonel here."

She paused to give them a chance to take in the good colonel and see if that was still how they sided themselves. He tried to stifle his frustrated whimpers of pain, but the yard was so quiet. Everyone could hear.

"Whether you wish or no, your lives are in my hands now, and so is

the rest of Balladaire. There's no time for you to act like spoiled children. You'll be dealt with just as swiftly. If you have any questions,
you'll take it up with my—" Shit. She needed an aide. "Take it up with
my aide. Dismissed."

Stunned silence hung in the air as the soldiers trickled back to their
tasks and drills.

"Are you sure that was wise?" Camille de Moyenne murmured
when they were alone in the field.

"It needed doing."

For the rest of the afternoon, soldiers who passed through the whipping field pretended to ignore their colonel strung up like a deer carcass, but almost all of them at least glanced from the corners of their
eyes. It was having the effect Touraine wanted.

She would claim her power the way Balladaire always did. The way
Cantic had wooed her as a child.

Whips and honey.

CHAPTER 5

OF WHIPS AND HONEY

Before the sun set too low, there was something else Touraine wanted to do. Something she wanted to find.

If she could just remember where she'd put them.

She left, alone, through the southern arch, acknowledging the on-duty soldiers who saluted her. She let her feet sink into habit, hoping that would guide her better than thought. The sky was orange and pink and the air was brisk. She kept her fingers curled for warmth. Her eyes glazed over the stones, looking for a mark, for something that would stand out, shout to her, *Here, here!*

When Touraine had stolen Tibeau's prayer beads, she had told herself she would never forget where she buried them. She had done it for his own good. After his first ones had been confiscated, the thong holding them together broken, the beads themselves scattered across their bunk and then swept away, she had thought Tibeau would stop. He'd been beaten. Badly. On that same Shāl-damned pole. Should have been enough to make anyone stop.

But he'd carved them again, out of wood and scraps of bone from their meals.

Unlike him, she'd been afraid. Was that the right word for the appreciation she wanted from Cantic and their other instructors? No. But she had been afraid for him. Afraid he'd be caught again. Whipped again. So she'd stolen them. She had enough sense not to give them to the instructor. Instead, she waited until she had a chance to bury them outside.

She stopped at a run of stone with a familiar crack like lightning forked in three branches. Seemed like the place she would have chosen—a fork for her, for Pruett, and for him. Were she and Pruett even friends at that point? She knelt in the snow and began to dig, clawing chunks out of the earth with a hunk of broken rock.

She'd been something like thirteen, with a half-cocked idea of how the world worked for people like them. She'd been so sure that if he *behaved*, they would treat them right. And they had. But Tibeau hadn't cared.

Tears and melting snow muddied the ground as she dug. When she came up for air, there was a hole the size of her head and nothing to show for it.

Above her, the sky had turned from orange to burning red, already darkening at the edges. Her trousers were soaked through the knees, her fingers numb. She didn't have time to dig in the dirt for bones like a dog. Especially couldn't let anyone catch her at it. Not after this afternoon.

She scuffed the dirt back into the hole. Brushed off her hands. She sniffed hard and twisted at Tibeau's grief ring on her finger. Wasn't that she needed something to remember him by. She couldn't forget him even if she'd wanted to.

She just wished she'd done things differently, was all.

She shoved her hands into her pockets.

"I'm sorry, Beau," she whispered to the place in the dirt that held nothing of her, and everything she was, all at once.

Back in the quarters she'd chosen—a clever aide offered to clear out Taurvide's rooms for her use, but Touraine had declined; she would be here for only the one night, and if she was honest, she didn't want to touch anything the bearfucker had—Touraine sat at her desk and pillowed her head on her arms. Her stomach growled. She'd smelled the food cooking in the mess hall as she walked back from her excavation, but she'd been muddy and tear-streaked. Instead, she'd pulled her tricorne low over her eyes and gone to wash up.

Someone knocked on her door.

"Enter."

The same enterprising aide who had offered to put her in Taurvide's room. Eager. Maybe too eager.

"Sir, will you take your dinner now? I can have it brought to you, and the marquise de Moyenne."

"When are the other soldiers eating?"

"They already are, sir."

"Oh. Why didn't you say earlier?"

"Euh, well, sir. The colonel—he requested a roasted chicken tonight. I had thought you might like that instead."

Her stomach growled again, even louder. The aide started to smile, then—

"No. Thank you, no. I'll eat in the mess. Have the duty cooks share it among the main meal. In fact, have them open one of the wine casks."

The aide didn't even blink. "Yes, sir. Shall I guide you to the hall?"

Touraine's laugh was rough-edged. "I know the way."

"Sir. I'll inform the marquise, sir."

Touraine had rarely gotten the privilege of drinking wine in the garrison itself. They were occasionally given weak ale, but if they drank so much it hampered their performance the next day, there were—as with everything else—consequences. They'd gotten wine on Longest Night, though. They'd gotten wine before they marched out to fight the Taargens.

Whips and honey.

The mess was crowded with the current shift of men and women. It smelled like she remembered. The peculiar blend of bread and sweat and hay and meat. A lump rose to her throat.

At the serving table, the soldiers on cook duty saluted sharply. One was so nervous, he splashed her stew as he doled it into the bowl.

"Thank you." Touraine tried to smile kindly at him.

By the time she'd turned to the rest of the room, they'd noticed her.

Making "friends" was going to be as difficult now as it had been when she was a child here, if for different reasons. She'd been "Balladaire's dancing monkey" then. Now the officer's table looked as if they'd rather be strung up with Colonel Taurvide. At the end of that table, though, she saw someone she did recognize.

She took her bowl and bread and sat next to Valmorin. The officers made room quickly, but their conversation didn't pick up again.

"Valmorin. I don't know if you remember me. We met once in the palace. I didn't realize you were a captain."

Touraine needed loyalty. A few skilled soldiers behind her and she'd have enough. He had been kind that day in the training yard.

Valmorin took her forearm gingerly, matching her soldier's clasp. "I didn't realize you were a general, sir."

"I wasn't." She smiled warmly and he smiled back, losing some of his hesitation. "I also had no idea you could shoot so well." Valmorin had been one of the keen-eyed soldiers in the shooting yard. "How did you end up here?"

"A long story, sir, involving, euh, do you remember Lieutenant Fougaire? The—"

"The asshole with the beard? Aye."

That got an appreciative chuckle from Valmorin and a sharp sniff from someone else across the table. Touraine noted their face, then ignored them.

Valmorin warmed to the attention. "Yes, well, he went out with Lord General Brice and the King's Own. Fougaire discouraged him from taking me along as part of the company." His face went bright red, maybe in anger, maybe in embarrassment.

"Luck in disguise," Touraine said.

"What do you mean?"

"The King's Own was lost."

"What?" Moyenne stood above them, holding her own bowl and bread. She jerked her chin for Touraine to scoot over, as casual as any soldier would to their comrade, but her stare was intent.

"Marquise." Valmorin's eyes widened. He looked as flustered as Touraine felt.

The officers stilled their utensils and turned to Moyenne and Touraine.

"Forgive me," Touraine murmured. "I thought the queen had spoken to you."

"I'm sure she will," Moyenne said stiffly. Then she tucked into her meal as if it wasn't her own brother's capture she was speaking of.

The mood was somber after that, and Touraine didn't know how to lift it. Luckily, she didn't have to. The quartermaster arrived, rolling a cask of wine. As the cask was broached, everyone waited on her.

Touraine stood and raised her cup.

"To Queen Luca. May her reign be bright."

The morning was a gray day, cold enough to make Touraine's breath mist in front of her face. Frost crackled on what patches of grass remained in the compound. The entire garrison was out in formation, three companies of career soldiers, all of them waiting to see discipline carried out.

Colonel Taurvide hung by his wrists on the whipping pole. He scrambled upright when he saw Touraine coming. He'd slept on his feet, perhaps, or maybe he'd tried to but failed, dangling to his shins until the pain woke him. His fingertips were fading from the deep purple they'd been, and color returned slowly to his wrists.

His lips were blue but he spat at her boots.

"Colonel Taurvide." Touraine pitched her voice to carry across the field. "For your insubordination and disrespect, you'll receive thirty lashes—"

Though no one was undisciplined enough to make a sound, there was a collective intake of breath that Touraine could *feel*. Officers didn't receive lashes. To strike a noble—

"You wouldn't dare," Taurvide snarled.

Touraine continued as if no one had interrupted her. "You will be henceforth discharged from Her Majesty's service. Your family will lose its commission. Further issues will be settled with fines paid direct to the queen's treasury or Balladaire's armies, at Her Majesty's discretion."

Taurvide purpled in silent rage, his meaty fists bunched and straining at the ropes that bound him. Touraine didn't look for reassurance in the security of the knots.

When Touraine had asked the aide this morning who handled the soldiers' discipline, she'd been directed toward Captain Laurelin, one of the captains she'd sat with at dinner the night before. The one who had sniffed when she and Valmorin talked about that asshole, Fougaire.

Captain Laurelin held the whip in her hand now, the leather curled against the handle and clenched in her fist. Her lips were pursed with distaste.

Touraine circled around behind Taurvide, took her belt knife, and slit the back of his shirt open. She wasn't sure if she should be the one to give the punishment or not. Or, no, that wasn't it—she knew if she could dole the punishment, their fear of her would stick. Their resentment, too, if they had liked Taurvide. The question was whether or not she *could* do it. She had never whipped anyone. Her stomach had churned all morning; she hadn't even eaten breakfast. If she asked for the whip, she couldn't hand it back.

What would Cantic do?

The answer came immediately, an echo in Touraine's own skin: if the offense was great enough, she'd dispense the punishment herself.

Then there was the anger. She was as hot with rage as Taurvide, so hot that it scared her, only hers had built up for years and years, though she hadn't recognized it until Qazāl. The same rage she'd felt when she found that headmistress in the Droitist school. Sky above, Touraine had wanted to kill her. If not for the children, she might have.

There were no children here.

Peace over all. That's what Aranen would say, wouldn't she? Or would she call this balance? The priestess's prayer beads at Touraine's wrist seemed to tighten, hidden there under her sleeve.

Maybe Taurvide loved his soldiers. Maybe he advocated for them to the queen. Maybe he even drank with them, like Touraine had last night. None of that mattered, though, because *Touraine* had decided he would be punished. *Touraine* had decided how and when. She had never had this power before.

She wanted to execute it herself.

"Give it to me." Touraine held an empty hand out to Captain Laurelin and jerked her head at Taurvide. "Something to bite down on."

She stared at the pale stretch of flesh before her, a tuft of hair at his lower back. It was mostly unmarked, except for a scar reaching around from his belly—maybe an actual battle scar. Men like him had made her own back ugly with pain. She'd been so afraid the first time Luca had taken off her clothes. She'd felt so hideous.

Her eyes pricked with tears. To keep them from falling, she gripped the whip and swung.

The whip cut the air with a whistle, cut off with a fleshy slap.

Taurvide grunted, biting down on the gag.

Again. Again. Again. By the time Touraine was at six, he was growling like a dog. The cords of his neck bulged. The muscles of his back and shoulders strained. Several stripes had split the skin, dripping blood down into the band of his trousers. At ten, though, he was screaming, the high-pitched sound only barely muffled by the cloth in his mouth.

Then it was over. Taurvide hung limply from the rope digging into his wrists. He spun slightly. The gag had fallen out, and drool dribbled from his lips onto the ground. The air around the two of them steamed. Her own back ached from effort and bitter empathy, her hand and forearm swollen and tense from her tight grip.

She handed Captain Laurelin the whip. She did not think she could do that again, and so she came to a decision. "Cut him down and tend to him."

Then she regarded the soldiers standing at attention before her. They were silent. Moyenne's expression was unreadable.

"Any one of you who cannot find it in yourselves to serve under a Qazāli, under your future prince, in the name of Queen Luca, leave now. In doing so, you abandon all rank and obligations as well as any reward. Leave your weapons and your uniforms. You won't be punished by me. But if you stay—" She gestured wide to Taurvide, who was on his knees, struggling to be led away. "If you stay and refuse my command, insubordination will be met in kind."

Then, to Valmorin she said, "Colonel Valmorin."

Valmorin stared in wide-eyed surprise. "Yes, General." He saluted.

Touraine turned crisply on her heel, and walked, back straight, face grimly bored, back to her room. She sat next to the basin, waiting for some sort of tell, like the nausea that had her vomiting in muddy ruts after her earliest battles against the Taargens. Something to show she felt guilt or shame or even the barest hint of regret. There was nothing there. Only cold, vindictive satisfaction.

She told herself she wouldn't do it again.

She told herself she wouldn't have to.

CHAPTER 6

THE SEED

Fili gripped the smooth wood of La Flottille's bar to keep her hands still. Sky above and earth below, but she was nervous. Her teeth fair chattered with it. The rest of the patrons in the public house—Fingers, all of them, or they would be soon—murmured darkly to themselves. It was after dinner hours, and they all clutched their mugs of ale or cups of wine. The bar staff flitted about the room, scooping up empty plates and bowls and refilling drinks, but their smiles were false and fleeting.

Fili ground her teeth into each other as if that could bolster her up. Alone, it probably wouldn't have worked. She'd wine of her own, though, and Brother Michel had ordered Joscelin the barkeep to keep her topped up.

To her right, Maître Gaspard leaned an elbow against the bar, considering the crowd almost as hesitantly as Fili was. Occasionally, he murmured something to Joscelin, who grunted in response.

Fili wondered how many of them knew she'd failed. If they knew she'd been tasked with a mission and now she was here before them, a failure. If they knew she put them all at risk, just by being here.

Brother Michel's presence was like a wave—people turned to follow his progression as he worked his way to the bar, their voices raising as they spoke to him and falling to an uncertain hush as he moved on. He stopped beside her and clamped a heavy hand on her shoulder.

This was what they had decided was best, Brother Michel and

Maître Gaspard. When Fili escaped the palace after her attempt on the queen's life, Brother Michel had been livid at first. Said she'd endangered the entire movement by coming back. She'd spent a few days in the cold, wondering if confessing to her mother was worth the shame if only she could sleep under a roof, in a warm bed again. Then Brother Michel found her, pulled her into La Flottille, and it was here she'd spent the last few weeks.

She learned of the queen's survival through the patrons' gossip. The death of the duke's son. The queen's coronation. She had failed. Completely. But Brother Michel saw it another way.

"You can become a legend, girl," he'd said, a hand on each of her shoulders, a glint of something in his eyes.

Hope, maybe.

That's what he called her, later, in his cups. Their hope.

At a signal only he knew, Brother Michel climbed atop the bar. Fili and Maître Gaspard winced at the dirty boots on the lovingly polished wood. So did Joscelin.

"The Fingers form the fist!" Brother Michel said into the hush, pumping a fist above his head.

"The Fingers form the fist," the room echoed half-heartedly.

"We will not break!" he said.

"We will not break." Even weaker.

Brother Michel nodded gravely, as if he had expected this dark mood, even though in the kitchens, he'd been fever-eyed with anticipation.

"Thank you all for coming," he said. "I can see you've heard the rumors from the west, and, aye, I'll tell you they're not rumors at all."

Fili looked to her master for an explanation, but his lips were pressed grimly together.

Brother Michel continued. "Mathien, the grocer on the corner of the Place du Bois—he's gone. Two days ago, his wife said, he came down with it. She turned to him and one side of him was shriveled up like an old apple, he could scarce breathe."

Only Brother Michel was brave enough to speak the words, and his voice was angry with it, instead of frightened like everyone else.

"The Withering is *in our city*. And what is the queen doing about it?

Planning a wedding to some Qazāli she brought back from the colonies! She probably doesn't even know, with her head so far up her own ribboned ass." Brother Michel's face was red now, his voice lowered dangerously. "She doesn't know how we suffer. But *we* do. *We* know the truth of it down here, don't we?"

He paused to gather in the reactions of the assembled Fingers, and their grim fear shifted with him to anger, to a different kind of muttering.

Then he turned to Fili. Beckoned.

"*I* know how you live. That's why I bring you hope, to go along with the ill tidings. Meet Fili, one of our youngest fighters."

He gave her a broad smile and helped her up onto the bar with his strong hands and clasped her to his side. The height combined with the wine made her dizzy. Gaspard's hand at her thigh steadied her.

"Thanks to Fili, the new queen is on edge. Fili, tell your brothers and sisters what you did for them."

Fili swallowed. She was afraid to speak the words aloud, but Michel had explained beforehand—among the Fingers, she was safe, and her deeds, from her own lips, would give courage to the rest. She would inspire them to take risks for their freedom, just like she had.

"I, um, I stabbed her?" she mumbled.

"Speak up, little sister, speak up." Michel's arm around her shoulder tightened as he shook her a touch harder than necessary.

She tried again: "I stabbed the queen." It was a heady thing to say, and she'd had to keep it in so long it was an almost physical relief to let it out. Her shoulders relaxed and she raised her cup. "I stabbed her!"

"Aye, she did!" Michel's approval was as heady as the wine. "Was she surprised?"

"Y-yes?" The line of questioning confused Fili.

The queen's mouth an O, her brow crumpling as she frowned at Fili.

"Was she frightened?"

"Yes?"

The queen's bright blue eyes wide and round as she fell, reaching frantically for a hand, calling for someone. Fili's stomach churned at the memory. Too much blood. Too much to drink. She swayed and Brother Michel held her upright. She clung to him.

"You see?" he said. "The princess thought she was safe from the wrath of the people, but Fili showed her even the palace walls are no sanctuary for thieves." He glanced at her, her last cue.

"We'll pull them out by the roots! Will you join me?" Fili's voice was loud and shrill, not a hero's voice at all.

A flush burned her cheeks as the Fingers cheered her. She wished she could tell her mother.

She realized she'd missed some of Brother Michel's words and heard him speaking out against the Qazāli.

"After Fili struck the blow, they say it was Qazāli who nursed her back to health. Vicious as wolves in their own country, but here? Nothing but lapdogs."

"No," Fili started, "no, that's just the ambassador—"

Michel pinched her arm and steered her roughly toward the edge of the bar, where Joscelin scooped her up in his large arms. He set her gently on the ground on his side of the bar and steadied her as she teetered. The next cup he placed in front of her was water.

Gaspard leaned over the bar to pat her shoulder. "All right, my dear?"

"Mhm." When the dizziness passed, Gaspard gestured her closer.

"Have you given a thought to telling him what else you can do?" he whispered in her ear.

Fili shot upright, stiff as timber. Though the room lurched, Gaspard's face was clear. Solemn, deep frown lines around his mouth and between his brows. No malice at all.

"What do you mean, maître?"

"You know what I mean." He rapped the wooden bar twice for emphasis.

Bile surged, burning and sour, into Fili's throat. She shook her head rapidly and lost her balance. Maître Gaspard clasped her arm from the other side of the bar.

"Surely you had to know I knew, my dear."

"I don't want them to call me uncivilized. I'm not like—*them*." The Qazāli and the Taargens with their gods. She didn't want to lose the respect she'd gained. Deep down, she didn't think it was a secret she could trust Brother Michel with. Not yet.

"As you wish." Maître Gaspard patted her hand once. Then he straightened as a young man approached the bar. Fili recognized Olivier, the leatherworker's apprentice. He'd helped her with the harness for her mother's wooden leg.

"You never told me you were a hero, Fili!" Olivier grinned, the apples of his smooth cheeks pink from the close warmth of the room. So many bodies, it was getting hard to breathe, and the chimney was due for a sweep.

"I only did what I could," Fili said, though she was pleased.

"More than I've ever done." Olivier stroked the fuzz of his mustache bashfully. "My master, he—he's not like Gaspard, here. Bit of a loyalist."

Maître Gaspard's smug look only made Fili blush harder. "Well, we're glad to have you, lad. Be sure you keep your head down. Don't want to give us all away." Then he patted Olivier on the shoulder and went to speak with a Finger Fili didn't recognize.

"Was it very frightening?" Olivier asked.

Fili wanted to tell him everything. How the queen had gasped. How hot her blood was, how afraid Fili was that she would miss, how she'd run so fast she thought her heart would burst, how more than anything, she'd wanted to tell the queen *she was sorry* as the blade went in.

She smiled instead, and said, "A bit. You find your courage, though."

Olivier was handsome when he blushed, and she liked the gentle way he held his cup of wine and the way his pale curls tumbled over his forehead. She liked his mustache.

Above them, Brother Michel still spoke. He had a way of tugging the mood of the room, from vigorous to relaxed, suspenseful to excited. Fili remembered the first time she'd fallen under his sway, even as she fell under it now.

Now he was calling for the next wave of volunteers in his next action.

"What will we do?" someone called.

Brother Michel shook his head. "We wait and see, my friends. I have eyes and ears within the palace walls, and we'll decide what comes next. In the meantime, we take steps to protect each other from the Withering, because the queen will not!"

The Withering. A sliver of fear wormed its way into Fili like a splinter under the nail. So many different people here, from almost every level of Chaisien society. Laborers and scholars, craftsmen and farmers in from outside the walls, even a few straight-backed types that might have been gendarmes out of uniform. Did one of them have it? Would she get it next? She had never lived through a plague year, but her mother and father had spoken of it in hushed voices, tight, grief-ridden eyes.

How could they bring revolution to Balladaire with the Withering cutting them down?

Michel made the call for volunteers again, and Olivier grinned at Fili as he raised his hand, waiting for Velte to come and take down his name in her shorthand. Though Fili smiled back, her cheeks warm and her belly fluttering, she couldn't help hearing Ghadin's voice in her mind:

Revolution is not a game.

CHAPTER 7

A WHORE

The afternoon Touraine returned to the palace, she knew she would have to face the two confrontations she'd avoided by leaving for the barracks immediately. She practically tiptoed to Aranen's rooms and knocked timidly when she arrived. She forced herself not to shift her weight from foot to foot while she waited. Instead, she clasped her hands at ease behind her back, legs wide.

"Aranen?"

Nothing. Maybe the infirmary. Touraine should have checked there first. She was about to turn when she heard a scratching inside, then muffled angry muttering before the door swung open. Aranen din Djasha, the high priestess of Qazāl whose act of faith had saved her country and gotten her exiled, who'd lost her faith and her magic with the death of her wife, raked Touraine up and down with disapproval.

"Are you lost?"

Touraine cleared the itch in her throat. "I deserve that."

"Hmph." Aranen rolled her eyes and swept into her rooms. Her Qazāli robes billowed after her in brilliant shades of green. "Come in, then."

A fire burning high in the fireplace warmed the room. Touraine couldn't help flinching. She wasn't entirely over almost burning alive a few weeks ago. On the low table in the anteroom, a sketch spread across multiple pieces of paper. Aranen knelt on a cushion beside it. A neat pile of notes in a tight, cramped hand was stacked beside the sketches. Touraine followed the branching lines, curving and splitting down the pages. It was...a tree?

"I never knew you were an artist," she said hesitantly.

"I'm not. I'm a doctor." Aranen straightened the papers so they aligned, and Touraine looked again.

If she tilted her head, let the splitting branches turn into roots instead...the roots followed a pattern, splitting into main lines that looked like—

"Fingers." Touraine knelt and brushed one of the sections with her own fingertips.

"A hand, yes. A leg. A foot." Aranen tapped another series of sketches. "I needed a diagram of the human nerves, and I didn't want to write in my own books."

"What for?"

"Many things. To help your friend the marquise for one. More importantly, I need to study the Withering. I've never seen it, and it's hard to get firsthand accounts."

Touraine frowned. "If you need Evrard or Ghislaine to talk to you, we can make them."

"It's hard enough to do this without their hostility. I don't need you to throw around your *queen's* weight. Or your own. Prince-General." The barb came with a wry smile, but it was no less sharp.

"I'm sorry. I should have come sooner."

"You should have. When is the wedding?"

"Winter festival. A month from now." Touraine kept her gaze trained on the illustrations in front of her. Her heart beat hard in her chest.

"That's not enough time to get a ship to El-Wast and back with a response. The council is going to bicker. They might even say no." Aranen looked up from the traceries of body and limb. Her golden eyes were steady and probing. "Would you walk away from her, then?"

"They're the ones who told me to use her." Touraine bristled. "To get what we needed however I could. I have."

Aranen cocked her eyebrow, a sad little half smile curving her lips. "You haven't slept in your own bed in days." She held up a finger before Touraine could try to pull some excuse out of her ass, which was good, because she had none. "I don't begrudge you whatever comfort you find. I've already given you my warnings."

Touraine had not forgotten. Luca was a flame with an insatiable hunger. She would devour everything, even Touraine, to get what she wanted.

What will you have to become, to withstand that heat?

The priestess closed her eyes then and shook her head, upset and bewildered. "But her *general*? You would take the Blood General's place?"

"I won't be another Cantic, I swear to you." And yet, she could still feel the slickness of Taurvide's blood on the handle of the whip. That dark thrill. But that wasn't her *becoming* Cantic. It was a blow *against* her, against all the Balladairan officers had done to the Sands. "Luca needs someone she trusts in command. I can do good."

"Slaughter?"

"Protection. And I can change things—open the ranks to the Qazāli. Infantry, cavalry, officers. Everything the Sands never could do, and with real pay."

Aranen tilted her head. "And that's progress to you, is it?"

Touraine frowned. "Isn't it?"

"And if she tells you to lead an army against us?"

"I would *never*. That's the point of marrying her—"

"Aranen!" Ghadin sang through the inner door joining Aranen's rooms to Touraine's—and thus, to Ghadin's.

Touraine flinched. Ghadin came in wearing Qazāli training clothes with the sleeveless shirt, draped in a blanket that she held closed around her.

The girl's face fell when she noticed Touraine. "Oh. It's you. I thought you'd never crawl out of the queen's—"

"Ghadin!" Aranen said sharply. "Show respect."

Ghadin and Touraine both jumped, then Ghadin jutted her jaw. "Why should I?" She cradled her arm close to her side in its sling as she sat. After Touraine's fumbling healing skills blossomed, it had been too late to do anything for Ghadin's arm but numb the pain.

There was more than one reason she'd avoided these rooms of late.

"Ghadin. How are you?"

"I thought we were leaving."

"No. I'm not, anyway. I take it you've heard."

Ghadin sucked her teeth. Nothing could have hardened Touraine against the disgust in Ghadin's face. "So you're a liar, too."

Touraine looked down at the table. Sky above, she was shit at this. Aranen's papers were suddenly very interesting. She curled the edge of one with her thumb.

"Luca keeps Qazāl—and the Qazāli in Balladaire—safe. We have to support—" No, she had to own at least some of the truth. "I *want* to support her. She's not the monster you think she is. She brought you back to us, remember?"

Luca had almost given up her crown to do so. Touraine's knees had nearly buckled when Luca showed up with Ghadin on a litter behind her. Fury and gratitude. Touraine had felt so helpless, and Luca appeared out of nowhere, achieving what Touraine never could have. She'd been jealous of Luca's power. She hadn't realized how much of Luca's power was hers. Ghadin certainly wouldn't understand.

"It's her fault I was there in the first place," Ghadin spat.

"I never asked you to come," Touraine snapped. "*You* wanted to follow me to Balladaire. I told you to stay. Was this the chevalier's adventure you thought it would be?" She included Aranen. "I knew this was a bad idea before we even set sail."

"I didn't want to be a chevalier!" Ghadin shouted back. "I *wanted* to be like the mulāzim who saved my city, but it turns out she's a… a whore for the Cripple Queen and the Balladairans who ruined our home!"

Touraine went still, still as she would under the rain of the whip's lash, trying not to show how deep each blow scored. Ghadin breathed heavily as she waited for a reaction, to see how far her own power reached. She was so young, just now testing the pressure she could exert on the world. Even Aranen was too shocked to rebuke her this time.

Touraine took a deep breath to steady her abrupt dizziness, to quell the anger in her gut. The anger leaked out anylight—she was out of the practice of bottling herself up.

"Don't ever call her that again."

A flush tinted Ghadin's pale brown cheeks. She knew she'd gone too far, but she only tightened her mouth and scowled harder. They sat like that, locked in a silent battle.

She was a child.

It didn't mean she was wrong.

It doesn't mean she's right.

Without another word, Ghadin spun on her heel and slammed the door between them.

Touraine pinched away the sting in her eyes. Aranen let her sit in the silence until the burning in her chest subsided enough for her to speak.

"Where did she get a mouth like that?"

"Not from me, I promise you."

"How do I make her understand, Aranen din?"

"Deep down, I think she does. But things are still very rigid to her. She grew up with a very different image of Balladaire than you. Luca is the living symbol of that Balladaire."

"Oh, they're the same Balladaire. Luca is all of it." And here Touraine was, thinking warmly of the way Luca's bare back felt against her cheek. "She also came here with a very different image of me."

"Our heroes rarely live up to our standards."

"You did." Touraine gave Aranen a wry, weary smile.

Aranen snorted. "Do you know how many people I let down when I touched Shāl's killing magic? And Ghadin has made no secret that she finds me, the slayer of the Blood General, insufferably dull." She clicked her tongue. "Heroes are best at a distance. Let them guide your path like stars, but don't try to touch them."

Touraine studied the priestess. Despite Aranen's impeccable posture, exhaustion sloped her shoulders. She had lost her wife to Balladaire—to Luca. Luca had imprisoned her, attempted to steal the magic of her god.

"Do you agree with Ghadin?"

Aranen's expression softened, as she understood what Touraine needed from her.

"Marry her, Touraine. At best, she truly will be that much more likely to honor the treaties we make. At worst, she goes back on her word and we can go back on ours. I believe most of the council will consider this a fair trade."

"It won't be the first time I disappoint Jaghotai." Touraine laughed to dispel the ache, but it only made the hurt worse.

"I'll write them. They won't get a better opportunity than this. Even if this weren't *political*..." Aranen stared pointedly across the table. "You're a grown woman. You can make your own mistakes, and this, at least, will do a far sight less damage than other things I've seen you do."

Touraine gave her a flat look. "You're too generous, Aranen din."

Aranen smiled broad and genuine, enough to smooth out the constant grief she wore. "What else?"

Touraine blushed. She did have another question, but the thought of asking made her stomach swoop with embarrassing giddiness. She held her hands in her lap, popping the knuckles joint by joint.

Instead, she asked, "What about Djasha's friend Roland? Can I speak to him? He'd be a good ally to have, especially if he can put a word in to his abbey."

Aranen was clicking her tongue *no* before Touraine even finished. "He left some time ago. He said he needed time for 'repenting and contemplation.'"

She trailed off with a faraway look, like she would have liked to spend some time repenting and contemplating herself. Still, Touraine couldn't make herself get up. If she was going to marry Luca, she wanted to do it right.

"Aranen, can I ask you something?"

Aranen was alert, scanning Touraine's body. "About the magic? Has something changed?"

Touraine knew what she feared—the same disease that had taken Djasha. Aranen and Djasha had believed it came from using Shāl's killing magic, but they didn't know for sure. It made the question even harder to ask.

"No, not magic. I wanted to know how you and Djasha were married?" Touraine hesitated. "I mean—how do you—" She blinked away, her face warm.

"Oh. The Shālan traditions." The look on Aranen's face was so tender Touraine couldn't bear it.

She found the edge of the paper again with her thumb and this time, she accidentally split it with her nail. She tucked her thumb in a fist. Started scraping the skin of her finger with the nail instead.

Aranen's hand covered hers. "You have a right to our traditions, Touraine. As much as any Shālan. It's only that I'm sorry. I wish you'd lived a life where you got to attend our weddings."

Touraine blinked rapidly to stave off another wave of burning in her eyes. She had never been to any wedding at all.

"What's a Shālan wedding like?"

Aranen smiled, her gaze distant again. "Noisy. So much music, dancing. Djasha and I couldn't hear each other for days afterward. I had to scream in her ear whenever we talked. Before she was sick, she was a beautiful dancer—so precise. I think that was the monks' fault. They sharpened her."

Touraine remembered the heady rush of Luca on her arm in the Qazāli dancing circle. The music in her ears, the rhythm in her blood. She'd never felt so free.

"There's also an officiant's component. It's necessary, if you want this to be a binding agreement in Qazāl." The seriousness of Aranen's tone brought Touraine out of her wistfulness. "If you're certain about this. If this is what you want."

Touraine held Aranen's gaze. "I am. It is." Her voice wavered only a little.

"Very well." Aranen stood and beckoned Touraine to her feet. Then she pulled Touraine into a hug. "I hope you find happiness with her. I truly do."

CHAPTER 8

THE TRUTH

The second confrontation seemed like it would go much more smoothly, at least at first. Touraine met Durfort in the salle at their usual training time. It helped them both to hold on to some sense of normalcy with the upheavals around them.

Durfort was already there, limbering up with vigorous calisthenics and stretching. She saluted Touraine when she entered, but finished the set of lunges she was making across the room. Touraine started her own stretches, trying to shake off Ghadin's fury and the anxieties Aranen had left her with. She rolled her shoulders and her neck, swept her arms in circles, squatted and rolled her ankles.

Durfort sauntered over. She clapped Touraine on the back. "Congratulations, Your Excellency. Or should I say, Your Highness?"

"I—" Touraine blew her breath out through blushing cheeks.

"I didn't take you for a nervous groom." Durfort smiled crookedly and shook Touraine's shoulder gently.

"I—I'm not."

"Liar."

"I'm not—"

"El-Qazāli. We're friends. We've fought beside each other—" They had not, exactly, fought beside each other, but Touraine would give Durfort credit that they *had* gone into danger together and Durfort had almost died for it—"plotted a coup together"—true—"and, among other things, we've spent hours in this salle together. All I ask is for you two to treat me like I have some sense in this thick skull of mine. Not a lot, mind you, but some."

There was a sharp edge to her humor, and her voice was almost a growl.

"You're angry with me." Touraine collected a training sword of her own from the racks.

"No," Durfort said tightly.

"Liar."

Durfort chuckled. "Touché."

"I'm not making any claim on her. You two can still…" Touraine waved her blade nebulously through the air between them. "Whatever it is you do."

Durfort's crooked smile widened. "You know very well what we do. How about a wager?" Bald challenge gleamed in her eye, a glimpse of a Durfort that Touraine had never met, appraising, even cruel.

Touraine hesitated. "For?"

"The first to ten touches, two-to-one ratio to you. If I win, you tell me a truth. If you win…" Durfort tilted her head from side to side. "Whatever you wish."

"What truth?" Touraine circled Durfort, holding her blade warily between them. Behind the challenge was a spark of light Touraine hadn't seen in weeks. Then it flickered away. She wanted to chase it. "Whatever I want?"

Durfort smiled and raised her blade in salute. "En garde, Your Highness."

The marquise settled into her fighting with an uncharacteristically grim expression, something beyond mere concentration. Touraine fumbled to get her parries up in time as Durfort came at her. Her feet almost caught on each other after a particularly clumsy dodge.

Durfort held back while Touraine righted herself.

"You're going easy on me," Touraine grumbled.

"And you're being reckless. Almost as if you can't wait to spill your secrets." Durfort twirled her sword in a useless but flashy series of loops.

"Do you want this truth of yours, or not?" Touraine lunged forward again. She scored a cheap point—Durfort was slow to get her blade in place after showing off.

Durfort's face darkened and she swore under her breath, shaking out her hand. "Six to seven. Again."

Seven times Durfort had touched her point or edge to Touraine's body, to Touraine's three. They weren't using the thin rapiers favored by most of the court; a long while ago, Durfort had decided it didn't suit Touraine. They fought with sideswords, delicate enough to look dashing on a noble's hip, and also good for cutting and stabbing, "If you insist on being coarse," Durfort had joked.

Another touch each and they were both sweating in their protective leathers. Touraine panted into the silence while Durfort inhaled smoothly through her nose. Her bare teeth were the only sign of her effort. Then another touch to Durfort.

The last touch happened too quickly for Touraine to stop herself. She aimed a thrust at Durfort's torso, an obvious blow but the best way to get Durfort to change positions. It should have been an easy parry. Durfort's hand shook, though, and the slight shake became an uncontrollable tremor and Touraine's blade sailed home unimpeded, right into the left side of Durfort's chest.

Durfort grunted in pain as her sword clattered to the ground. Her other hand went to her chest and she dropped to a knee.

"Fuck," she growled, staring at her shaking hand.

Touraine knelt beside her, one hand on her back. "Shit. I'm sorry. Is it bad?"

Durfort jerked away, turning her head as she grimaced. "I'm fine."

Touraine reached for her. "Let me look—"

"I'm fine!" Durfort yanked the hand out of Touraine's grasp and cradled it to her chest.

For a moment, they knelt on the floor in the salle, sweat pressing their hair to their faces, their strained breathing the only sound.

"It's getting worse?" Touraine asked softly.

Durfort hung her head. Slowly, she held her hand up. The tremors had stopped, for now.

The painful spasms and twitching had come after Durfort's second poisoning. Aranen said the toxin attacked the nerves, things that sent signals from the brain to the rest of the body, especially for movement and sensation. Touraine had never heard of this, and so, Aranen said, it was small wonder that Touraine's healing didn't quite repair all the damage.

"I'll never be able to duel again."

"Don't." Touraine pulled Durfort up sternly by the shoulder.

Durfort dashed away her tears with the back of her hand. "What good is a melancholy noble duelist? I can see it now! The fainting ladies, the swooning lords." She laughed bitterly. "I killed my favorite student, Luca is going to marry you, my people are dying of the plague, and I can't do anything about any of it. Especially not like this."

Touraine reached for Durfort's hand again, and this time, Durfort let her take it. It was warm, damp from sweating against the grip of her hilt. Hard calluses lined her palm.

"I'm sorry," Touraine said.

Durfort ran her thumb over Touraine's knuckles, staring at them as she shook her head. "It's not your fault. Sky above, look at me. I know that I should be dead now." She looked back up at Touraine. "I would be, without you. I'm not ungrateful."

Her eyes flicked down to Touraine's lips and she leaned closer. Her breath was warm against Touraine's face. Her cologne was strong, mingled with the clean smell of exertion. Touraine was drawn to her, and wondered how much of it was a desire to fix what she had broken—Durfort's feelings—Durfort with Luca—their easy friendship. Closing the space between them wouldn't make this less complicated, though. Like Durfort's damaged nerves, this tangle wouldn't be so easy to heal.

In a rough voice, Touraine asked, "Would you rather it were you?"

Durfort's jaw tightened. They were so close Touraine felt the tension in the rest of Durfort's body.

"Is that the truth you want?"

"Just tell me."

Durfort exhaled long through her nose. "I told you before. I'm only some of what she needs. There's sense in linking Balladaire with Qazāl. It's not as if she has to marry me to call the Durfort banner. When I leave—"

Touraine startled, Durfort's mesmerizing hold on her shifting. "You're leaving?"

"My people are dying," she said. "I'm going to them."

"But you can't, you'll—"

"Tchut. Luca already said everything and more." She reached up and brushed a thumb across Touraine's chin. "What truth do you want from me?"

Touraine shivered at the touch, or maybe at the weight of the words.

"Tell me what I need to know to be good for her."

Durfort's eyes widened. "What I really think?"

"Yes." Doubt made Touraine's voice shake.

"You hold back. Luca is too blinded by these dazzling eyes to see it, but I do." Durfort's hand still brushed her chin. "Is this another game for your council?"

"Of course it is." Touraine rolled her eyes, but her throat was thick. "All of it is a game for the councils and the courts."

Durfort's fingers slid from Touraine's cheek to grip her arm. A tremor echoed through. "Lie to everyone else, Touraine. Lie to the councils and the courts. But don't lie to yourself. Don't lie to her. She needs you to be *with* her, and she is *the queen*."

Touraine frowned down at Durfort's grip. "I know she is—"

Durfort shook her head. "No, you don't. I know how you see us. The nobility. You balk at the very idea of us. Of the crown. I heard what happened with Colonel Taurvide. You don't have the first idea what something like that means, what it will mean to Luca."

"He deserved it," Touraine growled. "You don't know what he did to me, what all of them did—"

"No. I don't know. But you don't know the people he knows, you don't know how he'll pull generations of debts just to hurt you, and by hurting you, hurt Luca. *You* humiliated him, but he'll make *her* pay the price. And if she pays, we all pay."

Touraine felt abashed and more than a little irritated. "That's not what I meant to do. I told her I would help and I will. I know I wasn't raised to it, but it doesn't mean I can't learn to manipulate and lie like the rest of you."

"There, you see? You don't think much of us at all, but you're about to become one of us. You can't fight us at the same time." Durfort's grip on her arm relaxed and she stroked it once, lingering on the seam over Touraine's muscled shoulder. "I'm not saying you're unfit. I'm saying that you need to commit. Figure yourself out, for Luca's sake."

The words left Touraine speechless and staring into the other woman's dark eyes. No matter how Durfort paraded in her mask as the court dandy, she'd cut Touraine to ribbons, peeling apart every secret guilt and fear she'd tried to hide.

After a long silence, Durfort squeezed her shoulder. "You did ask."

"And you?" Touraine asked. "You were going to win. What truth did you want?"

Durfort chewed her lip thoughtfully. "No claim on her? None at all?"

Touraine inhaled deep and held it. The truth? "I don't want to take her from you. But I won't lie to you and say none."

Gingerly, Durfort stood, pulling Touraine up, and then, as elegantly as ever, she bowed over their clasped hands. A single twitch pulled her face and Touraine caught disgust before Durfort smoothed it away again. Durfort pressed her lips to Touraine's knuckles and lingered.

"Thank you for your honesty, Your Highness. A pleasure, as always. Let me know when you'd like to collect your real winnings."

Swift as that, Durfort's court mask was up again. She winked and swaggered away.

CHAPTER 9

BARED FANGS

Everything *should* have been good. Everything *should* have been fine. But here Pruett was, freezing on the Shāl-damned wall of Samra', fighting the urge to scream into the night, to match the birds' caws or howl like the sky-falling dogs in the back of her head.

Touraine was choosing Balladaire. Balladaire over she. Days later and Pruett couldn't stop gnawing it like a fucking hyena.

Touraine didn't have the balls to say it plain in the letter, but Pruett could read it clear as day.

She could be telling the truth, a voice—a human voice—countered in her mind. *Or maybe she didn't dare confess anything in a letter that might be intercepted.*

Logical. Reasonable. But Pruett knew in her gut something was missing from that letter, and she had a feeling it was all to do with the new *queen.*

"Argh!" She slapped her palms on the cold stone and they bounced back up, stinging.

"Shall I come back another time?" a woman asked, speaking Balladairan with a heavy Taargen accent.

Pruett whipped around, pulling her pistol from the harness strapped across her chest, ready to use it as a bludgeon if she had to. A short, stocky woman stood before Pruett in a cloak of black feathers.

"Who the fuck are you?" Pruett tried to cover the tremor of fear in her voice. The cut of the woman's clothing, the animal mantle, the blond hair, half-shaved—Pruett had never been so pissed to be right in her life.

And to be caught alone, without Kiras or Noé nearby. She reached out for Sevroush and found him hunting in the distance. He was safe, at least. She winced at the sharp throb seeking him gave her.

"Well?" Pruett snapped.

The woman held out her empty hands and stepped closer. "My name is Lor. I come as a friend."

Pruett spat on the stones between them. "I can tell you one thing for sure, *Lor*, and it's that I haven't got a single Taargen friend. If I did, odds are even I'd toss her over this wall here."

Lor tilted her head as she considered the considerable drop. "An acquaintance, then, with an invitation of friendship. Or something more to your taste."

"An invitation of friendship. That's why you've been sneaking into my city and sucking out the souls of my people?"

"You worship the god as our southern cousins do. The Many-Legged."

The casual statement hit Pruett like a sack of red-clay brick. The bear god. The god of the Many-Legged. The fucking god of whatever was happening to her, the fucking *noise* in her head. She had never connected the two gods of beasts into one. How did the woman even know?

"Can't say I find much use for gods." Pruett tried to sound nonchalant, but her voice was high and strangled.

She could *do that* to people. She wanted to be sick.

Lor gave a small smile. "Like your old masters, are you?" She looked to the sky as if searching for something herself. Could she sense Sevroush, too?

"They're not my masters."

"They weren't just masters, true. And they never should have used you as fodder against us." Lor bowed over her hand against her chest. "I am sorry for the pain we caused you. When we realized you were conscripted against us, we were horrified."

Pruett studied Lor warily. Pretty words were cheap coin; sincerity could be faked. But it was a sincerer apology for what happened to the Sands during the Taargen Wars than any princess had given.

"Did you fight in them?" Pruett asked.

"I was too young. I lost a sister, though, and my brother was wounded."

"Not that I was all that old myself." Pruett folded her arms across her chest, holding tight to her pistol. "What do you want, *friend* Lor? It's cold and I don't have a fancy feather cloak."

A beautiful cloak it was, the feathers black as pitch until they caught the moonlight and shone with an oil-slick iridescence. Maybe it was a trick of the light, but Lor's eyes looked completely black, too.

"We share more than a god, Lord of Masridān. We have a common enemy. My queen would welcome you if you joined us, cousin."

"Lord of Masridān?" Pruett's laugh echoed down the wall. She couldn't say she *didn't* like the sound of it. "What do you want, then? My help fighting Balladaire this time? A flip of the mirror?"

"Yes—but we will not use you like the Balladairans did. You have the Bear Queen's word. We would take an army, though, what soldiers you can spare. An allied army. Not cannon fodder."

"Masridān is only recently liberated from Balladaire." Pruett hesitated over how much to reveal to the woman. "I don't have so many soldiers I'm willing to waste them."

Wind ruffled the feathers about Lor's face. "We understand. Our most important goal is to make sure we won't receive a knife at our back when we turn to her, but my queen doesn't offer you nothing in exchange for your aid or your abstention."

Pruett scowled at Lor. "What could I possibly want from her?"

"Vengeance. In return, we might also ask for information based on your history with Balladaire. And Shālan magic—your healers and Eaters would be invaluable."

"You know about the Eaters?" Pruett said stiffly. The Qazāli's healing magic had been a secret locked up tighter than an ant's asshole, and the killing magic tighter still.

"Unlike Balladaire, we in Taargen are not afraid of the gifts of other gods and maintain records, even schools of study. We would encourage cooperation and sharing between us. We sent word seeking an alliance with the Qazāli, as well, but perhaps your friendship could smooth that passage?"

Pruett snorted. Her "friendship" wouldn't smooth anything for anyone, especially not with the Jackal. She leaned her forearms over the stone, the cold rock seeping through her coat and into her bones. Only people she'd ever hated more than the Balladairans were the Taargens. She and the Sands hadn't survived the Taargen War without a good sense of how sky-falling brutal the bearfuckers were. And yet...it wasn't them that kept the Sands like trained monkeys with no purpose but to fight and die. They might have, if they'd gotten the toehold in the Shālan Empire before Balladaire did, but they hadn't.

Besides, Pruett found herself with a few problems the Taargens might help her solve. Problems in the form of Masridāni cities still under Balladairan control.

Lor waited for Pruett to come to the right conclusion. She almost reminded Pruett of that insufferable princess—*queen*—who had Touraine's fucking balls in a vise. Except Lor's carefully neutral expression was more patience than arrogance.

"Why now?" Pruett tossed over her shoulder. "Didn't we send you scurrying home with your tails between your legs?"

Lor's patient expression went cold but her voice held steady. "Balladaire is weak right now, weaker than it has been in decades. There won't be a better time to strike."

Pruett waited for her to elaborate.

"Surely you know of the new queen."

"Aye. Not enough to get me to go lose a war."

"Her allies are few and her rise to power turbulent. They say she was almost assassinated by commoners. Balladaire also has no more colonial conscripts if they cannot call on Masridān for aid. That cuts down their fighting force considerably," Lor said pointedly. "And... you know of the plague they call the Withering?"

Pruett froze, a sick writhing in her stomach. "What about it?"

"There have been cases of it in western Balladaire, and all our reports say it's spreading."

Even now, despite everything, Pruett's first thought was worry for Touraine. Then the other implications caught up to her—Touraine would definitely not be safe if Pruett took a war to her doorstep. War was one thing, though; sickness, undiscriminating, immune to bullet and bayonet—that was another.

Lor was right. There would never be a better time.

"What else?" Pruett asked, before she could stop herself. "If we help. What else do we get?"

Taking the question as an invitation, Lor came to stand beside Pruett. She rested her hands on the stone and pressed herself straight as she gazed out across the cold desert, to the south where Balladaire's other garrisons remained. Her nails were sharply pointed.

"Allies fight for one another. We have goods you might enjoy, as well, at preferential trade percentages. And for you . . ." Lor studied her carefully. "Lessons." Lor nudged her cloak, and the feathered mantle caught the starlight again.

The barbs of the feathers brushed Pruett's shoulder, and she felt the individual barbules pull apart and fall back into place like running fingers through short hair. The knot in the back of her mind thrummed with something else beyond the usual headache. She understood what Lor was offering, repulsed by the power and enthralled at the same time.

Pruett turned her back on the desert and leaned her hip against the stone, arms crossed, the better to size Lor up. She very carefully stayed out of reach of the feathers.

"We could use fighters," she said. "Might be you can get a head start on your campaign against Balladaire by helping us finish ours."

"Oh?"

"Aye." Pruett hooked a thumb south. "I won't leave if the other Balladairan garrisons can march on us. Nafoura is the nearest threat." Nafoura was the next proper city south of Samra' and, after Samra', had the most Balladairan soldiers.

"And if Nafoura is neutralized . . . you will."

"Might be we will. It'll also keep them from coming up on your asses. Win-win for you."

"I see."

"I won't make any promises until I've spoken with the rest of my people. You'll have an answer soon."

"Very soon. In a day. If I may borrow a horse?" At Pruett's narrowed eyes, she added, "It will spare one of your people. I'll leave a bird you can contact me by."

Kiras was still awake when Pruett entered the bedroom they shared. She was dressed in a dark robe, lying on the bed with one knee up, staring at the ceiling. Her gold bracelets gleamed in the light of the single candle. She sat up immediately.

"What's wrong?" Kiras's deep voice was husky with something Pruett couldn't trace.

Pruett didn't answer. She unbuckled her belt, then her pistol harness, and shucked it to the floor, followed by her trousers. She untied the neck of her shirt and swept it over her head. By the time she reached Kiras, the other woman had swung her legs over the edge of the bed and was reaching for her.

"What happened?" Concern, now.

Pruett dragged her hand through her own hair, and it snagged in the tangled curls. "I need to do something with this. Fucking rat's nest."

Kiras curled around her, eased some of the tangles out with her fingers. "It's wild."

"Wild?" Pruett laughed shortly.

Kiras, almost shyly: "I like you wild."

Pruett answered with a kiss, wet and open-mouthed, and Kiras didn't speak again. Instead, Kiras bit Pruett's lip until she gasped, tasting blood. She dug her claws into Kiras's back in response. They crashed into the bed, animal and hunger both. This was how they were. She snarled as Kiras held her down, howled into the pillows at the dig of Kiras's teeth in the back of her shoulder. When Pruett came, she sagged into the bed languidly, her skin stinging from the marks Kiras had left.

Heat and wet, metal and musk, tongue and claw—all of it and it still wasn't enough.

Kiras collapsed to the side of her and slipped an arm around Pruett's naked waist. The bed was soft beneath her, the blankets of the finest woven cotton, a specialty of Masridān. No wonder Yoroub had been so keen to hold on to it all.

"Pruett?" Kiras nuzzled into her ear.

Pruett didn't answer except to cover Kiras's hand with her own.

"Is it the people in the hospital?"

Pruett still didn't answer, willing Kiras not to ask more, not to push further. There were some doors she didn't want to open to the other woman. They had never talked much about past lovers, especially not about Touraine. It was just them and this desperate, fervent *thing* that happened whenever they were alone together. If Pruett cracked herself open even a little, anything at all could spill out. So she didn't.

Kiras understood. She *had* to. She didn't push. But her grip on Pruett slackened, and somehow, Pruett felt even lonelier, a thick lump forming in her throat.

"I was right," she whispered. "It is Taargens. They want us to join them against Balladaire. They're going to war."

Kiras's gasp was a swelling tide against Pruett's back. "And?"

Pruett sighed.

Until recently, she'd seen herself as careful and even-keeled. Especially next to Touraine and her impulses or Tibeau and his passions. She'd kept them both balanced. Tempered them. She'd had a lifetime of putting any grudge against the Balladairan captains and blackcoats behind her and getting on with the lot she had. The orders, the beatings, the war, the death. A lifetime accepting that fucking lot. While Tibeau daydreamed rebellion and Touraine danced for them all, Pruett had kept quiet and brined herself bitter like a fucking olive, because that was better than execution.

"I'm going to bring it up with the others at breakfast."

Kiras stroked Pruett's hip. "What do you want to do?"

To remind Touraine who she really owed her loyalty. Who her first and truest family was.

"Balladaire is weak." Pruett stole Lor's words. "There won't be a better time."

Kiras was silent for a moment, then she said, "If the others agree?"

"Then I'll send Unwah south with the Taargens to deal with Nafoura. Noé will stay here. Armande will go with some army or another, as she likes."

"And me?" There was something uncertain in Kiras's voice, something guarded in her sudden rigidity against Pruett. "What task do you have for me, Qā'id?"

Pruett remembered the odd distress in the woman's face from earlier. She turned into Kiras, their naked legs a-tangle. She liked the caress in the way Kiras called her "commander" in Shālan. The other woman's eyes glowed with a different kind of hunger, a need Pruett wasn't prepared for.

"Kiras."

At the sharpness in Pruett's tone, Kiras pushed onto an elbow. "Qā'id." No more caress. Better.

"Don't get attached. This isn't what you think it is. I don't want—that."

Kiras's steady breaths stopped.

Pruett wanted it to be a lie. In truth, it was herself she was warning.

"You're a good second." She stared down into the space between their bodies. "I'd like you to come with me. We can still…but don't expect anything more."

"Qā'id." Kiras's voice was so soft Pruett almost didn't hear the heartbreak. "Should I leave now?"

"In the morning will be fine. Get some rest."

CHAPTER 10

CONSORTS

Durfort's face fell the second Touraine entered the stables. "What are you doing here?"

Touraine cocked an eyebrow. "No *How may I try to get into your pants today, Your Highness?* You wound me." Touraine affected the clipped speech of the Chaisien nobility and pressed a hand against her forehead. It didn't hide the irritation curling her lip, though. She'd asked Luca to brief Durfort ahead of time because she *knew*—

"She won't thank you for it, sending me after her like a nursemaid," Touraine had told Luca when she'd asked Touraine to go with Durfort to Carleis, halfway between La Chaise and Premont.

"I don't care if she thanks me for it." Luca had been frantic, pacing about her study, one hand knotted in her hair in frustration.

The Withering had hit La Chaise. Commander Perrot had brought the news from the gendarmerie in the city, and it felt like the world had overturned. Luca's tasks were grim and interminable: buying food from every merchant to redistribute it; enlisting Aranen and Romanie, the palace physician, to set up a tent to nurse the ill; summoning every woodcutter for timber to start the never-ending pyres burning; calming the nobles who couldn't decide whether to flee the city or lock themselves in the palace; and every day a new calamity occurred.

"I thought I would have more time," Luca had whispered, covering her eyes with her hands.

Now, days later, Durfort scowled down at Touraine from her horse.

He was as handsome and well-groomed as his master, a reddish color with a gleaming black mane and shadowy socks. His polished leather saddle was worked with grape vines.

"Did she send you?"

Touraine glared right back before taking Cendre's reins from a stablehand. The teams for the wagons were already harnessed and servants were loading in the last baskets and barrels.

They were escorting food to the refugees.

"Does it matter?" Touraine asked.

"It does."

"Aye, she sent me. Of course she did."

"Does she not think me capable?"

"You would know better than me."

"You're rather closer to her than I am."

"Is that my fault?"

Sabine worked her jaw. "If she doesn't even think I can do *this* on my own, then there truly is no point in staying."

Touraine sighed in exasperation as she mounted. "I don't know what she thinks, Durfort. This is still your mission. I told her how you'd see it, and she told me she wanted a report. If you want to give her the report so badly, maybe you should stick around instead of running off at the first sign of trouble in La Chaise."

Durfort's gloved hand clenched hard around her reins, not in a spasm, Touraine was almost certain, but in fury. Durfort deserved it; Touraine hadn't done anything but follow orders. Instead of a retort, Durfort huffed from her nose and shook her head, almost exactly like her horse, then clicked her tongue and wheeled him away.

Riding side by side, they both led the column out of the city. With their plague scarves about their faces, they kept their eyes forward except to occasionally flick glances around the city—never to look at each other. The awkwardness stretched as they passed the middle wall separating the arts quarters and the gardens from the marketing districts, and then the duty wall where the merchants declared their goods for taxes. The layers of La Chaise reminded Touraine of El-Wast. The same human impulse to expand and to grow, to defend and pull back, driving them all no matter what god they kept or didn't.

The city was eerily quiet.

At the city gates, the guards looked sharply at those coming into La Chaise, but they waved the wagons through with a salute for the queen's crest.

Outside of the city proper, Touraine felt a sudden openness, as if she'd stepped out from beneath a shadow. She tried again.

"How long is the journey to Durfort?"

"Long."

Touraine stared at Durfort until she felt the weight of Touraine's annoyance. Cendre shied, upset by the shift in Touraine's weight.

Durfort grabbed the horn of Touraine's saddle as she righted herself. She pursed her mouth, unimpressed.

"It's far. Beyond Béson. Two weeks or so by carriage, depending on whether or not my mother is home."

"Is your mother home now?"

"She is."

"But you're going by horse."

"Yes. I'd like to arrive sooner rather than later. Circumstances as they are."

Circumstances as they are.

That dampened the mood even more, and Touraine decided it was easier to be quiet than to try to coax conversation out of a cranky Durfort, so she passed the day's ride trying not to let her mind spin on the end of the journey. She missed the marquise's usual chatter, though, and the loneliness burned in her chest. Outside of Luca and maybe Perrot, Durfort was her only friend in the palace. She understood now how Luca must feel.

By the time they reached the inn that was their halfway mark, with twilight purpling the sky and the setting sun stealing with it the last of the warmth, Touraine and Sabine were even more sullen and irritable than when they'd started.

As they both dismounted, the lieutenant of their escort squad approached. He stopped in front of Touraine and saluted.

"General, where should we—euh—the innkeep says she hasn't enough space to quarter us all; she's short two rooms. Shall I draw lots to see who sleeps outside?"

Touraine calculated quickly.

"Yes," Durfort said, at the same time Touraine said, "No."

A flush rose in Durfort's cheeks, but Touraine was too pissed to cede ground.

"Rotate the guard on the wagons overnight. Double bunk everyone else, triple if you need. Lord Durfort and I will share."

The lieutenant flicked an anxious gaze between them, a mouse caught between two tomcats.

"As the general said." Durfort narrowed her eyes at Touraine.

"Yes, General. Yes, Your Grace." He saluted again.

"Still my mission, is it, *General*?" Without waiting for Touraine's response, Durfort led her horse to the stables.

Touraine waited until Durfort was gone before making her own way in, and after handing Cendre off to one of the stablehands, she went inside. The inn was full and warm, and the smell of bread and roasting meat made her stomach growl. It wasn't hard to see the impact of rumor, though. The conversations between the patrons were subdued, and when they saw the soldiers, they were wary instead of curious. The food, when it came, was disappointing. The slice of bread was small and tasted more of dust than grain, and the meat was tough. Durfort was not in the common room.

Touraine found her in the small room they were meant to share. She sat on the bed in her stockings with her shirtsleeves rolled up, leaning against the wooden headboard with her knees tucked up against her chest. She glanced up when Touraine entered, but looked away just as quickly.

"Have you eaten?" Touraine asked.

"No. I wanted quiet."

"I'll go."

"Stay. It's your room, too. Sir." Durfort knuckled her forehead in mock salute.

Touraine tugged off her own coat and boots and climbed into the bed to sit beside Durfort. This close, she could see a shining tear streak sparking in the candlelight. Durfort caught her staring and scrubbed her cheeks with a handkerchief. She didn't say anything else, though, so Touraine didn't, either. She dug her finger into the blankets as the day's silence thickened between them.

It wasn't that Touraine didn't want to talk about the ways she might have hurt Durfort or caused her bitterness—from the wedding, to Tiro's accidental death, to the botched healing—though it was that, too. It was that she didn't know how or where to start.

"Touraine?" Durfort turned and Touraine was aware, too aware, of how the movement ate the hair of space between them. Durfort's wide eyes shone as she stared at her. It reminded Touraine that her own eyes were not her own anymore. They were Shāl's. She started to look down, away, anywhere else, as Durfort brought her face closer and—

Durfort's lips landed messily on Touraine's cheek.

They froze.

Touraine's hand was between them, not pushing her away, but not letting her closer.

"Durfort, are you . . . drunk?"

Touraine heard Durfort swallow.

"I am regrettably, bogglingly sober. I've not touched a drop since Longest Night." Her voice grew softer, sadder. "Lost the taste for it."

"Is this about Luca, then?" Touraine asked. "Because I told you—"

"It's not about her." Durfort pulled back, thunking against the headboard. "Or maybe it is." She sighed, covering her face with her hand. "Can't I want you, too, a little?"

Durfort met Touraine's eyes and then jerked away again. Her lips were parted in a self-deprecating half smile. The seam where their thighs brushed burned white-hot. It was all Touraine could feel.

What would it be like, sharing Luca with this powerful, charismatic woman who controlled every room she walked into with charm and grace? Touraine was nothing compared to that. They were so different—and maybe that's why Luca wanted them both. Maybe that's why Touraine wanted Sabine, a little, too.

She put her hand on Durfort's leg, heard the woman's breath hitch, then hold. She dug her nails into Durfort's inner thigh and the muscle tensed, hard as rock.

They crashed together, clashing teeth, biting at lips. Durfort's low groan sent fire straight from Touraine's belly and between her legs. Touraine swung a leg over Durfort's hips so she was straddling her, her fingers sliding up the marquise's neck and into her hair.

Touraine felt an urgency to fix the damage she had done to their easy friendship in the last month. To go back in time, before the engagement, before the poisonings. Back to the simplicity of riding through the grounds or sparring in the salle. To fix the rift she'd caused between Durfort and Luca, too, so Durfort wouldn't leave them both to chase down duty and death in her marquisate.

Then, unbidden, Pruett's face intruded, twisted in her familiar sneer. *Another one?*

Touraine banished the voice of judgment by pressing harder into Durfort's hips and flicking open the buttons of her chemise. At first, Durfort responded, rising to meet her pressure, and Touraine made a pleased sound in her throat. Then there was only air at her lips.

Durfort's face was flushed, her breathing heavy. She regarded Touraine with lucid wariness.

"Does Luca know you—this?" Durfort breathed.

"I thought you said you two didn't answer to each other?" At the slight pressure from Durfort's fingers, Touraine said quickly, "She does know. We talked. If anything, I'd wager she set us up."

In Luca's office, after she'd given Touraine her instructions, Luca had asked Touraine straight out.

"Has anything happened between you?" Luca had asked.

"No," Touraine had said too quickly. "Not exactly."

Luca peered suspiciously into her face. "Not exactly."

"Nothing, really." She hadn't been able to meet Luca's eyes. "An awkward moment in the salle."

"Will it bother you if I don't give her up as a lover?" Luca asked carefully.

"No. Will it bother *you* if I have other lovers?" Touraine had shot back, and she'd seen the sullen pout flicker across Luca's face.

Then Luca had smiled wryly and said, "I suppose it depends on whom."

"Huh." In the cramped little room on the road to Carleis, Durfort closed her eyes. For a moment, Touraine thought she had hurt her, but for the slight smile. Maybe she still had.

"I think you're right." Durfort ran her hands up and down Touraine's thighs with a longing look. "A pity. She won't manipulate me into staying like this."

Touraine thumbed the edge of Durfort's collar. "She's not manipulating me."

"Maybe when I come back." With surprising strength, Durfort hoisted Touraine off her and back to the other side of the bed. Then she stood and adjusted the crotch of her trousers with a wink before leaving the room.

Touraine woke early in the morning to find Durfort sleeping on the floor.

CHAPTER 11

THE SPROUT

Though Touraine and Sabine hadn't said all they needed to say, the next day's ride was comfortable. The quiet was companionable, and if they were both too lost in their own worries, at least the tension was no longer hostile. The silences were broken by Durfort telling Touraine funny stories of previous times she'd made the journey to Durfort, and her antics in the vineyards, including once when she'd escaped from a woman's angry suitor by hiding in one of the stamping barrels.

Durfort sighed wistfully. "I think that batch was an especially good one. I might even still have a bottle in the cellars." Mischievously, she added, "I was very attentive to those vines."

"There's still time. After the Withering passes, you can make another. You wouldn't even have to hide from me." Touraine crooked a smile.

"Was that a joke? Did Touraine El-Qazāli make a joke?"

Touraine kicked at Durfort's leg, and Durfort deftly maneuvered her horse out of reach, beaming.

"I think I'll turn to a new venture. There's quite a market in cheese, and in the Beaux, there's a lovely network of caves. Did I ever tell you the time I took a girl there and we were chased by a mountain lion? I had to convince her the wet on my trousers was from falling into a spring."

So the journey went, until there came a call from one of the soldiers up ahead.

"A man off the side of the road, Your Grace, Your Excellency," the lieutenant said. "Asks if we have a spare moment to help him with a repair."

The man in question was older, with a close beard, wearing a coat in fair shape and thick woolen gloves. A quick once-over of the wagon showed several casks inside and the broken axle in question.

"Please, my lords," he said, bowing and knuckling his forehead as Touraine and Durfort rode up. "If you could give me the use of a few of your men. My own boy can't do it on his own, but I've a weak back. I can't bend nor carry much weight." He indicated the young blond man who came around the other side. He ducked his head and kept his eyes downcast.

"Where are you headed?" Touraine asked him. "We have urgent business in Carleis, but we can give you a ride there so you can get help, stay somewhere warm, and be on your way the next day."

He shook his head quickly. "I couldn't leave my wine. We left Carleis for La Chaise, there's plague in Premont, you know. It's all the way from Durfort. And brigands—I don't want to be caught out after dark."

Touraine glanced at Durfort, with a hint of a smile, but Durfort was studying the man and then his wine barrels intently. Of course she was. The sun was setting, and quickly. Touraine had planned on getting to Carleis before the night set in, too. They didn't bring anything for camping, and the brisk day promised to turn to colder night.

It wouldn't be so bad, to travel in the dark. They weren't that far from Carleis. Plus, it could do Luca good if the queen's soldiers got a reputation for helping old men with their broken-down wagons in the road.

It would be nice to help someone and see the good of it right then, in the moment, instead of some decade later.

"All right." Touraine turned to the lieutenant. "Quick as you can, though. I still want to get to Carleis tonight."

The soldiers got to work, and Touraine did her best to stay out of the way. She didn't know the first thing about changing an axle. She did keep an eye on the sun's descent, though. They would need torches, soon.

Durfort was frowning at the barrels that had been unloaded, and flicking glances back at the old man, who was hovering uselessly around the soldiers fixing his wagon.

"What's wrong?" Touraine crossed her arms over her chest.

"These barrels aren't marked. All the wine that comes out of Durfort has a maker's seal. And I know everyone who sells Durfort wine. So he's either lying to people to inflate his prices in the city, or he's smuggling something else in the barrels." Durfort's nose was snobbishly turned up.

Touraine rolled her eyes. "Oh, sky above."

"What? I have my pride, and so does the rest of Durfort. You can't call any old slosh Durfortien."

"As you like, Your Grace." But as Touraine turned to leave Durfort with her counterfeit wine, she felt a prickle of unease up the back of her neck. Durfort had woken up her soldier's instinct.

The sun was just down below the horizon, but the sky was still light enough to see the road stretching east, back to La Chaise, and west, to Carleis and Premont and beyond to Durfort. No late travelers, rushing to get to town before full dark like them. It was quiet. Not even the sound of nocturnal animals nearby, waking to hunt or feed or scurry from one den to another. A creek ran in a little gully down the left side of the road, trickling.

She called out, "More torches!"

A soldier leapt to obey, but there was a sharp report of musket fire and he fell, groaning and clutching at his stomach.

"Cover!" Touraine looked immediately for the old man and his boy and instead found them wrestling with the soldiers who'd been fixing their wagon. One blackcoat already lay dead, a bloody rip across her throat. Touraine swore. "Highwaymen! Defend the carts!"

More scattered musket fire from the gully. No one could be accurate in this light. She willed them to give it up as she ducked behind one of the royal wagons. No sign of Sabine anywhere, and Touraine hoped she'd hidden well.

The bandits did not give it up. They rushed up from the ditch, steps heavy in the grass, crunching on the dirt of the road, coming around the wagon—

Touraine stepped out, knife first, and let the first highwayman rush onto her blade. She spun into the next, barreling them to the ground.

"The Fingers—form—the fist!" the second highwayman wheezed in Touraine's face. Each word flecked her cheeks with blood. She tasted it on her lips and shuddered as they died beneath her.

Not highwaymen. Rebels.

Others took up the revolutionaries' cry, but there was also the gallop of approaching hoofbeats. *Shit.* She had a squad of only a dozen—if not less—and they were too scattered to face down a mounted assault, even if they were just farmers.

"Durfort!" Touraine scanned the darkness for the marquise.

Luca would never forgive her if she let something happen to Durfort. She would kill Touraine herself.

Before Touraine could start going from shadow to shadow, though, the horsemen arrived, bearing torches that glinted off gold buttons and showed off the red halves of their coats. Travers soldiers. *Of all the shit luck…*

"Travers, to me!" Touraine called. "Protect the queen's wagons!"

There was no need. At the approach of the soldiers, the revolutionaries disguised as bandits broke away from the skirmish and ran. The Travers soldiers gave chase, and Touraine felt a shred of pity for the rebels.

It took only a few moments in the darkness to take stock of the skirmish. The old man was wounded, but not fatally. The boy had killed the blackcoat, but then huddled to the ground in fear, so he, too, was captured. The rest were dead, or judging by the fierceness of the Travers soldiers, would be soon. Durfort also emerged, looking pale in the torchlight. There was blood on her duelist's steel. Bodies littered the road, and one empty barrel rolled back and forth on its side like a broken toy.

"Who is in charge here?" The Travers captain rode into the center of the mess.

This time, Durfort waved her hand in a little half flourish, letting Touraine take the lead.

"I am." Touraine looked up at the captain. "General Touraine El-Qazāli. We're on business for Queen Luca."

"I am, of course, the marquise Sabine LeMarchal de Durfort." Sabine bowed, wincing as she flourished a bloody leg.

"Yes, I've heard of you, Your Grace."

"Have you indeed? You hear that, General?" Sabine preened. "Only the best things, I hope? Durfort wine, perhaps? My skilled sword work?"

"Sword work? In a manner of speaking. Do you recall a Lady Giselle Domrémy?"

Durfort's face went pale in the torchlight, her smile fixed as if with pins. "Ah."

The captain smiled, too, a baring of teeth. "I'm her elder sister. Captain Jeanne Domrémy, at your service, my lords. From the Travers garrison outside of Carleis."

Touraine stifled a snicker as Durfort cleared her throat awkwardly.

"Well. Mm. Ahem. Do remember me well to her. I think of her fondly—"

"I'm sure you do. When you think of her at all." The captain turned to Touraine and saluted. "General? You must be— You were lately the Qazāli ambassador? May I ask why you're on the roads?" She gestured with one gloved hand to their own wagons.

While the Chaisien and Travers soldiers gathered the bodies of the two soldiers who'd fallen and the rest of the highwaymen, Touraine explained their mission and the intent to get to Carleis by nightfall. Touraine didn't bother to explain that she was no longer the ambassador; news of her promotion to general and the betrothal would reach the town soon enough, and Domrémy, if stiff, wasn't forcing Touraine to pull rank.

"I see. It's a common enough trick of highwaymen, to offer vulnerable bait." She sniffed as if disappointed by Touraine's gullibility. "We'll escort you the rest of the way, and I'll send soldiers to escort you back to La Chaise, if it pleases you."

It was almost but not quite condescending.

"My thanks, Captain. The prisoners, as well. I'll have questions for them."

Captain Domrémy cocked an eyebrow. "Questions for highwaymen? Sir?"

"Yes." When no more detail came, the captain saluted and went to see to the arrangements.

Durfort was sitting on the back of one of the wagons while a lieutenant replaced the fallen goods.

"You're hurt." Touraine reached for Durfort's leg to see how bad the wound was. Blood darkened a large patch in her trousers.

Durfort shifted away, wariness in her gaze. "The graze of a stray bullet. You ought to teach your soldiers to aim better, Lieutenant. Could have been disastrous." Durfort laughed, the lieutenant laughed, and they all knew it was false, but the lie benefited everyone.

"You don't have to let me—" Touraine didn't say *heal it*. She didn't know how far rumor had spread about her gift. She didn't know how far she wanted it to spread. "At least let me look at it."

Durfort hesitated, then offered her leg. The wound grazed the outside of her thigh, but it was shallow enough that Touraine thought it would heal clean, even without magic. She had seen Sands heal from worse. Stitches would be enough.

"You can't ride to Durfort like this," Touraine said. "Come back to the palace. Aranen will sew you up and you can be out again."

"Still trying to keep me close?"

Touraine rolled her eyes. The lieutenant was failing to pretend he wasn't paying attention to them. "Lieutenant, bring me a bottle of spirits—yes, I know you have one, bring it, and a clean towel for a bandage. Then load the dead in the peddler's wagon. Search the ditches for any clues to who they were or where they came from. Move sharp. I still want to be in Carleis before it's too late."

"Aye, sir!"

Touraine turned back to Durfort, who was giving her an unreadable look. The lieutenant returned with a half-empty bottle of spirits strong enough to singe Touraine's nose hairs, and she dismissed him again.

"Pull your trousers down."

"Your Highness!" Durfort's mouth and eyes widened in mock scandal. "I never thought you'd be so forward."

"You wish. Pull your trousers down and don't you dare move."

"Do you ever talk to Luca this way?" Durfort asked as she obeyed, revealing muscular thighs covered in thin dark hair. She winced as she held herself against the wagon, clutching it for support. "Because I swear to you she'll like it."

Touraine's face heated involuntarily as she knelt and started to clean the marquise's leg. "Durfort, please. This is hardly the time."

Durfort gave a short laugh. "No, I suppose it's not. Well? What do you make of it?"

Touraine lowered her voice and leaned closer. "The girl who tried to kill Luca. You remember?"

"I don't remember the girl, but I'm not likely to forget that day as long as I live."

"The girl was working for someone else. The Fingers. Revolutionaries who want to bring down the crown. They're tired of the nobility."

Durfort raised her eyebrows incredulously. "Tired of me?"

"You can't win everyone with wine and a good kiss," Touraine deadpanned. "This was them. They might have been after the supplies, or maybe they didn't want us to get to Carleis. Maybe they saw the wagons with the queen's crest."

"What if they were after *us*? You and me? We *are* valuable targets."

"Huh." Touraine paused with the clean cloth poised over Durfort's legs. "We'll find out."

"I see. And if it was these Fingers?"

"Luca needs to know they're still acting against her." Touraine imagined someone getting as close to killing Luca as Fili had. Especially if Touraine were too far away to help. She tied the bandage off. "And then I have to do something about it."

"I'll come back with you, then. Long enough for Aranen to stitch me up. I can hardly ride halfway across the kingdom in this state, anylight." Another pretense.

"Good." Touraine slapped Durfort's other leg with finality and pushed herself to her feet, already looking for the next thing she had to do. She was in charge after all. She was one of the lords of Balladaire now. She had responsibilities.

"El-Qazāli," Durfort called from her perch on the wagon bed, kicking her good leg.

Touraine turned back. "Mm?"

"So you admit it was a good kiss?" Despite her pain, Durfort managed a cocky smile.

Touraine failed to smother her own smile. "Go fuck yourself, Durfort."

Durfort blew her a kiss.

CHAPTER 12

A SECRET

Touraine should have returned by now. She should have returned, and she had not, and Luca paced her anxiety across the length of her study. She must have been on her hundredth turn about the room when she noticed a letter on her desk that had not been there the day before.

"Adile?" Luca called. She picked the folded square up. The paper was soft and worn where it had been folded and unfolded again and again. The handwriting was an unfamiliar scrawl, messier than Touraine's painstaking penmanship. She sucked air through her teeth when she skipped to the closing.

"Where did this letter come from?" she asked when Adile arrived.

Adile furrowed her brow in confusion. "It's not yours, Your Majesty? I found it on the floor in the bedroom while I was gathering your clothing." Where, she did not add, the queen and her future consort tended to leave it in their amorous haste. "I thought it fell out of your pocket. I didn't look to see who from, Your Majesty."

"No." Luca ground her teeth until her jaw ached. "It is not mine."

"Your Majesty?" Worry colored Adile's voice behind her back. "Did I do—"

"It's fine, Adile. Thank you. Could you excuse me a moment?"

A rustle of skirts as she bowed. "Of course, Your Majesty."

Then she was gone and Luca scanned the letter again.

And then again.

The de facto ruler of Masridān, writing secret letters to Luca's *future wife* and *co-ruler*. Trying to coax Touraine to leave Luca and Balladaire, and to what? Turn on Luca?

She leaned over the desk, seething. Touraine was not here, however, so there was nowhere for her anger to go. Instead, it mingled with the worry that wound around her heart, squeezing tighter and tighter until she could sit still no longer.

"Adile?"

"Yes, Your Majesty?"

"Send for Lady Moyenne."

Luca met Camille above the training courtyard. The viewing corridor was mostly empty; a servant swept the stone tiles ahead of them of the dust and dirt that accumulated from the open space; a pair of young men stood at the opposite railing and pointed at a soldier below, hiding their mouths behind their hands.

Camille bowed graciously and fell into step beside Luca as they began their circuit, walking with her hands folded behind her back. Camille watched the blackcoats and the younger officers below with a trained eye but gave away little of her emotions, whether she was anxious about why Luca may have called her, or afraid for the future. She was a hard woman to read.

"Lady Camille. Or do you prefer *lord*?" Luca offered an apologetic smile. "I'm afraid I'm at a disadvantage. I've not had time to speak to you personally since we were children."

If Camille did not return the smile outright, at least her expression softened. "*Lady* suits, Your Majesty. I was only thinking myself how strange it is to be here now that I can see over the railings. If not by so much more." The joke was delivered straight, as Camille ran her hand along the rail that came just below her chest.

Camille LaVasse was shorter than Touraine, with the bearing of an officer. Even though she wore her noble's braid, she didn't act like the braggadocious nobles whose commissions were paid for. No, she was the kind of officer who favored economy and deliberation. Luca had every belief that she could order Camille to do something, but if, on the field, it went against her own wisdom, Camille would countermand it outright. Luca could respect that.

It made her regret what she was about to do.

A ruler does not have friends. Nor, apparently, were lovers sacred.

A ruler did need allies, however. And sometimes an ally needed a hook in the mouth to pull them close.

"Have you received any word at all from your brother's men?" Luca asked.

"Not in detail, Your Majesty." An empty response to a superior's question. Camille glanced over, questioningly.

"Then I am sorry to be the first to tell you, but glad that it comes from my lips. Brice and the King's Own have fallen to a— I don't even know what to call her. A warlord, perhaps. In Masridān."

If Luca had not been watching Camille's face carefully, she might have missed the dismay that pulled Camille apart for only a moment. She turned back to the courtyard with an intensity that belied her calm face, stopping to hold the rail. Her mask was like Touraine's: not a courtly mask at all with its false smiles, but a face that hid fear and pain and grief with competence lest your soldiers balk.

It was not the comparison Luca wanted to make right now. Some of the anger that had driven her to this meeting began to ebb, guilt seeping in at the edges.

"The prince consort told me," Camille said after a long silence. "Does he live?"

"I don't know," Luca said. The anger returned and she exhaled it out. "But as a gift, I offer you permission to keep an ear out for word of her. Hunt her, and seek vengeance for Brice. He was a trial, but I believe he was a good man."

"Brice is an ass, Your Majesty, if you'll permit me to speak so." Camille sighed. "But he is my brother. Why are you offering me this?"

Practical and clever.

"As I said, we've not had the opportunity to become close before. This is not how I would have preferred our relationship begin, but—" Luca smiled ruefully. "Such are the times."

"Such are the times. I already wrote to my sister. She'll have told the little ones. I must see to the rest of Moyenne. It's going to be a difficult season if the Withering makes it that far east. If word reaches the Taargens, they may see us as the cull of the herd and try to bite us off."

Luca couldn't help being slightly disappointed in Camille's equanimity. No sworn oaths against the lieutenant, no promise to seek her out the moment she could. The seed was planted, though, and there was no denying the new tension across Camille's shoulders. The harvest would come.

"Of course, Your Grace."

"I understand Lord Durfort has already left to see to her people. Shall I go now, as well? Or stay for the wedding?"

Luca stared down into the courtyard, where a particularly vicious duel took place between two blackcoats. In her pocket, she fingered the edge of Touraine's letter from Pruett. One of the women below cried out as the other bashed the pommel of her practice blade across her opponent's wrist, disarming her with a clatter. The aggressor wasted no time in pressing the blade against the leather guard at the other woman's throat.

The lieutenant bore no love for Luca, and no matter what platitudes she wrote to Touraine, the woman would never give Luca peace. Those storm-gray eyes had stared at her with hatred in Qazāl. It would only get worse if she found out Luca planned to marry Touraine.

Moyenne cleared her throat delicately, and Luca shook herself.

"Your . . . second brother is next in line, if I recall correctly?"

"Sister, actually. Her name is Étienne now. After the Queen Mother." Camille bowed slightly at this. "She is, yes."

"Forgive me. I didn't know. She's young, though, correct? Is she capable of handling this alone?"

"She's a Moyenne, Your Majesty." Camille didn't change her expression. She barely changed her posture at all. Her words, though, were wrapped in a subtle pride. "She'll have our advisors on hand, as well. I would like to go sooner, rather than later, however."

"After the wedding, then. You and your retinue will be permitted through the gates."

Moyenne bowed her head again. "Is there anything else, Your Majesty?"

"No, Your Grace. Thank you for spending some time with me."

CHAPTER 13

OF PRISONS

Touraine returned at dusk the next day. At her knock, Luca stood up behind her desk, that woman's letter crushed in her damp palm.

The road suited Touraine, with her well-fitted riding trousers, the handsomely disheveled chemise, and the long split riding coat. Even the smudge of road dust and the smell of horses and sweat wasn't unpleasant. It was the way she looked at Luca when she came in, though, that made Luca ease her grip on the letter: like she was a woman in the desert and Luca was an oasis.

"You're safe." Touraine's arms half rose as she approached, but Luca made no move toward her.

"You're late." Luca held herself rigid, afraid if she didn't hold her distance, she would forget the letter—*forgive* the letter.

Touraine aborted the embrace and clasped her hands behind her back. "We ran into Fingers masquerading as highwaymen on the way there."

She relayed the journey as a soldier would, noting casualties—soldiers, Fingers, goods, Sabine's pride—and the completion of the mission as if Luca were General Cantic. Cold and practical, she met Luca's distance with her own, along with a tinge of hurt and bewilderment.

Luca slipped the paper in her pocket.

"The prisoners?" she asked.

"In Le Fontinard. Neither of them is the leader. Fili wasn't there."

"Could any of them be...convinced to speak?"

Touraine grimaced. "Probably. These aren't soldiers, Luca. You don't need to be harsh with them. They'll piss themselves if I show them the knife."

"Good. See to it, then, General." Luca dropped her gaze to the desk.

She felt more than heard Touraine's footsteps circle round to her side of the desk. Hesitantly, she wrapped her arms around Luca from behind.

"I missed you. Has Evrard done something else?"

Luca shook her head, brushing against Touraine's own. "I missed you, too."

A week later, Touraine announced that one of the prisoners had given up the name and location of the head of the Fingers, and that Commander Perrot's gendarmes had captured the man.

"He's the one what gave him up," Perrot said as he led Luca and Touraine through the corridors of Le Fontinard. The cells were more full than Luca had ever seen them. At Touraine's orders, the gendarmerie had been busy. "Name's Olivier, a leatherworker's apprentice. Spends all his time sobbing fit to wake the dead."

Indeed, there was a continuous keening sound coming from behind the heavy door. The little viewing window was shut tight, but it didn't muffle the cries. Perrot waited for Luca's nod before unlatching it.

The man—sky above, barely more than a boy!—was dirty and tear-streaked. A fading bruise on one side of his face was only partly hidden by lank blond curls. He locked eyes with Luca and stopped mid-sob. Bright blue eyes. His face transformed as he realized who he was looking at.

He lunged for her, as far as the chain on his ankle allowed. "Your Majesty! Please, Your Majesty! Please let me go, I'm sorry! It wasn't my idea."

Luca stepped back quickly, wincing as her weight jarred her bad leg. Touraine was steady at her back, though. She searched her mind for the right passage from Yverte to armor herself against those blue-eyed tears. The boy looked nothing like Tiro, and was a decade older besides, but her heart wedged itself up her throat nonetheless.

Perrot had a protective hand in front of Luca, not daring to touch her but still trying to insinuate himself between Luca and the door, as if the pitiful child within could break the door down.

"He slit one of my women's throats," Touraine said. "Caught her by surprise."

Not so pitiful a child, then. Not Tiro. *But what might Tiro have become, raised to the crown by Nicolas Ancier? Raised to the crown by you?*

"Then he'll hang as a murderer."

The boy heard. "No, wait! Majesty, please! Wait!"

Perrot slid the viewing window closed.

Luca spun her grief rings on her finger. "Who else?"

"The lad says the other man is a carpenter, but he won't give his name, and the lad didn't know it."

"A carpenter?" Luca said sharply. She gave Touraine a questioning look, forgetting for a moment her mistrust.

"Mhm. They found the leader in his shop." Touraine lowered her voice. "It's the same one."

Luca drew a deep, anticipatory breath. "Show him to me. The carpenter."

Touraine's hand ghosted over her lower back.

At the second prisoner's cell, Perrot opened the viewing window.

"The door, please," Luca said.

Perrot hesitated only a moment—his glance past Luca to Touraine just a flick of his eyes—then unlocked the door. It creaked open to reveal a man sitting with his legs crossed, his hands on his knees. They trembled a little as he looked up at her.

"You're the carpenter."

"Aye," he said warily. He wore solid boots, and though his clothes were dirty, they were decent quality. What was he getting out of the Fingers' revolution? What was he fighting for?

Nothing, anymore. He looked like a man who knew he was dead.

"You sent your apprentice to kill me."

He inhaled sharply.

"Where is Fili?"

The carpenter lifted his chin. "I don't know."

Luca beckoned Touraine closer and held Touraine's arm as she lowered herself to a knee before the carpenter. She didn't hide the wince or the sharp gasp when a spasm of pain lit up her thigh. His eyes widened with uncertainty, and if he could have backed himself farther into the wall, Luca didn't doubt he would have.

"Is she all right?" Luca asked. "Her mother is looking for her. Did you know that?"

"I don't know where she is," the carpenter repeated, his voice unsteady now.

"Is she well?" It was an effort to keep her voice gentle. "I'm not going to hurt her. Her mother is a dear friend of mine. I owe her my life and more."

"I haven't seen her."

"There's no need to protect her. With your leader's execution, your ill-advised movement will be over. Fili will bear none of the guilt for the attempt on my life. Neither will you. I have a great many plans to change the way the nobility has taken advantage of the people. Ask General El-Qazāli."

Luca's hip was killing her, her knee bruising on the stone floor.

"She's telling the truth." Touraine stood above them with her arms crossed. "I've seen the new financial plans. She's helped my people, too."

"You see?"

The carpenter began to weep, long, slow tears. "I don't know where she is." He shook his head and closed his eyes. Over and over again. "I don't know where she is." He might actually have been telling the truth.

"That's all right, monsieur." Luca patted the carpenter's shoulder gently. "We'll keep looking. If you can think of anything, her mother will be grateful."

Luca reached a hand up, and Touraine was there again, strong and sturdy as she helped Luca to her feet. This time, Luca did hold back the gasp of pain, turning it into a disappointed exhale.

She ushered Touraine to leave the cell before her, and then turned back to the carpenter once more.

"You should know, in case she never told you—Inès Guérin was proud of the work Fili did under your tutelage. It does you credit."

The carpenter only cried as Perrot locked him away again.

That left the leader himself.

Perrot led them to the last door. Touraine's face was impassive and blank, as it was whenever she tried to hide her thoughts.

"What?" Luca asked under her breath.

"Nothing."

Even Touraine's impassivity couldn't fully deflate the swell of relief Luca felt as Perrot led them to the final door. As everything closed in on her—the Withering, the High Court, and now Pruett—at least she could put down the Fingers. Not forever, no; but without their leader, Luca could buy herself time to put her changes into place. To show her people she could be *good* for them. For Balladaire.

"You sure, Your Majesty?" Perrot said. "He's...a bit rougher than the last. The lad called him 'Brother Michel.' Far as I can tell, that's how they address each other. *Brother, sister,* the like."

"Open it."

The heavy door swung open on noisy hinges.

The man within was filthier than the boy had been, his greasy hair raked back over his head, ridged where his fingers had combed through it. He was a big man. He sat with his long legs folded in front of himself and clasped his hands to rest loosely on top of them, as if he were lounging in a garden and not in the prison reserved for traitors against the kingdom.

His head rested back against the stone wall, and he whistled a patriotic song Luca recognized—her father used to march her around the palace singing it, or hum it idly, as a bored afterthought. Bands played it during parades and coronations.

> *To the king, my strength and arms,*
> *To the queen, my life, my heart!*
> *For Balladaire, I'll ever march,*
> *Our empire, our glorious start!*

It was rather strident for Luca's tastes.

Abruptly, the whistling stopped and the man opened one eye, trained directly on her. She flinched at the intensity of his stare. She couldn't shake the feeling she was stepping into a beast's lair.

"Your *Majesty*." He stood when she entered, and he filled the space. "Finally worth your notice?"

"Brother Michel. Leader of the Fingers. A pleasure to meet you instead of your intermediaries."

"Heard my intermediaries did well enough." He bared his teeth, showing a crooked tooth here, a wide gap there. "Might have worked better if not for the sand fleas you keep round. It true you used your wild god to keep her alive?" The man sneered down at Touraine, who had followed Luca into the cell, a hand on her long knife.

This was not the flashy orator she'd expected. He didn't look like a charlatan or a mountebank, all slicked, curling mustaches, sleek clothing, and soft palms. He was a mannerless brute, with big, calloused hands.

Touraine's expression remained empty.

"Tell me," the man said in his low, grating voice. "That little Qazāli bitch is the one who told you about us, isn't she?"

Ghadin. Ghadin, who had stayed with Fili and the carpenter. Luca felt Touraine's energy coil in violence behind her. She held up a steadying hand without looking back.

"Where is Fili Guérin?" Luca asked. "The girl you sent to kill me."

Shock burst quick across the man's features before he sneered again. He hawked a glob of phlegm and spat. It splattered over the polished black leather of Luca's boot.

"She told you about us."

"You think she had to?"

He leaned against the wall and clasped his muscled hands. The muscles in his shoulders and chest bunched beneath a dingy linen shirt. Despite his nonchalance, he stared at Luca with a keen hunger that made her want to peel her skin off and burn it.

"What do you want with her?"

Luca tilted her chin up to better look down her nose at him, but didn't answer. He seemed the kind of man to fill a silence the way he liked to fill space. He met her, stare for stare.

Luca began to pace slowly in front of him. "What is it you want from *me*, Brother Michel? You gathered an entire cult of citizens to bend them against me, but you haven't even given me a list of demands. How do you know I wouldn't say yes?"

He grinned wide. "You'd say yes to the end of the monarchy? The fall of the nobility?"

"No. I would say yes to changing the nobility. I would say yes to raising the people. Yes to fairness."

"No fairness as long as the nobles exist. Look at them, then look outside your precious palace, Your Majesty."

"I know well what's outside my palace, perhaps even better than you. If you care so much about fairness, why did you have your people attack the food I was giving to Balladairans?"

"Food you stole from other Balladairans."

"Food I *bought*."

"Food *we* need. There are people starving in La Gouttière. What good's your coin if there's no food left to buy?"

Luca halted in front of Michel. "If you care so much about feeding the people, tell me where Fili Guérin is."

He snorted. "What's that girl got to do with it?"

Luca considered her next words carefully before deciding it was not so big a risk, to share a secret or two with a dead man. "You know the tales of the Chevaliers des Fruits?"

"Aye," Michel drawled. He cocked his head and smirked.

"If I told you Fili was the key to feeding Balladaire through the coming season, would you care enough for these hungry Balladairans that you'd tell me where she is?"

"Oh, is she? Going to make apple trees spring up in the middle of winter?" His smirk turned into head-back laughter.

Luca glowered. She did not like being mocked.

"I know what she is. Uncivilized, like your Qazāli." To Touraine, Michel said, "Fili said if it weren't for you, the queen would be dead."

If Touraine had looked at Luca the way Touraine was looking at Michel, she would simply never have spoken again. Michel didn't have that same sense of self-preservation.

"It true? You really a cannibal?"

Touraine tightened her grip on her knife. "Let's stab you a few times and find out."

Michel grinned again. "So I tell you where the girl is, she grows us some apple trees, and we all give thanks to the queen? I don't think so."

"You'd let the people you care so much about starve."

"No," Michel snarled, suddenly vicious. "I'd let them be their own hope. I'd give them someone else to look to, anyone else but you."

"How selfless of you. Tell me where she is and they'll have that hope."

"I never said I was a selfless man." Michel crossed his arms. "Go ahead. Execute me. You'll see."

The two of them could circle each other indefinitely, but Luca didn't think she could pry Michel open without help, and as much as she wanted to shatter his smugness, she wouldn't pin her hopes on torture.

"We're done here."

"Aren't you going to negotiate?" Michel said to her back. "My life for the girl's?"

"No."

Luca ushered Touraine out before her, but as she crossed the threshold herself, Michel spoke again.

"So you'd let the people you care so much about starve?"

Her own words hit her like an arrow.

"I don't negotiate with prisoners who want to kill me."

"What will you do with her if you get her, Majesty? Hold her in a cell like this? Make her follow you around, like that one? A little stable of uncivilized god-keepers so you keep all the power in *your* hands. How selfless of you."

Luca slammed the cell door.

"Was that smart?" Touraine asked Luca quietly as they left Michel's cell.

"Did you have a better idea?"

"I did. I said we should stab him."

Luca snorted and glared upward, through the ceiling of stone. This was all Nicolas's fault. He would have her build a state she didn't want. He would tell her, *If you are not willing to exercise your power, it will be snatched away by someone who is.* More Yverte. Luca would not let Nicolas snatch it away—not him, not Evrard, not the sky-falling Fingers.

Touraine followed her gaze. "When's the last time you spoke to him?"

Luca hadn't spoken to Nicolas since she locked him away. Perhaps she was a coward for not facing him, not taking the answers she needed. She thumbed her knuckles, feeling the grief rings on her fingers. The thinnest one on her smaller finger.

"Never mind," Luca said.

In the carriage back to the palace, her thoughts returned to Michel and the carpenter. She wouldn't loose Michel back into the world just for the girl. No matter what Fili could do for Balladaire. Luca would get her another way, and if not...she would find something else. *Or you can free the man and risk your life and your crown, all to help your people.*

Not if the god itself appeared waving wheat stalks in her face. Better to end one problem, then face the next, instead of juggling them all.

How selfless.

"How did Perrot find Fili the first time?" Luca asked.

Touraine startled out of her own brooding. "I don't know. Asked around for carpenters, I expect. Eventually, he pointed me at the right door and there she was."

Luca grunted. "If we've hounded them out of one den, we can find another. In the meantime, the Traitor's Corner will have to be deterrent enough."

Touraine's beautiful lips thinned, pressed tight together, her thick, dark eyebrows low as she stared at the empty bench across from her.

"You disapprove."

Touraine kept her gaze in her lap, running her thumb along her knee. "Quieter would be better. And quick."

"A quiet death isn't a deterrent."

"It could be. Show them you can be merciful, even if you're firm."

"*Brother* Michel doesn't deserve my mercy. He wants me dead." Luca had felt it whenever his gaze slid over her, like a foul slick of oil.

"So you'll martyr him instead?" Now Touraine met Luca's eyes. There was disappointment there, but challenge as well. "And Fili? When you find her? You told the carpenter you wouldn't kill her. You told Guérin."

"I wasn't lying when I said I owe Guérin my life. It doesn't mean I can let all of them go."

"Then you'll make her join your magical menagerie?"

The words snatched Luca's breath away, leaving a throb of pain in its place. "That's not fair, Touraine."

"Isn't it?"

Luca growled in frustration. "Even if Michel manipulated her, I can't give every would-be assassin clemency. I'd never be able to sleep again."

"You already don't sleep," Touraine muttered.

"Exactly," Luca said coldly. It was easier than holding the pain in her chest. "Trust me to know what's best for my rule."

Touraine laughed, short and sharp. "What kind of partnership are you promising me, Luca?"

"What kind of partnership?" Luca faced the window. The rage she'd stuffed away—hidden, as that woman's letter was hidden in Luca's desk—threatened to burst out of her. In a flat voice, she said, "This isn't the place."

"No. I want to know." Where Luca's anger was cold, Touraine's came hot, her voice rising. "Maybe I'm not your pet witch, but you dismiss me out of hand—"

Luca snapped around. "How am I supposed to trust you when you're hiding letters from my enemies?"

"What letters?" Touraine frowned, confused. "What enemies?"

"Adile found a letter from your *friend* on the floor."

Touraine's expression went utterly blank, her body still.

"Are you writing her everything that I do? Are you going to run off and help her break my empire into smaller and smaller pieces? Would she have you compromise our treaty?"

The muscle in Touraine's cheek ticked.

"What else does she want from you?" Luca's anger flooded her like a torrent of ice, but this feeling overwhelming her was more than anger. Her chest ached.

"I'm sorry I didn't tell you about the rest of her letter," Touraine said in a low voice. "But I'm not going to her, and she knows that. You should, too."

"I would have doubted you far less if you'd simply told me."

"Pruett's not a piece on your game board, Luca. She's my friend. She was more than that once, and there are some things—" Touraine looked away and exhaled sharply. "Some things deserve to be private. If she wanted anything that jeopardized Balladaire, I would have told you." When she turned back to Luca, shifting her whole body on the carriage bench, she seemed to expand, like Michel had in his cell. "If you expect me to trust that you know what you're doing for *our* people, Balladaire and Qazāli both, you have to trust me, too. *Together.*"

Touraine's words, coupled with the closeness of her body, the biding strength of it, shifted Luca's anger slightly off course. Luca shouldn't have liked how Touraine looked when she was angry—but the sharpness of her jaw, how she filled out her breadth, the fierce twist of those lips—Luca had particular weaknesses. She took Touraine's chin and stared her down. A gratifying spark flashed across golden eyes. The carriage jostled over the cobbles, pressing them together. Touraine glanced down to Luca's mouth. Luca still wasn't used to Touraine reacting—letting herself react—to her this way. She wasn't used to Touraine *wanting* her.

"Together, then." Even though her words were low, pitched in that way she knew made Touraine desire her even more, Luca felt something else, too—something softer. All the things she worried would pull them apart didn't matter if they could face it all *together.* And then, spite: *The lieutenant will not take you away.* She traced Touraine's lips with a thumb, gripped her chin tighter. "You are *mine.*"

Even though it was Luca who held her, Touraine controlled the kiss, pressing Luca back into the bench of the carriage. The hand cupping Luca's throat was almost bruising in its force.

Luca flinched, held herself taut, and with her hesitation, Touraine paused, holding still above her.

For a moment, neither of them moved, not even to breathe. Then Touraine pulled away.

"No," Luca said quickly. Too quickly. Needy. "No." She put Touraine's hand back where it was, against her breast.

The next kiss ripped the taste of copper from Luca's lips. Touraine hissed in Luca's ear, "Are you mine?"

Yes. Luca shuddered, squeezing her legs tight together. Yes, she was. And it terrified her.

CHAPTER 14

BOUND

Touraine transformed in the mirror as Aranen and Ghadin buttoned and tied her into her wedding finery. She both did and did not recognize the woman staring back at her, with creases at the corners of her golden kohl-rimmed eyes and a hard-set jaw.

Sands didn't marry. It wasn't that they had more important things to do. Not that they were too jaded by their shit lives to love someone, or to envision a future stretch out with a person at their side—though there was all of that. It wasn't that watching a lover die was hard enough and claiming them as spouse would only make it worse.

Touraine had thought about all these things when she was with Pruett. She had imagined, vaguely, like a fever dream, what it might be like to be a general in the Balladairan army, to have Pruett as a wife in another branch, or gone from the fighting entirely if she wanted. (She could never picture Pruett without a rifle in her hand.) She had imagined them having a home together. What a house looked like, what they did in it, was also fuzzy, except for the nights they spent in bed.

There was nothing else there, because Touraine didn't know then what a life outside of the conscripts looked like. She hadn't known what it meant to share a life that wasn't *being a Sand*. Most importantly, though, if marriage was an agreement to share a life, what could the Sands give each other? They owned nothing, not even their bodies. The Balladairans cared nothing for their feelings; you could be separated from a spouse for the rest of your days if they were stationed in the wrong battalion, and what cruelty was that, to inflict upon someone you loved? And so the Sands didn't marry, and in that way, they belonged to everyone and to no one.

Aranen took Touraine by both arms, cutting off her view of the mirror.

Touraine realized she was shaking.

Aranen kissed her on both cheeks. "It's time."

They led her to the Grand Hall, past the waiting nobility, and all the way to Luca, who waited in front of the dais. A pedestal with a piece of gilded paper, a quill, and a pot of ink. Two thrones. One of them was *hers*.

Touraine had definitely never imagined marrying someone who wasn't a Sand. Two years ago, she'd never even known someone outside of the army. She would never have been able to imagine standing here, beside Luca Ancier, queen of Balladaire, before the witnesses of the High Court and the Middle, while she signed a marriage contract in shining black ink. A dark pearl bubbled at the end of Touraine's name.

Here she stood, in her surcoat cut Qazāli-style, long and square, over a Balladairan chemise and cravat. Balladairan trousers and a Qazāli sash. Soldiers' boots. Everything she was, beside Luca, who was everything that *she* was: haughty, elegant, and beneath it all, visible only to Touraine and perhaps Durfort—uncertain. Doubting.

Touraine caught her eye and smiled. Luca's shoulders straightened a hair, and the slight tension around her eyes relaxed.

Are you ready? Luca mouthed.

"Yes," Touraine whispered around the lump in her throat. It was her duty. And if there was a flutter in her stomach or a stinging in the corners of her eyes as she walked into this scene she was never supposed to imagine, let alone live—so what?

On the dais, before all the assembled nobles with the High Court fanned out around them, Touraine held Luca's hands as they made oaths to each other, to defend and supply each other's nations and people against all enemies, known and unknown. As they spoke the words, an orchestra played quietly in the background.

Luca stopped speaking and squeezed Touraine's hand. Ran a thumb across the scarred knuckles. A page presented a second crown on a black silk pillow tasseled in gold, and Touraine knelt for Luca to place the circlet on her head. Then Touraine rose as prince consort. A royal of Balladaire.

The Balladairan part of the ceremony was done.

Aranen and Ghadin climbed the dais from where they'd waited as Qazāl's representatives in their ceremonial clothing. Ghadin held a bowl in both hands. A candle burned inside it.

"Your Majesty." Aranen bowed. "Your Highness. As you are married in the eyes of Balladaire, so you must also be married by Qazāli law for the union of our nations." Her clear, sonorous voice surprised Touraine. She did not seem so quiet and humble anymore.

Aranen looked Touraine and Luca in the eyes and took each of their hands. Ghadin's surliness at least managed to look like somber intensity as she held the bowl with its lit candle beneath Touraine and Luca's hands. Aranen waited one more breath, as if giving them a chance to change their minds.

It was far too late for that.

Aranen took the knife at her belt, and Touraine felt Luca tense. Touraine wasn't the only one, then, to remember another time a Qazāli had pulled a knife on Luca. This knife was jeweled, more ornate than any Touraine had seen Aranen with. Two quick strokes across each of their palms. Neither of them flinched.

The priestess pressed their palms together over the flame, Touraine's right hand looping beneath Luca's left, their wrists locked. The lick of the candle flame took only a moment to become painful, and she felt Luca notice it, though she didn't look to her face. Touraine tried to turn their hands imperceptibly so that more of the heat would fall on her, but Luca tightened her grip, her thin wrist like an iron bar. Their blood dripped into the flame and spattered into the bowl. It sizzled and smoked.

The hall was so quiet that Aranen's voice echoed.

"You will touch and be touched.
You will change and be changed.

You will become two things and one thing,
You will become everything and nothing."

Behind them, all the audience watched Touraine and Luca's blood mingle and burn. Though Touraine couldn't see them, she could imagine the disgust on their faces well enough. *Uncivilized.* This was what she and Luca were changing. This was *how* they would change it. She took a deep breath and waited for Aranen's nod. There was pain in the priestess's eyes, and Touraine wondered if it was because she couldn't complete the ceremony herself, or if memories of her own wedding haunted her.

Luca wore her court smile, small and aloof, but her eyes... There was the truth. The tightness of hope at the corners. The glistening sheen of them. Touraine focused on their hands. The prayer she uttered under her breath was short, but she felt the accompanying wave of dizziness as the flesh of their palms knit back together. Luca's tight grip steadied her.

When Touraine opened her eyes, Aranen returned to them, and Ghadin, with her bowl of fire and blood, stepped aside. Aranen folded an ivory cloth embroidered with gold around their hands and held them still as she spoke the last of the ceremony.

"Your flesh is now her flesh,
Her blood is now your blood.
By fire and flesh are you bound
Until fire takes all flesh away."

In silence, Aranen wiped their hands with the cloth until the pristine white was streaked with red. Then she folded it, bowed, and stepped off the dais, with Ghadin following behind.

Touraine and Luca turned to face the hall, and then unclasped their unmarred hands—no knife cuts, no blisters from the flame, only dried blood lining the seams of their palms and one fresh waxy scar on each. Only then did Touraine focus on their audience. She heard them gasp. Whisper. Some craned closer to get a better look, as if they'd missed a street trick and they only had to get close to see how the illusion was made.

Now Touraine understood what Aranen had meant, asking if Touraine was sure—this ceremony had felt more intimate and much more binding than the Balladairan signing of contracts. She took Luca's hand again, and when Luca met her eyes, a hint of her true smile threatened. *We can do more.*

As music swelled around them, though, Luca's attention jerked sharply toward the orchestra. "I told them not to play that song today."

While everyone else was clearing space or claiming a partner, Touraine caught the comte de Travers's eye. He stared directly at them before ducking into the crowd.

"What is it?"

"Tradition," Luca muttered with an edge of panic. "The spouses dance after the ceremony. Always. I thought if the song was skipped, we could glide past it and no one would remark upon it. I can't— The steps are complicated and even on the best of days—"

And now that the song was playing and people were preparing to join it, Luca couldn't stop it without calling attention to the very things she'd tried to hide.

Touraine's stomach plummeted. "I don't even know the dance."

"Someone's trying to humiliate us. The cripple queen and the foreign rebel." The music curled upward, cresting like a wave about to break. "Touraine, are you angry with Sabine? Is she angry with you? Tell me the truth, quickly."

Travers, Touraine was thinking, before Luca's words caught up to her.

"What?" Touraine instantly recalled the hot press of Durfort's lips on the way to Carleis. The solidity of Durfort's thighs beneath her, their weight digging into the bed. Heat climbed her neck. "No."

Luca stared her down, hunting for a lie.

"Truly. We're fine."

Satisfied, Luca marched Touraine down the dais to Durfort, where she'd stood as witness to both ceremonies.

Durfort looked up to Luca, brow crinkled in worry. "It's the Chasseur and the Buck. Are you going to dance?"

"Are you sober?"

"Unfortunately, yes." She blinked between Touraine and Luca. "Ah. Aha." Her cheeks went pink. "Are you sure?"

"Of course I am. Touraine, I need you to dance with Sabine."

Up to this point, Touraine was only barely following Luca's trail, left behind to fall into a great gap she could barely understand the shape of. Now she understood. She didn't dare say no. Too many people were watching them now, confused. They had probably missed their cue.

"I don't know how," Touraine whispered, pleading.

"Let her lead you, and you won't falter." Perhaps no one else in the room could see the desperation in Luca's eyes, but Touraine could.

"All right." She turned to Durfort. "All right."

Luca took both of them by the hand and led them to the space in the center of the room. Then she folded Touraine's hand into Durfort's, and kissed them both once on the lips. Then, as stately as she ever was, as if she had not been scrambling desperately a moment before, Luca returned to the dais. She raised a hand to the conductor, and at her signal the song stopped and restarted. Then she sat on one of the two thrones, and nodded to Touraine and Durfort.

"Trust me." Durfort took Touraine's hand in hers and let the other slip behind her back, just barely touching. "May I?"

"Yes, whatever you need. I mean it, though, I *really* don't know—"

"Shh. It's like sparring," she murmured in Touraine's ear as she pushed her backward into the first steps, her hand now firm against the curve of Touraine's body. "And I have seen you move. You truly are a wonder."

The flattery threw Touraine off guard, and she let herself sink into the messages Durfort's body gave her own.

It was the complete opposite of the last time Touraine had been made to dance at a Balladairan party, from Luca's blessing to the delicate skill with which Durfort maneuvered her. Then there was the rushing heat of her body every time Durfort brought her close, turn after turn and turn again.

But she was as terrified of humiliating Luca now as she was then.

Touraine saw the first spasm cross Durfort's cheek before it reached her hand, turning Durfort's hand for one second into a painful claw.

Durfort didn't miss a step, flawlessly taking Touraine into the next round. "Forgive me."

"Are you all right? We can stop—"

"We can't stop. I can do this for her."

A pregnant pause where Durfort drew both of them upright and torturously close together. They stayed there for a beat before Durfort directed them again.

"She's manipulated us again," Touraine said, feeling breathless and not from the effort of the dance. "Does that bother you?"

"Not as much as I wish it did."

"She is who she is," Touraine said, unable to keep the fondness from her voice. "And you are...a very good dancer."

"Don't think about that," Durfort warned. "Eyes on me."

Stupidly, Touraine looked right up into playful dark eyes and a handsome, crooked smile, and Durfort had to make up for her stumble.

"Then again, maybe don't." Durfort traced a subtle thumb up and down Touraine's back. "I do have that effect on women. Some men, too."

Out of spite, Touraine refused to falter again.

Together, apart, together, apart. Touraine had been focusing so hard that she hadn't noticed the other couples had joined them on the dance floor, turning and weaving around them. The song itself seemed endless, and she was afraid it would last all night—until Durfort drew her to a sharp stop in the center of the room.

"You did wonderfully," Durfort said softly, unexpectedly tender as she bowed and kissed Touraine's hands. She was barely breathing hard, but her cheeks were flushed.

"I'm sorry you had so little to work with." It was all Touraine could do to keep her voice steady.

Durfort smiled like she wanted to say something dirty but was holding back.

They were joined a moment later by Luca, however, and all the room's attention was on them.

This time Luca kissed them each on the cheek before turning to the expectant nobles.

"Forgive us for not staying long," Luca called in her court command. "You understand, I'm sure, that we have a long night ahead."

Some polite laughter broke out, but Luca didn't wait for any further reaction. She glanced at both Touraine and Durfort and strode toward the doors. Touraine tried to look just as imperious, pursing her lips with contempt before falling in behind her. Durfort flanked Luca's other side, and together, the three of them exited the hall.

CHAPTER 15

CONSORTS (REPRISE)

Durfort sighed as soon as Luca's door was pulled behind them. They'd been silent during the entire walk, not willing to trust the fullness of their feelings to the echoes of the corridors or a chance servant.

Luca set her cane aside, then undid her braid and tossed her long hair, but she didn't speak. She chewed her lip without looking at either of them.

"Are you okay?" Touraine asked, taking a step forward.

"Who did it?" Durfort said. "I thought you—"

"It doesn't matter," Luca said. "Thank you for your help, Sabine."

Durfort took it as a dismissal and cleared her throat awkwardly. "Of course. You're welcome." She stepped backward toward the door and was beginning to make one of her stupid bows when Luca gripped her by the collar and pulled her to her lips.

Someone—definitely not Touraine—*probably* definitely not Touraine—squeaked in surprise.

"But—" Durfort said in the gap Luca left her to breathe.

"Shh."

Luca deepened the kiss and Durfort forgot her own surprise; she wrapped her arms around Luca's waist, pulling her flush against her body, and Touraine—she watched.

The heat that lit her was complicated. There was jealousy, yes. Luca and Durfort had known each other for decades—and *known* each other at least half as long. Watching the sure, familiar way Durfort's hands traveled Luca's body, Touraine was reminded exactly how new and fragile *this* was.

But Touraine couldn't deny the other flare of heat in her belly, the one that made her lick her lips. The one that was tied to the press of Durfort's hips against Luca's. How Durfort's hips had almost but not quite, never quite pressed against her own while they danced the Chasseur and the Buck. "Uh."

This time the sound was definitely Touraine, an undignified little moan that somehow held all those feelings in equal weight.

Luca smiled against Durfort's mouth and pulled away. Then, holding Touraine's gaze, she wiped the wet of her lips with her thumb slowly. The look in her eyes was dark and intent and hungry and—

Touraine felt like prey.

Luca grabbed Touraine by the chin and forced her mouth up to meet hers. Her mouth was open and hot. Luca was greedy. What she wanted, she took. She tilted her head to give Touraine access to her bare neck, and Touraine traced her tongue obediently down the curve of neck and shoulder to place a sucking kiss.

With her mouth pressed against Luca's neck, she locked eyes with Durfort. Durfort's lips were parted, glistening. She stepped closer. Closer. Touraine rose from Luca's neck, and without releasing Touraine's gaze, Durfort pressed her mouth to the glistening red mark Touraine had made on Luca's skin. Between them, Luca gasped, clutching Touraine closer with one hand and Durfort behind her with the other.

With Luca pulling her in, her face was a finger's breadth away from Durfort's. Her cologne mingled with Luca's, a dizzying combination of woods and roses, earthy and floral. Touraine was already wet.

Somewhere, a tiny voice wondered if this was impolitic. Impolitic for a Qazāli. It worried about Pruett and her letter. It nagged about the comte de Travers and his false support, and then about Aranen's disapproval and Ghadin's scorn. A chorus of reasons she shouldn't obey the hot throb of her cunt.

With her right hand on Luca's waist, Touraine slid her left hand up the back of Durfort's head and kissed her, drinking her in while Luca held her close. Durfort pressed into Luca, pushing Luca into Touraine.

When they broke the kiss, Durfort murmured into the close space, "Is this all right?"

In answer, Luca took each of them by the hand to the bedroom. Touraine and Durfort both moved to undress her, but Luca jerked her head to Durfort in a silent signal, then turned on Touraine instead while Durfort slipped away.

Touraine fit her hands against Luca's waist while Luca unbuttoned her chemise for her.

"I liked watching you two," Luca murmured as she worked.

"You did?"

"Mhm. Do you want her to ...?"

"To what?" Touraine glanced over Luca's shoulder. Durfort was bent over in Luca's armoire in the corner. She gripped Luca harder.

"To fuck you."

Touraine swallowed. "Does she want ...?"

Luca paused with her hands on Touraine's trousers. "What do you think?"

"Do you want—?"

"What"—Luca undid a trouser button with each word—"do—you—think?"

And then her hand was pressure at Touraine's center and Touraine's eyes fluttered shut, breath hissing out between her teeth.

"Your Majesty? Your Highness? Who's wearing?"

Durfort's voice was smooth and low. Touraine cracked open her eyes. Durfort was smiling smugly, dangling the false cock and its harness from one hand.

"Sky a-fucking-bove," Touraine swore.

Luca was still stroking her through her trousers, her mouth at Touraine's neck. Her tongue at Touraine's ear. "Do you?"

"Mm." Touraine couldn't get a word out to answer either of them. She rubbed harder against Luca's hand.

"Hm? What was that?" Durfort asked, closer this time.

"Y—" Touraine started, but Luca slid her hand inside Touraine's trousers, fingers steady and circular against the wet of her, and her voice came out strangled and high. "You."

"Oh?"

Durfort's open-mouthed surprise burned Touraine's cheeks. A bashfulness she hadn't felt in a long time. She turned from it and into Luca, who was unbuttoning her own chemise with cunt-slick fingers. A thin strip of pale skin, a mole beneath her collarbone. Touraine took control of Luca's buttons, but she couldn't ignore the sound of Durfort's trousers shucking down her thighs or the jangle of the harness belt like horse tack, like her and Durfort's riding lessons, like the easy roll of the other woman's hips in the saddle, and—Luca's hand against her again.

Touraine slid Luca's shirt off her shoulders. The fabric fell to the ground in a heap of fine silk, and still it was not more fine than the skin of Luca's lower back as Touraine hoisted her up and carried her to the bed. She lay her down. Gently. They had an audience.

The bed. This bed, *their* bed, full of soft feather. An open-jawed trap.

Touraine climbed in, covering Luca's body with her own, mouth, breast, hand, neck, until the bed dipped with Durfort's arrival. Touraine rolled onto an elbow, her thigh still pressed between Luca's, to see Durfort on her knees.

"And who...?" Durfort asked wryly.

She was naked, except for the leather cock dangling awkwardly between muscular thighs. She looked between Luca and Touraine, and stroked herself idly, the leather length. Suddenly it wasn't so clumsy. It was real, all of this was so real.

Luca cleared her throat and the rake of her nails pulled Touraine back to herself with bright pain. Touraine rose and covered Durfort's hand with her own, the twist of her wrist, in tandem, their bodies pressed close, their eyes locked and Durfort's breathing growing more desperate. Behind them, Luca hummed in appreciation.

"El-Qazāli, you still have your trousers on."

It wasn't a command, but Touraine's hand froze. For a moment she considered it: pushing Durfort onto her back, ripping the harness off or, better still, sliding her hand beneath it, taking Durfort instead, with her other hand snarled tight in Durfort's hair, tight enough to rip, making Durfort writhe beneath her instead.

"El-Qazāli?"

The hesitation rippled through all three of them and with it, a change in the mood. The wryness disappeared, devoured by their hunger. With her hand still on Durfort's cock, Touraine pulled Durfort's mouth to hers. She let Durfort lay her down on the bed, soft, she didn't roll her, didn't wrest control away. She let Durfort slide the trousers down her hips, sword-calloused palms rough against skin. Touraine's chemise fluttered open to either side of her, barely clinging to her shoulders. She let Durfort nudge her thighs apart and settle between them, settle above her. She took Durfort's cock in hand again.

"Wait." Beside them, Luca watched with avarice, her tongue pink against her bottom lip. Her trousers were undone, her chest flushed pink, her stomach rising and falling with her breath. She and Durfort shared a glance that Touraine was not a part of, and something passed between them that made her certain they had done this before. She didn't think she liked it. Then, she wasn't sure she cared.

"Sit up."

Touraine obeyed. Luca slid behind her, legs to either side, kissed Touraine on the shell of her ear, behind it, below it, to the soft meat of her neck where her pulse had also lost control. Then Luca let her down, pillowing Touraine's head with her thighs. She felt the pressure of Durfort's fingers, two first, too easily. She sighed into it, and then directed Durfort's cock and she groaned into Luca's leg, biting but unable to find a hold, her mouth working wordlessly.

When she'd thought about Durfort and about Luca, about Durfort *and* Luca, she hadn't thought about it like this, hadn't thought of Durfort inside her while Luca's hands played against her chest. Luca's knuckles rocked beside Touraine's ear, she could feel Luca's short grunts in the clenching of her belly. It was a heady power, being wanted by these scions of Balladaire. How they craved her. How it turned her on, how she desired them both in turn.

"Harder, Sab. You won't break her. I've tried."

"Is that true, El-Qazāli?"

"Fuck—you—Luc—ugh—"

The thrust of Durfort's hips grew faster with the hitch of Touraine's breath and the rock of Luca's knuckles and when Touraine's pleasure came, a crest that brought tears to her eyes, she drew Luca's mouth to hers over her shoulder. Luca's gaze was soft but focused.

Then Touraine closed her eyes, lost as the wave of it knocked her under again.

CHAPTER 16

THE SCOURGE

The cool night air hummed with drunken tension while patrons of La Flottille watched Fili climb to the top of the Place des Oreilles fountain. She struggled to slot her feet into the crooks of the water-spouting acrobats' bodies, afraid the sculpture was too delicate to hold her weight. It did, though, and when she straightened, secured by the lock of her shins against the stone, she could see them all. It was like being on the table in La Flottille while Brother Michel told them all she would be a great leader, one day.

Only Brother Michel wasn't here. He'd been locked in Le Fontinard. No one came out of Le Fontinard until it was time for the Traitor's Corner.

Word spread about the raid on the queen's carriages. The food had only been going to Carleis to help the refugees from Durfort and Champs d'Or. That didn't sound as bad as Brother Michel had made it out to be, that Luca was stealing their food to throw it into the nobles' larders, but maybe there was more to it that Fili didn't know and he did.

No one had come back, though, not even Maître Gaspard. Velte had heard that the gendarmerie had raided the carpenter's shop. (Fili didn't tell Velte the queen already knew Maître Gaspard's workshop was connected to her.) Fili also hadn't seen Olivier. She wondered if Velte putting his name on that list had killed him.

Revolution is not a game, she reminded herself even as her eyes watered and her throat went thick.

"You ready, kid?" Velte said below.

No, Fili wasn't ready. But it had been her idea. The barrels of wine that showed up at La Flottille had been a gift from the queen, to celebrate her marriage to that Qazāli soldier. Casks of the finest Durfort wine to every inn and tavern on both sides of the river.

Fili had wanted *something* to be done. She just hadn't expected Velte to make *her* do it.

"The Fingers form the fist!" Fili punched her fist in the air.

The response was scattered. Though a few were drunk enough to call out, to wave their own fists back, the others who had followed her and Velte and Joscelin from La Flottille, rolling the queen's wine up the road in a parade of laughing and shouting, were now uncertain. The Fingers had never acted so boldly in public, and not everyone had put their name down in Velte's book.

Quick, say something else.

"Congratulations to the queen!" she shouted. Velte handed up a cup of wine from the barrel Joscelin had opened. "May she get everything she deserves!" Instead of tipping the wine back into her mouth, Fili poured it in an arc into the fountain and slammed the cup to the ground.

More of them laughed, shaking off some of the uneasiness.

"Why should we care who she weds when we're hungry?" Fili shouted, reaching for the lines Brother Michel used, though she had never gone hungry, not with her mother, nor with her master. She knew others who had, though.

A few shouts of agreement.

"Why should we care who she sleeps with, when we sleep ten to a room and the landlords gouge us?" Fili shouted, though she had never lived in a tenement. She knew others who had, though.

The crowd grew louder. She tried to remember what else Brother Michel said in all his speeches. Up and down the road, people came out of their homes, poked their noses out of another nearby tavern. A shiver ran up her back. She didn't belong up here. She started to climb down, but Velte, standing ankle-deep in the fountain, held her there with a hand on her leg.

She hunted for something else to say and settled for what she'd said to Joscelin and Velte in La Flottille.

"The queen thinks getting us drunk will buy our silence. Will it?" Her voice lacked the strength to carry the anger, and it showed in the lukewarm "No" the crowd gave her.

Fili deflated even more. The fountain's spray soaked her cold. She wanted to cry.

Then Velte climbed up the fountain with Fili, hanging from one of the acrobats' arms as if she were part of the statue herself. "Will it buy our silence?"

"No!" Louder this time. Having Velte on the fountain with her bolstered Fili's shaking knees.

"Jos, show the queen what we think of this piss!" Velte called, even though Fili knew Velte very much didn't think the Durfort was piss because she'd looked sadly at the barrels before agreeing to this.

The big barkeep upended the barrel into the fountain. It poured in deep-red glugs, turning the water beneath Fili's feet pink, then purple. Velte gave Fili a meaningful look and jerked her head back to the crowd. *Now*, she mouthed.

"Will it buy our silence?" Fili yelled, her voice shrill.

"No!"

This time, the answer was resounding, and while Joscelin emptied the one barrel, others went for the other two barrels they'd rolled from La Flottille. Wine flowed through the streets, turning the dirt between the cobbles into sour mud that people danced in. Others jumped into the fountain, splashing the wine-water into the air and cursing the queen.

Fili clambered down and joined the rest of the crowd, a drop of spray rejoining the river. This was better than being the one to stab Luca. This was better than when Brother Michel pulled her up on top of the bar. This was what she'd wanted the whole time. She didn't want to be a leader. She wanted to be a *part* of something. A clenched fist, not one pointing finger, singled out. She felt safe. She felt like it was all possible. Together, they could bring down the queen.

"Gendarmes!" The warning cut across the merriment. Two gendarmes jogged up the street.

Maybe it was the wine they drank before leaving La Flottille, or maybe it was the heady dizziness of telling the truth out loud, without hiding, but when the gendarmerie arrived, instead of running, one of the Fingers took half a stave from a broken barrel and swung it at a gendarme. Fili froze in horror as the woman let the blow glance off her shoulder, then slammed her baton into the Finger's arm with a crack.

It was like a stage cue. Another woman punched the gendarme in the face before she could bring her baton back around. Then, chaos.

Velte tugged at her arm. "Time to go, kid. Jos! Come on!"

They turned back for Jos, who sagged, seated on the rim of the fountain.

"Jos?" Velte grabbed him with her other arm, and he staggered after them.

The gendarmes' shrill whistle for backup cut through the night.

Jos struggled to keep up as they loped back toward La Flottille by the dark side streets. He slowed to a shuffling walk, his hand on his chest.

"We're almost there," Fili said, doubling back to him and Velte. "Come on, Jos. Are you hurt? What happened?"

Joscelin's quiet rumble was little more than a whisper as he struggled to get the words out. They led him a few more steps until they passed beneath a street lamp to better see what was wrong. Fili's eyes traveled from the feeble, trembling hand and up, up to the gray, skeletal face.

Fili couldn't help it. She screamed.

Luca woke up to the pale dawn light peering through the curtains, a sliver of dullness, bright only by comparison to the dimness of the bedroom. She lay there a moment, letting her eyes adjust to wakefulness, letting her leg adjust to the untwisting. The steady breathing of the other women in her bed fit the languid feeling in her body. She was tired and spent, contentedly so. She rose onto her elbow and regarded the two of them: Touraine's scarred back to Luca, curled into Sabine's chest while Sabine lay on her back, snoring softly.

Sky above, but they were beautiful. And last night—Luca shuddered with pleasure at the memory. Maybe they would start again after breakfast. Perhaps make a change or two.

She sighed back into the pillows.

It was done, then. They were married. The newly sovereign nation linked again with its former conqueror.

A heavy thought.

She lay there, listening to their breathing before determining no amount of comfort would seduce her back to sleep. She wrapped herself in a robe, wincing as her leg cramped at the first use, and tiptoed into the anteroom, delicately avoiding the false cock and the rest of the clothes scattered about the floor.

The anteroom was still cold, and dark. Adile hadn't come in yet to rekindle the fire. Luca pulled her robe close around herself. She went to the trunk in the corner where spare blankets and cushions were kept in case the fire was not enough. Atop the blankets in the chest was the wedding gift she had commissioned for Touraine. A slender sword with a decorative twist of the steel about the hilt—fit for the court but clearly a soldier's weapon. Not like the gaudy thing Sabine had gifted her. It reminded Luca of a hand unfolding, and it shone, even in the dim light of the room. The leather scabbard was equally fine, etched with a pattern of climbing vines with delicate thorns.

Her heart caught in her throat the same way it had yesterday, as she and Touraine made their marks on a new contract. As she'd placed the consort's crown on Touraine's head. As they'd clasped their bloody hands over the flame. *Would this be enough?* Would this truly make the empire stronger, or had she, as Evrard was so certain, made a grave error?

Had her parents' marriage started like this? Full of uncertainty and fear? Had Gil been there when they made love for the first time as a married couple? She laughed to herself and tried to push the awkwardness of the vision from her mind. In its place, a longing for Gil swept over her like cold water. Swift as it had come, she forced that away, too.

She had thought her parents loved each other as a child, but in the last year, she'd learned many things she'd thought as a child weren't as they seemed. She didn't know if they had chosen each other, for each other's sake and not for the politics.

Luca closed her eyes, and there, waiting for her, was the memory of Touraine, seeking Luca's eyes, saying Luca's name, digging her fingers into Luca's thigh.

"Luca?"

Luca gasped and jerked around, sending a shard of pain into her hip. She held on to the trunk and caught her breath. She smiled and righted herself. "Good morning, wife."

Touraine smiled. She had dressed in loose trousers and a sleeveless Qazāli tunic that fell to her knees. She rubbed her bare arms, covered in goose bumps. "Good morning, wife. Well done." She tilted her head wryly back toward the bedroom.

"Did she tire you?"

Touraine raised an eyebrow in challenge as she came over. "I think I've recovered."

And casually, so casually, she stroked Luca's arm and leaned in to kiss her cheek. The gentleness of it tightened around Luca's heart even as something else in her eased. Then Touraine looked into the trunk.

"What's this?"

"It's—" Luca swallowed, lost for words. She'd had a speech planned out for this moment, but all those questions crowded in her mind. She picked the sword up and held it flat in both hands. "It's for you."

Touraine took the weapon in both hands, thumbs tracing the pattern of vine and thorn.

"It's a—a sword, a—your wedding gift." Luca held her hands awkwardly at her side.

Touraine unsheathed the sword halfway and gasped a little as she marveled at the gleam of it. Then her face fell.

Luca rushed in. "It's a wedding gift, but—if you prefer not to think of it like that, it's all right, I don't— You needed your own sword, not a hand-me-down from one noble or another and even if you don't feel— I would like you to keep it. My power is your power now." Luca snapped her mouth shut so hard her teeth clicked.

Touraine slid the blade back home, without taking her eyes off Luca. There seemed always to be a pinch of sadness at their corners, and they were tighter now as Touraine's brow creased anxiously.

"I don't have one to give you—"

"You don't need to. I don't expect—"

"—yet." Touraine cupped a hand against Luca's cheek. "It's not finished. But I do hope you'll like it. I'm sorry it's late."

"Oh." Luca covered Touraine's hand with her own. "That's all right. Thank you."

She was afraid to say what she felt right now—even now! With Touraine's eyes a soft, warm gold, with that tentative smile, as if she were afraid to let it grow.

"Touraine, I—"

There was a fumbling sound at the bedroom door, and Touraine and Luca both whirled around to find Sabine, half-dressed, standing in one boot while she tried to slide into the other, cradling her waistcoat and surcoat in one arm. Her dark hair was messy. A deep blush rose from her neck to her hairline.

"Leaving already?" Luca asked.

"I—" A tic twitched Sabine's eye. She cleared her throat, then bowed with as much flourish as a half-shod woman laden with her clothing could. Which, for Sabine, was an impressive amount of flourish. "I was afraid I'd overstayed my welcome. After I commandeered your wedding night, I thought I would give you the time to yourselves. It seems I was right."

Luca hadn't imagined the strain in Sabine's expression.

"You're always welcome here, Durfort," Touraine said formally. Then, she cracked another of those half smiles. "Especially after last night."

Sabine grinned, straightening. "There's more where that came from, my prince."

Touraine had said exactly what Sabine needed to hear. With the interruption, however, Luca and Touraine's own moment had evaporated like frost under the bright light of morning.

"We should call Adile back from exile, then," Luca said. "Have breakfast so you can get up your strength."

"And other things besides," Touraine said under her breath with a wry twist of her mouth.

Heavy knocking shook the door of the anteroom.

"Who is it?" Luca called as Touraine stepped in front of her, her new sword drawn.

"Commander Perrot, Your Majesty."

The door opened and Deniaud stepped in, keeping the door discreetly slit as she slid through, eyes downcast for their privacy. "Forgive me, Your Majesty, but it's—urgent."

"We're decent, let him in." Fear sharpened Luca's tone. She tried to work saliva back into her mouth.

Commander Perrot bowed once as he strode in and said, without waiting: "Your Majesty. It's the Withering. It's hit the palace."

PART 2
BY WILD BEASTS

CHAPTER 17

CARRION

The Qazāli Council was no less infuriating than Pruett remembered, with the Jackal leading the charge for most likely to make Pruett pick the lot of them off, one by one, from the highest rooftop.

Pruett exhaled in a sloppy, lip-flapping puff of air. She propped her head on her hand, which was propped on the old Balladairan war room table. Wasn't really her place, was it? First time she'd even been invited to it. First time since the beginning, anylight, when they'd dragged her in there after the Balladairans had been kicked out, to see if she was actually loyal. Touraine had vouched for her. No Touraine here, though, and even if she were, she sure as the sky above wouldn't like what Pruett was about to do. That pleased her more than it should have.

"All right," she snapped at the council members. "You're fucking right, okay? No one told me to 'sack the city.'" In a barely audible grumble, she added, "Not in so many words." Then at normal volume: "You wanna cut my balls off about it, or do you want to hear what came next?"

Pruett made a show of pulling out her stolen cigarette case and stretching back to light a cigarette off the candle hanging from the wall behind her.

"Honestly, I'd rather cut your balls off." The Jackal leaned back in her chair, her arms folded across her chest. She waved her amputated forearm magnanimously, though, for Pruett to continue. "But let's have it anyway."

Pruett bowed her head. "Thank you, honored council member." She ignored the flutter of huffs around the table. Even Malika, who was younger than the stuffy heads around the table, glared at Pruett. Usually, they got along. Well, got along as well as Pruett got along with any of the Qazāli. Assimilating wasn't her strong suit. Pruett had always gotten along best by staying out of the way.

Not anymore.

"Shortly after I took Samra' back from the Balladairans," she said, exhaling a plume of smoke, "I was visited by an ambassador from Taargen." She explained the offer of troops and sustained shipments of food while the Shālan nations sorted themselves out in their regained independence, and conveniently left out the part about finding Masridāni with no souls in the ghettos of the city.

"So, we make her enemies our friends," Pruett concluded with confidence and her fishhook smile, holding her hands out wide.

The council members reacted first in silence, looking unreadably between each other. The Jackal's mouth was grim and disapproving, so that was a loss immediately. The bearded man—she'd heard his name but couldn't remember, sounded something close to *Bastard*, anylight, so she went with it—looked constipated, lips pursed together like he was trying to hold something in that would have been better off let out. Dina, the council member from El-Tarīq, only glared at Kiras, who sat quietly, face neutral, idly tracing the gold designs on the holy dagger at her hip. The woman from Atyid, named Istam—Pruett had marked her because Kiras had spoken of her representative with respect—was the only one who looked at Pruett with anything other than irritation.

"What will the Taargens want from us in return?" Malika frowned, deepening the scar on her chin. "What will keep them from sweeping back in where the Balladairans were?"

"They won't—" Pruett started.

The Jackal cut in. "If we burn our resources for them, we'll be even worse off than we are now, and we'll be dependent on another would-be empire in the north. Why should we do that? For revenge? I say no. We have a chance with a new ruler who has reasons to keep us happy and has thus far proven herself trustworthy. Trustworthy as any politician, anyway. Better a sickness we know than one we've never seen."

"Balladaire can't keep you happy. A plague is spreading through the country, and the queen is too weak to manage her own people." Pruett used the same points Lor had used against her. "They've been sending you grain. When's the last time you got a shipment?" All the council members but Jaghotai shared a worried glance. "The Taargens have promised meat and furs and funds and timber enough to help you rebuild."

"Only priests eat meat," the Jackal said flatly. "And if they have all of that, what do they need from us?"

"Soldiers. Healers." Pruett looked pointedly at Istam.

The Jackal leaned back in her chair. "Doesn't matter. You're late." She smirked, but not in a condescending way for once. More like she was laughing wearily at a joke she'd heard too many times. "If you'd arrived when that flea-bitten hyena Nicolas was on the throne, you might have convinced us."

"Now we have an alliance," Bastard added, stroking his thumb and forefinger down his black mustache to his gray beard. "A signed treaty."

"A signed treaty sealed by marriage." Malika stared hard at Pruett. Too hard.

"Marriage." The cigarette burned between her fingers, forgotten. "Whose marriage?"

"Whose indeed? My daughter married the queen of Balladaire, and now she's the prince consort. Can you see now, Qā'id, why going to war against Balladaire is off the table?" The Jackal swept her hand over the war table to illustrate her point. "And can you imagine, she didn't even wait for her poor mother to attend, or bring the bride here for a Qazāli celebration?"

Pruett fell back into her seat, all the air sucked out of her. Touraine. Married. To that fucking insufferable—

From the corner of her eye, she saw Kiras watching her, concern tugging her mouth into a deeper frown.

"That's how important sealing that alliance was," Jaghotai continued. "So, no. We're not going to break it now."

Then, as if on cue and that cue was how to make this situation even worse, Dina said into the silence, "Especially not beside abominations."

Dina frowned down her nose at Kiras even though Kiras could easily have picked her up and gutted her without even breathing heavy.

The Jackal gazed down at Pruett where she slouched, still too shocked to speak, then to Dina and to Kiras, whose golden-eyed glower smoldered one step away from burning the old woman alive.

"A recess. Seems we've all been given a lot to think on. Have a drink, a walk, a smoke. We'll meet in the morning. Start fresh and figure out what to do with Masridān and the rest of the Shālan Empire. Council dismissed."

No one moved.

Then, slowly, the council members from El-Tarīq and Zanafesh and Atyid left. Istam the Atyidi squeezed Kiras on the shoulder and beckoned toward the door. Kiras looked to Pruett for permission, then followed Istam. Malika trailed out a moment later, looking between Pruett and the Jackal.

When it was the two of them alone, the Jackal said, "I told her to get that alliance any way she could. She only did what I asked her to."

The Jackal's voice was low, and if not tender, most of the usual combativeness was gone.

Pruett laughed, rough around the odd lump in her throat. "You and I both know that's not true."

"I'm not going to war against her, girl. Not again."

Pruett wasn't sure whether the Jackal meant Touraine or Luca. She pushed herself away from the table and stood.

"You remember when I said you come back here and it's my orders or you leave?" The Jackal tilted her chin up at Pruett.

"Sure, I do." Pruett spun on her heels and flicked her cigarette over shoulder.

Pruett tried to suffocate her fury in her favorite smoking den. The broad-shouldered serving woman from before Pruett had left Qazāl was still there, but this time, Pruett didn't try to catch her eye.

Touraine had gotten *married*. *Touraine* had gotten married. For "an alliance." Pruett scoffed even though there was no one to hear. That woman didn't have the self-preservation of a fucking dog.

She took a long drag on her water pipe. It tasted like rose, sweet on the tongue, going down smooth into her lungs.

"Why couldn't you have kept your sky-falling head down?" she muttered.

It wasn't that Pruett wanted to marry Touraine. Maybe if Sands could have married, and none of this Qazāl shit had happened, they would have. Their world had been so small then: they had the barracks, the battlefields, the Balladairans, and each other. In a world that small, of course they were everything to each other.

Pruett bit the wooden stem of the water pipe until it dented between her teeth. How could Touraine still want to dance for them after fighting so hard to get free?

"May I join you, Qā'id?" Kiras's warm, quiet voice was followed by the brush of an equally warm hand across Pruett's shoulder.

Pruett made room on the cushions beside her and pulled Kiras down by the hand.

"I wasn't sure how long you'd want to be alone," Kiras said.

"You knew where I was this whole time?"

"I had an idea." Kiras took in the alcoves curtained with beads or cloth for privacy, the room lit by lanterns covered in colored glass and dimmed by hanging smoke. "This is where I met you for the first time. You were sulking then, too."

"I was not! And I'm not now."

"Hmm." Kiras leaned over and kissed her.

There wasn't hesitation, exactly, in the gesture, but Pruett could almost taste the next question on the other woman's lips.

"So. The Jackal's daughter." Kiras took the pipe from Pruett and settled against the wall, one leg curled beneath her and one arm propped on the cushions behind Pruett's neck. "You were lovers."

Pruett snorted. "Aye. For a while."

Kiras's grunt came out in a rush of smoke. "And we've known she was in Balladaire all this time."

"Mm."

"Is she why we're doing this?" Kiras's voice was hard. "Tell me the truth. Are we going to war because the queen fucked your woman?"

Pruett pulled the pipe back from Kiras. Tapped it on her lips before taking a long drag and letting it out in slow rings. Concentrating on the shape was easier than forming a proper answer.

"Would you be disappointed if I said yes?" Pruett traced the hard ridges of Kiras's kneecap through the woman's trousers with her empty hand.

Kiras huffed and looked away, her eyelids low. Her lashes were so long, so thick. "Yes. You're better than that."

"No, Kiras. I'm really not." Pruett felt the bitter fishhook smile pull her face into a sneer.

"Then maybe I'm jealous, too." Kiras's hand found the back of Pruett's neck and traced the short hairs there. There was something desperate in Kiras's touch. "If she chose to leave you—let her. It's her loss."

Kiras searched Pruett's face, her lips parted. *I'm here, she was trying to say. She is gone, but I am here.*

Pruett cleared her throat and turned away. "It's not about Touraine. It's about Balladaire. You don't know what they did to us."

"You're right. They didn't take me," Kiras said, ducking her head to the side in acknowledgment. "They fucked up my city, same as El-Wast, same as Samra', but nothing like the Sands." She caressed Pruett's neck with the side of her fingernails, catching Pruett's skin with the edges on purpose. "Whatever you want, you'll have me."

Pruett shivered into the touch.

"The more important question is whether or not we try to convince them tomorrow." Pruett sighed. "The Jackal is stubborn as a fucking rock, but she's not an idiot. That's why she's still in charge." The Jackal was practical and knew where to put a knife; she could even be cruel if Touraine's stories about how they met were true. But she had a frustrating and inconvenient integrity. "I won't let her take Masridān from me."

The door opened in a rush of cool afternoon air. Heads turned and people whispered. Pruett craned her neck around disdainfully as she could—only to see Istam and Bastard from the council standing in the middle of the room, squinting around as if looking for someone.

Pruett ducked down and pulled Kiras lower as they spoke to the owner. "What did Istam say after the meeting?"

"She seemed glad about Masridān. Wanted to talk to you. Don't know why she brought Basim, though. Only person she hates more than him is Dina."

"No one likes Dina," Pruett grumbled as the two council members walked toward her alcove. So much for a little peace.

She straightened as they arrived, propping her own arm carelessly against the backrest cushions, one leg crossed over the other in a hedonistic sprawl.

"Council members!" The fishhook grin, showing teeth and a curled lip. "I thought we weren't reconvening until tomorrow."

"Up," Bastard—Basim said sharply. He jerked his head to one of the cloth-curtained alcoves, and when Pruett followed his gaze, she saw the proprietor of the shop tidying it up.

Pruett sharpened the edge of her smile, and Basim pulled back a little. Istam, on the other hand, bowed.

"We'd like to speak privately," she said below the rumble of chatter picking back up in the café.

Kiras's pointed look decided her.

Pruett picked herself up, letting her limbs swing loose. "Since you asked so nicely." She ducked into the new alcove, which was curved in a steep U shape. Kiras slid in beside her.

The serving woman followed with Pruett's pipe at least, and then a round of strong, dark coffee. Then she pulled the curtain closed, and the rest of the café was muffled almost into silence.

Pruett took a fresh drag, exhaled slowly. "Where are the rest of your friends?"

Istam and Basim exchanged a look.

"Jaghotai does not believe in the fight, and Dina does not have what it takes." Istam bit the last words off. She held Kiras's golden eyes and Pruett understood. The woman from El-Tarīq hated the Eaters. *Abominations.*

"To be clear," Basim added, with a surly glare at Istam, "I also do not believe in this fight. For once, Jaghotai might be right. If Balladaire is as weak as you say, though—"

"They are," Pruett said.

He grimaced into his cup. "We need *reliable* allies. Food from Masridān and Taargen would not go amiss if Balladairan aid ceases."

"It will." Pruett rushed to fan this new flame of possibility. "Masridān's stores are as deep as we expected them to be. We could help." A quick count, though, and she frowned. "What about Malika? If she's with the Jackal, you're still outnumbered."

The council members shared another look.

"We don't have much in the way of soldiers, but there would be volunteers," Istam said. "I will send more of my priests."

"Not many of us heal," Kiras murmured to Pruett, "but we're worth more than a few men in a battle."

"We'll also give you coastal access if needed," Istam added.

Pruett tapped the pipe on her teeth, the clack of wood loud in the quiet alcove. "All you want in return is food?"

Istam's smile showed sharp eyeteeth. She didn't have the golden eyes of the ākilīn, but that didn't make her any less dangerous.

Basim hunched over the table, his excessive caution replaced with rabid hunger. "Get rid of the Jackal. I want her off the council. You said it yourself. We're outnumbered by that bitch and her pups, and she's never listened to an idea that wasn't her own."

"She thinks what's right for her people is what's right for everyone," Istam agreed. "But the Atyidi do not forgive so easily. Nor do our neighbor cities. Do this for us, and you'll have what little we can offer."

"But," Basim said, glancing down into his coffee, "as far as anyone else is concerned, we are neutral. We've sent nothing. The rest of the council will know nothing. We—we cannot afford another war. Jaghotai is right about that."

Pruett sucked her teeth. Basim was a cautious man. Or a coward, however you saw it. Fair enough. Not everyone could be raised from childhood to face death for a living; some people were just lucky. She passed Kiras the pipe and picked up her coffee instead. Bitter but warm. She tongued the grit against the roof of her mouth. It wouldn't be hard to get her out of the way. Take some of the Masridāni, catch her by surprise. She'd been a right bearfucker to Pruett last time, ordering Pruett out of Qazāl with no choice in it.

Was that worth getting the woman killed? Accidents happened when bad feelings were involved. When *power* was involved. Pruett held no illusions that the Jackal would enjoy her time in jail, not with how Basim's lips twisted in distaste whenever he said her name.

Touraine had married the sky-falling queen of Balladaire, but even so, Pruett didn't think she could hurt her like that.

"Won't it be hard to explain where she's gone to Dina? Or Malika? If they think you're not supporting the war?"

Istam smiled her sharp-toothed smile again. "That's not war. That's politics."

"No one will complain." Basim scowled. "Not if you deal with her allies, too."

Pruett took the pipe back from Kiras and considered. Wasn't really her business if Istam and Bastard couldn't hold El-Wast properly once the Jackal was gone. Or what they'd do if the Jackal ever came back.

"I'll send my fighters to get her. I'll send her back to Masridān to wait out the war."

Istam glanced to Kiras. "*Your* fighters? The ones *we* lent to the cause months ago?"

"What do you mean, *wait out the war?*" Basim said. "You need to *take care of her.*"

Pruett bared her teeth. "The Jackal stays with me until we get what we want. Deal or no?"

The council members' shared silence spoke loudly. Pruett got the distinct sense they thought of her as a necessary filth they had to sully themselves with. Just like the Balladairans. Funny how some things never changed.

But this was what she was good for. She'd learned that, she'd accepted it, and now she was going to use it.

"Agreed," Bastard said.

CHAPTER 18

OF A FEATHER

The night sky a million leagues above.

That was one thing about the desert Pruett had grown to love. Being a small speck in the vastness of the world. She liked to be alone in it. Alone, plus or minus whatever creatures she could feel nearby, throbbing in the back of her head. Soon, after the moon set, after the city and the slums and the compound slowly ducked their heads into their blankets, she and her new allies would move on the Jackal. Seemed right, to take a moment to herself.

Her ears—sharper now than they used to be—caught the crunch of a boot on the sand. She stilled, not turning, but her hand drifted to the knife on her belt. Her pistol wasn't loaded. She sought the ball of activity in the back of her mind—*claws scurrying in the dirt, burrow in the sand, cool, cool, hunt*—then she found Sevroush in that ball, and focused on it until she could feel the vulture flying overhead and coming closer. That gave her a sense of ease as the steps continued, steady and unhurried until Niwai, priest of the Many-Legged, stood beside her.

"May we run together beneath the sun," they said, looking up at her.

The priest was very short, coming up only to Pruett's shoulder, but they moved with the same confidence and grace as the massive lioness padding silently by their side. Pruett had not felt the lioness in the activity around her. A frightening thought.

"That how the Many-Legged say hello?"

They smiled, a gentle curve of their lips that creased the slight folds of their eyes. "It is one way. Particularly from one priest to another."

As if on cue, Sevroush's wingbeats grew louder. Out of reflex, Pruett shot her arm up, the one with the bracer for his claws. So did Niwai. She glared balefully at him when he landed on Niwai's arm instead of hers.

"Don't be disappointed," Niwai said to her, trying to feed Sevroush a piece of dried meat.

"He doesn't like it." Pruett felt peevish.

Sev clacked his beak at Niwai, not taking the offering, and the priest smiled again. Unlike Pruett, they didn't seem hurt by the rejection. "You've spoiled him."

"So, you know about this." She tapped the side of her head, then crossed her arms sullenly. Jerked her chin at Sev. "Have you known the whole time? Did you...see it through him?"

"Partly. When you bonded—"

"Bonded?"

"We sent Sevroush to try to bond with you. It is how a priest opens their mind to the community of life within all of us—"

"Sent? You did this to me on purpose? Can I close it?"

"You would cut yourself off from the rest of the world? We are strongest when we move in concert."

Pruett pulled up short. She didn't believe in this "connection to the world" shit. But she would miss feeling Sevroush soar with contentment.

"I don't want to get rid of all of it," she corrected. "Just...a thousand dicks, my head hurts all the time!" She pressed at her temples. "I can't even control it. Can you teach me?"

Niwai placed their empty hand behind their back and began to walk through the night desert. They didn't seem like they should be strong enough to hold Sev's weight on one arm.

"Tell us what your plans are with the Taargens."

The question caught Pruett flat-footed. She strode to catch up.

"Are the Many-Legged allied with them? Will you fight against Balladaire with us? You worship the same god, don't you? How come they can—" Pruett swallowed. "Do what they do. To people."

"The Many-Legged have already fought against Balladaire, and we succeeded. What more is there to do?"

She almost said it out loud, *make them pay, hurt them back*, but that wouldn't move the priest. What more *was* there to do, if she did not want that?

Pruett laughed at herself, this small spark in a world of night. Who had she become?

You never wanted to lead anything, let alone an army, said a snide voice deep inside. *So why* are *you sticking your neck out like this? Because some woman hurt your feelings?*

It *wasn't* because some woman hurt her feelings. It wasn't Touraine, it wasn't Luca. It was sky-falling all of them. Never, in all her life up to now, had she let herself feel the anger that constantly threatened to devour her. Not in the barracks back in Balladaire, not in the quiet nights on the Taargen killing fields. It was as if someone had opened a floodgate and decades of rage were rushing at her in a torrent. Lor had only given it direction.

Not Pruett's fault that Touraine happened to be in the path of that torrent. She'd chosen Balladaire. She could take the consequences.

Niwai stopped abruptly and faced Pruett. They pushed Sev into the air, and the vulture flew around them in a tight circle before settling on the ground beside the lioness. The great cat sat on her haunches and stared at Pruett with golden-brown eyes that reminded her of Kiras and Touraine both.

Niwai held their empty hands up, palms facing inward, gesturing for her to come closer. Pruett obeyed. Niwai held her face in their hands, middle fingers pressed against her temple. The gesture was so intimate that Pruett held her breath, staring at the priest with wide eyes.

"Close your eyes," they said.

She obeyed. As usual, her awareness went first to the presence in the back of her skull. Desert lizards. Snakes. Mice. Predators and prey. Sevroush, patient and, somehow, she knew, sarcastic. He'd been a friend, as much as Kiras and Noé had been ever since that disastrous first night outside of Samra'.

Then he was gone.

Pruett jerked away from Niwai's hands, shoved them. "What did you do?" She looked immediately to Sev, who croaked loudly and flapped his wings. He looked unhurt, but now she could only assume. She didn't *know*.

She probed again. It was empty. Not of all the feelings, but of Sevroush.

"What did you do?" she asked again, her voice shrill. She stepped toward the vulture, but Niwai stepped between them. "Put—put him back."

"Your bond with him is no longer needed. You may bond with a companion of your own."

Their voice was soft and Pruett could tell the priest was trying to be kind, but how could they be so sky falling *connected* to the world and not know what they had done to her?

"Sev," she moaned. He chirruped, fluffed his feathers, and walked around Niwai to rub against Pruett's leg. She knelt to brush her knuckles across his chest. He cocked his head, but she couldn't feel his contentment anymore. Her eyes stung with sudden tears.

She swallowed down the lump in her throat so that her voice was steady when she spoke again: "How do I do it? Make a . . . companion?"

"A small exchange of blood."

"How did you know that I could—that it would work?"

Niwai looked fondly down at the vulture. "We didn't know for certain. But a presence lingered at the edge of Sevroush's mind that was not ours, and so . . . we let him go to you."

"And the other animals? The ones in my head?" It came out more of a growl than words, and it was met by a warning rumble from the lioness, her head propped on her paws. "I just— Don't you ever—want—quiet?"

"Ah. You haven't learned to separate yourself from the other beings that you are. While you can never separate yourself from the great will that is all the creatures of the world, here—imagine that all those voices, those calls, wherever you store them in your mind, are in a cage. They won't like to be put there, but do it anyway. And then, cover that cage with a blanket."

Niwai cocked their head expectantly, their eerie eyes staring. Pruett closed her own eyes and tried to visualize the scurrying ball in the back of her brain and . . . covered it with a blanket.

The sudden silence of her thoughts was deafening. She had gotten so used to the constant *noise* that, at first, she thought she'd been cut from everything like she had been cut from Sevroush. But then, as she tongued it like a missing tooth, she could feel the different beasts, as if muted from under water. She pushed harder still, and then the cacophony came raging back, louder than before. She hunched over, hands pressed to her ears, but she couldn't escape. She threw the mental "blanket" back over the cage, and she was alone again. Almost alone.

Breathing shakily, Pruett straightened. "Thank you. For that, at least."

Niwai bowed their head. "We don't like to see one of us hurt. The Many Legs run best—"

"When we run in concert, yeah, I got it. But you won't come fight with us? In concert and all?"

Niwai shook their head this time. "It is not our place. An animal defends its territory. It doesn't hunger for more than it needs to survive."

"We're people, not animals."

Niwai hummed, considering. "And yet we breathe, eat, rut, and make waste like every other beast. Tell me why we should not adhere to these other laws as well?"

Pruett snorted and scratched her cheek. She wondered if it had been the connection to the animals that had . . . increased . . . her enjoyment of Kiras over the last month or so.

The lioness rose from her spot on the ground, growling at the dark outline of the city. Pruett could make out Lor's shape.

"Many-Legged." Lor bowed when she was close enough to them. The feathers on her cloak fluttered in the cold night air.

Niwai bowed back. "Bear-child."

"Will you be joining us, cousin?" Lor asked them.

Niwai held Pruett's gaze, searching with their odd eyes, as if they were the one who had asked Pruett, and were waiting to see if she would join *them*.

But Pruett had already made her choice. As Touraine had made hers. As the Jackal had, and Luca had.

With the animals in her head muted for the first time in weeks, her headache slackened. She was thinking as clear as she had in ages.

Niwai sighed as they saw the answer in Pruett's face. "We're afraid not, cousin. We're needed elsewhere."

"Then it's time," Lor said to Pruett. "We hunt."

As Pruett turned her back on the Many-Legged priest and their beasts, she heard one last croak from Sevroush.

Goodbye, feather-fuck.

Pruett strolled down the streets of Qazāl like she used to after the Rain Rebellion. What a silly name, for something that had cost her all the people she'd loved.

The streets were more alive than they had been when she left on the Jackal's mission to ally with Masridān. The city's scabs were flaking off, the scars beginning to stretch.

Though the people riding in rickshaws were now Qazāli—if there were rickshaws at all—the people sitting had cheeks almost as hollow as the people carrying them, and the people carrying them had shoulders as knobbly as nags. Laughter spilled from more than one smoking house or café, but the fights that overflowed into the street were vicious enough to leave bodies in the gutters. Pruett didn't check if they were unconscious or not.

"It won't take much to push them into a war," Lor murmured.

Pruett cut her eyes sharply at the Taargen woman. Even though she'd been thinking the exact same thing, there was something calculating about the way she said it.

The Jackal hadn't taken advantage of her lofty position on the Qazāli council and commandeered one of the well-appointed riads left vacant by the Balladairans (who had, of course, commandeered them however many decades before). She chose to stay in the building that Aranen din Djasha had lived in. The priestess had lived there with her wife, and all three of them had been close, according to Touraine.

The building stretched up, its pale clay brick easily visible in the night. The upmost windows were dark except for one at the front, which flickered soberly. The Jackal was in, perhaps reading, perhaps already gone to bed. She had it on good information that the bitch was probably alone. Not surprising.

Pruett turned to Lor and Kiras. "We'll go in from the top. Lor, wait down here in case she runs."

Pruett left the Taargen woman with the handful of Masridāni soldiers who'd been most eager to prove their loyalty—or to claim some taste of power. Then she led Kiras to one of the side ladders that would take them to the roof.

Climbing the ladders up the outside of the building was comforting in its familiarity. Pruett had spent so much of her time in the year after the rebellion on these rooftops, watching the Qazāli pass by in the streets below. Up here, separate from them all, it felt like she was doing the rejecting, not them. She hopped over the lip, boots landing silently, and cast a glance back over the city. Nothing had changed.

"Qā'id?"

Kiras's soft murmur and the tender brush of her hand over the back of Pruett's bare arm pulled Pruett's attention back to their mission. They crouched low, skulking to the hatch that opened into the house. Over the worn rug that she and Touraine had sat on, remembering Tibeau and Aimée. Past a couple jugs of that potent Qazāli liquor that Pruett had helped herself to on more than one occasion. She paused at the hatch, listening to the sounds below. It was quiet, but that candle was still burning.

Pruett pressed her finger to her lips and lowered herself silently down.

More threadbare rugs muffled her footsteps. Pruett pulled her dagger from her belt, holding it low so it wouldn't catch the light. She didn't intend to use it to hurt the woman—she *didn't*—but it would be important for persuasion.

The fitful illumination was coming from the front room, where the kitchen was, and the low table that Pruett had eaten at with Touraine and the Jackal and the priestess. Those early days had been awkward, at first, but the priestess at least had been kind.

Pruett went straight for the light, Kiras tight at her shoulder.

A candle flickered on the table, guttered down into a puddle of wax. Forgotten, as she'd expected. She started to backtrack, to check the darkened room she'd passed by where the bed pallets were, but a familiar *craa* arrested her.

Sevroush puffed his feathers on the windowsill. He tilted his head at her, and before tonight, she would have known exactly what he meant by it. Now Pruett couldn't feel him at all.

Kiras was rigid at her side, and had pulled out her non-ceremonial dagger. She glanced between Pruett and the vulture in confusion.

"Pruett?"

"She's gone," Pruett said thickly. "Sev warned her."

"What?" Kiras lunged for the bird, and Sevroush flapped his wings aggressively, though he couldn't spread them fully in the window. Pruett pulled Kiras back.

"It doesn't matter." Pruett glared at her old companion, and Sevroush turned one orange eye upon her in return. How could a bird make her feel ashamed of herself?

Despite her words, Pruett reached for the first thing she could find. The melting candle wax burned her skin, and even that pain was satisfying as she hurled it at the vulture in the window. It flew at Sevroush in chunks, some of it still soft when it collided into his dark feathers. He squawked in alarm and flew off.

"Fuck you!" she shouted after him.

"What's going on?" Kiras's turn to keep Pruett from the window.

"I don't need him. I never did. I don't need him, I don't need Touraine. I don't even need you, Kiras." Pruett jerked her arm away. "Don't try to coddle me."

Kiras's jaw clamped shut tightly. "I'm not trying to coddle you. I'm trying to keep you from giving away our position."

Pruett flushed and took a shaky breath.

"What do we do now?" Kiras had gone cold and professional. She would be angry for a long time. Pruett would have to make it up to her. Or maybe she wouldn't. Pruett didn't care.

"If she's fled the city, Bastard and the rest get what they want. If she hasn't run, she's an idiot."

She stomped down the stairs to tell Lor the news, leaving Kiras behind. Beneath the pain of Sevroush's betrayal, though, Pruett felt something else.

Relief.

CHAPTER 19

A LEGEND

The next days brought only bad cold and worse moods. Fights broke out in the ration lines, and the gendarmes enforced order with their batons. Half the doors Fili had seen that day had already been daubed with the white X of quarantine. Including La Flottille. She hunched deep in her coat and stamped her feet in the last of the slush, then knocked on the door of the inn.

"Velte?" She pounded with her fist, more frantic. "Hello?"

When no one answered, she tried the door. It was locked.

"What're you doing, lass?" someone shouted at Fili on the street. "Don't you know it's the Withering?"

She didn't turn to face them, and they didn't stick around to berate her. She shivered in the cold a little longer before banging the door again. The broadsides in her hand rattled with her shivering. She needed her gloves and the rest of her warm things, but she didn't dare go back to Maître Gaspard's. Not anymore.

"Velte?" she called, and beat the door again.

The door swung open, white X and all. Velte stood, haggard, in the doorway. She raked her greasy hair back messily from her face.

"Oh. It's you." She looked Fili up and down, lingering on the broadsides in her hand. "Thought you'd gone for good."

"I've only been gone since the morning," Fili grumbled. She kicked her boots as dry as she could and pushed inside. "Got our rations." She dropped the basket on a table.

"Morning? Sky above. What time is it now?" Velte massaged her eyes with her fingers. "No, don't tell me."

"They're going to hang them." Fili thrust the broadsides under Velte's nose.

Velte's eyes shot open.

"Maître Gaspard. Olivier." Belatedly, she added, "Brother Michel. What do we do?"

"When?" Velte snatched the paper, scanning. She sagged. Her voice shrank. "A week?"

Fili followed Velte up the stairs to Joscelin's room. It didn't tell much about the man; there was a window with a pot of wilting herbs on the sill, and a small table with a single rickety chair that shouldn't have held Velte, let alone Joscelin. Velte took the chair and buried her head in her arms, mussing the card game spread on the table.

"When are we going to get them out?" Fili asked.

"They're in Le Fontinard," Velte said, voice muffled. "There's no 'getting out.'"

"But what about Maître Gaspard?" Fili asked in a small voice.

"Fili. It's over. We have no leader. We have no goal—"

"Saving them is a goal—"

"No goal that won't get us all killed. Worse, we have no food that doesn't come through the queen now, and I don't even know how many Fingers have been—" Velte swallowed thickly as she stared at Joscelin.

"Is he any better?"

The night of the wedding, the strong man couldn't even make it up the stairs to his bed. Fili had been scared to touch him, but Velte couldn't get him up the stairs on her own. When word spread about the queen's hospital tents in the Parc du Coeur, they'd silently agreed not to take him. Fili waited days for her own skin to shrivel up, or Velte's, but nothing had happened. Yet.

"Same as before." Mostly unconscious, not speaking, barely able to swallow down water or broth.

"At least he's breathing. In the ration line, someone said people get so weak they can't even pump their lungs."

Velte shot Fili a dark look. "Wonderful." She twitched the curtain open and looked down at the street, like it was some faraway world. "It's over."

"I'll do it. Let me lead a group."

Velte snorted, but didn't turn back from the window.

"No. Really. I know what I'm doing." Fili didn't know what she was doing. But anything was better than nothing, wasn't it?

"Lead a group to what?"

"To get my master—and Brother Michel—out of Le Fontinard."

"I know it's hard to lose Gaspard." There was pity in her voice. It made Fili feel like a child. "We lost a lot of good people and will lose more in the fight. He and Michel knew the risks."

"You just said you won't keep fighting without Brother Michel."

"Aye, well…" Velte sounded hopeless and ashamed at the same time.

"I have connections to the palace. That's how I got close to the queen." Fili marched over to the table and slammed her fist on it. Velte jumped. "And we have people in the palace, too, don't we? Members of the guards? What about the scholars' halls?"

Velte and her shorthand came from the scholars' halls, where she studied on a bursary. Her favorite topics to speak on were economics, and that was what had drawn her to the cause. She'd grown up counting cards in gambling dens across La Gouttière. She liked to show off those skills by reaping Fili and Jos's quart-sovereigns like harvest time.

Before this.

Velte shook her head. "No one who can help us with this."

Fili studied her hands silently, and the wood of the table beneath them. There were other things Fili could do. Her master had asked if Fili wanted to tell Brother Michel about her gift. She'd kept it a secret for so long. She didn't know how Velte would react if she showed her. Knowing Fili kept a god. It had to be something they could use.

Velte slid off her stool and patted Fili on the back.

"Stay here as long as you need. If you don't mind staying in the plague house, anylight. For the rest…we'll figure out…something."

"I can do things, Velte."

Velte's brows met in confusion. "Hein?"

"Magic."

"Fili, please." Velte scrubbed her forehead with the heel of her palm. "I know you want to get him back, but this is life. Growing up means accepting some things don't work out the way you hoped. Get some rest."

"You know magic exists. That's why the queen is still alive."

"I don't know any such thing. Brother Michel likes to exaggerate."

"If I show you, will you hear me out?"

Velte narrowed her eyes. "Show me what?"

"My magic."

"You're serious. Sky above." Velte blew her cheeks out. "All right. Show me your little street trick."

"It's not a street trick."

Fili grabbed the plant on the sill. It was in poor shape without Joscelin to care for it. It stretched feeble leaves toward the watery daylight, but most of them were browned at the edges. Fili took her whittling knife off her belt and pricked her thumb. She squeezed until a throbbing red bead wobbled there, then plunged it, bloody, into the soil.

Velte leaned away in the chair, unnerved.

Fili concentrated until she felt the leaves like an extension of herself, straightening. She straightened with them, eyes closed until she stretched tall. When she opened her eyes again, she felt alive in a way she hadn't since she'd been away from the workshop. The brown leaves had gone green and plump again, the stems taut. The smell of tarragon and chervil and rosemary filled the room. Fili exhaled slowly.

"You should water them more often," she admonished Velte.

"What the sky-falling fuck." Velte stared at her open-mouthed. She stroked a leaf hesitantly. "It's real."

"I told you."

"My great-grandmam, she used to tell me this legend she had from *her* grandmam." Velte watched Fili carefully. The look made Fili nervous.

"What did she say?"

"Don't really remember. I got a bit cruel and stopped listening to her." Velte's accent tilted toward the Gouttière. "Thought I'd got too old for tales. Then she died. The way of things, like I said. But one of them was a legend about a Balladairan queen who could rip the earth out from under her enemies' feet or raise a forest with a touch. That she raised the forest that separates Balladaire from Taargen."

"Those are just stories. I can't do any of that." Fili picked up the pot to hide her nerves. She moved it to the little bedside dresser next to Joscelin's bed, thinking it would cheer him. If he was ever awake enough to see it. She tried not to think about that. She stroked his hand hesitantly. Velte's eyes bored into her back. "I could try something else, though. I'm really good with wood."

A rasp from the bed made Fili and Velte both jump.

"Velte?" The word was faint but unmistakable.

Velte leapt from her chair to Joscelin's side, urging Fili out of the way. She hesitated before taking his hand. His whole forearm had withered to the bone, but there was no mistaking the squeeze he gave her.

There was a new light in Velte's eyes when she turned back to Fili. An itch prickled between Fili's shoulder blades. She didn't think of the right word to describe it until she was lying in her own bed later that night.

Reverence.

CHAPTER 20

A THREAT

Panic spread through the palace more quickly than the Withering itself. Middle Court and Upper, friend to Luca's rule or foe, servant to lord, lord to servant, it struck them all. Some tried desperately to leave the palace, and the hostlers were run ragged preparing all the mounts and coaches. Others barricaded themselves and their servants into their palace rooms or their town houses in the city; some locked their servants in with them, and others dismissed their servants as if they'd brought the plague in themselves. Those who remained brought their panic into the Chambre des Graines: throw the ill out of the city! No, execute them!

And then, of course, there were those who took ill. Their bodies were dumped into the plague carts with as little ceremony as those of the civilians down the hill.

And, of course, those down the hill had been rioting in the streets. All the wine she'd given as a gift, dumped in rivers while they cursed her name.

But there was one benefit: all the fear and chaos silenced—for now—all talk of Tiro's murder and Luca's legitimacy. Even the announcement that she'd apprehended the leader of the Fingers and his upcoming execution had been swallowed up. The court had something else to be afraid of now.

It was during one of the useless meetings in the Chambre des Graines that Luca and Sabine locked eyes. Sabine didn't smile or wink or share anything other than a weighted, silent look. After the meeting, Luca caught up to her exactly where she hoped Sabine wouldn't go.

Sabine crunched through the snow toward the stables, a saddlebag slung over one shoulder. Watching her strong body, Luca couldn't help remembering the way that body had arched beneath Touraine's tongue on their wedding night. How Sabine had twined her fingers with Luca's in pleasure. Luca recalled, also, though she wanted to forget it, the hurt in Sabine's face when Luca reached for Touraine instead of her, a moment gone so quickly that Luca still wasn't sure she hadn't imagined it.

Sabine was a courtier, though. Like Luca, she wore many masks.

Luca limped faster.

"Coward!" Luca shouted at Sabine's back.

Sabine froze midstep. Without turning around, she said coolly, "Your Majesty. That's beneath you."

"Then why are you running away?"

"I'm not running." Sabine raised an eyebrow at Luca. "I'm leaving. As we discussed before your wedding."

"I hadn't considered the matter settled."

"Of course you hadn't. Must you always have your way, Luca?" Sabine asked wearily. She continued into the stables, where her bay stallion was already saddled. She slid her saddlebags off her shoulder and began to attach them herself.

The rebuke caught Luca off guard. But this was a matter of state.

"If you go, it will be harder for me to deny Ghislaine."

Sabine locked eyes with Luca above the horse's saddle and raised her eyebrows high. "Then don't."

"She'll muster an army against me as soon as she's in Champs d'Or!"

"An army?" Sabine threw her empty hand into the air. "She'll be lucky to get a few men with rusted swords forged during the first Taargen War at the rate the Withering is cutting us down. Sky above! Like it or not, I am the lord of Durfort—"

"And what will you do for them that your seneschal cannot?"

"Whatever I must." The stubborn determination and righteousness in Sabine's expression would have looked right at home on Touraine's face. "Food, hospitals. Whatever it is, they will see me by their side, not playing the popinjay in the capital."

Luca went to Sabine's side and pressed Sabine's hand still between the horse's flesh and Luca's own.

"I need you."

"You have El-Qazāli. She's just as loyal. She loves you as much as I do. She'll keep you safe." Sabine took her hand back and finished securing her bags.

"Won't you miss her?" Luca tried to laugh.

Sabine took pity on her and grinned, tilting her head back, and groaned in satisfaction. "Perhaps you should be asking her if she'll miss me."

Luca swallowed at the sudden block in her throat. She closed her eyes to keep the tears back. She saw the pyres in her mind's eye, their black smoke streaking the sky. So easy to imagine Sabine's body thrown atop one with brutal efficiency. Not even the ashes to keep.

Sabine cupped her cheek and thumbed away the tears Luca hadn't managed to stop. Sabine didn't bother to hide hers. Instead, she pulled Luca into a deep kiss, as much of a goodbye as either of them could stand. Then she hugged Luca close.

Luca gripped Sabine's coat as hard as she could. It was plain brown leather, a workman's coat, with none of the flashy embroidery Sabine usually favored. A caution for the road. So was the rough black tricorne.

Without giving Luca a chance to respond, Sabine bundled Luca's hands in one of hers, kissed them, then swung up into the saddle. She didn't look like the fop of the court now. She was a chevalier come right out of the tales, straight-backed and resolute. Luca wanted to believe that Sabine would come back, like the heroes in the stories. That was the problem with stories, though. They made you crave impossible things.

Sabine gave the hostlers a two-fingered salute and tossed them a couple of demi-sovereigns. As she spun her horse around, though, she let out a low whistle. "Speak of the wolf..."

Luca turned to see the comtesse des Champs d'Or striding toward them in a walking dress of red and gold, with a rabbit-fur cloak about her neck.

"Lady Ghislaine." Sabine bowed in her saddle. "Between the sun and your beauty, I can't say which shines brighter today."

The day was thick with gray clouds, not a hint of warmth in the air.

"Lord Durfort. You seem to be leaving." Ghislaine stared at Luca. "Would that we could all ride away to safeguard our homes."

Sabine gave Luca a questioning glance, offering to help. Luca almost took it. But Sabine was leaving. What sense in clinging to her like a child clings to her father's belt?

"Travel safely, Your Grace. I expect to see you again." Luca raised her hand in farewell.

Sabine's dark eyes held Luca. "As you command, my queen."

Then she wheeled her horse around and galloped away to the west.

Luca ignored the hollowing of her chest and faced Ghislaine.

"Your Grace. What do you want?" Luca didn't have the heart to coat her words in politesse.

"I walk for my constitution, Your Majesty. One of the physicians says fresh air and vigor will keep the Withering off."

Like many in the palace, including Luca, Ghislaine had taken to wearing a scarf around her face—hers was glaring crimson, and Luca remembered the wedding cloth stained with her and Touraine's blood.

"Do not let me disturb your contemplation." Luca made to step around her.

"Not at all, Your Majesty. Please. Join me." Ghislaine looked up at the clouds. "Back to the palace, at least."

"As you wish." Luca braced herself for the *request* she knew would come. No matter what Sabine said, she would not let Ghislaine go.

It would be more expedient to kill the comtesse. It's what her uncle would have done. Sky above, it's what Yverte would have done. But she was not her uncle. She did not *have* to be.

However, if she had to have this conversation once more, Luca would, perhaps, reconsider.

She was, therefore, surprised at the words that came from Ghislaine's lips.

"Congratulations on your wedding, Your Majesty. You and the prince consort make a handsome couple."

The kindness was off-putting. It even sounded half-genuine. "Thank you, Your Grace."

Ghislaine smiled softly, her face upturned as if the clouds above were the warmest summer day, green fields surrounding them instead of snow. "It's delightful, being in love. Nothing in the world matters so much as the way their skin feels against yours in the morning, and all the pain of your life is halved by the way their eyes catch yours."

Luca remained wary. "Your late husband?"

The comtesse's laugh was as melodic as shattering glass. "Oh no, not him." She winked conspiratorially. Then she sighed. "I had to give that love up. Luca. I understand at least some of what you must deal with right now. New love. A new throne. New grief." She looked pointedly at Luca's collar, where Gil's grief ring rested beneath her coat. Luca fought to keep from reaching for it reflexively. "The plague. A rebellion. *You were nearly assassinated*, by the sky above. You are a brilliant young woman, but even you are woefully out of your depth. Set aside your search for the old magics. Abdicate. Let your uncle take the reins. Go off and live your fairy book life with your wife and your lover. Take a stipend and give all the rest up." Ghislaine looked east, toward the pyre smoke vanishing into the storm clouds. "The Withering will pass, as it did before. Go and be happy, for as long as any of us have left."

Luca bit her tongue as Ghislaine unspooled Luca's secret heart between them. So secret that Luca had refused to admit to herself what she wanted more than anything.

How easy it would be. Ghislaine was right. *Abdicate.* Properly, this time. Let it all go.

"I will not abandon my duty, Your Grace."

The same sad smile, this time with an edge. "I see how well you understand your own duty, and yet you begrudge us ours. What about your wife? What about your duty to her?" Ghislaine's gleaming, manicured nails clacked as she tapped them against each other.

Luca looked sharply from the woman's hands to her face. "You presume much, Your Grace."

"I presume little. I speak only with the experience of years. Secrets are a rot in the marriage bed."

"I beg your pardon? My marriage bed is none of your business."

"Perhaps not. But perhaps it is. What secrets do you keep from your wife, Your Majesty?"

Luca could think of only one secret she kept from Touraine. Moyenne had left immediately after the wedding and was not here to betray Luca to Touraine, but Ghislaine couldn't possibly know.

"Our business is our own," Luca repeated coolly.

"Ah. I see. So she knows that you've given your permission to have her fellow soldier *dealt with*? That is perhaps a touch ruthless, even for a student of General Cantic."

Luca's court mask must have slipped—a crack, nothing more. But Ghislaine was a master of the game. She grinned beautifully.

"Oh, my dear. Don't behave as if this is a surprise. You are not the only one in the palace who enjoys a bit of . . . research."

A fat, wet snowflake landed on Luca's cheek, warm compared to the chill down her spine. She surrendered.

"You will vote in my favor for the reforms. In advance. Before you leave for Verlieu. And—" Luca stopped to steady her voice. "You will tell her nothing."

Ghislaine curtsied, an elegant maneuver that had never in history been so condescending.

"Your Majesty. You are kind. You have my word, on both counts."

Luca led Ghislaine back to the state rooms where the seneschal prepared the voting tokens, and while Ghislaine selected the token that meant "yea" and it was wrapped for the illusion of secrecy, frustration pricked at Luca's eyes.

When Ghislaine finished, she handed the wrapped token back to the seneschal and took Luca by the shoulders. It was almost motherly, the look in her eyes. She kissed Luca on both cheeks, their scarves brushing. Luca flinched. Then she left to prepare for her upcoming travel.

Later, after some of the desperation had fled and she had time to think, Luca decided that if she had no choice but to let Ghislaine leave, she did not have to let Ghislaine *go free*.

Touraine didn't return to their rooms—well, Luca's rooms, though a small part of Luca had begun to think of them as something shared—until the evening. Luca stood at the small mirror at her dressing table, examining her face for new lines, a change in complexion. She touched her cheeks, molded the skin, but it was firm. A healthy flush blossomed wherever she pinched it. At Touraine's first call, Luca returned to her study. The candle on the desk had burned down. The forest-green paper on the walls made the room feel darker than it really was. Normally, she liked the feeling; it made her feel blanketed. Tonight, it felt almost claustrophobic. She slouched into her chair.

"Luca?" Touraine was already talking as she entered the anteroom. "Aranen wants me to visit the healing—" She took one look at Luca's face and said, "Durfort's gone, hasn't she?"

Distantly, the words made Luca ache, but she couldn't register the feeling, not with Touraine standing right here. Touraine wore a soldier's blacks; however, in deference to her position as prince consort, her coat was gold. In one hand, her black tricorne. The other rested on her new sword, which hung well at her hip. She was perfect.

"Touraine," Luca started. She stopped. Started again. "I have to let Ghislaine leave La Chaise."

"What? Why?" Touraine lunged into the study, as if Ghislaine were there.

Luca couldn't fit her tongue around the truth. "In exchange, she has given me her vote for the reforms. That's her and Sabine in my favor." And hopefully Moyenne. Her vote was still a secret. Together, they would be enough.

"But the Champs d'Or militia. You trust her?"

"Of course not." Luca laughed bitterly. "I need your help."

Touraine unclipped her sword and sat opposite Luca. She rested the sword on her lap.

"Whatever you need."

"It's dangerous, traveling right now. Bandits on the road." Luca held Touraine's eyes as understanding came.

"You know I'm not good at lying."

"You're getting much better at it."

Touraine frowned down at her sword, idly stroking the scabbard with her thumb. Already, she cherished it. There was nothing like the warmth that gave Luca.

"It's true," Touraine said at last. "The roads are unsafe. I know it firsthand." She stood. "If you'll excuse me. I need to make arrangements." She sounded like a courtier.

She came around the desk and kissed Luca on the forehead. Then she left Luca alone again, with nothing but her own self-loathing.

And Luca had dared to call Sabine the coward.

CHAPTER 21

BALLADAIRE'S HEART

The day after arranging for the comtesse to have an unfortunate encounter with bandits, Touraine went to the hospital tent. She went in plain clothes and was glad for it. The portable ovens that kept the winter chill away from the patients turned the air hot and cloying. Her breath against her skin, kept close by the scarf Jaghotai had given her, wrapped around her face, was hot and damp. Her coat and gloves, which she kept on for protection, were hot and clammy.

Aranen and Luca had come up with the idea together: a place to tend the sick as the Withering spread, especially those who couldn't afford care and seclusion in their own homes. If a doctor deigned to see them at all. They'd chosen the Parc du Coeur, the great garden in the center of the city with eight corners and a statue in each, celebrating Balladaire's values. A place everyone would recognize and remember. At first, no one came. Touraine sent the gendarmes to follow rumor and gossip, trace the ill to their homes, and then daub the buildings with the white X—*this house is infected.*

It was as if the infections in the palace had lit a flame in the lower city as well. Word spread that Queen Luca and her Qazāli prince offered help, and if not everyone came—because they didn't want royal help, or because they didn't want Qazāli help—there were patients enough to fill the first tent less than a week after the wedding.

Now, two weeks after the wedding, she was kneeling beside a young man while Aranen dabbed a rag soaked in tepid water against his brow.

"When he came in, he was—he was big," Aranen said, gesturing with her hands. Her face sagged with sorrow. "Shoulders like this, ruddy face, a healthy belly. He even told me about a Qazāli he works with at the docks. He was learning to stand on his hands."

"What's his name?"

"René."

René moaned. His muscular arms and shoulders had atrophied in days. His belly was gone, his eyes and cheeks hollowed out like a skull, and he'd taken on the same gray pallor as the other victims. Even the living looked like corpses sucked dry.

"I want you to try healing him," the priestess said tentatively. "The most I can say is what anyone can see—it's degenerative. I can't tell how it spreads, either. There's no coughing or hemorrhaging, there are no rashes or pustules."

The man's eyes fluttered open. Blue, like Luca's but without her keenness. He probably couldn't even see her. Then the corner of his lip twitched. A spasm? The start of a smile? He closed his eyes again. Surely he was dead.

Touraine pressed her gloved fingers to René's neck. His pulse flicked against her. The heat of it called to her. She slid off one glove and hesitated, her bare flesh hovering over his. Would touching him be a death sentence? She imagined him laughing with a handsome Qazāli man. She thought of kissing Luca in the snow.

Shāl, protect me. She pressed her bare hand to his neck. There, the call that Touraine almost thought she had imagined. Throbbing against her fingers. She matched it with the heat of the meat in her own belly: cold sliced chicken that she'd eaten over bread. A sacrifice as much as any other. Then she prayed, asking Shāl for the power to help him.

She searched for the wounds in his body, for anything she could ease over with Shāl's gift, and found nothing. So she reached for *everything.* She bolstered his failing muscles, his faltering lungs, and felt a surge of triumph as his breathing steadied. She opened her eyes to see a slight flush in his cheeks where he'd been sallow before.

Aranen inhaled in awe. Touraine sank back on her heels.

"It worked." Touraine hardly dared believe it.

"Thank Shāl." Aranen set the bowl of water down and squeezed Touraine's hands. "Can you spare the time to heal a few more? I've triaged the worst cases—"

A horrifying, choking gasp interrupted her. Aranen and Touraine sprang to hold René's jerking body by the shoulders, but nothing could be done.

Where René had been shrunken before, now he was truly *withered*. The skin of his hands and face bunched like puckered flesh that had wrinkled in water, but it was as dry as leather. His blue eyes, crumpled like dates, stared at nothing. He wasn't breathing.

Touraine's stomach lurched and she turned aside, desperately forcing her bile down. As she took a shaky breath to get control of herself, she noticed that the Withering stole even the stench of death. The hospital tent was less like a battlefield than she'd first thought—none of the copper tang of blood, the voided bowels and ruptured guts. The only vomit was going to come from her. She pushed herself to her feet and hunched, hands on her knees, heaving and swallowing sour spit.

Aranen followed, raising her hand to flag another pair of aides. She put the other on Touraine's back and stroked soothing circles until the nausea passed. "The deaths are sudden. Too weak to carry on pumping its fluids and breathing its breaths, the body simply stops." To the aides, she said, "Take him out." To the corpse wagons.

A young Qazāli woman came up beside them. Her eyes were bloodshot above the scarf that covered her face. In Shālan, she asked, "Will we catch it next?"

The woman's many braids were pulled back beneath a kerchief. Touraine understood what she was really asking: *Is this a Balladairan disease, or will we die for helping them?*

"I can't say," Aranen whispered, watching as the aides rolled René in his blanket and carried him out. "You may go home, if you wish."

The woman closed her eyes and took a deep breath. She pushed back her shoulders. "I'll stay."

"Thank you," Touraine said. "Queen Luca and I both thank you."

After the woman left, Touraine turned her own hands over. Had she broken her own magic? Had she accidentally worked to *unknit* him instead? *Impossible.* She hadn't made the necessary sacrifice. But who was she to say what was impossible to a god?

He should have had more time.

Touraine itched to wash her hands. She wished that she were back in the palace. She wanted to press her head against Luca's chest and hide. Replace the nothing-smell of the Withering with the smell of Luca's hair, her skin.

"Your Highness!"

Touraine straightened and pressed the moisture out of her eye with her wrist. A Balladairan calling her, this time, raising a hand for attention near the entrance.

Aranen made an uncharitable noise. "There's at least one of them a day."

"I'll handle it." Touraine threw back her shoulders and went over, exuding as much calmness and authority as she could. Soldiers took their cue from their officers.

There was a queue outside the tent. People left their loved ones or struggled over alone before the sickness sank its hooks in, hoping for a bed or even a meal. The pallets within were full, and patients were dying quickly, but not quickly enough. Wails came from outside the tent as well as inside, and the corpse carriers filled the wagons by walking up and down the line.

Which was why, when she saw the guards in some noble house's green-and-silver livery shoving another Balladairan out of the way, Touraine stormed over to the noblewoman overseeing the harassment.

"Ah, yes. You're *here.*" The woman looked Touraine up and down. Certainly she must have recognized Touraine for who she was. "*Attend* me. I woke up feeling not *myself* today."

The woman had come in an elegant gown that showed off her figure and her finances—there was no mistaking her even for a wealthy merchant. Touraine couldn't recall her name, though, not for her life.

"You look fine to me." Touraine jerked her head toward the queue. "Wait at the back of the line like everyone else."

The woman's round-eyed, open-mouthed shock was gratifying. Then the woman smoothed her hands over her dress, calling attention to it and to the two expensively jeweled grief rings on her fingers.

"I'm sorry, perhaps you do not recognize me. I am Lady *Théophane* Barthelme de *Font-Sec*." Lady Théophane had an odd way of emphasizing her words as if you might not understand her importance if she didn't. She stepped toward the tent. "I was at your *wedding* to the *queen*. I saw you perform your *magic* and would like you to do the same to *me*. Where shall I *sit*?" She waved her hand with barely disguised disgust at the idea of Touraine's magic.

"You can sit on your ass at the back of the line. Or on the back of one of your guards. Or back in the palace. I don't really care." Touraine stepped closer. "I promise you, though, no one here will see you until every last one of them is seen first." She pointed at the queue. They were all Balladairans, most of them laborers or craftsfolk. She felt their eyes on her skin like an itch.

Lady Théophane didn't even spare them a glance. She sniffed and tilted her head up to look down her nose at Touraine. The gesture reminded Touraine of Lady Ghislaine, but Lady Théophane didn't have the elegance or the gravitas for it to feel like a threat.

Beneath Font-Sec's condescension, though, was the nervous shift of her eyes, the tightness in her forehead before she smoothed it. She was afraid, like everyone else. If she wasn't, she wouldn't be here, bullying the world for some kind of miracle.

Théophane de Font-Sec glared a minute more, then spun away, her guards tramping behind her. She'd find some chemist hawking the most expensive cure, and she'd buy up all the bottles to make sure she'd be safe. Touraine wished silently that it was all dyed piss and gutter water.

Cold winter air cooled the adrenaline burn of her skin. Half-frozen mud slushed beneath her boots as she went to sit on the plinth of the great statue for which the park and the nearby Parc du Coeur were named. A farmer with a regal brow and a set jaw holding a pitchfork in one hand and a sickle down at his leg. At his bare feet, carved in painstaking detail, lay a bundled sheaf of wheat. Above, the sky was dull gray, a wall of clouds with no hint of sky.

How long would the Withering cut its toll out of Balladaire? Would it spread beyond the borders, to Taargen? Across the Triaume, all the way to Qazāl? To Pruett, in Masridān?

She brought her gaze back to earth to find Ghadin watching her from inside the tent flap. She stood with her hip cocked. Though Aranen had declared it fit to use, the girl still favored her left arm, sheltering it with her body. Guilt, constant now, burned at the bottom of Touraine's stomach. The first time she had ever seen Ghadin, the girl was doing handsprings to launch kicks into other children's faces. Ghadin was like Touraine—they had the same urge to fight, to move, to clash against someone. They hadn't been able to train together for weeks, and she could tell that urge was trapped. It needed somewhere to go.

When Touraine passed her to reenter the hospital tent, Ghadin muttered, "That's why the Fingers are fighting."

Touraine halted, hand tight on the tent flap.

Ah. The hanging. If it wasn't the Withering, the execution was the talk on everyone's lips, though Luca had only announced the crimes as high theft, murder, and attempted assassination. Nothing about sedition.

Touraine closed the tent flap on the next Balladairan's face with a grimace of apology. His weary eyes didn't change as he sat onto the ground. The pallor already had him. There was nothing more Touraine could do.

She bowed her head over the tent toggle gripped between her fingers. "What they did was treason, Ghadin."

The girl snorted with disgust and left Touraine there.

"No, no, no—" Aranen's voice, desperate and pleading as a tray clattered to the ground, glass bottles shattering against each other as they fell.

Touraine caught up to Ghadin as they raced to the priestess. Aranen hadn't dropped the bottles. She knelt at Romanie's side. The palace physician, one of Aranen's few friends, lay sprawled, her age-spotted hands no longer wrinkled with age, but with plague. One was wrenched backward, as if the weight of the tray itself had broken it. Her mouth gaped with horror.

"Aranen," Romanie choked. "Please."

Aranen closed her eyes, her face twisted in anger. "Shāl, preserve us." The prayer was bitter. "Touraine, give me your knife." She took

Romanie's hand and, with the other, beckoned Touraine. She held Romanie's gaze and did not look away.

"What—"

"Give me. Your knife."

Ghadin's eyes were wide as she looked between them, holding her arm close. She was not the only one who had stopped to watch them. Death and despair, hope and fear were all around them, physicians and aides, patients and their loved ones. They all waited for Touraine to show them what to do.

She unsheathed the knife and handed it to Aranen.

CHAPTER 22

A FAMILY, BROKEN (REPRISE)

Y ou married her," Nicolas rasped.

Luca had barely opened the viewing window to her uncle's cell in Le Fontinard. She limited her surprise to a stiffening of the neck. He was getting news from outside the little prison island. It could have been anyone—gossip from the guards' loose tongues on patrol. Other visitors, though she didn't know who would dare. Perhaps Ghislaine, before she'd left. She had a reason to stay close to him. Or perhaps his dear friend Evrard.

"My dear uncle. It's been a long time. How are you?"

"My dear niece. Your prevarication is charming. The niceties, then, if you wish. I'm well: I've been sitting in a cell for— It's hard to say how long. I used to track the food as it came in, you understand, but I noticed that deliveries were inconsistent. Was the variation your idea? Clever."

Luca made a noncommittal noise in her throat. "I came with a gift for you, Uncle."

The paper packet in Luca's pocket crinkled almost soothingly between her fingers, and she hesitated to pull it out. There never was a good time, a right time, to apologize for murdering your cousin, was there? There was only *too late*, and with the Withering scouring the city like some holy vengeance, Luca had a feeling that *too late* might come sooner than she expected.

That, and she needed Nicolas's advice, no matter how she curdled with shame.

"A gift?" Nicolas's hoarse voice brightened with false giddiness, but it was interrupted by a rough, wet cough. "You shouldn't have."

Luca felt like she'd climbed those despicable stairs right into a trap. But the whole world had backed her into this corner, and she didn't know another way out. Her uncle was the only one who might help her see the board more clearly. She unlocked the cell door and stepped in.

Nicolas winced at the light of the lantern. She hung it up and closed the door behind her. Deniaud and Mareau waited outside, and down the stone corridor, another prison guard. She was safe.

The cell was dim and sparsely decorated. Not for usurpers the prison of the palace walls, with silk pillows and spiced wine. His lot was now reduced to a few blankets on a cot in the corner. The chamber pot had been removed prior to her arrival. *Considerate.*

Nicolas stood to greet her, his arms held wide and magnanimous. He was much changed. He had lost an unhealthy amount of weight, and his skin was pale and papery. He was clean, though, and clean-shaven.

"You seem well informed of the outside world, dear Uncle. I take it you also know the Withering has hit La Chaise? It's in the palace now. We might have been better prepared if you had told me sooner."

Nicolas's close-lipped smile left his eyes cold. "We were rather busy at the time."

"So busy we couldn't have spared a moment for the sake of the empire? I wasn't." Luca crossed her hands over the head of her cane. She suppressed a shiver. It was cold amid all this stone.

"You put it all at risk." He paused for another deep cough, rattling wet in his chest. He cleared his throat and said, more shallowly, "You insisted you knew the full shape of the board."

This was how Nicolas fought. Homing in on her doubts and her guilt. She *knew* this. And yet, it scraped close to the bone.

"You're not well, Uncle. Can I send for something? The Qazāli healer has a tea that will help."

"Spare me." Nicolas moved to his cot, slippers scuffing on the bare stone. He settled heavily on top of the blankets, his hands cupping his knees. Luca took in a deep breath and exhaled slowly. Her leg was sending sharp pains into her lower back.

"The people will starve if I don't do something. I've proposed a new tax plan to the Courts, but it's...audacious. What would you do if you were in my place?"

For a moment, Luca felt as if they were as they once had been, sitting over an échecs board while she waited for her uncle to evaluate her moves. But this was not that.

"I'm not in your place. I've been locked in a prison by my dear niece."

"Do not punish our people for your pride." Then, with an effort, she added, "Please. I've swallowed mine by coming here. I wasn't lying when I said I would keep your counsel if you gave it."

"You expect me to have a solution for you?" Nicolas's voice rose incredulously.

Perhaps she had. Perhaps she had only wanted to speak aloud to someone who understood her. To be told that she was *not* a failure, that there was still a way out of the mire if only she looked at it the *right way*. Perhaps she was hoping for someone to tell her what that *right way* was.

"You're right. This was foolish of me. I'm sorry to have disturbed you." She reached for the lantern to leave.

"Now, now, my dearest niece. I thought you brought me a gift."

Luca thought about keeping the ring. Walking away again. But she didn't want to have to come back. And with a cough like that, the time to do it might be *very* short.

"Was my company not enough?" She pulled out the packet and limped over to him, careful to show no fear. He had lost some of his physical presence, yes, but she didn't doubt that he could still harm her if he caught her unawares. He showed no aggression as she handed it to him, but she stepped back quickly, flexing her hand where her own grief ring for Tiro sat.

He took the paper slowly, all his bluster gone. He looked like a man opening a box of scorpions as he tipped the paper out onto his hand. The small ring fell onto his waiting palm, pale gold against his flesh. It caught the light of the lamp in occasional flare. His breath came out of him in a rush, and Luca watched him deflate into his cot, curling over the small ring in his hand.

"I'm sorry," Luca whispered. "I know you will never forgive me, but I am so sorry."

He balled the ring up in his fist.

"I would have chosen him as my heir."

He didn't look up but he chuckled darkly. "So you did marry the Qazāli."

Luca's silence was admission enough.

"Congratulations, dear niece. I wish you both every happiness." He blinked and tears slid down his face, but he smiled. "At least, until she turns on you again. I hear she likes to do that."

"You think I haven't taken precautions?" Luca said callously. "You must know you taught me better than that."

Luca had taken no precautions, because she was a fool.

"Ha! Good. For a moment I thought you were going to mewl at me, tell me how she wouldn't do such a thing because she loves you."

Oh yes, Nicolas knew what he was doing. Every word he said, calculated to make her bleed. It was all Luca had thought of since Ghislaine's threat: if Touraine, in her stubborn self-righteousness, would give Luca up to Pruett. What Touraine would do if she found out Luca had sent Moyenne after her friend. How far could one stretch a thin thing like love?

"I came to you in peace, Uncle, with a gift, to ask for your help—"

"My help? A *gift*? You call it a gift, this trinket that's all I have left of my dead child? While I rot here in this prison?" He laughed and fell into another fit.

Her own rising tears made her voice waver. "You took someone from me that night, too. This accounting of grief is between us, not our people."

"What do you know of grief, Luca?" Nicolas buried his face in his hands, the paper packet crushed within. "You cannot know such loss at all."

Luca couldn't stay any longer. His pain cracked her open, and she refused to cry in front of him. She closed the door behind her and mourned him, too. Endless, this grief. Her friends. Her family. An entire empire to grieve, and the losses had only just begun.

In the stone corridor, Luca took a moment to gather herself, away from the sound of her uncle's weeping. As she made to leave, the guard standing attention at the stairwell made a slight gesture with his hand.

Luca paused. She glanced at Deniaud, who approached him instead, with Mareau at her back.

"What do you want, gendarme?" Deniaud had a high voice, but it was hard.

The prison guard saluted, then spoke so quietly that Luca didn't hear. Mareau beckoned Luca.

"Commander Perrot set me to the duke, Your Majesty," the guard said with a bow. "If it please you."

Luca reevaluated him dubiously. He was young and soft around the edges, most likely a farm boy who didn't do well enough in the training intake to have a proper guard's job in the palace or as a soldier. What made Perrot trust him enough to be an informer in the prisons?

"What's your name?"

"Guard Cloche, Your Majesty."

"You have instructions?"

"Yes, Your Majesty. Watch who visits the duke. Listen. Check his food for notes and sharps and the like. Your Majesty."

"Were you paid?" Luca asked more softly.

"Yes, Your Majesty," he repeated, eyes wide. If it was a matter of coin, or fear, her uncle and Ghislaine were as capable as she was. She looked him over again.

"How is your family?" she asked. "Are they well?"

The young man's face went pink, and because his light brown hair was cropped close, she could see the color went all the way to the tips of his small ears. "I don't have much in the way of family, Your Majesty."

"Ah. I am sorry. No one to provide for? No sweetheart?"

His face turned pinker still. "No, Your Majesty. Not as yet, Your Majesty."

Luca smiled slightly, just enough to siphon off the young man's fear.

"I want to make sure you do have prospects enough for your future. Serve me well here, now, and I will see to it. Thank you."

Cloche's eyes brightened, his imagination unspooling right before Luca's eyes.

She left him there, that innocent young guard, thinking of Yverte.

Know a man's desires and you have an extension of your will.

She had thought that once before.

CHAPTER 23

THE TYRANT

Another hanging. Another crowd of discontented citizenry, brewing another revolution that Luca needed to crush. Another step in solidifying her hold on her crown. No sandstorm threatening on the horizon, this time, blowing grit into her eyes and mouth. Only a wind blowing from the mountains in the northwest, making Luca shiver as she alighted from the carriage.

Immediately, she knew something was wrong.

The crowd was hushed instead of partaking in the usual festivities surrounding a hanging. The stalls that offered street foods and warm drinks were shuttered, even though Luca had tried to supply as many as she could. There were no jokes, no rowdy groups of children.

Beside her, Touraine scanned the crowd warily. "This doesn't feel right—" She inhaled sharply, and Luca followed her gaze up the gallows and to three nooses, where there already hung a victim.

"Ah."

"I'll go get it."

Touraine started toward the gallows stair, but Luca caught her wrist and shook her head.

"Let me. You were right. I'd rather have you down here."

Luca had protested at first, when Touraine said she would stay on the ground with the civilians; she'd wanted the people to see them as equals. Touraine preferred to stay at the rear with a contingent of the gendarmerie who were there to ensure the people's safety—and to keep an eye out for any suspicious behavior that could lead to the Fingers. To keep an eye out for Fili.

Touraine turned her hand until she was subtly holding Luca's, squeezing before she joined the gendarmerie. Luca's chest swelled as she watched her go. Touraine looked every bit the prince consort, with her gold circlet and her gold coat. It layered over Luca's first ever memory of her, at that first hanging. Her new sword hung at her hip with the long knife Luca had given her in Qazāl. An unmatched pair, but beautiful nonetheless.

Luca led Deniaud and Mareau up the gallows. Every thunk echoed in the quiet square. The murmuring grew as people noticed her, the whispering and pointing. She ignored them and focused on the noose, putting on the mask of a sardonic smile.

In the center noose was a doll with hair made of dirty straw and smelling of horse. It wore a noble's coat cut from a tailor's scraps, with blue button eyes sewn on so crudely that one dangled off the doll's face. Someone had sewn the left leg to be intentionally wrinkled, almost as the ruching of a dress or shirt. The wrong leg.

Luca freed her miniature from the rope and smiled at it. She held it up beside her and faced the crowd. "A remarkable likeness. However, I did not think I was quite so short."

She chuckled and nervous titters echoed from below, but the tension only tightened. She stepped closer to the edge of the platform, her cane in one hand, the ragged doll in the other. She forced her grip on them to loosen.

"My people. People of Balladaire. People of La Chaise." Luca's voice rang across Traitor's Corner with certainty she did not feel. *There are so many of them.*

"I know that I am a new queen and you feel uncertain about the future. But Balladaire's future isn't something I create alone. It's one we make together." She took another step forward, holding up the doll. "I can only ask your patience. No leader, no queen nor council, can make change immediately, but I swear to you it is coming. However, we struggle against greater things. Feeding and sheltering all throughout the Withering is my first priority."

She glanced to the gendarmes at the rear of the crowd. If something happened, Touraine was here. Luca should have kept her closer.

She can't save you from a shot to the head.

Luca quelled the thought. She was meant to care for these people, not fear them.

"When I sent aid to those who, for your own safety, I could not admit within the walls of La Chaise, there were those who sought to take those goods for themselves. Food for the children, blankets and tents for those who could not shelter in someone else's home. I will not stand for it! As your queen, it is my duty to make sure *all* my people are fed and sheltered, no matter what side of the Nervure they were born on, no matter if they were born in Balladaire at all!"

She turned to where other guards waited with the prisoners, below the gallows, out of sight from the rest of the crowd. They brought them up, all three of them hooded. Michel, large and broad and straight-backed, with his wrists and ankles shackled in irons, and held on either side by men as large as him. The carpenter, only slightly smaller, shoulders hunched in resignation. The boy, who hadn't had the chance to fill out the shoulders cramped tight around his ears.

If Luca were writing her own text and not reading from Yverte's, what would she write of this moment? If she got it wrong, there would never be another chance to do it right. She tightened her grip on the poppet. As the blackcoats lined the three men up along the nooses, Luca held her hand up to stop them.

"Only him." She pointed to Michel, and gestured the others aside.

The blackcoat fought the rope around the sacking covering the man's head and cinched the rope tight. No chance for last words. No martyr's speech. She went to the carpenter and the boy herself and lifted the sacking from their faces. The carpenter had been allowed to groom his beard, at her order. The boy's face was red with his sobbing, snot in the pale fuzz of his mustache.

"To these two, I offer mercy. To the others who would have followed the man who calls himself *brother* against your fellow citizens, I offer this chance to work with me, not against me, in the difficult times to come. I promise, you will never see a Balladaire so bright."

Would her uncle have ferreted out all of Michel's followers before killing him? Would Gil have offered mercy to them all, Michel included? Would her father have killed them all and saved the moral quandary for lesser men who were too afraid to *act*? Too late now to second-guess. None of them were here. None of them would write this passage in the histories.

Luca raised her hand. She let it fall.

The executioner threw the lever, and the doors beneath all three nooses, even the empty ones, swung open. One rope snapped taut.

There. It's done.

As she waited for Michel's death struggles to cease, however, the neck of the gallows bent, bowing and creaking like a weak branch before—

The gallows snapped with a crack like thunder. Luca staggered back and Michel caught himself, half on the wooden floor and half in the hole that should have been his doom, while the scaffolding crashed down around him. It felt as if the whole world gasped, and no one breathed but Michel, desperate and squealing as he scrambled, blind, onto the platform and clawed the hood off and the rope loose from his neck.

A sharp line of pain whistled across Luca's cheek. She blinked sudden grit from her eyes. Her attention snagged on the scrambling motion at the corner of one squinted eye. The audience surged toward the gallows platform. Luca turned immediately to Michel, afraid to find him orchestrating this from his own noose.

He was halfway to his feet, breathing in ragged gasps. A raw pink line smiled beneath his chin. He locked eyes with her, then traced the chaos that had become of Traitor's Corner. Despite what it had seemed at first glance, it was not the entire crowd that surged up toward the gallows. But it was enough. Enough climbing the stairs at either end of the platform, enough throwing the rocks that clattered at Luca's feet or forced her to duck. Luca couldn't see Touraine anymore, but the gendarmes in the back fanned wide to surround the square as other civilians fled.

Michel's grin was nothing short of triumphant.

"Seize him!" Luca yelled.

The blackcoats on the gallows were too busy pushing back the tide of civilians trying to reach *her* with their makeshift weapons. Even the carpenter and the boy were taking advantage of the moment. In their shackles, they had crawled to the edge and were preparing to leap off. She stepped toward them—but they were not important.

Michel's triumph didn't waver. He was barely steady on his own feet, but that smug expression—*no*. Another stone crashed into her back and Luca winced. Michel laughed as he stepped toward her, alone and powerless with no guards to do her bidding. He didn't know it yet, but that was not her. *No*. Luca steadied herself through the pain shooting up her leg. The doll was still in her hand. Behind her, the sound of the Fingers being pushed back.

"I told you it would close round your throat," Michel rasped. He charged at her, his lurching gait shaking the boards beneath them.

Luca threw the doll in his face, and in the instant it took Michel to knock it away with his manacled hands, she unlocked the catch of her cane with a twist and drew out the thin sword hidden within. It took only a sidestep at the right angle, and there—the blade caught Michel by surprise, sliding into his thigh. He stumbled and Luca lunged again, this time piercing him through the chest. The blade sucked as she pulled it back, and Michel grinned up at her with bloody teeth. He staggered to one knee.

"Around whose throat?" Luca growled.

Michel's laugh was blood-soaked and horrible from his crushed throat. Her next lunge took him right above the rope's burn, and when the laughter didn't stop, only bubbled again, Luca didn't give him a chance to spit through his red teeth at her. She simply straightened her arm once more, sliding the blade into his eye without hesitation.

He crumpled to the ground and didn't move again.

The sound in the square rushed back on Luca in an instant. Like a physical thing, it made her stagger.

"Your Majesty!" Deniaud, rushing up from the stairs where the rest of the blackcoats still held the civilians. "You must go back to the palace."

"How?" Luca glanced around frantically. They were surrounded. Deniaud's urgency only made her panic burn brighter.

Deniaud took a stone aimed at Luca in the shoulder just as an opportunistic civilian slipped past the line of blackcoats on the stairs. He had a knife.

Nicolas had taught her to pause. To consider. To linger over a problem without seeming to give it a thought, until the perfect solution came, no matter how long it took to enact.

Gil had taught her the precision of a quick strike. He had taught her how to protect herself.

Luca did not hesitate.

The Finger was dead before he'd fully clambered onto the gallows, Luca's blade darting across his neck.

"Shall we fire, Your Majesty?" one frantic gendarme shouted.

This time, Luca did hesitate. Below, her perfect plans unraveled. The Fingers would not take her, and they would not take her throne.

"Fire at will!"

Touraine had never been to a hanging that hadn't carved something out of her. She listened to Luca speak, wondering what she would lose this time.

Then she watched, horrified, as the gallows beam cracked beneath Brother Michel's weight. She watched him scrabble up to his knees, and she thought she knew. She ran for the stage, not caring that she ran with the crowd. Anything to get to Luca before the worst happened. She made herself stop. Ordered the blackcoats around her to fan out, to let those flee who fled, and close the square tighter around those who fought.

"How are we supposed to know the difference?" the lieutenant asked.

Touraine bit her lip. "If they're really scared, you'll know. But if you can't tell, hold them and we'll figure out the difference later."

Then she ran back into the crowd, dragging people aside. Beside her, they pulled stones from pockets, knives from skirts, spiked sticks that had been disguised as litter on the ground.

Shit, shit, shit.

She did the first thing she could think of. The next person she saw pull back to throw a rock, she grabbed their raised arm with one hand and punched them in the face with the other. There was a look of surprise on their face before Touraine's fist collided and they crumpled to the ground.

As she fought her way forward, they recognized her for what she was—one of the queen's, and not just anyone. Touraine remembered too late that she wore her prince's circlet to match Luca's today. It had been a smart idea at the time. A chance to show herself.

She tried for another glimpse at the stage, but clawing fingers at her eyes drew her back. She wished she had her baton, something a hair less lethal than a sword. Instead, she lashed out with her fists, ducking past makeshift weapons, breaking arms and knees as a last resort. Another glance up toward the stage, and she thought she caught a familiar young face, a flash of blond hair—

A volley of gunshots made Touraine freeze, half-crouched like a rabbit before the dogs. Pain punched her in the thigh and took her all the way to the ground. Above her, the chaos heightened. The rush of the crowd turned, and Touraine fell beneath their trampling boots. She covered her head and curled up tighter, so tight that her knife and sword dug into her ribs.

Be here, Touraine told herself. *Breathe. Be here. Breathe.* Cobblestones. Shouting. Crying. Wet. Something wet in her hands, and sticky. Gunpowder. Sweat. Coppery blood. The full fire raging in her leg.

She unfurled, leg protesting as she rolled to her hands and knees, and in the sudden gap of fleeing people, Touraine saw her. The Rose.

Fili supported the carpenter in his shackles, leading him out of Traitor's Corner and down a side street. Touraine struggled to her feet. Her left leg buckled under her weight. She'd been shot. She laughed. If she didn't, she would weep. She limped after them, matching the pace of the carpenter's chained shuffle.

Most of the crowd had already fled, or else been kettled up by the gendarmes. Some, though, the most dedicated or maybe the most angry or the most desperate—hadn't the Qazāli been all of those when they fought the Balladairans?—fought to reach Luca on the gallows stand.

She watched in mingled pride and horror, a mix that made her sick as Luca fought her own people with Deniaud at her back. Touraine should have been up there, not down here.

But Fili was getting away.

It didn't take Touraine long to find Fili and the carpenter. They'd stopped running. He sat against the wall of a weaver's, and Fili knelt beside him, holding his hand and clutching him close as she sobbed.

Despite her anger, Touraine stopped. Her own heart squeezed. She hadn't wanted—not like this.

Fili flinched at the scuff of Touraine's boots against the cobblestones. "You did this," Touraine said. "To save him? To save Michel? Or to have another chance at the queen?"

The carpenter's beard had been trimmed, and he was clean, in fresh clothes—or he had been. His hand rested on his middle, and a dark stain spread from beneath that hand to the rest of his shirt.

The girl's back shook under shuddering sobs. When she turned, though, her mouth was a flat, determined line. "To save my country."

"You're tearing your country apart."

"You wouldn't understand."

"Wouldn't I? I've been where you are, at the bottom of a ladder, with the top so far away. She let him go." Touraine gestured to the carpenter. She edged closer. Her leg made her clumsy, but she accepted the pain. "You looked for someone to blame your unhappiness on and you found it, but did you know what you would do when she was dead? When *Brother Michel* sent you off as his puppet, without caring what the palace soldiers would do to you if you were caught?" Touraine snorted. "I've been that puppet, Fili. I've been the piece people like him play. You Fingers don't have any better idea of how to fix this broken world than the rest of us. Work with us. She wants to, you know."

"She wants to use me."

"She wants you to help her save Balladaire."

"I know what happens to people who try to kill royals."

"She won't execute you."

Doubt curled through Touraine at the image of Luca on the gallows, a furious storm. The gendarmerie firing on the citizens. Firing on *her*. They wouldn't have done it if Luca hadn't ordered it.

She looked over her shoulder. No one had followed them. No one would know.

Touraine imagined Ghadin's face if Touraine dragged Fili to throw at Luca's feet. She would lose Ghadin, without a doubt.

This was Luca's throne at stake, though. Without Luca and her throne, Touraine was nothing here. She'd be less than nothing. Again. She stopped herself from reaching automatically to trace the crown on her head.

Touraine braced herself against the wall and reached over the dead man to put a hand on Fili's shoulder. The girl jerked out of the way and leapt to her feet.

"Come with me, Fili. I swear to you, I won't let her hurt you."

A lie. She couldn't swear it at all, not least because a part of her was still furious that Fili had gotten so close to taking Luca away from her. But Touraine had made Luca bend before. Fili was just a girl.

A girl Touraine was trying to arrest. A girl Touraine might have to kill one day.

Sky above, what am I doing?

Fili shook her head and stumbled backward. With one last look at her master's body, she turned and fled.

Touraine sprinted after her. She made it several steps before the muscle in her leg remembered it had been ripped apart and she fell to the ground, scraping her hands and face on the cobblestones. She drew herself back on all fours and saw Fili at the other end of the side road, away from Traitor's Corner.

Touraine could do it. She could bite down on the pain, swallow the nausea, and at least *try.* She had done harder things before. But with every breath, every moment of hesitation, the distance between them grew greater.

Fili, whose power Luca needed. Fili, who had tried to kill Luca once for the sake of revolutionaries. She was getting away. Touraine was letting her.

The realization came slowly, like freezing in the snow. She felt her whole body go numb, except instead of little by little, it came all at once and started from the inside. She even shivered with the knowledge of what this meant. She hadn't just failed Luca. She had wanted to.

Touraine pushed herself to her feet and found that her knees were shaking. She felt for the gold circlet and pulled it off. It had bent a little. She held it in one hand and supported herself on the wall with the other.

Traitor's Corner was a nightmare. One of Touraine's personal nightmares. The bazaar square massacre in Qazāl, all over again.

What made Touraine shudder as she stepped over one body, a middle-aged woman in plain gray skirts and an apron with staring green eyes, was that they were civilians. She was used to dead soldiers. She'd eat a bayonet if a single one of these people had trained for combat before going up against the gendarmerie.

What made her sick was how some of them had fallen on their fronts, facing away from the gallows, clearly trying to flee. How many of them were Fingers? How many had only come for the spectacle of a hanging? How many were there by chance? The boy prisoner lay twisted in his irons, blond curls matted red.

Touraine swallowed the bile burning her throat. It was quiet now, not even the moaning of the wounded, and the air smelled bright with blood. She winced at the tackiness sucking at her soles.

At the center of it all, Luca stood, her cane sword bloody, her hair messy in its braid beneath her slim crown. More bodies lay at her feet, crimson pools soaking into the wood. One of them was Michel's.

"Oh, Luca," Touraine whispered to herself. "What have you done?"

CHAPTER 24

A ROT

It would have been an exaggeration to say that Traitor's Corner was covered in blood. Several bodies lay prostrate on the cobbles, unmoving, and yes, blood did pool beneath them, but it didn't stream like proverbial rivers through the mortar. People knelt beside the wounded, stanching blood with coats or scarves, but that blood, too, was mostly contained by the confines of flesh and bone. And there were not so many of either, dead or wounded, that Luca could not tally them quickly in her head. Twelve. The number was twelve. This was not a battlefield. This was not a massacre.

And yet, nothing could possibly be worse.

From a child, Luca had been taught the excruciating perfection of control. Control of expression and gesture. Control of word and weapon. Deliberate action and considered manipulation. Tactical patience. Most importantly, she had learned how to hide her weaknesses until it seemed she had none, even to herself. Pain. Fear. Anger. Sorrow. Love. Because if she could not control them in herself, someone else would control her with them.

So Nicolas had taught her, and so he had been right: Luca was not ready.

Luca had just shown them everything.

Luca had just lost everything.

A small part of her in the back of her mind had known it, even as she gave the order to fire, but it was not greater than the part of her screaming *survive!*, as any beast would. Not greater than the part of her filled with contempt for the Fingers who thought they knew better than her what her nation needed.

Now that she had survived, however, she came back to herself and she knew. She had done more to further the Fingers' cause than anything they could have.

Something moved in the corner of Luca's vision and she turned stiffly, her grip tight on her cane's sword. Touraine limped toward her, her weapons sheathed and her circlet gripped tight in one hand. Luca took an unconscious step backward, almost tripping over the body of a man who had mounted the gallows to get to her. Thirteen dead, she corrected.

"Luca?" Touraine's voice was hoarse and uncertain, but it was her expression that made something inside Luca crack. Horror, turning into fury. "What did you do?"

Control.

"The gallows broke."

Grateful for an excuse to turn her back on Touraine's accusatory stare, Luca stepped over Brother Michel's body where it lay face down in an ever-widening pool of blood. Fourteen. One end of the broken beam had fallen into the trapdoor, the nooses dangling into the darkness below. The other end jutted upward, jagged splinters biting the air. It looked like a branch that someone had broken in half with brute strength.

"It was rot, Your Majesty," said the blackcoat nearest, nervously, expecting to be punished for his negligence.

Luca pressed her thumb tentatively to the wood near the break. It was soft, and the splinters crumbled at her touch. She felt Touraine behind her. "Do you think it's rot?" Luca asked her softly.

"Luca—"

Luca knocked on the beam with the head of her cane, pressing her ear to the wood. "From the outside, all the wood looks fine. But here, look." She broke more of the splinters beneath her fingers. "If it was rot, the rest of the wood would be just as weak. There aren't any holes where an animal bored through, and if it were weather damp and age, it would be more consistent."

"Luca." Touraine's voice was low and gravelly behind her. "Is this really what's important to you?"

Luca spun on her heel to see the set jaw that presaged Touraine's temper.

"If it leads me to Fili, yes. Did you see her? Was she here?"

"That's it?" Touraine was rigid with disgust.

As if I haven't counted the dead myself a hundred times over! Luca wanted to scream herself hoarse.

Luca bent, haltingly, to pick up the doll in her likeness. As she rose, she saw the hole in Touraine's trousers, and the darker black of the bloody fabric. "You're hurt."

Touraine scoffed in disbelief and stumbled down the stairs, brushing off a guard's help when they offered her an arm. Luca followed her to the carriage and climbed in after her. A moment later, they were moving.

"Did you order them to fire into the crowd?" Touraine asked, taking her sword off her belt. She leaned into the corner of her bench and propped her leg on the length of it, then unsheathed the long knife.

"They were waiting to attack me, Touraine."

"With rocks. And sticks." Touraine placed the knifepoint with careful consideration at the entrance of her wound.

"Shouldn't you wait until Aranen din—"

"She has enough to deal with." Blood surged slightly at the pressure, and Touraine winced.

Luca pulled the small knife she always wore in her boot. It had been a gift from Gil. She offered it to Touraine.

"They had knives," she said softly. "They almost got to me on the gallows."

Luca felt for the cut on her cheek that had started this. It stung but it had already begun to dry. Paltry compared to the wound leaking in Touraine's leg.

"Rocks and sticks, Luca! They had rocks and sticks, and not a one of them had military training. We could have held them off! Instead, I'm trying to get to you and you know what happens? Your blackcoats shot me!" Touraine pressed Luca's slim blade—more like a needle than a knife—to the hole in her skin. Again, blood bubbled and she bit down on the pain, her breath coming quick as the small knife dug deeper. Then the carriage jounced and Touraine growled with pain. "They could have sky-falling killed me! Did you think about that? Then I was almost trampled to death, and do you know who I see? Sky-falling Fili, dragging her half-dead carpenter, who was also shot. He died. And the boy you meant to free? Dead."

The idea of counting Touraine's body among the cobbles was enough to keep Luca from asking, *Where is Fili now?* But she also couldn't give Touraine the response she wanted. She had promised Touraine better. That she had learned from the regrets of Qazāl. That she would be a royal worth loving. Luca could see in Touraine's face how badly she had failed.

Luca took her throne with blood and poison because she wanted to be a good queen. Now, a few months later, she wasn't sure that a person could be good and also *rule*. Every theorist knew it, every sovereign who had come before her. What did she know that they didn't? Seeing the bodies in Traitor's Corner had felt like killing herself—like killing the girl she'd been. The girl who loved chevalier tales and rode on Gil's shoulders. She'd plunged the rapier into her heart as sure as she'd stuck it in Michel's eye.

"Let me." Luca moved to Touraine's bench and pulled Touraine's leg over her lap. The warm weight was familiar, but Luca was afraid to look into those eyes as she took her knife back. Afraid to see more of that horror. The disappointment.

"Are you sure?" Touraine's tone was guarded.

"I'm a musician. I have precise hands." Luca had never needed this type of precision.

Touraine snorted. Then she put her hands on either side of Luca's, holding her thigh still. She moved Luca's empty hand closer to the wound.

"It might be too far in— I'll wait for Aranen—" She groaned through her teeth as Luca dug the knife deeper.

It was all a mess to Luca, and the blood— She clenched down on her nausea, but she felt the *tink* of the knifepoint on metal. "I have it."

"Good. Fuck. Good, now just find the edge of it and—"

Touraine cut herself off with a louder growl as Luca scraped the knife and the musket ball up. Luca's stomach wanted to heave but she fought it, focusing only on her connection to the lead through the steel in her hand.

Control. Control. She had caused this. She would fix it.

"Steady," Luca whispered. Maybe to herself. Maybe to Touraine. "I'm almost there."

Then the glint of bloody gray metal. One last squeeze. Then the ball rolled from the hole in Touraine's thigh and into Luca's palm. Luca sighed in relief but Touraine took the knife back and, ashen, dug into the wound again until she fished out a small circle of blood-soaked cloth the size of a pea.

Touraine retched, then collapsed back in her seat, leg still draped over Luca. Her face shone with sweat. Luca's own hands trembled. Then, she watched with awe as Touraine pressed her fingers to the wound and the flesh pulled itself together again. Her magic would never cease to astound Luca, nor cease to disturb her. This time, when her stomach turned, she had to turn away and swallow down bile.

Control.

She focused instead on the knife tipped with Touraine's blood.

Luca wished she could not care. She wished that she could be another Ancier the First, raze the country to rebuild it in her own image. She wished she could say, *I'll do better. Forgive me.*

She wished, she wished, she wished.

Across from her, the doll stared at her with its drooping blue button eye. The ends of its arms were red brown where it had fallen into someone's blood.

Fili wept alone in her little room in La Flottille. Her ears and her nose were stopped up, muffling the world. A relief. It was good to be away from the rage in the common room.

The Fingers had ignored the white X on the door and come in anylight, because where else was there to go? The streets were crawling with gendarmes. If Fili stayed down there, though, with the railing and shouting against the queen's violence, her own hatred would eat her up. She was already burning white-hot with it, her tears scalding on her cheeks. What good was their anger? What could they do against blackcoats and their guns? All the Fingers had were rocks and tools, and a few had had rusty knives and old guns that didn't even fire properly. Not an equal fight. Never an equal fight.

Fili and Velte had come up with the plan to sabotage the gallows, to make the wood too weak to hold up to the weight of a dying, thrashing man or three. Fili still didn't think they believed she could do it until the wood cracked under Brother Michel's body. It didn't even matter. Brother Michel was dead. Maître Gaspard was dead. Olivier was dead.

Was it you? Did you do that? her master had asked at the end, gutshot and bleeding against the wall. Before the queen's hound showed up. *You're a wonder, my girl.*

Tears and snot burbled up again, and Fili buried her face in her soggy pillow. The sharp rap on the door sounded distant.

"It's me," came Velte's voice from the other side.

"Come in." Fili tried to sound less pathetic, but judging by the pitying look Velte gave her when she came in, it failed.

"You hungry?" Velte said. "We've been worried—" She glanced over her shoulder to where Joscelin was scowling, arms crossed.

"She's barely well herself."

Velte bared her teeth at Joscelin. "Look who's talking. You should be in bed."

Since that day he'd spoken, Joscelin had recovered slowly, every day a little movement. He was still thinner than he had been. The gray pallor in his cheeks lingered.

"Anylight, it's not my writing arm, so I'm fine," Velte said. She waved her right hand, but her left arm was wrapped tight in a sling. She'd been shot at Traitor's Corner.

The seamstresses and the backstreet cutters in the Fingers had done their best to sew up the injured—Fili had heard Velte's swearing all the way downstairs—but there were no doctors to look after the group. Not unless they had money to spare, and there weren't many of those types in the Fingers. Not all of them had connections like Fili had. Not that she could reach out to her mother anylight.

Velte pulled Joscelin in with her uninjured hand and closed the door. She helped Joscelin into the only wooden chair and then hopped onto the foot of Fili's bed, one leg curled beneath her, and regarded them both with her steady student's squint.

"Now that we're all awake, we need to talk." Velte grinned, eyes bright, almost feverish with excitement. "The plan worked perfectly, Fili. Perfectly."

Fili blinked, surprised. *Perfect* wasn't how she would have described any part of the day.

"It doesn't make sense," Joscelin said skeptically, his voice low.

"How does it work? Is it—" Velte glanced back toward the door and lowered her voice. "*Is* it a god?"

It should have been easy to say no, to claim it was only the wind and the roots, the rain and the earth that moved her. But what Ghadin had said ages ago rang true—what is that if not a god? Now that she wasn't hiding the magic anymore, maybe she could share that, too? She wanted to tell someone who would understand *her*.

She sat up on the bed, propping her chin on the damp pillow clutched against her stomach. She focused blankly on the planes of wood that made up the wall of her room, tracing the distant whorls and streaks.

"The god speaks through me. Through the earth and the trees and to me, and I can talk back."

"It's not right...to have a god," Joscelin mumbled. Speaking was still a labor for him. "Uncivilized."

"And if her god saved you?" Velte countered. "Magic means power, and power means we have something to use against the queen. Besides, she has her own magic, doesn't she? That Qazāli what brought her back from the dead like Fili said, isn't it? Why shouldn't we have the same?"

"Did it save...me?" He stared at Fili from sunken eyes.

"I—I don't know. I don't think it's like that," Fili stammered. "I can't fight her with it, and she can't fight me with her Qazāli."

"Have you ever tried?" Velte asked, intensely.

Fili broke their gaze again.

"What? You already tried to kill the queen. You've got a pair on you. Think what else you could do!"

"What else?" Fili tightened her fingers on the pillow.

"With Brother Michel gone..." Velte's mouth thinned. "He pulled us together. You saw what it was like when he was gone. We were shiftless. Even I'd given up. *You* roped us back. *Your* plan. Your...*god.*" Fili's plan at the gallows *had* worked. So had her plan with the wine. She clutched the pillow even tighter.

Maybe this power had been given to her for a reason. Maybe she could do more than play with wood in the back of Maître Gaspard's shop. Gaspard, who was dead because of Queen Luca.

"Our god," she said quietly. She raised her head, looked at them both. "*Our* god. My magic comes from Balladaire's god. The queen knows, and the queen is scared of it. She wants it and can't use it. So we should—" Fili swallowed. There would be no going back after this. No going back to her mother. No going back to being a carpenter's apprentice. No running back to their home in Durfort. If she chose this, she would make an enemy of the queen and die for it, or she would win. She almost laughed, because she wished she could ask her mam for advice. Her mam knew the royals, her mam knew war. She laughed bitterly at herself. "I don't know what we should do."

What did she know but plants?

But plants were life. The cycle of growth and death and dormancy, patient stillness and grasping roots.

"Let the people follow us instead. *We're* Balladaire." Velte was flushed and triumphant. "We'll be true to our roots if the queen won't."

Joscelin looked ill at ease in his seat. "We got rid... of the god... for a reason."

"No." Velte danced the fingers on her good side over her knee. "Learn your history, Jos. The *royals* got rid of the god. Whatever they didn't want, it's got to be good for us. I say we go downstairs and show them we're not beaten." She sobered. "Otherwise it's going to be well hard to get them back."

"But I don't—I don't know what to do with it," Fili said. Then, more honestly, in an even smaller voice: "I don't want to tell everyone what I can do."

"They—*we* need someone to rally around, Fili. Something to give them hope."

"I can't give anyone hope if I don't know what to do!" Fili buried her face in the pillow, hiding from Velte's insistence.

It was hard, to know that Velte was right. She might be able to say the right words, and thanks to Brother Michel, people knew her. But wasn't she too young? *She* didn't know how to lead a revolution.

"There is one thing we can gather them around," Velte said cautiously.

Velte and Jos shared a glance. Only Jos's slow, heavy breaths broke the silence.

"Me... the Withering."

"But—but I didn't do anything." Fili looked frantically between the two of them. "We don't know if my magic had anything to do with that, or if it was my pa's herbs, or—maybe it wasn't anything! What if we can't make it happen again?"

"They don't have to know whether it's true or not." Velte shrugged, then grimaced in pain, her hand going up to her wounded shoulder. "They just have to believe."

Fili didn't want to lie, but what if she *could* fight the Withering? It was the one thing she could do that Luca couldn't. Everyone wanted to be safe. Everyone would come to the Fingers.

Luca would have to surrender.

Fili straightened and looked Velte in the eye.

"We're agreed, then." Velte smiled widely. She hopped up from the bed and swayed a little, trying to catch her balance. "Come on, then."

Downstairs, the inn was quieter. There were empty chairs where regulars once sat. Fingers whose blood had stuck to the cobbles in Traitor's Corner. Fingers who'd shriveled up and been thrown onto the plague pyres. Fili felt like she was full of gaps, too. A mouth with half the teeth knocked out.

Velte ushered Fili to the center of the room where everyone could see her. Slowly, using the bar and the tables for support, Joscelin came up beside her. Joscelin, who everyone knew had fallen to the Withering. They gasped.

"Brothers, sisters. Family," Velte started. "We've lost so much already, fighting for justice in our own home. But what if I said we had something even the queen desires for her own? Something the queen can't touch?"

Joscelin's voice was a harsh whisper, but that didn't matter. All the attention was on him.

"We have...a miracle."

CHAPTER 25

A PATH

Had Luca been so naive to think that this truly could not get any worse? How silly of her. She would not make that mistake again.

As Adile dressed Luca before the vote in the Chambre des Graines, a messenger arrived bearing an unmarked letter. A folded note written on thin military scrap. She flipped it open to find Touraine's careful slant.

You were right. The roads are unsafe.

Ghislaine had been apprehended. By "bandits."

That was one worry dealt with. For now.

"Thank you, Adile," Luca said as the woman straightened Luca's collar and cravat once more. Today, Luca needed to look the part of queen.

She did not wait outside of the Chambre des Graines, steeling herself. She barely gave the herald time to announce her before striding in, her guards on her heels. Judging by the fullness of the seats, most houses had sent someone to represent their vote. Of course they had. It was about money. Today, the High and Middle Courts would vote to accept or deny Minister Beaufoi's financial reforms.

A carved wooden pedestal waited in front of Luca's chair with a vine-painted vase atop it. It was old, older than Luca's father, this vase, and the slight chips in the paint were telling. This was tradition. Twined among the painted vines the three flowers of the vote: yellow iris, the flower of bold lovers, the flower of action, for yea; pink oleander, poisonous, native to southern Balladaire, for nay (though it was said by some that it was chosen for nay because it represented the Shālan Empire); and a furled red rose, tight in its bud, for abstention.

Luca took her place before her seat, but did not sit.

The nobles of Balladaire were just as much her people as the civilians of La Chaise. Here, in her palace, they nursed the same fears—death, illness, powerlessness. But, as Touraine had told her once, they would never know what it was to have nothing. That speech would not go well here. Instead, she struck where she hoped they would be motivated. Their own safety.

"My lords. My ladies. Esteemed companions." The crowd of scarf-wrapped faces was difficult to read, but Luca continued, voice somber, head bowed. "Some of you may know that the comtesse des Champs d'Or was eager to return to her estates and I was reticent—I thought that her place was here, and after the attack on the prince consort and the marquise de Durfort, the road no longer seemed safe.

"It's with my deepest grief that I inform you, the Lady Ghislaine was recently captured by bandits on the road. Possibly by the Fingers themselves, a last vengeance for executing their leader."

Hushed murmurs filled the room. The court knew of the revolutionaries; how could they not, with the very public catastrophe that was the massacre at Traitor's Corner? Luca brushed her fingertips over the cut on her face. Touraine had not offered to heal it, and Luca had not asked.

"We all know the source of the bandits, and even the unrest in these so-called revolutionaries. The people down the hill struggle even more than us. Can we blame their desperation? I will send my best to deal with those who have turned to violence—you know I'm well versed in dealing with their sort." Grim, uncertain chuckles. "But for those who remain loyal servants of the empire, we're gathered here to do what's best for them—to protect both them *and us* from the desperation that leads to villainy. With that in mind, I give the floor to Minister Beaufoi."

Luca bowed her head graciously to the smattering of applause as if it were an ovation, and then sat back on her throne that was not exactly a throne.

First, Minister Beaufoi enumerated the terms, including, most importantly, the intended taxes on the nobility's land holdings and to what ends. In short, they summarized, the crown needed more money to care for people as the Withering swept through the nation, to feed them with the low crop yields, and to alleviate the burdens on the citizens to appease their restlessness.

"Lady Théophane Barthelme de Font-Sec," Luca said, after Minister Beaufoi finished. "You've requested to speak on behalf of the negative. You may."

Lady Théophane was eloquent and sure-footed as she navigated her points, but Luca couldn't help but think that she'd been fed the words by one of the High Court. Ghislaine, before she left, or Evrard. She simply appealed to the nobles' current fears: that the taxation would beggar them, leave them no better than the common folk, and if the commoners were invited to the decision tables, why, soon there would be no difference between them at all. She even had the temerity to say, at the end, that the Withering was perhaps a gift in disguise that would ease the strain on the crown's purse, if it was indeed so desperate.

Luca pressed the pads of her fingers into the arms of her chair. It was less obvious than digging her nails into them like claws.

It was only made worse when Lord Joffre Vestin des Beaux stood to speak to the positive vote. Sabine had sworn he was loyal, that she'd given him a list of arguments to make that would help convince the nobility, especially the Middle Court, which had always felt poorly used by (or jealous of, depending on who you asked) the High Court, but Lord Joffre was no orator. He refuted none of the arguments that Lady Théophane made, only spoke the points he had clearly memorized, stilted as a novice actor reading a script for the first time. Luca pitied him, but oh, she pitied herself more.

If Sabine had been there, she could have given this speech instead. She could have swayed them, with her charisma, with her irritating but useful skill of argument. Resentment curled in her chest, not so dormant as Luca would have liked. Sabine should have been here. Balladaire needed this vote to pass. Luca needed this.

At last, Joffre sat down, mopping his sweating brow with a kerchief. Luca gestured with one hand. "Let us have the vote."

The nobles filed to the front with their chits closed tight in their fists. The *tink* of the chits falling into the vase filled the room, louder than the muffled mutters of those who had voted speaking to each other behind their scarves.

The seneschal dumped in the absentee chits without looking. Then began the arduous process of pulling out all the chits and separating them. Though the stack of irises started strong, the stack of oleanders grew alarmingly, and despair weighted Luca down in her chair. Finally, the larger chits of the High Court members were also arranged: two iris, one oleander, one closed rose.

Luca barely breathed.

The vote was clear.

It had succeeded.

She had succeeded.

Luca rose, legs unsteady with relief. Everyone went quiet, taking their places.

She beckoned. "Minister Beaufoi."

Beaufoi stood to the side, holding their satchel with their ledgers close to their body, protective. They were pale and wide eyed. They looked up from the stacks of voting chits and came to stand before Luca.

"Your Majesty." They bowed.

"Thank you for this well-thought-out plan. You have convinced the Courts." Luca kept her voice level, as if she had not helped develop the plan, as if hope didn't leave her dizzy. "Together, we will make sure the execution of it achieves everything we wish and more."

Minister Beaufoi smiled tremulously and gave a sharp, birdlike bob. "Thank you, Your Majesty."

"You are dismissed. All of you may go. Balladaire will thank you all for this service you have done her."

Luca waited until everyone in the room departed, careful to make neutral eye contact as they left. Then she went over to the stacked chits and braced herself over the wooden pedestal, shoulders sagging. She covered her face with one hand and wept.

Someone knocked on the heavy door of the Chambre des Graines. The sound was small on the thick wood. A moment later, with no announcement, Touraine stepped in and closed the door behind her. She took in the scene, and the confusion on her face turned to grim understanding.

Touraine was handsomely dressed, not in her military uniform but a gold-and-burgundy formal version of the Qazāli vest over a Balladairan chemise. A cravat ruffed her neck. She held herself rigid as she approached.

"It didn't pass," Touraine said when she stood before Luca and the empty vase.

"It did."

"Then what...?" Touraine trailed off, her gaze lingering on the tearstains that streaked Luca's face, on the defeat in her stance.

How could Luca explain? So she simply shook her head. "Did you need something?"

Touraine frowned. "I've had a letter."

Luca felt a skip in her heart. "From Pruett."

A terse negative. "From Moyenne."

Luca's throat closed. Before she could ask for an elaboration, Touraine flicked a letter out. This was addressed to Luca. "You opened—"

Touraine scowled. "Should I have?"

In the week since the hanging, Luca had felt Touraine pulling away from her. She didn't know how to pull her back. She didn't think she could. Touraine had banked her angry fire to glowing coals, but Luca could still feel the heat.

The three Moyenne pines stamped in the wax seal were intact.

Luca unfolded it hastily, slitting a sliver of skin as she did. Had Moyenne found Pruett and taken her revenge? Luca didn't know what she wanted the answer to be, anymore. If Pruett had been killed and Touraine found out Luca had a hand in it—

Luca sagged in relief though she shielded the letter from Touraine's gaze as subtly as she could. Moyenne's connections had not found Pruett in Masridān.

Her relief was tempered almost immediately by the rest of the letter. According to the Moyenne gossip network of merchants and hunters, the Taargens were unusually "busy" for the season. Taargen hunters and trappers were taking more kills than usual—*they usually like to let the herds flourish, Your Majesty*—and their merchants were buying up Balladairan grain even at their inflated prices—*this was before the order to restrict the sale of it, Your Majesty*—and Moyenne was not sure, could not guarantee, but thought that it would be prudent if Luca prepared for war.

"War." Luca's voice was hoarse.

Moyenne was not sure, though. She could not guarantee.

"Aye."

Luca closed her eyes and crumpled the letter in her fist.

"Can I have nothing?" she whispered. "Not one untainted victory?" Rage beckoned like a refuge from the despair yawning open inside her.

"We'll find a way—"

"I cannot afford a war! Even with the vote in my favor!" The emptiness of the platitude, the utter impossibility of it made Luca slam her fists onto the pedestal. It felt good, the pulsing heat in her palms, the pain. To let it out. To stop holding it all behind the mask. She swept her arm into the vase and its pedestal. Generations of tradition shattered on the floor and the base wobbled. Luca yelled over her own breaking, "My people will starve, my court will overthrow me, and I'll be hanged by next winter if I survive this one!"

The pedestal finally tipped and landed with a crash that shook the room, its ancient wood cracking in a single line across the top.

Touraine grabbed Luca's arm. "I'll write to Jaghotai. We'll ask Qazāl for money."

Luca jerked her arm away, stepping out of reach around the pedestal. "You have no money to give, especially not to us." Even if they did, Luca wouldn't ask for it. She had *some* shame.

Touraine circled with Luca, crunching the painted shards beneath her boots. This time, her grip on Luca's arm was rough and inescapable. She yanked Luca close and pinned both of Luca's arms at her sides.

"Isn't that why we did this?" Touraine was breathing heavily.

Somehow, she loomed over Luca. Her breath was warm on Luca's face, and her eyes were as cool as the gold circlets they both wore.

"I promised you before." Luca licked her bottom lip. "I will not break Qazāl to save Balladaire. Not again."

"Not breaking. Give. Take." Touraine's grip on her tightened. Pulled her closer.

Time seemed to stop and hold them there. If Luca kissed her now, if she pulled her down onto the floor right here, would it close the new distance between them? Would it put things right? Just *one* thing right, *please*—

Luca extricated herself and pushed Touraine away. Gently, while taking hold of Touraine's vest, but away.

"No," Luca whispered. "I won't."

Shattered ceramics crunched beneath her as she shifted her weight. She coughed, embarrassed, and this time released Touraine completely.

"Forgive me." Luca knelt with difficulty and picked up an iris from the floor, remarkably still whole. She held it. "I have a meeting with Guérin."

"She's in the audience chamber." Touraine, too, seemed to be seeing the results of Luca's temper anew. Her voice dispassionate as she took in the mess. "I came to get you. I'd like to be there."

Touraine offered Luca her hand to rise and Luca took it, but she released Touraine as soon as she was on her feet. The cracks between them, spidered out. Waiting to shatter, like the vase.

"As you wish."

As they walked side by side toward the door, Touraine asked in a low voice, "What are you going to do with her?" There was a plaintiveness in it. Luca knew what Touraine wanted her to promise.

In her mind's eye, Luca watched herself step onto the path that Nicolas had carved out for her. It wasn't the path she wanted, but it was clear, and it led, if not to a flawless rule, to a rule that was still *hers*. Her name and a position to do good work from. She was already doing good work—the vote had *passed*.

Or the other path: Balladaire broken in a new Taargen war because she was killed by the Fingers; a war for succession and a revolution tearing the empire apart while the people trapped in between suffered.

"Luca?" Touraine caught her wrist, forcing Luca to face her.

"Touraine." Luca couldn't meet her eyes. She looked down instead. Touraine's fingertips were cooling against the delicate skin of Luca's wrist. Touraine's thumb flicked over the veins. Another question. The same question.

Or a third path: Nicolas, in Le Fontinard. Free him and he would make the choices Luca was unwilling to.

Touraine ducked into Luca's vision, stealing and holding her gaze. "What are you going to do?"

Better to face it like a queen. All of it. "What I should have done the first time."

CHAPTER 26

A STEP UPON THE PATH

The audience chamber was the same place they'd last seen Guérin, just after Luca's coronation. The lofty ceiling was painted with the titular scene of the chasseur and the buck, the deer's antlered head turned toward its pursuer, a princess on a black charger, hounds baying at the horse's hooves. There was no fire to keep all that space warm. No place for a petitioner to sit, and the dais where the two chairs sat—new, that second chair—was high enough to make sure the queen looked down on everyone else. The rest of the room was covered in gold and black: gilt fixtures, alternating black tapestries depicting the Balladairan horse or Luca's personal device, a crossed quill and rapier.

It was a place to impress and intimidate. It was not the place to greet an old friend.

Luca signaled, the servants at the doors flung them open and announced Guérin. Her prosthetic leg clicked on the marble floor as she approached the dais.

"Your Majesty. Your Highness." Guérin had aged in the months since. "Has there been word?" She spoke like a woman who didn't know if she wanted to hear the answer or not.

"You mean have I found your daughter."

Despite the heat Touraine had felt against her moments ago in the other room, Luca's voice was frigid. An uncomfortable tickle itched Touraine's back. The temper Luca had shown in the Chambre des Graines was locked beneath the surface, but how far down had Luca managed to bury it?

"Yes, Your Majesty."

"Like you were supposed to find her."

Guérin hung her head, her proud shoulders slumping. "She hasn't come to me, Your Majesty. I thought she would, if she were in trouble. She hasn't been in any of the places I knew her to stay. No one's seen her. She wasn't even at the carpenter's house and now he's gone, too—"

"You heard about the hanging last week?" Luca interrupted, her head cocked.

Guérin closed her open mouth. Frowned. "Hard not to have heard, Your Majesty. I'm glad you're safe." She gave a collegial nod to Deniaud and Mareau, Guard Lanquette's replacement.

Luca smiled, tight-lipped. "Did you hear who was to be executed?"

Fear crept into Guérin's face line by line, the sinking curve of her cheeks, her mouth, the knit lines at the corners of her eyes. Touraine was sure she'd even stopped breathing. "Who?" The word was barely a whisper.

"Traitors."

Of course Guérin couldn't ask what she wanted to ask. That was too dangerous. Luca drew the moment out in silence, made Guérin stew in her fear and preemptive grief, made Guérin weigh that fear against loyalty.

It was a cruelty too far. Guérin deserved better than this, no matter who her daughter was. But Luca's mouth was a hard line, and she didn't veer to look at Touraine at all.

"It wasn't Fili," Touraine blurted. Luca turned to her, blue eyes cold. Touraine stared back, then in a more formal voice said, "But she was there. Working with the Fingers."

"She used her magic to start a massacre," Luca said, "and free the man who ordered my assassination."

The relief on Guérin's face was conflicted, but still, she tried: "She wouldn't, Your Majesty—"

"Wouldn't she? I have scars that prove otherwise." Luca caressed her own stomach. Subconscious or intentional, it drew Guérin's eyes. "I begin to think that you don't know your daughter as well as you wish. I also wonder if I can trust you as I once did."

"Please, Your Majesty—"

"You asked my permission to find her, Guérin, and because of the debt between us, I said yes. But you failed. Because you failed, I failed. People were killed and my kingdom is at risk." Luca leaned back against her chair. "My own soldiers will look for her now, under the prince consort's direction."

Touraine twisted in her chair, surprised. Luca only regarded her calmly, eyebrow patiently crooked as if daring Touraine to disagree. And Guérin looked up at Touraine—on her new royal seat, with her new royal circlet—pleading.

What will you have to become, to withstand her flames? Touraine had avoided answering, even in her own heart. Now she couldn't escape it. It was Touraine's own fault that they were all there, the three of them. If Touraine had sprinted after Fili, the girl would be in Le Fontinard now, waiting for Luca's justice. Touraine had made her choice, and it wasn't Luca.

No matter how much Touraine cared for her, she hadn't chosen her.

In the quiet nights awake, Touraine had realized something else. She saw herself in Fili. Brought into the Fingers by Brother Michel, offered a dream in exchange for a few things she would regret along the way. Fili was young. She could change, like Touraine had changed.

"I'll help." Touraine held Guérin's eyes.

Luca took Touraine's response for herself. "When we find her, Guérin, I cannot promise she will have the mercy she would have had if you'd found her earlier."

If a woman could break without folding in half, Guérin did. A tiny sound, a hitch in the chest, like she'd braced for a kick and had every rib broken. But she kept standing and bowed low.

"I understand, Your Majesty."

"You may go."

Guérin left, and with every step she took, Touraine trembled. When the door slammed shut and they were alone with only their closest guards, Luca let out a deep breath. It was only then that Touraine noticed the way Luca had been digging her nails into the wooden arms of her throne.

"You didn't need to do that," Touraine said hoarsely. "Guérin is—"

"Guérin is the mother of a traitor. I did precisely what was necessary." Though Luca's voice sounded cold and unaffected, a rapid pulse ticked in her throat. She hadn't drawn her eyes away from the spot where Guérin had stood. They were still red with her weeping.

Touraine gripped the arms of her own chair to ground herself. The fear that had held her when she saw Luca standing bloodied over her own people held Touraine in place again. Now it was Guérin, whose daughter *was* a traitor. The viciousness, though, toward people who were on *their* side—that was new. Touraine could practically smell Luca's desperation. How far would Luca go?

How much farther would Luca take her? How far was *Touraine* willing to go? Because if she stayed, she couldn't pretend she didn't know what Luca was doing. She couldn't wash her hands of this and claim it was all Balladaire's fault. She wore a crown now, too.

Touraine exhaled slowly and closed her eyes. "I'll go speak to Perrot."

Before she could get too far, Luca called, with a hint of the vulnerability she had shown in the Chambre des Graines, "Will I see you for dinner?"

"Fine," Touraine threw over her shoulder.

When dinner came, though, the meal was quiet and tense. They took it in the private salon, as usual; with its deep-red wallpaper and the gold accents, the small wooden table, it was intimate and warm. Now, the closeness only underscored the silence between them. Their knives and forks clinked gently on the fine porcelain plates. They chewed and swallowed and glanced at each other when they thought the other wasn't looking, before jerking their gazes back to their food.

"So," Luca started. "You gave Commander Perrot the orders?"

Touraine swallowed her food, then said tightly, still looking at her own plate, "Yes."

Luca stilled her utensils and gathered herself up. The haughty tilt of her chin, the tight pinch of her mouth, the imperious eyebrow. It was the disapproval of a queen, not the irritation of a lover. A different Luca, not Touraine's Luca. The scabbed cut on Luca's cheek only enhanced the effect.

Touraine put her utensils down and crossed her arms. "Guérin. She's—she was my friend once." They had trained together in the mornings in Qazāl. She'd been a friend when Touraine no longer had the Sands. Touraine didn't have many friends anymore.

"I told you, I did what was—"

"Necessary," Touraine scoffed. "*Ghislaine* was necessary. *Hanging Michel* was necessary. Guérin deserved better than whatever the fuck you did today."

"I know," Luca said evenly. "Unfortunately, I don't have time to coddle her. With the Taargens coming—"

"That was coddling? What will you do next, cut her fingers off one by one?"

"As a source of information, torture is highly unreliable. What would you have preferred I do?"

Touraine scrubbed her hand over her head, then pressed her hands flat against the deep cherry wood. *What indeed?* "Not treat her like a criminal. Trust her, at least."

"Trust her? I did trust her, and now look." Luca kept her voice low and measured. "It's her daughter, for the sky's sake. How am I supposed to trust her when it's me or her child? I wouldn't even choose me."

"You were cruel to her for cruelty's sake today. And I—I don't want—" Touraine had to drag the admission out. "I'm scared for you, Luca."

It sounded pathetic, but it was true. Afraid for her. Afraid of her.

"For cruelty's sake? You think I'm doing this for cruelty's sake?" Pain thawed the edges of Luca's ice. "Do you have so little faith in me, then? After all this?"

"I don't know what to think anymore," Touraine said. "I picked my mother once and you let your general execute me. Would you do that to her, too? Even though she's saved your life sky above knows how many times?"

Luca paled, stricken. The wound on her cheek stood out. Her mouth twitched with the answer she couldn't bring herself to say.

Deny it, Luca. Tell me I'm wrong.

As Touraine pleaded silently, Luca's face hardened and she pressed her lips tight. Her grip on her silverware was vicious.

Touraine's heart squeezed painfully and she closed her eyes, exhaling sharply. She'd gotten this far by telling herself that Luca was decent. Not perfect, but decent. That there were lines Luca wouldn't cross. At the thought of being wrong—

"This isn't you, Luca. The Luca I love is better than this." Touraine's tongue froze. It was the first time she'd said the words aloud, and now she wasn't sure there was anything left of that Luca. Anything Touraine could still keep. Someone she wouldn't make herself sick serving.

Luca's eyes homed in on her as she traced the words Touraine had finally said.

"No. She's not." Luca's voice wavered and her mask crumpled. "She's scared, she's crippled, she has all the power in the world but she's powerless. She's one wrong move away from sending her country into civil war or famine if they don't all die of plague first. Probably both. I can't see any way out that *isn't* unspeakably cruel."

There she was. The Luca Touraine was searching for. Still in there. Still fighting. And so, so scared.

Touraine pushed away from the table, and panic flashed across Luca's face—Touraine knew what she was thinking; it wouldn't be the first time Touraine had walked away from her. Instead of leaving, she walked slowly around the table and took Luca by the hand. She rested the other hand on the high back of Luca's chair and knelt beside her.

"There must be something between tyranny and chaos, Luca. Your vote today. It worked. You're going to help people. *You did that.*"

"It was a peacetime hope. It won't stand up in war." Luca looked from Touraine's eyes to their hands to the plate of mostly eaten winter vegetables and pheasant. "There is no other way than this, Touraine. I've tried. Every theorist from Yverte to Pêcheuse says so. I was supposed to be smarter than this. He taught me to be smarter than this."

"You don't need to be like Nicolas, you don't *need* to listen to the—"

"I know you wanted better than this from me. So did I. But this is what I am. What I've always been." Luca's eyes were wet with tears when she looked up at Touraine. It wrenched Touraine's heart.

Then she realized what the note in Luca's voice was. A note she'd never heard there before.

Defeat.

"Fuck the theorists, Luca. We keep trying. Otherwise, I—I don't—I don't know if I can stay."

Luca's sigh blew across Touraine's lips. "I'll do what it takes to keep my throne, Touraine. With you or without you."

Touraine dropped back on her haunches, shaking her head. A thousand protests bubbled to her lips.

"You promised me, Luca."

Luca looked down her nose at Touraine. "What promise did I make you that I have broken?"

"You said you would be *good*."

"I said you make me want to be good. I would not make you a promise that I did not know I could keep."

Touraine pulled her hand from Luca's and stepped back. Luca's hand reached after her, as if of its own accord, before she brought it back to her thigh.

"Will you go back to Qazāl?" she asked, unable to look at Touraine.

Touraine exhaled a shaky breath as she backed away. "I have work to do. I won't leave my people so easily."

"'Your people.' Are they yours now?" Luca was looking for a place to wound, and Touraine ignored the bruise of it. Were the Balladairans hers? No, of course not. They didn't love her any more than she loved them. And yet...

"They became mine when I married you. Qazāli and Balladairan alike will be vulnerable in the days to come."

"You told me once that you were good at the hard math," Luca said raggedly to Touraine's back. "But you are so naive. We can't afford that anymore. Not with a war coming."

"Naive?" Touraine chewed the inside of her lip, hands on her hips. "Naive. All right."

At the door, she glanced over her shoulder. Luca sat with a fist pressed to her bowed head. Touraine hesitated on the words, sensing in them the last thing that might pull Luca back.

"Is this what Gil died for?" Touraine's quiet voice carried. "For you to become this?"

Luca's mouth twisted in a perfect, soundless snarl, and she stared at Touraine, completely still.

"Get out."

CHAPTER 27

A SECRET (REPRISE)

After their fight, Touraine didn't return to their rooms. She spent her time with Perrot and what maps hadn't been burned in Nicolas's temper tantrum, and when she had exhausted the commander but not her own spinning thoughts, she went to the hospital tent to work with Aranen and Ghadin, tending the dying and comforting the living. At least the work in the tents kept her body too busy to think.

There were so many patients now that they'd spilled past the bounds of the tent and slept outside in the cold. Where possible, they'd erected new tents or made rough lean-tos with spare canvas, but those filled, too, and so they covered as many as they could with blankets and coats and cloaks and hoped it wouldn't snow.

Touraine took turns with the physicians and volunteers, sleeping in shifts, napping a few hours at a time before returning to tend to the sick. There were fewer of them, too. It was uncertain how the Withering spread, but spread it did. It took no care for money or station. It even struck Qazāli. Rarely—too rarely—a patient's symptoms reversed. Their gray skin grew fuller, their lips moved of their own accord. Those who were spared didn't question their luck, only thanked the caretakers profusely. Touraine questioned, though. She just didn't have an answer yet. Neither did Aranen.

Day into night and night into day, they wiped brows and pressed soaked bread against parched lips, dripped water and broth, and when it was too late, with no miraculous recovery near, they called for the corpse bearers, who came in their gloves and scarves and carried the dead to the wagons that bore them to the pyres on the outer edges of the city.

Sky above, the city was thick with smoke. Even with the pyres so far from the hospital green, Touraine smelled it constantly. Knowing it was charred flesh that flaked through the air as ash only gave her another reason to distract herself with the work.

It was almost a relief when Luca sent a courier to find her in the hospital tent. She didn't deign to come herself. They hadn't spoken in over a week. The note was terse, no flourish, no apology, as if Touraine were just another officer—or worse, a servant.

Bring her back. —L

Aranen raised an eyebrow and tightened her lips in knowing disapproval. She was spooning the broth Touraine had just brought her into a barely conscious patient's mouth.

Touraine folded the letter up before holding it over a lantern flame. It caught, flared, disintegrated.

Aranen raised both eyebrows this time.

"General's business." Touraine sent the courier back to the palace with word for Perrot to have a squad meet her at the gate, along with a carriage, a small purse of sovereigns, and her own horse.

An hour later, she was leading the squad out of the city, the empty carriage trundling along behind them. She was glad to be away from the smoke, away from the claustrophobic misery of the hospital tents. Away from the aching dance of avoidance that she and Luca were performing so well.

There was no chatter between her and the blackcoats as they rode. She was their general, their prince, not their friend.

She missed having friends.

She missed Tibeau and Aimée. She missed Pruett. The prospect of war without the Sands by her side felt strange, like going into battle without one of her limbs. And now she was responsible for the lives of not just her squad or her company, but the whole army.

Tibeau would have encouraged her, as he often had. He would remind her that she had studied all those stupid Balladairan books for a reason. At least, he would have, if it weren't Balladaire's army she was fighting for. Aimée would have asked if Luca was a good lay, and when, exactly, it would be her turn. She and Sabine would have gotten on well. Touraine chuckled to herself through the sting of grief, drawing a side glance from one of the blackcoats riding nearby. It would have been nice to have a friend to talk about her frustrations with—frustrations not with Luca the queen, but with Luca her lover.

They rode southwest through the cool, crisp morning and into the afternoon until they found the first waystone jutting up out of the side of the road. The marks were worn with age, but they told passing travelers that it was three hundred miles to Chazac, down on the southern coast. A single man leaned on it, picking his teeth with a stick beneath a black scarf that covered his lower face. When he saw Touraine, he flicked his stick away and straightened, looking her up and down.

Touraine thought she recognized the man. He should have been one of Perrot's lieutenants, Forgeron. This man had Forgeron's short, wiry stature and deep-set eyes. A slouchy cap tugged low cast it all in shadow. A good choice, for the theater of it; he had the hungry look of a man who'd fallen on hard times. Last time she'd seen him, he had a beard. Hopefully it was enough of a disguise.

"Where is the comtesse?" Touraine barked.

Forgeron held out an open hand. *Where is the money?*

Touraine unclipped the purse from her saddle and shook it. Forgeron considered the enticing clink, then ran off the road a ways. A group of "bandits" huddled around their prize. At Forgeron's urging, they came, stopping short of Touraine's squad.

All of them were masked and variously disguised, their blackcoats replaced with patched cloaks, dingy shirts. They even smelled like bandits. The Lady Ghislaine was smudged with dirt but unharmed.

"Prince Consort," the comtesse said tartly. "How good of you to come and fetch me."

"Release her." Touraine dismounted and carried the pouch of coins to Forgeron. Rustling behind her as the blackcoats readied themselves for treachery that wouldn't come. "From the queen, with a warning: do not get comfortable."

Forgeron snatched the coins from Touraine and dipped a mocking bow. Though she couldn't see his lower face, he did a good job of sneering with only his eyes as he backed away.

"Are you well, my lady?" Touraine asked as she led Ghislaine to the carriage.

The comtesse sniffed. She didn't take Touraine's offered hand to climb inside.

"I've been held hostage by bandits while the queen took her sweet time deciding whether or not to ransom me. Do you think I am well?"

Touraine took a long, slow breath. "The queen has much on her mind. Be glad she saw fit to ransom you at all." She closed the door and found her own mount.

Touraine rode beside the carriage back to the city, the dread returning with every step. Those walls would close around her again soon. She pretended to keep an eye out for bandits and lost herself in the fretting.

"Is something amiss, Prince Consort?"

Touraine startled at the comtesse's voice. The older woman had pushed aside the curtains to speak to her.

"All is well, Your Grace. There are provisions in the carriage if you're hungry."

Ghislaine made a small sound of dissatisfaction. "Yes, thank you. Are you sure you would not like to join me? You seem in poor spirits. There is enough Durfort in here for two."

It was only to be expected that Ghislaine would try to lure Touraine into exposing some confidences. Touraine wasn't good at keeping her face schooled at every moment, when any expression could be used against her or against Luca. Belatedly, she realized that those in court had probably noticed how she had avoided Luca for the past week. Courtiers noticed those details, exploited them.

Which of course made Touraine scowl, because as far as she was concerned Luca and the rest of them could all go hang in fucking Traitor's Corner.

Ghislaine chuckled. "She is rather difficult to deal with, isn't she?"

Touraine smoothed her face again. "I'm not a dog you can set biting at her heels, my lady."

"Of course not." Her voice was laced with conspiratorial understanding. "She's as stubborn as her father. There's so much I could tell her about Balladaire's past, but she refuses to listen to anyone else."

"You mean she won't give up the throne like you want her to." Touraine glanced around them, but other than the driver who was Luca's personal coachman, no one else was in earshot, and it was difficult to hear over the clatter of the wheels.

"Among other things. She will crack under the strain. Ah," Ghislaine said at something else she read in Touraine's face. "Is already cracking, then. I heard things, among the bandits. A massacre in Traitor's Corner."

Touraine's grip went white on her reins. She would kill Forgeron herself, and every last one of those blackcoats for opening their mouths—

"Even before your wedding, I could tell."

It was bait. Touraine knew it was bait and ground her teeth together to keep herself from swallowing it, but the hook had already caught her deep, where she was already hurting.

"What do you mean?" Touraine refused to turn her head, but from her periphery, she saw the comtesse studying her.

"Oh, nothing you wouldn't already know." Carelessly, Ghislaine tucked back a strand of her disheveled dark hair. The streaks of gray had grown more prominent, and despite her misadventures, she carried herself as if this were a pleasure jaunt. "But when I heard that she sent Moyenne off like that, to hunt down the upstart Masridāni rebel who stole Samra' from her—well, I knew something was wrong. All those noble words she'd given at the court about reconciling with you Shālans..."

Touraine wasn't listening anymore. Pruett. Luca had sent Moyenne after Pruett. A part of her said that this was a trick, this was a lie, Ghislaine was *doing this on purpose*. Luca would never do this to Touraine.

Luca wouldn't lie to her.

But the other part saw Luca, standing on the gallows over dead civilians. Luca, over the shattered vase. Luca, dispassionate as she watched Guérin buckle between love and loyalty. Beautiful and without pity.

What else would she do?

What *wouldn't* she do?

This is what I am. What I've always been.

"Oh. Oh dear. You *didn't* know. Surely this wasn't a compatriot of yours from your conscript days? I would have thought—"

"Excuse me, Your Grace." Touraine spurred her gray roughly, and Cendre leapt ahead. From the front, no one would see her fury.

Somehow, she needed to protect Pruett.

Touraine was still riding at the front of the train as they approached La Chaise's western gate. Traffic was thick; a holdup at the gate. She flicked a signal to one of her blackcoats, and the soldier rode ahead of her and Ghislaine's carriage.

"Make way," called the blackcoat. "Make way for the prince consort."

The crowd split fitfully. As Touraine rode through it, she watched as the upturned faces changed from Balladairan farmers and laborers with their hollow-eyed expressions to weary Qazāli, with packs on their backs and their shoulders tight around their ears like they'd been hunted.

"What's going on?" Touraine asked when she reached the front. "Who's on duty here?"

The guard on duty at the gate had blocked the path with a squad of blackcoats. Above, more blackcoats trained their rifles on the Qazāli below.

"Answer me." Touraine glared. "Did the queen order you to stop Qazāli at the gate?"

A woman with a lieutenant's stripes on her sleeve came forward and saluted.

"It's not that, sir. I mean—Your Highness, sir. They asked to see the queen, sir. To be taken to the palace." The woman swallowed so hard her throat bobbed. "It was irregular, Your Highness. We sent for you direct. Didn't realize you were gone."

Touraine frowned and scanned the group of Qazāli on foot until she found a familiar face.

Jaghotai stood at the front, feet planted, her arms crossed over her chest, staring right at her. Touraine felt awkward on her royal horse, in her prince-general's coat. If Touraine had thought the old rebel would be impressed, she was badly mistaken.

"Your Highness." Jaghotai gave Touraine a mocking bow.

CHAPTER 28

THE JACKAL
AND THE WOLF

Luca rode to the gate on horseback, and so she was already in a poor mood. Her horse whickered and shifted beneath her, and she gripped the reins tighter. The messenger who'd fetched her said a Qazāli ambassador was at the gates demanding to see the queen. That was urgent enough for Luca herself to go investigate. Qazāl had assigned no new ambassador since the wedding; Luca and Touraine had heard nothing from the council at all. On her way to the gate, Luca had thought the worst—this was a trick. A ploy of Pruett's.

Her mood soured further when she saw that a group of Qazāli were already filing into the city.

She stopped her horse in front of them and looked for the lieutenant on duty. "What is this? Halt and explain your business."

The Qazāli woman closest to her had a martial look that made Luca uncomfortable. Soldiers, ready to infiltrate—

Luca smothered the irrational fear. "Do you have an escort?"

"Me."

Luca hunted for the source of Touraine's voice. She stood by the gatehouse door with the lieutenant. Luca urged her horse through the crowd. It wasn't just the newly arrived Qazāli but Balladairan civilians, too. They pressed in. She half expected them to drag her from her saddle and try to kill her again. The cordon of guards nearby didn't make Luca feel any safer.

At the gatehouse, Luca dismounted and met Touraine's blank, stony expression with cool. "Is it your place to grant *anyone* the right to see me, my lord?"

"Do I not have the right to see my daughter's wife, Luca din Touraine?"

Luca froze with her face in her mount's shoulder. She wasn't sure what startled her more—the Jackal's voice, or hearing her married name in the Qazāli fashion.

To cover her falter, she patted the beast's shoulder before ducking under its neck. Jaghotai emerged from the group of harried Qazāli.

The Qazāli rebel stood beside her daughter, and Luca could not imagine how anyone had missed the blood shared between these two. Their mirrored noses, the tilt of their eyes, the same broad shoulders and thick arms. Jaghotai was fuller compared to Touraine's lean muscle, and gray rose from the roots of her dreadlocks, but only a fool would think Touraine was the more dangerous of the two. They even stood the same, with their arms crossed, wearing the same dubious scowl—Touraine's was pointed at Jaghotai; Jaghotai's was aimed at Luca.

The jackal and the wolf.

Perhaps some things simply were in the blood. Luca couldn't help the quirk that tugged at her lip.

"Jaghotai. It's good to see you again," Luca said, speaking in her over-formal Shālan. "You're Qazāl's new ambassador?"

"Is that why you're here?" Touraine frowned. "I've been keeping you up to date. You shouldn't have come. There's a plague." She jerked her head at the gate, at the soldiers in their scarves.

"You think I would come to some uncivilized plague city for a tour?" The Jackal snorted. "Is this where the great leaders of Balladaire conduct their business? In the street, with no refreshments for their guests?" She clicked her tongue, and Luca wasn't convinced the disgust was a jest.

Touraine leaned over to say in Luca's ear, "Ghislaine is in the carriage." Her voice was tight, and no wonder; Jaghotai had a way of putting Luca on edge, too.

The unmarked carriage surrounded by guards waited to be let through. The curtains were pulled closed, but Luca had no doubt that Ghislaine was noting everything she could.

"Have her escorted to her rooms and kept there. For her own safety, of course."

"Of course."

Touraine exchanged a quick word with one of her blackcoats, and in moments, the carriage was bustling toward the palace. Then she came back, leading her gray mare by the reins. Funny, how things had changed. Luca remembered how afraid Touraine had been of that sweet horse before the parade last autumn.

"Do you want to ride behind one of us—" Touraine started.

"I can call a fiacre for you," Luca said at the same time.

The Jackal looked between the two of them, smirking. She scoffed and shook her head at a private joke. Then, without warning, she grabbed the horn of Cendre's saddle with her good arm and swung herself up. The gray was too well mannered to do more than dance sideways in surprise, and she turned readily at Jaghotai's direction.

"My best friend was a Brigāni," Jaghotai said to Touraine's shocked face.

"Hein?" Touraine was dumbfounded.

"Here." Luca offered her a hand. Touraine eyed it for a long moment before grabbing it and pulling herself into the saddle. Luca tried not to show the strain it took to lever the woman up. She also tried not to show the flutter she felt with Touraine pressed against her back, thighs wedged against hers. For a moment, she forgot her irritation. "The Brigāni tribes—Djasha din Aranen—were renowned horse breeders. Quite a few of the palace's horses come from Brigāni stock."

"And how do we think that happened?" The Jackal shot Luca a flat look.

Luca flushed. Touraine snickered behind her. Just like that, the irritation returned. With a small burst of pettiness, she clicked her horse forward abruptly. Touraine yelped and clutched Luca's waist.

"Ass," Touraine grumbled against her shoulder.

She didn't release Luca, though, and Luca relaxed against her. Some of Touraine's words had been unforgivable. Some of them, however, had been no more than Luca expected. Inevitable, even. Luca wouldn't hold Touraine against her will, and Luca would miss her if she left. Quite possibly, her heart would break. But she had meant what she said.

"Did you invite her here?" Luca spoke just loudly enough for her voice to carry over her shoulder above the clatter of the horse's hooves on the cobbled streets.

"No."

"Do you know why she's here?"

"If I did, I would have told you."

"Would you?" Luca guided the horse around a commotion on the side of the road, a screaming match between a family, perhaps, or a merchant and customer. No—someone was screaming, but someone else was dragging out a body.

A plague death. The door was unmarked. The people touching the body had their faces wrapped, but—had they been living with the victim? Luca swallowed the sour spit of her fear and urged the horse on.

"It's getting worse," Touraine murmured. Luca felt her scoff. "Some of them won't bring their sick to us because...we're Qazāli. So they stay out here, maybe infect more people. Die."

Though quiet, her voice was thick with aching frustration.

Luca covered Touraine's hand with one of hers. Laced their fingers together.

Luca and Touraine met the Jackal in a private sitting room. The old rebel's entourage had chosen to go to their new rooms—most of them in the palace guards' quarters. One of them, however, remained. It took Luca a moment to recognize the young blond woman at Jaghotai's side. Aliez LeRoche looked much older than she had over a year ago. Sun had creased her eyes and freckled her tan face. She sucked her dry bottom lip into her mouth and bowed to Luca.

Jaghotai took the whole room in at a glance, her hand on her hip. Balladaire's rich landscapes woven in tapestry, the art of its carpenters in the wood of the furniture, its sculptors in the flourishes of the stonework, all of it taken in and dismissed with the sucking of her teeth.

"Welcome to my home," Luca said, bowing her head, one ruler to another. "Coffee is on the way, and something to eat. I'm afraid we're rationing somewhat given the circumstances, but if you wish it, only ask. We'll do our best."

Jaghotai grunted.

Leaning against the door, Touraine folded her arms across her chest and cocked one foot over the other. "We weren't expecting you, Jak. Why are you here?"

The Jackal sighed. Her shoulders sagged. She looked less like a rebel leader and more like a middle-aged woman tipping to old. Not weak, but tired. She dropped down on a thickly cushioned chair, stretching her legs. She rubbed idly at the left one.

"I'd rather only tell it once."

The refreshment came before Aranen. When at last the priestess arrived, they were finishing their second cups of steaming coffee.

Aranen's mouth fell open when she saw Jaghotai. "Jak. What are you—"

"Aranen." Jaghotai's voice was thick with emotion as she stood and gathered Aranen into her arms.

Luca flicked a glance at Touraine. Touraine had almost certainly not been greeted like that, but that was not Luca's business.

"Well?" Touraine said after the two friends broke apart.

Jaghotai returned to her couch. There was a hesitancy in her now that Luca would never have imagined in the woman Touraine spoke about.

Never forget your enemies have more facets than sides of a die, Yverte wrote.

She's not my enemy now. But, oh, how quickly those things could change.

"El-Wast has fallen. Qazāl has." She held her head in her hand before looking up at Aranen from beneath her fingers. "I tried. I'm so sorry."

"Fallen?" Aranen echoed, her voice faint.

"To whom?" Luca said sharply.

Touraine was silent and still, waiting.

Jaghotai jerked her head at Touraine. "Your sharpshooter. She came with a raven bitch from Taargen."

"Who?" Luca asked Touraine, even though she already suspected the answer.

Touraine closed her eyes and exhaled sharply in disbelief. "Pruett."

A burning hollowness spread through Luca's chest. "Please, tell me you didn't know."

Touraine turned to Luca, and for a moment, Luca could have sworn she saw hatred there. Then it was gone and Touraine looked away again. "Of course I didn't know."

"So she didn't take Masridān at your command?" Luca asked Jaghotai. "Has she joined the Taargens?"

Jaghotai bared her teeth. "Not at my command, no. I'd say she's on no one's side but her own. Me and the rest of the council refused, but next thing I knew, strangers were knocking at my door in the middle of the night."

"What about Malika and Saïd?" Despite Touraine's new court habits, her anger was plain in the cant of her dark brows. At least Luca wasn't Touraine's only disappointment.

"Fine, as far as I know."

"What do you need from me, then?" Luca asked. "Refuge? I might have mentioned, my city is besieged by a plague. And perhaps soon by Taargens. Or do you need soldiers to take the council back?"

"*No.*" All three Qazāli women spoke the word immediately, all spinning on Luca, their expressions running from exasperation to contempt to horror.

Touraine kicked off the door, clasping her fist in her palm and tapping her lip. "She must be coming with the Taargens. Or she knows they're coming and she's taking advantage. We need more soldiers."

Luca bit back her sour retort and crossed her hands over her cane. Of course they needed more soldiers. But how? To pay them all with money the banks had loaned Luca for food? To feed them and their horses with the last of the empire's grain?

In a slightly more measured tone, she said, "A levee of plague victims is hardly the most intimidating military force."

Touraine scowled over her fist. "You know what I mean. Pull the soldiers from the High Court houses. I'll lead them."

"No," Luca said immediately. "No. You're not going."

"Why else am I wearing this coat?" Touraine plucked angrily at her golden breast.

"No. We need you here. Aranen and I need you—" Luca looked to the priestess for support. Aranen's eyebrows knit low as she frowned thoughtfully, but she didn't answer.

"She's my friend." Touraine swallowed and stared down at her clasped hands.

Touraine wouldn't be able to fight Pruett. Luca read it in her hesitancy.

"We have messengers." Luca tried to keep her voice level and cool. As if the idea of sending Touraine away, sending her to *Pruett*, sending her *to war* wasn't filling her with panic.

Touraine, on the other hand, spoke with resignation. "Messengers take too long, and they don't have enough authority to act. I'll go."

"Touraine—"

Jaghotai cleared her throat loudly. "It sounds like you two have something to discuss. If you don't need me here for your lover's quarrel, I'd like some real food and a nap in a bed that doesn't move."

Embarrassment flared hot across Luca's face. She'd forgotten the older women entirely.

"We all have plenty to think about," Aranen said diplomatically. "We won't make any decisions tonight."

"Of course. Forgive me, Your Excellency." Luca bowed in her seat. "I forgot you only just arrived. I'll leave you to your rest. We'll speak soon. Touraine?"

"I'll stay a bit longer," Touraine evaded. "If you have another minute, Jak."

Jaghotai didn't protest, so Luca left the sitting room, already replaying the mistakes she had made while simultaneously hunting out a new path to victory on a game board that had drastically shifted.

Instead of resting like she'd told Luca, Jak asked Touraine where she could stretch her legs. They said their goodbyes to Aranen and Aliez, the Balladairan girl who had been born in Qazāl and never left, and then Touraine took her to the training square in the palace courtyard.

It was good to spar with the Jackal again. Good to remember the other ways of moving her body, the motions she had learned in Qazāl. The palace soldiers stopped to watch them in fascination. It was the closest thing, Touraine thought, to what other families might call a hug. But now the sentimental bit was over and Touraine was no longer the estranged daughter, just another rebel under the Jackal's command.

"You married her."

Jaghotai sipped water from the cup a servant had brought her, swilled it through her mouth, and spat it into the dirt. She mopped her stump across her broad brow, sweating even in the cool winter air. Touraine sat on the wooden bench beside her, elbows propped on her knees, hands dangling, empty, her head bowed as she caught her breath.

"I did."

"A condition of the treaty?"

"No."

"Because you're lovers?"

"How did you know about that?"

"I have eyes. Was it?"

A second of hesitation. "No."

"Then why?"

"You asked me to play her. To *use* her. Now we have everything we wanted, don't we? For Qazāl." The words came out more bitter than she meant them to, hiding the truth as they were. It wasn't entirely a lie, though.

"*Play* her. *Use* her. Not *marry* her."

"It's already done, Jak. Both sets of customs and laws. Aranen did the full Shālan ceremony." Touraine held up her scarred palm at Jaghotai's questioning eyebrow. "Touraine din Luca. Hardly seems like you're in a position to make any promises about Qazāl besides."

"So you're not coming back?"

Not the question Touraine expected.

"No. I don't know." She gestured vaguely at the sky. "Maybe if we make it out of whatever's coming."

"We'll fix it," Jaghotai insisted. "After this, you'll come home."

"Stop." Touraine spoke with such iron in her voice that Jaghotai leaned away from her. "Why do you care so much, anyway? You afraid what I'll get up to if you can't watch over my shoulder?"

"Why shouldn't I be? Look at the cock-up you've made here." Jaghotai's words were cruel, but they sounded forced.

"I'm asking you to trust me," Touraine growled.

"How am I supposed to do that when I barely know you!" The Jackal's breath heaved. "I send you to do one thing and you go running back to *them* without even thinking about what you commit us to! What do we do now if we want to get out of this mess with *your wife* and the Taargens? Eh? What?"

Touraine couldn't answer the question. She was still reeling from the first gut punch of a sentence. *Those* words did not sound forced. If it had been anyone else, she might have rationalized her way out of it. *Ah, she's angry. She didn't mean it.* It might even have been true. But this was Jaghotai. She'd carried a rock into the desert to memorialize Touraine. To mourn her loss. The daughter she'd had—*Hanan*—gone. Never coming back. All that was left of her was captured in that stone.

"You'll never forgive me for not being her." Touraine balled her hand into a trembling fist on her knee.

"What? Who—"

"I'm the most powerful person in Balladaire." Touraine stilled the angry quaver in her voice. "Do you realize that?"

Jaghotai snorted. "Second most, last I checked."

Touraine shook her head. "She loves me. I made her bend for me once. I could do it again." She'd felt it, in the squeeze of Luca's hand, on horseback.

"Do you love her back?" the Jackal snarled. "Because if you do, if you'd get on your knees for her, then you haven't won us anything."

"People have been passing me back and forth so long, how would I even know what love is? Good to see you again, Jak." She stood.

"Wait."

Despite herself, Touraine turned.

"Aranen. The hospital. She's been healing the Balladairans? They know...about us? About Shāl's gifts? Both of them?"

"Aranen hasn't told you?"

"Told me what?" Jaghotai said flatly.

"It's not mine to tell—"

"If it has any bearing on how we move forward, you'll tell me now and not make me chase the two of you around this Shāl-cursed palace."

Touraine sighed. "She doesn't have her magic. Not since...Djasha. I'm the only healer here."

Jaghotai processed this, her eyebrows low and her lips pressed together. Twice, she inhaled sharply, as if she were about to speak, and twice she let the breath whistle out of her nose without saying anything.

"She kept it quiet all this time." When she finally spoke, Jaghotai's voice was soft and surprised, and if Touraine didn't know any better, she'd say the Jackal sounded hurt. But she cleared her throat roughly and said, "If you can heal, we still have a priest."

"That's it?" Touraine said, incredulously. "That's all you have to say about it?"

"What else do you want me to say?"

"I don't know! First, I'm a filthy dog of the empire, now I'm your last priest. Isn't there something—argh!" Touraine gripped the air with hands like open claws. Trying to make Jaghotai understand was a waste of time. "Never mind."

"But the Balladairans know about it?"

Touraine grunted.

"It was your princess, wasn't it?"

"Of course it was, but no one believed her until I healed her beneath a chandelier in the fucking Grand Hall after someone tried to assassinate her. I did it, Jak!" Touraine threw her hands up in the air. "That's my fault, too! If I hadn't, you'd be here falling on Duke Nicolas's feet and begging for *his* mercy. I can tell you, you'd have been better groveling for LeRoche than the duke. So yes. I made choices, Jak, but Shāl take my eyes if I'm not doing my fucking best. If I fuck the queen on my way, what is it to you? I've done everything else you asked of me. What more do you want?"

The Jackal raised her head slowly to look up at Touraine, standing above her. Her eyes were the same brown that Touraine's used to be, and Touraine felt a stabbing sense of something like homesickness. A homesickness for herself. For who she'd been once.

"A loyal child." Jaghotai pushed herself up. The slope of her shoulders told her age in a way her body hadn't when they were sparring. "Seems too much to ask, though."

She turned then, leaving Touraine, when Touraine had meant to be the one to walk away. Leaving Touraine with all her own fear and hesitation still locked up tight in her chest.

She hadn't even been able to tell her mother that she had missed her.

CHAPTER 29

THE HUNTERS

The next morning, Luca invited Aliez to her private salon for lunch. She had much to tell the young woman. Before that appointment, however, Luca needed to pay a visit to Le Fontinard.

Though they were speaking again, however tersely, however briefly, Touraine did not come to bed with Luca. If anything, Touraine seemed even colder toward her. At first, as her thoughts spun with nothing and no one to distract her, Luca thought it was the residual anger from their fight over Guérin. Then, she thought it was from her friend Pruett's betrayal. It wasn't until she turned her mind to dealing with Ghislaine that Luca realized—they had arrived together. Luca had never intended Touraine to fetch Ghislaine herself. Had Ghislaine gone back on her oath, and told Touraine what Luca had done?

In the end, Luca had only been able to placate herself with the unfortunate logic—if Touraine thought Luca had tried to hurt Pruett, Luca would have gotten much more than cold looks.

Not a single step that she climbed in Le Fontinard improved her mood, nor did the sight of her uncle standing in his cell instead of huddling piteously against the wall.

"War is coming," she said with no preamble. "With the Taargens."

"Mm. Taking advantage of the instability you brought."

She opened her mouth to say that she wasn't the one who had usurped the throne, nor did she cause the Withering single-handed, but passing blame back and forth would change nothing.

"Thank you for the extra blankets," he added. "And the medicine. That was you as well, I presume?"

The blankets in question were folded in a precise stack on his bed. Tiro's ring winked at her from his finger.

"I'm surprised you didn't think it was poison," she said flatly.

"To the contrary, my dear niece." He was calmer than when she had last seen him, his grief buttoned away again. "I hoped it was. Imagine my surprise and dismay when, hours later, I was not only still breathing, but breathing better." Nicolas patted his chest.

"Next time, I won't bother. Will you continue to hold the empire hostage, or will you tell me what you know about Balladaire's magic?"

"How could I hold anything over your head? You have all the power. Use it. Squeeze the fist and it is yours."

Luca gritted her teeth. "I'm not you, Uncle."

"You've said. And as I've said before...that is a great pity." He paced back to his bed and stroked the thick blankets. "Has she left you, then? Your half-civilized Qazāli? You seem especially desperate today."

As usual, he dug unerringly into Luca's cracks, and she felt like nothing more than shattered porcelain.

"Who will you replace her with? One of the Bear Queen's children? A tidy solution, though they're as uncivilized as the Shālans."

Luca dragged hard on the reins of her badly frayed temper. Damp crawled into her leg, aching in the joints and the seams where the bones had healed. The odor of mildew hung like a dense fog.

"I am still married to Touraine."

Touraine, who was the prince-general of her armies. Touraine, who wanted to parlay with her oldest friend, a woman who despised Luca. A woman who had more ties on Touraine's loyalty than Luca ever could.

Her uncle chuckled with genuine mirth, a sound Luca had not heard in years. It felt like a thing he'd stolen from her himself, that laughter. Yet another thing she'd deserved, something she'd loved, taken.

"Tell me, Uncle. If you ever loved me—if you ever loved your brother or even this sky-falling country, Uncle, just *tell me*. How can we use the magic against the Taargens?"

Nicolas chuckled and shook his head. "Maybe you are more like your father. So incompetent that the only path you see to victory is to put your reliance in chevalier tales and uncivilized magics—and then, when you fail, you'll give these same gods the blame for it, won't you?" He paced the small cell as if it were his private library. "Not your fault, never yours. You were never the wrong choice, you were never unsuitable."

Luca held her tongue until she thought she would bite it off.

"If you want it so badly, dear niece, take responsibility." Nicolas grinned as if he had made a daring play and was waiting for Luca to realize she was a few inescapable moves from checkmate. "Show me you have what it takes to rule. Or let me out so that I can do what you cannot."

It would be so easy to do as he said. Nicolas. Her dear uncle. She *had* done as he said. And sky above, the way that Touraine had looked at her... Touraine didn't understand what it was to rule, not like Luca.

But there were lines.

"No."

"I won't stoop to insult your pet—your wife, rather, whatever you wish to call her. She was an excellent specimen; I told her so myself. But if I did, would you? Would you finally *act*?"

There were *lines*.

"Deniaud, come here."

Deniaud stepped inside. Her dark queue was neat. She still wore her gloves.

"Your Majesty."

"Close the door behind you, please."

Deniaud obeyed.

"Nicolas Ancier has something he'd like to tell me, but he wishes to be persuaded."

"Your Majesty?" Deniaud glanced from Luca to her uncle.

If Nicolas looked more vivacious this visit, pacing his cage, he still looked diminished. His skin sagged papery at his jaw and neck. It aged him, and the thinning of his brown-gray hair only made the change more pronounced.

Weren't there? Lines?

"Persuade him."

"Your Majesty." Deniaud bowed her head. If the request shamed her, she gave Luca no sign. "How would you prefer?"

"Start with your hands. If he asks for more, we can oblige."

Luca locked eyes with Nicolas and saw the triumph on his face right before Deniaud's backhand caught him across the cheek. He stumbled onto his bed. Bright pink splotched the pale skin. His grin widened, a smear of red across his teeth.

"Again. Use your fists. Stop us when you're ready, Uncle."

Deniaud rained blows upon Nicolas, ceaseless. Luca's own fists dug into her palms until she broke skin.

"Enough," Luca called out when she could bear it no longer. Nicolas had long since curled himself into a ball, his knees close to his chest, his hands over his head. He had not cried for mercy. "Are we ready, yet?"

From the bloody heap on the floor came a raspy chuckling, bubbling and wet from her uncle's squashed face, soggy with blood and spit. He uncurled himself slowly, his gasps of pain mingling with his laughter as if each were its own part of a breath—mirth and agony, mirth and agony.

"No, my dear niece. You are far from ready. But this is a start."

Aliez arrived at Luca's salon in Qazāli clothing, from the hooded vest down to the soft, low boots, though she wore a long-sleeved shirt beneath the vest to account for the cold. Her hair fell in a loose flaxen sweep, so different from her brother's tidy braid.

"Your Majesty." Aliez LeRoche bowed before sitting. "It's a pleasure to see you again."

Luca gestured to the crusted bread, the thick slab of cold butter, the small jars of fruit preserves, the cold meats, but ate nothing herself. Her stomach was leaden with the news she had to deliver—and what she had just done in Le Fontinard.

"I hope you traveled well? How was it with the Jackal?"

Aliez ignored the food, picking up the delicate cup of strong Qazāli coffee. She smiled wryly behind the rim of the cup.

"About as you'd expect. Is my brother in the city, then? He hasn't responded to my notes, but now I know the city has been under plague, that's not so strange. I wanted to tell him about Father. He—"

"Aliez," Luca interrupted softly. She rubbed her fingers together nervously. If she could have put this off longer, she would have. The right words hadn't come overnight.

Aliez didn't need the right words. Her hand and mouth went slack at the same time. She set the cup down and frowned at the breakfast table, blinking rapidly.

"Was it the Withering?"

"It was not. It—"

—*claret-red blood, thick, throat gaping*—

Luca closed her eyes tight against the squeezing ache in her chest.

"What happened?" Aliez whispered. Her hands balled into anxious fists.

"He was murdered." Luca's voice cracked. She cleared her throat. Tried to speak firmly. "Duke Nicolas had him killed. To make me surrender. It was— I held a funeral."

"How?"

"On the royal pyre grounds, with every hon—"

"How was he killed?" Aliez asked through gritted teeth.

"He— Are you sure you want—"

"How was he killed, Your Majesty?"

"His throat was slit."

"The duke slit his throat?"

"I believe an assassin was hired."

Luca reached hesitantly across the table and gripped one of Aliez's trembling fists in her own just as the other woman's tears began to fall. Aliez's grief summoned Luca's own, already close to the surface, and they wept together in silence.

After a few minutes, Aliez seemed to remember whose hand she held. She released Luca and wiped her eyes with the heels of her hands. The sudden coolness left Luca feeling bereft.

"Where is the duke now?"

"I've made him pay for Bastien's life twice over."

Luca didn't tell her that that price had come out of her own heart, too.

"Whatever it is," Aliez said, her voice dull and raw, "it's not enough."

"Perhaps not."

Luca let Aliez sit with her anger a moment longer, then she wiped her own cheeks.

"This isn't the only reason I wanted to speak with you."

Last night, as Luca had considered how much to tell Aliez, she'd come up with a way to deal with Ghislaine and any other malcontents the comtesse would stir now that she was back in the palace. She laid out her proposal.

"So you see," Luca finished, "the comtesse will welcome you as her daughter's dear friend, back from the wild desert. All updates could be passed on to me discreetly. We won't let her help my uncle back to power. Will you do this?"

"I will." Aliez sniffed. Despite her watery eyes, her mouth was set in anger. "Why haven't you hanged him? I was glad to see my father drop."

Luca envied Aliez her certainty. She didn't know if it was youth, or the sheer force of Aliez's hate, but the young woman didn't waver. Luca and Bastien had never spoken of the things his father had done. They'd toed around the spot, even when they were regularly sleeping together. A wound she never probed. She thought it had been out of her own kindness, but maybe it was not.

Luca leaned her elbows on the table and studied her clasped hands. The gleaming grief rings, especially the smallest one with the twinkle of sapphire. She thought of striking him herself, the ring cutting into his lip. Even now, it wasn't unpleasant to imagine.

She sighed. "I'm afraid I may need him a little while longer."

Or perhaps she was simply . . . afraid.

CHAPTER 30

AN EXCHANGE

Within days, Fili became a legend.

Or at least, it felt like she'd become a legend. As much of a legend as you could be when it was only a few quartiers that knew your name, and only those in the quartiers who were part of the Fingers.

Word was spreading. The people who came to La Flottille with its white X across the door—it had become a badge of pride, that X—stopped being people that Fili recognized, and even if they didn't all put their names in Velte's ledger, they listened, rapt, while Velte and Joscelin spoke their piece against the rule of the nobility and the queen's useless promissory notes.

Without fail, they all lined up after to touch Fili's hand or have her touch them, or touch their little babe all swaddled up. If they had it to spare, which happened more and more often as word spread up from La Gouttière to the merchants across La Chaise, they'd drop a demi- or quart- or even a cent-sov in Velte's upturned cap. (First time it happened, it was an accident. Then Velte started leaving it out every night.)

Fili didn't let Velte use the money on overpriced wine, though. Not all of it, anylight. She made Velte source more of the herbs Fili had gotten for Jos when he was sick. Some, they kept for Fili to grow in her room. Then they sold those for a few coins, too. It was going so well that they'd decided not to show everyone Fili's magic; it was safer, Joscelin said, even as they experimented little by little to see what exactly Fili *could* do.

"We can't keep doing this here," Fili said, up in her room about a week after the hanging. "If the queen is still looking for us, she's bound to notice."

"What do you suggest, O Mystic One?" Velte asked. Her usual sarcasm came out weak. She sagged on the foot of Fili's bed again. Her wound was inflamed and weeping beneath the bandage, and it pained her.

Fili flushed.

"Girl's right," Joscelin said from his post at the doorframe, where he leaned with his arms crossed over his now-thin chest. "Not that I'm keen to traipse all over the city." He still moved slowly, like every movement was a giant's effort. "But we have friends enough. Plenty would host the Lucky Hand."

Fili and Velte winced. That's what people had started calling Fili. Velte moaned that it was uninspired, not the name for a legend.

"Anylight," Velte said quickly, cocking her ear toward the door. "Sounds like the Lucky Hand's adoring public awaits. Shall we?"

The noise grew louder as the three of them walked downstairs to the common room. Fili let Velte and Joscelin lead the way.

Plants grew in every corner of the inn now. Herbs near the kitchen and the bar, pots with shrubs and small trees lining the walls, and blooming flowers on the tables that had no business perfuming the air with winter still bitter and not shy about coming in through the open doors. It was odd, even a little off-putting. Velte said it made a statement.

The full common room went quiet as soon as Velte and Joscelin split apart to reveal Fili behind them. They'd gotten good at the performance, and no one was more shocked at herself than Fili. Ghadin said revolution was not a game, but maybe it was a bit of street theater.

Velte whistled sharply. "Who will plant the seeds?"

This chant was new, but everyone had caught on well: "The Fingers!"

"Who will reap the dream?"

"The Fingers!"

"Who will reap the dream!"

"The Fingers!"

Velte's eyes were bright but unfocused as she stared out into the room, and Fili waited for her to launch into her introduction—a well-honed and oft-practiced tirade against Queen Luca and her ilk—but the short scholar only swayed on her feet.

"Velte?" Joscelin muttered under his breath.

She fell to the floorboards like timber.

Fili had two choices: the hospital tent, or her mother. The hospital tents for the Withering were run by Qazāli, and Ghadin had said Qazāli priests could heal. But the Qazāli tent meant the queen's dog, Touraine El-Qazāli.

If Fili took Velte to her mother, at least Fili could beg. Even after everything, her own mother couldn't want her hanged in Traitor's Corner.

Sidonie, a fiacre driver in the crowd, volunteered, pulling on her jacket before Fili even told her where they were going. With an effort, they managed to get Velte into the cab. Joscelin climbed in, too. Fili didn't argue.

Sidonie looked to Fili for a direction, and Fili hesitated only a moment. "Number eighty-five, rue Pont de Vis."

Pont de Vis was the bridge that crossed from the lower city to the upper. Sidonie's eyebrows raised, but she said nothing else.

Her mam's new house still intimidated Fili. Four columns supported a pediment carved with racing horses, and it stretched up two stories. She didn't know the neighbors, whose houses jammed close on either side. In the dusk light, she tripped up the unfamiliar stone steps to the door, and Joscelin and Velte both groaned with the extra effort of staying upright. She helped them to one of the columns, and they sagged against it.

The columns were cracked in places, and the frieze of horses above was worn. This was no hastily constructed home but old and venerable. Fili could feel the history behind it. Who had it belonged to, before the queen gave it to her mother?

With one last glance at Joscelin and Velte, Fili girded herself and knocked on the door.

Silent seconds stretched. Maybe it was better if her mother

abandoned her after all. She turned to call Sidonie to help them back down, when the door opened. In the shadow of the doorway, a man she didn't know blinked at her. Fili gaped. She started to back away, but her mam's familiar clunk-step froze her in place.

Inès Guérin arrived behind the stranger's arm, backlit by the warm light of a fire. She pushed the stranger's arm aside and stepped onto the porch.

"Fili?" Her mam tilted her head, wary and incredulous.

Fili's eyes welled up with tears involuntarily. She'd prepared a whole speech on the way here to convince her mam of the right thing to do.

All that came out was "Maman, I need your help."

Her mam came closer, eyeing Joscelin and Velte at the column. She looked down to the street, where Sidonie was still waiting, with her two nags who looked past ready for the knacker.

"Come in. Quickly, come in." Her mam turned to the stranger. "Get them something warm to drink."

The doctor arrived not long after Fili's mam sent for him. He worked on Velte in one of the bedrooms upstairs, with Joscelin hovering the whole time. Fili also lingered, long enough to see the curious way the doctor eyed Joscelin. She could tell he recognized the mark of the Withering, and wanted to know how he'd survived. But Jos never took his attention away from Velte, and so the doctor, too, stuck to his work.

Fili returned downstairs, to the sitting room. Her mam beckoned Fili to join her at the table before the fire. A cup of tea and a cup of chocolate waited on the table. The man, her mam's butler, waited in a corner. With a subtle gesture, her mother dismissed him.

The house was quiet. They were alone for the first time since her mam had visited her at Maître Gaspard's shop. Fili hid behind the chocolate, touching the warm sweetness with her lips. Her mother didn't seem to know how to start, either. She turned her own cup in one hand while massaging the thigh of her amputated leg with the other.

"I'm sorry about Gaspard." A peace offering.

Fili only nodded.

"Are you making anything new these days?"

Fili shook her head.

Her mam exhaled slowly, already losing her patience. "Might be a good way to honor him."

Fili set her cup of chocolate down. "I'm honoring his memory as he would want."

Her mam tightened all over—at the corners of her mouth, the hand around her cup, the line of her brow.

"That how your friend got hurt, is it?"

"If I say yes, will you turn us all out?"

Her mam turned toward the fire, her jaw working. The hard lines of her face that Fili remembered had softened even more.

The same old fight, no matter how Fili tried—

The doctor saved them from knotting themselves in the tired threads, emerging with his satchel of tools over one shoulder.

"She will be fine. I left her friend with a poultice. Administer it daily for a week."

When he gave the price for the medicine and the service, Fili's mouth dropped open in outrage, but her mam merely counted the full sovereigns out and added extra.

"For your discretion," her mam said.

The doctor bowed, tucking the coins into a pocket of his bag. After the butler escorted him out, Fili turned to her mam, unable to resist.

"Do you know what that kind of money could do for the people across the bridge?"

"Aye, it's doing what it just did." For the first time, a flicker of doubt crossed her mam's face. She rubbed her thigh again and said, "Your da and I grew up on sheep farms a thousand miles away from anything like this life, Fili. We had lean years and flush ones. We learned to save in the flush so we'd have enough for the lean. When Queen Luca sent me back, I told your da to sell the farm and move here, to be with us. He said no, better to keep it, just in case." Her mam chuckled sadly. "Now that case has come. He's got food, shelter, and aye, he may be far from me, but he's safe. I won't give away what the queen's given me, not when we may yet need it." She broke off, as if she wanted to say something else but couldn't find the words.

Someone knocked on the door, hard, firm raps.

"The doctor?" Fili stood up so her mother wouldn't have to, before remembering the butler.

Murmuring voices, then a chorus of heavy soldiers' boots approached. Inès Guérin stared into the fire and refused to look at Fili as Prince-General Touraine El-Qazāli entered the sitting room flanked not by the gendarmerie but by palace soldiers.

"Maman?" Fili whispered.

"Inès Guérin. The queen thanks you for your loyalty."

Slowly, her mam rose and bowed. "Your Highness."

Something unreadable passed between the two women. Then, at a signal from the prince, Fili was being cuffed.

"Maman?" Fili turned frantically to her mother as her arms were wrenched behind her.

"Go quietly, Fili. Please." Her mam held her eyes for only a moment before turning aside. "It'll be all right."

"Maman, please!" But she knew there was nothing else her mother would do, could do now. As the soldiers led her out, she saw Joscelin, clinging to the railing as he struggled down the stairs. His eyes went wide with horror, but he could do nothing, either. What would happen to him, and to Velte?

They dragged her past the strange columns and down the unfamiliar stone steps.

"Will she remember her promise?" Fili heard her mam ask the prince behind her.

The prince answered with a voice as cold as iron: "I'll make sure she does."

CHAPTER 31

BY THE ROOTS

L e Fontinard was stark against the pale sheet of the sky. The wind whipped Luca's coat tight against her. Guérin stood in front of the fortress's heavy wooden doors, holding her cloak tight against herself with her free hand, squinting against the bluster.

"Let's get this over with," Luca muttered. She climbed down from the carriage and Touraine followed.

Uncertainty cracked the other woman's stony expression. "You sure?"

Luca snorted. "You should never ask a queen if she's sure."

"I wasn't asking you as the queen." Touraine fell back into her dark mood.

"It was a joke."

Touraine grunted and walked ahead.

"Your Majesty." Guérin bowed deeply, her eyes searching Luca's face for a hint of mercy. Luca turned away.

The fortress seemed darker than it ever had, every shadow a lurking sin. By the time they arrived, Luca's body ached from the sole of her right foot to her shoulder. She'd lost her sense of charity and mercy somewhere around the thirtieth step. When they arrived on the fourth floor, she bade Guérin wait in the cylindrical stairwell while she and Touraine went onward.

Fili did not wear chains well. She was bound heavily, with little room to maneuver, so she sat with her knees close to her chest, manacled hands dangling at her side.

"Hello again, Phillipette."

The young woman—girl, really—glared up at Luca from her knees. "This isn't the relationship I had hoped to have." Luca gestured to the jailer, who brought a chair this time. She sat.

"I don't want any relationship with you."

"A pity. You have one. Right now, it's rather antagonistic." Luca leaned forward, resting her elbows on her knees. "It doesn't have to be."

Fili's gaze tracked between Touraine and Luca, occasionally drifting to the royal guards arrayed behind them.

"Phillipette Guérin. Do you really think you're in the position to bargain with your queen?"

"Fili."

Luca raised an eyebrow. "Fili, then. You worship Balladaire's god."

"No, I don't."

"No?"

"I'm not uncivilized."

"No one said you were."

"Gods are uncivilized."

"Not among us, I promise you."

"Then what?"

"The magic."

"What about it?"

"We'll be at war soon."

Fili paused. "With who?"

"The Taargens."

Bewilderment drew Fili's pale eyebrows together. "I don't understand. I thought we were allies."

"Precisely. You don't understand."

Fili reclaimed her forced bravado. "What's it to do with me?"

"You and your friends are rebelling against the crown at the very moment when I am trying to save our empire from an invasion, a debilitating plague, and the worst food shortage we've had in a century. If you truly believe that you're fighting for the good of the people I've downtrodden, then I would strongly suggest you stop and think about what that means."

"I think it means we should fight harder."

It had the air of a rehearsed line, fed to her by someone else.

"Can you fight against a fully armed Taargen military, with their beast priests? Where are your cannons, your cavalry? Your *trained* soldiers?"

It was hard to say if the pallor in Fili's face was a trick of the flickering lamplight, or if it was fear. Luca pressed, hoping it was the latter.

"Together, with my research and your...practical understanding...we can use Balladaire's god to protect Balladaire itself. Instead of undermining me, you and the Fingers can fight the Withering. Your mother protected me, once. She believes in Balladaire."

"You took my mother from me." Fili glared at Luca from behind her knees, her nails digging into her legs.

"I didn't take her from anyone." Luca clasped her hands to quell any unplanned impulse. "Your mother made her choices, and she was honored for them. If you can't tell the difference between an adult's choices and my coercion, then you're not ready to even contemplate the meaning of revolution."

"You made her betray me."

"She put the good of the empire before herself."

Surprising Luca and Fili both, Touraine knelt beside Fili. She rearranged the chains so they pulled less tightly on Fili's shoulders, allowing her an extra inch to straighten.

In a deep, calm voice, she said, "Before I was the ambassador, before I became the prince consort, I was a conscript for the Balladairan army. Did you know that?" Touraine chuckled to herself. "I don't think many people do now. Not here. I forget it myself, sometimes. But Balladaire wasn't kind to us. The conscripts. The Sands. You're right. The empire chews up everyone it can and spits out their bones. Sky above knows it does. When I met Luca—" Touraine turned, met Luca's stare with golden eyes, and Luca's stomach flipped. Then she turned back to the girl and continued in that same steady voice. "When I met the queen, before she was the queen, she was...different. Not completely different. She was still a royal. But she was honest. She made me promises—made my people promises. Promises that have cost her, but she made them anylight because they were right. They were *good*. Qazāl is independent in part because she made a choice. I'm here now, using my magic to help Balladaire because I believed in her more than any Balladairan I've known. Don't you owe Balladaire as much? Luca will take care of her people. All of them. But you have to let her."

A thick lump formed in Luca's throat.

"I swear to you, Fili," Luca added. "I only have Balladaire's best interests in mind."

Fili looked between Touraine and Luca. Then she spat on the ground of her cell. Touraine's fist clenched and unclenched slowly.

Fili had been aiming for Luca's boots, but fell woefully short. A thin splash of spit landed not far from her own shoes, and a thin line of spittle clung from her lips to the spatter, until it broke and trailed to her chin. Luca felt a rush of pity for this girl. Young woman, old enough to make her decisions, Luca reminded herself. Like Guérin had made her decisions.

"What's your plan, Fili?" Luca surged to her feet, ignoring the spike of pain that shot through her knee. The girl had to crane her head all the way up if she wanted to look Luca in the eye. "When you've deposed me, how will you govern? Do you have another queen lined up? Will you rule, like some god-chosen master of old? Or will you try to win the war on your doorstep with a half-fledged committee?"

The questions backed Fili into the wall, but the set of her jaw didn't soften.

"I *was* helping people," Fili said. "We *were* fighting the Withering. If you care so much, let me go!"

"How were you helping people? You've been stealing food and dumping wine in the streets! How is that helping?"

"I'm not my mother. You don't get to control me like you control everyone else." Fili stared pointedly at Touraine. "I don't want to fight your wars. But if you let me go, *I* will save *my* people in ways you can't."

Luca gripped her cane to keep from shaking the girl by the shoulders. *How?* she wanted to scream. *How?*

"Bring her," Luca called over her shoulder.

"Fili?" A frantic, pleading voice accompanied a noisy shuffle. Inès Guérin burst into the corridor ahead of her escort, like a dog being let off a chain, her crutch skidding on the stone.

Guérin looked fearfully into the cell. At the sight of Fili, she balked, her free arm reaching toward her daughter, as if she didn't know if she could—should—still embrace her. The uncertainty as she glanced between Luca and Fili. Luca could practically hear the ticking of Guérin's thoughts as she calculated the cost of her loyalty. The older woman's eyes were rimmed red.

"Maman." Plaintive and accusing at once. Fili's chin wobbled as she tried to keep it jutted and proud.

"Please, Your Majesty," Guérin said. "She's only a child."

"This child is part of the rebellion against my crown, Guérin."

Guérin bowed her head low. "I understand." Then, before Luca understood what she was doing, Guérin lowered herself haltingly to both her knees. The crutch clattered, and she braced herself with flat palms on the frigid stone. Her face twisted with the pain of it. "But I beg your mercy, Your Majesty. She's my only daughter, and I've wronged her."

Luca felt despicable.

"I've offered her clemency," Luca said, cold, calm. "Make her take it. For her own sake and ours, convince her to help me save this kingdom."

Seeing her mam humiliate herself on the ground for Queen Luca made Fili want to weep with rage.

Touraine El-Qazāli offered a hand to help Fili's mam stand, but Guérin shook her head and waved her off. El-Qazāli looked between her and Fili both before sucking her teeth and following the queen.

That left Fili chained up with her mam and her jailers.

"I hate the way she makes you bow and scrape for her." The tears—angry ones, only—dripped fat down Fili's eyelashes.

"The queen didn't make me do anything. You did." Her mam sounded angrier than Fili had ever heard her.

"You turned me in!"

"You put your life in danger with this—these Fingers. I told you to let it alone!"

"I can't, Maman! It's not right!"

"Queen Luca is a good woman, Fili. Can you say the same for all your friends? Did you think to who rules in her stead, after you've done all you want?"

Fili hesitated. The queen had asked that, too, but Fili had no answer. That used to be for someone else to think about. Brother Michel had, she supposed, and then Velte and the rest when he died.

"What will you do with them? My friends. Did you pay the doctor just to throw them in jail, too?"

Guérin looked away.

"What did you do with them, Maman?"

"Nothing," Guérin hissed under her breath. "Cadroux will see them out when your friend is stable."

That gave Fili pause. "There'll be people like us in charge. We'll share Balladaire's wealth, us what make it. No one to hoard it all at the top."

Guérin snorted and rolled her eyes. "There's always someone to hoard it at the top, girl." She sighed and shook her head. "Queen Luca said she offered you clemency. What's she want from you?"

"She wants me to use my magic."

"How?"

"I don't know."

"What...?" Her mam licked her lips nervously. Fili had never seen her nervous before. "What can you do that she might want?"

"Only what you already know about. The wood. I can make some plants grow, too. And..." She hesitated. "People come to get blessings from me. So they don't get sick."

Her mam pulled back reflexively, and Fili flinched at the unveiled fear in her face.

"Blessings?" her mam said with effort. She slithered closer to her, her bum rasping on the stone floor. She reached out, hand hovering over the chains that held Fili in place. An apology. "She doesn't want to hurt you, Fili. You've got to trust me."

Fili's throat choked up, and she couldn't hold herself up anymore. She bent double, sobbing, and her mam caught her against her chest and wrapped Fili up tight. Her arms were so strong, and Fili surrendered to feeling like a child again. Her mam smelled like Fili remembered from those too-brief visits home to Durfort: leather and steel and that out-of-place hint of eau de parfum.

"I'm sorry I wasn't the best mam to you," her mam murmured into Fili's dirty hair. "That'll go with me to my grave, it will. Might be that means you don't know me or trust me as well as I'd like. But I'm still your mam. I want you to live." Her voice wavered and she stopped to swallow. "What do you want from her, you and your...friends? What if I spoke to her?"

"Nothing less than her gone. I don't want to live under a queen's boot."

"Oh, child." Her mam tilted her chin up to stare at the ceiling, blinking furiously. "Oh, my own heart. *I* want more time to know you, if you'll let me. *I* need you alive. And the Taargens *are* coming. The queen is scared. Everyone's scared. The only reason more people aren't scared yet is because they don't know what's coming."

Fili leaned out of her mam's embrace. "People are plenty scared. There's the Withering. They're hungry to death. What's a Taargen to all that? 'Stop your rebellion and pledge allegiance to me, to your country.' It's a trick. But we don't need her, Maman. I'm telling you!"

Her mam scrubbed her hand through her hair. It was down to her shoulders now, longer than it had ever been.

"You want to do something big, don't you, Fili? You want to help the people in the city. You want to make a difference. Sky above, think!" Her mam's voice rose, and she swung the flat of her hand through the air. "There are bigger things than you, and me. You don't have to love the queen to see her sense."

"Why don't you go run after her, then?" Fili shot back. "Maybe she'll get your other leg, too. Then maybe you'll listen to me."

That left her mam breathing heavy in the sudden silence. Fili's remorse was nothing against the burning in her belly. Clumsily, her mam climbed back to her feet, gathering the false leg beneath her.

She turned back to Fili before the guards closed the cell door. Fili waited for her to say something, but her mam only looked at her with hopeless frustration. Then Fili was alone in the dark.

CHAPTER 32

AGAINST THE STORM

Did you mean that?" Luca asked when they'd reached the point in the palace corridors where their paths diverged to their separate chambers. "What you said to Fili?"

Touraine faced her wearily. "Which part?"

"All of it."

She took Luca's chin between her thumb and forefinger. Stroked a hot line up her jaw, across her lips. She pressed her own lips on Luca's and breathed against them: "Yes."

The sensation left Luca hungry for more, but as she tried to deepen the kiss, Touraine pulled away.

"All of it, I said." Her voice was hard again, with that keen edge of anger. "You're royal. You're clever. You're used to getting what you want because of it." She waved away the protests Luca didn't even have time to form. "I'm sorry about—about what I said. About Gil. But I mean it. When people don't see things your way, it gets messy."

Luca grabbed Touraine's hand before she could turn away. "I know. I know. I'm sorry."

"You can't apologize to the dead we left in Traitor's Corner." She started to say something else but stopped.

"I know," Luca said. "But without Fili's help, without her and the Fingers agreeing to an armistice, it's going to get worse. I can't split

Balladaire across this many fronts. There's a reason it's called Traitor's Corner."

"I know."

"We'll have to make hard choices—"

"We do. They're just not the ones you think they are."

"We'll have to see, won't we?"

Touraine chewed on her bottom lip. "Guess we will." She glanced down at their hands, then back up. Her eyes were tight and wary at the corners.

"Touraine, will you stay tonight?"

"Luca, I—"

"Please?"

"It's not that I don't want to," she said quietly, though she didn't meet Luca's eyes. She sighed and shook her head. "It's been a long day. A hard one."

"Take a bath with me, then. We'll rest."

Touraine exhaled a sharp chuckle. "Rest?"

"I mean it." Luca made her most solemn face, and it was worth it to see Touraine roll her eyes and smile, however briefly. It was nothing short of a miracle, for her to be able to do that to this woman, of all the women in the world. There was no reason Luca deserved the privilege.

It was another miracle entirely to watch the woman strip beside the large copper tub of steaming-hot water. Touraine's broad shoulders and strong arms had filled out with her time at the palace; so had some of the hollowness in her cheeks. Her hard edges, softening.

Luca loved having Touraine in the palace with her. She loved knowing the other woman was, if not with her, nearby. Within a messenger's distance. She liked knowing Touraine was safe, or as safe as you could be as a royal. (Which, admittedly, was not safe enough for Luca's liking.)

"Are we going to get in or are you just going to stare at me?"

Luca realized with a start that she'd stopped unbuttoning her waistcoat, lost in admiration. Her face flushed hot.

Touraine snorted and tiptoed to Luca on the cold marble tiles, her shirt on the floor, her trousers undone.

"You'd think you had servants dressing you all your life." She knocked Luca's fingers off the buttons and began to undo them herself, only fumbling once: when Luca grazed the edges of her fingernails absently across the curve of her back. The hitch in Touraine's breath made Luca want to do it again.

Touraine was right *here*. She wouldn't always be. Luca could indulge herself.

As Touraine started on her chemise, Luca skimmed her nails down Touraine's back again, this time going down to her waist.

"Luca..." Touraine chided. She raised an eyebrow but didn't stop unbuttoning Luca's shirt. "A bath. Rest. Isn't that what you said?"

But her voice was deep in a way it got only when she was aroused; Luca knew this because Touraine was in the palace, with her. What else would she know if Touraine stayed? If they had years of this?

"This is relaxing," Luca said as Touraine kissed her.

She slid her hands into Touraine's trousers, thumbs dipping into the creases of Touraine's hips, and pulled her close. She hummed at the feel of Touraine's bare chest on hers. The warmth, skin grazing sensitive skin, while Touraine's hands slid beneath waistcoat and chemise to glide over Luca's own naked back.

It wasn't the frenzied kiss of their first night; it couldn't be. The world around them had changed too much—could change even more in a moment. They kissed slowly, deeply, until Luca had, on second thought, had enough of savoring. She released Touraine's neck and started unbelting and unbuttoning her own trousers.

"Boots," Touraine murmured into her neck.

The tender brush of Touraine's nose against Luca's neck tore right through her with longing for the very thing she had right here—only it wasn't her, now, who wanted it, but a future her who would miss it so, so much.

"Fuck them." Luca tried to push her trousers down anylight, but Touraine grabbed her hands. Her long fingers were gentle, but firm.

"Sit down," Touraine commanded. Gentle, but firm.

Luca obeyed, taking the upholstered wooden chair by the tub that she often used to get dressed or undressed.

Touraine knelt on both knees and took off one boot and then the other, her grip strong on Luca's calves. She met Luca's eyes and held her gaze as she ran her hands deliberately up the outside of Luca's thighs. There was a mournful longing in her eyes, possessiveness in her hands. Could Touraine also feel what was coming?

With her fingers hooked into the waist of Luca's trousers, Touraine simply said, "Up."

Luca lifted her hips and Touraine slid the trousers down her legs and off with torturous slowness.

The cold raised goose bumps on her skin—or maybe it was the trail Touraine's mouth was marking from her knee to her inner thigh. Luca noticed then, with astonishment, that Touraine had a single white hair growing at the crown of her head. It sprang out oddly, straighter than the rest of her dark curls. Luca brushed it with her fingers and wondered what Touraine would look like when she was older—if the world would grant her that. If the world would grant Luca the gift to see it.

A sharp bite on her inner knee brought her away from that impossible future, and then Touraine's mouth was warm and wet against her and she was pulling Luca's hips to her face and Luca was sliding down the chair, one hand gripping the back of Touraine's head and holding her there, the other holding on to the back of the chair. Not that she needed to worry about falling off; Touraine had propped Luca's legs over her shoulders, had one hand looped behind Luca and gripped the seat of the chair. The other hand—

"Oh, sky above, Touraine—*fuck*."

"Mmm." Touraine hummed against her, but she didn't stop working with her expert fucking tongue or her perfect fucking fingers.

With Touraine in the palace, Luca could have this.

She gasped silently when she climaxed, her legs locked around Touraine's head.

The sudden spasm of pleasure also sent a spasm of pain up Luca's bad hip, and she hissed as she righted herself gingerly.

"Ah. Sorry." Touraine sheepishly wiped her chin with the back of her hand.

Luca wiped the rest of Touraine's face with her own thumb before kissing her. The taste of herself on Touraine's lips sent another wave of tightening through her.

"Do you feel rested, Your Highness?"

Catching the glint of danger in Luca's mood, Touraine smiled, but that melancholy remained. "Not quite yet, Your Majesty."

She kicked out of her trousers and settled over Luca, straddling her hips in the chair. Luca slid her hands up Touraine's strong thighs, letting her thumbs glide up the taut inner muscles until she reached Touraine's muscled waist and dug in her nails. Touraine smirked, shook her head, and leaned down to kiss her, one hand behind Luca's neck. With her other hand, Touraine guided Luca's fingers inside her. She grunted a little against Luca's lips and Luca closed her eyes, luxuriating in the sound.

Luca reveled, too, in the knowledge that her body was still whole. The Withering had not taken this from her. This was still *hers*.

She opened them once, to memorize the sight of Touraine above her, eyes screwed tight, brows knit, head tilted forward, knocking against Luca's as she moved to the rhythm of Luca's hand. The sheen of sweat along her collarbone.

Luca was not the only one saying goodbye.

After, with more than a little guilt, they called for Adile to send for another kettle of hot water to keep the bath from being completely frigid when they got in. After they'd bathed, Touraine settled between Luca's legs, resting her back against Luca's front. The candles were burning low and she was pleasantly drained, her eyes drifting shut as the tepid water lapped against them. Luca couldn't rest easy. Not yet.

"Touraine?" She spoke softly.

"Mm?"

Luca felt the hum of it in her chest. Touraine pulled Luca's arms tighter around her, and Luca nuzzled into the crook of Touraine's neck, to memorize also the smell of her, the feel of her in her arms, of the short hairs against her nose, her cheek.

"You didn't know, did you?"

"Know what?" Touraine said drowsily.

"It was her. With the Taargens."

Touraine went rigid between Luca's legs. She didn't turn around.

"I know what you would do for your Sands. I'm not so foolish to think I rank above them in your heart." She stopped Touraine's protest with a gentle squeeze. "I don't ask to. I only ask—can I trust you now? You had nothing to do with this?"

"Trust is a choice, Luca. Faith is a choice."

"I know. I'm making that choice now. Did you mean it? If I sent you after her now, as my general—to parlay or defend us against her—you would go?"

The silence stretched long. Luca would have given anything to know Touraine's mind. Instead, all she could do was surmise from the minute tremors that rippled the water and the rapid beat of Touraine's heart through her spine, flush against Luca's breast.

Luca had no one else she could trust. No one else as well suited to the task.

"You don't want me to parlay, do you?" Touraine's voice was devoid of emotion.

It made Luca feel cold inside after their intimacy.

"I want you to end the threat to my kingdom," Luca said carefully. "However you can."

"But?"

"But. I have an idea."

"Another lie for you." Touraine shook her head. "I can't lie to her, Luca. She knows me too well."

A flare of jealousy. Luca suppressed it. "That's why we aren't going to lie. You're going to tell her the truth. Tell her how I've let you down. Tell her how I've disappointed you."

Luca felt Touraine's deep breaths as if she were taking them herself, each one as steady as the last. She would miss this, too, if Touraine were gone. This steadiness. Touraine, her bulwark against the storm.

The answer, when it came, was so quiet, though, that Luca didn't even hear it. Like those steady breaths, she felt it in Touraine's exhalation, in the sudden sagging of her body against Luca's chest and the scrape of her nails against Luca's thighs.

"Everyone always sends me away. To turn someone's love for me against them." Touraine glanced over her shoulder at Luca, and Luca's heart squeezed painfully at her miserable expression. The sorrow in the lines of her mouth, her low-lidded eyes.

"I'm sorry." Luca reached to trace the lines with her fingertips, as if she could press them away as quickly as she had put them there.

Touraine turned away, leaving Luca to caress the empty air.

"Don't be." Touraine climbed out of the tub and dried herself with a towel. There was no rancor in her words, only listless fact. "You and I both know how well it works."

CHAPTER 33

THE STORM

Pruett felt like she was marching backward in time as Lor led her to the Taargen tents. The cold air, the sloping Balladairan plains with the dense forests drawing a sharp line at the eastern horizon. Draped in their hides against the wind, the tents looked like a herd of grazing animals, the Taargens' gruff, staccato language an odd kind of animal call.

The sense of déjà vu made Pruett hesitate. Lor looked up at her. The blue-black feathers of the Taargen woman's cloak fluttered against her cheeks, which bloomed patchy pink with the chill.

"Well?" Lor's breath came out with a puff of smoke.

"Well, it's too sky-falling late for second thoughts, isn't it?" Pruett turned to Kiras on her other side. "Ready?"

"I am, Qā'id." Kiras was dressed in what she said the old Qazāli warriors used to wear. The hooded vest and loose trousers gathered at the ankle. A red sash around her hips was the only nod to the color of Pruett's own coat, the color they'd claimed for their flags. Her holy dagger jutted from the cloth along with a more mundane one. The side of her head was freshly shaved, the rest of the curls left to blow free.

Pruett's own hair flopped, shaggy, into her eyes. She pushed it back and straightened her coat. She'd had it made before they left Masridān, red as a scab and down to her knees, thick enough to handle the last of the Balladairan winter and cold snaps of early spring. Her high boots gleamed with polish. Her pistols were belted across her chest.

They were ready for war.

When she saw the two men standing over the table in the Taargen command tent, Pruett understood the term *bearfucker* in an entirely new light. A young man and an old one, both of them twice as wide as she was, and half again as tall, their small eyes peering out over thick beards. It didn't help that they were both covered in great fur cloaks.

If their mothers hadn't fucked a bear or two to get *that*, she'd eat her own guns.

"Hello, gentlemen." Pruett stuck her thumbs beneath her gun braces and smiled her hooked smile.

The two men straightened and looked to Lor, who stepped forward and bowed.

"Your Highness. Your Grace. This is Pruett El-Masridāni, qā'id of Masridān, commander of the Shālan armies, here to aid you in the reclamation of your rightful land." Pruett grunted at that, but Lor ignored her. "Qā'id, I have the honor of introducing you to His Royal Highness, Prince Roric of Taargen, and His Grace, High Priest Albric, beloved of the Bear." Lor bowed again and retreated to the side of the tent with the other aides or guards or whoever they were.

It was not the prince but the graybeard who approached Pruett first. He studied her with orange-brown eyes. Pruett forced herself not to step back even as he loomed closer.

"Qā'id. You know us, I think." Like Lor, he spoke in Balladairan. It was the one language they all had in common, including Kiras.

Pruett jutted her jaw. In Taargen, she said, "Aye. Killed more than my share of you, not too long ago." From the corner of her eye, she saw Lor wince and the other men reach for weapons. Then Pruett grinned, showing her teeth. "Don't worry, boys. We have a new enemy in common."

The high priest was not provoked. He tilted his head to the side. "And more than that, I think."

Internally, Pruett rolled her eyes. Just like Niwai. "Many legs, all that."

The knot of awareness in the back of her mind was quiet now, and for the most part, had been ever since she'd left Qazāl. She'd experimented briefly over the Triaume, but the assault of a million tiny fish was mind shattering. She'd shut it away almost immediately, but for the rest of the trip, she was certain a curious dolphin had butted up against her mental walls, following their ship all the way to land. Pruett had been disappointed to leave it. She missed Sevroush.

"Indeed," Albric rumbled with gruff amusement.

Pruett swaggered around him to better see the table he'd been standing over. A map of Balladaire and western Taargen, with the Moyenne lands marked out with carved stones—different parts of the army, she guessed, or enemies spotted. Pruett pointed to a large stone near Balladaire's southeast coast, east of the River Diminue.

"This us?" She switched back to Balladairan so Kiras could understand, too.

The young bear grunted affirmative. The sides of his head were shaved, the skin pale, the occasional red pimple. The rest was pulled back into a braid down his neck. His beard was less impressive than Albric's, russet brown and short. The hazel green of his eyes made Pruett think of a forest under the afternoon sun, but his gaze was all arrogance. None of the careful consideration of his older counterpart.

Pruett jabbed another stone not too far away from their position. "Then who the fuck is this?"

The two bears shared a glance that included some of the other men in the tent. Prince Roric beckoned one. The man approached the table, hands clasped behind his back. Pruett almost jumped when he turned his back to her—a wolf's head dangled upside down, the hood to his fur cloak. Its teeth were sharp and yellow. Pruett jerked away. When she leaned her hands on the table, they were trembling. The prince noticed, and a smile twitched at the corner of his mouth. Pruett curled her lip in an answering snarl.

"Here is a small company of Balladairan soldiers," the young man said with a thick accent. "They are farther away than they seem, but they are not very strong in numbers. We think they are looking for us."

"And you are?"

"Henrir, sir. I believe you would call me *lieutenant*."

"Henrir is one of my battle-brothers. You will respect him as me." Roric also spoke with an accent, lighter than Henrir's, though his

Balladairan wasn't perfect. It made Pruett think of Luca, and her flaw-less but formal Shālan. No doubt her Taargen was as perfect.

Pruett turned her smile on Henrir. His dark hair fell about his face in untidy waves, and his beard was more closely trimmed than Albric's and Roric's. Where the other men were thick and broad, Henrir was leaner. He looked quick. She would be careful around him.

"Hard for them to miss an army this big, isn't it?" she asked.

"Precisely why we are going to find them first." Roric crossed his arms over his chest in self-satisfaction.

"Come with us if you wish, Qā'id," said Albric. "We will show you how we plan to scythe the wheat."

"If you can keep up," Roric added.

Kiras stepped to Pruett's other side, caressing the pommel of her holy knife. "We can keep up."

The Balladairan camp was a day's march north, nestled between two hills that resembled a pair of half-green tits. They waited until full dark to advance. The Balladairan campfires made the darkness seem deeper, and it was easy to watch them go about the evening routine of a soldier: the polishing, the mending, the washing, the eating, the gambling, the laughing.

The Taargen company dispersed around the camp in a wide circle, then slowly tightened the noose. Interspersed among the Taargens were some of Kiras's Eaters and Pruett's own Masridāni, about a hun-dred all told, not including the beast priests. Pruett almost shat her pants when she caught sight of a massive wolf stalking in tandem in the grass not fifty paces away from her, jaws already bloody.

"Shāl take my eyes and stop my ears," Kiras swore under her breath, staring at the creature.

The wolf turned its yellow eyes upon them, steady and knowing. Then it turned back to its task, so Pruett squeezed Kiras's hand once and they kept moving. When the wolf stopped, so did they. They waited.

A soldier's startled shout from the direction of the camp. Pruett held her breath as a bear lumbered into the camp. Bigger than any natural bear had a right to be, it still pretended. It sniffed a sack, pawed at a tent, flinched away from the torch one soldier in a blackcoat waved at it. Cowed by the shouting men and women, it backed away with a pitiful moan: the food here was not worth the trouble.

Pruett felt a sick sympathy with the Balladairan soldiers. She knew their fear, the same fear she'd picked up in the Taargen War for any wild animal. She knew their relief when it left—a wild bear, a true bear, nothing more. She knew the easing tension as they turned back to their chores, their meals, their comrades. The nervous laughter. The teasing. Their guards dropping.

The wolf and the other Taargen animal priests crept forward. The circle around the camp tightened further still. Pruett and her soldiers followed. This time, when the blackcoats heard more noise in the darkness, they ignored it. *There goes that bear again.* Not worth the worry.

Until three bears and two wolves growled at the edges of their camp and rank upon rank of soldiers circled them.

The Balladairan soldiers stood, some with swords in hand, others with no more than their dinner knives. The wolves howled and their cries were echoed by other wolves in the distance—true wolves or priest wolves, it didn't matter. The effect was the same.

Some of the Balladairans dropped their weapons without being asked.

At the center of the camp, a woman stood, blade drawn. She wasn't wearing an officer's coat, but she pointed her sword at each of the animals in turn.

"Show yourselves, beasts," she said.

Pruett joined Roric and Albric as they walked through the center of the camp. The rest of their soldiers closed in with them, and the Balladairans were squeezed tighter and tighter, until they were a dense cluster of frightened men and women in their shirtsleeves, their swords and bayonets bristling outward like a Shālan porcupine. The few who still held guns didn't know whether to point them at the giant wolves or the bears or the humans in the center.

"Hold your fire," the woman snapped.

"Wise," Albric said. "We've come to take your surrender."

Pruett watched the woman's gaze flicker between Albric and Roric, and the animal priests. Toward the soldiers she was meant to lead.

Weighing the price of surrender. Every Balladairan knew that price. Pruett had whispered about it with the other Sands before they went to their first battles, and she'd had nightmares about it after.

The woman threw her sword on the ground.

It was a bloodless anticlimax to the tension coiled in Pruett's body. The wolves herded the blackcoats out of the camp like great sheepdogs, steering them toward the Taargen-Masridāni encampment. As their commander's gaze passed over Pruett, it snagged. She halted, and one of her men bumped into her back.

"Lieutenant Pruett of the Balladairan Colonial Conscripts," the woman said calmly. "Qā'id of Masridān."

Pruett narrowed her eyes. "Do I know you?"

"I'm the marquise-colonel Camille de Moyenne. You killed my brother."

Pruett had, in fact, never been happier that Brice de Moyenne was still alive. She had brought him along in the hopes that he could be ransomed, or failing that, a source of information about the latest organization of the Balladairan military. Having his sister was twice the bounty.

Unfortunately, it was also twice the trouble.

It took time for Pruett and the Taargens to find the best arrangement of the two armies. Took time for the bearfuckers to stop ordering Pruett and her soldiers around like lackeys. One Taargen had almost gotten his hand cut off after grabbing an Eater's ass; one of the Masridāni had almost lost an arm after taunting a dog that was, in fact, a real war hound and not a Taargen priest. More than once, Pruett had stormed into the command tent to find Roric and Albric with their advisors, devising plans without her.

"Your little messenger bird told me you needed me," Pruett snarled across the table to Albric the third time this happened. She'd stolen more cigarettes from one of the prisoners, and one burned between her knuckles as her fingers splayed over the map. Ash fell from the glowing tip, and the priest frowned. "If you don't, I'll leave, and I'll take all the Shālans with me. Including the Eaters."

The young bear glanced at Albric, uncertain. Albric only looked down his sharp, narrow nose at her.

She met his subtle contempt overtly. "Two *equal* armies, or you're on your own."

"Of course, Qā'id."

The chaos of the new alliance left cracks to exploit.

Outside the command tent, soldiers began shouting in three languages throughout the camp. Pruett and Kiras were the first ones out. A streak of prisoners raced for the northern edge of the camp, toward the Diminue and a small forest that would shelter them. At the front of the line were the siblings Moyenne. Even Brice, who'd been imprisoned for months, found new vigor with freedom a few footsteps away. Behind them, two tents burned like beacons—a fire that could rip through the camp. Soldiers from both armies leapt for the blaze.

Pruett crushed her cigarette and sprinted after the prisoners, but Kiras was faster still.

The wolves were even faster.

By the time Pruett and Kiras caught up to the wolf priests—Henrir was the dark gray one with the black muzzle, she knew now—the siblings Moyenne were on their knees. Brice de Moyenne lay on his side, howling in pain and reaching for his shredded leg. He got off lucky; one of the other prisoners lay motionless in the dirt a few paces farther. His throat was a ruin. Henrir stood panting over the corpse, his gory tongue lolling. Moyenne the younger glared murder at Pruett.

"Didn't want to wait for ransom?" Pruett asked her.

Camille de Moyenne breathed heavily, saying nothing. They waited like that, staring at each other while the two wolves stood sentinel, trapping the rest of the prisoners. No one wanted to become the next dead soldier in the grass.

When Albric and Roric arrived, Pruett gave them a bored look.

"Gentlemen, I'm glad you could make it," Pruett said, more casually than she felt. "I think we only need one Moyenne, don't you? What do you think about showing the rest of these blackcoats why they won't be running away again?"

The high priest considered Pruett with a new appreciation and a slight smile behind his long beard. He moved toward Camille de Moyenne first.

"Apologies, High Priest, but she is the one I want." The woman knew Pruett, and that meant her orders had come from the queen herself—or from Touraine. Pruett wanted to know who.

Brice de Moyenne crawled away on his elbows, dragging his mangled leg behind him. "No, no! Stop! You can't do this to me, I have a seat in the High Court—" The pale-furred wolf growled, baring sharp teeth as long as Pruett's hand. Two Taargens grabbed him and held him in place, and still he fought.

Pruett beckoned Kiras and went to hold the colonel's arms, but Camille de Moyenne didn't struggle. She stared at her brother as Albric bent his head close to Brice's. The general wept into his unkempt red beard, begging, "Please, please, no, please, anything, I'll give you anything"—Pruett wanted to close her own eyes. She wanted to throw up.

And yet, she was fascinated. This was her god, too. Could she do this? Would she?

Albric whispered his prayer to the bear god, and Brice's begging trailed into one long, jagged moan. Then it cut off. Albric dropped Brice limp to the ground. The priest's shape elongated, his human features swallowed up by the bear cloak over his shoulders until there was nothing left of the man and a great brown bear raised up on its haunches, blocking out the thick clouds above. It roared. The sudden smell of piss filled the area as more than one of the prisoners wet themselves. Pruett didn't blame them.

In their grip, Camille de Moyenne sobbed once. On her other side, Kiras swore again.

Brice alone did not react. He lay on the ground, eyes staring blankly in his sister's direction, his breathing steady. He no longer cared about his ravaged leg, his seat on the High Court. His sister, his command. He no longer cared about anything.

"Will you at least kill him?" Camille de Moyenne snapped as Pruett dragged her to her feet. "Is there no mercy among you monsters?"

A mercy.

Pruett made herself look at Brice. She thought of the family in Masridān, when their own brother had been taken, probably by Lor.

Rouh, Kiras had called it.

Before Pruett could give any order, Kiras was kneeling before him. Her ceremonial dagger flashed once, over the throat. She closed the general de Moyenne's empty eyes.

Kiras gave Pruett a long, disappointed look before returning to camp. "I don't like waste."

A storm was coming.

The air was cold and smelled of home, a home that shouldn't ever have been home, but what else was Pruett supposed to call the sudden blur of familiarity as she wandered off into the fields of dead grass? Qazāl didn't have winter like this. In Masridān, the grass never died of cold.

Far from the tents of the Taargens and her Masridāni, far from the new Eaters, far from Kiras, who was still angry with her, Pruett walked in the cloud-scudded moonlight. She walked till she couldn't hear the noise of the people at all or smell the acrid smoke from the burnt tents. Till there was nothing but the clean rustle of the wind picking up, flapping her coat. It eased the nausea that had roiled her stomach since Brice de Moyenne was... taken.

But it wasn't just that. Now that Pruett was back in Balladaire again, there was a whirling in her heart that she couldn't articulate, not even to Kiras. Especially not to Kiras. It left her feeling lonelier than ever. Even keeping the cage of beasts in her mind quiet felt as isolating as it was peaceful. She really had shut herself off from the whole world. So she walked until the loneliness felt intentional.

Nature was quiet in winter. Dormant. If you didn't know where to look.

Pruett felt for the cage in the back of her mind. She whipped the imaginary blanket off, and the noise crashed into her. She stumbled to a knee, groaning.

hide hide, this is food, this is—hunt, hunt, hold, wind against feathers, silent—food, warmth in the den, out of sight—hold, look, hold, waiting, a storm on the wind, hold—food, burrow, food, burr—DIVE.

Pruett felt the rodent die like a spasm in her chest even as she soared with the raptor's elation. She seized that feeling, used it to pull herself aloft, too, and then—she *called*.

She felt the bird's confusion. Felt it hesitate. Pruett called again. But food in between her claws was more urgent. She resisted, flying away, but the strange grip *pulled* again, and so she turned and saw in the field a strange creature. It was not like her, but she met its eyes in the darkness as she hovered. It pulled again. She dived again. A storm was coming. She felt it in the wind against her feathers. Home. Back home before the storm. A nook between the branches of her tree, a hollow, home. *Pull.*

The bird crashed into Pruett's chest, and they both fell to the ground, dazed.

"Hello there." Pruett gingerly picked up the stunned little kestrel. It still clutched the remains of a vole in its tiny claws. When the little ball of feathers came to, it glared at Pruett, dark beady eyes fierce and angry. A kindred spirit.

She considered the ritual Niwai had described to her before she left them. She still had the scar on her hand where Sevroush had bitten her. She let the bird stand on her open hands and thought to the bird what she intended, not sure if it would understand or not. Whatever it thought, it bit quickly enough when Pruett held her finger out.

Pruett swore, then stuck the bleeding digit in her mouth as she had with Sev. Probably she was supposed to pray or say something profound about the unity of human and beast like Niwai always did, but Pruett didn't have the head for it. She barely had the head for poetry these days.

She stroked the fluffy breast of the little kestrel, and it studied her until it was satisfied she wasn't going to do anything else. Then it proceeded to tear into its dinner and eat it in Pruett's hand. It was disgusting.

Her loneliness receded almost immediately, replaced with affection for the tiny predator.

Pruett wouldn't be isolated soon. Soon, she would dash herself upon the world, unexpected as a flash of lightning, inescapable as thunder, fierce as the wind buffeting her wild curls.

Be the rain, went the Qazāli rebellion's poem. Oh, how she would be.

"I'll call you Tempête, then, eh?"

The kestrel glared at her with entrails dangling from her beak.

As the first drops of rain pattered across Pruett's shoulder, Tempête shat in Pruett's hand.

PART 3
BY FAMINE

CHAPTER 34

MOTHERS

The faint smell of mildew and smoke still pervaded Luca's parents' rooms, but the worst of the mess had been cleaned: the damp carpets removed, the soot scrubbed away. Her parents' items, however, remained. Her mother's violoncelle, useless now; her father's sword. An upholstered chair remained, too, and was one obvious source of the moldy smell, but the servants had clearly not been sure what Luca had meant when she said "clean it all but touch nothing." She hadn't been in her sharpest mind at the time. She would ask them to remove it. Even if it was the chair her parents had sat in.

Poor sleep had left her exhausted; pulling herself from bed each day became a greater trial than usual. She told herself that it had nothing to do with Touraine's absence from the palace.

It had everything to do with the problem of Fili. Fili the Rose. Fili, touched by Balladaire's god. Fili, the infuriating child who *refused to see*—Luca raked her hand through her hair, making it more disheveled than it already was. She'd been too lazy to braid it and too disgusted with herself to let Adile do it for her.

Luca had been half tempted to ignore Fili's claims until Aranen confirmed them yesterday. Fewer people were coming into the hospital tent, and some of them *were* walking out—especially those whose loved ones had given them clutches of weeds. Not everyone survived or recovered, but it was more than nothing, Aranen said, and worth investigating if Luca could. She didn't say it was worth making any deal, but the judgment in her golden eyes said all.

Aranen had grown cold after Touraine and Luca's true falling out and their public harshness. It was a necessary subterfuge, not to explain their tentative reconciliation, yet it stung.

The Withering had not eased among the nobles in the palace.

Luca didn't need Fili. She needed only the magic. She needed the god. And may all the gods take Luca if the only way to get to them was through an entitled teenager. So Luca returned to the one thing that had never betrayed her in her life: books.

Her uncle had burned her father's library, and with it, all the Ancier records of centuries of rule, up to the war against the kings Fontinard and beyond, when the lords Ancier were just petty landowners with a little wheat and far too much ambition. How much of that history did Luca not understand? How did Balladaire's god weave into the motivations that toppled one family and raised another?

She didn't expect to find these answers here, but Luca had taken books from their home shelves and never returned them; perhaps her father had, too.

Luckily, the shelf that held the handful of books had been far from the fire and the blasting water of the pompiers. They smelled musty, but the leather was intact—and so was the glue when, smiling, Luca picked up her copy of the tales of the Chevaliers des Fruits.

Other books she was familiar with: Yverte's texts on rule, though Luca would have been surprised if her father had ever read them; Carlwic's on warfare, which was well thumbed—

A smaller volume slipped to the floor as Luca pulled down the theorists. It landed splayed open on its pages. The cover was unmarked, and it was slimmer than Luca's finger.

The first page Luca opened to was a mass of scribbled text—no, *scribbled* was inaccurate. The handwriting was immaculate, written with care and a steady hand with an attention to even spacing of the lines, to the delicate curve and precise connections of the letters. It was someone's account of their day—one of her parents. Luca barely breathed. She skimmed the page until she saw—*Roland went out riding*—her mother's, then.

At first, she was disappointed. Then she caressed her mother's lines with her fingertips. How many times had her mother been left alone in the palace while King Roland and Gil were away, gone to make war? Perhaps this was exactly what she needed tonight.

Luca scanned the shelf for any more of the small volumes—two more. Not nearly enough for the years of her mother's life spent here. She sat there on the clean patch of floor in that dank room, and surrounded by the last moldering pieces of her parents, she read her mother's journals.

It wasn't until her leg was throbbing beyond the point of distraction and the sky was lightening behind the cloth that covered the gaping hole in the wall that Luca stumbled across a paragraph that gave her pause. She wiped the wetness from her cheeks and read it again.

I want to marry Roland in the old way; Guillo lies and says he doesn't care, but when I told him he should marry him, too, he almost dropped his sword. That man blushes so prettily. Roland doesn't think it's in keeping with his position, to have an "uncivilized" marriage. Guillo and I will convince him. A secret.

Luca ignored the pain in her hip and knee and now the present urgings of her bladder and skimmed through the rest of the journal. There was no other mention of the marriage, "old way" or "uncivilized" or anything else. There was only a pregnancy—which might not even have been Luca. Then the journal ended.

She slumped back against the shelf, unsure what she was dreading most: the grinding pain of pushing herself back onto her feet, or the inevitable journey back to Le Fontinard to visit the one person who might have the answers to her new questions.

Luca rolled to her knees, but her leg refused to cooperate. Even her good leg was numb from sitting all night. She clutched at the edges of the bookshelf and inched her excruciating way up, dragging her legs beneath her, waiting for her good leg to wake up and take her weight. A little higher, and she reached for the shelf itself, to help—

The wood cracked beneath her, splitting and sending her and Carlwic and Yverte crashing to the ground in a heap of pain that she could barely feel.

Before she could call for help, Deniaud and Mareau were in the room. Mareau swept the books off Luca and turned her gently while Deniaud scanned the room for a threat.

"I'm all right." Luca's breath came short, but she was fine. She was *fine*.

Framed in the doorway, watching Luca with concern, was Inès Guérin.

"Guérin," Luca said from the floor. "What are you doing here?"

Guérin bowed, supporting her weight on her crutch. Luca recognized the flinch of pain on the other woman's face. She'd made it herself often enough, whenever she was made to stand too long on her bad leg. The light coming through the makeshift curtain was barely enough to make full morning. Luca's own eyes were gummy with tiredness.

"Please, Your Majesty. I needed to speak to you."

"Who told you I would be here?" Luca glanced to Deniaud and Mareau, unable to mask her suspicion. "How did you get in?"

Mareau shook his head and wedged himself beneath Luca's armpit. Together, he and Deniaud lifted Luca to standing and carried her out of the room.

"I was your guard once, Your Majesty." Guérin bowed again, more shallow. It sounded like a reminder and a plea both at once. "Are you...all right?"

"I'm fine." Even though she still struggled to find her footing. "What do you want that could not wait for an audience at a decent hour?"

None of the guards, not even Guérin, reacted to the cold in Luca's voice.

"My daughter, Your Majesty. I want my daughter."

"Have you convinced her to help us?"

The downward cast of Guérin's features spoke loud enough, but still, the woman said, "I can't make her understand, Your Majesty. Please. Have mercy on me."

"Mercy?" Luca's hand strayed again to the scars Fili's attack had left. The healing had done its work well. Luca didn't think she would ever forget the piercing pain, though, and the certainty that everything she'd worked for was lost. "Do you know what she's doing that's helping the city? How she's doing it?"

Guérin turned her hands up helplessly. "She says she can't explain it to me."

"Can't or won't?"

"I don't know, Your Majesty. I don't understand what she does, I never have. Please."

Guérin began to lower herself, sliding down her crutch, and Luca remembered the woman kneeling on the stone in Le Fontinard. How impossible it had been to face her then.

She lunged forward and yanked Guérin up by the collar, her hand a claw in the larger woman's coat, fingers twisted painfully by the weight of her.

"Do not try to manipulate me," Luca snarled in Guérin's face. "Do you think me a tyrant? Or do you think I'm a fool, softhearted? That you can tug at my heart just so, ply our old debts so that I will risk my throne for you? For a daughter you barely raised, and so she despises me for it? Her hatred of me is as much your doing as mine, but I will pay the price for it. Do you understand, Guérin?"

"I do, Your Majesty." Guérin scrambled to get her weight beneath her, but Luca didn't release her. Tears fell down the woman's cheeks, tears she had never shown Luca, not in one day of service, not even the day she'd had her leg mangled by a crocodile in Qazāl.

Unbidden, a moment from that time came to her: Touraine, shouting her down in the town house in the Quartier. *Guérin almost died for you. I'd bet she wishes she had.*

You will never have nothing. Not like we have nothing.

I would have nothing if Fili had her way, Luca wanted to growl at the memory. She knew, though, as she'd known then what she owed Guérin. The guilt had almost eaten her then, and it hadn't stopped. It had never stopped.

Luca loosed her cramped fingers from Guérin's coat, and the woman stumbled upright. Luca sagged into Mareau's support. She could barely stand.

"Guérin, how did you marry your husband?"

"Majesty? I don't—" She frowned, bewildered by the sudden shift.

"I know more of you keep the old god in the north. Even if you keep it quietly. How were you married?" Luca ran her thumb along the scar on her palm, where Aranen had made her wedding cut. It was silvery smooth across the natural lines.

A gray pallor leached through her pale skin, too rapidly aged, too thin, the tendons and bones of her wrist suddenly stark.

"*No*," she whispered.

Guérin's gaze followed Luca's. Their eyes met.

"Your Majesty," she whispered. "You're sick."

Luca felt Mareau stiffen against her. She braced herself for the crash of the ground. She wouldn't have blamed him for dropping her.

"What does it mean, Guérin?" Luca insisted. "What does it mean to be married in the old way?"

Guérin gathered her crutch beneath her and straightened. She considered Luca and the two guards at her side, one holding Luca by the waist, one free to draw her weapon. A calculation.

"My daughter, Your Majesty."

"You want. To bargain. With me?" Each breath was a labor, and with it, Luca knew the laughability of her position.

"Without her, you'll die, Your Majesty." Despite everything, Guérin looked truly grieved. "Fili can help you, and I will tell you all I can."

Though Guérin's face and body had softened in the two years since her service, the soldier was still in there. The soldier who had sworn to give her life for Luca's. The mother who had turned in her own daughter, and now—regret.

"If I do this thing, this thing for you—" Luca bit the words off. It was madness. Utter insanity.

Her legs gave out, but Mareau held her.

"Take me," Luca ordered. "Le Fontinard."

"Leave us the keys," Luca told the jailer from the cradle of Mareau's arms.

Fili Guérin and the jailer both looked at Luca with blank surprise. The jailer took a noticeable step backward.

"Leave us and say nothing of what you've seen."

"Without protection, Your Majesty?" The jailer looked as if Luca was the one she wanted protection from.

"My guards are protection enough, you'll find."

The jailer took in Deniaud's muscled form, her pistol, her sword.

Even Guérin, whose determination made her look formidable. The jailer gulped and handed Deniaud the keys, then bowed herself out. Deniaud closed the door.

"Set me down."

Mareau set Luca down on the stone floor, propped against the wall so that she could see Fili. Luca tried to pull her lips into something like a reassuring smile, but it snagged on the effort of moving the muscles of her mouth. Now she couldn't get the words out.

"You're sick," Fili said.

"Yes." That much Luca could say, letting it escape in the rush of one labored breath.

"Help her, Fili." Guérin swung into the room on her crutch. "Help the queen, and you come home with me, today. She promised." She looked to Luca for reassurance.

"Yes," Luca breathed again. Death crept through one side of her body. One hand still flexed, its flesh full.

"No. You can die like you were supposed to." The petulant glare from beneath her dirty hair made Luca appreciate how young the girl really was.

"Fili!" Guérin snapped.

"What?" Fili tugged at her chains. "You want me to save her? Look what she's done to us, Mam! To me, to you!"

Luca struggled to work her mouth, and each word came out halting, half-slurred:

"If I die—you both die—with me." She raised her head to Deniaud and Mareau, almost expecting to see them balk, but they both put their hands on their weapons.

There was the fear Luca was waiting for, Fili's mouth slack as she looked to her mother. But the fear hardened to resolution.

"If I help you, you surrender to the Fingers."

"Help me and you live," Luca growled.

"Please, Fili. Help her." Guérin quailed beneath the hatred in her daughter's glare. Luca had never seen her falter in any fight, but she shrank before her daughter. "Do it for me."

Fili shook her head at her mother. "If I give you a blessing, you don't touch the Fingers. No more hangings."

The girl was no masterful bargainer. No matter what promise she extracted from Luca, she should have known Luca couldn't, wouldn't stop, not so long as the Fingers threatened her rule. A problem for tomorrow. Today, Luca had to live.

"Then you will stay—away from them. Stay with—your mother."

Fili's mouth tightened. She glanced at her mother, whose eyes were pleading.

"Fine."

"Then you have my word." And now they were both liars.

With her good hand, Luca gestured to Deniaud, and the other guard unlocked Fili's chains. Fili took her time, shaking out her wrists, rubbing the bright red rings where the cuffs had chafed. As Fili loomed above her, Luca couldn't help but laugh. It was raspy, and the muscles of Luca's stomach struggled to match the force of the irony.

"What?" Fili looked at Luca with suspicion.

Luca closed her eyes and shook her head, a monumental effort. All her hunting, all her research, and it had still come down to this. Her life in the hands of someone who would rather her dead. When Fili put her hand to her forehead, to her cheeks, Luca remembered Aranen. The certainty that Aranen would unknit her. Unlike then, there was no feeling that told her the magic was working. This could all be one of the many uncivilized delusions the court had accused her of. At the brush of Fili's thumb across her lips, Luca fought her eyes open.

Fili's own eyes were closed in concentration, her thumb still pressed to Luca's mouth.

Luca's next breath came more easily. So did the next. A sob of relief escaped her, and her hand found Fili's arm. She held it tight.

Fili's eyes shot open. In a brief unguarded moment, Luca saw satisfaction. Tenderness. Then the real Fili came back, and she shook herself out of Luca's grasp and went to stand by her mother.

"Now let us go."

"A promise is a promise. You're free." Luca tried to push herself to her feet, but her legs were still weak. With Mareau's help, she made it to her knees, but she would not be walking back to the palace. Her mouth moved more easily, though the words still came tilted, as if she were drunk. "Know this, Fili. I loved your mother for every moment of her life that she gave to me." Then she turned to Guérin, pausing to catch her breath. "But if your daughter comes for me again, I will kill her and I will kill you. This is my debt to you both discharged, Inès Guérin."

CHAPTER 35

THE GENERAL

Halfway through the third week of marching, as Touraine and her army passed the tip of the Diminue and its hilly country, the first blush of spring caught them. After being snared by the tail end of winter, quartering in nearby villages during snowstorms and freezing in tents, it was a balm to everyone's mood, even Touraine's. Soldiers doffed their caps and unbuttoned their coats and collars to bask in the sunshine. Touraine even taught them some of Pruett's old marching song, "Jolly Soldier." They hesitated, at first, and no wonder; the prince-general was hated by the queen. But Valmorin encouraged them and they took to it with a good will, if not a good ear. Above, a bird glided, hunting.

Touraine and Luca did not have to pretend their falling out. Not exactly. Despite the day in the bath, the distance between them hadn't fully closed. Even though Touraine volunteered to go after Pruett, she hadn't forgiven Luca for sending Moyenne in secret.

People noticed. Jaghotai and Aranen—Aranen, who pulled her aside and asked if she was all right—the nobles of the court, who turned their shoulders now that she hadn't the protection of the queen. Even Perrot had his misgivings, though he obeyed Touraine without question.

And so when the queen did not even show up to see off her wife, the prince consort, before she rode to war, no one was in any doubt that something had gone ill between them.

Touraine tried not to let herself stew over the rumors that would spring up in the palace while she was away.

It's no worse than they already believed.

Beside her, Colonel Valmorin hummed placidly along to "Jolly Soldier."

"How did you get into the army, Colonel?" Touraine unbuttoned her own collar and took off her tricorne, the better to feel the sun on her skin.

She rode with him at least part of every day, getting to know him and what he knew about the Eastern Division, coordinating the campaign. He was a quiet man, and thorough in his thinking. She had been surprised that day shortly after she arrived in Balladaire, when he attempted to befriend her in the palace training yard. Now she saw he treated almost everyone that way, even the new Qazāli soldiers, who were usually given a wide berth.

"I fell into it. Like your horse did, I think." He smirked at Cendre, Touraine's gray from the palace.

"Whatever do you mean?" Touraine said in mock offense, pitching her voice higher and imitating the court accent.

"I'm not a warhorse, either, but my parents have an heir for the estate, and I can do better for myself—and for them—here. They're rather old-fashioned. Still believe in that old law, 'one for the land, one for the crown.' And so here I am, for the crown." He raked his fingers across his thickening blond stubble self-consciously. He was growing out his beard; not a popular fashion for most nobles.

"But you shoot so well," Touraine said.

"And not much more than that. Rather, not much martial. I took my commission hoping to handle logistics," he said, a soft wryness in his voice. One day, the beard might suit him. "I'm very good at logistics." He'd taken on much of the administrative burden so that Touraine wouldn't have to, and she could have kissed him for it. His smile wavered, though.

"But?"

He looked anxiously toward the horizon. "It—the Taargens— What was it like, fighting them?"

"It was war." Touraine rolled her shoulders in her coat. It suddenly felt too small. "It wasn't good."

"I've heard they're monsters. They fight with evil, uncivilized magic."

Touraine leveled the full weight of her golden-eyed glare on him.

"Apologies, Your Highness."

Touraine grunted. "It is magic. Some Taargen priests—they can turn into beasts."

Valmorin smiled again. "I know I've never been into battle, but I'm not *that* gullible. Every drunk who came even close to fighting in the Taargen Wars has some fairy story about giant bears terrorizing the countryside."

"Wonder why they're drunk," Touraine said sarcastically.

"You're not serious."

Another flat look. His smile faded.

"Sky above." He put his tricorne back on his head and held it there. "Sweet sky above." Then he turned to her, wide eyed and pale. "And we're going to fight them?"

"Aye."

He stared back at the horizon, whimpering some variation of "sweet sky above" over and over in different timbres of fear and amazement.

"This doesn't change our plan, Colonel. We parlay first. No matter what."

Valmorin gaped at her. "How do you parlay with beasts?"

"Most animals have good hearing. You just have to avoid the teeth." She bared her own.

Thundering hooves alerted Touraine to a scout riding in hard down the grassy hill, horse lathered and blowing.

"Sir." The scout saluted her. "I found an abandoned camp outside an empty village. It had Balladairan materiél. Little to no sign of struggle in the village. Camp was two weeks old? Maybe more?"

An abandoned camp. None of the other scouts had returned today. The hair on the back of Touraine's neck raised.

"Moyenne," Touraine said to Valmorin. "Have you heard from her?"

Colonel Valmorin shook his head, worry creasing his gentle brow. "It might not be them. If they're on the move, it can be hard to spare a messenger too often."

"Call a halt down the rest of the line," Touraine ordered. "Stay ready."

Valmorin passed the hand signal to his captain, and it traveled to the drummer, who rapped out the sharp tattoo. He looked to her, anxious and trusting.

This was power, too. This weight. The trust in Valmorin's eyes, the faith in every step her soldiers took. This was what she'd wanted Cantic to give her. What she'd wanted Cantic to find her worthy of.

"Colonel, give me twenty of your best. We'll ride—"

"With all due respect, sir," he said softly, "you shouldn't ride anywhere. Your place is here, with the rest of the army."

Touraine frowned. Her body was buzzing with anticipation just this side of fear. She had never been good at stillness, at being left undirected. Add to it now the uncertainty that she *could* do this anymore— she hadn't forgotten how she'd lost herself when Luca's carriage was attacked, and how she'd lost Ghadin as a consequence.

"I need to see it for myself."

"The army needs you." Valmorin sidled his horse closer. "The queen needs you."

Touraine glanced sidelong at him. Had he seen through their anger? They had decided to trust no one, and so she had told her second-in-command only what he needed to know. The rest was in a letter he would find in his saddlebags.

Attend to your orders. Do not come after me.

Whatever else you hear of me, I act under the queen's authority.

Touraine exhaled long and slow. "Thank you, Colonel." To Valmorin's captain she said, "Your best lieutenant and twenty soldiers." To the scout: "Get a fresh horse and lead them back to the camp. Check the area for bodies or survivors."

"Yes, sir."

When they were gone, Touraine surveyed the terrain again. The river came down from the hills to the northeast, little runnels that merged over time into the Diminue—not as big as the Nervure, but formidable enough a crossing here that most would simply spend the extra half day going north to the bridge at Argenvoil. Touraine didn't want her soldiers trapped against it with nowhere to run, but she also didn't want to leave room for anyone to get behind them.

These choices she had asked for. The hard math. Still, she could not help but think, *Are these Pruett's soldiers? Will they be Sands?* Shālan or Taargen? Masridāni or Qazāli? Did it matter to Touraine which, if they attacked?

She ordered the rest of the soldiers into squares with the river at their backs, and the cavalry in a wedge at the front. Faster than she would have expected, the army groaned into position, a neat little grid of infantry and chevrons of cavalry. She also sent another pair of scouts north and south, just in case.

Then they waited. Above, another bird cried out and dived for its prey.

Then, cutting sharp through the sound of the army's nerves, the pawing and snorting of the horses, the clink and the shift of rifles in slick grips, Touraine heard the screaming.

She held her hand up, her golden sleeve glittering in the sun. *Hold.* She hunted for the source of the sound. Behind them, the river gurgled and rushed. To the north and south, nothing she could see.

The Balladairans came first, galloping from the east, horses straining their necks forward. The dread of certainty hollowed Touraine's stomach like a pit before the Taargens even appeared.

Bears. Great bears, larger than any bear deserved to be, running on all fours after the blackcoats. As Touraine watched, one bear caught up to the slowest rider. The horse rolled its eyes as it smelled the predator, its mouth frothing with foam. It couldn't run any faster, no matter how desperately its rider goaded it.

The moment stretched, pulled tight and tighter still. Touraine held her breath.

It snapped.

The bear shouldered the horse's hindquarters, sending horse and rider down, hooves flailing in the air— She closed her eyes against the end.

No. Open them. This is what you always wanted.

Taargen infantry followed the bears, spilling down the hill that had hidden them from view, taking advantage of the fear they knew the bears would evoke. In their dark greens and leather, it was like watching the forest itself racing at them.

"Balladaire!" Touraine urged them back to themselves. She ordered the captains to spread the infantry wide. "Leave a gap in the middle, they're running straight at us. Open up like a jaw, then we close them against the river. Fire when they're in position!"

Dangerous, maybe, with the hazard of friendly fire, but the best way to make the most of the soldiers she had and turn the river into an ally.

The first volley of shots fired. Touraine couldn't help the full-body flinch that took her. Few hit the targets. The bears seemed to shrug off any bullets that landed.

"That's not going to be good for morale," Valmorin said, voice strained. He pressed his tricorne lower onto his head, as if that would protect him.

"Excellent observation." It took everything in Touraine to keep her seat as Cendre pulled nervously.

Breathe. Breathe. You chose to be here. Breathe.

They peeled off the main body of the army, riding out of the way, toward what was now the rear of the southern jaw of the trap Touraine was trying to form. She turned in time to see the cavalry split around the charging Taargens and wheel around on either side to crash into their flanks.

Touraine felt a thrilling hum in her chest. Men and women were dying, but *it was working.*

A snarl behind her froze her blood, and Cendre shied beneath her. Touraine fought hard to turn the gray, only to see a pair of wolves skulking toward her. Giant fucking wolves. She fumbled her sword out of the sheath at her hip. Someone fired at the wolves, but with eerie intelligence and speed, the wolves dodged in synchrony.

Touraine couldn't get control of her horse; it was backing up on its own, trying to get away from the growling, slavering beasts with the jagged, huge teeth—then the wolves lunged, and Cendre, Touraine's first horse, her only horse, the horse she'd been so terrified of once, reared and dumped Touraine on her ass in the dirt.

This is how I die. Touraine rolled away from where she thought Cendre would go next, arms covering her head. She thought of Luca and her leg, trampled in a sky-falling parade. She scrambled to her feet, grabbing her sword. Shāl's own miracle she hadn't skewered herself with it.

The wolves focused on her, and with the army focused on the bears and the Taargen infantry, Touraine was alone. She sheathed the blade.

"I want to speak to Pruett," she told the wolves-that-weren't-wolves. "The Masridāni. I'm Touraine El-Qazāli. The prince consort."

She expected the beasts to turn and lead her away. Instead, the second wolf leapt. Touraine didn't dodge fast enough—she screamed as the wolf's jaws clamped on her forearm, bearing her backward with the momentum of her own leap. She punched with her free arm, gritting her teeth through the eye-watering pain. The first wolf sank its teeth into her shoulder and shook, warning.

White spotted her vision as the wolves' teeth scraped against bone. They held her, but didn't tear her apart. She stopped struggling, and they dragged her away from the battle. Away from Valmorin and the others. Right to where she wanted to be.

The journey was an agony of uncertainty, but that was quickly eaten up by the true agony of her raw back scraped against the ground and the jerking and jouncing of her pierced shoulder. At one point, she might even have passed out, the blue sky above turning into a dreamless swirl of clouds and formless pain.

Finally, they stopped. Touraine closed her eyes to keep them from rolling back into her skull. She was Touraine El-Qazāli, prince consort to Queen Luca, prince-general of her armies, and a royal sky-falling idiot. She rolled onto her knees. The wolves growled when she tried to stand.

Touraine raised her head wearily. A ring of bristling bayonets also discouraged getting to her feet. She sagged onto her haunches and stared down at her hands in her lap, chuckling.

"It's been a long time, Lieutenant."

The familiar voice made Touraine jerk up against her will. Pruett stepped through the ring of guns and beasts. A cigarette dangled from her lips. The tip burned bright as she inhaled.

Touraine cocked the crooked smile that used to charm Pruett, once upon a time. Nothing like Sabine's, but it had worked.

"It's *General* now." She held her arms out wide as she could, showing off her gold coat. Every breath sent daggers of pain into Touraine's shoulder. Blood soaked warm down both arms.

"Among other things, I hear." Pruett didn't smile back. She held out an arm with a leather bracer, and a small falcon landed gracefully. She fed it a scrap of something from a pouch on her belt.

Touraine relaxed the smile and stepped into the role she'd claimed in the palace, no matter that she was ragged on her knees.

"I'm here to parlay."

CHAPTER 36

CAPTIVES (VARIATION)

It shouldn't have been so frightening to kneel at Pruett's feet, in Pruett's own tent, out of sight of other soldiers, Taargen or Shālan or Sand. She shouldn't have held herself so stiff as Pruett examined her forearm and shoulder, gently washing them with a cloth. Just the two of them, like it had been so often, for so long. It should have been comfortable. Touraine should have felt safe.

They'd bound her wrists behind her with irons, and the rope around her ankles was looped through the irons so she couldn't stand, couldn't even sit up straight without straining her bitten shoulder beyond bearing.

"You're in no position to parlay." Pruett stared down at Touraine from her travel stool. Her storm-cloud eyes were brewing with darkness. Her lips and eyes were both tight at the corners. She put aside the bloody rag and started to roll a cigarette on her leg.

"You look tired, Pru," Touraine said tenderly. As much to remind herself as to remind Pruett. They'd been on the same side, once. "Why are you doing this?"

"Why are *you* doing this? I asked you to come with me."

"You never said anything about war."

Pruett rolled her eyes. She licked the cigarette closed, then lit it from the candle on her desk, and took a drag.

"If I'm not in a position to parlay," Touraine asked, "what are you going to do with me?"

Pruett tapped her rolled cigarette on her knuckles. "The Taargens want to send your head back to *the queen*." She sneered the words. "A warning of what's coming."

"That's stupid. Didn't they think about the ransom they could get for sending me back?"

"I know." Pruett's hand stilled. When she spoke again, her voice was hard, no trace of humor, bitter or otherwise. "What would she pay, do you think? For her wife?"

Touraine closed her eyes. "I had to, Pruett. For Qazāl."

"For Qazāl or for a place?" The glowing burn at the tip of the cigarette streaked across Touraine's vision. "You've finally got your general's coat. Cantic would be so proud of you."

The words hit Touraine like a blow in the gut. "You can't say anything, not while you're running errands for the Taargens after everything they did to us."

"We have a common enemy."

"Look, Luca and I— It's complicated. We…didn't leave things well. But she's not your enemy."

"What is she, then? She conquered our homes, she's trying to steal our magic, and all in the name of the empire that stole us and fed us to the wolves because they thought we were less human than them. If she's not my enemy, who under the sky above is?"

"Do you have to have an enemy?"

Pruett's mouth gave a rueful quirk and she took another pull. "I think so."

"There's more to us than this." Even though Touraine still asked herself the same question. It had felt *right*, making Taurvide pay for the sins of his compatriots. He was one piece of the whole rotten fruit, and Touraine had had the power to right at least one wrong in her past. She couldn't—completely—blame Pruett for this.

"She sent me to offer you, if you'd listen, the same deal she made with Qazāl. Generous reparations, support for rebuilding. She said she already sent you an offer."

Pruett frowned as she took another drag. She exhaled a thin stream before saying, "Shame. We must have crossed each other."

"But why?" Touraine tried. "Qazāl can't afford to fight right now, I don't care what you told them—"

"How do you know what I told them?" Pruett narrowed her eyes. "The Jackal is with you."

"She told me what you did. We could have had peace, Pru. For the stars' sake, *peace*."

"You don't want peace and neither do I," Pruett snarled. "We're no good at it. Tell me, what were you doing in that pretty little palace of hers, hein? Dancing in your pretty slippers? Learning to play a delicate little instrument? We're soldiers, Touraine. We fight, we kill, we win. I can't change that about myself, but I can stop doing it for other people. Not surprised to see that you can't. They always did have you well trained." Pruett looked like she wanted to spit.

"Fuck you," Touraine growled from the floor, her voice rising. "You self-righteous bitch. I'm doing what I can for *my people*. To keep them alive and give them something better than they had before—"

"Like you gave Tibeau? He's fucking dead, Touraine, because you thought you could help the Sands by getting in bed with the Balladairans. Look where that's got you!"

"It got us a treaty."

"Aye, and a bigger fucking bed, I bet. Is she good at least?"

"Don't."

"Does she make you kneel for her? Does that get you off? Or does she like you to slap her around—"

"Shut up!" Touraine roared. Her face burned and her eyes stung and if she couldn't place exactly where the pain was, did it matter really? In a matter of seconds, Pruett had flayed her as thoroughly as Touraine had Taurvide.

She didn't know what hurt worse: that Pruett was right on every count, still able to strip Touraine down to the deepest secrets she kept even from herself, or that her relationship with Luca was such a raw place that every finger poked into it was lemon in the wound. If she didn't get control of herself, this would all be over before it even started.

But Pruett did shut up. Her eyes were red and her voice as raw as

Touraine's. She looked as shit as Touraine felt. She sat that way, look-ing off to the side as her cigarette burned out, her jaw working.

Then she left the tent without a word.

The flap opened again, and a pair of Masridāni soldiers in Balladai-ran blackcoats sewn with red patches on the sleeves stitched and ban-daged her wounds, then dragged her out of Pruett's tent.

Dusk had come, and with it, the warmth of the day had gone. Touraine wondered if Valmorin had gotten the companies away. If he had found her letter. If he was even still alive. The camp was quiet, almost subdued. Touraine reckoned there would be more celebrating in the enemy camp if her army had been broken. Small favors.

They didn't drag her far, just to a tent next door. A small one, fit for a pair of soldiers bunked tight. Like the cheap ones the Sands had got-ten. Pruett wanted her close.

The Masridāni threw her into the dark tent without ceremony, then left.

Touraine rolled off her face and onto her side. She had to laugh to keep from weeping. Sky above, what a fool she was.

"A visitor?" came a hoarse but distinctly aristocratic voice from beside her.

Touraine jumped, barely stopping herself from screaming from shock and then pain. "Who are you?"

A pause. "Prince-General?"

"Lady Moyenne?"

Touraine didn't know if it was good or bad luck that her tent mate was Camille de Moyenne. Since their visit to the barracks and the display with Colonel Taurvide, Camille hadn't been overly friendly, but she'd treated Touraine with the distant courtesy of a peer. Then Luca had sent her after Pruett.

That wasn't her fault. Touraine tried to quell the rush of fury. It wasn't Moyenne she was angry with.

"What are you doing here, Your Highness?" Moyenne asked. She sounded guarded, but her shock won through.

Touraine laughed at the contrast of her title while she was tied up in an enemy camp, smeared in dirt and blood. "Same as you, I expect. Do they just leave us in here like this?"

Touraine could barely see the other woman in the dark of their tent. A pause that Touraine was sure had been one of Moyenne's crisp nods. "They do. Though I'm usually fed around this time." There was an edge of amused annoyance when she said, "I suppose I have you to thank for the disruption. What have you done?"

"They ambushed us."

"Who is 'us'?"

"Eastern Division. We found a camp outside of Goppes. It looked like it was one of ours, but it must have been a trap."

"Mm. That will have been ours. I was out with one of my patrols, checking on the situation with food in the town, and the Withering. The aid I'd ordered hadn't arrived. I suspected brigands, of course." Her voice turned bitter with a familiar cast of guilt—the feeling that, as the commander, she should have known better. "We were settling in for the night when we were surrounded. Wolves and bears. Uncivilized."

Touraine chose to ignore the insult. She was too busy wondering if the brigands were an excuse.

"Are you the only prisoner?" she asked.

"From my patrol? I wasn't, but who's to say now? Better we had all died."

"And outside of your patrol?"

"My brother...was here."

"He was?" That was the last thing Touraine had expected to hear. "Yes."

Moyenne didn't have to explain the thickness in her throat to her. Touraine had been one of the Taargen prisoners once before. She knew the holding pens they would keep prisoners in until one of their priests needed a sacrifice.

"How has it been in here?" Touraine asked instead.

"I don't know if they'll ransom me back to the crown or if they hope to get information out of me."

"Torture?"

"Some," Moyenne said nonchalantly.

They chuckled into the silence that followed, quietly thinking about what would come next. Sharp knives and rough hands. Touraine's eyes got used to the dark, and she could make out the silhouette of Moyenne's head. Her noble's braid was a rat's nest of grease and dirt. The proud, sharp angle of her nose was skewed.

Iron rattled and dirt scuffed as Moyenne scooted closer and closer to Touraine until they were just touching. Touraine felt her hot breath on her face and recoiled.

"Shh. Don't worry, I'm no Durfort. But"—Moyenne lowered her voice even further—"I would certainly promise you that they're listening. Tell me what's happened outside since I've been here."

"How long have you been here?" Touraine whispered back.

"I don't know. A few weeks, perhaps. Start from when I left the palace?"

Touraine caught Moyenne up on the progress of the Withering since the wedding, and then the preparations of the soldiers, leaving Moyenne with a dismal view of the whole situation. She swore when Touraine finished.

"Hopefully Colonel Valmorin survived. He's good at logistics." Touraine allowed herself one smile.

Moyenne made a thoughtful sound in her throat. Then she said, "He'll do better than Taurvide."

Another long, dark silence.

As she stared at the slope of the tent above her, she could almost see the pieces of her and Luca's plan moving, like they were playing an échecs game.

An échecs game they couldn't possibly win.

"Any thoughts of getting out?" she asked Moyenne.

The marquise snorted laughter, then jangled the irons that looped around her wrists. Her ankles, too.

"I've been rescued out of worse," Touraine said. Rescued from a Taargen sacrifice pen by none other than Pruett her-sky-falling-self.

"How lucky for you."

They were so quiet for so long that Touraine could hear the sounds of some couple nearby very noisily fucking, and she smirked. "Good for them."

Then, with an embarrassing wave of heat, she recognized one of the women's cries—the louder voice, in fact.

"Oh, fuck you, Pruett."

Moyenne laughed darkly. "They're like rabbits. Every night." She cocked her head. "Not usually so loud, though. Maybe a win stoked her fire."

"Who with?" Not that it mattered.

"A golden-eyed one, like you. The qā'id calls her Kiras."

"Kiras," Touraine repeated. The name was surprisingly sour in her mouth. *Like me.*

"I'm sensing a history here."

"Something like that."

"Enlighten me, if it pleases Your Highness. I have nothing but time."

There was a bored camaraderie in Moyenne's voice, like two soldiers on watch. Touraine was torn between that likeness and the desire to ask her point-blank—*Did Luca tell you to hunt her down, or was Ghislaine lying?* What would be the point? Pruett was alive and Moyenne was in chains.

"Let's just say, I used to be in Kiras's place."

Moyenne groaned. "Sky above. And now you're with the queen?" She swore again, somehow managing to remain stiff and dignified. "We're never getting out of here alive."

The point, Touraine told herself, was that she needed to know if she could trust Luca. If not...

If not, will you turn on her? Is Pruett right?

Was Pruett *worth* that?

"Did the queen send you to find her? The qā'id? Is that why you were really down here?"

Touraine could feel Moyenne's hesitation in her body. Then, in a choked voice, she said, "Her Majesty gave me leave to hunt my brother's killer."

"I see." Touraine felt sick to her stomach. She could imagine how Luca would have phrased it. How she would have coaxed and convinced Moyenne into it, so that Moyenne didn't even realize it was Luca's own will she was chasing.

"Why?" Moyenne asked warily.

"Do you trust me?"

"I— Do I have a choice, Your Highness?"

"Then have faith. If not in me, then in the queen."

Touraine could practically hear Moyenne slitting her eyes in skepticism. She closed her own eyes, trying and failing to block out the sound of Pruett and Kiras, but the harder she tried, the less it worked. So she tried to remember Luca beside her during their last night together, fitting the noises over each other. The way Luca's lashes fell dark on her pale cheeks. The quiet curve of her lips in sleep. She was so soft then. Almost kind. Touraine couldn't help but wonder what Luca might be without all of this: a crown, a plague, a war. But it was Luca's hardness that drew Touraine. That unyielding, unrelenting, uncompromising drive. Like Cantic. Like Jaghotai. Like Djasha. Touraine admired it. She craved it.

They slept together again, and if she had imagined Luca was telling her goodbye in the bathing room, she was not imagining it this time. They'd clung to every kiss, unwilling to break away, pressing close, constant.

It had left an aching fullness in Touraine's chest, as she held Luca and traced her fingers through her long hair.

She was wondering when she would come back, if she would come back, when Luca had looked up at her. Touraine realized she had stopped awkwardly mid-stroke, her hand hovering over Luca's head.

What will you have to become to withstand her flames? Aranen's words, a lifetime ago.

What will you make me, Luca?

"What?" Luca had asked, her blue-green eyes dark and sated in the half-gone candlelight.

Had Touraine said those last words aloud?

"Nothing." She shook her head.

"Liar. I can tell when you lie."

"You cannot. How?"

"Why would I tell you?" Luca pinched Touraine's naked hip. "What?"

Touraine swatted her hand away, then grabbed it back. She brushed her thumb across the knuckles one by one.

"I'm going to miss you," she said.

"I'm going to miss you, too."

Luca sniffed in the dark, and Touraine raised her thumb to Luca's cheeks. They were damp.

"Don't. It's all right."

"People die in war."

"People die in war. Even if they don't fight. People die in peacetime. Queens and princes are assassinated—"

Luca squeezed Touraine's wrist hard. "You're not making me feel better."

"No?" Touraine twisted her arm free and wiped Luca's face again. "If I don't come back—"

"Come back." Luca gripped the short hairs on Touraine's head.

Touraine hissed sharply, teeth bared.

"That's a command from your queen." Not so sated, then.

That feeling rose in Touraine, the thing she'd thought she'd laid to rest after the first time they'd slept together—properly slept together, not frantically finger-fucked against the infirmary wall—and then again after she'd bruised the aroused flutter of Luca's pulse beneath her thumb. Anger and frustration and the fierce ache to watch Luca surrender beneath her hands. Give. Take.

"Yes, Your Majesty." Touraine flipped her, and bore her down, face-first into the pillows.

And then, with her hand snarled in Luca's hair:

"Are you mine?"

"Yes."

Fingers tighter, nails digging: "Are you *mine*?"

"*Yes.*"

Later, when Luca thought Touraine was sleeping in the pale hours of the night, she'd whispered again, lips against Touraine's back.

"I am yours, Touraine. Come back, my love. Please."

In the prisoners' tent, Touraine spun her memories until the weave of them fell apart, long after Moyenne's breaths slowed to sleep. Then, instead of sleeping herself, Touraine tried to figure out how to lie to the one person she'd never been able to lie to.

CHAPTER 37

OF HOUNDS AND HINDS

Twenty days. Twenty days since Touraine had marched away to meet her old lover on the battlefield, for peace or for war. Twenty days since Luca had kissed her goodbye, wondering if she would return.

Ten days since she'd found her mother's journals. Since Guérin had explained the old marriage rites, binding lovers to the land. Ten days since she had felt the touch of the Withering. Felt her own body failing. Ten days since Luca had traded her own life for Fili's. One last time.

She had spent three days in her chambers, turning away everyone until she was certain the Withering had left no sign on her body. Nothing visible, anylight. She had to switch, for a time, from her cane to her crutch.

Four days since Touraine's last messenger: the weather atrocious, the soldiers amiable. Nothing to report.

Nothing to report. It seemed impossible that so much could loom over Balladaire and yet *nothing.* Luca told herself it was the way of war. The way of life. A hunter stalks in silence until—the crash of quarry through the brush, and off go the hounds! She tried not to think of herself as the quarry. She had her own game to hunt, weak as she still felt.

Does the wolf not hunt the deer, only to be brought down by the hunter?

Today, her quarry was Evrard. More specifically, it was Evrard's money. Despite the vote turning in favor of her reforms, the need for money had only grown with the Taargens' approach.

She was on her way to meet him in the gaming salon that afternoon when Aliez de Beau-Sang came striding toward her. The young woman was dressed head to toe in Qazāli fashion, vibrantly colored, layered despite the surprise warmth. Her eyes were wide with urgency, and she reached for Luca, as if Luca would pass her by.

"Your Majesty, it's Lady Ghislaine—"

"What now?" Luca growled under her breath. She had hoped to be in the gaming salon before Evrard so that she could exert her presence.

"She's holding a salon—in the conservatory. There's an officer there and he's . . ." She trailed off, her face going pink.

"What? Speak, my lady." Luca adjusted her steps to the conservatory instead. She cursed. The two rooms were not near each other, and the effort of walking was still more of a strain than she wished to admit. If she was quick, though, she could handle this and move on.

"He's talking about the prince consort, Your Majesty."

Luca stopped in the middle of the corridor. It was hard to say what motivated the skip in her heart—anger that Touraine was very likely being gossiped about? *You knew that would happen. This was part of your plan.* Or mounting dread of what Ghislaine had planned? Luca started off again, leaning heavily on the crutch wedged beneath her arm.

The conservatory was bright with light thanks to the pride of the room: a great roof of glass let in the sunlight of the clear winter day. It had been unseasonably warm the last couple of days, and those who were not out riding were clearly enjoying the sun however they could— the room was crowded. Almost all the courtiers piled on the couches around one speaking figure, enraptured. A few had even unwrapped the scarves from their faces. Luca could see only Taurvide's back, in a military coat with a gold-striped black sleeve—and Ghislaine's beside him.

"—and when I spoke out against her disastrous ideas," he was saying loudly, "with all my experience in battle, she set her men on me like dogs until I was subdued, a dozen of them!"

Luca walked slowly, quietly up behind him, and Aliez followed her lead, hanging a step behind. The courtiers facing Luca closed their mouths and sat back abruptly. The colonel didn't notice. Ghislaine did.

"They dragged me to the pole and had me whipped! Me! A peer of the empire." His voice grew steadily louder. "The queen gives that beast too long a leash!"

Luca gave Ghislaine a small smile. The comtesse cleared her throat delicately as the colonel drew breath for the next verse in his tirade. The large man jerked like a marionette as he realized something greater had stolen his audience's attention. Hesitantly, he turned. Luca had never seen the color drain from a man's face so quickly.

"Your Majesty." He stood and bobbed, wincing, even though it had been months since Touraine had had him whipped. "Forgive me, I cannot bow, my injuries—"

"Lord Taurvide." Luca stepped closer. "I realize things have changed since you first met my wife, but I will tell you now: you may refer to the prince consort as 'Her Highness' or 'Prince-General' and nothing else, in my hearing or without."

Taurvide's bull-like face purpled. "Of course, Your Majesty. Forgive me." Somehow, he found it within his injuries to bow this time. "It was only in my frustration, and if only I could have some redress for my injuries, Your Majesty—"

"As my general and my consort, Touraine El-Qazāli speaks with my own tongue. Were you insubordinate, she is allowed to mete out what punishment she deemed fit." Luca cocked her head, aware of the utter silence. You could have heard a pin drop from any of the noble braids. "Were you insubordinate, Lord Taurvide?"

Taurvide cleared his throat several times before he spoke. His face shone with sweat. Luca couldn't deny the thunder of her own heart, knowing that every move she made right now would set up difficulties in days to come. The others in the room didn't move, not even to leave: rabbits frozen at the sound of the hunter's tread. From the corner of Luca's eye, Ghislaine was, if not petrified, the still of a scavenger, waiting for Luca to leave the carcass behind.

The colonel found his voice. "My passions for Balladaire overgoverned me. I think only for the empire's good. Forgive your loyal servant."

"Mm." Luca let her mask slip further into disdain. Not so much a mask, today. "You would do well to think of your own good before you speak. All of you."

Without warning, Luca turned to Ghislaine. "An interesting move, my lady."

Elegance to the last, Ghislaine stood and curtsied low, raising the hem of her emerald dress.

"Your Majesty, forgive me. I had only invited the esteemed colonel because we have always been friendly, and I had heard he had returned to the palace. It was only tea, Your Majesty, but he has a flair for storytelling."

"Apparently, the idea of Le Fontinard was not enough. Perhaps the noose?"

Ghislaine laughed her stage laugh, the one certain to gather all the attention in a room.

"For me?" she said. "I've done nothing wrong."

"Gathering your friends to titter over treason is nothing? Ghislaine Bel-Jadot, your lands and titles were given by the crown in trust. I now strip them away. Guards, take her to Le Fontinard."

The pair of guards who chaperoned Ghislaine snapped to action, flanking the woman on both sides. When they reached to grab her arms, she snatched them out of reach and strode toward Luca.

Deniaud was between them in an instant, her sword pointed at Ghislaine's décolletage.

Ghislaine glanced down at the blade and sniffed. "Arrest me, then. But Colonel Taurvide isn't wrong. Do you think your pet doesn't hold this same ill will toward the rest of us? Toward you? Especially now that she knows what you've done. Your quarrel has not gone unnoticed."

Luca's heart stopped cold. She wanted to shake the woman and demand the truth, but she was keenly aware of the balance she needed to strike. She couldn't appear to be another mad king, like Ancier l'Atroce. Then the nobility would gather their strength together at last and pull her down. Balance, like Aranen din Djasha preached.

But Ghislaine's bluff cast the last weeks she'd spent with Touraine in a new light. The distance. The hesitation. The goodbye in Touraine's kiss. Had Touraine finally learned how to lie?

"She brought you home. We ransomed you from bandits. I would have expected more gratitude."

With the guards around her, Ghislaine gave Luca another narrow-eyed once-over. "Are you well, Your Majesty?" A knowing curl of her lips. "You look rather gray."

Luca kept her cold mask in place. "Take her away."

"Yes, Your Majesty. And the colonel?"

Taurvide cringed, as if he could hide his broad body among the cushions.

"Please, Your Majesty—" he began.

"Lord Taurvide, if you call my wife outside of her titles again, I will finish what she started." She flagged the pair of guards at the door of the salon. "Escort him to his rooms." Taurvide let one of the men help him gingerly to his feet, and he followed them meekly out.

The rabbits didn't dare move as Ghislaine and Taurvide were taken away. The rush of the power she held over them was an intoxicant in the blood. Perhaps there was something to l'Atroce's madness.

Balance.

Luca bowed to Aliez, who startled. Luca replaced her icy court mask for a slightly warmer one but all formality. "Lady LeRoche, comtesse des Champs d'Or. Thank you once more for your loyalty."

Aliez's eyes went wide. "Y-Your Majesty." She stammered and bowed at the same time. "I— Thank you. Of course."

"I hope the rest of you pass an enjoyable afternoon," Luca told the courtiers who remained. "There will be precious few of those to come. Think well on how you wish to spend them."

Luca left them there and rushed to the game salon, while trying not to appear as if she were rushing. She prickled with a febrile sweat beneath her clothing. She did not know how long it would take her to fully recover—if she ever would. This new weakness on top of the old was yet another insult, and she pushed herself with dogged spite. She collected herself before she entered the games salon, straightening her waistcoat and smoothing the escaped strands of her braid.

The room was near as full of courtiers as the tea room was, though instead of crowding all around one couch, men and women lingered over tables of échecs and tarot and a host of other games; for some, the games were an excuse to gossip or flirt, for others, true contests. If news of Ghislaine's arrest hadn't reached the room, it would soon.

Evrard stood as she approached. The échecs board was already set, the white pieces toward the empty seat waiting for Luca. One cup of tea and one cup of coffee steamed on either side of the board.

"Your Majesty." He bowed. "While I waited, I took the liberty of sending for a coffee. I've heard your time in Qazāl gave you a taste for it. Are you well?"

Courteous, while not failing to point out that Luca was late.

"Thank you, yes. I'm looking forward to this game."

As she settled in, however, Luca realized how true the words were. Her body eased with the comfort of familiarity, the pieces in her hands, a warm drink. The steady hum of conversation. She had not known how much she would miss this when she chained her uncle in a cell.

Luca played her first move, then sipped her coffee.

"Has something happened?" Evrard asked, taking his own turn. Age-spotted skin bunched around his knuckles, but it was not the Withering.

"There was an incident with Lord Taurvide."

"The colonel?"

"No longer."

Evrard raised his white eyebrows, his dark eyes sharp. "I take it he did not agree with the prince consort? I told you, Your Majesty, this marriage would only have consequences—" He must have seen Luca's expression freezing over. "Forgive me, it is done, as you said. Please." He gestured at the board.

"We're going to war, Your Grace."

"On the word of your foreign friends, yes, I've heard."

"Those foreign friends are our allies."

He tutted, finger against his lips as he considered the board or her words. "It sounds like an internal power struggle. Best not to get involved in those. Better we focus on our own borders. Balladaire cannot afford a war with the Taargens, not in coin and certainly not in blood."

It couldn't. Which was precisely why Luca was there. No one could

do anything about the cost in blood but Touraine. Coin, however…
She gave the room a casual glance, noting how many people had come
into the room since she'd arrived. How many players played, or pretended to play, and how many watched her and Evrard with no pretense at all.

"Are you hesitant because of your son?" Another move.

She watched him carefully, catching the barest hesitation as he
placed a chevalier on a black marble square. Then he held it there,
thoughtfully. She realized he was staring at the thick gray stone set in a
gold band he wore on his index finger.

"We all have our griefs, Your Majesty, from the wars and the
Withering."

"That is precisely why I cannot avoid the truth."

"The truth?" The comte made a small choking sound in his throat.
"The truth is that my son's body was so destroyed that his comrades
scarcely found enough of him to burn."

"They told you that?" Luca forgot to hide her shock.

"There are some things a father needs to know about his child."
Evrard used his chevalier to fork her keep and a scholar.

Luca focused on the game board, trying to choose her next move so
that she wouldn't think of Tiro.

"If the army has the money they need for supplies and arms, they'll
stand a much better chance."

"What about food for your people in the cities? This band of revolutionaries in the city…the Fists? Whatever they call themselves. Why
not turn your attention to feeding the people?"

"The crown's coffers reach only so deep. Thanks to the new reforms,
the banks have agreed on a loan to the crown. We'll buy as much food
from the great houses' stores as we can."

Evrard's next move allowed Luca to take one of his scholars. He
gave a rueful laugh when he realized what he had done. Several turns
later, and he laughed again. He sat back in his seat and took off his
spectacles, eyes crinkling.

"I'm an old man, Your Majesty. I've lived through three Wither-
ings." He waved his hand at his uncovered face, his wrinkles, his hoary
eyebrows and white mustache. "An uncivilized person might say that

I was spared for a reason." He gave Luca a sharp look. She wondered if he could see the disease's mark upon her. If he knew why *she* had been spared.

"It's only chance," he continued, smiling warmly, "and occasionally, generosity. Out of respect for that, I will make loans to the crown so that we may do some good for Balladaire. Use my funds for food, and divert your sovereigns to the war effort. I know we have had our differences in opinion, but look."

He opened his hands out over the board. Luca's last move had placed him in checkmate.

"I have high hopes for you, my queen." He stood and bowed.

Luca studied the board as he'd left it. Too many careful mistakes. Too much generosity.

CHAPTER 38

A PRINCE'S RANSOM

The map Luca had commissioned for the war room stretched from one corner of the right-hand wall to the other. She traced with her fingertips the town of Goppes, the River Diminue flowing near it, then down to the southern coast, where the Diminue fed into the Triaume.

When this was her father's war room, weapons had hung on the dark green walls and enemy banners had hung from gold gilt rods beneath the golden filigree, bloody and burned, but her father had never been one for waging war from the royal seat. Luca barely remembered him in here at all, and the first Taargen War had been fought before she was born.

She had loved this room, though, when it was her uncle's war room. During the second Taargen War, she'd sat to her uncle's left, and even though it was his commands the generals obeyed, she'd thought herself a queen. Her uncle's war room had been one of ledgers, sheaves of correspondence, the inaudible scratch and stamp of lives changing hands by royal writ. The era of the conscripts. She'd even been present when General Cantic was reinstated from training the young Shālan soldiers to return to the front.

Luca pressed her thumb against Goppes again, remembering the last press of Touraine's mouth against hers, before she sagged into her seat—not her old seat at the corner, but her new one. Her uncle's. Her father's. Hers.

The Jackal sat to her left. In Luca's old seat. The Qazāli woman stared around the room, taking in the centuries of Ancier rule, the decisions made here that upended her life, her nation. However Jaghotai felt to be sitting at this table now, the grim set of her mouth offered no nuance.

"Lord Evrard. Lady Aliez." Luca didn't stand when the only two members of the High Court in La Chaise entered. "Please, sit. Lord Evrard, have you met the acting ambassador of Qazāl, Her Excellency Jaghotai...?"

Luca trailed off. She didn't know Touraine's mother's full name. The Jackal provided no correction or addition, however, only sat there in a gifted Balladairan coat with one sleeve pinned close to her stump and both arms crossed over her chest.

Aliez adjusted slowly to her new station; she seemed hesitant to enter, glancing about the room as she took one of the high-backed velvet-lined seats. Evrard had made no mention of the change in the few days that had passed since Ghislaine's arrest, and this morning he entered the war room without his usual patronizing smile.

Commander Perrot also sat at the table, a sheen of sweat on his forehead. He shifted against the black cushions and adjusted and readjusted his coat. He'd been the one to deliver the ransom letter to Luca late last night.

With all of them gathered, it was hard to find the words. Harder still to speak them without giving away her true feelings.

"A few days ago, we had our first engagement with the Taargens. Just outside of Goppes. The Eastern Division was ambushed, and though the army remains largely intact"—Luca paused to swallow—"Her Highness was captured in the fighting. Lady Camille de Moyenne has also been captured. The enemy has offered to ransom them back to us."

"Ransom?" Aliez put a hand to her throat. The gesture was uncannily Ghislaine's. "How much?"

"It will hardly be a trivial demand," Evrard said, "not while we already suffer under the Withering."

As if Luca needed the reminder. She had already taken Evrard's loan and put it in the hands of her seneschal and Minister Beaufoi to disperse it accordingly, but buying food fairly was difficult, and it wasn't as if she could buy it from outside Balladaire anymore. All the while, the plague fires still burned, and Luca avoided passing the windows of the palace at night lest she see their glow upon the dark sky. Her people died and she knew the one person who could help them. Some of them, all of them. She had taken that succor herself, and yet, she would not offer it to them. She could not.

"The cost is too high," Luca said. To herself and her war council.

"Your surrender," the Jackal said softly.

Luca let her silence answer. Better that than show her quiet triumph at this one success. Besides, more than a little doubt remained. What if Touraine was wrong, and Pruett let the Taargens torture her, drag out even the information Touraine wasn't meant to give? Bad enough that Luca could *see* Touraine biting her tongue bloody on the pain, refusing to answer. Unless of course, Ghislaine was telling the truth. Touraine could have turned her coat in truth, vengeance for Luca's own cruel pettiness.

Luca had to trust her.

Like she trusted you?

Evrard cleared his throat delicately and stroked his white mustache. He wore the onyx cloak pin Luca had given him months ago, as a reminder of their mutual benefits.

"My lord?" Luca prompted.

"It is hard to lose such valued members of the court. Another loss for the lords Moyenne, so soon after losing Brice—perhaps there is some compromise."

Luca tightened her mouth at his tone, the optimism showing through the dismayed apology, like metal below the flaking gilt. "Yes?"

"I know we said it was done, Your Majesty, but a marital alliance with the Taargens..."

"I am already legally married, my lord, by the customs of two nations, and the Taargens are holding the wife in question hostage. It does not warm me to them."

"I'm sure they would be willing to overlook certain technicalities, if you were, too."

The Jackal coughed a laugh. "Let them kill my daughter to keep their place secure?" She spoke Balladairan with a Qazāli musicality.

Evrard looked distastefully at Jaghotai, and Jaghotai gave him a lopsided smile, showing a crooked incisor. Aliez looked between the two as if afraid that she would be caught in the middle of a brawl. Poor girl. After a life in the colonies, she wasn't prepared for the slip-daggers of the Chaisien court.

"I will consider it," Luca said, forestalling a diplomatic incident. "Touraine's failure is a disappointment. We may yet need a bloodless path to peace."

"Thank you, Your Majesty. To protect Balladaire, surely we must make some sacrifices."

"What do any of you know of sacrifices?" the Jackal growled.

Luca shivered. Before the ransom letter came, she had thought of nothing but sacrifices. About what Guérin had told her. The old Balladairan weddings, the blood of the couple mingled and dripping into the earth. It called too readily to mind the sacrifices Ghislaine had spoken to on her estate: children thrown to their deaths for the sake of the harvests. When she was strong enough to get out of bed again, Luca had sat at her desk with Bastien's golden coin and the clay coin she had found in Champs d'Or. The skull on one side, the wheat or the apple on the other. She was missing something, something about the balance between growth and decay, pestilence and bloom, something important, but she couldn't put it together. Bastien would have known. He would have seen it.

Luca, on the other hand, could barely concentrate on the question without the intrusion of her failing empire.

"What will they ask for, Lord Evrard? What are their terms if I marry? That Balladaire become a vassal country to the Taargen Empire? That all her goods and taxes go to the Bear Queen, to be spent through her?"

"How terrible that would be," muttered the Jackal in Shālan.

Luca shot her a glare. *Not helping.*

"That will be the last sacrifice I make, Your Grace. I'm not so afraid of the Taargens that I'll surrender before the battle is begun, but perhaps there are other arrangements."

"If you don't accept their conditions, will you go get her?" The Jackal looked at each of the Balladairans from beneath low lids, unimpressed and unhurried. She stopped on Luca, her dark brown eyes steady.

"You mean the army?" Luca asked. "They'll expect that, I think. Hope for it, perhaps."

"Probably. It would leave your flank open. Unfortunately for you, your flank is your city."

"Unfortunate for you as well." A probe, to see where the Jackal's own loyalties would lie.

The older woman ducked her head in concession. "It could be an opportunity. Make it seem like you are throwing all your weight at them. They would believe it if you made very much noise about it."

"A lure." Luca cocked an eyebrow. "What about the Qazāli contingent?"

"I don't know. My guess is some will come upriver, but I cannot tell you if they've mixed the armies or not. So it depends where your navy stops them. I did not see so many ships when I came in myself."

Luca's face warmed at the subtle rebuke. "The Withering has kept us occupied. I trust the captains who see them to act expediently. In the meantime, send scouts south, Commander."

"Aye, Your Majesty," Perrot said. "Who will command the armies now?"

"Who's the ranking officer?"

"A Colonel Valmorin, Your Majesty."

"That's fine."

"Forgive me, Your Majesty, but—" Perrot bit his lips into his mouth as he stared at the table. "He's green wood, Your Majesty."

Luca frowned. "I need you here." She needed someone she trusted close to her. The duke's man had proven himself surprisingly loyal—if not to her, then to Touraine.

"Not me, Your Majesty. Could—I know things are—but could you not send Taurvide? Conditionally? He's got the experience and he's at least familiar with the soldiers. And the Taargens."

Luca stared at him, mouth half-open, stunned at his audacity. The thick knob of his throat rode up and down beneath his beard as Perrot stalwartly met her gaze. Then Luca remembered Evrard was there and she closed her mask back over her face.

Perrot wasn't strictly wrong. If Touraine had not intended to leave Colonel Valmorin in charge, Luca would have preferred someone with experience to lead the fighting in the east. As it was, Taurvide would probably disrupt Touraine's own instructions to the young colonel. She also couldn't help but wonder if this was a trick of Ghislaine's, her reach extending beyond her cell. Considering it made Luca feel filthy. Like she was stabbing Touraine in the back, undermining her in the very ways she'd promised not to. But Luca needed to be beyond suspicion.

A line from Yverte decided her: *No one is so grateful as an enemy spared.*

She kept her resignation from showing, sitting up straighter. "I will reinstate Colonel Taurvide, conditionally. Let him know his debt to me and behave accordingly. He is to work *with* Colonel Valmorin in an advisory capacity only."

"Yes, Your Majesty. I'll make it clear to him." Perrot saluted and left.

That left Evrard and Aliez.

"We're at the bottom of what we've requisitioned from within the city," Luca said. "What about the Travers and the Champs d'Or stores?"

Evrard pursed his lips. "I'll write to my seneschal to inquire. I previously informed him to dole it out to my people as necessary. We might find ourselves depleted. I suspect it is the same across all Balladaire." Luca could hear the unsaid: an alliance to the Taargens would also give them the breathing room to feed their people instead of their armies.

Luca would not give up Balladaire, by marriage or otherwise.

"I'll write, also," Aliez said. "We'll contribute what we can. As soon as . . . things are in order in Champs d'Or." She smiled apologetically.

The two nobles left.

"You sit in a basket of cobras," the Jackal said in Shālan when they were alone. She scrubbed her face with her palm.

"I know. The only mistake Touraine made was not flaying Taurvide to death."

Jaghotai made an odd grunting noise that Luca realized belatedly was a chuckle. Then it cut off.

"The old man. Why don't you put him in your prison like the woman?"

"He hasn't done anything wrong. Technically. It's one thing to show my teeth. Another to go on a paranoid rampage. The nobles *and* the people at my throat?" Luca shook her head. "I may as well hand the crown over to the Taargens, then. Without evidence..." She flipped her hand and blew the air out of her cheeks.

"You sound as if you are ready to give it over." Jaghotai turned her glass on the table. "Are you really going to give her up?"

Luca searched Jaghotai's face, her posture, for a threat, but found weary sadness. Luca wished she could confide in her. Touraine had told Luca to trust Jaghotai, but Luca found herself clutching her secrets ever tighter.

"I'll figure something out."

"It seems like marrying my daughter has been more trouble to you than it's worth. That's all."

"You have no idea what she's worth to me," Luca snapped.

Jaghotai raised an eyebrow slowly and tilted her head.

"I'm sorry." Luca leaned on the table, resting her lips against her folded hands. "You know better than anyone that our arrangement isn't purely political. She told me you sent her here to capitalize on a certain weakness."

The Jackal's eyes crinkled in a smile, smug. "It worked."

Luca started to smile beneath her black scarf, but she remembered that the woman they'd played between them was now a captured piece on a different board.

Then more soberly, Jaghotai added, probing again, "I know you two fought. Before she left."

"Understand me, Jaghotai," Luca said, offering some truth. "No matter what happened between us, if I can bring her back safely, it will be done. But Balladaire cannot afford my weaknesses."

Touraine's calloused palms against hers. The press of her nose against Touraine's neck.

"I understand more than you might think. When I lost her that first time..." Jaghotai sucked her teeth and grunted. "Never thought I'd see her again. Then I did, and she was yours."

"Is that supposed to make me feel better?"

The older woman tapped her fingers on the table and stared intently at her hand. Touraine's mother wasn't old, exactly, probably not more than fifty years or so. Younger than Gil. The years of her life, though, had worn on her. Her brow was lined in a permanent scowl, her cheeks sagging around her downturned mouth. Her nose looked like it had been broken at least once. Her dreadlocks were long and shot unevenly with gray from the roots.

"I don't know, princess." Jaghotai said it like a sobriquet, not a title. "Don't care if it does, really. I guess I mean to say I'm waiting and hoping, same as you are."

"I have been...comforting myself with the fact that she's with her old sergeant. The way Touraine speaks of her, I don't think she would hurt her."

"Pruett? The sharpshooter?" Jaghotai snorted. "Not sure I'd trust that hope. Something's twisted in that girl, and if I know anything, it's you and yours that did it."

The Jackal pushed herself to her feet with a sigh. There was a weariness in the way she carried her powerful body. As if she wished she could put it down. She patted Luca awkwardly on the shoulder on the way out.

"Jaghotai," Luca called before the woman opened the door.

"Hm?"

"Trust me. Trust her."

The Jackal laughed out loud, and the door slammed shut behind her.

CHAPTER 39

ON FRIENDSHIP

The days passed slowly. Touraine and Moyenne usually woke to a breakfast of congealed porridge. Occasionally, Pruett would look in on them, dour and silent. More often, she didn't.

Touraine waited to feel the great beast that was an army lumber to its feet around her, but it lay dormant. With every visit, she felt Pruett's restlessness. It was a good sign, she told herself. They weren't moving, and it was probably her fault. Something had gone wrong in their plans. She wasn't surprised, then, when Pruett came in a few days after Touraine's capture with a key.

"Don't you two look cozy."

Touraine woke groggily, her eyelids gummed. Sleeping on one wounded arm in the dirt was a far cry from the palace beds. Moyenne lay beside her, mirrored, and curled into Touraine's stomach as Touraine had curled into hers for warmth. Moyenne stirred, sat up, then put on a grim expression that gave nothing away except distaste.

"You always did have a thing for authority figures," Pruett said derisively.

"We love the old jokes, don't we?" Touraine said.

"Oh, please. Don't pretend you weren't rubbing it off to Cantic for years. When you left me for the princess, that's what surprised me the most—I thought for sure it would be for our dear general."

"And you have a thing for cannibal witches." The retort didn't have the impact Touraine wanted, croaky as it was.

Sky above, she was thirsty. And hungry. The morning serving of porridge wasn't enough to fill her belly on a good day, let alone since she'd tried to heal her shoulder on the last meat she'd eaten with her Balladairans. It hadn't been much of a sacrifice; the wound still wept beneath the stitches, and she hadn't been able to do anything for her forearm at all. She wondered if she'd be able to use a sword again.

"Maybe we're not so different after all." Pruett went thoughtful as she knelt beside Touraine and unlocked the manacles and untied the rope around her ankles. The relief was immediate. "Both of us getting hard for power. Different kinds of power, is all. The power you get from authority or the power you have when you don't give a sky-falling shit what people think of you."

Touraine rubbed the feeling back into her wrist. "Do you? Not give a shit?"

Pruett eyed her sharply as she helped Touraine to her feet. "Come with me."

Touraine blinked under the brilliant sunlight. It was the bright cold of false spring, and she shivered as the wind cut through her coat. Her limbs were sluggish, her fingers and toes stiff. The camp stirred, soldiers striking tents, eating one last meal before the road, stowing cook pots and supplies in wagons, polishing weapons. The beast was alive, and Touraine shuddered to feel the comfort it gave her.

"How's your arm healing?" Pruett asked as she led Touraine through the camp. Her belts and the twin pistols at her chest clinked as she walked, the hem of her red-and-black coat swaying at her calves. Touraine was not the only one who'd upgraded her wardrobe and weapons. There was no sign of the bird who had perched on Pruett's bracer that first day.

"It's fine." Touraine pulled away from Pruett's reaching hand.

"I'm not going to hurt you." Pruett chuckled sadly. "I'm sorry we started off so poorly. That's not how I ever envisioned our reunion."

"Me neither." Touraine gave her a cautious, sidelong glance. "I'm sorry about what I said."

They meandered along the borders of different squares that marked different divisions of the army, marked by different flags that still flapped and snapped in the wind. It seemed to be an aimless tour of the grounds until Pruett spoke.

"It's the biggest coalition of independent states in recent history. So many sky-falling flags to pull together." She waved her hand vaguely at a standard Touraine didn't recognize. She sounded awestruck. She sounded proud.

"And it's all too big," Touraine said.

"Aye. Too fucking big. So many sky-falling things to go wrong. They're all in your hands."

"I know the feeling."

"I know." Pruett accepted the salute of a Masridāni in their red-patched black coat, then glanced at Touraine. "I'm glad you're here, honestly."

"Why's that?"

"You're better at this shit than me." Pruett stopped them at one of the last warm cook fires and got Touraine a bowl of warm porridge. Only her aching arms kept her from wolfing it down.

"You don't have to buy me," Touraine said, mouth full. Even if Touraine hadn't wanted to be bought, another bowl and Touraine would've been cheaper than either of them expected. "I mean it. I should have come when you wrote."

Pruett gave Touraine a long once-over, as calculating as Touraine had been. "What happened?"

Touraine shook her head. More pieces on the échecs board in her head moved. It could be easier than either she or Luca expected, if only Touraine said the right things. If only she could wear her old self like a mask.

You're going to tell her the truth.

"Would you believe me if I said I came looking for you?" she asked Pruett, keeping her voice level.

"Ha!" Pruett barked before deadpanning, "No."

Touraine watched their boots scuff through the grass that had been worn to patches. "Right before I left—I found out that she sent Moyenne to hunt you down, without telling me. I knew I couldn't stay. She'd never lied to me before. It soured everything between us. Then she asked me to leave. To fight you. It was the easiest way out. I said yes."

Touraine wasn't faking the anger that gritted her teeth or the tremor in her voice.

"You married her. You and your duty-and-honor bearshit. You didn't come here to turn coat."

"Aye, I did marry her. Then I watched her order a plaza full of civilians slaughtered."

"You would have known who she was if you ever listened to me." Pruett's stormy eyes were full of reproach.

"I didn't like the person I became with her."

"What do you mean?"

Touraine shook her head. That was enough truth, maybe. She'd picked a bit too much of the still-healing scab that held her and Luca together.

"She made you feel special," Pruett answered her own question. "Then she made you do her dirty work on her little échecs board."

Touraine flinched. Truth was a gun they could both fire.

"The Taargens don't trust you. To be honest, I don't trust you. But I want my friend back." Pruett tugged the sleeve of Touraine's golden coat. "Give us what we need to pull her down. Help me lead. If you prove yourself—"

"I'm not going to hurt her. She was—we were—" Touraine broke off as her heart sped. There were lines she wouldn't cross, even for this.

Pruett grimaced. "Would you swear your loyalty to me? I could at least let you walk around the place."

"You would?"

"Should I not?" Pruett narrowed her eyes.

"I'm an enemy in your camp."

"But you could be a friend." Pruett jerked a thumb toward the Taargen side of the camp. "Course, if you run away, we'd have the wolves on you again."

Touraine thought of those muzzles. Their keen noses. The thick sharp teeth. Her shoulder ached with the memory. She traced her fingers over her bandaged forearm.

"There are other ways I can help," Touraine said. "I can tell you the villages where the army cached its supplies. I also picked up some new skills."

Touraine pulled gingerly at her coat and shirt collars to show Pruett the half-healed flesh of her shoulder.

Pruett gasped. "You can do it now?"

"Not as pretty as it could be. You don't feed your prisoners enough meat."

"That's how the queen survived the attack," Pruett said, almost to herself.

Touraine jerked up sharp to meet Pruett's eyes. "How did you know about that?"

Pruett waved a vague hand and put on an airy voice. "Many legs. Many eyes. Many ears."

Touraine tucked that slip of information away. "We have a deal, then? I heal for you, you let me walk the camp?"

"If you heal for us, I won't let the Taargens kill you. We'll see about the rest. I'm not looking for a knife in the back."

"I won't. Never. You know that."

"Then come with me. We'll get you some meat, and then you'll show us what you can do."

Pruett entered the room after Touraine and pulled the tent flap closed around the toggles. Even though the afternoon sun was bright outside, they needed lanterns to illuminate each other's expressions. The room smelled like pine and animal musk, fresh and familiar. It eased the coiled tightness in her chest.

"Qā'id. Prince Consort." Prince Roric sat with his forearms on the table, hands folded together, imitating the high priest.

For once, both Roric and Albric had taken off their cloaks, folding them over the backs of their chairs. She still didn't fully understand the significance, though she knew wearing a full cloak meant you could... change... into the animal that had made your cloak. It was a part of them, somehow. She hadn't gotten the courage yet to ask them if they could teach her the same kind of magic. She and feisty little Tempête were getting to know each other slowly. She felt the kestrel snoozing somewhere dark nearby. She wondered how long it had taken Sevroush and Niwai to learn each other.

"Prince Roric," Touraine said, bowing her head slightly, one prince to another. "High Priest Albric. It's a pleasure to see you again."

Hearing Touraine speak with court manners and the edge of a court accent was as strange as if Tempête had started speaking from her beak. Another reminder of how different Touraine was now. *Good.* Pruett needed that. She couldn't afford to trust Touraine like she once had. No matter what she could offer. No matter how badly Pruett wanted things to be like they once were.

"We heard congratulations were in order." Albric's voice tilted with irony, as twisted as the smile he gave within the thicket of his long gray beard. The freshly shaven sides of his head were stippled from the razor.

Touraine smiled back. "A marching army is an odd wedding gift from an ally."

Pruett stepped in. "And this is Kiras." She swept her hand to where Kiras picked at her teeth with a twig, making a show of slouched insouciance.

Touraine raked the woman up and down with her gaze. "I've heard."

"You didn't tell me your old lover was an Eater, too, Qā'id," Kiras said in Shālan, her smile wry. She didn't take her golden eyes off Touraine. "Was she as good as me?"

Touraine's mouth fell open—then she laughed and turned to Pruett, waiting for an answer. The casual exchange caught Pruett off guard. She covered her unease with a wiggle of her eyebrows.

"Ha!" Touraine saluted Kiras. "Touché."

"Welcome, sister." Kiras saluted with her twig.

Roric cleared his throat.

Pruett brought the conversation back into Balladairan.

"Touraine has offered us a deal. Show them, Touraine."

"I need meat," Touraine said.

Pruett followed her gaze to the Taargen sausage on the table. "Is that enough?"

"It'll do."

Pruett raised an eyebrow, and Albric slid the plate across the table. The sausage wobbled obscenely, but everyone tracked the knife as Touraine reached for it. *Don't be stupid, Tour. Please don't be stupid.*

For once in her life, Touraine did the smart thing, cutting the sausage into manageable bites instead of lunging at someone. She sat the knife down deliberately, looking Albric in the eye. Pruett sucked her teeth. Touraine never could resist picking a fight with the biggest fucker in a room. She ate the whole thing, even gestured to the cup in front of Albric to wash it down. She wrinkled her nose at the thick, dark beer. Pruett could have told her she wouldn't like it.

Then Touraine stripped out of her coat and shirt, down to her bandeau, so they could see the wound in her shoulder and the one on her forearm. Deep puncture marks in the shape of wolves' maws, half-scabbed, still oozing.

Roric smirked. "Henrir does good working."

Pruett hissed him quiet.

Touraine plucked the stitches out of the still-raw wounds, wincing as she worked. Then, she pressed her hand to the bite in her forearm, lining her fingertips up almost directly with the individual marks of each tooth. She closed her eyes and mouthed something silently to herself.

Pruett glanced at Kiras, only to see the Eater entranced, leaning across the table to better see. Despite her jealousy, Pruett couldn't help herself, either. It was amazing. The skin was sealing, going from raised and red and weeping to smooth brown skin, leaving a series of waxy scars.

Touraine opened her eyes with a gasp and she stumbled, barely catching herself on the edge of the table. Her eyes were glazed and searching until they met Pruett's. That seemed to steady her.

"Are you all right?" Pruett stepped close, hand outstretched. Whatever Touraine had done, it had cost her.

"Can you do that again?" Albric asked thoughtfully. "To how bad a wound?"

It took Touraine time to answer either of them. "Not yet. I need food and sleep. And meat. It takes from you—the healer and the healed. Even more when you're both." Her legs threatened to buckle, and Pruett caught her about the waist. She felt Touraine shaking against her, and—sky above, her skin was burning hot.

"You can ask her more questions later." Pruett dragged Touraine to the guards outside the tent and gave them instructions to lock her back with the marquise. Better safe than sorry for now.

Back in the command tent, she put her hands on her hips. "Well? Worth having with us?"

She expected more enthusiasm than Roric's scowl and Albric's pensive beard-stroking.

"We can't trust her," Roric said. "She'll never give us more than—"

Albric cleared his throat and spoke over Roric. "Do you have any surety other than your past relationship?"

"She's too smart to get herself killed by running away. And she's got her own disagreements with the queen. Your little palace source told us that much, so I know she's not lying." They still refused to tell Pruett who was feeding them information, but so far, it had all been good. "In the meantime, she mentioned caches. We can test those easily. If it's an ambush, we'll know she lied."

"It's not worth it," Roric said. "If you can't trust her, she's useless—"

"We're going to war," Pruett snapped. "A healer is worth fifty soldiers. A hundred! If it takes letting her walk around the camp to have her on our side, I'll pay that price willingly."

"I agree with the qā'id," Kiras broke in. Her accent rolled smooth and assertive through the Balladairan syllables, making them hers. "My people don't heal well. She can teach us. Then there will be more."

"See?" Pruett said. "No, she's not ideal. Sleep with wolves, you get fleas, sleep with vipers, blah, blah, I know. She stays. I'll keep her under my eye, and if she isn't who I think she is, I'll deal with her myself. That good enough for you?"

Roric glared at her, but he looked to Albric for guidance. When Albric nodded, so did the boy.

"Kiras?" Pruett asked.

"I follow you, Qā'id," Kiras said in Shālan.

CHAPTER 40

FROM THE TREE

Living with her mam for the first time in almost all her life felt like Fili's most false performance yet. She was a puppet on a stage with nothing inside her, no thoughts, no motivations but the hand moving her from bedroom to dining room to sitting room and over again. The town house up the hill was a beautiful stage bought with Queen Luca's money, the stage dressing—the fine upholstered couches, the dining sets, the shelves half-full already with books, even a small bench and table and tools so Fili could practice her carpentry, all bought with Queen Luca's money—!

Her mam was her main audience, but not her only, oh no. It was bad enough feeling her mam's morose eyes on her, making her feel like she should be livelier, smile, pretend to be grateful that her mother had gotten her out of Le Fontinard. People didn't just get out of Le Fontinard.

No, there was also a handful of servants. Fili had never had servants before, not with Maître Gaspard and not with her pa in Durfort. Whenever they came to tidy after her or brought her a meal, she felt a sick wash of shame, like she was pretending at airs to be better than them when she hadn't asked for it at all.

Besides her mam and the servants, though, there were the guards. Not the gendarmerie but proper soldiers from the palace with white piping along their short cloaks. A little bushel of them at the door, inside or out, staring at her hawk-eyed, waiting for her to put a foot wrong.

She sighed into her breakfast. Two weeks gone like this. She prodded the boiled egg with a silver spoon.

"Eat," her mam ordered. "You know as well as I do there's not food to waste in this city."

"I'd bet I know better than you," Fili muttered. She picked the egg up with her hand and bit into it as she would have with Maître Gaspard. The egg tasted like ashes wrapped in boot leather.

"You don't want to know what I've eaten when I needed to." Her mother picked up her own egg between her fingers and finished it in two bites. She wiped her hands in her lap, and the servant waiting on their meal flinched visibly before offering her mam a cloth. Her mam waved him away apologetically.

"Maybe I do. Something to distract me in my new cell."

Her mam looked stricken, cheeks sagging as she frowned. Fili's own face went hot with fresh shame, but she was so angry and so tired of pretending. And anylight, it wasn't as if she knew what to say to her mam, so how could she apologize?

"Do you want—" Her mam hesitated. "Do you want to go out? With me. Get a bit of fresh air?"

Fili eyed her mam warily.

"You're right. I don't mean to keep you cooped up in here." Her mam closed her eyes and bent her head. She sighed. "I wish your pa was here."

Fili didn't want to talk about her father. She didn't know what he would think of all of this.

"Does he know? Did you tell him?"

"And tell him what, exactly?" Her mam's eyes were hooded.

Fili looked away. "I'll go. Where?"

"To the market, I suppose. Not that there's much there. But we can pick up tomorrow's rations."

They took a fiacre down to Le Four, sitting in awkward silence, her mam, herself, and one of the guards. Another guard rode with the driver. The streets were near empty, and people went about their business in their scarves—some of them. A surprising number of them didn't, and she stuck her face close to the glassless carriage window. They went bare-faced through the city with sprigs of stoneweed pinned to their coats and dresses like little sprays of snow. She couldn't tell if they were talismans against the Withering or badges of pride, the way some of them stuck their chests out.

"What?" Fili's mam looked out of her own small window, and a frown line deepened between her eyebrows.

Fili craned her neck around the guard sitting beside her to see what her mam saw, but her mam blocked her with an arm. Then her mam knocked on the wall of the fiacre until the driver stopped.

"Stay put." Her mam slithered out of the carriage.

Fili tried to follow, but the guard gave her a warning look and raised an arm, ready to grab her if she went for the open door. Fili glared, but the guard remained impassive, her eyes dark and mouth set.

Her mam swore, then Fili heard a ripping sound.

"Take us home," her mam commanded the driver as she climbed back into the cab.

"What?" Fili asked. "Why are we turning back? You said—Le Four—" Excitement buzzed through her. There was a current like a river, and Fili thought if she could get outside, walk through Le Four, she would understand it.

"Be quiet, Fili." Her mam's tone caught Fili by surprise.

Her mam took one gloved knuckle between her teeth and frowned out the window, her gaze distant. Her face was etched deep with—with fear.

"What's that?" Fili pointed to the piece of paper balled up in her mother's fist. Fili went to her own window, but there were no broadsides she could see. "Maman? Let me see."

"You heard the queen." Her mam's voice quaked with anger. "I am your mam, Fili. I would die for you, and gladly. As I would have for her. For our country. I will give my life for a cause I believe in. Do you know what it is to ask that? Queen Luca knows. You're with me now because she knows the debt you owe to those who sacrifice for you. Are you ready to ask that of other people? Or are you a child throwing a temper tantrum because you can't have your way?"

"I— What do you mean?" Fili reached for the paper, confused, but her mam held it out of reach.

"What do these people give you? For your 'blessings'? Money?"

"Only them as can afford it. Everyone else—" What was it that they gave? It wasn't *nothing*, but it wasn't tangible, either. "They give what they can."

"And if you take the little money they have? Their last hopes?"

Fili's confusion shifted quick to frustration. "Whatever they put their sky-falling faith in me to do, I can't do it here where *you're* keeping me."

Her mam huffed and crumpled the broadside tighter.

After a long silence, when they were closer to home, her mam asked in a whisper, "Is it real? What you do?"

Fili met her gaze. "You know it is, Maman. You saw what I did for her."

Her mam shut her eyes tight and covered them with her empty hand. When she emerged again, she was pleading. "Then why won't you work with her?"

It was easy to fling her anger back up, anger at Queen Luca, anger for the years she'd spent away from her mam. But now she had her mam, and it wasn't anything like she wanted it to be. Even that short time they spent together while Fili made her mam's new leg, the happiest memories she had of them together, they felt impossible to get back.

It went beyond that now, though. Fili had spent time with the Fingers. She knew the tenement families crammed into drafty rooms smaller than the armoire she had now; she knew the dock laborers who drank themselves into a stupor because then they didn't have to worry about finding a place to sleep for the night; she'd pressed her hands to the foreheads of people who'd lost one child to the Withering and were afraid to die and leave the rest orphaned.

"It's so much more than Queen Luca now," Fili whispered, more to herself than her mam. "More than you and your leg or me and my... my magic. Maybe she's as good as you say. But who comes after her? Who came before her? We shouldn't have to live like this, Mam. I don't mean the Withering, I know she can't control that. There's got to be a better way, and maybe I don't know what it is, but it's not this." Fili hooked her thumb over her shoulder, toward La Gouttière. "We might be fine with her as a patron, aye, but my friends who don't have that? They work themselves to the bone, and for what? A landlord to throw their families on the street the minute they're short on the rent? We can't all put ourselves in service as queen's guards."

It all came out in a rush, the most she'd said to her mam since leaving Le Fontinard. She expected her mam to defend the queen again, or call her a child. Instead, her mother watched her steady, and when Fili was done, she only turned her gaze back out the window.

The dismissal hurt more than the years apart.

At home—not home, Fili corrected, there wasn't anything for her there, not like there was at La Flottille—her mam threw the crumpled broadside into the fire. Fili went straight to her room and curled into herself on her bed. A true bed with thick blankets and feather stuffing and pillows silky against her skin. She thought she would cry, but she didn't. Her mam knocked on the door once, but Fili didn't answer. A softer knock later, one of the servants with dinner, and Fili ignored that, too.

She didn't mean to fall asleep, but when she woke, her mind was clear. She ignored the growling of her stomach and went to the window. It faced away from the streets, overlooking thick hedge that separated all the homes from another road. The night was as clear as her mind, the stars bright splinters of light in the distance. She could see the pillars of the palace from here.

Fili wished that her room was on the ground floor, but the window below hers would make a good foothold. If not…it wasn't so far to fall, she told herself. The guards kept watch at the front door. As long as she was quiet, she could be free.

She looked around her room for anything she could take with her. There was only her whittling knife, which had been returned to her on her release. She tucked it in the pocket of her trousers.

The wind bit when she opened the window and climbed onto the ledge. *It's like climbing a tree.* She'd done it all her life in Durfort, which her mother wouldn't know. She waited for the regret to prick her as she clambered down. Something that would make her stay. It didn't come. Her mam had made her choice. Fili could make her own.

Despite her fears, she touched down lightly on the ground below. She sighed out some of the tension.

"Goodbye, Maman," she said softly, resting her palm against the wall. At a clink and creak of metal and leather behind her, Fili spun around. Her mam stood in her trousers and shirtsleeves, looking wearier then ever in the starlight.

"I bargained my life for your freedom," her mam said, coming closer. Her quiet voice carried amid the hush and rustle of the hedges. The first buds tipped the branches. "Don't make me regret it, Fili."

Fili swallowed at the lump in her throat, but it wouldn't go. Her mam would die if she left. Another thing to lay at the queen's feet. But it wasn't Fili's fault. She hadn't made that bargain.

"You gave your life to her a long time ago," Fili said, voice trembling. "What difference will it make, if you'd died in her service or die now? I'll give my life to the people." Her choice. Not her mam's, not Brother Michel's, not Maître Gaspard or Velte, either.

She searched her mam's face for the anger that had been there before, but all the fight was gone from her.

"Will you tell her I've gone?" Fili backed away, ready to run.

Her mam said nothing, and Fili took another backward step. Still, her mam said nothing.

Fili ran, into the night and toward her own future.

Fili shivered in the cold outside of La Flottille, staring at that white painted X. It was the middle of the night, and other taverns were still doing a raucous trade—nothing like before the Withering struck the city, but it was still *life*—occasionally spilling out drunk patrons and ushering in others. The noise inside the tavern pulled to her. Warmth and familiarity. Was it so different from the stage she walked on in her mam's house? If not, she could at least say she preferred it.

When you worked with wood, it could be generous with mistakes—especially if you started out with a big enough piece. Long as you cut little by little, you could go back if it wasn't enough, or turn it to other uses. Cut too much, though, and the wood was ruined for its purpose. Cut further still and it might not be good for anything but kindling a fire. Fili felt like she was about to make a risky cut, the kind Maître Gaspard warned her against. The kind you couldn't come back from.

"You said it yourself, Fili," she muttered. "You're giving your life to them."

The door opened onto cheerful chatter, a roomful of people in good spirits despite the meager offerings on their plates. Someone sang a bawdy d'Orséan song about a farm boy and a soldier girl over a flute, and the patrons kept time with their palms on the tables or their boots on the floor.

Do you have time for a farmer's boy,
oh, do you have time for me?
I haven't got time for a farmer's boy,
unless he has time for three!

The song reminded her of Olivier, and the sweetness of the music made her ache. The ache pushed her forward another step. For Olivier and Gaspard, she would do this. For her pa. For her mam, even if she didn't want it.

Her heart jumped into her throat when she thought she saw Ghadin, but an incredulous voice called her attention.

"Fili?"

"Velte!"

Fili raced through the maze of tables, ignoring the stares and gaping open mouths, and flung herself into Velte's arms. The woman clasped her back tightly, both arms strong around her.

"You're alive," Fili said into the scholar's hair. She hadn't really believed her mother would let Velte and Joscelin go free.

"Course I am, thanks to you." Velte pushed Fili to arm's length. "Sky above, that was a stupid thing to do. How'd you get out?"

Fili glanced over her shoulder at the room. All the people were wearing a sprig of woolwort or stoneweed pinned to their clothing. They were all looking at her.

"What's that?" Fili stumbled over to a broadside pinned to the board on the wall.

Velte followed, hands on her hips. "Seems you have an admirer. We didn't have aught to do with it."

Someone had drawn a likeness of Fili on the gallows, like they'd made one of Queen Luca in the days after Brother Michel's hanging. They'd given Fili a crown of weeds, and instead of a bloody sword, one hand held the frayed end of a noose. The other was empty and outstretched, reaching for the viewer.

"These are all over the city?" Fear raised the pitch of her voice. This was what her mam had seen.

"Sure they are. This room's never been so full, or didn't you notice?" Velte jerked her head toward the patrons. "Went up after you got taken by the queen's wolf."

"Has she seen them?"

"Don't know if she saw them before she left, but she's off in the west now, with the queen's army. Taargens. Anylight, sounds like we should talk somewhere quiet."

Fili had heard about the war, but her mother didn't speak of it with her. She followed Velte behind the bar, where Joscelin gave her a tight hug. He'd gotten back more of his strength since she was gone, though it was still odd to see him so much smaller. Gray grew in his hair where it hadn't been. Jos took over from the cook and chivvied her out of the kitchen so they could have a moment's privacy.

"How did you get out?" Velte asked again.

Fili hesitated. All this time and she'd never quite told them the truth about her mam and the queen, and where she came from, how she had access to the queen's palace in the first place. But that old fear was a child's fear.

She told them everything, from her mam's absences from their home in Durfort, then losing her leg at the queen's whim. Fili told them how she escaped the queen's garden and how she'd gotten close enough to kill her the first time. Then she told them how her mam had promised the queen her life if she'd free Fili. How Fili had given the queen the god's blessing.

Velte frowned, her nose all wrinkled up. "So you've just been play-acting the poor apprentice—"

Jos put a hand on Velte's shoulder and squeezed. Velte looked up at him, then back to Fili and shut her mouth.

"We're glad to have you, Fili," he said. "Doesn't matter how you got here."

"Aye," Velte said, begrudging. "There's soldiers out there, and more than a few I'm pretty sure are half-noble themselves. It's you most of 'em came here for anylight. But why didn't you let her die?"

Fili looked at her hands clasped together. She had asked herself if she should have been braver. Brother Michel would have told her to die, and take her mother with her. But she was scared. Even now, she was scared to die. Scared to watch her mother die. The guards' swords had seemed so permanent. So painful.

Jos squeezed Velte's shoulder again, and Velte sighed. "You got energy to show your face? Touch a few hands?"

Fili felt exhausted just thinking of it. "I can. We should think of what's next, though. When I... helped her, she promised not to hurt the Fingers. No more hangings. We can use that against her."

"Promised?" Velte raised an eyebrow.

"Aye. It's the perfect time if there ever was one."

They both looked taken aback by her fervor, but Fili had nothing else to lose.

Joscelin patted the air. "We'll talk about it tomorrow. For now, let's show everyone you're back. Enough for now?"

"All right." Then, as they were headed back into the common room, she said shyly, "Do you have any more of those broadsides? I'd like to keep one."

Velte laughed softly. "No, but they're on every wall from here to the palace, I reckon. We'll pluck you one down easy enough. Who would deny a legend?"

Fili stayed in the common room, greeting people, touching them and letting them touch her hands until dawn's light creaked through every time someone shuffled off to the work that still needed working even with the Withering. Exhausted, she unbent from her chair to see the last supplicant.

Ghadin stood before her with one hand cocked on a hip.

"What are you doing here?" Fili asked.

"Can't you tell?" Ghadin whipped her long braid over her shoulder with practiced ease, revealing the pinned woolwort on her heavy coat. "I joined the revolution."

Fili eyed her up warily. Ghadin had given her away to El-Qazāli once.

"I thought you said revolution isn't a game."

"I am not playing." The girl was younger than Fili, but she was fierce and certain.

"Can I trust you?" Fili asked bluntly.

Ghadin's face fell. "I owed her."

Fili chuckled wearily. She was feeling every wakeful minute of the night.

"I know how you feel," she said. "If you mean it, we'll have you."

"I mean it."

Fili held out a hand and Ghadin took it. There was no turning back.

CHAPTER 41

IN THE WAR CAMP

The Masridāni blackcoats outside the prisoner's tent looked Touraine up and down with a sneer as she approached with Moyenne's breakfast. Moyenne looked up when Touraine ducked in. The sun's pale light lit up the tent from the outside, and as her eyes adjusted, the disgust on Moyenne's face grew clearer. Every morning like this, since Pruett had given Touraine these minor freedoms along with the distasteful chores. Today, Moyenne said something.

"You've betrayed your queen."

"I may have helped her take the throne," Touraine said, "but she is not and never has been my queen." Luca had been both more and less than that, but she had never ruled Touraine. Never commanded her. Was it better, or worse, then, that Touraine had always done her bidding?

She knelt in front of Moyenne and held a spoon of porridge out to her. It was the dregs of the day's breakfast, half of it burnt leavings and the other half already congealing. It was food, though, and judging by how long Pruett had left them without food before, Moyenne would be smart enough to take what she could get.

Or not. Moyenne pressed her lips tight together and turned her face.

Touraine exhaled slowly through her nose. "Eat." Quietly as she could, she added, "You're going to need your strength when you get out of here."

"What?" Moyenne turned back around so quickly that she knocked the spoon out of Touraine's hand. Touraine caught it before it hit the ground.

"Tchut. Eat and listen."

Unlike the other members of the High Court, Touraine could tell that Camille LaVasse had not been born for a life in the marble-tiled halls of the court. She'd been raised for the military and had spent more time in barracks than her brother had, despite his place at the head of the King's Own. Luca had explained a little about them as a house—proud of their military prowess, staunch believers in protecting the border between Balladaire and Taargen; they provided the largest number of soldiers through both the Balladairan permanent army and their own militia. Where Brice LaVasse preened almost as much as Durfort, Camille de Moyenne was simple and understated, even when she'd come to take Brice's place in La Chaise.

She locked eyes with Touraine and, without blinking or saying another word, opened her mouth.

Cantic had also been from Moyenne. How well had they known each other? Had Moyenne the sister idolized the dead general like Touraine had? Would Moyenne have gone on to become another Blood General, if not for the Rain Rebellion, if not for Luca's coup against Nicolas and the loss of Brice de Moyenne?

None of that mattered. It was a different world, and because of that, Touraine and Moyenne were different people. Or at least, they had the chance to be.

"Pruett—the qā'id—said there will be a party before they march. Tonight, tomorrow, I don't know." Touraine shoveled a spoonful of oats into Moyenne's mouth. The spoon clanked on her teeth. "I'll take out the guards, then you're going to beat the shit out of me and take everything you can."

"How?" Moyenne said with her cheek stuffed with food.

"Take a knife, slip out the back of the tent—"

Moyenne gulped the food down. "No, how are you going to make it so that I'm not recognized?" Then, with an undeniable quaver that Touraine couldn't fault: "And the wolves?"

Touraine shoved another spoonful in, wishing it would stop

Moyenne from asking the kinds of questions that would poke holes in the little confidence Touraine had in the desperate plan.

"Move fast. Before anyone realizes you're gone. The Taargens drink that sky-falling awful beer like it's tea. Maybe even the priests will be slower—"

"Ya, hurry up!" One of the soldiers guarding the tent ducked his head inside.

"She's being stubborn." Touraine grimaced as if this were the worst duty she'd ever been given.

"If she's too stubborn to eat, don't feed her."

Moyenne opened her mouth quickly, looking sheepish if not contrite.

"It's toilet next," Touraine said. "Be done in a bit."

Touraine dragged over the chamber pot, and the blackcoat ducked out quick.

"Absolutely not," Moyenne growled. "I'm not doing this with you. I'll wait until tonight. I can hold it."

"You've already been doing this. If I come out with an empty pot, they'll have questions." She smirked, but her tone was grim. "Do you really want to escape to your army wearing a piss-soaked, shit-caked uniform?"

Moyenne let Touraine unlock the binding that kept her ankle irons and wrist irons together and didn't protest as Touraine pulled down her trousers and held her steady over the pot. The other woman's knees trembled with the effort of hovering while she used it.

"This is humiliating," Moyenne said through her teeth.

"Well, it's not the best time I've ever had, either." Touraine kept her head turned purposefully to the side. "When you're out, divide the army. You can trust Valmorin to take the other half. He has his orders. Come for the rear and take bites out of their ass where you can. Valmorin should look as inviting as possible—small enough that the Taargens think he'll be an easy fight."

"It *will* be an easy fight. Haven't you seen their numbers?"

Touraine frowned as she helped Moyenne pull her trousers back up. She *had* seen the Taargens' numbers. That was why she was so desperate to get Moyenne out of here. They needed to thin them out before they reached La Chaise. And there was no doubt that they would reach the capital.

If you can't stop them, delay them. That's all Luca asked.

"*Don't* let it be an easy fight."

The second guard came in this time, and Touraine kicked the back of Moyenne's knees. The woman fell with a grunt, narrowly missing the chamber pot. Touraine locked her wrists and ankles back together while the soldier watched. Then she hoisted up the slop in one arm and the empty porridge bowl in the other hand and led him out. She didn't look back at the marquise.

"Where's the spoon?" one of the guards asked.

"Told you. She was being a shit. Knocked it in." Touraine sloshed the chamber pot. She tried not to breathe.

"Should have made her eat from it," the other said.

"You think I was going to fish it out? Fuck that."

They laughed appreciatively behind her back as she went to dump the pot and wash the bowl.

Winter was an odd time to be on the march, even when you could smell spring on the air. The nights were still cold and silent, the buzz of summer bees and the song of autumn crickets long gone, but it was too early for spring insects. Most right-thinking armies didn't risk it. Too early and you'd as soon freeze your soldiers or starve them if the weather turned back. The Taargens hadn't thought that way, though, and so Balladaire couldn't afford it, either. Which meant the Sands. Now, it meant Pruett.

There was a festive mood in the war camp. Touraine sat beside one of the cook fires with a few of the Sands. She wasn't bound, but she wouldn't get far if she tried to escape in this crowd. Armande, her old artillery sergeant, sat on her left side, making coins disappear in between her fingers. Armande had been one of Aimée's closer friends and, at least some of the time, her lover. Belligerent when she was drunk, she would challenge everyone to a fight until she ended up blubbering in a corner, asking for Aimée. The year in Qazāl after the rebellion had taught Touraine a lot of new things about her old family.

The spot to Touraine's right was conspicuously empty.

It had been half a year or so since she'd been away from the Sands in Qazāl, and Touraine didn't feel as at home with them as she used to. Some of them jerked their heads in greeting at her, but Pruett was their commander now, and Touraine had showed up in a Balladairan uniform again, a prince's golden coat.

Pruett stood near a different fire with Kiras. Touraine watched as Pruett snaked an arm around Kiras's waist, smiling into the Eater's eyes. Something in Touraine softened, even as a sadness came over her. A longing. Nostalgia. Another part of her, the part that had been in the court too long, thought: *a weakness.*

One of the other Sands—Sidonie, from a different company, Touraine didn't know him well—cleared his throat pointedly, and Touraine realized she had been staring.

Touraine laughed into the awkwardness. "So...Kiras, huh?"

Armande guffawed aloud before stifling the sound with her fist. She pointed two fingers at Touraine, holding the coin between them. "From what I hear, you can't talk."

"What?" Touraine held her hands wide. "It's not like they're shy." Lewd whistles from the Sands around the campfire. "Anylight, I was just going to say, it's weird to meet...another one."

Some of the Sands looked queasy.

Armande scratched nervously at her temple with the coin in her hand. "What's it like, fucking the queen of the empire?"

With that transparent shift of the conversation, it was Touraine's turn to be the butt of the whoops and jeers. There was an edge beneath the humor, though, and she felt the pressure of their gazes as they waited for the answer.

She forced a chuckle. "Luca was more than adequate, thank you."

Armande pulled a face. "She put her tongue in your mouth, that's sure."

If Touraine focused on the warmth of the fire, on Armande and her coin, Sidonie and his trousers, she could pretend they were only gossiping about old, inconsequential lovers they'd once taken, lovers whose time had passed because they'd outgrown each other, or been stationed in units too far apart to maintain the dalliance. Not Touraine's wife, the leader of the Sands' enemies.

"She wasn't as bad as you think." *Not always.*

A part of Touraine really wanted to convince them. She wanted to smile a bit moon-eyed over the Luca who giggled and threw snowballs at her back. She wanted her friends to be happy for her.

Another Sand snorted.

"No, really. She never understood me like—like you all, but when I was with her, I didn't feel like I was being torn apart. She never made me feel like I had to choose one part of myself. Not like Cantic or the Jackal. She knows what it's like to want everything and not be afraid to take it."

It was something Touraine came back to, whenever she tried to explain—to herself, if to no one else—why she felt pulled irrevocably toward Luca, the dry tinder that caught her desire. Yes, Luca was beautiful, and if she cared for you, she was generous beyond imagining, but mostly—there was something greedy in Luca that called to the hunger inside Touraine.

"And you like that?" Pruett said, dropping onto the log next to Touraine.

Touraine jumped. She wet her lips, uncomfortable with the honesty this conversation was pulling out of her. "It's true. Aye, she's been cruel. But that same cruelty in her is in me. We're cruel in the same ways, even if it comes out differently."

"You're nothing like her," Pruett said.

Touraine laughed darkly and gestured to the war camp around them. It might have been at rest, but it was only violence contained. A lion in wait. She included the rest of the Sands in her words. "What's all this for, if not to take something?"

"I'm taking something *back*. It's different."

"Beside the Taargens?" Touraine muttered. She turned a pointed glare to everyone around the fire. "After everything they did to us?"

Uncomfortable glances, hastily dropped. But most of them looked to Pruett for their answer, and that told Touraine enough. It would be hard to sow dissent among the ranks unless it started with Pruett first.

Pruett hummed thoughtfully. "No different from what Balladaire did to us. You forgave Luca quickly enough."

"Did I?" Touraine said sharply.

But in her head, she wondered. Maybe she had forgiven Luca. If she couldn't, even a little, how could she forgive herself? What she'd done. What she let happen. What she would do. Touraine might have been blameless when she was taken, but she was old enough now to take responsibility for the shitty decisions she'd made. Sky above, there were enough of those. She'd done her own damage in Qazāl, and she'd tried to atone for it after Balladaire left. She'd have to work until she died for Jaghotai to see her as anything other than a Balladairan dog. Then there was Fili, and Guérin. She couldn't put all of that at Luca's feet. She couldn't even put the lies she was telling now at Luca's feet, for all that they were for her. Touraine was choosing this, as she'd once chosen to face Cantic's firing squad.

Touraine tilted her cup over her mouth, washing down the last of her meal with that foul dark beer, when there was a rustle behind her. The Sands went quiet as they looked up.

Touraine twisted round. "Prince."

"Consort."

Touraine sighed. She'd known this confrontation would come sooner or later. She'd been banking on later, hoping that Albric would keep the young man in line a little while longer. At least until Moyenne had gotten away.

Roric stood over her, legs spread wide as if he were bracing himself against a squall, arms crossed over his chest. He wasn't as broad as he would be when he was fully grown, but Touraine reckoned he was only twenty. In ten years, he might be massive.

"You want to be part of the Taargen war camp, come." His accent was as dense as Taargen bread. "I'll show you how a Taargen warrior moves."

Armande raised her eyebrows. "Lucky me, right before my watch."

Touraine heaved herself up, but before she could follow Roric, Pruett pulled her aside.

"And you mean it?" Her hand was tight around Touraine's arm, digging painfully into the thickness of muscle. "You're done with her?"

"I—"

"Promise me." In Touraine's ear, Pruett's tone was pleading. "If you don't want to fight with us, I won't let them kill you. But for the love of the sky above, tell me you're done with her."

"I promise," Touraine said thickly.

"Say it."

"I'm done with Balladaire, Pru. I'm done with Luca. I promise."

Pruett stepped back, her grip loosening slightly. She looked relieved, and surprised to be relieved, as if she was surprised Touraine had actually said it. "Okay. Okay." She released Touraine with a hesitant smile. "Go show that hairy brat what you can do."

CHAPTER 42

A DANCE

Roric waited in a cleared area in the center of camp near the food and beer. Touraine scanned the crowd quickly for the high priest, but Albric wasn't within the immediate glow of the firelight. The camp stools and soldiers had cleared out to the edges to watch a line of Taargens dancing in a series of low squats and jumps over a line of spaced swords. Touraine watched in admiration for a moment before studying the pattern. Just when she thought she'd figured it out, a different set of soldiers twisted the blades on the ground, changing the spacing and crossing the blades.

The dancers changed their steps to match effortlessly. At least, it looked effortless. The careful placement of boot to narrowly avoid stepping on the blades. The depth of the squat and the power in the spring. As the music grew faster, so did the steps, until their feet were a blur.

"We call it the Dance of the Wolf," Roric said. "A great warrior is strong, agile, and can endure. What about you, Consort?" His smile stretched, his teeth gleaming amid his beard.

Touraine suspected she didn't have a choice. She'd be lying if she said she didn't want to test herself. Her body itched for it. There was a roughness, despite the skill, something more visceral than what she did with Durfort in the training salle. It reminded her of home.

How ironic to find it in the camp of her old enemies.

New enemies.

Touraine bared her teeth. "Show me how, bear cub."

He led her to the path of swords. The other dancers hopped away from them, and the second set of soldiers straightened the swords into clean lines again. He threw his bear cloak to one of them, and they held it reverently.

The musicians started a fresh round with their drums and their pipes, and Roric beckoned her close. "Like this and like this," he said, demonstrating each of the main steps when the music called for them.

She imitated him. "Good enough?"

He huffed begrudgingly.

She turned to the sword path, but he clapped a hand on her shoulder and pulled her back around. "One thing, though, Consort—" He gestured with his other hand, and someone came with two large wooden mugs. He handed one to her. "To your steps."

"To your steps," Touraine echoed.

Together, they bottomed up the cups while the whole of the crowd goaded them. The heavy, dark beer churned in Touraine's stomach. She would try to keep her head steady. Not just for Roric's challenge; there were other things she needed to do tonight. Things that required clarity.

When they both tilted their empty mugs over the grass, the music kicked up in earnest.

"The first to fall or falter loses," Roric said, taking his place opposite her. "Keep up."

Touraine made no boasts. She didn't need to win to get what she wanted tonight. She needed to get to know Roric. To understand his strengths, his weaknesses, what his people thought of him. Who he was away from Albric's watchful eye.

As the sparks snapped and the logs crackled and soldiers from all the countries watched and cheered and drank, Touraine and the Taargen prince danced across a path of blades.

Time disappeared. She matched him, her thighs burning as she dipped low again. She waited anxiously for the soldiers to change their blades. From the corner of her eye, she could see them, hands hovering over the hilts.

Concentrate.

Touraine met Roric's grin with one of her own. The rhythm of it was in her now. When the blades shifted, she adjusted with only a few stumbles—and she never knocked the blade edge.

There were hoots in Shālan—she didn't know if they came from the Sands or the Masridāni.

Without warning, Roric kicked one leg out. Touraine saw the flash of movement and leapt back instinctively, ready to dodge a blow. She tripped over one of the swords and fell to her ass in the cold grass while Roric kept dancing, now on one foot but as strong and agile as before. The last measure of the music repeated itself slower and slower, and Roric slowed with it until it stopped completely, with him standing gracefully on one foot, with the other leg bent up beside him as if he were a heron.

It told Touraine much that she'd needed to know and more than she'd expected.

Roric held out a hand to her, gracious and condescending at once. Touraine took it with a smile anylight and clapped him on the back as hard as she physically could.

"An impressive game, bear cub," Touraine said. "In Qazāl, we do it a bit differently."

"Oh? I haven't had the privilege." He glanced at some of the Shālan faces curiously. "Show me."

Touraine took her turn to show Roric some of the moves she'd learned from the Jackal and her fighters. She pulled one of the Sands who'd also learned, and together they dance-fought their way through the fires. Roric didn't try any of the flips or twirls; he only smiled tightly, with his arms across his chest.

That, too, taught her something.

By the time the night was truly underway, Touraine was more than half-drunk. The prisoner's tent—and Pruett's beside it—would be a dark journey through a network of tents that Touraine could barely navigate sober.

"I have to piss," she told the soldiers sitting around her. "Then I'm going to sleep this swill off."

She pushed herself to her feet and swayed, blinking her vision steady. A chorus begged her to stay as she staggered away from the warmth of the fire, the warmth of newfound camaraderie bought and old bonds restored with drink. Alcohol could make friends out of almost anyone. Their groans of disappointment made her feel fiercely wanted. Like she belonged, however briefly, however falsely. It made her feel good, to be a soldier. To pretend for a moment that these soldiers would have her back no matter what, and that she would have theirs.

She stumbled into the darkness, weaving through the tents, using her drunkenness to her advantage. It was mostly silent as she pretended to meander aimlessly. There were the telltale grunts of soldiers fucking, and a few other drunken people on their own secret missions, but none crossed Touraine's path.

She hummed the Taargen dancing song as she approached Moyenne's tent. Touraine focused her vision first on Pruett's tent: it was dark, no figures moving within it. None of that Shāl-forsaken cat-yowling. Then her gaze slid back to the guards, and her heart seized up in her chest. A Masridāni blackcoat and…Armande. Her old artillery sergeant. Her friend.

Touraine ducked between two smaller tents before they saw her, and tried to calm the panicked beating in her heart. Fear sobered her.

She hadn't planned on killing Sands. There had only ever been Masridāni and Taargens guarding Moyenne, and she'd already resigned herself to the fact that she'd have to kill whoever was on duty. There couldn't be any witnesses, and she couldn't afford to trust that someone would stay silent just because she asked. Why would they, if they saw her freeing the enemy? They'd call for Pruett, and Touraine would be shot for certain—or worse. Armande, especially; she was close to Pruett now, one of her officers. She swallowed as hard as she could, pressing down the lump in her throat.

They chose to be here, she reminded herself. They could have stayed in Qazāl.

What if it was Noé? a cruel voice asked. She owed Armande a chance, didn't she? But her chance to live was Touraine's chance to fail, and if she failed here, *now*, there would be no saving herself. No saving La Chaise. No saving Luca.

Her fists bunched at her sides. Her throat closing off her air. Making her dizzy.

She had chosen the Sands once before, and gotten more of them killed than she'd saved, and too many other Qazāli besides. Freeing Moyenne almost guaranteed more Sands would die.

You can't count them all. They're soldiers.

It was just one person. *One person.*

Fuck. Touraine closed her eyes against pricking tears. It was that, more than anything, that told her she'd already made the decision. Now all there was to do was follow through. Forgiveness wasn't— couldn't be—a thought. Someday, though, she would be judged for it.

First, she had to live long enough for that to matter.

She lurched toward the tent, pasting on a lopsided smile and acting like a drunk trying to act sober. (She wasn't quite sure where the act ended and the truth began.) She staggered into the Masridāni guard; she'd already marked the short blade at his left hip, closer to a dagger than a sword. Armande was armed with two knives at her belt, and they both held rifles at their sides, butts resting on the ground. Armande was lazy with it, tired at the late hour and irritable because she'd drawn the short straw to leave the celebration early. Their bayonets were still stowed.

"Steady, yeah?" the Masridāni said in Shālan, righting Touraine.

"Lieutenant?" Armande said, bewildered amusement tilting her voice. "Early night, then?"

The Masridāni held Touraine up, her face brushing against his stubbly cheek.

Armande grunted. "You've got to be careful with that Taargen bear piss, Lieutenant."

It was gentle, almost kind.

"Should we toss her back in there, let her sleep it off?" the Masridāni asked.

"Lemme sleep...off..." Touraine slurred. She kept a tight hold on the Masridāni's coat, her hand on his waist above the dagger. If she missed this chance, there wouldn't be another.

"Aye," Armande said. Then: "Get the irons, though."

"Aye—"

Touraine didn't give him a chance to finish. She slid his knife out of his belt and stabbed it up through a slit in his ribs, yanked it out, and thrust it through his throat. It spurted hot and red, coating her fingers, but she gripped the handle and turned to Armande. She was shocked but already reacting. The point of her rifle gouged into Touraine's hip, and she gasped in pain. She ignored it and tackled Armande to the ground, and her aborted shout turned into a breathless whumph. The rifle lay between them, digging into Touraine's chest as she tried to press her elbow against the other woman's throat while the blade in her other hand found flesh.

They snarled and snapped at each other like dogs, and Armande's breathing turned into wheezing. She raked a clawed hand across Touraine's face right before Touraine's blade hit home. Touraine stared into her eyes until the burning furious life went still beneath her, and Armande's grip on the rifle went slack.

"I'm so sorry," Touraine whispered. But Armande couldn't hear her anymore, and no one would believe her. She dug around for the keys to Moyenne's cuffs and staggered into the tent.

"Sky above and earth below, what happened to you?" Moyenne gaped from her knees on the floor.

"No time. I'll be...fuck." Touraine cut off a sob in her throat. She knelt—fell to her knees—behind Moyenne and unlocked her binds. "Here. There's a bit of food for you outside the tent. Take this, too." She handed her the Masridāni's bloody knife. "Whatever time we thought you had, you have even less."

Moyenne was intelligent and dutiful and probably courageous and all that other shit a soldier was supposed to be, so she didn't ask any more questions until she realized what Touraine said.

"You're not coming with me?"

Touraine shook her head, wincing. "I need to stay."

And even if she didn't want to admit it, it wasn't only her and Luca's plan holding her here. She'd felt it at the fire tonight with Pruett and the Sands.

"They'll kill you if they find out."

"So hurry."

Moyenne took the knife from Touraine, looked around the tent for anything else, and started to walk out.

"Wait," Touraine said, pushing herself up achingly to her feet.

"I thought you said—"

"You need to hit me. Really beat the shit out of me."

"Pardon me for saying, Your Highness, but someone already has."

"Just knock me fucking unconscious, Moyenne. I need a reason I couldn't sound the alarm."

"Ah."

"Aye. Good luck." Touraine planted her feet and gave Moyenne a soldier's clasp. "And if you see the queen, tell her—" She licked her split lips, bright with the taste of metal. Moyenne didn't make her finish, just squeezed Touraine's forearm in grim solidarity.

Touraine stuffed a wad of handkerchief between her teeth. She watched Moyenne's windup, the twist of her foot in the dirt, the swivel of her hips, the hook of her arm. Her pale, dirty knuckles.

CHAPTER 43

OLD BOOKS

The Royal Oak was bare of leaves, the detritus below long swept away. The turned patch of earth that marked where Luca had buried Gil's ashes in the golden coffer was just more bare earth beneath the tree, nothing to distinguish it from the rest. Luca knew where it was exactly, though.

She sat on the stone bench and dug her cane between her legs. She stared at the patch of dirt until she felt tears well, which wasn't long at all, and then she pressed her forehead into her hands on her cane.

"You are dreadfully beautiful when you're sad, Your Majesty. Have I ever told you that?"

Luca's heart skipped in terror, then elation. She was halfway into Sabine's arms before her dignity caught up with her.

"You never have." Luca pulled up short. "You're losing your touch."

Sabine's mouth went wide in mock horror, and she stroked her thumb along Luca's jaw. "You've grown cruel, my queen."

Luca bowed her head. "I have."

Sabine sobered. "Sit. Tell me what I've missed. The Taargens can't be all."

"You've heard?"

"Oh, yes. Even the sheep in Béson have heard by now." Sabine urged Luca back to the bench, but Luca shook her head.

"What's this?" she asked, running her hand over one of Sabine's heavy saddlebags. Sabine was still in her travel clothes. "What's so important you haven't cleaned off the road?"

"Surely you are?"

"For you to appear with a week of dust on your neck, smelling of hay and horseshit and only"—Luca sniffed for effect; it felt good to lose herself in banter after so long—"a trace of cologne? No, I am not. Come. I'm cold. Explain."

"I thought I looked dashing," Sabine grumbled, but she obeyed.

As they walked back to Luca's rooms, Sabine caught Luca up on her adventures in Durfort. Her levity proved as much a mask as Luca's. It fell to reveal a sobriety that suited her handsome features well. She gravely described directing Durfort's own hospital efforts, from overseeing the administration to carrying water from fountains for patients. She also told Luca how the Durfortiens had hung certain herbs all over the hospitals, and Luca recalled Guérin mentioning Fili doing the same. How the Fingers wore their allegiance in herbal corsages. She said as much, and Sabine's eyebrows rose. Sheepishly, Sabine opened her coat. Sprouting from an interior pocket was a bundle of yellow-flowered weeds.

"So I shouldn't wear these on my lapels?"

"Absolutely not." Luca almost told Sabine about her own brush with the Withering, but stopped herself. *It will only make her fret.*

Instead of following that trail to the revolution burning beneath Luca's feet, Sabine indicated the saddlebags as Luca let them into her rooms.

"I brought these." Sabine set the bags carefully on the table in Luca's sitting room and opened them.

Books. Old books.

Luca gasped, horrified. "Did you ride with them in your bags like this?" She reached into the bag and picked one up gingerly in her gloved hands. Very old. She glared. "Jouncing up and down on your horse? It's a wonder the bindings are still intact!"

Luca expected Sabine to grin, crooked and charmingly abashed. Instead, the other woman remained somber. "I thought you'd want them as soon as possible. While I was home, I asked my mother about the old ways. She let some things slip."

A catch in her voice and the delicate, almost too careless way Sabine brushed a thumb across the nearest book made Luca pause in her careful unloading of the bag. "Is she well?"

"She's lonely in that castle, all by herself." Sabine had a faraway look. None of her usual disparaging laughter at her mother's expense, no insult. "For my father's sake, at least, I wish…I wish that she had more."

Luca put down the book in her hands with all its secrets and held Sabine close. Sabine was so different from Touraine; she didn't stiffen at the tenderness, but collapsed into it, hunching to bury her face in Luca's neck.

"Forgive me, Your Majesty," Sabine said, extricating herself a moment later. "I intended to bring you a gift, not the maudlin regrets of an undutiful child. I do believe I'm the most loyal and trustworthy Durfort to the Ancier crown."

Luca gave her a flat look.

Sabine gestured toward the small library she'd smuggled. "These are texts from before Ancier the First's purges. I saddled up as soon as I realized what they were."

From her brief glance, Luca could already see that Sabine was right. The book was a recounting of all the significant dates of a year well before the fall of the lords Fontine. The beginning of harvest season, the beginning of calving season, a date marked only by the cryptic "Gifts given to ——" where the final word had not been written at all but simply marked by a dash, as if redacting a word. A name.

"What are you going to do with this?"

"Find a way to save my empire, I hope."

"No, I mean…there was a reason, wasn't there?" Sabine asked dubiously, even as she brushed her coat where the weeds were hidden. "That we got rid of it. Look at the Qazāli magic. Even with the good—"

"Touraine saved your life," Luca said coldly. "Without her magic, you wouldn't be here to hold a sword at all. *Neither* of us would be here."

"You're right. Forgive me. You're right." Sabine folded herself into the corner seat. "I'm an ass."

Luca sat down at the table so she could study without the burn of her hip demanding all her attention. Engrossed as she was, it didn't stop Sabine's next words from tuning her pain to an astounding pitch.

"And where is our soldier?" Sabine's old smile was back, teasing and handsome. "I would be lying if I said I wasn't hurt that she hasn't come to greet me personally."

"Gone." Luca tried to focus on the words of the book in front of her, on the events she didn't understand. Holy days, perhaps, that had no current analogue. There was something there, if Luca could think of it, and not Touraine. But Luca had not expected Sabine, and so she had not decided whether or not to tell her the truth.

"Ah. You sent her to live up to her training?" Luca could hear Sabine's smile fade. "I'm surprised you could stand to let her go—"

"She was taken captive." From the corner of her eye, she saw Sabine's expression shift. Rather than leave their lover to dwell in the same pain or fury or helplessness that Jaghotai and Aranen must feel, she continued. "I...sent her. To get close to their leaders." Luca beckoned her over and explained the broad strokes of her and Touraine's plans while Sabine's mouth dropped lower and lower in horror.

"Are you—are you two insane?" Sabine exclaimed. When Luca hissed her quiet, she ducked her head close to Luca's ear. "What if they catch her?"

Luca met Sabine's outrage with a steadiness she did not feel. "They'll probably kill her."

She had returned the ransom letter with what she considered was an admirable amount of restraint, without making her seem too disinterested. They hadn't sent back Touraine's head in a box, at least. She had dwelled too long in her room thinking about the severed fingers of Balladairan citizens she'd been sent in Qazāl. The stench of them. The grizzled gray of the flaps of flesh, the jutting knuckle bones, the flaking blood. She had wondered too often in the emptiness of her bed how many pieces they might send of Touraine, and how slowly.

"Luca—" Sabine's empathy was more than Luca could bear.

"Please, Sabine. Please don't."

She pulled the books closer to her. These she could control.

In the Durfortien seneschals' logs, she was able to find the sacrifice days—those "gifts" given to an unnamed mark. It fit. In other, more personal books that looked like an old Durfortien lord's journal, she noticed the trend of dashes redacting a name, and it fit the pattern for it to refer to the god. Perhaps there was a taboo against writing the god's name, or a superstition. Other notes in another seneschal's log, years later, recounted the journey to a coronation, saying, *My lords swore to the queen by blood to —— own oak*. It could only mean the Royal Oak. It *fit*.

By the candlelight, eyes throbbing but unable to stop in the rush of a mystery being almost solved, Luca opened another book and another, even though her vision began to blur and yawns cracked her jaw. A book of tales, next, or perhaps a history in which the author or illuminator had taken copious liberties, including but not limited to a rather embarrassing, inaccurate, and improbable depiction of what was probably meant to be a cat carrying a penis.

One illustration, however, stopped her breath in her chest with its beauty. A golden-haired youth sprawled at the base of a great tree, the leaves of which were painted in green ink and flecked with flaking gold gilt.

Before she could delve into the story, however, a messenger arrived with Lady Aliez des Champs d'Or's urgent request to convene the High Court's war council. Luca's "basket of cobras" stood when she entered the war room, including Touraine's mother. Only half the candles had been lit; the dark room was darker than usual. So were the shadows beneath everyone's eyes. She scanned the great wall map as she passed it, skimming for the place Touraine and the Taargens had last been reported. A small ritual. A superstition. *Uncivilized*.

She took her seat and her war council followed suit.

"Lady Aliez? What's happened?"

The young woman was pale beneath her tanned skin. Before she could speak, Sabine entered on a wave of earthy cologne, freshly dressed in sleek brown trousers and a simple—for her—night-blue coat. A damp curl fell around her forehead.

"Forgive me," Sabine murmured, taking her place unobtrusively.

"Lady Aliez?"

"Yes, Your Majesty. I— Forgive me, I know we weren't to meet, but I thought you would want—"

Evrard cleared his throat, and Aliez blushed deeply. Luca glared at the comte, but gestured for Aliez to continue. Quickly.

"Someone— The grain in Verlieu has been stolen."

"The grain stores are gone?" Luca repeated. "All of them?"

"Yes, Your Majesty." To her credit, the young woman didn't quail under Luca's glare. "Raided. My soldiers checked all the granaries on the estates and even the nearby villages. If the comt—if Ghislaine hid them, or had them dispersed, we haven't found them."

Luca's stomach opened like a pit. All that food. Champs d'Or was Balladaire's grain basket, and if that basket was empty...

"Sky above and earth below," she swore aloud, forgetting herself. Aliez chewed her lips.

Evrard tapped a single finger against his mouth. "She could have sold it to brigands to spite you, Your Majesty. One last blow, in retaliation for her humiliation, perhaps."

"Perhaps."

"The family Bel-Jadot have many secrets," he added with a pointed eyebrow. "You know as well as I. I could send some of my soldiers to investigate."

Luca gave him a sharp look. "Are your people not occupied enough in Travers? Because if so, we have need of fighters in the south."

"Indeed they are, Your Majesty." Evrard lowered his head, contrite. "I only meant to offer what few I could spare."

She couldn't see what he was angling for yet, but she mistrusted all of it, and the threads holding her together right now were already pulled to their breaking points.

"Is there anything else?" Luca growled. "Since we're all here?"

She listened to the rest of their updates with half a mind, the other half circling about this new problem. Deaths were easing in the hospital tent, but they hadn't stopped, the Jackal reported; like Luca, she suspected it had more to do with activity from the Fingers and not with anything Luca had done. By contrast, Evrard assured her, nobles in the palace and on the hill continued to sicken, including Lady Théophane, and it would be a strong gesture if she paid a visit to some of the ailing courtiers. There was also an army coming up from the south on the western side of the river, flying Taargen and Qazāli flags; it looked as if it were also heading toward La Chaise, but it was too early to tell.

They were barely finished when she was ushering them out, so that she could make another trip to Le Fontinard. The Durfort library would have to wait.

Luca arrived at Ghislaine's cell along with a servant from the palace who bore a tray of food and a bottle of wine. The jailer knocked once and unlocked the cell. Ghislaine wore a simple white shift that clung and draped in such a way that she seemed an apparition. The two grief rings on her fingers fit more loosely than they had before. Her eyes flickered alert, but she didn't rise from the cot where she sat.

"Ghislaine Bel-Jadot," Luca said as the cell door swung open. "How do your accommodations suit?"

Her cell was much like Nicolas's; cold stone dankness permeated the room. Though the rigid cot was a far cry from a quilted bed stuffed with feathers, and the simple sack dress had nothing on her elegantly layered gowns, Ghislaine carried herself like the comtesse.

"You're looking remarkably well, Your Majesty. A miraculous recovery."

Luca remained silent. *The nobles in the palace continue to sicken.*

"What do you want, Luca? Surely you have greater priorities than taunting a poor old woman you've already brought low?"

"I brought you a gift, my lady." Luca set the tray down on the foot of the cot, Ghislaine's gaze following her all the way.

"Alas, I am no longer a lady."

"I'll be frank, then. The grain is missing from the Champs d'Or stores in Verlieu. Evrard has accused you of selling it to brigands. How do you respond to that accusation?"

"It doesn't deserve a response."

"Then where could it be?"

"How would I know? I've seen nothing but this musty stone since you sent me here." She gestured with one delicate hand around her, then turned to the plate of food and wine Luca had brought her. "How long has it been?"

"That time could be over," Luca said to Ghislaine's back as the woman poured her own wine from the carafe. "If you tell me what I want to know."

Ghislaine stiffened. "Which is? How someone stole *my* grain off *my* land while I was imprisoned?"

"No. I want to know the secrets of your family, Ghislaine."

Because it was this that she had come back to. Evrard's pointed look in the war room. Luca was certain it had everything to do with the d'Orséan claim that they'd been the first to eradicate the god, its priests, its texts, all. The skull and coin they had found on Champs d'Or land months ago.

"Tell me what your family knows, or if you've secreted it away like the other houses. *Balladaire needs it.*"

Ghislaine leaned away from Luca's vehemence, but scanned her once more, lingering on Luca's exposed flesh.

Luca exhaled slowly. "I am well. I want the same for Balladaire. All of Balladaire."

Ghislaine picked up the goblet of wine. She swilled it around, studying its contents before savoring a long drink. She closed her eyes and sat on her cot, making a delicate smacking sound with her tongue. "A Durfort. You are generous, my queen."

"Have you no care for your people at all?" Luca asked quietly.

"I have nothing but care," Ghislaine returned, just as somber. "That is why I will not let you do this. You have ruined Balladaire. You would turn this empire as uncivilized as your whore's homeland, and you deserve to fall. King Roland would turn his face from you. If you are at an impasse, perhaps it is meant to be. The god's will," she added with a perverse smile, taking another drink.

Ghislaine smiled into her wine when she saw her words hit their mark. She tilted the goblet carefully, drinking the last of it. A spill of wine colored her lips like the paint she used to wear in the palace, until she licked it away, quick and darting. She took one of the pâté-covered crackers.

"These are my favorite." She crunched it with relish.

"I hoped you might appreciate it," Luca said through her teeth.

"Oh, I do. More than you know." Ghislaine dabbed the crumbs from her mouth with a single finger, then dropped them onto the tray.

Luca kept her hands still on her cane, hiding her impatience. "I take it that means you won't tell me what I need to know in exchange for your freedom?"

"The secrets of Champs d'Or. Ah, but every noble house has its secrets, even if Champs d'Or more than most. They're better off that way, I think."

The former comtesse settled against the wall, pulled her legs onto the bed, and clutched them to her chest. It was a girlish thing to do and so unexpected that Luca's heartbeat quickened. She relaxed the sudden pressure she'd placed on her cane and waited.

When Ghislaine spoke again, though, it was only a whisper. "I will not fall with you." Then she closed her eyes and said nothing else.

For a long breath, Luca considered yet again bringing Deniaud into the room with her. Breaking the soft, pale shell of Ghislaine's cheek. There was a pallor there, but it was not the plague pallor. She did not yet have Nicolas's cough. But that loss of control in her uncle's cell had won Luca little and cost her much, much more.

Luca left, slamming the cell door behind her.

She was wasting what precious time Touraine had sacrificed herself to gain.

CHAPTER 44

STRANGERS

How has she been with the soldiers?" Pruett murmured, leaning her head back into Kiras's touch. They were in their tent, and she sat on the ground between her lover's legs while Kiras massaged Pruett's temples, trying to ease away the headache that plagued her even with Niwai's guidance. With the way things were going, it probably wasn't the animals causing the pain.

It was hard to get two armies to behave as one when half—at least, the Sands—didn't trust the other half. Then there was the Withering. They hadn't expected it to hit their camp, but it did. Didn't help morale, waking up to soldiers shriveled up in their blankets when they'd been healthy the night before. It was horrifying. Touraine said there was no healing it.

Then, of course, there was fucking Touraine.

"What do you mean?" Kiras asked without pausing her ministrations.

"I don't know, does she—" Pruett exhaled sharply and let her head fall completely. She stared at the tent ceiling. "Does she seem suspicious? Does she ask too many questions?"

After Moyenne's escape, the Taargens had demanded Pruett lock Touraine up until they could prove that Touraine had nothing to do with it. As if Touraine getting the shit beat out of her wasn't proof enough. And Armande. Touraine might have done a lot of fucked-up shit in her life, but she wouldn't kill one of her own Sands. Not on purpose.

Then they sent a contingent to the village Touraine said held a cache of foodstuffs for the Balladairan army. Henrir had prowled around the village, sniffing for a trap, but there was no army in wait, only a few guards on the barn where it was all stashed. There was even Balladairan wine—d'Orséan, not Durfortien, but still.

Pruett wanted so badly to believe. That desire was precisely what made her suspicious.

Kiras ran her fingers gently back through Pruett's curls. "Not that I can tell. It's...amazing."

Her hands stilled, and Pruett looked up to see Kiras lost in thought. Pruett could write poetry about that face. Like a hawk herself, with those golden eyes, her fierce brows, and the proud hook of her nose. And she looked awestruck thinking about Touraine.

"What do you mean 'amazing'?"

Kiras ignored Pruett's petulance. "I wish I could do anything close to that." She held her hands open beside Pruett's ears, in some sort of supplication. After a heartbeat or two, she asked, "Do you think she would teach me? Could you ask her?"

"Shall I ask her if she'd like to have a drink with you as well? And a fuck after?"

Pruett felt Kiras stiffen behind her, the tension where her thighs and forearms met Pruett's shoulders. Despite Pruett's warning back in Samra', Kiras kept digging her way deeper into Pruett's chest. Anything that held Kiras at a distance was a good thing.

"Pruett—"

Pruett twisted away from Kiras's warmth. "I'm trying to figure out if we should trust her, and you're ready to become her Shāl-cursed acolyte?"

"That's not what I said, Qā'id," Kiras said softly, but she didn't meet Pruett's eyes, which made Pruett feel like a smear of shit on the bottom of a shoe. "We'll need all the healers we can get, you said."

Pruett crossed her arms over her chest. "I'm sorry," she said to some spot off to Kiras's left. Kiras's hands were still upturned, open.

"When I was young," Kiras started, her voice soft and distant the way it got when she spoke about her past, "with the priests, we had to prove we could be trusted, too."

Pruett cocked an eyebrow.

As she spoke, Kiras caressed her stomach, and Pruett saw vivid in her mind the scars beneath Kiras's clothes.

"Touraine is *not* going to let us cut her open."

"No. But trust went both ways. Let's see what she's willing to do to one of her own. We can take one of the Balladairan prisoners, and..." She tilted her head from side to side.

Kiras spoke so calmly of what was done to her, and what she'd done to others in their school of young Eaters. Pruett frowned, open-mouthed. All she could think to say was "But you hated that."

"I did. But it bound us all together, even when other Shālans would have called us blasphemers."

For a second, Pruett considered it, which was long enough to make her feel more ashamed than she already did. She cut her hand sharply. "No. I'm not going to do that to her."

"Then *trust* her."

Pruett wanted to. Sky above and earth below, she wanted to. *But*— she crushed the doubt. "You're right. You're right. I will. She deserves that much. Besides, she never could lie for shit. Couldn't even fake an orgasm."

Kiras chuckled, her shoulders relaxing. She held a hand out for Pruett to come back. Her arms were inviting, and Pruett felt too good in them.

"I'm going to get some air. Check on Tempête." She pretended not to see Kiras's face fall as she left.

The air was cool, a relief after Kiras's seeking attention. It was all so fucked. She didn't know if she should sneak Touraine out under cover of dark so the Taargens wouldn't kill her, or if she should do the job herself. Instead of make the choice, she ran from it, into the back of her mind to brush the tips of the clouds with her wings.

Peace, up here in the sky, where she could see everything for what it was: tiny and unimportant. You couldn't place anything against the infinite stretch of the night sky and say it mattered at all.

The respite of the brisk, mighty wind was short lived. No matter how she pretended, there were still things on the ground that mattered to her, and through Tempête's sharp little eyes, Pruett could see it all.

Hunting, wings outspread, gliding. Below—men like mice, too big to steal from their burrows, too big.

Pruett followed the falcon's attention. Fighting in the east, at the tail end of camp.

The wind rippled beneath her as she turned for another pass over the fighting. Furtive shadows sprinted into tents and just as quickly slipped away.

"Attack!" she shouted, slamming back into her own body, lurching sideways into the tent, almost dragging it down.

Kiras was already outside and reached to steady her.

"Alarm!" Pruett called again. "Attack from the east!"

A drummer boy beat the signal a moment later, bleary eyed, coat unbuttoned, his nimble hands a blur.

Pruett strode to Touraine's tent, stomach leaden. She half expected Touraine to have magicked her way out of the tent, leaving her fetters on the ground to mock them all, like the marquise had.

The guards outside Touraine's tent were still alive, though, and Touraine was still inside, hands cuffed to her ankles. She was awake and alert.

"Tell me you didn't know about this." Pruett grabbed Touraine by the collar. "Did you plan it? Are you working with them?"

Touraine glowered at her with her puffy eye. The bruise was only just fading from blue black to yellow green. Scratches on her face, scabbed. The other eye wore a shadowy bag of exhaustion. *Trust her.*

"Did. You. Do. This."

"No," Touraine growled through her teeth. "What did you expect? You're in enemy territory."

She threw Touraine down with a sound of disgust. She hated what the two of them had become. Fucking cats in a sack. They used to be better than this. Then Qazāl happened and Cantic happened and Luca and—

Pruett heard Roric bellowing. She left Touraine in the tent.

"Where is she?" Roric stormed down the path between the tents, barreling down on Pruett as she stood, arms crossed, outside of the prisoner's tent. His unsheathed sword had blood on it. If Pruett couldn't calm him down, she knew exactly where it would go, and however complicated her feelings were about Touraine right now, she didn't want the woman spitted like a sky-falling sausage. Albric followed close behind.

"High Priest, if you'd be so kind as to call off your prince." Pruett held her ground. "I've already spoken to the prisoner, and we have reason enough to believe her."

"Yes, you have a reasoning," Roric said, his accent even stronger with his anger. "The *reasoning* is that she is your friend. Do not be so weak!"

It wasn't his insulting words or his condescending tone that made heat rise to Pruett's face. Petty training-yard barbs never killed anyone. It was how close he struck to the truth that rankled. How he plucked out the fear she gnawed raw every night, the reason that even she couldn't allow Touraine to have free rein over the camp anymore, the reason Touraine was just another prisoner.

"I said *we*. Everything she's told us has held true, or did you drink so much of that wine that you forgot? She has no way to send messages in secret because she's always watched. Always. If she were delivering orders from here, I would know."

"Who's to say you don't already know?" Roric stepped closer, his teeth bared. He smelled meaty, but not drunk.

She stepped to him until their chests were touching, and though she had to look up at him, she didn't flinch.

"I already told you. I'm going to kill the queen. I'm going to sack her city. I'm going to make Balladaire give back everything it's ever taken from me and more. If that's what you want, you have me. I won't grovel and beg for your help. You came to *me*. You try to put me on my knees and you'll go right after the Balladairans."

Albric put his hand on Roric's shoulder and pulled him gently back. The high priest's amber eyes studied her. What was he looking for? Some sign that Pruett was lying through her fucking teeth? She matched his stare right back.

"Set extra guards around the camp," she said. "Extra shifts, too, so they stay fresh. Can your priests keep their animal forms? Those are as good a deterrent as any."

Albric shook his head. "They can't hold them that long, nor so often. I won't risk them losing themselves. Then they're as much a danger to us as to the Balladairans."

Pruett sucked her teeth. "Regular soldiers, then."

"We'll also send one of our own to help guard the prisoner," he said, in his deep voice. "Just to be sure."

"Be my fucking guest."

Another attack came the next night, from the north. It wedged through a crack between the Shālan troops and the Taargens. Even though Pruett had set birds to keep watch, by the time their fierce cries sounded, the Balladairans had already killed a handful of soldiers and melted back into the night.

A few uneventful but sleepless nights passed. Just as the soldiers began to feel like the danger had passed too, the Balladairans attacked again, this time from the south, near the front of the train—Pruett's command.

She was ready for them. Not all the Balladairans escaped into darkness. One of her Masridāni brought a trussed-up blackcoat to the command tent. The man's pale face was smeared with blood streaming from a crushed nose and a cut on his forehead.

"Ah! You caught one!" Roric said.

"Aye, now come with me," Pruett muttered. She met Kiras's eyes and saw a flicker of understanding. "We're going to take two birds with one shot."

Roric and Kiras took the captive under each arm, dragged him into Touraine's tent, and threw him on the ground next to her. The captive squealed as he landed on his broken nose.

"Kiras, unlock Touraine." Pruett plucked the key loop off her belt and tossed it to Kiras. Kiras caught it deftly but hesitated, one eyebrow raised in question. Her golden eyes gleamed in the lamplight, like Touraine's. It almost made them seem like sisters. *Are you sure?*

She didn't have a choice, did she?

"Kiras," Pruett said firmly. Then to Touraine: "You're going to get us answers."

The irons clanked as they fell to the ground. Touraine shook her wrists out, grimacing. Pruett offered her a knife, handle first. Touraine looked from the naked blade and back up to Pruett. Then down to the blackcoat in the dirt beside her. Understanding flattened her mouth into a grim line. She didn't take the knife.

With a painful effort visible on her face, Touraine crawled over to him and pushed herself up to one knee. The blackcoat had worked his way onto his side, and his eyes widened as he watched her approach. Pruett wondered if he recognized her. If he was one of hers, like Pruett had once been one of hers.

"Who's your commander?" Touraine asked.

Before he could answer, Pruett bent over and dragged him upright by the hair. He spat at their feet.

"Tell them what they want." Touraine licked her scabbed lip. "I don't want to hurt you."

"Bearfucking traitor." He geared up to spit again, but before he could, Touraine backhanded him across the face.

Touraine sighed and glared at Pruett. "I already told you, it's either Moyenne or my colonel, Valmorin. Unless Valmorin fell when you captured me." She turned back to the Balladairan. "What's your current deployment?"

"Fucking sand fleas," he gritted.

This time, Pruett felt the anger in the blow that cracked against the man's face. Touraine held her hand out for the knife and pressed the point of it beneath the man's chin.

"Say it again," she growled.

The man's eyes were even wider than before, and his bloody lips trembled, parted. He was going to tell them. Touraine had done it.

"Fuck you." The last brave act of a dead man.

With a roar, Touraine spun the knife and buried it deep in the meat of the man's thigh. He screamed, Touraine screamed, Pruett screamed.

"What the fuck, Tour!"

And then the knife was back under the man's throat, painting him with more of his own blood, dripping it down his neck while his bloody thigh seeped into his lap. And Touraine with her hard jaw, her quick hands, the other one snarled into his hair to hold his throat bare.

"Where—are—they?"

Maybe he had believed they were bluffing before. Maybe he'd reconsidered his position now that he'd had an actual blade in his body.

"We divided the army," the soldier blubbered. "I don't know where the others are, but I'm with Marquise-General LaVasse. They divided us into three, the others are somewhere in the north, I don't know, we haven't been in cont—"

"Three?" Touraine pressed the blade harder into his throat. Tears rolled fat and wet down his face, cutting into the old, dry blood and swirling with the fresh, bright stuff.

"Taurvide. Colonel Taurvide is going to be near Cinq-Tombeaux, but I don't know why—" His pitch rose in a squeal as the tip of the knife broke skin. "I—I don't—I'm only an infantryman, sky above, please, have mercy. Please, have mercy."

Touraine nodded slowly and the man started to relax, his cries turning into whimpers. She shoved the blade up into his jaw and silenced him.

Pruett's mouth dropped open. Kiras's mouth was twisted in surprised disgust.

"We could have used him." Albric was calm, but there was a note of irritation in his voice.

"He had more to tell us." Roric's face was red as he stepped farther into the room, his sword out and ready.

Touraine eyed the point of Roric's sword. It was hard to tell her expressions on her swollen face, but Pruett had known her through a lifetime of bruises and wounds. When Touraine looked down at the dead Balladairan, she looked sad and bone-fucking weary. Only for a second, though. Then she was expressionless again.

"He was half a second away from telling me about the first person he ever kissed, and he definitely pissed his trousers." Touraine wrinkled her nose. "They're harrying you. Keeping you awake, keeping the soldiers on edge. Whittling you down." She threw the knife onto the ground. It landed in the sticky puddle of blood, splashing smaller droplets in the half-dead grass.

Pruett made herself look away from Touraine. "What's this about Cinq-Tombeaux?"

"I don't know," Touraine muttered. "Something's wrong. Taurvide shouldn't be anywhere near here. I decommissioned him."

"Then you are not so useful after all, if your information is so late."
Roric crossed his arms over his chest. "I'll take a company of my own
and meet them. This Taurvide will not expect it."

"Don't. This doesn't make sense," Touraine said. "Cinq-Tombeaux
is two days out of our way to the west. It leaves the way to La Chaise
too open."

"You do not order me, Consort."

"They'll have scouts, same as we do," Pruett cut in. "They'll see you
coming. Besides, we shouldn't spend that many soldiers—"

Roric jutted his jaw forward. "It's better than having two separate
enemies at our back. I will crush them and come back."

A snuffling sound came from Pruett's left. She glanced over and—
Touraine was snickering to herself.

Touraine brushed away Pruett's disapproval. "He said they split
the army up. They know your numbers. Why would they do that if it
wasn't a trap?"

Roric's face reddened. "You'd know, wouldn't you?"

"Aye, I would, so I'm telling you. Don't be a child, princeling. We
should avoid them. Keep the hills between us."

"Touraine," Pruett warned, "don't be a dick."

"If he's going to get a chunk of his army killed, he deserves to know
about it."

"So we take more soldiers. Victory will be defined!"

"Definitive," Pruett corrected out of habit. "If you're so certain this
will fail, what should we do? Because Roric's right. We don't want
them catching our flank."

"I believe the prince-general is volunteering to go with the prince."
Albric had been hanging back, but now he stepped close enough to
look down on Touraine, the toes of his boots in the dead man's blood.
"Make sure it does not fail."

"What? *No.*" Touraine glared at Albric, then at Pruett. "I'm not going
to fight a fucking suicide battle just to stroke a spoiled princeling's ego."

"I didn't think you minded stroking spoiled princelings," Pruett
said acidly.

Touraine's lips curled back from her teeth. "What are you going to
do, kill me? Strap me to a horse?"

Albric leaned forward. "I think you'll find we can be quite persuasive."

Touraine went stiff and finally shut her fucking mouth.

"If it looks like she'll run back to the enemy," Albric said, "shoot her. Qā'id?"

Pruett turned to Touraine, who was staring at her, mouth agape, eyes pinched in betrayal. "That's acceptable, High Priest. Take her as your captain, Prince Roric. She may be an ass, but she knows the Balladairans." Pruett stared at Touraine pointedly. "She'll help you look for where the trap might spring."

"And"—Albric held up a thick finger—"if Prince Roric does not return alive, then we will take the qā'id as sacrifice."

The outrage from Touraine and Kiras was immediate, Kiras launching herself between Pruett and the Taargens, while Touraine swore, already reaching for the knife she'd dropped to the ground. They were both going to get themselves killed. Idiots.

Pruett understood Albric's intent. Test her and Touraine at once, get rid of a thorn in his paw if Touraine proved false. She knew Albric wasn't bluffing, either. If Touraine ran, or tried to kill Roric in the chaos of battle, Pruett would die. Her skin was hot with the certainty, her palms damp.

"I agree," she said. Only Albric heard her. His smile was slow, teeth appearing in his hairy face. She shouted, "I said, I agree!" When Touraine and Kiras went quiet, she looked at everyone in turn. "I accept these terms."

Pruett, Touraine, and Kiras left the Taargens in the tent to make their way back to their side of the camp. Kiras was a silent bundle of fury—she kept her eyes straight ahead, didn't even look at Pruett as she walked away. They would work that out in their own tent. Touraine on the other hand—

"You shouldn't have done that," Touraine hissed in the falling darkness, once they were out of earshot.

"No? Can I not trust you with my life?" Pruett scoffed. "This is the only fucking way you're still alive. I've pushed them this far—but if you go with him—if you *fight* with him, then maybe you can finally, *finally* just be here where you belong."

"Where I belong, huh?" Touraine held her hands out in front of her, her pale palms painted red and darker red in the cracks. "Can I at least wash my hands before you chain me up again?"

"I'll bring you a basin. And stop goading Roric."

"Or what?"

"You want to know what happened to the last marquis de Moyenne?"

The hard lines of Touraine's face softened in the darkness. "She told me."

"The other one? Aye. They made her watch. Then we cut his throat."

Touraine turned her golden-eyed gaze back to Pruett. Pruett's lip curled at the judgment she saw there.

"Power doesn't let go of power, Tour. Balladaire won't surrender until we've broken everything by force. Including her."

After a moment, Touraine bowed her head. Heartbreak. Exhaustion. Tonight had shown Pruett how much Touraine had changed since the last time they'd seen each other. Even more since the last time they'd battled together. She didn't know the ruthless woman who had stabbed the man in the jaw, and yet, there was something familiar in the eagerness to please. In the strength to do a thing when it needed doing. Then there was this—this sorrow, this weight upon her. That was new.

"Fine."

"Good." Pruett looked Touraine over one more time, to see if she'd handed her life over to a stranger. She couldn't tell. "I'm counting on you."

CHAPTER 45

A COAT OF MANY COLORS

Roric's fastest scouts confirmed the dead Balladairan's intelligence before the sun broke past dawn, and his soldiers were marching a hair after, Touraine with them. They approached the spot the scouts had indicated without as much caution as Touraine would've liked. Not that you could disguise a company and a half of fighting men marching in column. The scouts assured Roric there couldn't be more than a hundred Balladairans coming from the northwest. A hundred plus five cannons.

They didn't know where Moyenne's contingent was, or Valmorin's— Touraine assumed he was commanding the third leg of the Balladairan army. It was troubling, but not as much as Taurvide's reappearance. Did Luca change their plans? Or had Taurvide wormed his way back in with some sky-falling intrigue, and this was his way of flexing his "experience"? To top it all off, a blanket of pale gray clouds clung to the sky.

"I mean it, Roric. If they left a company out here, dangling like bait in front of our noses..." Touraine trailed off.

Shāl take Pruett's eyes for this. Shāl damn the fucking Taargens. Shāl damn idiot princelings. She frowned, remembering Pruett's snarky comment. Luca and Roric did have some unfortunate commonalities. Arrogance and entitlement, for a start. A way of looking down their noses that had become a fond irritation in Luca and made Touraine want to kick Roric in the stones. If Pruett hadn't agreed to be a hostage, this would have been the perfect opportunity for that and more.

"Wolves do not cower," the prince rumbled.

Touraine rolled her eyes. "They also don't have thumbs. So what?"

"What?" He blinked in confusion.

"It means I don't give a shit." The ground ahead of them—well ahead; the infantry in front would reach it first—seemed sturdy, no dug-out pits patched over with dirt, no hidden spikes to trip horses—not that Touraine and Roric had much cavalry, just that half company, and the only beast priests in the bunch were Roric and his wolf friend Henrir. Her shoulders prickled with unease, but the Balladairans were too far away for her to spot them.

A scout's whistle warned them first, some native Taargen bird call that made Touraine's whole body cringe. It carried, though, and that's what mattered.

There they were, less than a third of the army Touraine had marched toward Moyenne, marching toward her now. Only infantry and some of the cannons, parked ahead of the infantry and to the side. Touraine looked up again at the sky. Rain would be shit for the muskets, but it would make it harder to set the cannons off, too.

She tried to cough away the dry scratch in her throat. Her palms were slick in her gloves. She tried to catalog the panic away. The discomfort of the saddle beneath her. The damp in the air. The smell of gunpowder, though no one had fired yet. She closed her eyes tight and tried to breathe.

In Taargen, Roric called the command to move from column to line, and the soldiers seamlessly spread themselves out two deep instead of Touraine's familiar three, advancing all the while. He also said something to his captains—his real captains—but he spoke too fast for Touraine's rudimentary skill to understand. She grimaced at the spittle that hit her face. Then she felt another drop. On the other side, the pitch of the Balladairan voices turned frantic.

Another fat drop hit her in the eye.

"Fuck," she muttered. "Roric, it's now or never. If we want a volley before the rain—"

"First rank, fire!" he shouted.

Balladaire's cannons cracked like thunder, a bright flash of light and smoke, as if obeying Roric's command.

Touraine supposed the Taargens fired, too, smoke billowed in front of them, but she was too focused on the canister shot poking holes through her soldiers—*Roric's* soldiers—like lethal gravel. Her breath came short and black spots threatened her vision. She focused on the leather of her gloves. The creak of the reins in her grip. The horse's heaving lungs between her legs.

"Second rank, fire!" Roric called.

Above the musket fire, thunder rumbled.

Touraine coughed again. "Will you...turn?"

"No," Roric said grimly. "If I embrace the god, I will not be able to command my men. Henrir will suffice."

Touraine noticed with a start that a great wolf had loped up beside them while she was trying not to lose herself in the battle fear. *Sky above and earth below.* What was she doing here?

There's still time. Fight through the Balladairan line and surrender. Go back to the palace. Tell Luca you tried.

And then—what? The two of them, circling, blades pointed at each other's throats, only barely able to meet the other's eye?

No. She wasn't going back.

Besides, there was Pruett. That was a line she could not cross.

As the Taargens fired and reloaded again, the first and second ranks still alternating as best as they could, return fire opened up holes in the line.

The shhhh of rain falling on the grass snuck over them like a blanket. Musket shots fizzled out or misfired; soldiers dropped slick barrels or musket balls; powder turned to gray mud in their hands.

"Fix bayonets!"

Here we go. Rain dripped from Touraine's tricorne in a curtain.

"Charge the dirt-eating bastards! Charge!"

Henrir's howl ripped chills up Touraine's spine. It was a sky-falling wonder that the Balladairan infantry screamed and charged back. On both sides, soldiers yelled, "For the queen"; "For the prince" from the Taargens; and a lot more wordless defiance of their own sky-falling fear than the drinking songs would ever honestly admit.

Roric sidled his mount close to hers so their legs bumped. "Do not try to flee."

"I'm with you," Touraine gritted.

"What are you doing?" Roric asked incredulously as she slid down the side of her horse.

Given how well she'd ridden in her last battle, going on foot seemed like better odds. She drew her sword. Luca's gift. Pruett had returned it to Touraine before she rode off.

"I was trained as infantry." *Might as well die as one.*

She shook the rain off her tricorne and charged.

Minutes stretched like hours, every second a miniature eternity. Touraine had been fighting for a thousand lifetimes when thunder pealed again, so loud it seemed to shake the ground. A feeling in the base of her spine made her shiver. Blood spattered, she turned, expecting someone behind her. What she saw was even worse.

Horses riding up from the south, some coming from the left and some from the right. They would hit Roric's company from either side and smash them against the Balladairan infantry. There'd be no way to escape. Another Vauteur's Field, that infamous defeat, but played out against the Taargens. And this time, Touraine was with them.

"Fuck, fuck, fuck, fuck."

She looked for Roric. He had to call the retreat. She had to get him out. She'd do better to kill herself here than go back to Albric without even a corpse to show him.

Besides, there was Pruett.

Fuck it. "Retreat!" she shouted in Taargen. One of the Taargen soldiers looked at her with disgust and shouldered his way into the press of the melee, but she jerked another around by the sleeve and pointed at the incoming cavalry.

"Cavalry!" she shouted. "Fall back!"

A few heard her, and gave her panicked looks. Sky above, she understood the fear too well. If they ran, they were just as like to die as not, run down one by one. There was nowhere else to go.

"Roric!" she yelled.

The cavalry hit.

Touraine felt the crash of horseflesh and steel as the mass of her soldiers—*Roric's* soldiers—fell, trampled or cut down or trying help-lessly to flee into their fellows in front of them. All the while, the Bal-ladairan infantry rammed forward, bayonets fierce and shining.

Please, Shāl and every god that's listening. She didn't know what she was praying for at this point, though living might be nice. She prayed that the casualties for Balladaire would be small. She prayed that she wouldn't blow her cover to the Taargens.

Then there was no time for prayer because she was shoving her sword through another person's guts and trying to keep her own guts where they belonged.

For a few everlasting moments, that was all there was, until her arms ached and her back ached and her legs ached. She was soaked with warm blood and cold rain and everything chafed raw and she struggled to keep the grip on her weapon. Miracle enough that she managed to keep her feet—

Then Touraine wasn't on her feet anymore, but face down in the mud. She yowled as someone stomped on her hand, trying to keep their own balance. They fell anylight, in a heap next to her. She pushed herself to her elbows and saw the slit throat, the head half off the body, and the cavalry soldier with their blade still aloft as their horse reared.

She ducked down, hiding her face and hoping the soldier didn't notice. When that particular danger passed, she crawled on her belly, arm over arm, slithering in the mud, away from the fighting.

She gulped in air. She wiped her face with her forearm, clearing the wet from her eyes only to have the rain stream down her face again. Her tricorne was gone. A shame. It had reminded her of Cantic. Some tiny part of her knew she wasn't supposed to like that, but Cantic had taught her *this*. Touraine had gotten good at war so that Cantic would *see* her. Love her. And here she was, alive. For now.

From her belly, Touraine surveyed the field. The Balladairan cavalry had collapsed the Taargen lines inward, hacking at them from the rear, forcing the Taargens into the jaws of the Balladairan infantry.

She found Roric in his white bear cloak, in a broken-off pocket of fighting with a trio of blackcoats.

Touraine sprinted for him, heedless now of the rain streaming down her face. She ducked around one attempt to bash her in the head with a rifle barrel and kicked the blackcoat in the side of the knee. Just enough to make him slide in the slick grass—she hoped. Then she was running again, eyes on Roric. He'd taken one Balladairan down, but he'd been wounded. He staved off the other two Balladairans from one knee.

One of them got a lucky jab into Roric's shoulder, and Roric bellowed as he pushed himself farther onto the bayonet to cut deep into the man's arm.

Touraine hesitated. For the hundredth time that day she thought: *Let him die.*

So what if there was Pruett?

Right before the second blackcoat speared Roric through the neck, right before it was too late, Touraine dropped low, sliding on the grass and slicing the back of his knees. As he fell, she checked the one whose arm Roric had cut. He was sobbing on the ground, but alive. For now.

She hesitated, then bent down low and whispered a prayer to Shāl as she put a hand on the writhing man's forehead. He closed his eyes and quieted, and Touraine made the veins and arteries seal themselves. Then she clambered over him to Roric.

"Come on, man, call the retreat!" She dragged the sodden fabric of his coat, snarling in pain as a nail tore. There were barely any soldiers left to retreat.

"No!" he shouted. "We can still—"

"Get your head out of your ass!" Touraine jabbed behind them with her sword.

The field was a sky-falling mess, with soldiers slipping and dying in the mud through luck more than skill. The scream of horses, mud flying through the air with every strike of their hooves.

His face went paler. "Fuck," he whispered in Taargen. Then, louder, he ordered the retreat.

It was odd to hear these words that were familiar to her a lifetime ago. To recognize them was almost to feel like she was a different person, remembering someone else's life.

"Can you walk?" She hoisted him up.

He gasped in pain, holding his hand against his hip. His trousers were soaked with blood.

"I'll take that as a no." She threw his good arm over her shoulder, and they hobbled.

"I can still dance on one leg. You saw."

"Shut up and hop, then," she grunted beneath his weight. "And be thankful they missed your balls."

"Your soldiers are very poor to miss so very big a target." He grinned.

"I'm going to leave you here to die."

"But then you would not have your friend. Or a horse." Roric whistled a sharp pattern, and then another.

Touraine's horse came galloping up to them, sodden mane lank, flanks heaving and mud-spattered. It was not Cendre, but Touraine had never seen anything so beautiful. The beast allowed her to throw Roric onto the saddle.

Roric held his good hand out to her, and she met his eyes. His face was smeared with blood. So was the hand.

She had gotten him this far. She could turn back now, fall back into the shit that was this battle. Take her place back as general. Get back home to Luca—

The thought startled her. Home. Luca. As if they could possibly be one and the same. If she left now, Balladaire would probably fall. She didn't let herself think about the part of her that had agreed with Pruett last night, the doubt that coiled like a noose around her heart. *Power doesn't let go of power.*

"I'm not going to stab you, Consort, but I am not going to attend you."

On the field, the Taargens were being slaughtered—or they had surrendered, falling to their knees and locking their hands behind their heads.

A Balladairan figure on horseback seemed to look directly at her. Broad as a bull and golden sleeved. Taurvide.

Could Touraine let go of the power she'd taken? Let go of Luca? Of Shāl's gifts? The Qazāli Council, the Balladairan courts? Not a pawn or a chevalier, not a priest or a prince—but leave the board entirely?

Roric misread her hesitation. His eyes tightened at the corners as he looked back at the field of dying and surrendering Taargens. "I know. My soldiers. My people. I cannot afford to stay. Come."

Touraine took his hand.

*   *   *

When High Priest Albric asked for Touraine's irons to be brought, Prince Roric stopped him. Prince Roric, who raised a toast to Touraine at the fires:

"To the Traitor Prince. A true friend of Taargen."

They got her drunk. They got her stupid, stumbling drunk. She let them. They were angry and grieving, but she had brought back their prince. Touraine and Roric and Henrir, the only survivors to return— so far, the soldiers said. *So far.* The hope of the hopeless. They needed to celebrate. She was angry and grieving, too, and as she leapt the swords with Roric, holding him up on one side while his beloved Henrir held him on the other, the arms of the army opened up to embrace her. She remembered Roric calling her his battle-sister. Remembered healing him, knowing all the while that she should have let him die. She remembered kissing him on his cheek, his beard scratchy against her face. She remembered the toasts they made, shouting the names of the dead to the darkening sky. She remembered her own dead, quietly. (She thought the other Sands remembered, quietly, too.) She remembered returning to her tent with help from Kiras, remembered wondering if this was the moment, if Pruett had given in and sent Kiras as the knife in the dark. It wasn't. The relief and the astonishment in Pruett's eyes. Kiras laid her down and set a guard. Touraine remembered wanting to cry, sprawled in a heap on her tent floor, but nothing came.

The next morning, full of grief turned vengeance, the conquering army razed the small town west of the Taargens' defeat, where the cavalry had hidden, quartered by the people.

Touraine watched beside Pruett. Listened to the cries. Traced the smoke through the now cloudless skies. A hole yawned open inside her, but Touraine said nothing. She did nothing. When the Taargens and the Sands and even a few of the Masridāni had had their fill, they turned their sights back on La Chaise, and Touraine turned with them.

CHAPTER 46

A MATTER OF FAITH (VARIATION)

Luca and Touraine's plans were working all too well. The Taar-gens' strike on Pont-de-bois had engendered few casualties; for that, Luca was grateful. The Taargens' unfocused path toward La Chaise was giving Commander Perrot time to shore up the Chaisien defenses—repairing the walls, upgrading the practically ancient artillery on the battlements, constructing chevaux-de-frise to slow the enemy advance up the plains outside of the city, and even more importantly, rebuilding the strength of the armies with new recruits. However, it had also created a flurry of fear in the surrounding villages. Frantic farmers crowding other cities or, worse, crowding the roads to La Chaise. Luca did not like their chances if the Taargens encountered them there. Some of them would be good for the city, adding to the ranks of the willing fighters. Others would only be more mouths to feed on an already stretched purse.

The rest of the war council also disliked it.

"If you let them take one village, they will take another, and another," Jaghotai growled. "They won't all be deserted."

"And we cannot afford to lose more food." Aliez's eyebrows were knit with worry.

"I understand—" Luca began.

A firm trio of knocks interrupted. Colonel Taurvide was ushered in by a servant. He was in a clean and sharp officer's coat, his right sleeve striped with gold from shoulder to wrist.

Taurvide bowed over the tricorne he clutched in both hands. "Your Majesty, I had news I thought you would not want me to trust—nothing but the gravest—"

"Or you took the first chance you could to come running home?" Luca said, her hard voice belying the sudden lurch of her stomach. *Touraine.* But the worst had already happened—she was already a "captive." Unless she had been—killed?

"There was an engagement with the Taargens. I led us to a decisive victory, but General El-Qazāli—" He hesitated, glancing around the room, but he found the nerve to puff up his chest. "She was fighting with the enemy. The prince consort is a traitor."

Luca froze, her whole body abruptly cold. This was what she had sent Touraine to do, she reminded herself.

Sabine laughed, loud and disbelieving. She looked to Luca, as if expecting her to join in.

"Thank you, Colonel," Luca answered coldly. "A messenger delivered the news of this battle this morning. That is the job of a messenger. The job of a colonel is to lead an army. Do you not have an army to lead, Colonel?"

Taurvide bristled, his face purpling. "The marquise de Moyenne escaped the Taargens. She has taken the charge."

Judging by his sudden discomfiture, Luca expected that there was something more in his dismissal from the field. She couldn't even find pleasure in that thought, though.

"Did Moyenne see her? The prince consort?"

"No, Your Majesty. She was stationed elsewhere. But I saw her with my own eyes. She saved the Taargen prince's life and rode away with him."

Publicly, it would be difficult to frame that as anything but treachery. It was necessary for Touraine's role in the Taargen camp that she remained unquestionably disloyal to Luca, by the Taargens or any spies they had in Luca's own court. But Touraine should have killed Roric. The whole point of the subterfuge was to cut the head from the snake. They had agreed. What they had not agreed on was the utter destruction of Cinq-Tombeaux and the slaughter of its people, which had also been in the report.

And so Luca wavered.

What if Taurvide was right?

"We'll send a messenger." Sabine was still incredulous. "We'll discuss terms."

"We will not." Luca clenched her fist tight as if her grip would hold her pieces together. "This changes nothing." *It might change everything.*

Sabine shared a glance with the Jackal, and Luca wondered when Sabine had had a chance to work her charms on the stony woman. Aliez's eyes were wide, absorbing all even as she looked lost. Evrard, thoughtful but too tactful for once to point out that Touraine was not so strong a marriage alliance after all.

"That's enough for today." Luca flicked her fingers dismissively, and Evrard and Aliez left, followed by a surly Taurvide. Jaghotai also stood, but she hesitated, gripping the back of her chair and looking down at the black velvet cushion, its golden rearing horse.

When Luca, Sabine, and Jaghotai were the only ones in the room, the other two shared another knowing glance and then looked at her, as if waiting for the mask to fall.

"I told you," Luca said, "*nothing* is worth my crown. *Balladaire.*"

Jaghotai grunted. "He's a fool. I spoke to Touraine before she left. She wouldn't even leave you for my sake."

"It doesn't matter what I am to her." Luca stood, steadying herself on the table. "The only thing that matters is the line she's crossed."

The older woman tongued her teeth, dissatisfied, as if she would add something. In the end, though, she just grunted again, and then left.

"You don't think this is real, do you?" Sabine murmured when they were truly alone.

"She has higher loyalties than to me." Luca laughed bitterly. "She's proven it more than once."

Or, maybe, something had gone wrong. Maybe Touraine had learned something, something too valuable to let Roric die. Luca didn't know what it could be, but there could be something, couldn't there?

Was it worth pinning her crown on that hope?

"She wouldn't do this, Luca." Sabine raked her hand through her hair, shaking her head. "This is *not* El-Qazāli. That woman is so loyal she couldn't tell you it's raining when the sky is blue. You would trust Taurvide? Over her?"

That was what it all came down to. Luca dug her thumb into the scar that crossed her palm. *You will become two things and one thing.* Did Luca trust Touraine? Could she afford to, with her empire at stake? Touraine had made no secret that she loved Luca, not her empire. Luca had thought that nothing could hurt worse than sending Touraine away, and she was so, so very wrong. Because she had trusted Touraine, trusted her with everything. *Everything and nothing.* Trusted her enough to let her lead Balladaire's army, trusted her enough to send her straight back to that woman—

"I'll prepare for the worst case."

"Luca, don't—"

"She crossed a line, Sabine," Luca repeated. "I don't know where she stands anymore."

Trust is a choice, Touraine had said.

So is betrayal.

Luca's thoughts still spun in bitter circles when, a few days later, after she had retreated to her rooms for the evening, Commander Perrot arrived, knocking urgently.

"Your Majesty," he said, saluting briskly. "It's the comtesse des Champs—pardon, Ghislaine Bel-Jadot."

"What does she want now?" Exasperated, Luca pulled her robe around herself with one hand.

"She's—dead."

"The Withering? Why wasn't I told? She would have showed—"

"Not the Withering, Your Majesty. Not that we could see." Perrot glanced sideways and added, "My guards say it was...sudden."

Luca narrowed her eyes. "Sudden."

"Perhaps poison."

"Take me."

Le Fontinard was quiet. Calm. Night had settled deep, casting the perfect shadows. Within, however, the gendarmes were ill at ease.

Word of the death had spread. When they saw Luca, they saluted skittishly.

Ghislaine's body lay neatly on her cot. Her hands were folded over her stomach demurely, two grief rings glittering. In death, Luca could see the fine wrinkles on the woman's dry skin. Everything about her, from the thick, dark hair and her olive skin to her lips—no longer painted—was duller. How quickly death made its home. She wore the same shift she'd worn when Luca last saw her. On the floor beside her bed was a tray of food. A few pâté-covered crackers. Another carafe of wine, half-empty.

"We found her like this, Your Majesty," said the guard who'd opened the cell.

"Who brought her these?" Luca gestured sharply at the food and wine.

Perrot glared at his man, who swallowed.

"I—I assumed you did, Your Majesty. The servant brought it, and it was the same as last time. I didn't think to ask."

"You didn't think—" Luca cut herself off mid-snarl.

It wasn't fair to hold him responsible—his logic was reasonable—but now—! The "family secrets" Ghislaine had denied her were gone. Maybe they would have helped, maybe they wouldn't have, but now, Luca would never know. Answers within reach, snatched away once more.

A pressure built in Luca's chest and it rose like fire, burning through her lungs and throat until it came out of her mouth in a wordless scream. Her body uncoiled like a whip, and she lashed the tray onto the floor with her crutch. The carafe of wine shattered, dark Durfort red seeping across the stone like blood. The crackers crumbled, and globs of mushroom splattered into the wine.

Luca spun, ready to stomp her boot into the glass and wine and crackers, full of a fire that could only die by burning itself out, but as she whirled, she saw Perrot and the jailer, and another who had come at the noise. The roaring in her ears had drowned out the sound of the jailer's boots. All three of them stood in the door, staring.

The sight doused the flames quicker than any water, and shame rose up in their stead.

"Prepare the body for burning."

The guards hesitated.

"It's not the plague. She was given poison. When you're done,

Commander Perrot, you will determine personally how she was able to get poison in her cell."

Luca turned back to Ghislaine's poised body, now beyond Luca's rage. The woman had expected this death. Welcomed it. Perhaps Ghislaine still had many friends in the court, but Luca believed only one person had the audacity.

Luca took the steps to her uncle's cell faster than her bad leg could tolerate, but her fury burned brighter than the pain and lent strength to her recovering body.

She looked through the small viewing grate and found the duke sleeping, eyes closed and jaw slack. The bruising on his face had faded pale yellow. His nose had not been set well. He looked vulnerable. Any other time, Luca would have turned away in embarrassment.

She pounded on the door. "Wake up, Uncle!"

The jailer opened the cell and Luca burst inside. Nicolas jumped, startled awake, clutching his blankets about him as he pushed back into the wall, away from Luca's advance.

"What a pleasant—"

"What did you give her!"

"What? Give what? To whom? My dear niece—"

"Don't toy with me, Nicolas! What did you do to Ghislaine?"

Nicolas raised his eyebrow at the crutch Luca leaned on so heavily, taking in her trembling body, her shallow breaths. "I did nothing."

"Liar. What does she know that you don't want me to find out?"

Nicolas furrowed his brow in confusion, then laughed. "You think I killed her to keep information from you? About what? The god?"

"And why wouldn't you?" Luca snarled. "That's all you've been doing! Blocking me at every turn!"

"That is between you and me. I wouldn't kill a member of the High Court for that." Nicolas met her raised voice with quiet amusement.

"Even if it's her house that holds the secrets?" Luca gripped her crutch tighter, fighting a sudden faintness. "What does the family Bel-Jadot know?"

"Are you well, niece?" His knowing satisfaction made Luca feel sick.

"Tell me."

"It's nothing so important as you imagine, dear niece. Just two sisters and a river. The sort of thing tragic songs are made of."

"Sisters?"

"Yes. Ghislaine Bel-Jadot had a sister. Did you know?"

"No." Luca frowned. It had never been on any of the family charts and lineages that she studied as a child. "Why don't I know this?"

"She died when they were girls. Drowned in the bit of the Vidant that crossed their estate."

"Why does no one speak of her?" Luca asked, anticipating the answer. "It's a normal enough tragedy, for youth to drown."

"It is." Nicolas tilted his head back and forth. "No one speaks of it because they suspect, I suppose, what Ghislaine's parents refused to conscience."

Dread curled in Luca's stomach.

"Did... Ghislaine push her? Why?"

Nicolas sniffed. "I cannot say. I was not there. But I know there are things that the House Bel-Jadot was particularly adamant about. Things they would not stand for."

"Sky above." Luca sagged into her crutch. "She killed her because she had Balladaire's magic? Her sister was a believer?"

Nicolas hummed the possibility. "That's what most think. However... I suspect it went the other way. I think that Ghislaine's sister— Valère was her name—caught Ghislaine working some uncivilized magic, and Ghislaine wanted to keep it secret. She can be—pardon me, could be—quite ruthless, you know."

"She'd been able to use—all this time—"

"Oh, I doubt it. A pity she's gone now." The lines at the corners of Nicolas's eyes deepened as he smiled. Then wryly, he added, "Be glad you were an only child. There is something cursed about siblings in this land, all the way back to our beginnings."

Ghislaine and Valère. Nicolas and her father. How much worse would the question of succession be if she had to add a sibling to this war between her and her uncle?

His words tickled something in her memory, though. Something urgent.

"Thank you, Uncle. This conversation has been elucidating."

She left Nicolas laughing to himself in the darkness behind her.

Back in her rooms, Luca returned to what she had begun to call the "Durfort Library." She found the book she was looking for beneath a stack of Durfortien ledgers. She'd meant to return to it, but had become distracted by the years of records. The chevalier tales didn't seem as important.

She turned to the page with the golden-haired youth, his limbs splayed against the great tree, and this time, she read his story and then she read it again, letting its meaning sink into her bones.

A pious, beloved, younger prince; a cruel heir with poor judgment; a bloody plea for mercy at the feet of the god.

It made her think of a moment when, during that too-brief idyll between her coronation and their wedding, Luca had asked Touraine, head buried in her hands, how Touraine did it.

"Do what?" Touraine had asked, warily.

"Find your god. How did you find...?"

"Faith?"

"I tried. In Qazāl. After Aranen showed me how Shālan magic works." She had shown Touraine the thin scar on her forearm. "Nothing happened. Gil used to say faith is believing in something unquestioning, but you—you're skeptical of everything, aren't you? You must be. I would be, if I were you."

Touraine had laughed then, softly. "I don't trust most things." Luca also heard the unspoken *I don't trust you*. "So I don't know if that's it. But..." She went quiet, her vision unfocused. Luca had no idea what she was reliving. When she spoke again, her voice was gentle but the words cut. "You've never had to surrender in your life, have you, Luca?"

"Of course not. I don't lose—" Then Luca paused, smirk frozen on her face, the humor frozen on her tongue. How could she even joke that she never lost, when she'd burned Tiro's body, and Gil's and Lanquette's so recently? She shuddered. "I surrendered a colony," she said, as if it had been not a loss but a strategic retreat. "I surrendered a throne."

Touraine had grunted, considering. After a thoughtful silence she said to Luca, "I don't know how your god works, but maybe you should stop fighting so hard to grasp it."

Like I grasp at everything else I want. Luca had walked that path of conversation with Touraine before.

"You have to have faith in something." With the cold winter sun illuminating Luca's study, Touraine's golden eyes were hooded and dark, almost brown again. "Something that's not yourself."

The next morning, after a sleepless night, Luca went to the healing tent to speak to Aranen din Djasha. She regretted leaving the palace immediately. She could smell the pyres burning, all the way from here.

The healing tent as Luca had last seen it was gone, swallowed up by the smaller tents bubbled around it. A mass of people wearing scarves around their faces rushed between them all.

"When we spoke some time ago, you asked me what I was willing to sacrifice." Luca walked at Aranen's side, making the circuit of the Parc du Coeur. "For the gifts of the gods. For Balladaire."

"I didn't expect you to return with an answer."

"I...haven't. I've been studying what I can of Balladaire's old magic. Its god and how we came to this point."

They left the healing tent in their wake as they passed by the great statue of the farmer with his square stone brow, the gentle slope of his chin. A determined but kindly visage. No coaxing chatter from Aranen to ease the words out. Aranen was patient. Abiding. No small amount of silent judgment.

"I don't think I can do it. I can't ask my people to make the sacrifices they once did. And I—"

The beautiful painted youth, the gilt flaking off the page. The carefully rendered torment on his face. He reminded Luca of Bastien, beautiful and butchered, sprawled out upon the grass of the queen's maze. If he had died a little closer, over the roots, would that have been enough to spare Luca from her own decision? She glanced at Aranen and unexpectedly met the priestess's eyes, golden and probing.

"I can't do what I know I should, Aranen din. Even if I can somehow turn back the Taargens, I will fail my people."

Aranen hugged herself close. "If it were easy to do, it would not be a sacrifice."

A simple answer, one Luca had come up with herself.

"Did you know," she said bitterly, "that Balladairans were once so afraid of the god that they never wrote its name? The fate of my empire is under siege by some plague-riding deity, and I don't even know what to call it!"

Luca breathed in the cold air, the charnel smoke, letting it cool her temper back to ice, tightly shaped. They passed another statue, a woman with a hand outstretched, her mouth wide open in song, her eyes closed. Her other hand had broken off a long time ago. It had held a bird.

"What a thing, to be so afraid of your god that you cannot even speak its name."

"And who spoke Shāl's name to you?" Luca said defensively.

Aranen tilted her head back, unbothered by the mystery or Luca's attitude. "Perhaps it was whispered into the ear of a great prophet. The First Healer, or his sister, the First Scourge. Maybe it was simply a pleasing combination of sounds. I don't think it truly matters what we call them."

"The healer, the scourge? I haven't heard of them."

"We're discovering a great many things you haven't heard of, aren't we?"

"Please, Aranen din." Luca bowed her head. "I'm only curious."

Aranen ticked her tongue against her teeth. "If Djasha were here, she would tell it better, but I will give you the short of it.

"There were two twins, lost up one of the great mountains in Briga. They were traveling through a pass too close to winter. A storm stranded them. The sister was injured, Shāl spoke to them, and her brother was able to heal her. They remained trapped, though, and with no food. He gave his life so that she would not starve. Then, alone, the sister was set upon by bandits as she tried to return home. She found herself with a vicious power and slew them."

Luca digested the tale quietly as they passed a statue of an athletic youth, nude, gracefully tense, her every muscle carved in sharp relief. A dancer or a fighter. "Is it true?"

"Does it matter? It's served as origin of our religion and cautionary tale alike for so long that that is all the truth it needs."

"Apparently, we have a story like that, too." The fallen prince. His sacrifice for his sister's reign. Perhaps siblings truly were cursed. "It seems we had many things in common, once. Like our marriage rites." She hadn't realized she was going to confess this until the words were already coming out. "Before the purges, we used to cut our palms, too, but we spilled the joined blood into the earth. We had no healers, though, so the couple took the time away while the wounds healed. I think that's part of the sacrifice we made to the god. Before."

"Were your parents wed that way?" Aranen asked keenly.

"I don't know. My mother's journals . . . She was trying to convince my father, but I don't know if she ever succeeded." Luca gestured backward, toward the healing tent. "Perhaps this is the consequence."

"You believe you need to wed in your god's fashion to end the Withering?"

Luca's face warmed. "It's hard to say. It might be too little. Anylight, Touraine is gone—"

"What about that charming marquise of yours? The girls are all a-titter in the tents, so I know she's returned to La Chaise." The smile in Aranen's voice coaxed a matching one to Luca's lips, briefly.

"I've asked too much of her already."

"And you haven't asked too much of Touraine?" Aranen's laughter vanished as soon as it had come.

"You think less of me for denying her ransom."

This time, the silence was long. They were circling upon the healing tents and the unspoken agreement that this conversation would end when they returned. Not for the first time, Luca considered confessing their secret to the priestess. Aranen halted. She tucked her graying curls behind her ears.

"Jaghotai told me what Touraine did." She sighed. "There are many reasons for me to think less of you, Luca din. This, at least, I understand. I was also sacrificed by my wife on the altar of something greater."

Luca wasn't sure if it was the cruelty of the words, or the kindness tucked within them that left her eyes stinging. For once, it didn't sound like castigation.

Aranen inclined her head. "Here. Take this. To be safe." Aranen pressed something from her pouch into Luca's hands. Without waiting for Luca's leave, she returned to her work.

Luca opened her hand to find a sprig of woolwort. She inhaled its fresh sharp fragrance, then tucked it inside her pocket.

CHAPTER 47

THE KNIFE

Riding through Balladaire's countryside as an invader gave Touraine new eyes. Every village a source of hostiles or resources for the beast of an army lumbering behind her. Only, she couldn't shake the familiarity her body felt in the coolness of spring. The chill air in her lungs was home, the springy grass beneath her boots was home, the bubble of the stream was home, the wind rustling in the green trees, home. Home, all of it.

And she led an army to destroy it.

Whoever wrote Balladaire's histories would call her traitor, or worse, a piss-poor general, captured in her first engagement without the courage to die. A liability to her queen. But then, the Balladairans had always thought her a liability to the queen.

Or this would work, and maybe, just maybe, they would call her a hero.

With each step closer to the city, these facts loomed larger in Touraine's heart. The path she was on. She wouldn't know if it was worth it until it was too late.

That's what faith is for.

Touraine laughed darkly to herself as she picked her way to the stream to bathe. El-Ākilah was there, as she'd expected. The Eater took her bathing time alone, and short of ambushing her at the latrines, her bath was the best time for Touraine to get a private word. The joint Taargen-Shālan army would reach La Chaise soon. Then Touraine would be out of time.

Kiras waded barefoot, naked except for a Shālan lunghi tied so it hung above her knees. She scrubbed one long, muscled leg with a wedge of soap. The muscles of her back and waist twisted and rippled magnificently. Her holy knife lay on a pile of clothing.

Touraine scuffed a stone to alert her and raised empty hands.

Kiras jerked her head around and curled in on herself, hiding her soft spots. Then she saw Touraine and let out an exasperated huff. "I bathe alone on purpose, El-Qazāli."

"I want to talk to you about something that no one else wants to hear. El-Ākilah." Touraine had never heard Kiras given a second name, but the title had slipped from more than one mouth.

Slowly, the other woman straightened, but she kept her back turned to Touraine, shifting as Touraine got closer.

"I can wait for you to finish, if you want."

Kiras hung her head so Touraine couldn't see her expression, but she heard the woman's sigh over the burble of the stream. Then Kiras turned around, her chin held high, her shoulders not proud and rigid like Luca's but upright in resignation. Like a bloody-nosed brawler who refused to stay down.

"El-Atyidi, if you must." Kiras spoke Qazāli Shālan, but with a slightly different accent than Aranen's or Jak's. "I am not only what I do. El-Khā'in." *Traitor.*

Touraine inhaled slowly. "I take your point."

Kiras El-Atyidi was a fiercely stunning woman with lightning-strike eyes, and since she seemed to be inviting Touraine to look, Touraine did. From her eyes to her mouth to her collarbone, the split between the muscles of her chest, her breasts—and below her breasts, leading all the way down below the edge of the lunghi and into a trail of dark hair, was a network of waxy scars crosshatched across her belly.

They weren't random like Touraine's scars were. She recognized the pattern. She had seen them in Aranen's anatomy books. The incisions where the anatomists had cut the body and pulled back the skin to examine the internal organs. Those illustrations and sketches had all come from cadavers—Touraine had thought. Maybe these were from an operation. Whatever they'd come from, the scars all had the same melted-wax texture that came from Shālan healing.

Touraine pulled off her coat and her shirt and her own chest wraps, stepped out of her boots, and rolled her trousers up to the calf. She waded into the stream with Kiras, gasping at the first touch of frigid water, and slowly turned around.

Goose bumps sprang all over Touraine's body, raising the hair on her shins. She closed her eyes and tried not to shiver.

Kiras, very close behind her, whispered, "I know these scars."

Touraine turned, eyes drifting to Kiras's belly again.

Kiras made a considering sound in her throat. "We have much in common, I think."

Touraine saw then a sharp loneliness in the other woman. The turn of her mouth, the downcast gaze. Touraine knew that feeling. It was the kind of thing that Luca would pull at, to get what she wanted. It was the weakness in the front line that Touraine had been waiting for. A place to break through. It was a heady thing, to feel recognized in a world when you thought you were alone.

"How do you do it?" Touraine asked. "The magic. The killing magic."

Kiras cocked her head. She pressed her hand flat against the scarred sections of her belly. "You've already done it."

"That was an accident. I haven't tried since. I haven't needed to." That wasn't strictly true; she could have used it to fight in the palace, against Nicolas and his guards. She corrected: "I haven't been willing to."

"That's good." Kiras went back to her bathing, soaping under and along her arms and over her torso. "Shāl willing, you'll never be desperate enough for it."

Touraine sighed and turned a little, her heart knowing better than her body the direction of La Chaise. Less than a week away, if the weather held and nothing bogged down the artillery wagons.

No more time.

"I think we'll all be desperate enough to try a lot of stupid things soon."

"Then what's your question?" Kiras offered Touraine the soap.

Touraine took it, held it up to her nose. Argan oil. Oud and orange blossom. A sharp pang of longing for Qazāl cut through her thoughts before Kiras brought her back to them.

"Oh. You want to know how…here?" Kiras tapped the side of her own head. "How to get around the thought of eating human flesh? There's no getting around the sacrifice."

Touraine's stomach turned, mouth flooding with hot spit. She swallowed it down and focused on scrubbing the dirt off her legs. "But there are rituals? Something to make sure it works? I watched Djasha do it once. She wasn't sure that she would be able to, but it worked. I just don't understand *how*."

Kiras's mouth dropped open. "You saw Djasha din Aranen make a sacrifice for Shāl?"

"I— Yes? You know her?"

"I know of her. She brought the other half of the magic back to us."

"They called her the Apostate."

"And yet, you described the truest act of faith. She inspired my teachers."

Touraine straightened. "Your teachers?"

"They taught us that to kill we had to be ready to give up our own lives. We sacrifice someone, yes, eat their flesh or take their lifeblood, yes, but *we* are the sacrifice in the end. If we haven't surrendered to that, then Shāl will not hear us."

"That's the secret?"

"I think it is gullshit, is what I think. I was a child. I wasn't ready to make that kind of sacrifice."

"Neither was I." Then, it became clear. Touraine pointed at Kiras's stomach. "They did that to you."

Kiras chuffed heat into her arms. "They gave me a purpose. *That* I do believe in."

"What purpose?"

Kiras bared her teeth, a vicious grin that made Touraine step back, slipping on the algae-slick stones beneath her feet. Sikīn el-qā'id, the army also called her. "To fight Balladaire."

"Then why didn't you come fight in El-Wast?" Touraine covered her awkwardness by splashing water on her arms and chest and soaping herself. "We could have used your help."

"*They* told *us* not to come. They scorned us. Called us blasphemers. Abominations. Perversions. So we sent no one."

Touraine thought of the handful of golden-eyed Shālans in the camp. "The other Eaters. They all grew up with you? With your teachers?"

Kiras grunted assent. "Some are with the others in the west."

"Are there many of you? There were a lot of Sands, once."

"Maybe a score." Belatedly, Kiras gave herself one last rinse. "Not as many as I would like."

"You should tell Pruett to let me go over to them. I'll teach them what I know about healing, too."

Kiras looked west, toward the Nervure. The rest of the Taargen-Shālan coalition was marching toward La Chaise from the other side of the river.

"I'll speak to her. It could be useful."

They both turned at the sound of yet another visitor. Pruett swaggered down the hillock that blocked the creek from view of the army camp.

"Sky above. Shāl take my eyes. Tits of the fucking Bear." After swearing in each language, Pruett gave a low, appreciative whistle. "Say whatever you want about me and my faults, but you can never say I don't have exquisite fucking taste."

Touraine snorted and Kiras smiled quietly, her eyes crinkling at the corners. She really was beautiful; Pruett did have exquisite fucking taste.

"Did you come to ogle?" Touraine flung water at her.

"Well, I am feeling a bit dirty all of a sudden and in need of a good wetting, but no—word from the west. They think the queen will engage them tomorrow."

"They're that close?" Touraine's heart lodged in her throat.

"Aye." Pruett made an irritated sound. "But we won't be able to reinforce them. No way we can reach the city in time, and we can't afford to split the eastern forces if we want to keep the bitch walled in from the south. Especially not with the others still on our asses. All we can do is march like the war depends on it and hope the others kick 'em in their holes."

Kiras frowned. "Why doesn't Istam hold and wait for us?"

"The longer they sit still, the more vulnerable they are," Touraine answered before Pruett did. "The fight may go to them."

Pruett sucked her teeth. "Aye, that. Get dressed and meet us back at the command tent."

Touraine and Kiras dressed in amicable silence, but there was a dangerous new undercurrent now. They could both feel it; they were fighters. Their purpose would be spent soon.

And so Touraine was surprised when Kiras asked, "Has she always been so angry?"

Touraine cackled on the ground as she tried to slip her damp foot back into her sock. Then she noticed Kiras looking embarrassedly at the ground.

"Oh. Sorry. Yes. She has."

"I would like to make her smile."

Touraine blinked at her, nonplussed. The other sock dangled, forgotten.

"You're serious."

"I am."

"Take her some of those." Touraine nodded toward the wildflowers growing by the streambed, shocks of yellow and red and purple. "And listen to her poetry. The dirty stuff and the rest."

She smiled to herself, but it was a confusion. Where there should have been the memory of warmth between her and Pruett, there was an empty shape that the rest of Touraine's life had to fit itself around. There were new memories now, and those were much harder, with jagged teeth.

Kiras finished getting dressed before her, and was carefully plucking some of the flowers by the streambed when a protective urge overwhelmed Touraine.

"Do you love her?" she asked.

Kiras plucked another flower and unbent. She twirled the stem, smiling to herself, not the vicious smile with sharp teeth, even though the hardness of the woman remained. "I want to wake up beside her. Fall asleep beside her. Fight beside her. I would follow her anywhere, I think, and break every tenet of Shāl if she asked."

Heat rushed to Touraine's face at the sincerity of the answer. She covered it awkwardly, snickering and saying what so many had said to her: "What are you, her pet?"

"You more than anyone should know that love is much more complicated than that." Kiras stared at Touraine hard, unfazed by her shitty barb, like she could see through it to the truth beneath:

Once, and not that long ago, Touraine would have answered the first question not only *yes*, but *yes, more than anything.*

More than everything.

CHAPTER 48

THE REAPING

Luca stood in front of the war map, twirling the dead rose between her fingers. The white petals had long since dried, browning at the edges before shriveling and holding their place. The unnaturally long thorns remained sharp, however. Her hand was already bloodied. She closed her eyes and tried to pray to the god whose name she did not know. If Fili could do it, if Ghislaine once had done it, surely she could, too.

Grow, she thought, squeezing her bloody fingers tighter around the stem, cupping the head in her other palm. *For Balladaire's sake, grow!*

"It's still not working?" Sabine said, breaking Luca's concentration.

Sabine had been weaving gracefully through her sword forms between the chairs she had arranged as opponents. If she faltered at all, she hid her spasms well.

"No, it's not," Luca said tersely.

She glared at the castle on the map that was La Chaise, pressing her fists against the map on either side of the city. The battle for the western side of the river had begun. Reports from Colonel Taurvide were corroborated by Perrot's men; halfway up the Nervure between Marticourt and La Chaise, they'd engaged the other arm of the combined Taargen, Qazāli, and Masridāni forces. Perrot's scouts estimated two battalions, easily matched with Travers and Champs d'Or troops and the Chaisien company.

Luca was not there. Luca could not be there. Luca would not

imagine what she would see if she were there. She would not imagine the hordes of the enemy nor what would happen if she rode in the charge; she would not imagine what it would feel like to have her horse shot from beneath her, nor what it would be like to fight on foot through hundreds of soldiers while trying not to get stabbed by a rusty bayonet. She would not imagine Touraine leading that enemy army against her.

A streak of red marred the war map. Luca swore.

"You two are going to kill each other. You and her." Sabine leaned against the opposite wall, arms folded. As if she could read Luca's mind. Then again, Luca probably wasn't so challenging a cipher at the moment.

"Maybe we will," Luca whispered, giving voice to the fear for the first time.

Sabine came around and tucked a free strand of hair back into Luca's braid. "Write to her. Get the truth before you condemn her. If nothing else, buy us time."

"It's too late, Sabine."

"Too late for what?" The Jackal flung the door open, and a servant wafted in behind her with the smell of mint and sugar. Qazāli tea. Aliez came in a moment later, looking as harried as fox in a hunt.

"Parlay." Luca glared at the rose in her hand before throwing it down.

Jaghotai grunted and took a cup of tea from the tray. After a moment's thought, she placed it in front of Luca and took another for herself, then sat to her left, as usual. Sabine took a cup and inhaled deeply, sighing with relish as she took her seat at Luca's right.

"Jaghotai."

"Mm."

"Why are you here?" Luca asked. "In my city, fighting with me, and not with them?"

Jaghotai sipped her tea. Swirled the glass cup and watched the sediment at the bottom spin and settle. "Do you know about Emperor Djaya?"

Along with her strong accent, the Jackal had a rough voice that almost reminded Luca of General Cantic. They were cut from the same cloth, dyed in different patterns. Luca still couldn't stop looking for Touraine in Jaghotai's features. Wondering if Touraine would have those same lines, if she would soften in the cheeks and the stomach and the hips in the same way.

"Of course. The last emperor of the Shālan Empire and the reason for its downfall."

"That's how they taught it to you here?"

Luca snorted. "It most certainly is not."

"Tell me, then, princess. How they teach it here."

Luca looked up at the tightness in Jaghotai's voice. The older woman's face was pinched around the eyes and mouth. She pulled one dirty boot onto the black velvet seat, right arm resting on her knee.

"Empress Djaya crossed the Triaume for greed of our bounteous land." Luca felt for the dry woolwort in her pocket. "Fertile, green, beautiful. She came with her cannibal witches, and they churned those fertile fields to mud with the blood of our innocent people. They ate the hearts of children in front of their parents, fed on spouse in front of spouse, and scattered the remnants for the crows."

"Pretty detailed for a tutor to tell the royal whelp."

"I was a curious pupil and a morbid one at that. My interest was deemed inappropriate. They tried to deter me. It didn't work."

"I see that."

Luca flicked the edge of her nail over a thorn on the dead rose. "I'm beginning to suspect that we used our own god to fight back, but that is not something we're taught. We are taught, however, that it was in response to this savage violence that Ancier the First revolted against the kings Fontine to live in a nation that abhorred uncivilized worship of the gods. They didn't want to become like the empress.

"From then on, we've been at some kind of war with our neighbors, either trying to take their land or bend them to our beliefs. Ta, you see? Is your version of the tale very different?"

Jaghotai grinned without mirth. "The way we're told it, the emperor was trying to save her people, but she got arrogant. Thought she knew better than Shāl. The Brigāni teach it even more differently still—they say she was betrayed. Ah, but you're right about one thing. There was a lot of blood."

"What's that have to do with you being here?"

Jaghotai's shoulders rose and fell heavily, and she took another drink of her tea, savoring it before smacking her lips. "I can see why Touraine got so comfortable here."

Innocuous as it was, it felt backhanded. "You're here because of the tea?"

"No. I'm here because Touraine is here. Was here."

"And now she's gone again."

The Jackal gave a rueful smile. "She does that, doesn't she? Up and off she goes, never quite where you expect her to be when you turn around."

Maybe she should have trusted Jaghotai with their secret. It certainly would have been kinder.

"Will you be joining her, then?"

"I suppose not. Aranen's here. And the girl. I didn't give Pruett the fighters she needed when she asked because I was tired of fighting. Peace over all. That's what I wanted. Even peace with you, if that's what it took." She paused, swirling the mostly empty glass around again before upending it over her mouth. "I thought maybe Touraine had been right."

"About what?"

Jaghotai took one of the extra cups of tea. "Who did your tutors say won that war?"

Luca didn't have the chance to answer. Someone pounded on the door. Deniaud opened it onto a young runner holding a message tube.

"From the western front, sir," the youth said, saluting Deniaud, then bowing to Luca. "Your Majesty."

Luca's hands shook as she opened it and took out the tightly rolled paper. "Jackal—you tell me. Do the Qazāli say Emperor Djaya won, or lost?"

Jaghotai inhaled sharply. "She lost. Everything."

"She was victorious," Kiras said. "Empress Djaya swept through Balladaire like a scythe." Kiras made a tiny motion with her hand, slicing down grain. She sat her horse with a gentle sway as they rode toward Balladaire's capital, as if expecting the rolling gait of a camel.

The hawk-nosed woman was telling stories again, and Touraine and Roric listened intently. Roric rode on Touraine's right; ever since Cinq-Tombeaux, he spent at least part of his time riding with her instead of his other battle-brothers. It had even softened him toward Pruett, who rode on Kiras's other side, sweeping the sky with her gaze. Touraine never knew which eyes she was looking through—her own, or the little kestrel that sometimes deigned to perch on her forearm.

The walls of La Chaise rose far in the distance. They weren't more than a day or so away for a single rider. Touraine could make it to the palace, plead to be let inside the walls. Some of the gatemen might recognize her. At the very least, they'd send for Luca. If Touraine wasn't hit in the back by a certain sharpshooter, or hunted down by Henrir the wolf. She was trapped in the noose of Luca's plans.

"That's not how I heard it," Touraine said. Djasha had told Touraine about Emperor Djaya. How, thanks to her, the Brigāni had lost their magic and been cursed from their homeland, forced into a nomadic life. It had been the beginning of the end of the Shālan Empire.

"The Qazāli betrayed her. She could have taken all of Balladaire then. She almost had. Right up to their grand city walls."

"You're Qazāli," Touraine pointed out with raised eyebrows.

Kiras tilted her head from side to side. "In Atyid, we weren't all so... dogmatic about Shāl's teachings. We sheltered a lot of the Brigāni, you know."

"No, I don't. I don't know most of what I need to about modern politics and recent Qazāli history, let alone ancient bickering."

Pruett chuckled from Kiras's other side. "Kiras likes to tell us poor Sands about everything we missed. Don't you, love?"

Touraine wasn't sure if Pruett meant to sting or not these days. It felt like they were constantly dancing over the Taargens' sharp blades. She might trust Touraine enough to keep her close, but there was still a wound that wanted healing, and Touraine wasn't sure even Shāl's magic was strong enough to mend it.

"What happens if we win?" Touraine asked, just as Kiras asked, "You don't want to know?" There was hurt in Kiras's face, but Pruett didn't turn to see it.

"Eh." Pruett shrugged one shoulder. "If we win, we take the palace."

A win meant the Qazāli in the western companies would survive. Some of them were surely people she knew. There was some justice in it, too, a Qazāli victory on Balladairan soil. As prince consort, Touraine wasn't supposed to want that. But sky above, if there wasn't a little thrill of hope that the Qazāli would prove the Balladairans wrong—show them how strong, how fierce, how *human* the Qazāli people were.

A win meant losing Luca.

If Touraine had been on the other side of the river, she would have turned them back. Disengaged, delayed. When she had asked to help, though, Pruett had laughed and sworn and said there were captains enough, and Eaters, too. People the Qazāli would listen to, not foreigners like them.

"You aren't nervous, are you?" Roric asked. His Taargen accent was even thicker in Shālan than it was in Balladairan. Unfortunately, his dogged attempts to speak in Shālan were also endearing. He laughed through his errors, even when he tried to explain Taargen religion and ended up accidentally talking, at length, about the complexities of Taargen chickens.

"Of course I am." Touraine gestured to the walls in the distance. "What if we don't win? You won't get anywhere near the palace."

"A woman of little faith." Pruett turned her snarl of a smile on Touraine. "If we lose . . . we take the palace. Don't worry." She cackled and Roric laughed with her.

"They will win," the bear prince added. "I am told they have even more . . . you call them Eaters? And Hannis Grigor, one of our greatest bear priests, fights with them."

None of that settled Touraine's stomach, and yet, was it wrong for her to be a little excited that the soldiers who'd scorned her, who'd forbidden to let her rise in the ranks, would be undone by the very thing they called uncivilized?

"What about the emperor, then?" Touraine asked. "What happened next?"

"She captured all of this." Kiras gestured expansively. "The spoils fed the entire Shālan Empire for months, from the rivers east of Lunāb to the seas west of Briga. It was a time of plenty."

"She didn't hold it, though?"

Kiras shook her head. "Couldn't. The magic stopped when Shāl was displeased. She'd gone with an army of warrior priests, but without their magic to knit and unknit, the Balladairans could fight back."

Touraine shuddered.

"Are you still so afraid of what you can do?"

Touraine looked sharply at the scorn in Kiras's voice. "No?"

"Good." Kiras didn't sound like she believed her. "Part of having faith is believing in the gift. Believing you were given it for a reason. You can misuse it like any other gift, but it's not something to be ashamed of." Her golden eyes flashed fierce in the gloaming.

"I'm not," Touraine said, even though the knot in her stomach turned to queasiness.

"Some people at the... temple where I was raised. They said that Shāl was jealous of Djaya. That she was too mighty."

"So Shāl had to bring her low again."

"Exactly."

They set up camp as the sun set. The walls of La Chaise were clear now. The Nervure was a rush of northern snowmelt and city sewage on their left. Somewhere beyond that, a battlefield full of new corpses. She waited with the others in tense quiet around a cook fire for word from the other battalions.

Word came in the form of Lor, a Taargen messenger. When she transformed out of her raven form into a woman cloaked in feathers, she still had a few mannerisms that struck Touraine as out of place: the way her head cocked sideways, the piercing black of her eyes. They never quite went normal. Someone had lost their soul for this message.

Roric jumped to his feet and caught her as she stumbled. He helped her to a stool, plied her with water and spiced sausage.

He murmured to her in Taargen, gentle and chiding, and she snapped back good-naturedly after chugging the cup of water.

No one uttered the question that was at the front of all their lips.

Touraine rested her forehead against her clasped hands. Whatever happened, she would make her next choice, and her next choice, and she would walk like that until she died. That's all a life was. Step after wrong-footed step until you died. What a life she'd made, that it should come to this.

"We won," Lor said when she'd recovered. Her pale hair was lank, and baggy shadows dragged down her bright eyes.

"We won?" High Priest Albric repeated.

"By what margins?" Roric asked. "How many losses? What was the state of the enemy?"

"We won," Lor repeated, this time with triumph. "The farmers ran with their tails between their legs."

Pruett sagged on her clever little hide folding stool. She swiped her fingers through her wild auburn curls with a laugh of incredulous relief.

"We did it," she said. "We'll take the city together. We did it!" She shouted the last, and whooped. The cry was picked up by the other soldiers, Shālan and Taargen alike. Like a chorus of drunken wolves.

Touraine fought hard to keep a matching smile on her face. She took a cup of that dark Taargen beer with everyone else. Raised it high with everyone else. But while everyone else drank and celebrated, she let her beer sit beside her in the dark. Her stomach churned, her head spun.

It was time to tear herself apart.

CHAPTER 49

UP THE HILL

Is this what it feels like to go to war? Fili thought as she stood before the Fingers gathered in La Flottille. On the table in front of her, Velte had made a map of their targets with cups, some still half-full of watered wine. Each cup represented the exclusive meeting houses and wine merchants of La Chaise that catered to those who despised everyone the Fingers stood for.

This had been Velte's idea, inspired by the queen's wedding night, when they'd rolled the barrels of Durfort red and dumped them into the fountain.

Fili looked to the crowd that was looking back at her, hopeful and hanging on her every word, and she could only think, *See, Mam? I'm doing right by them.*

In answer, her mam's sad, disappointed face bobbed up in her mind like an apple in a barrel.

She shook the memory away and raised one of the cups from the table. When everyone else raised theirs, she turned to Velte, who was better at speaking than she was.

Velte held her own cup high. "The god has given us a sign! Sending us Fili—when we were at our lowest! I remember when she showed up—put her name in my ledger. I felt something even then!"

Fili didn't know if that was true, but she remembered that moment, too, clear as anything that had happened since. Her life had changed the night Maître Gaspard brought her to this little inn for the first time.

"A miracle! While the Withering strikes down the rich in their palaces, we are safe! Thanks to our miracle! And when they locked Fili in Le Fontinard, where no one escapes, the god delivered her back to us!"

At this, a cheer rose up from those crowded in so tight—they really were like a balled fist. With the door flung open, noise from the crowd outside, those what couldn't fit into La Flottille, came like an echo. The noise clamored against her ears, and Fili let it wash over her. This was part of it.

"She is favored!" Another cheer. "She is blessed!" Another. "With the god's blessing, we will climb up the Queen's Bank and drag the nobles screaming down it! Will you follow our miracle tonight—when we show them—what we think—of their tyranny?" Velte punctuated her phrases with her breath, crescendoing to her conclusion.

The sound that followed fair shook the building.

Mere months ago, Fili had been hiding her gift for fear of being called uncivilized. Now she had resurrected a—a religion. She was at the center of it.

"Then go! Soldiers of the sky above and the earth below! We will make them see us! We will make them hear us! We will make them *fear the power we wield*!" Velte bellowed, an enormous sound from her small form. Then she took her raised wine cup and slammed it to the table, spilling what was left in a splash of watery purple.

That was the signal, the general's horn, and at her command, their army marched into the warm evening.

They hit the targets that had been circulated—only shops on the Queen's Bank, none of the places owned by friends of the Fingers. Glass shattered and wood splintered and angry shouts followed, but no one fought against them emptying the wine stores—who could fight against a host so large?

Not that it was so large, Fili thought, seeing them all spread before her, up and down the street. It was only that after the emptiness of the first plague months, it seemed so many. Even untouched by the Withering, they were shadow eyed and hollow cheeked by shrinking rations. It was unnerving, and just as troubling when they kicked in a door painted with the white X and no one protested from inside at all. The first time it happened, the great organism that was the Fingers shuddered to a halt and turned to one another, and it felt exactly like a tree going still after a wind. The silence. Then someone shouted that they should have followed Fili the Miracle, and because they hadn't, they had got what they deserved, and someone ran in and ran out with a bottle they declared was d'Orséan white and upended it over their mouth gleefully before passing it along.

It went like that, and Fili took her share of bottles handed round and joined the chanting. The gendarmes that they passed were few and scattered—they hesitated. Was it because they were outnumbered, or because the queen had ordered them to hold? Regardless, she was swept away by the feeling of being bound together like a bundle of sticks. Ghadin marching beside her, Velte dragging her forward, Joscelin's steady presence behind.

"The Fingers form the fist!"

Their lockstep had turned into a swaying, stuttering shamble by the time they approached l'Hauteur, the hill on the Queen's Bank where the lesser nobles and the greater merchants and other crown favorites had their town houses, the hill that stretched all the way up to the palace grounds—the hill where her mam lived. The houses loomed and tilted on their slope.

The sounds turned from joy to distress, but it was not *their* distress. It was *someone else's*. That was important. *Important.* Not only wine bottles dragged out, but people in their nightgowns. The wine was sticky in Fili's mouth, but when a bottle was passed back to her again, unwatered and bold, she drank. She was warm. Ghadin hung on one arm, Velte tugged at the other, and—someone was at her back. She looked up. It wasn't Joscelin but the jailer from Le Fontinard. The one who had told them tonight was the best night, while the queen was distracted. With war. Fili was relieved. The jailer was solid and Velte had vouched for him.

Her boots sucked at the cobbles, sticky with wine like her mouth. Like the hanging. Blood staining the cobbles for days.

The memory shook her when it hit and she fought back, shouting, "This is for Traitor's Corner!"

The words tumbled from her thick tongue, her dry mouth, only to be picked up and carried, then transformed.

"This is for Traitor's Corner!"

"Traitor's Corner!"

"For Brother Michel!"

And the names continued to change as they shouted their dead, from the plague or the queen, or if not the queen and her empire, close enough as she could be blamed.

"For Maître Gaspard," Fili slurred to herself. "For Olivier."

Velte's arm looped around her shoulders. "Aye, for them, and for them what come after us."

What would come after them? Fili wondered as they marched up l'Hauteur, the houses growing greater with the import of the owner the closer they got to the palace.

They would be noticed. They would get justice.

What would that justice look like?

A loud shriek from one of the houses caught Fili's attention. A skinny young man in a nightgown fought tooth and nail against the Fingers who had broken down the door of his home. A nice home. Pillars at the top of stone steps, like Fili's mam had. The young man screeched when one of the bigger men tossed him onto one shoulder, and he punched feebly at the Finger's back while those surrounding them laughed. The lad sobbed, his long, dark hair hanging on end.

It sobered Fili. With sobriety came shame.

But what could she do to stop this beast writhing all around her?

You are the miracle. You are their miracle.

"Stop!" The people nearest to Fili sluggishly turned, bumping into each other. She shouted again, and the ripple spread. Unsteadily, she pushed through the crowd until she reached the edge, where the big Finger and his friends were still laughing.

The laughter petered out as Fili approached.

"Friends. My friends." She swallowed and glanced around her, but Velte wasn't there. Nor was Joscelin. She had only her own voice, and it was shaky. "Put him down. Please."

"He's one of the sov-stealers, isn't he?" The large man looked to his friends for confirmation, then gestured toward the pillars and the inside of the house beyond the open door. "What's a little roughing up compared to what we've had to live through?"

"Put him down," Fili repeated.

Begrudgingly, the man did, muttering, "Shoulda known she wasn't one of us."

Fili glared at the man and he flinched back. Then she steadied the boy, an arm across his back, and helped him up the stairs.

"Are you all right?" she murmured.

The young man looked around her own age. He eyed her with disgust. He shook her off when they reached the door and started to close the door in her face when she noticed the white X on it. The paint smelled fresh.

"Wait!" Fili flung her hand against the door before it could slam shut. The youth glared, tried to push the door harder, but he wasn't strong.

Fili glanced back over her shoulder. The crowd of Fingers watched her. It was so big that farther up and down the road, she knew the Fingers were still breaking glass and hunting for wine to spill into the streets. She might be the miracle, but she couldn't control it all.

"Is someone here sick?" She pointed to the sprig of woolwort pinned to her coat. "I can help them."

His glare turned to a sneer. "Uncivilized gutter—"

"Who is it?" Fili pushed harder on the door, gaining another inch. "Your mother? Your father?"

The youth's dark eyes tightened at the corners, his mouth twisting as he held more tears. His damp cheeks shone in the light of the street lamps and the Fingers' torches.

"Take me to them," Fili whispered. It was the right thing to do. She could feel something building within her, the same feeling that had come over her as she faced the dying queen, a shell of herself at Fili's feet. "I can promise you a miracle."

"You'll make that rabble leave? All of them?"

"They're not rabble."

"They're savages. You saw what they did to me."

"Do you want my help or not?"

Another glance toward the street. "Come in."

Fili addressed her people from the top of the stairs. "Wait for me." She raised a hand at their dismayed protests. "He needs a miracle, like you all needed a miracle. I'll be back soon."

Fili followed the boy inside and he locked the door behind them, giving her another dirty look. His house was not unlike her mother's on the inside, either, but it had the look of lifetimes spent in it. A family. A single Shālan carpet on the floor, beautiful wooden furniture that might even have come from Maître Gaspard if Fili took the time to look for his mark.

But there was also an emptiness. Too much of the life vacated too soon, deflated like a bladder. He picked up the one lit candle in its holder and led her through the dark, up creaking stairs, and into a bedroom.

"Papa?" The boy set the candle on the windowsill and stood anxiously at the foot of the bed. Fili saw his hesitation—he wanted to go closer, to comfort his father, but he was afraid. "Papa, there's someone here to see you. She says she can help."

He raised his eyebrows at Fili, haughty and impatient.

Fili went to the man lying in the bed. He had his son's dark hair, but it was tangled and matted with sweat. The Withering was well advanced—wrinkled fingers on the coverlet, sunken cheeks, parched lips. He did not open his eyes, but the blankets occasionally rose and fell.

"I'm Fili Guérin, leader of the Fingers. We fight so that all in Balladaire can benefit from her plenty." Fili touched his forehead with her thumb, and then each cheek, and then his mouth. "I carry the blessing of Balladaire's god, and I pass that protection to you." She unclipped the sprig of woolwort, tucked it into the man's hands, and closed his fingers around it. The skin felt so dry and brittle, she was afraid she would break him.

Fili didn't know how much of this was a performance and how much of it was truly the god speaking through her, but it had come to her as she touched supplicant after supplicant in La Flottille. Maybe it didn't help the magic, but the ritual gave the people something to cling to. Something to believe in. She was making up so much of it as she went. Sometimes, she felt like a fraud. Sometimes, though, a sensation pressed over her, refreshing as summer rain over her face.

"Is that it?" The boy stepped forward gingerly, skepticism plain on his face. He had a small mouth, and his eyebrows were sharply plucked.

Soft and sneering, like the queen. His hands were pale and smooth as he put one over his father's. He couldn't have been more different from Fili, or the world she lived in.

"He'll wake, or he won't." Fili stood. "If he does, a donation wouldn't go amiss. Send it—" Fili hesitated. If he betrayed them to the palace, it would put all her followers in danger. "Send it to the healing tents. Tell them it's on behalf of Fili the Miracle. Then join us. This is what we can do for you that Queen Luca can't."

Even as she spoke, the man beneath the covers took a deep, shuddering breath. His dry fingers stretched, then closed around the plant.

"Papa? Papa!" The boy dropped to his knees at the bedside and clasped the man's hand in both of his. Feebly, his father's fingers twitched against his.

Despite herself, Fili felt tears on her own cheeks as the boy pressed his face against his father's hands, kissing them, pressing them to his forehead, over and over.

"What are you?" He looked at Fili over his shoulder. "A...a priest? Isn't that what they used to call them?"

Fili looked down at her hands, turned them over. Their scars, their calluses, weathered as a young oak.

"I suppose I am."

Many of the Fingers remained outside, obedient. Fili went to the front of the crowd this time, and she led them, not in breaking and burning, but finding the houses with the white Xs. She no longer felt drunk, but clearheaded, and it spread to those around her.

This was what Fili was meant to do. Not robbing carts or assassinating the queen. That was Brother Michel. He was gone now.

The Fingers belonged to her.

CHAPTER 50

THE EMISSARY

The emissary arrived in the midst of the celebrating. The waning moon was high and the camp was noisy with drink and dancing. Everyone stopped to watch him ride in, the white flag streaming behind him as he held the reins with one hand. They whooped and jeered as he passed them.

His black-and-gold livery was rumpled, and his legs shook after he dismounted before the commanders, but he stood with as much dignity as he could muster. Though Touraine waited at the end of the line, with Pruett and Roric at the center and Albric and Kiras beside their leaders, the emissary found Touraine's eyes immediately and held them. She hid her discomfort with a disinterested stare.

"State your name and your business." Roric folded his large arms across his large chest. The white bear cloak across his shoulders made him even bigger.

The emissary swallowed, the knob in his skinny throat jerking up and down. His hands were balled in fists at his sides. They trembled.

"I speak on behalf of Queen Luca, Her Imperial Majesty, Empress of Balladaire."

"Lot of titles for someone who's about to lose her country," Pruett muttered, not so quietly that it didn't carry over the hushed camp. It was met with appreciative chuckles from those near enough to hear.

"Her Majesty bids you welcome to Balladaire and extends her hospitality." The emissary met her eyes boldly. "She invites you to send two representatives to the palace, where you may discuss the terms of your surrender with her."

Pruett laughed out loud, another of those shrieking cackles. Roric joined in, with his joyful baritone and a hint of a boyish giggle. Albric and Kiras did not.

"Giving *us* surrender terms? When she doesn't have a leg to stand on?" Pruett hooted again.

Touraine's teeth creaked with the effort of suppressing the urge to punch her.

The emissary blushed scarlet in deepening dusk. "She proposes to allow you to retreat peacefully provided you do no more damage to the townships you pass as you return beyond your respective borders. She will not renege upon the Qazāli treaty, and she's prepared to meet Masridān with similar terms. As for the Taargens, she would renegotiate the terms of the Taargen War treaty since you have broken it and thus reparations are owed."

High Priest Albric made a huffing growl in his throat. His orange-brown eyes glinted under his gray-black brows.

"How would she like it if we sent your head back for her reparations owed?" Roric's accent was thick in his haughtiness. Pruett's smugness was contagious.

The emissary sniffed, his shoulders back. "I daresay Her Majesty would find it insufficient."

"Let him be." Touraine moved in, bumping Pruett's chest with the back of her hand. "The terms are insulting, but it's not his fault."

"You take all the fun out of things, Tour." Pruett turned back to the messenger. "On your knees, then. Beg for your life. Some of us have softer hearts." Pruett smirked at Touraine, not unkindly.

Pruett was so assured in her position. There would be no negotiation with Luca, here or otherwise.

Without hesitation, the emissary dropped to his knees and crawled to Touraine's feet. "Please, Your Highness."

Instead of humiliation, there was a hard set in his jaw, like he knew this might be the last thing he did, and he wanted to do it right. What had Luca done, to put such loyalty into this man? Touraine almost snorted at the thought. How, indeed, did that woman earn such devotion?

The soldiers jeered and laughed, some of them cheering, "The prince consort! The prince consort!"

Touraine had grown used to the title-turned-insult-turned-nickname, like she had with *mulāzim*. The soldiers' faces were backlit by crackling fires that pushed away the darkness of the night. The heat of the fires, the pressure of everyone's gazes... There was something monstrous about them, their laughter, the darkness of their open mouths, the gleam of their teeth. It reminded Touraine of a line from one of Luca's philosophy books: *War makes beasts of men, and blood alone will slake their thirst.*

The emissary crawled closer still, reaching for Touraine. "Show mercy."

He clutched her hands to his lips, to his forehead almost prayerfully. Touraine's eyes went wide as she felt the sharp, unmistakable edge of a folded piece of paper pressed against her palm. She tucked it into her palm and ripped her hand away from his, swiping the fist backhanded at him to cover up her own surprise. Her heart raced. She didn't dare look over at Pruett or Kiras or the Taargen men.

Touraine kicked the emissary down, her boot connecting with the soft flesh of his side, hooking beneath the ribs.

"Tell your queen this: we are stronger than she thinks." Touraine spat on the ground in front of his face. "Her philosophers won't be enough."

Only then did Touraine manage to find Pruett's eyes. Pruett's fox-like smile was fixed. She snapped her fingers at the nearest soldier, a Taargen woman. "Get him a meal. See to his horse, too. Poor things. Rode all this way for nothing." Then she walked off, Kiras following behind her like a deadly shadow.

Touraine ducked inside her own tent, relieved to feel all those eyes blocked off when the tent flap fell shut. She lit the one candle she snagged from the quartermaster and slumped onto her small bedroll, flat on her back. She pressed the back of her hand, the one still clutching the piece of paper, against her forehead. From Luca. It had to be. She could barely breathe with the longing and yet, she couldn't prize her fingers out of the fist that kept that paper secret. Safe. If she opened it, she wouldn't be able to hide from what was coming.

The corners of the fold dug painfully into her hand.

Luca wouldn't write unless it was important. A change in the plan. A request. An order. A goodbye.

Longing won.

Wincing, Touraine uncurled her hand and flicked the little strip open with her thumb: *"And so the young prince, for love of the faithless one, plunged his dagger into his breast, that the world's pain would be undone."*

Touraine read it again, trying to parse the meaning. She didn't understand. Deep down, though, she knew. Luca was undoubtedly the prince, and so Touraine was the faithless one. She balled up the letter and pressed her fist against her mouth, forcing her breathing to slow.

There was no pleading, no callback to their time together. Touraine didn't know what story this had come from, but the line was a slap to the face, even without context. It was condescension and pain in a single sentence.

Something had changed. Was it the deviations Touraine had made from their plan? Was it Cinq-Tombeaux?

Was it so easy for Luca to lose faith in her? That wasn't fair, though. Touraine had doubted Luca more than she cared to count, even as she infiltrated Pruett's camp. Even now.

But if Luca hated Touraine, she would have spelled it plainly. The only benefit of a cipher was to prevent it from falling into the wrong hands. What would she care if Pruett read her curses, if the Taargens ripped out Touraine's soul and threw her body to the wolves, the bears, the ravens?

Touraine could still do what Luca had asked. It would cost her her life, but if Roric or Albric died, the Taargens might hold their attack, maybe even return home. Especially if Albric died. Roric was well loved, but the army looked to their high priest, not their prince.

If Pruett died...

Touraine pushed the thought away. She told herself that it was a stupid idea. That Luca should never have asked her for that, of all things. That it wasn't fair. The truth was more complicated.

Or, maybe, achingly simple.

It was the same choice Touraine always had to make.

A note, then, via the messenger. She owed Luca that much. But her candle was already half-melted. She'd been in her tent longer than she realized. The messenger would already be gone. Her veiled warning would have to be enough.

She uncrumpled the paper to stare at Luca's handwriting again. She could see Luca, hunched over her desk, the brisk scratch of her pen—how many times she had probably written and discarded other scraps of paper before settling on this note. Was this the perfect one, or had she only run out of time?

Touraine balled it up again, small as it would go, and popped it into her mouth. She chewed, softened it as much as she could with her spit, and swallowed it down.

There was only one way she would see Luca again.

CHAPTER 51

THE MONSTER

The war room. Again. Luca's books and correspondence strewn over the table. The wall map covered in flag pins and charcoal marks crossing out towns in the Taargens' paths. Some of the pins were scattered on the table, some scattered on the floor. Gold horses on black flags for Balladaire. Brown bear paws on green flags for Taargen. Black wings on red for Masridān. Gold hand on red for Qazāl. The blanket that someone had covered Luca with, now pooled on the floor where it had fallen. Luca pushed herself upright, rubbing the fog out of her eyes as a servant entered to light the candles around the room.

"Good morning, Your Majesty." Sabine came in next, her hair damp, smelling of the training salle.

"What time is it?" Luca croaked.

"Time for you to freshen up. Your audience approaches."

"Kill me now—"

Sabine took a towel from a servant and dunked it in the basin they carried, and scrubbed it over Luca's face. She spluttered, but Sabine held her firm. Then, for good measure, she flicked water in Luca's face. Then Sabine moved to her hair, redoing the braid into something less ornate but much tidier.

Another servant placed a bowl of oat porridge before Luca, then whisked the blanket from the floor. The smell of honey wafted from the bowl.

My people are starving for grain.

"Do I have to feed you, too?" Sabine pushed the small cup of coffee in front of Luca. "Eat."

Luca started with the coffee, and not a moment too soon. Evrard entered just as the fog in her mind began to dissipate, followed shortly after by Aliez and the Jackal.

Commander Perrot entered last, his face gray. He didn't take his seat.

"Your Majesty," he started.

The door behind Perrot burst open, bouncing off his broad back, as a nobleman from the Middle Court ushered himself in. He wore a velvet-lined coat and deep-purple scarf around his face. A noxious smell wafted off him, and Luca wondered what charlatan had swindled him a cure for the Withering.

"Your Majesty! Is this where your subjects should come if they wish to be heard? For you have not held a formal audience in weeks, and we have a right!"

Luca struggled to place him. He had the perpetually red face and pugnacious nose of the Brebis family, and the arrogance to go along with it. They were newly raised, married into a minor house in the Travers lands, if Luca was correct. Her head was throbbing, and every one of the nobility was another nuisance she longed to be rid of. The Fingers were right.

Evrard frowned, his wrinkles deepening in displeasure. "You forget yourself before the queen, Lord Brebis."

"The queen forgets her duties! Our homes have been invaded by these filthy cretins! They've been looting and burning all up and down the Queen's Bank! Our shops—"

"Do you think I haven't heard?" Luca let her spoon clank back into her bowl.

She'd been in this same sky-falling room when the news came. She'd asked for wine and felt the irony of it as she tried to figure out what to do next. Marauding Fingers, led by "a miracle." Fili had gone free again. The girl wasn't even hiding anymore—Perrot had found their headquarters, a little inn in La Gouttière called La Flottille.

Luca wondered if she'd only gotten drunk so she wouldn't have to think about throwing all her citizens into Le Fontinard. Fili had broken her word, and it was time for Luca to break hers. Then she would arrest Guérin. Some promises, a queen had to keep.

But not yet. She couldn't bear it yet.

"Then you will do something about this?"

"It will be taken care of, as soon as we've dealt with the plague and the army and the famine—"

"You have already taken our coin for their sake!" Lord Brebis's scarf fell down around his chin in his indignation. "And—and we know that you have been sick! You have been sick and yet recovered, while our families have not. You are hiding a cure from us!"

Luca stared into the congealing porridge in her bowl. Then she looked up to Lord Brebis, with his pink cheeks and tailored silk, puffing up his chest at her.

"I have no cure for the Withering, Lord Brebis. I am not a physician but a queen, and generations have not cured this plague nor understood its whims. Did you think this was going to be easy, my lord?"

She wasn't sure if she was asking him, or asking herself, but the lies were oh so easy to tell.

"These changes will take time, and I cannot promise a single one of us will be alive to see it. If you don't have the stomach for it, go back to herding sheep."

Gasps around the table. Lord Brebis's mouth hung open in apoplexy.

"You will regret this, Your Majesty."

Commander Perrot and Sabine both straightened, Perrot quite close to Lord Brebis with his hand on his sword.

"Will I?" Luca laughed. What was one more regret nestled among the many piled at the foot of her throne? "There is room in Le Fontinard with the other traitors, if you prefer."

Lord Brebis's face pinched in on itself, and he glanced at Commander Perrot stepping toward the open door.

"No, Your Majesty. Forgive me." He straightened his coat and pulled his scarf back up over his face.

"Commander Perrot will see you out."

Perrot cleared his throat. "Forgive me, Your Majesty, but there's something else." He gestured to one of the two guards waiting outside the war room. "Niles will see it done."

When Guard Niles and Lord Brebis were gone, Luca raised her eyebrows at Perrot, who shifted from foot to foot.

"What is it, man?" Sabine gestured impatiently with one hand, head propped on the other. "Come now, can it be so bad as all that?"

"The emissary—an emissary from the Taargens."

Luca straightened, alert. "Bring them in."

A Taargen woman, head high and proud as two guards marched her into the room. Perrot preceded them with a basket and carried it to Luca's side.

"She came under a flag of truce, Your Majesty. With this." Perrot's voice was strained with a mix of emotions—rage, disgust, grief.

The war room was silent. Luca didn't need to open the basket to know what was in it. She could smell the reek of blood and rotting flesh. They all could, and they waited silently. Aliez buried her face in her own scarf as the basket passed her. But Luca felt a duty. She flipped open the lid and clamped down on her urge to vomit, trying to make her stomach as hard as her heart. Then Sabine peered over Luca's shoulder, only to heave noisily and turn away, covering her face. Evrard's lips were a thin line. The Jackal's face was grim.

One of the servants in the room, who wasn't even close enough to see, did vomit, noisily. That strained Luca's control further. Sabine retched again.

The Taargen watched them. Her cheeks were soft and pink, her brow smooth. She met Luca's eyes unblinking. Her head was not shaved, so she was not royal, nor was she an animal priest. Did she know what Luca might do to her, with this grisly gift in hand? How could she not? It was far beyond insult.

Sabine leaned close to speak directly in Luca's ear. "Maybe we should surrender."

Luca turned slowly and glared. Sabine's skin had gone gray green.

"Look in that basket, Lord LeMarchal."

"I don't—"

"Sabine LeMarchal de Durfort, look in the sky-falling basket!" Eyes blurring, Luca pointed at the ill-used remains of her emissary until Sabine looked again. "Look inside and tell me we are surrendering to the people who did that!"

Eyes closed and cheeks wet with tears, Sabine said, "We're not surrendering to them."

"No, we're fucking not."

"No, we're fucking not," Sabine repeated, eyes still shut tight.

"Please," Luca said to Commander Perrot. "See he's burned with every dignity and that his family is provided for." Then she jerked her chin at the Taargen woman. "Lock her so deep in Le Fontinard that I can't get my hands on her."

When they were gone, the Jackal grunted from Luca's other side. "I would have had her head right here."

After hiding in the gardens as long as she could, Luca went to the salle. Like the war room, like the garden, it was full of memories, and even the good ones brought nothing but pain. She went through her exercises anylight, hoping that the movement would fortify her—and failing that, that the pain and exertion would distract her.

She had sweat through her shirt by the time Deniaud admitted Sabine to the room.

Sabine hesitated in the doorway. "Your Majesty. I didn't expect to find you here. May I...?"

"Don't be an idiot, Sabine. Come in. I could use an opponent."

Sabine shrugged out of her coat and rolled up her shirtsleeves. She looked Luca up and down before turning to the practice swords. "Seems like you've already put in your time."

"I needed a diversion."

A diversion. Sabine with her strong shoulders, her thick forearms, her long legs. Luca followed her to the sword racks.

Sabine exhaled sharply. "As did I."

Luca pulled Sabine's mouth to hers, kissing her fervently. With her other hand, she started unbuttoning Sabine's shirt.

"Luca, what—" Sabine turned away, but Luca chased the kisses down Sabine's neck instead. "Luca, stop—"

"You know it's all right," Luca murmured, still seeking. "Touraine—"

"I don't want—" Sabine stopped Luca's hands where they worked on her shirt. She pushed them down and held them there. "I just—I saw a man's body in a basket today, Luca." Her voice cracked. "I— Are you—" Sabine stared at Luca in horror.

Am I what? Luca wanted to make Sabine finish the question. She was afraid for her to finish the question.

She dropped her head against Sabine's chest. "I know. I know. I just need—" She closed her eyes and clenched her fists in Sabine's grip. "I can't do this. I can't do this, Sab."

"Is it true? Were you sick?" Sabine tilted Luca's chin up and searched her face.

"I was. Fili—the...leader of the Fingers. I had her in custody, and she...gave me her god's blessing."

Sabine sucked air through her teeth.

Three sharp bangs sounded on the salle door, and Deniaud and Perrot both came in. Perrot was breathing heavily and Deniaud was already flushed.

"Commander Perrot, if you're bringing me more bad news—" Luca started through her teeth.

"A militia has stormed Le Fontinard, Your Majesty."

Luca pushed herself off Sabine. "The Fingers? Now this is too bold—"

"No, Your Majesty. It's the duke."

Le Fontinard. Again. The prison fortress's gray walls loomed in the bloody sunset, making a corona out of the orange-and-pink-and-purple-hued sky. It sat on its little island within the Nervure, but the thin spit of land that bridged its moat was swarming with blackcoats. Some of the gendarmerie were shoving gawkers away, but Luca's attention was on the fighting.

Rifles fired back and forth—a contingent trying to get into the prison and another trying to stop them? *Or trying to get out.*

Luca got out of her carriage as if she were walking through honey, ignoring Perrot's shouts for her to come back. She'd told Sabine to stay in the palace, and she was glad.

"Where is he?" Luca shouted over the din, heedless as she strode toward the bridge. She hunted through the crowd of the fighters—some of them were dressed in the official black and gold of the palace soldiers and the all black of the prisons, but many of them were in plain clothes, despite their weapons. They were not the same rabble she'd fought in Traitor's Corner.

Perrot jerked her back roughly, pulling her behind him. "Militia from the houses, Your Majesty. Stay back. We'll take care of it."

Luca yanked her arm out of his grip. Lord Brebis. Ghislaine's little salon, listening to Taurvide's stories.

"Tell them to hold their fire, Commander."

"Your Majesty—what?"

Luca pushed him away and marched toward the bridge, her own guards racing in front of her.

"Uncle!" A bullet whizzed past her and she flinched, but she was not afraid. She was furious. "Uncle, show yourself! By order of the queen, drop your weapons!"

It helped that reinforcements from the palace marched up behind her. The traitor militia retreated toward the doors of Le Fontinard, and Luca was unsurprised to find that some of their number wore jailer blacks.

Behind them, protected by the half circle of their formation, was her uncle.

She stopped at the end of the bridge, keenly aware of the range of their rifles. Deniaud and Mareau flanked her. The sun was sinking quickly now, and this close to Le Fontinard, they, too, sank rapidly into shadow.

"My dear uncle. I did not expect to see you here."

"I had hoped to greet you in the palace, dear niece." Nicolas gave his soldiers a slow dissatisfied look that Luca knew all too well.

"Command your men to lay down their weapons, Uncle. There's no need for anyone else to die here today."

"Today." Her uncle pushed through the protective circle of his men, stopping on the other end of the bridge. "In exchange for what, dear niece? A slow, rotting death in a dank cell?"

"Did you prefer something gentler after you tried to usurp my throne?"

"I heard that you were making a mess of things. I thought we could perhaps exchange places for a time." Nicolas pitched his voice to carry as best he could. His cough was gone, but his voice was ragged. Prison had left his body as wasted as any Withering victim's.

It went against everything Luca wanted, this confrontation before so many witnesses. She'd felt naked enough alone in his cell. Power was nothing without witness, Yverte wrote, but a public weakness was a certain death.

"Maybe I did make a mess of things." Luca took another step forward, boot and crutch clicking on the stone paver. "But you could not have done better."

"Balladaire need not fall with you." Nicolas matched her step with haughty gravitas, despite his diminished state.

"For King Nicolas!"

A gun report tore open the night. Deniaud pushed Luca behind her and readied her sword as Mareau started forward. Behind Luca, a clicking as the palace soldiers lowered and cocked their own rifles.

"Don't shoot him," Luca cried. "Arrest him! *Arrest* him!" Luca struggled to see what happened next as her soldiers ran forward to obey.

When she had a clear line of sight, she saw Duke Ancier kneeling in a dead soldier's blood, yanking the knife from the dead man's belt.

"To me! On, on!" He rallied his traitors.

"Don't let them off this bridge, or I'll pickle your fucking balls!" Perrot roared.

The few chanced shots were lost in the melee of sword and bayonet, and Mareau pressed Luca tight behind him. He grunted at an impact, and fell back against her. She tried to catch his weight but could not, and he dropped to the stone, a dark stain spreading across his coat.

"Behind me, Your Majesty." Deniaud pulled Luca away protectively.

"But Mareau—"

"Behind me!"

And then it was over, as quickly as it began. Nicolas's soldiers were dead or on their knees. Nicolas himself was pinned on the ground, his hands stretched behind his back. A grisly sight, with his filthy clothing and unshaven jaw. Blood tracked into his mustache from his nose or his lips, and his hair hung in stringy clumps across his face. Luca went to him in slow, uneven steps.

"Finish it here, then, dear niece." Her uncle's words were a wet wheeze as he craned his neck to look at her.

"It doesn't have to be like this, Nicolas."

Luca found the traitor soldier's knife and kicked it off the side of the bridge and into the river. She couldn't see the weapon fall, but she heard the splash.

"What should it be like, then, Luca?"

Blood speckled the dead traitor's face. Blood leaching up the white shirt beneath the black coat and soaking into the mortar between the pavers. Luca knew what she had to do tonight. Balladaire needed its god, and she knew how to bring it back.

Nicolas laughed into the silence of Luca's realization. "I'm proud of you, dear niece." He smiled then, bloody and begrudging.

"Commander, take him back to his cell."

They dragged him to his feet and began to lead him away, and Luca tried to think of the right last words. Something pithy, about sacrificing her queen. *Never do that*, he'd warned her as a child. She thought to say thank you, for all he had taught her, for the love he *had* shown her, in his way.

Why not hang him, Aliez had asked. No one could question her now—this was treason. *Why not?*

Because of the honey cakes. Because of the stern corrections and satisfied approval. The way the weight of his hand had also felt like her father's. How he resembled her father, despite their differences. How *she* resembled *him*. But she had not been able to unsee the gaping wound in Gil's chest. And once, in their quiet moments, Touraine told Luca how he'd humiliated her in his office, made her feel like an insect pinned to a board. And now Mareau. She glanced back to where her second guard lay unmoving on the bridge.

Luca had no one else. She had Nicolas and Sabine; Touraine was gone. Everything else had been stripped from her: a city of plague and anti-royalists, two god-touched armies outside her walls, and a court full of people who wanted to tear her off her throne. She could not face this on her own.

Nicolas limped between the soldiers, held up by his armpits. He tried to walk on his own, but his leg gave and the soldiers had to yank him up again.

He wouldn't be the one to help her. He'd been waiting for her to fall, all this time.

"Wait!"

The soldiers halted and Nicolas looked over his shoulder at her.

All this grief she had wasted. All the chances she'd given him, denial. She hadn't been able to fix it, only delay this moment. When she was no longer here, she didn't want him to claim what remained in the ashes.

"Let's have done with this, Nicolas. Commander Perrot, shoot him."

Perrot went rigid, his face a pale substitute for the absent moon. He pulled his pistol obediently and turned it on his previous master.

Luca turned and walked toward her carriage, waiting in the street.

"Luca!" her uncle yelled. "Don't walk away from this. Watch your orders done."

She felt Perrot waiting for her and wished he would carry out the sentence. But he didn't and so—she turned.

She met her uncle's eyes across the length of the bridge. Honey cakes and the scars on her wife's back.

Commander Perrot shot Duke Nicolas Ancier in the head.

Luca closed her eyes on a shuddering breath and locked the memory away, tucking it beside Gil's.

CHAPTER 52

A BANDAGE

Touraine slipped from her tent when the night was deep. The fires and the celebrations had carried into the morning, and into the next evening. Now it all burned low as the soldiers found their beds and prepared to march to victory tomorrow. The air no longer carried winter's bite, but summer's heat was still distant. Touraine walked through it all feeling that odd steadiness she'd found before— the gray peace where the outside world was muffled but her thoughts were clear.

She skirted the outside of the camp until she was at the northern edge and could watch the last sliver of the moon rise over the city. The Shālan-Taargen camp had grown as familiar as any army she'd marched with. She could find the mess tent, the latrines, the horses, the smith, all of it in the dark with her eyes closed and her ears stopped up. Say that for the Taargens; they were even more regimented and well organized than the Balladairans. It filtered into the Masridāni; they were as green as the grass they trampled, but they'd picked up field discipline quick.

"Where are you going?"

Touraine jumped and spun around. Outside of the calm, gray peace, Touraine's heart beat too fast. Pruett approached her in the dark, her boots silent.

"For a walk." Touraine shoved one hand in her pocket, rested the other on her pommel. "Needed the air."

Pruett's gaze went pointedly from Touraine's head to her boots, lingering on the moonlit gleam of her weapons.

"Fully armed?"

"Enemy territory," Touraine grunted. "Besides, it's not like I'm universally beloved in camp."

"Best to have company, then." Pruett tucked her thumbs in the crossed braces over her chest, where her pistols hung. Her dagger gleamed at her hip.

A sharp whistle broke the night and Pruett raised her forearm. Tempête dived from the sky like a musket ball to land on the leather bracer.

"Fucking terrifying," Touraine muttered, shaking her head.

"The thing about animals is...they don't judge you." Pruett pulled something out of a pouch to feed it. "Or, they do, but not for the same things as people. They think we're so strange and hairless—or featherless—and terrible at finding food, but somehow, they love us anylight." Pruett stroked the kestrel's downy breast, and it tolerated it.

"I used to hate horses." Touraine reached a finger toward the bird, gingerly, looking to Pruett for permission.

Pruett brought Tempête closer, and the bird tilted its tiny head suspiciously at Touraine, dark pupils devouring the night.

"Until I started getting lessons from—" Touraine broke off as an image of Durfort surfaced. The marquise riding jauntily beside Touraine, making suggestive corrections to the placements of Touraine's thighs, laughing and hooting as she took off at a gallop and left Touraine to plod hesitantly on. She wondered if the Withering had caught Durfort in the cold north. At least she was far away.

"Here." Pruett pulled something out of her pouch and put it in Touraine's outstretched hands. It was cold and slimy and smelled awful. "You get used to it. Hold it out." Pruett moved her arm a little closer to Touraine. "Lessons from who? Your queen?"

"Luca hates horses. A different noble. A friend."

Touraine held out the offering, and Tempête sidled down Pruett's arm to investigate before snapping it up. Touraine couldn't help her gasp of surprise, and Pruett smiled, a warm smile, a true smile. Tempête looked up at Pruett, and something passed between them.

The kestrel fluffed up its feathers and looked like nothing so much as an angry dandelion seed. Then it made an irritated chirrup and flapped off Pruett's arm and onto Touraine's.

Its tiny claws dug into her flesh, but not painfully. Tempête looked between the two humans as if to say, *Are you happy now?*

"She's beautiful." Touraine stroked a finger along the bird's back. "I never knew you liked animals so much."

As she spoke, though, Touraine remembered Pruett feeding scraps to Qazāli street cats, taking special care for the littlest, saddest-looking ones, the ones that were probably better off drowned.

"You mean..." Pruett closed her eyes, and when she opened them again, they were falcon yellow, the pupils massive, gathering in all the light the night had to offer.

Touraine yelped and stumbled back. Tempête shrieked at the indignity and took wing.

"Sky above, I don't think I'll ever get used to this." Touraine tried to catch her breath.

"You should talk."

"Can you...change like the Taargens?"

"No. I keep asking, but they won't teach me yet. One day. So it's the way of the Many-Legged for now." Pruett followed Tempête's circling above with her eyes.

"You would take someone's soul?"

"You would eat someone's heart?"

"Kiras told me to go for the liver if I have to eat it raw. Easier to chew."

"Ugh. Fuck. Don't tell me anything else." Pruett retched. "Really. Don't. I still want to kiss her."

"Why birds?"

"You know why." Pruett sobered, her voice taking a wistful turn.

"Tell me." Touraine began to walk, and Pruett fell into step beside her. Even though she looked, she couldn't see Tempête in the dark.

"The freedom. No matter where I am, I can always be somewhere else. The rush of the wind against my body—her body—the heights, the speed, the kill. I have a way out."

"Albric says his priests can get trapped if they stay animals for too long."

"Aye, maybe." Pruett sounded not like she didn't care, but like she wouldn't be upset if she did get stuck like that. "Fucks my head if I'm in Tempête too long. Screaming headache, and mice start to look like a good snack. Can't imagine killing her to get my cloak, though."

"It's all changed so much."

"It has." Pruett squeezed Touraine's shoulder. Their first friendly touch since Qazāl. "It's been good. To have you back."

"It's been good to be back," Touraine said around the tightness in her throat.

Touraine hadn't felt this alive in so long. Being with people who had grown up with her... There was home in that. There was home in not being the only god-touched one. Luca could think of magic only for what it offered her, Sabine was terrified of it, and Touraine hated to drag Aranen back into the grief of her loss. Here, though, Touraine was one of many.

Their circuit had taken them around to the horse pickets, where they dodged piles of manure. Pruett patted a rump here and there. As Touraine followed, she recognized the emissary's horse and pointed.

"He hasn't gone back?"

Pruett frowned a moment, then understood. "Ah. Roric sent her a message this morning. Bloody bastards, those Taargen lads. Not surprised the Balladairans went to war with them." She wrinkled her nose. "He was right, though. We needed to send her a warning."

"A warning?" Touraine said sharply. "What's more of a warning than thousands of men and women pointing bayonets at her door?"

"I'd like her to be a bit scared, personally." Pruett halted among the horses. "Touraine. I need to know that you're with us." Her tone was cold and sharp as a blade. "With me. When we break into the palace, I need to trust you at my back."

Touraine sensed more than saw Pruett's hand stray to her belt. Despite all the time that had passed, despite the other people there had been, Touraine still knew Pruett's body around hers. They'd spent their whole lives together. Touraine had known the shape of Pruett's absence as well as she'd known the shape of her body beneath her fingers.

A hand drifting toward a knife in the dark. They were alone, no hostlers, no soldiers. Two old friends in the dark with nothing but a lie between them. Which one of them was faster, these days?

"You can." Touraine brought her empty hands up. "You always can."
Pruett's hand went from her belt to the emissary's horse, stroking its
sleek flank.

Touraine sighed, the tension ebbing from her body. "Promise me
one thing, Pru?"

"Hm?"

"If we can spare her, we do."

Pruett laughed loudly, incredulous, then smothered her mouth with
her hand. "You're serious."

"I am. I know it's hard for you to understand, but . . . you see someone struggling, fighting so hard every day for something. It's hard not
to admire that. Not to love it, a little. That strength." Touraine smiled
ruefully. "Even the way they fail."

"Like you and me?" Pruett said, suddenly bitter, weeds of anger
growing over the inroads they'd made on this walk.

Touraine turned Pruett around by the shoulder. She cupped Pru-
ett's neck with both hands, forcing her to meet her eyes. This close,
Touraine could make out the sullen cant of her mouth, her eyebrows.
"Yeah. Like you and me."

Pruett closed her eyes, and for a moment Touraine thought that
maybe Pruett understood.

"Would you believe me," she continued, "if I told you she made me
feel like I was more than this? More than just blood?"

"More than blood? They think we're fucking savages, Touraine."
Pruett's body went rigid with the force of her words. Her voice shook.
"They treated us like animals. They *made* us with blood. Blood and
steel. I'm still so—I'm so angry all the time, Tour, I don't know how I
can ever be anything else! I want to burn them all down, all the time,
for making me into this!"

"I know." Touraine pulled Pruett closer, wrapping an arm around
her shoulders, pressing Pruett's head against her. She smelled the cigarette smoke on Pruett's breath, in her clothes. Gun oil and animal
musk. "I know. I know."

"You love her," Pruett said, muffled against Touraine's jacket. The
gold one.

The ache hit Touraine so hard that it felt like a bruise in her ribs.

"Something like that," she said hoarsely.

Pruett shook her head against Touraine's chest, then pushed her away. "It's like Cantic all over again."

"What do you mean?"

"You hero-worshipped her, and she manipulated you, manipulated all of us. You were a kid. You didn't know any better."

Touraine recalled the pride she felt when Cantic appraised her, her eagerness. Touraine couldn't say why it had happened, but she knew how she'd felt.

"I loved her, too. And I think in her own fucked-up way, she loved me. Or there was something close enough to love that I latched on. Fed off it. It kept me going."

"Better you didn't go on, then. Better you died than mistake what Cantic gave us for love. You deserve better than that. We all do."

Pruett's ferocity made the horses whinny. She turned from Touraine, hands on her hips. Then she turned abruptly back. "Do you even know what love is?"

The question surprised Touraine, and she let it fall into silence. Felt it settle in the crack in her heart.

"Aye. It's me, here. At your back."

Pruett scoffed, but she didn't meet Touraine's eye. "Love can't fix what Balladaire did to us."

Touraine couldn't argue with that. There had been moments in Luca's arms when Touraine forgot everything bad that had ever happened to her, forgot everything but pleasure and the warmth and safety of Luca's chest beneath her ear. There had been nights when she couldn't forget, and Luca had been there then, too. None of it could be undone. It wouldn't fix Qazāl or Masridān. It wouldn't help Fili and the Fingers. Touraine had thought it could, but then had come Traitor's Corner. Luca's lie. The war. Love was such a paltry bandage.

"I know it can't." Touraine grabbed Pruett by the upper arm, squeezed. "But we can. Come on. You seem like you need a smoke."

CHAPTER 53

A QUEEN'S LIFE

Luca paced before the Royal Oak, willing with all her might for Touraine to come to her. For Touraine to stalk through the maze and emerge at its heart to sit beside her beneath the full foliage above. It was the perfect night. The heart of the Rose Maze was fragrant with fresh roses blooming in the hedges. The sliver of a moon was high; it would vanish tomorrow. Stars twinkled between scattered cloud cover.

Touraine was *supposed* to come. She had promised, before she left, to leave the Taargens before they attacked La Chaise.

Too much, it seemed, had changed in their time apart.

Luca knelt at the roots of the great tree. Deniaud waited at the entrance to the garden's heart. Luca tugged out the slim boot knife she'd worn almost every day since Gil had given it to her. It was so small, she often forgot it was there. The steel gleamed. She pressed it against her thumb, and it sliced off skin without drawing blood. Her blood would be a match for Bastien's, that gruesome red scarf more precious than silk. She clutched his grief ring on her finger.

If she made this sacrifice, here at the foot of the oak of kings, her grief rings would stay with her body. That was tradition. It was courtesy. She had made her decision before she'd even got to the garden. The iron weight in her stomach when she read the story of the second prince.

It wasn't until she was in the garden that she realized Nicolas was as much a prince as she was. His blood could have watered the tree instead of hers. And so, in the end, he was right, was always right—she wasn't thoughtful enough, wasn't careful. Perhaps he was right about all of it.

Where did a queen's life hang in the balance of her kingdom?

It was nothing, compared to the safety of her people. Touraine was nothing. Sabine was nothing.

It was everything.

And so what, if another part of her thought, *Yes, yes. It would be so much easier. So much better to be gone.* So what, if that voice had sung to her for weeks? *For months.*

Luca had put together the old texts: the slit palms joined together in the wedding ritual, the children sacrificed for good harvests, the golden prince. Long ago, there had been a ceremony every year during the harvest where the king or queen shed their blood over the Royal Oak, and the nobility followed suit, swearing fealty. That hadn't happened in generations—maybe centuries. But she couldn't be sure her theories were correct, that the Withering was the god's debt come due. She had only this desperate prayer, so she offered it here.

Luca touched the rough bark. The Royal Oak was centuries old, at least, older than the lords Ancier for a certainty. Fed by the blood of kings and queens, it had grown strong, tall, thick. She wished she could say the tree thrummed with power, with an unnatural warmth. A promise that this was the right choice, and some magic of Balladaire would kindle into being. She felt nothing.

But the crown, another part of her protested. *All she had sacrificed!*

Her sacrifices had kept her here, for this moment. How much blood she had spilled already, to be stronger for this kingdom—the blood of Qazāli rebels in El-Wast, Touraine's and Djasha's and all the Balladairans who fought in her name, like Cantic and even that shit of a man, Rogan; all the Balladairans who'd fled for safety as sickness spread through the colony; Bastien, whom she did not love, but who had helped her with so little thanks; Tiro, sweet Tiro who had never done anything wrong, innocent of all his father's crimes until perhaps one day, the day he might have learned to pick them up; Madame Béryl and Nicolas's schoolmistress both, gone to their royal game of échecs as easily as pawns and forgotten almost as soon; the woman Luca had killed with her own red, sticking hands to take her throne from Nicolas, and Lanquette, who had given his life to save Luca's, and Gil, who had given his life to save Touraine's, which was very much like saving Luca's, and now Ghislaine, and now Mareau, now Nicolas himself. Luca had even shed her own blood for this wretched, beautiful place that was hers, choking on it, coughing it up on the dais as she abdicated for the good of the empire.

Nothing was worth more than her kingdom. Not even her.

With that acceptance, Luca embraced the silence of the night. The solitude. The damp earth seeped into the knees of her trousers. Deniaud checked on her and Luca sent her back. She toyed with the blade, letting it hover over the bare skin of her wrists. The blue green of her veins pulsed, quiescent. Her forearm was already ribbed with scars from her failed attempts to call forth Qazāli magic.

Luca was stalling.

She wished she could see Touraine again.

Footsteps crunched on the dirt path behind Luca.

She startled and turned, grimacing at the spasm in her hip. Through the manic, half-awake blur of her vision, she brought her dagger up before her in an ungainly crouch. It wasn't an assassin come to slay her the night before the siege, nor was it Touraine. Above, the sky was the empty gray of pre-dawn, just pale enough for her to see that she'd been out here all night.

"I was looking for you." Sabine approached tentatively, as if afraid Luca would bolt.

"What for?" Luca asked, hoarse.

"You weren't in your rooms." Sabine knelt beside Luca and took the dagger out of Luca's corpse-stiff fingers and folded Luca against her. She held Luca's arm up to the light. A thin score of red crossed her wrist where Luca had almost but not quite committed to her course of action. Smaller lines, where she had shivered and jerked.

Sabine hissed. "What are you doing out here?"

"I killed him. Nicolas. He's dead."

Luca felt Sabine's breath stop in her chest. Then, after a long moment, Sabine let it out.

"Good riddance. But why are you here? With this?" The dagger was hilariously small in Sabine's large hand.

Luca laughed at the absurdity. "Praying for a miracle."

"Did you get it?"

"No."

Sabine ran her thumb along Luca's wrist gently, then took Luca's hands in both of hers.

"Don't leave me alone with this, Luca." She looked away, blinking rapidly. "The thought that you might have been gone when I got back to La Chaise—"

"It's the only way to save Balladaire."

"From what?"

"From the plague. The Taargens. I understand it now. The god wants blood." Luca looked down at her wrist and then at the rich dark earth at the base of the oak. "My blood."

"It— By the sky ab— *Your* blood? Ugh!" Sabine threw her gaze to the sky in exasperation, to the splayed branches above. "You two are so alike, it's infuriating. Who said you were so special, hein?"

"I'm the queen—"

"If this is real, Luca, *if*, why would the god give a steaming shit who you are? You aren't even the first royal house of Balladaire, so I doubt you've been chosen by the god as some— What did they used to call them? Saint? How would the god know your blood from one of the hostler lads?"

"I— Saint. Hm." The word was odd on Luca's tongue. She had seen it once or twice, in the old story books Sabine had brought. To be holy, to be as kin to the god. "Maybe it doesn't matter who I am. It only matters that I'm willing."

"Willing to what? Abandon your country when we need you most? I'm quite certain a queen on the throne when the bearfucking army arrives is going to be a lot more important than bleeding out in the sky-falling royal gardens."

"You just said I wasn't special." Luca raised an eyebrow pointedly and crossed her arms. "And in case you haven't noticed, my city is rioting in the streets right now against my name."

"Not—not like that," Sabine said. "You are still the queen. We need

a leader. No, don't look at me. We both know I'm not fit. But you are."
She put a hand to Luca's cheek.

Even as she countered Sabine, Luca's resolve ebbed away. In its place
rose her fear of facing the magnitude of all that Sabine described.
Luca closed her eyes against Sabine's palm. It twitched, then steadied.

"I thought she would come back, Sab," Luca whispered past the
ache in her throat.

"There's been no other message?"

"Nothing since...the emissary." Luca pushed out of the embrace.
"We need to continue the evacuations. Get the servants to safety, send
Aliez to the hospital tents—"

"Of course. I—should say—I was looking for you to tell you, I was
having a drink with Aliez. She's not handling any of this well."

"Is anyone?" Luca muttered.

Sabine huffed softly. "She was visiting some of the d'Orséan
wounded, and they told her that the Travers soldiers weren't there.
They never arrived at the battle, that's why they were so badly outnumbered." Sabine's gaze was dark and steady. "That's why they lost."

"Travers," Luca breathed. "We have to arrest him."

Was he a traitor, or simply saving his own skin, a coward, unwilling
to make the sacrifices?

"He's already gone."

Luca swore.

"Shall I hunt him down? He can't have gone far, he was at the war
council this morning." Sabine glanced at the pale sky. "Yesterday
morning, rather."

Luca inhaled slowly. Exhaled.

"Let him go. We need everyone we have for the assault. Assume the
palace is compromised."

"They'll come today?" Sabine's beautiful dark eyes were tight at the
corners and shadowed beneath. Luca missed the mischief that once
played so readily there, when the lines came from laughter instead of
worry.

"Today. Tomorrow." Luca pushed Sabine's hair back behind her ear.
"It's so long now."

Sabine smiled and shook her head so that her dark hair fell back across her brow and into her eyes, her old charm glinting through. "Do you like it?"

In answer, Luca toyed with the hair at Sabine's nape and kissed her gently, fondly.

Leaning on each other for support, they returned to the palace to face a day Luca hadn't thought she would see.

PART 4

BY THE SWORD

CHAPTER 54

THE TRAITOR

They attacked in the dark of the new moon.

The walls of La Chaise stretched up against the night sky, the old stone blocks so thick that weathering barely seemed to have taken a toll. Nothing like the ancient walls in Qazāl. These fit together so tightly that, if not for treachery, it would be impossible to get in. Treachery, though, had given Pruett and Roric the discreet wooden door in the eastern wall, for messengers on royal duties to make their way.

They were met at the door by a Balladairan in dark, nondescript clothing. Touraine didn't recognize him, but he spoke with the cultured accent of a noble's servant. He wore no livery, bore no soldier's stripes. Even his face was plain: dark hair, dark eyes, dark beard close to his chin.

Pruett pressed a coin into his palm, and he made it vanish, quick as a street magician.

"Follow slow." The man held up two fingers. "Small groups."

Roric gave his orders to his squads of Taargens, and they trickled through, silent as wolves padding on the forest floor. Some headed toward the gate towers in the wall; they would take the Balladairan guards by surprise and open the gates to the rest of the Taargen army. By morning, the city would have fallen.

The rest of them broke into ragged bands of twos and threes, the better to look like friends staggering home in the middle of the night.

Touraine kept close to Pruett and Kiras, but she couldn't help stealing glimpses of the city she'd grown to know so well. La Chaise had changed since she arrived on that boat from Qazāl.

The wild nights of light and laughter were gone. Lanterns guttered outside homes and shops only sporadically, and no lamplighters ran up and down the streets to keep them on. Almost all the doors were slashed with great white Xs. No music in the streets, no performers in the squares. The Withering had taken more than the people; it had sucked the soul from La Chaise sure as any Taargen priest.

New broadsides had been pasted on the walls, too, replacing the insulting drawings of Luca and the hanging. Touraine stopped to skim one.

A girl on the gallows with a crown of some kind of flower, holding a noose in one hand and beckoning Touraine closer.

"Come on." Pruett yanked Touraine's vest, and Touraine stumbled after.

Fili. The girl had to be Fili.

"Pruett," Touraine started, when they were close to the palace. There had been too few guards.

"Shh."

Touraine gripped Pruett's shoulder and pressed her mouth to Pruett's ear. "We need to be careful. Balladaire has a god—we don't know what Luca's capable of right now."

"We have it under control." Pruett shook her off and pointed between the two of them and jerked her thumb back at Roric. He was walking arm in arm with Henrir. They'd tucked their animal heads away so that the cloaks looked less Taargen, but in the late-spring warmth, they hardly blended in. "Between us, I think we can take anything she's got. What's she going to do, tickle us with rose petals? That what you two got up to?"

"Don't start," Touraine muttered.

Pruett waved her off.

At the palace, their escort led them around to another suspiciously unguarded entrance onto the grounds and into a servants' door.

It shouldn't have been this easy.

The man knocked a pattern on the door and waited.

Nothing happened.

The man frowned and knocked the pattern again.

"Something wrong?" Pruett fingered the bayonet at her hip.

The stranger glanced over his shoulder, and Touraine saw the first flicker of worry on his unremarkable face. "Someone else is supposed to let us in."

"But they're not here." Pruett's voice hardened.

Touraine pulled Pruett back by the arm. "I told you. We should go back. Something isn't right. Isn't this why you wanted me here? I *know* Luca."

Pruett glared at her. "Roric, help us out, would you?"

"It is my happiness." Prince Roric ushered their escort out of the way with one large arm, then kicked the door by the knob.

It rattled loud enough to call every guard within a hundred yards, but none came. Again, and the wood began to crack. Face flushed, Roric kicked once more. With a crack like thunder, the door splintered at the handle and swung open.

"After you, Qā'id, Prince Consort." Roric grinned and bowed smugly.

Pruett rolled her eyes and stepped inside the dark servants' corridor, holding one of her pistols ready. "Pleasure. *Pleasure* is the word you want." She looked to the stranger. "Now where?"

The man ducked his head. "I wasn't supposed to go farther than this, sirs."

Pruett scoffed. "Go, then."

But Roric exchanged a look with Henrir, who caught the man with a forearm around the neck, squeezing him to his chest. A silent gasp, and the man struggled, kicking his feet against Henrir's shins as he suffocated. The wolf priest didn't flinch, his face impassive for the long moments it took for their guide to go unconscious.

"I may need him," Henrir said in Taargen, as he tossed the man over his shoulder.

Pruett scowled at the men, then turned to Touraine. "If she knew she'd been betrayed, where would she be?"

The question made Touraine's heart beat heavily in her throat, a lump she couldn't swallow around.

If Luca were frightened, she might hide in her rooms. She hadn't been frightened in a long while. Not like that. Since her coronation, she'd marched brazenly into the places that scared her, chin held high. Traitor's Corner, Le Fontinard, even the court—

"Touraine?" There was a warning note in Pruett's voice.

"In her office, probably."

Touraine started to lead them, but Pruett pulled her by the back of her hood. Pruett's eyes closed, and she flinched as if in pain. The line between her thick eyebrows deepened. Then she sighed and shook herself like a wet dog.

"No, she's not." Pruett looked around her as her eyes came back into focus. "Follow me."

"What was that?" Touraine whispered.

"Rats. They're nosy fuckers and they know everything."

Touraine shuddered. She and the others followed Pruett into the main corridors. The Taargens and Masridāni crept as quietly as they could, but it was hard to hide the clatter of a platoon's worth of guns and swords and clicking boots and muttering, and still no one came to stop them. Soon, she realized where they were going, and it made sense. If Luca knew she'd been betrayed, she would go to where she felt strongest. She would want to make a point—that she wasn't scared and held all the power she needed.

Outside the Grand Hall, between the two plinths with their rearing horses that framed the tall doors, Touraine hesitated. She could imagine the scene within: Luca, pacing in front of the throne. Her soldiers arrayed before her. The way she'd glance at the oversized clock on the wall, waiting and waiting and waiting.

"Pruett." Touraine wedged herself between Pruett and the gleaming gold door handle. "This is a trap."

Pruett raised her pistol and Roric his sword. The others leveled rifles and blades alike. Some faced the Hall doors, but others faced the corridors. Henrir was already rippling and shifting, their traitor guide limp on the marble floor, eyes staring. The short man grew taller and hairier and hunched—as if the cloak around his shoulders were devouring him. Then there was no sign of the man, only the wolf.

Finally, Touraine heard the sound she'd been dreading. Boots, dozens of marching boots behind them.

"Aye." Pruett smirked. "We've already sprung it."

Confused, Touraine held her hand up, about to speak, when Pruett shoved her out of the way and pulled the door's handle.

Touraine saw, for one brief moment, a tableau different from what she expected, but also the same:

Luca in front of the throne, gold circlet gleaming in her golden hair, soldiers fanned around her. Sabine, at her right hand.

Gunshots tore through the air from the throne room and from their rear. Touraine hip-checked Pruett to the side, out of the line of fire, ducking and rolling for cover as gunfire tore through plaster and bounced off marble. With her back against the left plinth, she paused to catch her breath. Beside Touraine, Pruett devolved into swearing in every language she knew. Henrir the wolf launched himself onto one of the soldiers in the Great Hall as Roric and the Taargens followed. Then the shrieks of horror and confusion.

"Sky above," Touraine swore under her breath.

She could spare them none of her pity. The palace guard had them surrounded, clogging up the corridor from both ends. Pruett's squads of Masridāni couldn't hold their own against a dozen of the palace's best, let alone two dozen. Touraine poked her head out. Commander Perrot led them, shouting orders as the guards ran forward, swords drawn, half cloaks fluttering. A noble charge. For a moment, Touraine locked eyes with Perrot. Her friend. His lips twisted in disgust and he came for her.

Kiras was not waiting. Under cover of Henrir's transformation, she'd snuck to the poor guide and pulled him behind the plinth opposite Touraine and Pruett. The guide's stomach was open, his entrails spilled.

"With me?" Pruett's hand was tight on her wrist. Stormy eyes waited for an answer.

"Always." Touraine stood and drew her sword, and together, she and Pruett emerged from the plinth, Pruett's pistols discharging one after the other. Touraine met Commander Perrot's charge with a wild yell. He was not a good swordsman, but neither was he the coward he'd once told her he was. As he cut down at her, she caught his blade on the hilt of her own sword and angled her point at his throat.

"Surrender, Perrot."

"Kill me," he snarled.

She hesitated, and in that hesitation, he dropped his sword and pushed Touraine's aside. A moment later, her own sword clattered to the ground and he was on top of her, his bulk stealing the air from her lungs, impossible to move. Touraine swung her leg up into his groin and he wheezed, curling in on himself. She rolled away as he fell aside, and snagged her sword off the ground, then clubbed him in the side of the head.

The Masridāni had been forced backward, into the Grand Hall. Within it, Henrir's snarls and the sloppy wet crunch of bone were matched by the snarls of Roric's human soldiers. No battle cry could cover up the high-pitched scream, abruptly cut off, or the triumphant howl that followed.

CHAPTER 55

BOUND (REPRISE)

The great wolf was upon Deniaud before Luca understood what she was seeing.

"No!" Luca screamed.

The guard barely made a sound before the wolf's jaws clamped upon her chest and shook. Then it threw Deniaud limp to the ground and snarled at the rest of the palace guard fanned out before the dais. Another desperate round of fire, every shot trained at the beast, while Roric's soldiers came at them, swords raised. The blood flowing down its flanks didn't slow it.

The bear god's magic, as real as anything Touraine had ever done.

Outside the Grand Hall, the fighting was just as pitched, and the palace guard pushed the invaders into the Hall on their heels.

Luca had guessed that the Taargens would use their traitor to sneak into the palace. Still, she wanted to keep as many soldiers as possible on the walls, the better to protect her people from the greater army. Perrot had offered to stop them at the servants' exit, but when he told her how small the force was, Luca had chosen to wait, like a spider in the heart of a web. Entice them. Trap them. Her guards had begged her to flee, but she refused to surrender the palace. Where would be safe if the Taargens defeated La Chaise?

If Luca had hoped that Touraine would stop this, she was paying for that hope now.

"Are you with me, Sabine?" Luca unclicked her rapier from her cane and stepped down the dais, willing her legs to hold. She still did not feel as strong as she wished.

"Always." Sabine's voice trembled, but Luca felt her close behind. She was grateful.

Luca joined her guards in the line they had made, sticking her narrow blade through the gaps between them, finding the unprotected necks and eyes while Roric's soldiers wrestled with the palace guards. Sabine stayed close, her flash and flourish traded for deadly economy. They couldn't hold. The palace soldiers in the corridor couldn't break through to help, not with Roric's wolf guarding the door.

Then a gap opened up in front of Luca. The Balladairan soldier she'd been hiding behind lay on the ground, his skull split across the eyes.

"Oh, sky above." She backpedaled until she felt the dais at her heels. The Taargen in front of her grinned.

He thrust his thick sword at her and she countered, barely catching the edge of his blade on the strong of her own and redirecting it. Enough leverage to hold him away as her own point found his throat. He went slack in surprise, and she thrust twice more to make sure he would stay dead.

It was Traitor's Corner, all over again.

It had been a mistake, not giving herself to Balladaire's god last night. She would die here, her blood pooling on the marble, like Deniaud's, like Mareau's and Nicolas's had on the bridge. Useless.

Roric and his soldiers pushed the dwindling palace guard closer together. Sabine was at Luca's side now, her eyes wide and breath heavy, but when Roric advanced on Luca, Sabine intercepted him without hesitation.

Luca focused on protecting Sabine's flank from another Taargen in a dun-fur mantle laced with bits of antler. The Taargen cut in with his bloody saber and Luca parried and lunged into the gap below, but the antlered man curled his sword back around before she could pierce him. He swept her blade aside—or rather, he tried. As soon as his blade was displaced, she flicked beneath his and lunged again. This time, the thrust took him in the stomach.

Luca looked for Sabine, for Roric. They were making a dance of it, the two of them, but neither of them could take the edge. Sabine was quick, her blade work clever, but Roric was too bullish for her cleverness and she was too quick for him to catch with his strength. Sabine's face was taut with the effort.

The antler man's bellow of rage pulled Luca back. He swung his sword down, a cleaving blow too strong for Luca to parry. With her cane to balance her, Luca staggered aside, pulling her left leg back and leaving a void for his sword to find. She struck as soon as his powerful blow was too far for him to recover, sinking her rapier deep into his eye.

Luca pulled her blade from him, sagging under sudden exhaustion. The Withering had truly wrecked her, but she stumbled toward Sabine and Roric.

She saw the spasm take over Sabine's right side, jerking her face, her shoulder, locking her hand inflexibly around the hilt of her sword. Roric's parry knocked the blade free from her uncontrolled fingers, and Luca found the strength to run the few paces between them.

"Sabine!"

As Roric reversed his parry to cut down at Sabine's right side, Luca barreled into it with her guard high, putting herself between the two of them, shoving Sabine behind her.

"Luca!" Sabine yelled from the ground.

Luca stared down the blade of Roric's sword, from where the point hovered at her throat, all the way to his eyes. He was breathing heavily, triumphant.

"Balladaire! I have your queen!"

In the corridor, the fighting only intensified as the palace guard struggled to break through. Crunching bone and tearing flesh silenced more than a few battle cries as the wolf ripped into the brave who made it into the Grand Hall.

"Cousin Roric." Luca made herself appear cool and unbothered. She still had her rapier, and if she was going to die here, she would take at least one of them with her. "I found your traitor. Evrard."

"Cousin Luca!" Roric's voice was jovial and deep. It echoed through the chamber without cracking. Little Roric, not so little anymore. "I brought friends."

Just as Luca was about to angle her blade into the pit of his arm, he stepped back and to the side, gesturing behind him.

Luca's heart filled her throat.

Pruett, that bitch from Qazāl, sauntered in with a pistol in one hand and the other on a belt knife. She wore another pistol in a holster on her chest. To her right, a golden-eyed woman with shoulder-length dark curls on one side of her head and a shaved temple at the other. Her lips shone moist, a trickle of red staining one corner of her mouth. And on Pruett's other side—

"I'm afraid you're wrong, Your Majesty." Pruett gave a mocking bow. "Here's your traitor."

Touraine held the sword Luca had given her as a wedding gift as she came in, scanning the room. She was lean and wolfish again, her muscled arms bare in a black Shālan vest, a red hood. When she turned her hollow-eyed gaze on Luca, she gave her a sad, crooked smile. The hope inside Luca snuffed out.

"Hold," Luca called. The fighting at the doors faltered, then stopped.

"Bind the guards," Touraine ordered. "Arrest the queen."

Luca had never truly heard Touraine in her element. When she spoke, the Taargens gave only a glance to their prince, who nodded. They obeyed her, disarming the palace guard in the corridor and the few remaining in the Grand Hall.

This was how it was to be, then.

"Wife." Luca curled her lip and filled the words with all the court disdain she could. "You've been gone so long. Tell me truthfully. Did you enjoy it, burning down Balladaire? Was it all just vengeance?"

Touraine's mouth twitched, but her gaze slid over Luca like a stranger's. "We'll throw her in Le Fontinard until we figure out the best way to use her. Might earn us goodwill from the people; they certainly don't love her."

Honest, if brutal.

Luca pointed her rapier at the soldiers closing in on her. The wolf prowled close. Only Sabine stood at her back. Luca lunged and heard Sabine take her cue. Luca took one man in the groin before Roric and the others disarmed her, shoving her to her knees and wrenching her arms back behind her.

Chest heaving, she faced Touraine and the qā'id. She shook her head to reposition her crown.

"No." The asshole lieutenant who was now qā'id looked Luca over with disdain and stroked the butt of her pistol with her thumb. "Best way to use the bitch is to kill her. Show them her head if you need to. Royalty's like roaches, don't you remember your stories? Full of lost princes and true queens coming back all heroic. They can't come back if they're dead."

"That's not necessary, Pruett." Touraine's command seemed to falter. "The people love a spectacle. We'll give them one when the time is right."

Luca laughed darkly. " 'It's not necessary,' she says, offering her wife to the masses for sport." She wanted Touraine to look at her again. She wanted to scream at her. She wanted to say that she was sorry for Traitor's Corner. For Moyenne, for everything. It was far too late for apologies.

"Quiet," Pruett snapped. Then: "I think it is necessary, Touraine. Very necessary indeed."

The look Pruett gave Touraine was barely subdued rage, and Luca wondered if she hadn't misread this entire moment.

Touraine met Pruett with her own cold growl. "You promised."

"You made me a promise, Touraine."

"I've kept it. From Moyenne to La Chaise, I brought you here."

"Finish it, then. Here. Now. If not, I'll do it myself."

Pruett came over and pointed the gun to Luca's head.

Luca refused to piss herself. If she was—if she was going to die—
Oh, sky above. She jerked at the arms of her restraining guards, but they were like irons. She sought Touraine's eyes again, but Touraine had learned the lessons of the court too well. If Luca was going to die today, this dull-eyed mask was all she would see.

"Wait!" Luca said. "What about my people? What will happen to them? They don't deserve any of this."

"You self-righteous bitch." Pruett backhanded Luca so hard that Luca sagged in her captors' hands. "*Your people* are as guilty as you. Don't pretend they didn't know what you did. As if they didn't take every advantage of the colonies that they could. As if they don't look down on us."

Luca righted herself and spat blood on the marble at Pruett's boots. "What will you do, then? Raze the whole country? Turn them into slaves? How will you get your revenge, *Qā'id?*"

Pruett sneered down at her. "Touraine. Put me out of my misery."

"El-Qazāli, don't do it!" Sabine shouted from between the Taargens holding her.

"Shut her up," Pruett said, without turning from Touraine. "Well, *El-Qazāli?*"

Luca heard the thud of fist on soft body, the grunt of air rushing out to return only in wheezing gasps, but she didn't dare turn from Touraine, either. *Say no,* she begged Touraine silently.

Touraine joined them, looking Luca up and down. Indifferent. Maybe even disappointed. No help would come from this quarter; Touraine had barely blinked when Pruett hit her.

"I made you a promise," Touraine said under her breath.

She drew her knife, and more insulting than heartbreaking, it was the knife that Luca had given her in Qazāl. For a blissful, catastrophic moment, Luca thought Touraine would take the knife and plunge it into the qā'id's chest.

"El-Qazāli, you fucking bastard! Don't you dare—" Another series of thuds, longer this time. Then what sounded like Sabine dropping to the floor. Still, she groaned pitifully, "Don't. Please."

The cold steel Touraine put to Luca's neck was the realest thing there was in the whole world. It had been so long since Touraine's face had been this close to hers. Longer still since she'd seen her wear her face of blank, hopeless obedience. It was a tell if nothing else was. Touraine didn't want to do this. And yet, here she was, with Luca at her mercy. How many orders had she followed, precisely like this? She wouldn't even meet Luca's eyes. That told Luca enough.

She straightened and lifted her chin to give Touraine's blade more room.

"I would die at your hands before anyone else's," Luca said softly, aiming once more for a weakness in the armor.

Touraine inhaled sharp and shuddering.

There it was. A crack. Then her blade bit into Luca's neck. But if there was a crack, Luca could widen it.

"Wait!" Luca's throat bobbed against the metal. "Spill my blood in the garden. At the foot of the oak. Where you agreed to marry me."

Another spasm crossed Touraine's face before she closed herself off again.

"Let my death mean something for my people, at least."

Touraine frowned. "The magic?"

Luca nodded against the blade. The walk from the throne room to the heart of the Queen's Garden was long enough for Pruett and her mélange of soldiers to make mistakes. For Luca and Sabine to escape, with Touraine's help. She searched Touraine's face for a sign that she understood.

There was only an intense concentration that Luca couldn't read.

Pruett growled her irritation. "We don't have time for this shit, Touraine."

"We should do it." Touraine withdrew the knife. Tucked its blade against her forearm. "It's to do with the plague, I think. Sacrifices are important here, like the Taargens and with Shāl."

"It is." Luca couldn't help adding tartly, "Unless you want to take over a country with a plague that's eating up the population?"

Pruett sucked her teeth, considering. "You seriously believe this?"

"Yeah." Touraine sighed. "Yeah, I do. And our soldiers will keep succumbing, too, if we don't fix it." She jerked her head at the soldiers holding Luca and Sabine. "Follow me. Hold them tight."

This time, the soldiers didn't obey Touraine until they got firm assent from both the prince and the qā'id. The soldiers frog-marched Luca through the corridors, and without her cane, she was forced to limp awkwardly between them, missing whole steps where they scraped her along the ground. Beside her, Sabine struggled gamely until they hit her hard enough that she vomited and they had to drag her the rest of the way.

No signal came from Touraine, and anger, bitter as gall, soured Luca's stomach. At least, she consoled herself as they walked through the maze, her mother's roses were in bloom.

They stopped her in front of the Royal Oak. It was so large and old that even in the darkness the soldiers couldn't help but look up in awe. It held Luca, too, if for a different reason.

This is for you, if you're listening at all.

Luca took advantage of their distraction and jerked herself free. Not to run, though, no. She wouldn't be stabbed in the back or shot running. She was queen for a little longer yet.

"*Coward*," she snarled as she knelt at Touraine's feet.

She sought Sabine one last time. Her friend dangled from her captors' arms, her handsome face crumpled ugly with sobbing and swelling. A cut bled where the tip of Roric's blade had barely missed her right eye.

Then Luca bared her throat to Touraine. In that moment of surrender, her anger receded. Not all of it, but enough to see Touraine's chest rising and falling faster, to see her hand shaking on the knife she held.

"We always knew this was one possible end, didn't we?" Luca's voice was perhaps calmer than it should have been.

She waited, hoping that Touraine would say something, anything. She hated herself for it, but she still wanted to hear Touraine again. *Her* Touraine.

She was never yours. You never owned her, no matter your leverage.

But Luca had been *hers*.

Touraine remained silent and Luca wouldn't beg. She held her palms out to her sides, brushing the edges of her boots.

Touraine knelt in front of her, reaching with her empty hand for Luca's neck, as if to pull her into a kiss, as she had so many perfect times before. Luca wished she could remember them all. She wished she never had to think about them again.

Soon. But she was queen for a little longer yet.

Luca yanked the small knife from her boot and drove it up into Touraine's sides. Touraine roared, jerking away. As Luca pulled back and thrust again, the world went bright. A fist or a boot. Then a jutting root and more stars across her vision. She heard shouting behind her, but her world narrowed to the heavy, achingly familiar weight on top of her. She pushed and scratched, trying to get the knife back into position, but Touraine twisted her wrist until the bones popped and she wrested the blade away.

Luca's sight came back in a spotty blur. Touraine straddled her, pinning both of Luca's wrists above her head. The handle of Touraine's knife dug into Luca's forearm, and Touraine's knee crushed her thigh, shooting pain up and down the leg. Their chests heaved hot breath in tandem.

The shouts turned to jeering. Like this was a street brawl and all the odds taken were against her. She jerked her hips, enough to slide one thigh free and aim the knee where she had already stabbed Touraine. Touraine grunted, muscles tightening all over. Luca did it again, scrambling to get her hand between them, to push Touraine off and crawl away, but Touraine's grip was like iron. She wedged her forearm against Luca's throat and pressed it up, up into Luca's chin until she gagged. Luca's hands were trapped between their bodies.

"Stop, Shāl damn your eyes. Stop fighting me."

Luca was so surprised to hear Touraine's voice—*begging* her—that she obeyed.

"Touraine?" she breathed. "Why?"

Touraine opened her mouth, then grimaced. Her forearm pressed harder into Luca's throat. In the end, though, she said nothing.

Luca grunted against the grinding force on her windpipe. "Please, just...if you ever loved me at all, make it quick." Her eyes fluttered shut and she felt the shame of tears falling from her eyelashes to slide, scalding, down her cheeks.

The knife thrust into Luca without warning, so sharp that she felt no pain. At first. Her eyes shot open and her gasp came mostly from shock. She even felt the knife jar into the roots underneath her. Pain built like a wave: first sharp and burning, then deep and rippling like the cramps of her menses, until it was almost all.

Almost all. Because it was not pain alone that held her here. It wasn't her blood dripping from the blade, from her wound, and into the earth. It wasn't the metallic smell of that earth or the trunk of the god's oak. It wasn't Sabine's howl of grief. There was also Touraine.

Touraine, with a face of stone. Hard jaw, hard frown, hard eyes that shimmered like a mirage beneath a sheen of unshed tears. Her warm brown skin speckled with the red of Luca's choking breath. The touch of Touraine's hand, though, was soft despite the calluses. A warm caress at the bare nape of Luca's neck.

Luca imagined Touraine's voice whispering, "I'm sorry."

Luca pulled her close and held her tight. She shut her eyes and saw Touraine's face, upturned and laughing in the snow.

CHAPTER 56

A STAIN

Pruett itched for a cigarette.

"You fucking monster! You animals!" that blubbering noble screamed again, the cords of her neck taut as she sobbed at Touraine. Blood sheeted down one side of her face.

Touraine ignored it. She ignored them all, even Pruett. Instead, she sat on her heels, holding the queen's body in her arms. The knife had been plunged blade first into the dirt, the bloody handle gleaming ruby bright. The queen's circlet had fallen nearby. Touraine's face was dry, but her breath came in shuddering hitches. Call it the wound in her side, sure—that had surprised Pruett; seems the queen had a pair on her after all—but there was a tightness in her mouth and eyes that Pruett knew all too well. She'd loved Touraine once. She'd held her when she cried—and when she was trying not to.

Without warning, Touraine stood, lifting the queen with her. She winced, favoring her side as she carried the queen to the other noble.

Pruett kept close, pistol half-raised in case the prisoner went feral. Pruett also wanted to see—this woman who had given her so much grief. This woman who had stolen Touraine from her. This woman who had all the power in the world, who could have had anything else—but she'd taken the one thing Pruett had ever given a shit about. Pruett had never wanted a command. She hadn't cared if the Balladairans saw her as equal or not. She wasn't even bothered if they kept fighting. She'd only wanted her friends.

That woman was stiffening, growing paler by the second. Blood stained her lips, her blond hair, blood on her hands, blood soaking her cream chemise worth more than a year of a Sand's salary. Her legs flopped grotesquely with Touraine's swaying steps.

"You want her back so bad," Touraine grunted, "take her. Let her body keep you company until we're ready for you."

Touraine jerked her head at the soldiers holding the woman, and before the woman could run or throw a punch, Touraine dropped the dead queen in her arms.

At first, the noblewoman—and she was a noblewoman, Pruett could tell by the shocked outrage that anything dared go remotely against her wishes—stared open-mouthed, silent, at the closed eyes, the unmoving chest. Then she bared her teeth at Touraine.

"How could you? *How could you?* She loved you." She kept repeating herself, but her voice grew muffled as she pressed her face against the corpse's neck. She held the queen close, heedless of the blood seeping into her own fine clothes. *She loved you, how could you, she loved you. She loved you.*

If the words made an impact, Touraine gave no sign.

To the Taargens who'd been holding the woman, Touraine said, "Escort her to her rooms. Let her mourn a bit before the smell sets in. No one in or out but us."

"You sure, Tour?" Pruett muttered as Touraine brushed past her.

Touraine didn't answer. Roric tried to clap Touraine on the shoulder, a boyish grin on his face, but she dipped beneath his hand and went back to the tree. She yanked the knife out of the earth, scooped up the crown, then followed the soldiers and the noblewoman into the palace.

"What's wrong with her?" Roric said. He clapped once. "We were victorious! She struck the final hit!"

"You mean the final blow," she corrected. "Don't be a dick. That was her wife after all."

Not that Pruett's own back didn't shiver all up and down with the frisson of victory. *She* had beaten the queen of Balladaire.

But she'd broken Touraine to do it.

"Send a runner to the men at the walls. Tell them the queen is dead and offer amnesty for those who surrender. I'll check on Touraine."

"Amnesty?" Roric said, confused.

"Aye. Mercy, like."

"I know what amnesty means. I just don't like it. Not here. Not for enemy soldiers when we occupy their city."

"You're young, Prince. Trust me when I say, if you occupy a city, everyone's an enemy soldier. And you sure as shit can't kill them all."

Touraine forced herself to walk down the familiar paths to her own room. She didn't let herself follow Durfort and her Taargen guards. Didn't let herself look at Luca's body once she'd dumped her in Durfort's arms.

Step after impossible step. She flexed and unflexed her fingers, unsticking them from their bloody hold on the knife. Bloody mud soaked through her trousers from the knee down, and her clothes were soaked with a mix of her and Luca's blood. Copper and iron, she smelled like.

The crown was glued to her other hand, its leaves and decorative thorns sharp in the meat of her palm. The marriage scar was pale and glistening among the red.

Her rooms were empty. No Ghadin. No Aranen. She'd read in Luca's books that there were places, long ago and far away, where a person was buried in a room made to look like their rooms in life. That's what these rooms felt like—the life of a dead person, left unchanged while the corpse rotted away.

Surprisingly, there was still water in the jug by her basin. It smelled stale, fetid, like the edge of a pond. She poured it into the fine washbasin. Beautiful porcelain painted with an orchard of trees and a chevalier reaching up to pluck a tiny fruit. She wondered if Luca had had any say in that choice. It was the kind of thing she would have picked.

The tink-tink of the knife against the bowl was all that told Touraine her hands were shaking as she plunged her hands into the water. Soften the blood. She tried to steady them. Overcorrected. The knife and crown, loosened, both splashed into the water. She jerked her hands out of the way so she wouldn't cut herself—*what did it matter, a cut, after this?*

The bowl tipped, sloshing water everywhere as it rocked and spun. She tried to catch it. Clipped it instead, hands disobedient, reflexes too slow, coordination shot. Touraine clutched empty air as the bowl crashed against the ground, shattering the little chevalier to pieces. She followed, crunching the fine ceramic pieces with her dirty, blood-stained knees.

She stared at the shards between her clawed hands and tensed them harder, as if she could pull the fucking air apart. Better than letting out whatever this was that wanted to rip through her.

Touraine doubled over trying to hold it in, and gasped in pain as she was reminded, ha! Luca had gotten her, too, a few fingerwidths short of being fatal. It hurt. She pressed her fist into it, gritting her teeth, pressing harder and harder until it pulled a groan from her lips. Sky above, it hurt. She should clean it. She should heal it, but Shāl take her eyes, she deserved this pain.

She staggered to her feet and looked for something else to break. Something she could throw, something she could tear apart. There was nothing but the rumpled pillows on her bed, stuffed with royal fucking feathers. She lurched over, grabbed one. Left a pink smear of a handprint. Gripped with both hands, pulled with all her might against the cloth, until her side ached with the strain, and she pulled even harder because it felt good to strain against something that could take it, it felt good to *hurt*, and then she couldn't take it anymore, she just couldn't, and she sobbed into the pillow.

It felt like it would never stop.

She pressed the pillow harder against her face and screamed until her throat was raw and the only thing that came out was a ragged hiss of drool.

A pounding knock cut through the headache throbbing in Touraine's skull. That was all the warning Touraine had before Pruett sauntered into the bedroom.

She felt numb at the sight of her. It should never have come to this.

"What a state you're in." Pruett nudged Touraine's dangling boot. With her hands on her hips, she surveyed the room. The spilled water, the shattered basin, the pillow Touraine had thrown and the pillow she still clutched, soaked with blood, tears, and spit.

"What are you doing here?" She couldn't make her voice sound hard. It ached to form words above a whisper. No point, anylight. The whole room gave the lie to whatever facade she could fling up.

"I came to check on you."

"For what."

Pruett sat with her hip cocked on the edge of the bed. "You've changed, Tour, but not that much. My Touraine wouldn't kill someone she loves so easy as that." She blinked and shook her head incredulously. "When we were talking about love the other night—I didn't think you meant—you were serious."

"I betrayed one woman I love for the other. We have what we wanted." Touraine's voice cracked. She was no good at hiding her pain. Let Pruett think it was a simpler grief. "Why, Pruett? You promised."

"You lied to me," Pruett said quietly.

Touraine stopped mid-swallow, holding her breath.

"The messenger." Pruett knotted her fingers in the coverlet. "When Roric... questioned him, he said he delivered a message to you. Don't have to be whip smart to figure out what she said. Then I saw you sneaking out. I had to be sure of you, Tour. You understand, don't you?"

"Sure of me?" Touraine laughed cruelly over the secret rush of relief. "And if I hadn't"—*say it, you have to say it*—"killed her? What then?" It felt like thorns dragging up her gullet. "Were you going to kill me, too? You know I wasn't sneaking out. You *promised* me you'd let her go."

"I didn't." Pruett looked down at her fingernails. She'd bitten them down to the quicks. "She seemed too important to you. As long as she was alive, she was a threat."

The anger Touraine had been waiting for roared out, blazing hot. "Yes, Pruett! Yes! I never lied to you about that! I fucked the queen, Pruett! I fucked her, and I loved her, and I fucking killed her! I killed her anylight, *for you!*" She fell back, panting through her teeth.

"You're too good for her."

"I'm not good, Pruett. No better than you or any other Sand. And she's no worse. At least she tried." Touraine stopped to swallow moisture back into her cracking throat. "She tried to imagine something better when she could have sat back and kept what she had. Sky above knows it's all the rest of them wanted."

"She owned us! Her family has owned us all our lives!"

And she still owns me, Touraine didn't say. *But this time, I've chosen it. I offered, and she took, and I've taken, too.*

"Since when did you care?" Touraine asked. "Not like you ever fought back. Tibeau tried and you sneered him down just as quick. Now you want to lecture me?"

"I own that. It was a mistake. Half the living I do now is because of him." Pruett's gaze went distant and her shoulders sagged wearily. "Him and Aimée and all the rest. He'd be proud of you for this."

Another stab in the gut. She spun the grief ring on her finger with her thumb, the dark stone glinting with that red flash. The metal was tinted red with Luca's blood. Tibeau would hate her for what she felt. It was Luca who'd given her these grief rings, though. What would a grief ring for Luca look like?

Don't think about that.

Pruett followed her focus and reached hesitantly for Touraine's hand. "Are these for them?"

In all the time marching together, she had never asked.

Touraine yanked her hand out of Pruett's reach. The motion tore through her side, and she clapped a hand to the wound reflexively. It came away bloody.

"How bad?" Pruett asked, immediately concerned. "You haven't healed yourself?"

"It's not," she lied. "I just need to eat first. And rest."

"Roric will have food. He needs your help, too. His man was hurt."

Pruett reached for Touraine again, and again Touraine rebuffed her. "They've sent for Albric. He'll bring in the rest of the army so we can consolidate—"

"No," Touraine said abruptly. "I'm not letting them have the city."

The next steps of her plan, her new plan, coalesced into a shaky vision.

"What?" Pruett gaped at her from the other end of the bed.

"Balladaire is mine. I fought with you, I earned it. You keep Masridān, they keep Taargen. They can even have a slice of Moyenne if they like. I take Balladaire."

Touraine heaved herself to her feet. Dizziness almost pulled her to the floor. Pruett caught her arm. Held her steady, one hand on Touraine's chest.

Pruett frowned. "You never asked for this before. The Taargens won't like it."

"I didn't know I wanted it before," Touraine said. "Now I'm here, and—you may not care, but this is my home, Pruett. I'm keeping it."

She needed to keep the Taargens from getting comfortable on the throne. She had to buy time, and it would be easier if the soldiers didn't have a hold in the city.

"Why?" Pruett's eyes went doubtful and mistrusting all over again. "You had all this before, with her."

Touraine met Pruett's suspicion and this time told her the truth, the one that had made it possible to march all those miles with an enemy army, the truth that she'd held even as she plunged the blade home.

"I told you, I fell in love with a dream." She gingerly picked her knife up from the floor, swiped it on the cleaner thigh of her trousers, and shoved it home in its sheath. "The longer I stayed with Luca, the clearer it got. A dream is all it would ever be. I'm going to make something real."

CHAPTER 57

A CLAIM

Supported by Pruett's shoulder, Touraine returned, crown in hand, to the throne room where Pruett's Masridāni and Roric's Taargens were gathered. Some saw to the wounded, others gathered the dead; the Masridāni had been hit the hardest. Still others lurked, waiting for instructions. The remaining palace guards had been tied up to sit on their knees. Some wept, their sobs echoing in the high-ceilinged room no matter how they tried to muffle them. With a leap in her chest that she crushed immediately, Touraine saw Commander Perrot alive. The hatred on his face burned her even at this distance.

In the center of the room, Roric cradled the head of the great wolf. She limped over and, with an effort, knelt beside them. Blood pooled on the marble beneath them. Roric's palms were painted with it. When Touraine had walked into the Grand Hall, he'd had his blade at Luca's throat.

"How is he?" Touraine asked.

Roric's ruddy face was damp, his hazel eyes waterlogged. He shook his head. "He took the second round of rifle fire in my place. I didn't know... He didn't follow us."

The wolf's fur was matted with dark, slick patches along its heaving sides. The damage within would be worse. Touraine barely had the strength to heal herself, let alone dredge out the musket shot scattered through Henrir's body and seal every rupture they'd caused.

"My battle-sister. Can you?" Roric looked bleakly down at his comrade. The wolf lay on its—*his*—side, panting in Roric's lap, his long pink tongue lolling between sharp teeth. Yellow-green eyes rolled up at Touraine, wide and eerily understanding. "He is...near to me." He gripped tighter into the wolf's fur.

Dear, she wanted to correct him. *He's dear to you,* but her heart hurt to think it.

She set Luca's crown to one side, then held Roric's shoulder with one hand and reached tentatively to scratch the wolf between the ears, like Roric was. She waited until Henrir licked her hand before ruffling the fur gently. He sighed into the touch.

Touraine had left her room with all the conviction in the world, but it faltered now. It didn't feel right, to hold Henrir's life over Roric's head. But it did feel necessary.

It was what Djasha would do. When her own student had tried to kill Luca prematurely, Djasha hadn't hesitated before ending the girl. Roric was a strong playing piece, but he could change hands at any time. Cantic would never let an enemy walk away, and Jaghotai was the same. What was mercy to the Jackal? You couldn't eat it, couldn't drink it in the desert. Mercy was for those with leisure. Touraine couldn't afford leisure, not if she had any hope of saving the city Luca loved.

But peace? a voice asked, and it was Aranen's. *We can always afford peace. Peace over all.* If she healed Henrir, would Roric take his men and leave? Not if he was a smart man; but Touraine had done stupider things for the ones she loved. How long would a peace bought like this last? How tightly would Roric hold to his vows of honor if Albric called him to battle?

Beneath her hand, Henrir shuddered another breath, this one shallower still.

"If I try," Touraine said, "you have to promise me, as your battle-sister, one thing."

"Anything."

The tramping of boots and new voices echoed behind them as new arrivals strode through the palace.

Touraine pulled Roric by the coat as his attention strayed. "I heal him and you tell Albric that Balladaire is mine. The palace is mine, La Chaise is mine, its people are mine. All of it."

Roric's heavy brow crinkled as he understood the fork she'd put him in. He stroked Henrir's side again, knotting his thick, hairy knuckles in the fur at the wolf's chest. He bent over and kissed Henrir between the ears.

"Prince Consort!" Albric boomed, surrounded by his soldiers. "I hear you have good news for me."

Touraine ignored him, waiting for Roric's answer. Roric looked between her and Henrir, then to his mentor.

"Where is the queen?" Albric asked.

"Dead." Touraine turned toward him, but kept her hand in Henrir's fur. "In exchange for killing her and for healing the prince's companion, I will take Balladaire as my own." She turned to Roric and held his gaze. "Carve whatever you want off Moyenne and you'll have me as an ally. Are we agreed?"

A whimper escaped Roric's mouth, and Touraine watched as his first grief lines etched their way into his face.

He looked up at Albric's outrage. "What is a lord without the loyalty of his men, Albric?"

"This isn't loyalty, Your Highness, this is heart-pining foolishness," Albric snapped. "Don't be a child. We will give him the god's rites as befit his service."

Henrir licked Roric's fingers, as if in agreement. It had the opposite effect.

"Save him and you have my word," Roric said thickly.

"My prince, your mother—"

"My mother will understand. She wanted to topple the Ancier line and reclaim Moyenne. We've done that." Roric turned to Touraine. "Please. Quickly."

"Bring me meat."

Albric strode over and yanked Roric by the shoulder. "Your Highness, this land will be *yours*—"

Roric set Henrir's head tenderly onto the marble floor, then rose to his full height. He seemed to realize for the first time that he was near as tall as Albric and as broad.

"High Priest, I am your prince, and one heir to this land you propose to give me. I will spend it as I see fit." Then he shouted for food.

"Meat," Touraine shouted from the floor in Balladairan. "It has to be meat."

"We are not Balladairans." Roric knelt beside her again and ventured a smile as if the deed were already done. " 'Food' is 'meat.' "

She turned away from the warmth of his optimism.

So what? This is not for him. It was never for him.

"El-Atyidi?" She called the Eater over. "I need your help. Like we practiced."

Kiras hesitated. "Are you sure you want me?"

Without waiting for the other woman, Touraine dived into Henrir's body with her mind. Her magic was weak—she could feel her own body's strain in the sluggishness as it explored his wounds. Tendrils of the magic also sought her own wound, trying to knit her flesh together. She focused harder on Henrir. On the metal hunks lodged in the thick muscle of his beast form. She pointed and felt someone digging at them with a belt knife.

Someone else was at her hand, pressing sausage onto her and dried venison. She roused herself enough to take it and mindlessly shoved it into her mouth, already muttering a prayer echoed by Kiras beside her. Touraine's magic flared hot, searing into her own side even as it rushed into Henrir. The wolf snarled and spasmed and whined, and she matched him, growling through her teeth at the branding pain.

Then Henrir went still and Touraine collapsed onto his broad side. The smell of wild animal and dirt flooded her senses, and Henrir's steady breaths lifted her head up and down, lulling her into darkness. Her magic was quiet.

Roric jerked her awake, his hands clutching her by each arm. "You have done it? He is well?"

Touraine moaned.

"He's steady," Kiras said, staring awestruck at her hands.

Touraine gripped the front of Roric's coat and brought herself, swaying, to her feet.

Roric rose and steadied her. "You have saved me twice over. My debt is great." He glanced at Albric. "It will be." Then, to her surprise, he hugged her.

Touraine patted his back awkwardly. "See to your man."

She scooped up Luca's crown. Her crown. She had to pass Albric to reach the throne.

"You don't understand your situation, *Prince Consort*." He glanced meaningfully around the room, and Touraine could practically hear him counting the Taargens against the Masridāni in the room. "My soldiers have already taken the gates of the city. You'll find us hard to remove."

"I don't think you understand, Lord Albric." Touraine placed the blood-streaked crown upon her head. The heavy, cold weight of it. Sharp. She stepped back until she felt the throne against the back of her legs, the armrests at her fingertips. "Even ticks can be burned out."

He smiled knowingly. "A tick can burrow so deep within a deer that it never comes out."

"Aye, true enough. But the ticks that bury themselves so deep? They die there. The deer may die. It may not."

Instead of collapsing like she wanted to, she lowered herself leisurely onto the throne and watched Albric's face pinch in rage, turning from pink to red to deep purple. She stroked her palms over the smooth wood. Once, she had had Luca in it. There'd been something so thrilling about it then. Scandalous. It was all hers now. The crown, the throne, the city. All of Balladaire.

Another Emperor Djaya. As she imagined it, her stomach knotted. She gripped the arms of the throne to bolster herself.

"You once asked me if we could be friends, Your Grace. The answer is yes, if you will have me."

She saw the moment she won: the slight pulling back of his shoulders, the flare of his nostrils.

"Taargen does not wish to be your enemy," Albric said. A relieved rush of breath escaped everyone in the room. "However, a new accord will have to wait. The company of Balladairan soldiers we left in the countryside are closing in on the walls. I do not expect they will be pleased with the changes." He looked down his nose at Touraine.

To Touraine's surprise, Roric spoke, with none of the pleading of before. "I gave Touraine El-Qazāli my word that her battles will be my battles. Do not make a lie of my honor, High Priest. We will fight with you, Your Highness."

There, that was what he had in common with Luca. What it must be like, to know that all the world was meant to kneel at your feet. What was it like, to know that from *birth*? Touraine could sit in this chair for the rest of her life and never feel that certain.

"Your honor is my own, Your Highness." Albric bowed to Roric. Then, in a voice low enough for Touraine's ears only, he growled, "You are a friend like a cucklebird in the nest. We will see who sits here after this is done."

Touraine tilted her head back against the throne just enough to meet his eyes. She lowered her lids slightly, in a mask of disdain. "Do cucklebirds get ticks, too, I wonder?"

Albric left, snarling, not as a man snarls words but as a beast snarls at the back of the throat, low and rattling. Touraine thought of Henrir's finger-length fangs, his jaws dripping with Balladairan blood. She had avoided looking at the bodies, but she could guess who they belonged to. Deniaud and Mareau would not have let Luca go to the oak to die.

She held herself together, eyes glazing while Roric directed his soldiers to make a litter for Henrir and carry him away. He was a man again, covered in a wolf's pelt. Then she was alone with Pruett, Pruett's soldiers, and the Balladairan guards who had survived the slaughter.

She limped down the dais and went to Commander Perrot. A livid bruise colored one side of his face. "You. You will attend me."

"You sure?" Pruett folded her arms across her chest and eyed him up and down. "Take one of mine—"

"I know this man. He's a coward." Touraine held Perrot's glower as he looked up at her from his knees. "He fled Vauteur's Field. He won't cause me any trouble. He knows all about the way the friends we leave behind haunt us. Besides. He owes me a debt."

Perrot spat on her boots. The gob clung, thick and snot-like, to the leather. "I may be a coward, but I'm not a bearfucking trai—"

Touraine kicked him so hard that she almost fell over with him in her clumsy exhaustion. She made it look intentional, bending low to grab him by the collar with her bloody fists. Bloody again. Bloody still? Hard to say. Perrot looked down at them, and she knew he saw Luca's blood, like she did. He was trying so hard not to be afraid, and she loved him for it. *Forgive me, friend.*

She held him up to her face. "You will attend me, or you will die."

Oh, he despised her. Luckily, he wanted to live more than he wanted to spite her.

"I will attend you." He sagged in her grip, and Touraine struggled to stay upright.

"Good man." Touraine smiled, and it was dark and it was cruel and she wished it felt more unnatural on her face.

CHAPTER 58

A CORPSE

Touraine woke the next day feeling like she'd been trampled only by a small stable of horses and one small donkey instead of an entire cavalry. Probably because it was well into the afternoon when she dragged herself out of bed. Pruett had come by; she had a vague memory of her apologetically asking if she wanted to go with her to the hospital and speak with Jaghotai and Aranen. The older women were causing trouble, to no one's surprise. Touraine had been too tired to feel anything more than a quiet pride, and she'd fallen back asleep as soon as Pruett closed the door. She'd left more pack rations to eat, though. A peace offering. The Taargens weren't ready to trust the kitchen staff.

Which meant the plate of herbed grain and some cold roasted game bird must have come from Perrot. She tore into it ravenously, sparing only half a thought that maybe Perrot didn't trust her after all, and so the kitchen staff wouldn't, either. If it was poisoned, it was also delicious enough to bring tears to her eyes.

She'd explained to Perrot as best she could, whispering after the Masridāni had gone. He'd come around, and she'd given him instructions: evacuate as many as he could and tell the blackcoats to toss their uniforms and blend in, to stay ready.

Ready for what? he'd asked.

She didn't know, yet. Probably Moyenne. She didn't tell him that none of that mattered to her yet, that she couldn't think that far.

With Pruett gone, it was easier for Touraine to visit Sabine's rooms. Near two months she'd been gone, but the maze of the palace came easily to her.

Two Taargens stood outside Durfort's door. They didn't salute Touraine when they saw her, but chucked their chins up in greeting.

"Prince Consort," the shorter of the two said. He was blond with a fox mantle over his shoulder. The other man wore none; Touraine had slowly grown to understand the intricate language of rank the different animals and their pelts signified among the Taargens. "We are getting relief soon?"

"Aye," said the other. They spoke in Taargen to her, as much a welcome as anything else. "I am close to asking the prisoner for her chamber pot."

"I'll ask the prince. First I need to speak with the prisoner. We had unfinished business." Touraine flexed her fingers in and out of a fist to show them what kind of business she meant.

The short one smirked. "Don't be long."

They let her in and closed the door behind her.

"Fuck you and fuck your mother back into whatever dung den she crawled out of," Durfort shouted from another room.

Touraine followed her voice to the bedchamber, admiring the furniture and decorations as she passed. Durfort's tastes were very different from Luca's. And Touraine's for that matter. A tapestry of a duel spread across one wall—probably a famous one from Balladairan history that Touraine didn't know. Or maybe Durfort had had it commissioned, a fantasy. A bookshelf lined another wall, but unlike Luca's bookshelves, where the books were pulled down often and stacked haphazardly in an organization that only Luca could fathom and included history texts, political treatises, almanacs, and scientific theories, Durfort's only books were sword treatises and collections of chevalier tales, all of them neat upon their shelves. The wall of the sitting room outside the bedchamber was covered in swords displayed on racks—ancient swords, gleaming swords, gaudy swords and simple, some sharp and untouched and some well loved, longswords and sideswords, saber and rapier, dagger and knife. There were even a few wooden practice dowels of various lengths in a basket below the racks.

Touraine reached her hand out to brush one of the handles as the bedchamber door swung open, almost hitting her.

"Argh!" The gleaming point of a short steel came speeding toward Touraine's eyeball, and behind it hurtled Durfort.

Touraine yelped and leaned awkwardly out of the way.

Durfort recognized her. The steel clanked to the floor.

Touraine started to smile. "Durfort—"

"You bitch-whelp."

Stars flashed across Touraine's vision as the back of her head slammed against the wall of swords. Durfort's strong hands gripped Touraine by the throat, holding her in place. The blades dug into Touraine's back; some of the sharp edges pressed into her. She choked, gasping, trying to explain, but Durfort didn't let her.

"I should kill you right now." The marquise's cheeks were blotchy with fresh anger and stale weeping, eyes bloodshot, nose dry and red. The cut on her bruised face hadn't been stitched; it would scar, badly. Her fingers jerked against Touraine's neck, that sharp little bone inside it digging harder into Touraine's windpipe with each spasm.

"I know," Touraine tried to choke out. She'd wanted to die at least fifty times in the last twelve hours alone. She wouldn't get that bliss from Durfort, though. If Durfort were willing to kill, she wouldn't be talking herself up to it. She wouldn't have dropped the steel on the floor.

Touraine brought her arms up and broke Durfort's hold, then kicked the back of Durfort's knees as she twisted off balance. She hooked a forearm around Durfort's throat until the other woman gasped and clawed for release. Touraine shook her sharply once.

"I need to see her."

"You don't deserve to—"

"Durfort, she's alive! At least—she might be. I need to see her."

Durfort stilled. "What?"

Touraine threw Durfort to the ground and stepped over her.

Luca lay on the grand four-poster bed in the same bloody clothes. The curtains had been pulled closed, as if Durfort couldn't bear to look at her.

Touraine pushed the curtain aside. The thickness of tears in Touraine's throat threatened to overpower her.

Durfort came up behind her. "What do you mean she's alive?"

"Luca." Hands trembling, Touraine brushed her fingers through Luca's hair. Across her pallid cheek. It was cooler than it should have been, but...she pressed two fingers beneath Luca's sharp jaw and found the sporadic flutter of a pulse. She almost sagged to her knees in relief.

"Thank Shāl." She reached beneath Luca's bloody chemise to the skin beneath. Slightly warmer than elsewhere, which was reassuring.

"Are you going to explain what under the sky a-fucking-bove is going on?"

"Shut up. I need to concentrate."

Touraine sank into Luca's body as she had done only twice before— both times when she was feeling Luca's life slip away in her own hands. She traced the newly sealed skin and the tentative knitting of the organs and muscle that her own blade had passed through. With a prayer to Shāl, she reinforced them. It was like going over something stitched with rotted thread with leather instead—it would make it stronger, but it was also harder. She could feel Luca's body fighting her as she forced it to repair itself.

She also felt something else. The tissues of Luca's body struggled to obey her. They responded sluggishly to her command, and when they knit together, they still felt more tenuous than they should have. Confused, Touraine poured more of herself into the work.

When she had done as much as she could, she staggered back, faint. Durfort caught her before she crashed to the floor. Carefully, the other woman lowered her.

"*Now* will you explain?"

"What's to explain?" Touraine slurred. The sleep she'd snatched from the afternoon hadn't been near enough, and the meat from the bird felt meager, and long, long ago.

"Why you killed her, to start. Why you came marching in with the sky-falling Taargens for another! She told me about your plan and this wasn't part—!" Durfort stopped, gripping her head in her hand.

"It was the only way I could control what happened. The only way I could keep her safe. The only way I could come back alive." Touraine let her eyes fall shut.

Durfort laughed incredulously. "Oh, right. That sky-falling hero complex of yours. I told her, you're just alike. I spent the last few months thinking I wanted to *be* like you, all duty and no fun, but sky a-fucking-above. I told her, I *told* her, you'd be the death of each other. I didn't know it would be so literal."

"Would you prefer I got myself sent back in a basket?"

Durfort paled and turned away. "She thought you'd betrayed her."

Touraine saw again the desperate pain in Luca's eyes, begging her to do something, anything else. To pay the price to save her. Well, Touraine had paid the price, and there was more to come due yet.

"We need to get you and Luca out of the palace."

"Oh really? That's a wonderful idea. Funny thing, though—she's about as agile as a corpse."

"I know," Touraine said flatly. "She should wake up in the next day or two, though."

Durfort eyed the bed dubiously. "Last time, she was out for a week."

Touraine covered her eyes, panic welling in her chest again. She pulled herself onto the bed. Took Luca's hand. The pulse at her wrist was stronger, but Durfort was right; she didn't look like she would ever open her eyes again, let alone sneak out of a palace through an occupied city to a safe house that didn't exist.

"We don't have a week. I'll buy you as much time as I can, but they're going to expect her to start rotting. They're not always cruel," she added softly. "They'll want to take her from you. Insist on rites. Albric might insist on proof before they burn her."

"Take her signet ring. Or the grief rings."

Touraine twined her fingers through Luca's, tilting them so that her rings caught the light. Her own rings gleamed alongside them. She couldn't bring herself to take them off, or to imagine how Luca would feel if she woke and found them missing.

"I'll fetch her signet ring from her chambers if I need to." She took a deep breath, trying to inhale some sense of resolve. "Right. In three days, I'll make sure the room is unguarded and unlocked. That will give you time to build up your strength. Try to feed her if she wakes. She'll need it. Then I want you to go—"

"You're not coming with us?"

"If I disappear, they'll catch on that much quicker." Worst case, they'd find out and Pruett would fill her up with musket shot. "You can't pick a lock, can you?"

For a second, a glimpse of Durfort's old cockiness shone through. "Don't insult me. One day I'll tell you about a game I used to play with a minor comtesse—"

"One day, but not now." Touraine held up a hand. "Take her to Aranen, biggest hospital tent in the Parc du Coeur."

Durfort shook her head. No laughter now, only horror. "How am I going to get her that far?"

"Aren't you Sabine de Durfort, scourge of husbands and wives? Who can sneak through this palace without getting caught if not you?" Touraine's voice cracked with desperation, but Durfort only stared at her. "Look, I don't *know*, but you have to try, because if they catch you and they realize she's not dead, they will fix that and I can't—I can't—" She dug her hand into Luca's bloody coat, balling it in her fist until her knuckles were white. Dry blood crackled and flaked rust onto the white bedclothes.

"Fine. Fine." Durfort stood and draped her arm around Touraine's shoulder. She surprised Touraine by pulling her against her in a hug. Her warm body was a change from Luca's, her heartbeat strong against Touraine's ear. Her body sturdy and powerful. Durfort pressed firm circles across Touraine's shoulders with the heel of her palm like Luca used to, easing a tension that had cramped her for weeks.

Touraine sagged into the embrace. "I'm sorry I can't heal you. They'll know I was here."

Durfort chuckled softly, but there was sadness in her words as she said, "It'll only add to my charm."

"If I don't find you…" Touraine cleared her throat as the words caught. "You will."

Touraine shook her head. Truth to tell, she wasn't all that afraid of the dying. But dying now, like this…

"Tell her what really happened. I don't want her to think…"

"That you're a traitor?"

Touraine snorted and said heavily, "I am a traitor. It's just not her I betrayed."

CHAPTER 59

ON FRIENDSHIP (REPRISE)

And this is where you and she spent your days?" Pruett looked sidelong at Touraine as they ambled across the small lawn beyond the Rose Maze. "While the hungry masses cried out for justice?"

The small woodland ahead of them was lush and green. The grass sparkled with dew and nothing existed in the world but them, the trembling gamekeeper, and the single hunting dog he'd brought. Over the last couple of days, Touraine had rested, had eaten another quail or pheasant or whatever it was. She was wearing her finer clothing again, her arms bare to morning air, already warm with the promise of summer. It was nice, even with Luca's crown sitting heavier on her head than the thin metal should have.

"We spent one day out here, aye," Touraine said quietly. "I think she was trying to redeem the palace in my eyes. Maybe in her own. Last few months weren't all wine and dance cards."

"Right. The duke. Hmph. What about the children at those schools?"

Touraine winced. "The plague came so fast. Then..." She trailed off and raised a pointed eyebrow.

"Oh, so that's my fault, is it?"

"You sure didn't fucking help."

"Here is good, Your High—Majes—" The groundskeeper fumbled a knuckle to his forehead and bowed all at the same time. In his other hand, he held the collar of a sleek little hunting hound with floppy ears. "Whip, here, she knows just how to flush 'em, and she will. Should probably come up around...there." He jabbed his thick middle finger—he was missing the index—at some point in the sky. Touraine wasn't paying attention to that. She was watching Pruett.

Pruett tracked the man's gesture with those sharp blue-gray eyes, her thick eyebrows slanted in concentration. She licked her thumb and held it out on the air to gauge the direction of the wind. Her nostrils flared.

"Hold our friend Whip a moment longer, then."

Pruett knelt to ready her rifle, but she spared a moment to hold her fist to the hound. It sniffed, then licked her knuckles. Then it stilled and cocked its head curiously at Pruett.

"She's excited." Pruett grinned up at the groundskeeper. Touraine remembered teasing her about it, how anytime Pruett smiled, she looked like she was going to kill something. She regretted that now. She would miss that smile.

The groundskeeper, however, looked sickly. He scratched through his mostly white beard and smoothed his hand anxiously over his mostly bald head. "Should say, Your Majesty. It is nesting season, so maybe it's best not to take too many."

"Don't worry," Pruett told him. "I'll take care of them."

The groundskeeper didn't know what to make of that. Neither did Touraine.

"Does it bother you?" Touraine lowered her voice. "The birds and all."

"Why would it?" Pruett stood and raised her gun to her shoulder, sighting down the barrel. She peered at Touraine with one eye. "You going to have a go?"

"I'd rather watch the master." Touraine meant it.

Pruett rolled her eyes. "If you wanted to lick my asshole, you could have just said. Off you go, Whip!"

The hound broke free and darted toward the small cluster of trees, every part of its body fit to its purpose: nose reaching and scenting, claws furrowing the dirt for traction, body low to the ground, haunches bunching up with explosive speed. Watching the hound, Touraine understood how the Many-Legged and the Taargens could find something sacred in that perfect coordination. She felt the same when she fought, or watched a good sparring match.

Pruett's eyes were closed, gun to her shoulder and pointed up, just above the line of the trees. Her body was still, breath slow. A single eyelid twitched.

The pheasants burst from the trees in a crash of feathers and squawking. Pruett adjusted her body minutely, exhaled, then fired without opening her eyes.

Mouths hanging open, Touraine and the gamekeeper watched the flurry of birds. One dark speck fell to the ground. A falcon's cry came next, a new dark blur diving from above toward the little flock of game birds. It crashed into one of the birds, then flapped away with the still form in its talons.

"Sky above and earth below." The gamekeeper stepped back from them, watching Pruett as if she'd grown a second head.

Pruett smiled, then opened her eyes. When she turned to Touraine, her grin was wicked.

"How was my shot?"

"Not bad, if you're going to cheat," Touraine grumbled, trying and failing not to sound impressed.

Pruett thrust the rifle at Touraine's chest. "Your turn, then."

Touraine started to push the gun back at her when a streak of movement caught both their eyes. Someone was running toward them from the palace.

It's too soon. There hadn't been enough time for Durfort to get Luca away. Touraine tightened her grip around the rifle barrel. Through it, she felt the tension coiling in Pruett's body.

Touraine kept her mask of concerned confusion. Maybe it was some completely different catastrophe—

"Qâ'id, sir, the prisoner is gone."

Fuck.

"Which prisoner?"

"The noble, sir. She took the queen's body with her."

The look she leveled at Touraine was scathing. "Where's Kiras? Tell her to find them."

"She's hunting them as we speak, sir." The soldier saluted.

Pruett's frown was so fierce that her lips were twitching when she rounded on Touraine.

"What's a Balladairan noble want with a queen's corpse, Tour?"

Touraine considered lying. Drawing out the inevitable pain. But sky above and earth below, she was exhausted. She half smiled and jerked the butt of the rifle into Pruett's cunt.

Pruett grunted in pain, and Touraine stole the gun from Pruett's slack grip. She aimed her first blow at the soldier who'd delivered the message. It cracked into his nose, and he fell to the ground with a bubbly screech. She swung for Pruett's nose, too—at the last moment, Touraine pulled the blow and sent it toward Pruett's stomach instead of her head.

Shāl help her, Touraine still didn't want to kill her.

The gun met empty air. Touraine stumbled and caught herself facing down the barrel of one of Pruett's pistols. Those fucking pistols. No pretending Pruett wouldn't shoot her now.

Touraine loaded her weight into the balls of her feet, ready to slip desperately to one side or the other, but the anguished fury on Pruett's face slowed her. Made her want to stay and make peace with the woman she'd loved all her life. Running away felt cheap. Pruett deserved better. Touraine couldn't give her better, if she wanted to stay alive.

She dropped the rifle to the grass. It would only slow her down.

"Why shouldn't I pull this sky-falling trigger, Touraine? Is there any gods-damned reason?" Pruett's voice was as steady as her arm. She stood side-on, making her body a smaller target.

"Because if you miss, you'll only have one more shot." Touraine took a step back and slightly to the left.

"The bearfuckers were right. It was you. You killed Armande. You let the Moyenne free." Pruett curled her lip but didn't break her sight line. "Why, Tour?"

Touraine kept her eyes trained on Pruett's, letting her peripheral vision track the rest of her body.

"What? You going to tell me you did it all for love?" Pruett snarled. "She that much better a lay than me? 'Cause you've sure never done anything like this for me."

"That's not true and you know it." Touraine had fucked up in Qazāl, but she'd been doing it for the Sands. For Pruett. A long time ago. "I told you. She had a dream and it looked a lot like mine." If it was for Luca alone, Touraine would never have made it this far.

"A dream," Pruett repeated. "A fucking dream."

The shot started not in Pruett's finger, not in her arm, but in her face. In the harsh pull of her mouth, rippling down the tendons of her neck. Touraine leapt to her right as the gun went off, knowing that Pruett had probably guessed which way she would move, waiting for the bullet to hit.

A hot burning cut across Touraine's left cheek, and the tickle of blood followed.

That left them both staring at each other, Pruett's pistol spent and smoking. She looked disgusted, though Touraine couldn't tell if it was Touraine she was disgusted with, or herself for missing the shot. Or for taking it.

Pruett reached for her other pistol, and Touraine turned and ran. Another pistol shot and Touraine felt the burn of the bullet graze her right shoulder.

At the sound of rapid footfalls behind her, Touraine looked back in time to see the hound bolting, belly low, legs stretching as it leapt and sank its teeth into her calf. She kicked and swore and stomped, trying to send the dog flying, but it growled and danced around her. She saw the blur of Pruett sprinting for her, the flicker shine of a knife.

Touraine dropped to her knees, slamming all her weight on the dog's lean little body. Bones cracked. It howled pitifully, but Touraine was already reaching up to grab Pruett's knife wrist. She flipped Pruett down to the ground with her own momentum. The edge of the knife gleamed between them as Pruett tried to bring the blade home into Touraine's chest. Strength for strength they pushed until Touraine slammed Pruett's hand into the ground, once, twice, again until Pruett's fingers spasmed open and the knife skittered into the grass.

Touraine had lived this moment before.

Pruett bared her teeth. "Will you kill me for her?"

"What do you love that's worth all of this?" Touraine snarled back, letting out all the anger she'd held in for the long march back to La

Chaise. "Everything *you've* done? Or was it all because you're pissed that *your* parents didn't love you enough to fight for you?"

"You sky-fucking bastard." Pruett let out a wildcat's roar and punched Touraine with her free hand right into the half-healed wound Luca had made in Touraine's side. Touraine gasped into the black-spotting pain, and Pruett flipped her onto her back. Daylight was coming in bright, the sky clear and full of early-summer sun.

Pruett had a knack for finding Touraine's open wounds. But Touraine did, too. That was the problem with loving someone so long. They could hurt you better than anyone else.

Pruett tightened her fist around Touraine's throat. Touraine pushed and clawed at her with both hands, but Pruett had the leverage and longer arms. Dizzy from lack of air and burning with pain, Touraine's focus narrowed—the hot rush of Pruett's breathing and the throb of her pulse through her fingertips.

The heat. The blood.

She remembered a conversation she had had with Aranen once, about Luca.

"To touch is to be touched," Aranen had said. "Yes, you can get close to her. Maybe even change her. But she'll be just as close to you."

Touraine let her hands fall to her sides. She stopped struggling and held Pruett's eyes. Tears streaked Pruett's face. Touraine hadn't noticed. Her own face was wet with blood. Maybe more.

How had they gone so wrong?

"I'm sorry," Touraine tried to say. It came out a hiss. Blackness was collapsing her vision. The pulse in her head pounded harder. Her eyeballs were going to burst. The crown's thorns dug into the back of her skull.

"You can't just apologize, Touraine," Pruett said. She might have still been talking, but sound was dimming now, too. Touraine let it. She followed the trail of Pruett's hands, the heat, the blood, the spark of her—

Touraine snuffed it out.

Pruett collapsed on top of her.

Touraine checked her pulse. Still there, still strong, but unconscious. As if Pruett had fallen asleep caressing Touraine instead of throttling her. Touraine heaved her over, and limped to her feet. Every grateful breath through her bruised throat burned.

The Masridāni blackcoat was down. The groundskeeper had wisely made himself scarce. The dog still whimpered, scrabbling at the ground with its forepaws. The rear ones didn't move. She picked up Pruett's knife and slit the poor thing's throat.

She looked back at Pruett one last time. The last time she'd see her and be able to pretend they had ever been anything more than enemies. She didn't dare let herself wonder if Pruett would forgive her.

She didn't think she could forgive Pruett, either.

CHAPTER 60

ON DYING

Death was an empty place, and Luca's wounds had traveled with her.

Her stomach ached. Her cheek stung. She couldn't feel her legs, but there was the unsettling sensation of movement, as if she were being buoyed on a river. A knobby river. Instead of the sound of water rushing and lapping against the vessel that carried her, there was a muttering, whispering, and the shh-shh of something dragging.

Some people, in their platitudes to a young, grieving Luca, had told her that death was simply another journey, a long one.

She must not have arrived at that final destination. She closed her eyes and let the river carry her away.

She woke as death's boat jostled and crashed against the shore. The ground was solid beneath her, cold as marble against her cheek.

"Luca. Wake up."

One side of her face was cool, pleasant. A rapid slapping brought heat to the other.

Some people, in their platitudes to a young, grieving Luca, had told her that death was peaceful. An emptiness where no one felt any pain.

This was not that, either.

"Luca, by the sky above, please, wake up."

The whispering shh-shh of the river was also gone.

"Hello, Death," she tried to say. Her tongue was too thick. Too dry. A wordless rasp issued forth.

"Luca?"

Death rolled her over onto her back. Her eyelids were so heavy, but she pried them open. She was too curious. One of her great flaws. She wanted to know what Death looked like.

All was dark, shades of gray and black, and a figure above her, darker than the rest, closer, the outline of a tricorne blocking out the gray around them. Strange, that Death, that great universal, should dress like a Balladairan. Perhaps it fit its figure to its victim.

"Oh, thank the sky above," the voice whispered. Familiar.

Luca blinked. Blinked again. Her surroundings slowly sharpened into focus.

"Shit, shit, shit."

Death grabbed her arm and hoisted Luca onto its shoulders, dragging her feet beneath her. A ripping pain seared through Luca's middle. Death was not painless. The pain was so great that, for a moment, it sharpened every sense. As they passed a bright torch, she craned her neck to better see Death's face as it carried her.

"Sabine?"

Then all went black again.

The next time she woke, Death still wore Sabine's face, and Death was stuffing her into an—an alcove. An alcove with a pedestal. A pedestal with a statue. Sabine-as-Death muttered a holy litany the whole time:

"I am Sabine de Durfort, scourge of husbands and wives. I am Sabine de Durfort, scourge of husbands and wives."

Then Sabine-as-Death was whispering to Luca.

"Luca? Can you hear me? Stay here. Don't move. If I don't come back, wait here until—wait until—sky-falling fuck."

Luca grasped at Sabine's coat with feeble fingers. "No, stay—" Stay where? Why? She fought her way closer to the surface. With her other hand, she felt that same cold stone beneath her. "Where are we?"

"In the palace. I'm getting you out. Soldiers are hunting us."

Soldiers. Hunting. She had soldiers. Sky above, this would all be so much easier if she could *think*, but everything hurt and she was dead.

"My soldiers."

"No."

"Are you dead, too?"

"What? No. No, for the stars' sake, Luca. You're alive. Wake up. Look at me." Warm hands on both of her cheeks, tilting her head up to look into dark pools that must have been eyes. It was too dark to make out anything but the outline of a face, but Luca had slept beside this face. Had made love to it in darkness and woken up to it by moonlight. Sabine.

She wasn't dead.

Touraine and the qā'id, coming into the palace. Evrard's treachery. The qā'id, demanding Luca's death. Touraine, driving the knife deep, without hesitation.

Luca fisted Sabine's coat with a burst of fear-born strength. "I'm not letting...you go again...Shāl damn your eyes."

"What? You know I don't speak Shālan. No, shh, never mind. Shh. I'll be back." She looked behind her, up the corridor the way they'd come. Bootsteps and frustrated voices.

Luca fumbled for the words. Gripped tighter. "The last time...I let you...you almost died."

Sabine looked pained. "If I don't, they'll catch you."

"If they...catch *you*?" Luca hissed. "I won't let you...be used... against me. Not again."

"They won't. I'd rather die."

"Stop. Talking." Luca pulled with the little strength she had. It wasn't enough to move Sabine, who had her arms propped on either side of Luca, between the wall and the stone pedestal, her body hiding Luca from view. But there was enough room for them both to get out of the main line of the corridor if Sab would only come. Sky above, she *hurt*. She clutched at her stomach with the other hand but refused to unsnarl her fist from Sabine's clothing.

"You're all I have left," she whispered. Whined. "Don't leave me."

No one, in their platitudes to a young, grieving Luca, had told her that death was dignified.

Conflicted pain crossed Sabine's face. "No. I'm not. Touraine is still out there. She's fighting for you. Piss-poorly, but she is," she added in a mutter that Luca didn't think she was supposed to hear.

Sabine curled into the dark space, wedged her long legs on either side of Luca, and wrapped her up in her arms. They waited until the steps passed and the hallway was quiet again.

She woke once more, this time with her face against smooth, short fur. The smell of manure all around. A massive, excruciating weight pressing on her stomach—her own body. She retched.

"Luca? Sky above, you're awake. Can you sit up? Here."

It took Luca less time to acclimate herself to consciousness, this time. With the help of Sabine-who-was-not-Death, she slithered, nauseated, back down the horse's ribs. The stables were empty, no stablehands, no stable master.

"Up you get. Hurry." With deliberate gentleness, Sabine placed Luca's left leg on the stepping stool and hoisted her onto the saddle.

From the height, Luca swayed, still nauseated. Her vision dimmed and she felt herself tipping—

"Oh no you don't."

A hand grabbed her roughly. Held her in place. There was a dangerous lurch as Sabine swung into the saddle behind her, holding the saddle horn in front of Luca and wedging Luca against the strength of her arm and chest. She let her head loll on the warm steadiness behind her.

"Where are we going?" she murmured as Sabine nudged the horse to movement.

The brisk air on her face—that didn't feel like death. It shocked Luca's eyes wide open. She was in the same bloody chemise and waistcoat she'd been wearing when Touraine—

"Touraine said to go to the hospital tents. Aranen will take care of you."

The hospital tents. Luca was known there, if not respected.

She looked behind them as they passed from the stables. Behind her, the palace—*her* palace—rose in all its columns and stone, its pale beauty. You couldn't see the side ruined by fire. You couldn't see the invaders within. Somehow, as they rode, the building never seemed to get smaller.

I'll be back for you.

No one, in their platitudes to a young, grieving Luca, had told her that there was no coming back from death. They did not need to. She had seen the finality in her father's empty eyes. Had felt it in her mother's cold flesh, which she touched when no one was looking. She felt it now.

"No. Not the hospital tents. A tavern. La Gouttière. La Flottille. Take me there."

Luca woke with full lucidity in a shabby little bed made of rushes and a warm quilt pulled up to her chin. Within moments she was retching over the chamber pot beside the bed. She wiped her mouth on her arm. She was naked. The smear of sick on her skin was dark red, almost black among the pale hairs. Dark clots floated in the pot.

That wasn't promising. The heaving alone had made her insides feel like they were ripping all over again. She pressed her hand to her middle—then, with a bolt of memory, pulled the blanket away. Along with the little waxy knuckle-wide scars from Fili's attack at Luca's abdication, there was a single, short scar running diagonal across Luca's abdominal muscles. *Sky-falling fuck.*

Her clothes were folded neatly on the single wooden chair in the room. Luca calculated the odds of her being able to stand and dress herself without collapsing. Those were also not promising. But she couldn't wait for someone to come tell her what was happening.

She kicked one leg over the side of the bed at a time, then stopped to take another agonizing breath. She reached for the chair, the only thing she could use to hold herself up with. Her cane had not taken the long journey through death with her.

For once, it wasn't the clicking pain in her hip or the stabbing in her knee or up her thigh that took her down. The very motion of stretching her hand out and straining her middle that far made her cry out and double over. That, of course, was when her hip and knee gave out, and she fell to the ground, knocking over the chair.

The crownless queen, sprawled out naked like a broken puppet on a sticky, pocked wooden floor in the inn of the rebels who wanted to overthrow her. Oh, glorious reign.

She curled in on herself and waited for the bright spots of pain to dim.

Before they did, her door burst open and Sabine stood framed in the middle of it. Relief and horror mingled on her face. Luca hoped she had at least managed not to upset the chamber pot full of bloody vomit.

"Is the bed not to your liking, Your Majesty?" Sabine forced amusement into her shaking voice.

"Sabine LeMarchal de Durfort, shut the fuck up, shut the fucking door, and help me put on my fucking clothes."

"Your wish is my command." Sabine bowed so low her hair flopped over her eyes. With the door firmly shut, Sabine helped Luca to her feet. Instead of helping her back onto the bed or into her trousers, though, she wrapped Luca in a fierce hug.

"I'm so glad you're all right," she whispered into Luca's hair.

To Luca's dismay, fiery tears pricked the corners of her eyes. She dug her fingers into Sabine's back and scrubbed her face in her shirt. She smelled of horses and someone else's soap. None of her cologne with its autumn leaves and loam.

Luca held Sabine at arm's length. If she didn't, she would begin sobbing, and she was quite certain her body couldn't handle that. Still, she kept her hands tight around the other woman's elbows. She felt weak as a fawn.

"We're at La Flottille?"

"Yes. It was a trial getting them not to kill you on sight, I should say. Why did you tell me to bring you right into the revolutionaries' den? If I'd known you were raving, I would have ignored you. Here, sit."

Luca let herself be lowered back to the bed. "I have a plan."

Sabine looked down at her skeptically. "If this plan involves you being spitted again, let's pretend it didn't work and move to the next one."

"Help me dress. Then will you please bring me some food? And whoever passes for a leader these days." Luca plucked at her tangled hair. "I also need to do something about this."

Sabine bit the inside of her cheek, hesitant. Then she noticed the chamber pot.

"You're...all right, aren't you? She said you'd be all right."

"Touraine?" Luca's heart stuttered. "Is she here?"

"She's keeping up a front with the qā'id and the Taargens to buy us time."

Luca bit her lip. "A front."

"Mm."

"If I ever see that woman again, I'm going to..." She trailed off, unsure how to finish the sentence. All she knew was how much it hurt, the idea that she wouldn't see Touraine again. Even if it was only because she wouldn't get to scream at her, to punch her, to make *her* hurt the way Luca did.

Sabine made a knowing sound in her throat, but had the grace to say nothing as she helped Luca slide on her chemise. That effort was enough to leave Luca panting and out of breath, her body radiating pain. She gestured frantically for the chamber pot again.

"I'm fine." Luca wiped her chin with the back of her wrist and glared, daring Sabine to challenge her. "Food. Please."

Sabine inhaled sharply, nostrils flaring, then left. She returned with a bowl of warm broth and a handful of strangers. No, two strangers, and two people Luca had gotten to know in her own prison. Fili was there, along with a short woman and a tall man whom Luca didn't know, and—Ghadin.

"We should kill her," the short woman said.

Sabine stiffened as she bent over the bed to give Luca the bowl. Without looking at the Fingers, she said, "You'd be dead before you got close." She put a hand to the hilt of her sword.

"Sabine. It's all right. I want to talk. I'm sure they realize I'm more useful alive. A conquering army isn't going to listen to a bunch of civilians grumbling about their sovereignty. Trust me." Luca gave a cold smile, pretending confidence she didn't feel. She felt more like herself wearing her court mask.

What a thing that was, for a mask to feel more like your true self than being stripped bare.

"Fili. Have you considered... what we spoke of?"

"You can talk about it with them. They know about the god. About my gift." Absently, she fingered the plant pinned to her lapel. The others wore something similar.

"And?" Luca raised an eyebrow.

Fili gathered herself up with an effort. She didn't look back at the adults around her. "I won't do it."

"There's an enemy army in our city. This isn't time for pettiness."

"I won't do it," Fili repeated, "unless you surrender Balladaire to the people. These are our demands."

Luca barked a laugh and winced.

"She's laughing at us, see?" The short woman jutted her chin. "We're better off without her."

"Fili, Velte. Wait." It was Ghadin, pulling Fili's arm. Ghadin's voice started out low and uncertain, but it grew. "She was willing to work with Qazāl. And she saved me from the duke. I've been in the court. She can do things that you can't. People will take her seriously if she negotiates for us."

"They should be negotiating with the government of the people."

"And where is that government?" Ghadin put her hand on her hip and raised her eyebrows pointedly at the short woman, who must have been Velte.

A smile tugged at the corner of Luca's mouth, but she flattened it.

Velte glared at the girl. "It'll come."

"We need it *now*."

"The price is still the same," Fili said to Luca. "You get your life. You get my magic. We turn back the Taargens. You surrender the throne."

"You say that as if you can turn back the Taargens on your own. If I say no, you'll have no army. You'd spite yourself, just for this?"

"*Just?* This isn't 'just' anything. It's about our right to dignity." There was a new note in Fili's voice, and though the words had the air of something she'd practiced, they didn't sound like lines fed to her from someone else.

Luca had not sacrificed all she loved to give the throne up like this.

"And if I have other news for you?" she said. "How to stop the Withering? Will you see then that I am doing everything I can for you, for *all* my people?"

"We didn't need you for that," Velte said. There was a sharp glint in her eyes. "We picked it up ourselves. Friends of Fili don't get sick. The Fingers are safe. More people saw that, more people joined us. Might be our numbers picked up a bit."

Part of Luca leapt at that—she wanted to know everything. She forced that down. Reminded herself they were her enemies. Reminded herself, again, that they were *not* her enemies, they were her citizens. The people she was meant to care for. Like stubborn children. She exhaled slowly through her nose.

"Don't do it, Luca," Sabine murmured.

"I won't," she answered quietly. Then louder: "Deny me your aid. Let the Taargens win."

"One master is the same as any other." With that, Fili left, followed by the other Fingers.

Ghadin, however, lingered.

"Thank you for standing for me," Luca told her. "That was generous of you."

"Didn't do it for you." She absently rubbed one arm. The one that had been broken.

"No?"

"I didn't want Touraine to kill them if she found out they'd killed you."

"Oh." Luca had to swallow twice to work her throat clear. "Ghadin, about Touraine..."

"Is she coming back?" The girl's face lit with wary hope.

It crushed Luca. She opened her mouth to speak the truth, to say that she might come back, but it was more complicated than that, and that Touraine was in a dangerous position at the moment and even Luca didn't know, but Sabine beat her to the mark.

"She is. She's coming back. As soon as she can."

CHAPTER 61

THE RETURN

Relief, cool and sweet, washed over Touraine when she saw the hospital tents still stood. Pruett's temper after seeing Jaghotai had made Touraine certain Pruett had burned them all down.

Bloody and heartsore, Touraine had limped from the palace, ducking in between buildings and weaving through narrow side streets. She'd thought Pruett and Albric would be merciless, but Balladairans continued to mind their business. Yes, they kept their eyes trained forward, lowered, and yes, they hurried, and yes, there were fewer than there should have been—but they went on, living. It wasn't much, and it was everything.

Touraine slipped between a shuttered cobbler and a tailor, both with windows boarded up and walls smelling like piss. She sagged against the stone. Just for a second. Catch her breath. Reconnoiter. Her leg ached. She was afraid to sit, piss or no piss, in case she couldn't get up again, but the more she thought about it, the louder the pain grew. She slid to the ground. Just a minute.

Taargen soldiers—some in fur mantles, at least one priest in a full fur cloak—guarded the perimeter of the Parc du Coeur. They were alert, but not *hunting*. They couldn't know she'd run. How had Durfort gotten Luca past them? She prayed to Shāl that they had made it this far.

Harder would be to get herself in. They would recognize her, but they would know something was wrong by the Shāl-damned dog bite shredding her calf. Luca's crown was a misshapen lump beneath her shirt. The desire to be safe, to know Luca was all right, tugged Touraine forward from deep behind her belly button. So hard it made her nauseous. Aranen was in there, too. Jaghotai. Ghadin.

Touraine gathered herself for one more push. The sudden movement made her head spin, and she braced herself on the stone wall.

"Mulāzim?"

Touraine spun around. Her wounded leg cramped in pain, and she bit her lip so hard it split, an explosion of copper.

Ghadin, her deep-brown eyes wide with surprise. Her braid rested over her shoulder. The girl looked older. It wasn't that she was taller, though she was, though still a bit shorter than Touraine. The faint frown in her face had set, the down curve of her mouth, the knitting of her black eyebrows. The weary shadows beneath her eyes.

"Ghadin." Touraine opened her arms, lurching forward, and the girl rushed into them, burying her face in Touraine's shoulder. The crown dug into her skin, but both of them ignored it.

"You're back," Ghadin murmured.

Touraine's throat was too thick to speak, her eyes wet. She squeezed harder.

"You're good?" It was all she could bring herself to say.

"I'm good," Ghadin said into her chest.

Touraine held her out to arm's length to look at her. Touraine wanted to ask her more, so much more, but that could wait. "Is Luca with the others?"

Ghadin's face fell and Touraine's heart with it. "The blackcoats said you were fighting with the Taargens against Balladaire. Your friend with the pistols said, too." Ghadin's voice was flat, accusatory in that way only neutrality could be. Behind the accusation, Touraine heard the hope the girl had held and the disappointment that had taken its place.

"It's complicated." The excuse rolled easily off the tongue. Then she stopped, feeling the weight of Ghadin's expectations. She thought of the hero worship she'd seen when Tiro looked at Durfort in the practice salle. It had reminded her how she'd worshipped Cantic. Sky above, a few years shy of thirty and Touraine was *still* looking for someone else to tell her how to be, *what* to be. She couldn't blame Ghadin for seeking the same.

A part of Touraine wanted to be that for her. To tell the girl which way to grow. That was why it hurt so badly every time Ghadin saw through her mask of certainty. Every time Ghadin saw her fumbling mistakes. How many times had Touraine let her down? And yet, Ghadin came back, looking at Touraine like she held all the answers.

Cantic and Djasha, Aranen and Jaghotai. Luca and Pruett. They'd been given power or they'd taken it, and all of them thought they knew what to do with it. They'd each done what they thought they needed to to make the world right. Touraine had watched all of them falter. She'd watched some of them die.

"I'm sorry, Ghassa. I know you wish I'd chosen something else. Someone else. I know she isn't—she isn't good."

Look at her, begging this girl, this young woman not to hate her in ten years the way she herself hated Cantic and loved her at the same time. It was inevitable.

"I—"

"Maybe after all of this, I'll have a chance to explain. It might not make sense to you, but please know that I'm trying. One day, you'll have to make your own choices, the best choices you can, and they'll probably be half shit but maybe half good, too—"

"I know, I—"

"Let me finish. You don't have to agree with me." Though she hoped Ghadin wouldn't judge her too harshly under the clear light of time passed. "I just need…" Touraine didn't have the right to ask the girl for anything. She asked anylight, voice a cracking whisper. "I just need you to believe that I tried to do good."

"I know, mulāzim." Ghadin held her gaze steadily. The petulant kid Touraine had left behind had changed. "What makes you think I'm not already making my own choices? I don't need you to agree with me, either."

Her answer was so certain that it took Touraine aback.

"Oh," Touraine said. Pride and pain made the tears spill over. She wiped them away roughly. "Okay. Good."

"Luca's not in the hospital tent. I'll take you to her."

Ghadin offered Touraine her shoulder, and if Touraine was leaning more heavily on the girl than she should have, Ghadin was kind enough not to jerk away from her touch.

Ghadin knocked on the door of the tavern with a coded pattern Touraine was too groggy with pain to follow. The door opened and a woman looked sour-faced at Ghadin, and even more sourly at Touraine. The Finger growled something in her throat, but she went back inside, leaving the door open.

The first thing Touraine noticed was the warmth. The fire was low, and there were enough bodies within to stifle the air, but the windows were closed and someone locked the door behind them. Then she saw Durfort on her own, tapping fingers anxiously on the empty table. Then Durfort saw her. Durfort's eyes went wide. She stood.

Touraine staggered forward. "Is she—"

"Upstairs," Durfort said. "Second door, right—"

Touraine was already moving, and Durfort was at her side an instant later, an arm around her waist, helping her. Touraine forced herself up each stair, pulling the crown out of her shirt.

Durfort gasped. "How did you—"

Touraine shook her head. "Do you mind if I—if I do this alone?"

She waited for pain to shadow Durfort's face, but there was only understanding.

"Of course." Durfort traced Touraine's cheekbone, the slightest touch. "You're hurt. I'll make sure there's hot water and someone to see to you after."

Durfort's steps echoed down the stairs, and Touraine sagged against the door, resting her forehead against the wood. Finally, she dredged up the strength to pound her fist on the door.

"Come in."

It was her. Touraine had been half-sure it would be a mistake, but sky above! That fucking imperious, frustratingly haughty voice. It was her. *Luca.* Her. It was Luca.

Touraine's legs were shaking. Only now did she let herself stop to think about what this moment might be like. If she'd let herself think it

before, she would have hesitated. She would have doubted. If she'd hesitated, if she'd doubted, she would have fallen, she would have stopped,
she wouldn't have made it. Now she was here and she couldn't even put
her hand on the doorknob. She didn't have the strength to turn it.

"Hello?" Luca's voice again, this time colored with fear.

Touraine pushed the door open.

Luca sat in her bed, an open book face down on her lap. A thin
blanket covered her to her hips. Dark shadows ringed puffy eyes, and
her cheekbones seemed starker than they'd ever been, her collarbones
too prominent. As if something had been devouring her from the
inside. Her mouth hung open.

Her golden hair was cropped short, just below the ear.

"Touraine," she whispered.

"Luca."

Luca swung her legs over the side of the bed. Breathlessly, she said,
"You look like utter shit."

"Your hair." Touraine took a hesitant step toward her, arms swinging halfway up of their own accord.

Luca heaved herself to her bare feet. Pale toes gripped the wood. She
was wearing the same shirt Touraine had seen her in last. It had been
washed, but the shirt was more pale brown than cream. The hole in the
middle had been carefully sewn with tight stitches. Step by shaky step
she came, like a vengeful corpse returned from the grave.

"You lied to me." Touraine didn't know the words were coming out
of her mouth until they were there, between them.

Luca halted, frowning. "What?"

"You sent Moyenne after Pruett. You hid that from me."

Luca struggled to stand upright, reaching for that imperiousness
like a blanket. "And look at what she's done."

Touraine could not deny it. "You were supposed to trust me."

"You fucking *killed* me. You let them kill my people— I thought—"
Luca's anger faltered and she turned away. "I thought you'd abandoned me."

Touraine didn't tell her how close she'd almost come to doing just
that. Instead, she held out the golden crown. It was bent again, some of
the delicate leaves crumpled, and fallen off.

Luca brushed the crown with her fingertips, but didn't take it. She held Touraine's eyes. "Why did you come back?"

"It was the plan." Touraine pressed the crown into Luca's hands. "Remember? Things got a bit difficult is all."

Touraine waited, hoping despite herself.

Then Luca fell onto her, pulling Touraine close, burying her face in Touraine's neck. She smelled...clean. Like herself. No rose perfume, no ink.

"Just tell me you're here," Luca murmured, her breath hot against Touraine's skin. "Tell me this is real. Tell me the sky-falling truth, Touraine, because if you're going to stab me in the back—or the front—again—you had better make sure it keeps."

"I'm sorry, Luca. I'm so sorry. I'm here. I am. I'm here."

She pushed Luca away, just enough to meet her eyes. Luca held her there, cupping Touraine's face in her hands, thumbs tracing her cheek, her brow. Luca kissed her, lips firm and urgent, trying to learn the truth of it. With that kiss, the war outside disappeared. The war inside Touraine went quiet. For one moment, she had everything she needed.

Luca pulled at her vest and Touraine shucked it off, barely separating their mouths for a second. It fell to the ground. The sudden air raised goose bumps on Touraine's flushed skin. They shuffled in a desperate minuet to the bed, Touraine pushing, Luca pulling. Touraine was trying to lower Luca gingerly to the bed when the muscles in her calf seized, stretching the bite whose ache Touraine had forgotten.

She bit down on the scream so the only thing that came out was a tortured moan as she toppled face down into the bed.

"Touraine?" Beneath her, Luca searched the source of her wounds.

Touraine heaved herself to Luca's side and flopped onto her back. Luca's hands worked at her boots.

"Don't bother, I'll get it," she slurred as she sat up and reached to bat Luca's hands away.

"If you weren't so pitiful right now, I would let you try. I need a good laugh. Lie down."

Touraine obeyed. Had it only been this morning that she'd fought Pruett off? A few days since she'd broken into the palace? The bed was soft. Luca's body was warm beside her. The first boot slid off easily, but the second—Luca hissed, and Touraine groaned through her teeth again.

"What happened?"

"Do you know the gamekeeper's hunting dogs?"

"Not well."

"I do."

"Oh, Touraine." Luca settled beside her and pulled Touraine onto her chest. "Tell me what happened."

Touraine opened her mouth, fully intending to confess everything that had happened from the very first day she had left the palace up to this very moment, but she lost herself in the rhythmic stroke of Luca's hand on her back. Then there was nothing.

CHAPTER 62

ON SURRENDER

Touraine woke briefly while the wounds on her leg and face were cleaned, stitched, and bandaged, and slept immediately after. The next time she woke, she was naked and curled into Luca's hip, the bedclothes pulled to her shoulders. Sunrise gilded the room, and the smell of garlic and onion rose from below. It could have been a dream.

Luca sat upright in the bed with that same book. Her expression when she looked down at Touraine, though...

Touraine blushed. "Morning."

"Good evening." Luca scraped her nails across Touraine's hair, and Touraine leaned into it. "How are you feeling?"

Evening. Sunset, then. Explained a few things. "I'm starving."

"What a coincidence. Sabine brought this up. Told me to make you eat something. Can you sit up? Put this on."

Touraine moaned with the effort of putting on the proffered shirt. She'd put her body through the shit, and it was telling on her, loudly. She took the bowl Luca handed her next, and then watched the queen of Balladaire fall upon humble tavern stew as if it were the best thing she'd ever tasted.

"There's meat in it. They said it's rat," Luca said around a mouthful, "but I told them I didn't care as long as there was more." She smiled slyly and swallowed. "I don't think they were expecting that."

The food eased the ache in Touraine's belly and made her feel less like a strung-up carcass, but it also refilled something deeper inside.

She'd depleted herself so much trying to heal Luca, then Henrir, and with her body trying to heal itself...Her body was probably cannibalizing itself to find the strength it needed. Maybe that was why Luca looked so gaunt.

Touraine tilted the bowl up to swallow the last of the juices, then let the spoon clatter into the empty bowl.

"And you? Are you...all right?"

Luca scraped her spoon through the last of her own stew. "I'm not sure. This is actually the first time I've been able to eat properly since I arrived." She glanced anxiously over the side of the bed. "I wondered if you could...see if something has gone wrong."

"What's happening? What do you feel?" Touraine pored over Luca, trying not to think of Luca's body limp and heavy in her arms. Instead, she thought helpfully of Sabine's botched healing, and her failure to heal Ghadin at all.

"I would have been dead if you hadn't tried at all, Touraine." Luca pressed a calming hand against her shoulder. "However, I do think I was...vomiting blood yesterday."

"You were *what*?" Touraine said, strangled.

"I'm all right, I only want to make sure things are..." Luca tilted her head from side to side. Her short hair swung loose, and she raked it back.

"Here, let me see."

Luca put their bowls on the bedside table and lay back. The lines in her face eased—a little—as she closed her eyes. Touraine put a hand at Luca's hip, beneath the hem of her shirt.

"Can I?" she asked.

Luca hummed her consent, and Touraine slid her hand up Luca's stomach. Luca's breath hitched at the brush of skin against skin. Her muscles tensed.

"Hurts?"

"Cold."

"Sorry."

"That's all right."

Touraine closed her eyes and let her senses travel through Luca's body, the places where raw gashes were only barely sealed together with new flesh. Weak flesh, almost as likely to break as new stitches. Some places where the new flesh *had* broken.

Cold fingers wrapped around Touraine's forearm. It felt good on her flushed skin.

"Why does it still hurt so much?" Luca's voice was tense with pain.

"I didn't have a chance to work on it like I should have. And you've woken too early. Last time—"

Luca gasped and squeezed her arm as Touraine pressed too hard.

"Sorry. Last time, I healed you a little every day. I think you could heal on your own now, but it would take...weeks."

"Can you speed it up? I sincerely doubt the Taargens will wait on our pleasure."

A reminder that this wasn't a dream at all.

"There's something else. I don't understand it." The same sluggishness as before, Luca's flesh slower to respond to the healing. And it was warm, too warm. "Your body is...slow. I'm having a harder time than usual getting it to— Are you sure you're all right?"

Luca stared hard at the ceiling, lips pursed tightly.

"What?" Touraine paused. "Luca, tell me."

"While you were gone, I was sick."

Touraine's hands convulsed involuntarily and Luca winced. "The Withering?"

Luca nodded and explained the deal she had made with Fili and Guérin. Clearly, it had not gone quite as any of them expected.

"I understand," Touraine said when she finished.

"You do?" Luca held tight to Touraine's hand again, almost desperate.

"Aye." Then Touraine shifted from tenderness to practicality. "Get ready."

When she finished reinforcing the healing in Luca's gut and making sure there was nothing else wrong, Luca opened her eyes, her breathing ragged and shallow.

"What about you?" she asked.

"What about me?"

"Your leg. The gamekeeper's dog?" A crease of worry between her dark eyebrows. "What happened after I—after that?"

Touraine explained as best she could, from the day she'd marched off with Balladaire's army. She didn't tell Luca how all of it had happened because she couldn't make herself kill Pruett.

Luca stared at her hands in silence for a long while. When she did speak, it was quietly. "I'm sorry. I should never have gone behind your back. Ghislaine threatened to tell you."

"That's when you had her captured by 'brigands.'" Touraine exhaled sharply. "She did. Tell me. On the way back from her 'rescue.'"

She watched Luca replay those last days together in her mind, sadness deepening the lines around her mouth, at the corners of her eyes.

"She's dead now," Luca said quickly, turning aside to stare at the other side of the room. "Poison. So is Nicolas."

"What? Both of them?"

The cords of Luca's neck stiffened. "I killed him."

Touraine's mouth worked silently. As much as she hated the man, she'd never expected Luca to go that far. When Touraine still said nothing, Luca faced her again, her expression torn between defiance and shame. She expected judgment. Again.

"They were long months, Touraine."

Touraine covered Luca's hands with one of hers, without breaking eye contact. She could judge no one. "I know. Me too."

Luca rested her forehead against Touraine's, their noses brushing. "And now?"

Touraine sighed. "We should leave before someone downstairs decides we're worth the price of safety. I heard horses. We could leave La Chaise, lay low for a while, come back stronger—"

"No." Luca raised her head. "I'm not leaving my city. I will die—again—before I let them keep my palace."

"You'd have us all die fighting?"

"I would have *the world* die fighting to keep my city, Touraine. This is your home, too. Don't tell me you wouldn't fight for it."

The words struck at a knot of feelings deep within Touraine's chest. She'd traced the edges of them often lately, only to flinch away. She pushed them down again.

"You have another brilliant plan?"

"I had a plan—something like a plan—" Luca's mouth twisted into a sneer. Touraine startled at the uncloaked expression. "But I need the

Fingers *and* the soldiers, and Fili refuses to help unless I surrender the crown."

"So give it up. It's not worth the city."

"*No.* They're mad if they think I've fought all this way to throw it to the dogs."

"They're not dogs," Touraine said quietly.

"I— You know what I mean."

Touraine released Luca's hand and sat back, good leg curled beneath her and the other stretched out. The dog's bite still throbbed. She would see to it soon. She stared up at the ceiling, as if it could make the next words easier.

"What if the Fingers are right?"

"That I shouldn't be queen? That I should give up the throne?"

"Aye. Let the people have a say in their own lives. In the laws that govern them."

Luca scoffed. "I spent my whole life studying how to keep a country running. Have they?"

"You run this country with help. Seneschals and advisors and the like. Could it be so bad to let the people have a sort of council, like we do in Qazāl? Jaghotai was talking about expanding it, before I came here." She waved her hand to encompass the new war sprung around them.

"Gil died to put me on this throne. I will not waste that." Luca's voice was cold and barely restrained.

"It's not a waste," Touraine said, unable to bank the hot frustration in her own words, as gentle as she wanted to be. She let her head fall back against the headboard. "If Nicolas were on the throne, we wouldn't even have this chance. Gil died to give you the *choice.*"

"You don't know what he wanted. He was the bodyguard of a *king!*"

"It doesn't matter what he wanted. This is *our* choice. He's not here. *We* are. *They* are. I once fought you for the same things they're fighting for, remember?"

"Are you here to help me save my crown, or take it?" Luca shouted.

"Fuck the sky-falling crown, Luca!" Touraine twisted in bed to face her. "I'm here for *you.*"

"I *am* my crown!"

"No! You are *not*. You are a clever woman who was accidentally born to a couple of royals. You like to read about heroes who plant magical trees. You play échecs. You're my— You have too many lovers and not enough sense. Right now, you are still a woman people listen to. But you are *not* a shiny circle of metal. You are not a gilded chair.

"You've had so many dreams, Luca. I *know* them—you shared them with me. Think of how many you'll achieve if you let the crown go. Everything I did out there? It was for this chance. Everything you want for your people. *Those people downstairs.*"

"I—I can't."

Once, Touraine had thought that Luca would never bend. That she would shatter like a dropped glass if she were ever forced to hold on to her principles and her crown at the same time. Naively, Touraine thought Luca had grown past that.

But here Luca was, arms wrapped around her own body as if she could hold on to this last piece of herself.

"I can't, Touraine. I can't."

Touraine took Luca's face in her hands. "You can. The world will go on, maybe better than before. You'll still be part of the histories."

She tugged Luca forward, slowly, coaxing her like Durfort had taught her to coax a horse. Luca collapsed into her chest.

"I have to keep fighting," she sobbed. "I have to keep fighting."

"Aye." Touraine stroked Luca's hair. "We will. We will. But we need friends. We can fight for something better than we started with. Later. When we're stronger. I promise, this time, I'll be here."

It was a long time before Luca quieted, succumbing to the exhaustion of her healing. They settled against the headboard, with Luca still curled into Touraine's chest, nestled in the crook of her arm. Touraine's shirt was damp, and she was about to shift Luca up so she could get more comfortable when Luca spoke again.

"Remember when you told me I needed to have faith in something that wasn't myself?" A pained smile curled one side of her mouth. "I think I have."

Touraine stiffened. "Don't. Please don't."

Luca startled back, stricken. "Don't what?"

"Don't make me into a god. I can't live up to that."

Sadness tilted the corners of Luca's eyes, blue green and sparkling like the Triaume under bright sun, her fury burned out.

"No one can. That's what love is. We make our people into tiny, ruinous gods, and we act surprised when they let us down." She traced a thumb around Touraine's chin. "Yet we worship them all the same."

"Mm." Touraine kissed Luca once before tucking her back beneath her chin. "Is that what love is?"

"Rather underwhelming, isn't it?"

"Hardly."

Then, a short time later, Touraine asked: "If you had faith in me, why did you stab *me*? *Twice*?"

Luca turned a wry smile up at her. "I didn't say I was perfect."

Touraine laughed into Luca's hair and squeezed her tight. Breathed her in, as if holding on to even the smell of her would make this moment last longer and delay all the rest.

"Luca Ancier, last queen of Balladaire." Then, despite how much the overwhelming surge in her chest frightened her, Touraine whispered, "I do love you, Luca."

Luca tightened a fist in Touraine's shirt.

"It's not enough, though," Touraine said. "Is it?"

"Perhaps not." Luca traced the scar across Touraine's palm, and then the matching one across her own. "But can't it be a start?"

"Aye, it can. Or an end."

CHAPTER 63

ONE DAY MORE

A knock on the wooden door roused Luca from an uneasy sleep. It took her a moment to remember where she was, who lay beside her, what had happened. Touraine lay with her back curled against her, facing the wall.

The knock came again, more urgently. Touraine startled awake, reaching for a knife that was not there.

"Luca? Touraine?" Sabine.

"Come in." Luca rubbed the sleep from her eyes. "What time is it?"

"It's the middle of the night." Sabine gave them a once-over and snorted. "I hope you've made up, my doves. These *Fingers* have news." She faltered over the rebels' name for themselves. Luca didn't blame her. The way of things had turned all upside down. "The Taargens are going door to door through the whole city, looking for you. They're bringing their army in, squad by squad—"

"But they'll be trapping themselves in here—" Luca frowned, confused.

"Because without you dead, the next best thing is to occupy the city." Touraine scrubbed her face. "Besides, it'll be easier to hold the city against Moyenne from the inside."

"But surely they wouldn't want to face a siege? In a hostile city?"

"It doesn't matter what they want. It matters what they're doing." Touraine had regained her broad soldier's accent while she was away; Luca hadn't realized how much a stamp the court had left on her. "I need to speak to Perrot. He's our contact for the gendarmerie and the rest of the soldiers garrisoned in the city. We need to speak to Fili and organize them into some sort of defense—"

"Let me help." Sabine looked dashing in borrowed rough trousers with her shirtsleeves rolled up. No frills or lace, no cologne, but she still carried herself like the noble rake she had once been. The cut on her face had been stitched; it would leave a scar.

"Talk to Perrot," Touraine said. "I'm sure he'll find a place—"

"Let me ride to the Travers garrison," Sabine interrupted.

"Travers? He was a traitor—"

"I'm sure his soldiers didn't know that. There's a captain"—Sabine flicked a glance to Touraine, whose eyes narrowed—"she's competent, and I'm sure she's loyal. She'll ride south with me."

Luca frowned. "Even if you could get out of the city, what will you do? Lead them in a charge?"

Sabine crossed her thick forearms over her chest. "You need every person you can get."

To Luca's chagrin, Touraine was stroking her chin thoughtfully. "The Taargens' western army won't stand by and watch. They're probably marching on the West Gate now. Half the Travers garrison is cavalry, isn't it?"

Sabine nodded.

"Then you should."

"Don't I get a say in this?" Luca looked between them.

"Unfortunately for you, I don't think so." Sabine crossed the room in long, leisurely steps. She knelt beside the bed. "Luca."

Luca stared straight ahead, lips pursed.

"Luca. Listen to me." With gentle fingers, Sabine turned Luca's chin to face her.

"It's too dangerous." Luca scowled.

"Am I any less than either of you?" Sabine's dark eyes sought Touraine, who dipped her head in solidarity. Then she turned back to Luca. "I'll do this, and then when the empire is saved, we'll come back and I swear to you we will all three of us fuck until the leather on that cock unravels. How does that sound? My looks aren't so spoiled, are they?"

"Ha!" Touraine snorted. "You have a deal."

Sabine held Luca's eyes, waiting.

Luca sighed. "You'll wear out before the cock does."

Sabine clasped her hand to her chest and bowed her head over it, as if wounded. Then she smirked. "I'll take that as a challenge, Your Majesty."

Luca laughed despite herself. "Go, then. And for the sky's sake, be careful."

"Aren't I always? You two, on the other hand…" Sabine stood and half climbed onto the bed. She brushed Luca's hair behind her ear only for it to fall free again. "Be safe." Sabine kissed Luca, her fingers gently caressing Luca's ear and down her neck. Luca held Sabine's face close to hers. Then Sabine pulled away and glared at Touraine. "Both of you." She climbed over Luca and straddled Touraine. Their kiss was less sentimental, more growling competition; Touraine's fist was tight in the hair at the back of Sabine's head.

For a moment, Luca let herself imagine that they might survive this. That, if she were not queen, they could have all the time in the world, with no nation-ending crises to hollow out Sabine's laughing eyes or stoop Touraine's strong shoulders. She and Touraine and sometimes Sabine, with a library and a few swords, maybe a horse or two. A simple bed in a—well, perhaps not *too* simple a home, nor too simple a bed.

"Maybe I could stay a little longer—" Sabine said, mouth trailing down Touraine's chin to her neck.

Touraine shoved her off, laughing, but when she spoke, her tone was sober. "We don't have time to waste."

"Waste?" Sabine cried in outrage. "Waste? I'll show you waste—"

"Do you want to save the city or not, my lord chevalier?" Luca asked dryly.

At that, Sabine rolled her eyes and clambered off the bed. She stared down at them both for a long moment. "Good luck, my dears."

It was as if Sabine took all the hope with her, leaving only the weight of the duties ahead.

"Shall we?" Touraine asked.

"Delaying will only make it worse."

They dressed and went downstairs, following the muted voices to the common room. Gathered around one of the large tables were Luca's new allies. Fili and her two companions, Ghadin, Perrot, and—

"Guérin?"

The former guard looked at Luca as if she'd seen her own death coming. She stood, holding herself up on the table. "Your Majesty." Guérin glanced desperately toward Fili, as if even now she would protect her from Luca.

Luca smiled wearily. "It's good to see you, Inès. I'm sure Fili's told you by now."

"Told me what?" Guérin sat back down, relief sagging her features. To Fili, she said, "Tell me what?"

Fili's young face was smooth except for the slight wrinkle of concentration on her brow. "What do you mean?"

"I accept your terms. I will abdicate. However"—Luca held up a finger to forestall any exclamations—"if we survive this, I will not watch this country thrash around like a beast with no head. We work *together* to build what comes next."

Silence for a moment, as the Fingers regarded each other. One by one, they all turned to Fili, waiting.

"We accept."

"You'll fight by my side?" Luca said. "At my direction?"

"Are you a general?" snapped the short woman at the table. Velte, Luca thought her name was.

"I am." Touraine crossed her arms, her muscles flexing.

A sharp look from Fili, and Velte sat back, surly, tonguing her teeth.

"How do you propose we fight?" Fili asked. "We're not soldiers."

"I have some ideas." Ideas she'd gotten from the old chevalier tales in the Durfort books. "Do you know the story of Queen Isobelle?" The queen who had raised the earth in torrents to stop her enemies. Precisely the kind of power Luca had been looking for, but she hadn't been able to call even a hint of it to herself.

Fili's mouth tightened. "I do. But I don't know if I can do that. Definitely not alone."

"You won't be alone." Guérin put her hand on her daughter's shoulder.

"No." Luca felt a burning in her nose and a tightness in her chest. "You won't be."

They planned deeper into the night, and when they were finished,

Perrot sent one of his lieutenants in plain clothes to spread the word. One of the Fingers went, too, looking for bags of thorntree pods like they used to plant barriers between crops and grazing land. When they had done all they could, Touraine dragged her back upstairs.

"Come on." She yawned behind her hand as she tugged Luca's sleeve. "You'll want your rest come tomorrow."

Luca followed her, but in their small bed, she stared at the ceiling, unable to sleep away her last night as queen.

The next thing she knew, she was being shaken awake.

"It's time," Touraine said, stuffing a piece of dried meat into her mouth. She was already dressed in the same rough laborer's clothing as Sabine, but over it all, she put on her now-sleeveless gold prince-general's coat. She buckled her sword belt over it. She tossed Luca similar clothing.

"I can't wear this," Luca said, holding the plain blouse to her chest. "I need them to know it's me." *She* needed to know.

Touraine tossed her bloody, half-bent crown onto the bed. "That should help."

Before they headed down the stairs and into the commotion below, Touraine asked, "Are you sure you don't want to stay?"

"We talked about this," Luca said archly. "I'm not hiding in a rebel tavern while my city is sacked. Get me to the wall."

Touraine put her hand against Luca's chest, fiddling with a button on her blouse. "Luca—"

Luca covered Touraine's hand with hers. The nervous chatter downstairs was a low hum as Fili and her people prepared to go to their respective fronts. Her own stomach was a knot, tightening even as she glared Touraine down.

"These are my people, Touraine. For the time being, I am still the queen."

Touraine exhaled slowly. She brushed the edge of Luca's crown with her thumb, then the corner of Luca's mouth. "Aye."

Downstairs, Perrot was waiting, a youth bouncing on his toes beside him. When he saw Touraine, he saluted.

"Report," Touraine ordered.

"Your Highness. The Taargens are still fighting to get through the gate—the ones who are already in the city are fighting to hold it open. I've already sent men, but I don't know how long they'll hold it. The palace garrison was only a thousand strong, the gendarmerie twice that."

Touraine closed her eyes and exhaled slowly. "Do whatever it takes to shut it. Give me a hundred men for the walls and spare an escort for the Fingers going to the West Gate."

"Aye, sir." Perrot saluted, then they shared a soldier's clasp, holding tight to each other's forearms. A silent conversation passed between them that Luca was not privy to.

Then it was their turn.

The streets had emptied when the Taargens raced to their posts at the gates, the hunt for the dead queen on hold. Luca had no cane, but they got in a fiacre driven by one of the Fingers, and she drove them as close to the wall as she dared. Luca white-knuckled the edge of the seat. Touraine glanced at her.

"I'm fine," Luca said through her teeth.

Touraine squeezed her knee.

When the driver stopped them a few blocks from the wall, Luca heard the fighting. It was like the rushing of a river or the pounding waves of the ocean—every distinct moment becoming a wall of blended sound.

"We have to fight to the top," Touraine said, climbing out. "Don't come up until I give the signal."

"What's the signal?"

"When we've won the wall."

Luca caught Touraine's sleeve. "And if we don't? Win the wall?"

Touraine held her eyes. "You'll know."

Before Luca could call her back one last time, Touraine slammed the cab door and ran off.

CHAPTER 64

ON DIPLOMACY

Pruett fingered the bayonet in the belt at her hip. It was Taargen make, the angle of the point different from the Balladairan bayonets—a subtle tilt she could feel by running her finger along the edge. She didn't have the words for how strange it felt to be in Balladaire again. To be at war against it. She'd never been to La Chaise properly before, but she'd seen its walls stretching up.

No, she corrected herself—she had been once, to a hanging in Traitor's Corner. It had been a warning, not a pleasure trip. *Don't fuck up or you'll swing here, too.*

She was past that kind of fuckup. She'd probably die on this field, but whatever happened, she'd take Touraine down with her. Touraine hadn't just lied to Pruett. She'd killed Armande. She had reached into Pruett's body without permission and—whatever it was, Pruett felt… not dirty, not used, but something worse. Vulnerable. Violated.

After Pruett had let her back in. After Pruett had fought for her, protected her.

Pruett had woken up on the lawn, staring up at the purple-pink sunset, alone except for the corpse of the hunting dog and the unconscious Masridāni. Kiras had turned up nothing in her search; she didn't know the city, and her face marked her too foreign to get cooperation. She'd sent squads of soldiers through the city then, breaking down doors and searching rooms for anyone stupid enough to shelter the fugitive queen.

Now the fighting had begun, there was nothing else but to hope the people hated the bitch too much to rally around her.

The allied Masridāni and Taargen soldiers fired volley after volley against the packed groups of Balladairans marching from the south. There weren't many of them; chewing at Pruett's heels during the long march had cost them in numbers, but they were forced to clump by the Balladairans' own defenses. The chevaux-de-frise made choke points. When they were close enough, Pruett would call the order to charge through the clumps. Break and scatter them like a powder packet.

Behind her, the soldiers of the forward companies were marching into the city as organized as you could squeeze thousands of soldiers through one massive door. It was another dangerous choke point, but Roric was directing the flow from the walls above, keeping the Balladairans from reclaiming the cannons above. They had time. They had plenty of time.

Beside her, Kiras fingered her holy knife, like Pruett. Steady. Thoughtful. They caught each other's eyes and Pruett smiled. A faint blush darkened Kiras's brown cheeks.

"Tell me when, Qā'id."

Pruett sucked her teeth. "Hold a little longer. Another volley, if our infantry get their dicks and cunts in hand; you'll go cold waiting on them to reload."

Kiras's smile broadened, but it fell as someone shouted behind them.

"Qā'id!" A scrawny Masridāni came running, leaping over divots the army had dug into the ground with their marching. "Qā'id! They're trying to close the gates!"

Pruett jerked her gaze back to the wall. The soldiers pushing in were stalled, progress slowing. She flinched as another volley of rifle fire exploded behind her. If they didn't keep that gate open, she'd be crushed against the wall.

"Well, fuck me with a rusty bayonet," Pruett swore. "Taargens, ready cannons!"

La Chaise's walls were high and fortified, impossible to breach, especially when they were manned by scores of soldiers with fresh ammunition for their rifles and the cannons that would crush the armies who dared come against their walls. They were a relic from an older time, the era of the kings Fontine, of Empress Djaya and the first King Ancier.

Today, these walls were Touraine's.

The Taargens swarming the top like green beetles were her problem.

To the left, the fighting at the gate was thick, but the influx of Perrot's blackcoats kept the Taargens too occupied to bother with the squad racing for the crooked set of stairs to the right of the gate. Perrot was outnumbered, though. A snake of doubt curled around Touraine's ankle. If Moyenne didn't hurry, it didn't matter if Touraine took the wall; more Taargens would come from behind and slaughter her and her blackcoats to take it back. Take it all.

No use telling Luca all of that. She would find out soon enough. Touraine gripped the knife in her hand. *Stop dwelling. Go.*

"Up!" she roared to the blackcoats around her. "Take the walls, and we take back La Chaise!"

She stopped thinking about the gate and about Moyenne. No Luca, no Sabine, no Pruett. Just the tight stairwell, stone to her right and a drop back to the city cobbles on the left. The Taargens met them on the stairs with knives and hand axes, bayonets and pistols, tooth and nail.

Touraine snarled her knife into another Taargen's ribs and threw them to the left. They slipped on the blood-slick stone and never caught their balance, crashing into the empty storage barrels below. She sagged into the wall, fighting the dizziness that almost sent her after them. She had never had to fight so soon after healing as much as she had in the last week, and it showed in her body.

"Battle-sister!"

Touraine raised her gaze from her feet, blinking until her vision cleared. Roric blocked the path to the top of the wall with his bulk. Her battle-brother. Her unexpected, unsuspecting friend. His face was splotched red, contorted in bitter anger.

"You saved my life," he said gruffly, speaking in Taargen. "You lied to me."

"I told you." Touraine set herself against the stone wall, resetting the grip on her slick knife. "This is my home."

She lunged, hoping to force him backward, but he was nimble. She knew this, knew how swiftly, how truly he could place his feet. She had studied the Taargen dance, studied how Roric moved because she had *known*—had she known, or had she secretly hoped this moment would never come?—that one day, they would dance for their lives.

He swung down on her with his heavy sword and Touraine ducked beneath it, stealing another step, keeping her back to the wall of the stairs. Touraine wasn't fool enough to overestimate her skill with a blade, no matter how much time she had spent with Sabine de Durfort. Better to keep him in tight, to own the terrain. She jabbed her knife out again as another blackcoat thrust up at him. Roric parried the blackcoat's blade with his own and shoved the soldier down the stairs, taking several others with him, Taargen and Balladairan alike.

Touraine's own blow was caught in the bear fur, unable to bite through the thick hide. She took the opportunity to take the high ground, but Roric was quick. He pressed her and she stumbled back, up and up until—she found a dip on a stair, worn smooth by decades of soldiers. Her foot slid from under her, and she cried out as she landed on her tailbone. Roric pounced while she was dazed.

She rolled away from his thrust at the last second and stared down a fatal drop off the edge.

"Shit, fuck, shit." Without looking back toward Roric, Touraine kicked like a donkey. It connected with something hard as rock, but it connected. She kicked again, low, aiming for the ankle. Only glancing.

Beneath them, the stone rattled. The heavy door to the city slammed shut, and some unlucky sod screamed.

Above her, Roric raised his sword again. There was nowhere else for her to go. Nothing beneath her head but air. Touraine groped for her knife, but it was out of reach. The blow descended toward her face.

"Your Highness!" A Qazāli, half stumbling, half crawling up the stairs, yanked Roric by the ankle and the big man fell, his sword strike going wide. Touraine jerked to the side and took the blow in her left shoulder instead of her skull.

She looked over Roric's prone body to the man who'd saved her life.

"Mulāzim." He saluted her in the Balladairan style.

Shālan soldiers. It made Touraine feel like she'd done something right. It made her feel like she'd done something wrong.

With his help, Touraine scrambled to her feet. The prince didn't move.

"Help me get him up there." Touraine jerked her head up the stairs, and together, they dragged the unconscious prince to the top of the wall. She kicked his sword off the edge of the stairs. Her own knife dangled uselessly in her left hand; she couldn't raise that arm at all. Warm blood trickled down her chest, her elbow, soaking her golden coat.

When they saw their captured prince, the Taargens on the wall fought harder, but Touraine's blackcoats overwhelmed them. Soon, Roric was the only Taargen left alive. Henrir the wolf was not among the dead.

Standing on the wall, all of Balladaire stretching before her, Touraine couldn't believe it. The cannons were hers. Below, the milling mass on the ground churned the green grass to mud. Fields interrupted by pockets of flowering meadow. Dark patches of forest and the silver streak of the Nervure, running off into the distance, not knowing or caring how many bodies it would carry with it.

Touraine should have felt relieved.

Between their grips, Roric began to stir and then, when he realized who was holding him, to struggle to his feet. Touraine let him stand, just so that she could kick the side of one knee. It popped and he fell back down with a roar of pain. The other soldier bent the arm he held behind him until his shoulder joint cracked loud as musket fire. She put her long knife to Roric's throat and led them to the edge of the wall.

"Taargen!" she yelled from her painfully raw throat. She searched the crowd for Albric's unmistakable form. "We have your prince!"

"Taargen! We have your prince!" The bellow came down from on high, ragged but unmistakable.

Luca's relief almost made her knees buckle.

She alighted from the fiacre and followed the trail of corpses Touraine and the other blackcoats had left, up the narrow staircase. On the top of the wall, the noise was otherworldly, gunfire and screaming, a walking nightmare. Touraine stood on one side of the wall with

Roric. Her left arm dangled at her side, but she held a knife to Roric's throat with the other.

"Stay down," Touraine hissed when she noticed Luca. Then she bellowed to her soldiers, "Fetch a white flag!"

Luca ignored Touraine's instructions and strode tall to the patch of wall above the gate. Balladairans stopped as they saw her, and a half-distracted cheer went up. How many of them had believed her dead when the palace fell? She flinched as another volley of musket fire came from down below, but steadied herself against the crenellations. The stone was cold beneath her naked palms.

As a blackcoat waved a massive flag half the size of a coverlet, Touraine shouted that they had Prince Roric, and Luca felt the crush of fear closing tight around her throat, waiting for a musket ball to take her where she stood.

Instead, the gunfire sputtered to a halt. Silence. Then a voice boomed from below, within the city walls. High Priest Albric had a speaking cone to his mouth.

"Are you ready to speak terms of surrender?" he called.

"Aye." Touraine raised her eyebrows at Luca, as if to say, *Get your ass over here, Your Majesty.*

Luca crossed to Touraine's side of the wall and looked down. She pitched her voice to carry, and still it sounded too small. "High Priest Albric. The last time we spoke, you extended your hand in friendship. This is disappointing."

"You are more alive than we were led to believe. That is also disappointing."

"Do forgive me." Luca gave him a mocking bow. "We'll return your prince to you if you turn away now."

Touraine pressed Roric against the wall, so hard that he wheezed as the stone edge pressed into his chest. His white bear cloak distinguished him from anyone else, though the fur was bloodstained, matted, and musty. He snarled at Touraine, trying to get free. She met his growl with bared teeth. The other soldier held him firmly by his topknot.

"I will not go back!" Roric's words carried on the still air. It was not what Luca expected to hear. Nor, judging by Touraine's alarmed expression, did she. "I will die for the honor of the Bear and the Bear Queen!"

"There, you see?" Albric called up. "You are worthy of your pelt, Prince Roric."

Down below, the Taargens on both sides of the wall cheered.

"You don't have to do this, Roric," Touraine said urgently. "We fought beside each other once. Remember? You called me your battle-sister. We could end this together."

He looked at her with a boy's hatred and a boy's hurt. He spat. "Albric was right."

"Touraine," Luca interrupted. "Hand me your knife."

Touraine hesitated.

"Give it to me."

Touraine frowned and looked to Roric again. He held his chin up.

Luca took the blade. It was heavy in her hand. Roric had been a friend, in a way. She had watched him grow up, from a chubby little toddler to an overgrown teen. And now this strong, bearded man, ready to die for *what*? The futility of it all made her want to weep, and that made her furious. With that fury, she pulled the blade across his throat.

Cartilage crunched as the blade caught, but Luca jerked it through. Roric gurgled involuntarily as blood spurted hot and warm in front of them, splashing over the stone, dripping down his collar and over Luca's shaking hand.

A wolf howl, long and keening, came from far too close. It raised the hair on her arms and the back of her neck, a more primal fear than Luca had ever imagined herself capable of.

A roaring sound grew in Luca's ears, like a roll of thunder coming up the plains. She looked over the ledge, but the soldiers below weren't moving. It was within her. Roric's body slumped to the stone in a red pool. His dead eyes stared up at her.

One cannonball, then another, and another hit the wall and shook Luca to the ground.

"What about diplomacy?" Touraine helped her up, supporting her to the stairs as the world vibrated around them. Her hands were drenched in blood, her chin smeared with it.

"That *was* diplomacy." Luca's breath came raggedly and her heart beat too fast. "I learned it from Djasha. Brilliant woman."

Touraine started to say something, then shook her head in disbelief. A flush crept up Luca's neck.

"Now you've said your piece," Touraine said, "go to the hospital. Albric will be after you, and they're going to bring the sky-falling wall down."

"I know, I know. I'll go."

She couldn't make her feet move, though. Her hands were covered in blood, and already Touraine's shoulder was a gaping wound, cutting across her collarbone. The adrenaline rush of Roric's death left her shivering and terrified as she imagined the rest of the battle stretching out before them.

"You don't say goodbye before a battle," Touraine said. "It's shit luck. I'll see you when it's done." She pulled Luca by the front of her coat with her good arm and kissed her. "Be safe."

CHAPTER 65

WELCOME, JOLLY SOLDIER (REPRISE)

Touraine ran back up the stairs, still tingling with the press of Luca's lips. Before she reached the top, she paused to gather herself. She was general here. Her decisions would weave the fabric of Balladaire for the rest of history, and she'd be lying if she claimed she didn't feel lightheaded at the thought.

Luca believed in her. Not just Luca, but Sabine and Ghadin and even the Fingers who'd accepted the tasks she'd handed out to save the city. They'd given her a part of the city's fate to hold in her hands.

This is what you always wanted.

She emerged onto the top, ready.

"Balladaire!"

The soldiers looked to her. More than a few were Shālan. Despite all that had happened, she had more in common with these black-coats than she did with Luca and Durfort. More in common with the foot soldiers than the noble officers who would have otherwise ordered them to their deaths. Touraine was that officer now. She wanted to believe she had no choice, but she did. The problem was, the other choices were choices she refused to imagine.

She was too hoarse to raise her voice anymore, but when she spoke, they turned to her. "Those people down there have come for Balladaire. They want her fields. They want her orchards. They want her rich hearth and her wide skies, without the work it takes to earn it. They would rather water it with our blood than honest sweat.

"When they captured me, I watched while they raided our cities and burned down villages too helpless to defend themselves."

Never mind that she'd been fighting alongside the Taargens. That she'd as good as offered the villages as sacrifices for this bigger victory. Rumors that she was a traitor might have spread through the palace in her absence, but none of that showed in their rapt faces. She held them in her hands, as Cantic had once held her with her every declaration.

It was terror and ecstasy all at once.

"They've come for our home! Will we let them take it?"

"No!"

"Will we let them take it?" she yelled again.

"NO!"

"For Balladaire! Fire cannons at will!"

"For Balladaire!"

The response echoed up and down the wall, and the soldiers carried it with them.

Touraine stepped to the outer edge of the wall and peered over. The Taargens below had already turned their attention upward. They fired and missed, fired and hit. Farther along the wall, the stone shuddered with the impact of the Taargen cannons. And while the artillery kept Touraine and her people afraid, the Taargen infantry within the city would race to reclaim Balladairan cannons.

"Hurry up!" Touraine shouted. "Do we want the walls down before we get a single shot?"

Another soldier helped her wrap a swath of the white flag about the wound on her shoulder. She hadn't had a chance to heal it yet. To either side of her, the blackcoats prepared the massive cannons, loading them and loading muskets.

"No, sir!" chorused those nearest to her as they grunted everything into place.

Pruett might be down there. Some of the Sands, too, mixed with the Taargens and Masridāni. They'd made their choices. Touraine meant what she said to the blackcoats on the wall, no matter the impenetrable oil-slick layer that had kept her apart all her life.

Soon, every breath was full of gunpowder as her own cannons returned fire. Smoke and grit coated her tongue, and each tremor tested her balance. The iron barrels rattled in their brackets, water splashed as the soldiers sponged the cannons cool again. Sweat stuck her clothes to her back; the air was humid with the promise of rain that hadn't come. The dull gray clouds above were more like fog than towers of thunder. She prayed the rain would give them a reprieve.

Don't pray for rain. Be the rain.

It was new, this wholeness, and maybe Touraine only felt it because she knew she would die today, but she felt a certainty: home was as much about claiming a thing, a place—a person—as it was about being claimed. Touraine could claim Balladaire, and there it was— hers. All its faults, all its beauty—hers, and no one could take it away from her. She was a part of it; one of its darker parts, aye, but she was woven as deep into the fabric of this empire as it was in her.

"Sir! The cannons are failing!" One of the blackcoats struggled to shift a jammed lever while a lieutenant pointed out the angle, but the cannon wasn't moving.

The guns were new, large twenty-four-pounders, meant to be loaded from the breach in the back, with levers to shift it up and down or left and right in its bracket. A clever invention, but now it was another failure point in the weapon. Touraine glanced back over the wall. It wouldn't be precise, but there were enough soldiers down there that it would hit someone.

"It doesn't matter!" she shouted in the lieutenant's ear, trying to be heard through the cotton plugs the woman had stuffed in them. "Fire the fucking things until there's no one left to hit!"

Touraine missed Armande, the Sands' artillery master. She missed all her Sands. Even the ones down there.

Another soldier at her elbow: "Sir, we're running out of powder—"

"Get more from the magazine."

"But the Taargens—"

An explosion, the loudest yet, threw Touraine into the wall. She slid to the ground gasping for air, heat at her back. Her head spun. She couldn't hear a sky-falling thing, and her shoulder screamed.

When she was no longer seeing double, Touraine staggered to one knee. The lieutenant beside her had been thrown, too—her head had cracked into the wall, and she sat slumped at Touraine's side, eyes glassy and empty. One of their cannons had exploded. Taken a chunk of the wall and its whole team with it, in bloody, smoking bits amid the burning wood and twisted iron.

Maybe they wouldn't win here. Maybe she'd stacked her chits on the wrong cards, like Pruett said. Touraine would get what she deserved for playing the pet monkey one last time.

She wasn't dancing to Balladaire's music, no matter what Pruett said. Touraine didn't need to break herself to fit, ignoring the ways it cut into her flesh. She was changing it, not by erasing herself but by staying, by making them reckon with her presence. With what it said of their shared history and what shapes their shared future could take.

To have a future, though, they had to win.

"Sir, look!" The words sounded as if they were coming through water, muffled and bubbling.

Touraine took the offered arm and limped to the wall. She croaked, "Where?"

The blackcoat pointed.

Touraine could just make out the approaching mass if she squinted. "Who?"

Moyenne was already on the field below. Touraine had seen the Moyenne standard. She'd thought Valmorin was with her.

"Looks like a Balladairan flag, sir, but I don't think—"

"Give it to me." Touraine snapped her hand out for the lens. She hadn't dared think these pieces she'd placed were still in play.

Eye to the lens, Touraine found the Balladairan infantry below, pressing the enemy into the wall. To the side, where the soldier had pointed, she saw the standard—a bedraggled black banner with a golden horse, and the rumbling mass of Valmorin's cavalry.

"Sky a-fucking-bove," Pruett swore as the next round of cannon fire from above landed in the middle of her own army. "Shit shit shit-fuck." She looked for the drummer to call a new order—about-face,

form column, retreat, anything. Her soldiers were still spread long, the
better to hit the oncoming Balladairans from the field. More soldiers
waited in tight square reserves behind the line, and there the cannon-
ade from above fell.

There was only one way for them to go.

"Forward!" Pruett pointed toward the line of Balladairans to the
south. Her young drummer beat the tattoo. "Charge, you fuckers, or
get it up the ass by a cannonball!"

The combination of the drummed orders and Pruett's berating got
them moving, but they weren't moving well. Despite all the drilling
she'd done with them in Masridān and on the long march here, there
hadn't been enough time to make them *smooth*. Even veterans got
shaky in the open field, and these were not veterans. They were slow
and confused and they were frightened—*she* was frightened. With
every blast of the cannons behind them, they flinched, ducking round
to see if they were about to lose a leg, an arm, a head.

Welcome, soldiers. Welcome, jolly soldiers.

Those little shits of soldiers who'd bitten their heels in the dark had
turned into a solid company and a half of organized troops marching
straight at them, and though there were fewer of them, they knew what
they were doing. Past the obstacles now, the first row of the blackcoats
knelt down and fired one last volley.

It took Pruett's soldiers haphazardly as they charged. Some threw
themselves to the ground and fired with nothing more than a wish.
Pruett almost envied them. Commanders couldn't duck to the ground
and wait it all out.

This is all your fault, Touraine. I hope you choke on her fucking cunt.

Was it her fault, though?

Pruett looked up again. No rain fell from the gray sky. Unlucky. A
bit of rain might have muddied the cannons and the muskets, given
them a fighting chance.

To Kiras, Pruett said, "You ready?"

Kiras drew her knife and closed her golden eyes. "Yes, Qā'id."

When Kiras began to surge away with the rest of them, however,
Pruett held her back. "No, stay close."

She didn't need to watch her fighters running through Tempête's eyes. To watch them crash against the Balladairan line. To watch them fall. So she didn't see the cavalry coming until the thunder of their hooves gave the warning, and by then, it was too late. While her Masridāni grappled with the infantry in front of them, the Balladairan cavalry swept in from the east. There was no way under the sky above that she'd get her soldiers to form square when they were already fighting every person for themselves.

"Qā'id?" Kiras, unmarred by worry. "What do we do?"

Try not to die. But that was more optimistic than any of them had a right to hope for.

"Buy our artillery enough time to blast through the gate." She tried to sound calmer than she was.

Her men and women were falling back, closer and closer to the Taargens near the wall. She grabbed the nearest Taargen soldier and pointed to the line of cavalry.

The cavalry had two options. Smash the clusterfuck that was her Masridāni, who were already engaged with the Balladairan infantry, or crush the Taargen line and scatter them until they reached the cannons. The former would be easier, but it was unnecessary. Her soldiers weren't the threat.

"Protect the cannons!" she roared as the Taargens balked, looking for their officers to give them orders. She found the nearest one, with his fur mantle and braided whiskers—what was his name? She knew it, it was on the tip of her tongue, but it wouldn't come—and pointed out the threat to him, too. He got his soldiers into position.

She turned back to her own catastrophe to find the Masridāni falling back, their numbers dwindling. Where was Kiras?

Her eyes—or was it Tempête's eyes that gave her the ability to pick out her lover's figure, that blaze of ferocity, so quickly? Like a storm herself, Kiras fell on the Balladairans with her holy dagger and the blazing palm of her hand. Pruett watched in awe as the death priest left bodies ripped apart in her wake.

Except for one. One soldier wouldn't let Kiras get close, flashing sword keeping Kiras on her back foot. A soldier Pruett recognized, because she had kept her imprisoned in a tent next to hers for almost a month. *Moyenne.*

It was stupid to stop in the middle of the field while the cavalry rushed in on her left and the Balladairans pressed closer, gaining yard by yard. She stopped anylight, flinging her rifle over her shoulder. She readied it with the mindless speed of instinct and flipped it up to her face. Sighted down it.

She pulled the trigger, and everything happened at once.

The recoil slammed into her shoulder.

The cavalry slammed into the Taargen line behind her.

Roaring from soldiers, from riders. Shrieking, from humans and horses.

Pruett's bullet took Moyenne in the chest, jerking her off balance, but not enough to stop her sword from spearing Kiras through the middle.

Pruett must have screamed. How else would Moyenne have known to look up as she shook Kiras's body from her sword? Why else would she flick the blood off her sword and raise it to Pruett, some bastard of a salute as she staggered toward her?

As she yelled, her mind splintered into a million bodies—*she was scurrying scurrying flying rearing up lashing out screaming screaming screaming—*

Another Taargen cannonball slammed into the wall. Pruett wrenched herself back into her own body, her own throbbing head and breaking heart. Moyenne steadied herself on the shaking earth and looked with horror at the walls of La Chaise as chunks of stone fell. They locked eyes and made their choices.

"Balladaire!" Moyenne called, raising her gold-striped colonel's sleeve, sword high. "To the wall! Seize the cannons!" She took one lurching step, then another, and another before she fell to one knee. The Balladairan colonel collapsed.

Pruett could have ordered the Masridāni she had left to hold, to defend the cannons. She could have yanked the Taargens by the scruffs and made them hold the rear. She was losing everything for this city, and she was so close. Her coalition still outnumbered Balladaire. They only had to *outlast* them.

But what would she have when it was all over? Vengeance for the little girl whose parents had sold her to strangers across the sea? An old lover who hated her, and a sky-falling menagerie chittering in her head? The last time loneliness like that had torn her open, it was Kiras who found her, lured her in like the feral thing she was. Fed her, warmed her, loved her. Kiras had never let her down.

Pruett ran to her.

Kiras knelt, bent over, head pressed into the bloody mud. She clutched at her middle, holding herself together.

Pruett slid to her knees. "Kiras? Kiras, I'm here, can you hear me?"

Kiras turned her head just enough to see her and coughed a thick spatter of blood on the ground. Pruett laced her fingers with the claw Kiras was digging into the ground.

"Hurts," Kiras grunted.

"Thank fuck. Means you're alive. Don't cock it up now, eh?" Pruett forced a laugh. "Come on. Use your magic. We've got Balladairans to fuck over."

"You know... I can't."

Pruett closed her eyes. She knew Kiras couldn't. Not like Touraine, who could fucking kill the queen before their eyes and bring her back easy as pissing.

Touraine, who had thrown her aside again.

What was a favor owed between ex-lovers?

"Can you buy yourself a few minutes?"

"Uh?"

"Come on. We get to Touraine, we get you fixed."

"Fucking... mad."

"I can't lose you, too, Kiras. I need you. Okay? I need you. Please, try."

Even as Pruett held Kiras, a small throb of heat passed through the priest. She was scalding one second, normal the next. *Is that it? Is that what it feels like?*

"Okay? We have to move."

Their quaint bubble of solitude was breaking as the Balladairan infantry surged forward to smash the Taargens against the wall as the Taargens tried to fit themselves through the heavy oaken doors. Somewhere above that mess, Touraine was laughing down at them. Pruett needed to get Kiras to her.

Pruett slung her rifle over her shoulder and hefted Kiras to her feet, wedging herself under one arm. Kiras's tan tunic was soaked with blood. Together, they took a lurching step. Kira's legs buckled beneath her, bringing them down again. They would never make it to the wall, let alone through the fighting and the breach. The door they had slipped through in the night was too far away and sure as shit had soldiers manning it by now.

"Come on, Kirkousa." Pruett hooked Kiras under the armpits and dragged her. "Come on. Please. Do you know the things I still want you to do to me?"

Kiras chuckled dryly from the ground. Blood dribbled down her chin.

Pruett kept up a litany of the dirty thoughts she'd stored up, waiting for the nights—and days, Pruett wasn't picky—she and Kiras were free. With each future escapade more ridiculous than the last, her cheeks grew wetter. Tear tracks cut through the dirt on Kiras's face. They both knew the truth.

Pruett should have written the gods-damned poems.

Still, as she dragged Kiras toward the wall, she hunted through Tempête's eyes for Touraine.

Leowult. That was the Taargen captain's name.

CHAPTER 66

A LEGEND (REPRISE)

Fili approached the West Gate with almost two dozen Fingers at her back, last she counted. They picked up a few more as they ran through the streets. A dozen Balladairan soldiers in plain clothes followed, rifles slung over their backs, a few with swords at their hips. It was them that Fili looked to when she saw there were still Taargens atop the wall, guarding the gate so their army could enter the city from the west.

She turned to Velte to ask her what to do, but her mother gave a set of hurried orders. Several shots rang out and a few Taargens fell. Then the soldiers were racing up the stairs to deal with the Taargens still standing.

Her mam watched with grim focus until it was clear the Balladairans had won the wall, and Fili watched her—it was easier than watching the killing and dying above.

And what do you think will happen when you walk out that gate?

Fili made herself watch the last Taargen fall, a bayonet punching through her torso, hands scrambling desperately at the wooden barrel of the gun. Then the Balladairan shook her off the gun to the stone and out of Fili's sight.

Her mam squeezed her shoulder. "It's time."

On the other side of the city, cannons bashed the eastern walls, but it was so far away, Fili could almost pretend it was happening in another world. She couldn't ignore the storm in front of her.

When El-Qazāli was throwing around words like "company" and "battalion," Fili had conjured up an idea of what that meant. A lot of people, marching in some lines, rifles in hand—enough to fill the Place des Oreilles or maybe the Parc du Coeur. She had been wrong. The group marching toward them could have filled the Parc du Coeur four or five times over. An army of Taargens and Shālans, coming to rip her home away like everyone said the uncivilized would.

"You sure this'll work?" Velte stood at Fili's side, shading her eyes from the bright gray sky, the better to see their doom. She squinted at Fili. "My great-grandmam told me the stories, aye, but they might have been just that—stories."

Fili tugged the hem of her leather vest. "I can do this."

She and Luca had talked about those stories long into the night. *A Balladairan queen who could rip the earth from beneath her enemies' feet and raise forests with a touch.* Fili could scarce imagine it, but she had to try—*that's how any piece starts,* Maître Gaspard used to say. *You have to see it in your mind's eye so you can feel it in your hands.* It didn't work for Fili that way, though. More often, she felt the call of the wood in her hands, first, and then the shape emerged, as if it had always been there, waiting for her.

The thorntree seeds had already been planted, their gathered pods broken and scattered in the earth in front of the West Gate. Now all Fili could do was wait. Wait, and trust her hands.

"You can do this, my girl, but you don't have to." Her mam stood on her other side, her mouth and forehead creased deep with worry. "You haven't trained for war, none of you have."

Fili still hadn't reckoned with her mam showing up at La Flottille, not to drag her back home or to the queen's prison, but to see her. To stand with her. It felt good. Even if her mam did keep hovering and asking her if she was sure. It wouldn't have been so bad if Fili weren't asking herself the same question.

"I do have to." Fili stopped fiddling with her clothes. "You said yourself. I'm not going to waste anyone's sacrifice." And if Fili did this, the queen had promised to step down. So Fili would give whatever it took.

Ghadin and Joscelin were close by, and the other Fingers fanned behind Fili like geese, their woolwort pins on their coats and caps and collars. Behind them, the blackcoats. A few Fingers now held the wall, just in case.

Just in case Fili failed.

She wasn't alone. She marched out of the shelter of La Chaise's tall stone walls and down the road, through the shops and stalls that had long shuttered in the face of the advancing army, and through the shanty village of refugees who had come first to escape the Withering. The army had driven them away, too.

And then Fili's tiny army spilled out into the open field. Stone pavers forked west and south, cutting through green. The enemy army came from the south, dwarfing the road and churning all to mud as they marched toward Fili.

She stopped at a line of freshly turned earth and hastily stripped off her boots and socks. The ground was warm beneath her bare feet, alive with the end of spring and the turn of summer. It was the time for growing things.

"Do we do it now?" someone called from up the line.

"Aye, and how much blood do we let?" someone else asked.

Even her mam and Velte looked to Fili. *She* was the god's chosen. The miracle. And she didn't know. The weight of their hope was so much to bear.

Her mam said, "We trust you, Fili. Tell us what to do."

"It doesn't have to be a lot. There are so many of us, and so many—" So many had already died on the other side of the river.

Her mam and Velte passed the word down the line.

Fili closed her eyes and felt the grass beneath her feet. She could feel how the spring had woken the land and how it would spend the summer reaching higher and fruiting for the autumn to come. How the bugs beneath the soil turned it and made room for the air and the water. The wind on her face brought the smell of lilies and lilac. River weeds choked the banks, clinging on for their own lives. She reached farther and felt the blood soaking into the earth. So much blood.

Her whittling knife cut quick and familiar. She'd never made a cut this big before. Blood dripped down her palm before she realized that had been stupid. She wouldn't be able to hold a carving knife comfortably for weeks. Then she remembered, she may not have weeks at all.

She closed her eyes and thrust her uncut hand into the earth while the other one dripped over it. To her left and right, the others did the same, even her mother, even Ghadin, who accepted a cut on her forearm with Guérin's help, because Ghadin was smarter than Fili, had been since the beginning.

Where would she have been if she'd listened to Ghadin then? Probably not here. But Fili had gotten the queen to surrender to the Fingers. To the people. *She* had done that.

Fili waited. And she waited. Nothing happened. No quickening in the seeds, no waking of the earth. She opened her eyes and saw Velte and Ghadin looking at her, worry in their faces. Her mother watched the army come closer, blood snaking down her arm. They were beginning to doubt. Fili closed her eyes again, squeezing more blood from her fist.

Please.

The thunder of hooves made Fili open her eyes with a cry, but the noise came from the west, not the south. Her mother shoved Fili back, keeping herself between Fili and the new riders, but a moment later, the ready tension in her mam's body eased. Fili recognized the rider at the head of the small column of cavalry. The marquise de Durfort. The rest of the riders were wearing red-and-black Travers livery. By the blowing of their horses, they'd ridden hard to get here.

"Guérin." The marquise drew up beside Fili and her mother. "Any word from Queen Luca?"

Some of the Fingers grumbled and scowled at this, but Fili's mam directed the marquise to Fili brusquely. The marquise sized Fili up and down with an arrogant eye, lingering on Fili's bloody fist. A muscle tic crossed her face, tugging at the stitched wound down one side.

"Well?" the marquise said, without dismounting.

"It's not working," Fili said quietly, trying not to alarm the others.

"What's not working?"

"The god's magic!" Fili hissed.

The marquise inhaled sharply, her gloved hand spasming on the reins. The handsome bay shied beneath her, but she calmed it with the pressure of her thighs and a click of her tongue. Then she looked at the oncoming army, and her frown deepened.

The enemy was closer now, less than a thousand paces away from them and within the thorn barrier—or at least, within the area the thorn barrier should have been, if Fili had been able to grow it. Then, as they watched, a small contingent of the enemy broke off to the left. Fili couldn't make out who they were or what they were doing, but an instinctual fear shuddered down her spine.

Where there had been a group of soldiers, there was now a bear, and when it raised on its hind legs and roared, Fili felt it in her bones.

"Sky above and earth below," somebody swore.

"There, over there, look!"

Another bear on the right side of the enemy lines and a building war cry as the enemy picked up speed.

Fili turned to see two of her Fingers backing up, ready to turn and flee back into the safety of the walls.

"Wait! Stop!" she called. "Your city needs you! The land needs you!"

The two halted in their tracks, half-turned toward the gates. The others were barely any better. Only Fili's mam seemed unbothered.

"We can't stand against that," one of them said. "They're uncivilized. It's madness, isn't it?" And he ran. A moment later, his companion whimpered and followed.

"Please! Stay!" Fili begged. "I need more time!"

"How long do you need?" The marquise de Durfort's handsome face had gone hard, her dark brows low over dark eyes. She cut an elegant figure on her horse, and Fili couldn't help but think of the chevalier tales her mother used to tell her.

"I don't know, I've never done this before, I thought it would—"

Fili's mam interrupted her, voice stern: "As long as you can give us, Your Grace."

The marquise inhaled deeply, drawing her sword. She shared a glance with the captain of the Travers riders, and the other woman nodded solemnly.

"Luca needs us to hold these walls, and so we will." Then, under her breath, Fili thought she muttered something like "I am the scourge of husbands and wives." Then, louder: "For Balladaire and Queen Luca!"

The marquise raised her sword in the air and wheeled her mighty horse around, kicking it into a gallop. The cavalry streamed forward, a mass of snorting horse flesh and jingling tack, kicking up clods of earth, their manes streaming behind them. The shouts of the riders mingled with the pounding of the horses' hooves. It seemed like the Shālans and the Taargens screamed louder, too, raced faster to the inevitable crash.

"Fili," her mam grunted. "Don't waste this."

"Aye, right. But I don't know what's wrong, I don't know why it didn't work the first time—"

Fili couldn't help straying back to the charge, which had become a battle only a few hundred paces away. The Taargens would come for them next.

Fili shoved her bloody hand into the earth this time. She closed her eyes. *Please.*

Still, nothing.

A pressure on her shoulder and she turned to see her mam looking down on her. "I love you, Fili. And by the sky above, I am so proud of you."

Her mam was pale, and Fili frowned at her in confusion. Then her mam dropped to her knees, and Fili saw blood pouring from several clean lines across her wrist. Blood in uneven sheets pouring down her mam's thick, pale forearm and into the earth.

"No!" Fili cried. "Mam! No, no—" She yanked her hand from the ground, but her mam squeezed her shoulder again, the pressure weaker this time.

"I was already living on borrowed time, gifted by the god."

Fili jerked round to her other side to see Joscelin kneeling. He made the cut before Fili understood what was happening, then his blood, too, was leaking out faster than it should have.

"Stop! Please, no, don't, please!" She turned back to her mam, who laid herself down on the dirt, digging her bloody fingers into it.

Even as Fili begged her mam to stop, begged Joscelin to stop, she felt the surge of the earth responding to the blood muddying the ground around her. The earth seemed to suck her in, holding her fast, but she couldn't stop staring at her mother's eyes, closed now, at peace.

Don't waste this.

The wind ruffled Fili's hair and was cold on her wet cheeks. She probed deeper, hunting with her senses for the seeds they'd planted. Some now soaked with blood and the water deep in the earth. She urged them to grow beneath the boots trampling above them, the claws coming to claim Balladaire for their own. Pushing and pushing, she sensed the rapid press of green shoot from hard shell, through the tunnels of earth gifted by the worms, higher and higher until they burst from the earth and the green shoots all across the southern fields were green twiglets that hardened into woody stems with thorns as long as knuckles, as long as fingers, and the thorntrees burst through the pavers on the road and they reached out to each other, grasping and locking and her vision went white and there was screaming all around her, echoing and echoing and echoing as the thorns hooked into flesh and snarled around the marching bodies and the rearing horses, until more blood dripped into the earth and a matching pain pierced her own body and split her skull and the screaming grew louder and louder.

Somewhere, someone screamed something that might have once been her name.

CHAPTER 67

AT THE GATE

Valmorin's cavalry hit the Taargens below in a crash of metal, screaming horses, and crying men.

Touraine would have killed for quiet, but that cacophony meant victory. It meant hope.

"Disable the cannons so they can't take them back," Touraine ordered.

She'd clung to that hope as Moyenne smashed the invaders' rear lines. She'd been so sure Moyenne would break through the enemy and be able to offer support from within the city. Then, when Valmorin smashed into the eastern flank of the Taargen line, she'd hoped *they* would scatter the Taargens into a retreat. Instead, Taargens fled into the city in a desperate trickle, like ants from a tunnel. Perrot hadn't managed to close the gates after all—they were half-shut, half–wedged open with stone and bodies lodged between the thick doors. The Taargens' cannons had splintered a corner off. It was open only enough to let their enemies in, not their allies.

Hope was a fool's crutch in war.

Touraine raced back down the stairs, bringing a handful of soldiers to reinforce the blackcoats there. Her squad wasn't a match for the warriors Roric had handpicked to enter the city first. They weren't a match for Henrir, whose howl of grief Touraine had recognized when Luca slit Roric's throat on the crenellations above.

Oh, Luca. Maybe it was the right decision, maybe it wasn't. It was done, and Balladaire would lose what little advantage Roric's death had gained them if they didn't get more of their own soldiers into the city.

As she raced onto Henrir's killing ground, the wide boulevard that welcomed visitors and merchants into the city, a chorus of howling broke out from the street dogs in the city behind them. Touraine flinched, remembered pain throbbing in her barely healed calf. At the same time, birds erupted into the sky—soldiers exclaimed mid-fight and Touraine wasn't the only one staring, mouth open in awe as crows and gulls and sparrows left in a single flock that blotted out the sky. Her people didn't know what it meant, but Touraine did. *The Many-Legged.* Pruett.

Touraine didn't let herself think about what that meant. She couldn't spare any of that fool's crutch for Pruett.

She sprinted for the gate, ignoring the hails as the blackcoats called her out by name, by rank, calling for help. She ignored them all and fell upon the next Taargen to come through the giant doors, her sword flashing in the summer sun peeking out at last from behind the clouds.

"Highness!" This shout, practically in her ear. Perrot appeared beside her, breathy and bleeding. "What are you doing?! There's a fucking wolf-fucker!"

Touraine glanced behind in time to watch Henrir dodge another attack, too agile by far for a beast this size.

"And you have Taargens up your fucking ass! We have to get the gate open. We need Moyenne and Valmorin! Help me!"

Together, they turned the narrow gap into a death trap for the Taargens, while their own soldiers fell to Henrir's jaws. Touraine turned as he gave a victorious howl that made her bowels go soft.

"Behind you!" Perrot grunted.

Touraine dived through the crack between the gate doors sword first, ready to fend off the next wave of Taargens only to find someone altogether more welcome.

"Prince-General," Valmorin said gravely. His hair stuck to his head with sweat and blood leaked from a gash in his bearded chin. "It's good to see you well."

"Thank the sky above," Touraine said. "Help me get this gate open."

With her feet wedged on the fallen rubble, trying and failing to avoid stepping on the dead bodies piled up on either side, Touraine and Perrot and Valmorin and a handful of blackcoats pushed, step after step, grunting and cursing everyone from Luca to the Taargens to every single laborer who had built a sky-falling monstrosity of a gate that was four times her height and half again as thick as her own shoulders. She'd fumbled her sword back into her belt and heaved against the door with her good shoulder. The left one was still weak with pain; she'd mended it only enough. Sweat-soaked clothes chafed her skin raw and pinched it tight. On the other side of the door, Henrir's growls were broken by shrill screams. Touraine focused on the weight of the wood, weather-worn and too strong. Speckled and smeared with blood, like she was. Then the screams were quiet and only a growing snarl remained.

She felt Perrot's sigh beside her. A deflation.

"Perrot, don't! We almost have it!"

He looked down at her and there was sorrow in it, but also something else. He bent to pick up the sword of a dead man. The weight of the door increased as Perrot stepped away and Touraine and the others scrambled to redistribute their strength.

"You don't—have to—" Touraine grunted. Sky above, her back ached. Her legs burned with the strain. They were close. If she could just—

But Perrot was gone, roaring toward Henrir as the wolf readied itself to pounce.

She couldn't look, but she had to, peering between the doors.

Perrot didn't try to finesse the wolf priest. You didn't dance on the hunt. He charged like a boar rushing down a hill, and when Henrir snapped down on his chest, Touraine's gasp couldn't cover up the sound of crunching bone, but Perrot's final effort was silent: a blade angled just so, like a boar's tusk into a wolf's throat, unknitting the life Touraine had a few days ago held together.

Perrot wasn't the first friend she'd watched fall. Far from it. But the door slipped as her legs faltered.

"Push, for the stars' sake, General, *push*!" Valmorin snapped Touraine to and she closed her eyes against her blurry vision and pushed.

The gap widened, and as it widened step by painful step, other soldiers shoved rocks and weapons and whatever else they could to hold the great door open. When it was done, limp as a wet rag, Touraine ran to Perrot in his macabre embrace. The Taargen priests didn't turn human again in death, it turned out.

Valmorin came up quietly beside her. "Who was he?"

"He was the duke's man. Then he was mine."

She needed to find Albric. She needed to finish this. She couldn't stop looking at Perrot, though, mangled body cradled against Henrir's furry chest.

This was why generals fought from the rear in their little tents with their little tables and fake figurines carved of wood and stone. Those toys didn't bleed. They didn't sigh before they were cut down. If you were in your tent, you couldn't see them look at you one last time—with hatred or pain, affection or relief. You could go on making your decisions in the abstract, away from the truth of blood and tears and sweat.

Touraine was too close.

Once, she'd tried to read that philosopher Luca adored so much—Yevière or whatever his name was. *To Wage a War.* One line had stuck out to her because it made her ache for Luca. It had explained so much of the other woman's loneliness. Her desperation to be loved. When she'd read the line, Touraine had closed the book on her finger and sat for a long time. Then she'd gotten up and kissed a startled Luca hard on the mouth. She never told Luca why, but she'd made love to her then, intensely, trying to show Luca how wrong she was.

A ruler does not have friends. They can have tools and that is all.

She understood why Luca clutched it so tight.

"We have to kill Albric." Touraine forced herself back into the moment. "He's the last head of the Taargen army."

Only, he wasn't, not if they would obey Pruett. If she wasn't already—*Will you finally kill her, too?*

If I need to. If that's what it took this time, she would do it.

As if simply thinking of Pruett called the animal forth, Touraine heard a familiar high-pitched whistle, and a dark blur hurtled toward her from the sky. *Tempête.*

She batted the bird away, but the tiny thing dodged and pecked at her coat but not her face. She had seen the falcon take out a man's eyes with its lethal little claws. This wasn't an attack. It cried and cawed and flew away before flying back to peck and screech and fly away again. Always in the same direction. Always toward the open gate.

Still no sign of Albric.

Tempête didn't leave Touraine alone until she began walking toward the gate. *This is a trap*, a voice shouted at the forefront of Touraine's brain. She couldn't push the thought away, but she followed. Outside the gate, off to the side and too close to the wall to fall prey to cannon fire from above, Tempête rested on a bundle of clothing, and the figure kneeling next to it turned. Pruett turned to her, eyes yellow in the sunlight. As Touraine watched, they settled back into her natural dark gray blue.

"Touraine!" Pruett cried out at the same time as Tempête shrieked away into the sky.

A year ago, the pain in Pruett's voice would have broken Touraine. Even now, with all they'd done to each other, she staggered.

"Please!" Pruett clutched Kiras's body in her arms.

The Eater's brown skin was gray, and her front was covered in blood. It trickled down her chin, it soaked her tunic, it coated the hands clutching her belly. Her eyes were closed.

"I can't bring someone back from the dead."

"She's not dead." Pruett pressed her hand against Kiras's pulse. "She's not."

"Prince Consort!"

Touraine spun around at the rumble of Albric's voice at her back. She ripped her sword from its sheath. He approached with no weapons drawn, but he dragged a half-conscious blackcoat at his side as if they were a doll. Every step held the threat of his magic. The bear's head of his cloak covered his own head so the teeth framed his face. She could kill him now, if she were fast enough.

"Where is the queen?" Albric tilted his head up, and the bear snout mirrored the motion, as if it were sniffing her out. "Take me to her, and the rest of your people might live."

Luca, in the hospital tent. Ghadin and Aranen and Jaghotai.

"Touraine, please. She's dying." Pruett, begging. Her face was streaked through with tears and smeared red where she'd tried to wipe them away.

Albric smiled through his beard at Touraine's hesitation. He looked down at Pruett and Kiras. Laughter shook his thick chest.

"I'll find her myself."

Touraine lunged at him, but he stepped out of reach, laughing again. The blackcoat he was dragging moaned.

Pruett pressed her forehead to Kiras's, and Kiras reached one weak hand up to Pruett's wrist. She was alive, barely.

Touraine looked between Pruett, with her anguished, furious face, and Albric, chanting prayers in Taargen with his forehead pressed to the limp Balladairan's.

Touraine didn't know Kiras as well as she could have, but they had a bond of kinship, pulled tight by the god they'd killed for. More important than that, Pruett loved her. She could see it in the rictus of Pruett's mouth, in the harshness of the insults she hurled at Touraine's shoulder.

Albric was changing, like Henrir had. That slope-shouldered *wrongness* of stretching skin and snapping bones until he was no longer a man. Like a beast, he would hunt Luca down.

Pruett didn't let Luca live. Pruett made you kill her. Is that friendship? You would risk losing Luca now, for that?

Touraine would never forgive Pruett for forcing her hand, but whatever else she was willing to do, Touraine wouldn't hurt her like this.

Albric loped into the city.

Touraine dropped to her knees in the mud and tore at Kiras's clothing, hunting for bare skin.

The wound was clean, a straight line. Stabbed. A touch was enough to feel Kiras's life draining out. Touraine felt a few places where it seemed Kiras had started to heal herself, like a child painting a wall but not understanding you had to paint the whole thing in even layers. Touraine closed her eyes and went over the "walls" again, evening the coats of tissue in the body until everything vital was whole again. Enough that Pruett could get her to safety.

Touraine pulled her mind from Kiras's body and tilted in dizziness, falling to her elbows. Her own injured shoulder throbbed as her magic tried to heal that, too. She was too tired, though. She had spent all she had.

"Wait." Pruett held Kiras in her arms, but the other woman was unconscious, the healing taking its toll on her body. "Is she going to be all right?"

Touraine shook her head clear and staggered to her feet, falling back to a knee before dragging herself upright again. "Is anyone?"

She left them there and prayed she wouldn't be too late.

CHAPTER 68

OF HEROES (REPRISE)

Luca couldn't bear the weight of the hospital tent's silence. Even the ill held their breath.

While Touraine defended the city walls, while Sabine led a traitor's militia and Fili worked Balladaire's magic outside the walls, Luca sat on her hands in the Parc du Coeur. Or, more accurately, she paced along the aisles of the ill and injured while swearing under her breath. She neglected to consider herself one of the injured, despite the pain that yet radiated through her middle. She should be *out* there.

Luca may not have been a good queen and she may not have been queen for very long—the shortest reign quite possibly of anyone, including the Anciers who were executed—but she *was* Balladaire's queen. The last one.

She had had visions of a new world, one that she would help build. They would never come to be.

She'd never become the warrior she'd thought she would as a child. Even without her leg, the daydream wouldn't have held. She played her games on her boards and she was good at them, but she was no warlord.

"Can you sit down? Jackal's tits, you're making me dizzy."

Luca glared at the Jackal. She'd been avoiding looking at her, because looking at Jaghotai made her think of Touraine, and thinking of Touraine right now...no, better to not.

"Do you often talk about your tits like that?" Luca retorted in Shālan.

Next to the Jackal, Aliez giggled, smothered behind bitten lips.

"Turn of phrase." Jaghotai smirked. "I mean it. You're giving me a headache, princess."

Luca frowned and lowered herself gingerly onto an empty stool between Jak and Aranen. Her breath hitched as the pain shifted, then eased. The priestess sat on a cushion on the ground with her eyes closed, fingers folded together in her lap. Her chest rose and fell with her deep, steady breaths.

"Is she praying?" Luca whispered.

I don't know, Jaghotai grunted wordlessly.

"It's called meditation," Aranen said without opening her eyes. "Roland taught it to me. It steadies the mind. Or it *would* if you two could also find a way to settle yourselves."

"How can you sit so still? I can hardly stand it," Luca muttered. "I should be out there with everyone else."

"Doing what?" Jaghotai asked. "Getting yourself killed? Beg your pardon if I'm not so willing to die for your monster of an empire. I've got my people here." She nudged Aranen, who appeared to ignore them. Then she indicated the other Shālans who were seeing to the last of the patients in the hospital. "I'll be happy enough to see them safe."

"And Touraine?" Luca said tightly. "Ghadin? They're out there."

"They are. They have their own business. And if more of your friends make it through the gates, I reckon mine will take up arms, too. For you or for their own skins, only Shāl knows."

"What a tremendous show of sorority." Luca pursed her lips sourly. "Touraine signed a treaty on your behalf. That Qazāl and Balladaire would fight for each other in our hours of need."

"Hmph. About that. What army we had left after your little conquest seems to have decided that, actually, you don't deserve forgiveness for the...tremendous show of sorority you displayed before you decided you wanted to fuck my daughter."

Luca gasped indignantly and Aliez gaped. From the ground came a quiet chuckle; a small smile played on Aranen's lips. Luca sighed and leaned her elbows on her knees, letting her hair curtain around her face. The length would take getting used to. She combed it back with her fingers, and it fell again as soon as she leaned down.

Through the fall of hair, Luca met Jaghotai's eyes. Deep-brown eyes, brown like Touraine's had been before the change. Almost red brown. "If an empire is monstrous, so be it. I won't argue. We've done monstrous things in Balladaire's name. And if I am her queen, call me a monster. I've done monstrous things in my own name." Luca straightened and pushed back her shoulders. "But that doesn't mean I have to sit by and watch our people—both our people—suffer alone."

Jaghotai snorted. "You think you're a hero. You hear this, Aranen?" She shifted into a Shālan dialect that was too rapid to follow, but Luca could guess the intent. Aranen only hummed, mildly conciliatory, eyes still closed.

"No, I don't." Luca's cheeks flared in embarrassment.

Urgent voices at the tent's main entrance made all four of them jump to their feet, Aranen most alert of all.

"It's time" was all the priestess said, and then she was helping the new arrivals bring in the wounded and pointing out what pallets to place them on.

Luca picked out Ghadin first. The Fingers, fewer than she recalled leaving for the West Gate. That wretchedly irritating one, Velte. Two bodies came in, held by the arms and legs. One of them was Fili, eyes closed but cheeks still flushed with life. The same could not be said for Guérin beside her. The retired guardswoman's wrists were bloody and open.

Luca's breath rushed out of her. "What happened?"

"It worked." Ghadin trembled. True to her apprenticeship with Touraine, she gave her report like a soldier. "Fili did it. I was beside her. First, it didn't work, but the army was still advancing. The marquise de Durfort arrived and bought us time, but it still didn't work. So her mam..." Here, Ghadin faltered.

Luca took a shaky breath. She couldn't give the woman what she was owed right now. Jaghotai listened with a tight-lipped frown.

"And the army? The marquise?"

"I don't—" Ghadin struggled visibly now. Sky above, she was so young. But Luca needed to know.

"Please, Ghadin." She reached out to take the girl by both arms, then caught herself, hands hovering in the air around her.

"The marquise and the Travers soldiers charged. Then the magic started... it started growing. The cavalry pulled back, but some of them still got caught in the—and Fili— We had to come back." With wild, dark eyes, Ghadin begged Luca to release her.

Luca patted her shoulder awkwardly. "Thank you, Ghadin. Thank you."

Touraine's young protégé went immediately to Aranen and buried her face in the older woman's robes.

Luca began to pace again.

She cringed at the sound of a million animals crying out: seabirds cawing, gutter dogs baying, alley cats yowling.

"What was that?" she shouted across the tent.

"Fucking Many-Legged." Jaghotai took a few steps toward the exit, listening.

Luca remembered the mournful howl after she'd killed Roric. The Many-Legged perhaps, or the Taargens.

Fingers and Qazāli and loyalist alike held their breath. An age passed.

"Someone told the civilians to stay in their homes?" Luca asked. "Barricade their doors?"

"Aye, Your M—aye," one of the Fingers said, holding a cloth to his hand. "Cléophin and Josephine went—"

Luca didn't get to hear where Cléophin and Josephine went, though, because the speaker went quiet as the next sounds reached them.

The screams built like a wave. Battle cries drowned out by shrieks of terror. As they grew closer, Luca made out sobbing. Individual cries for people by name, *Amman, Papa, Maëtte, Claudot, please, my son*—

Luca screwed her eyes up tight against the pricking heat in them.

Jaghotai was on her feet. "If you can use a weapon, with me!"

A gaggle of the Fingers and the patients who'd been lying on the ground, stricken with something other than the Withering, mustered around her. They didn't look like much. The Qazāli who'd come to Balladaire with the Jackal, though, held themselves dangerously. But there were only a few guns between them.

Luca gathered herself. "I'm coming, too."

"No." Jaghotai held a knife.

"Those are my people!"

"And you are one woman!" Jaghotai snapped back. "You've no

weapons, you can barely stand, and without you, all of this falls." It looked like it galled her to say it.

"That's not true." Luca jerked her head at the Fingers. "They said so."

"Princess," the Jackal said, restrained though everything about her presence screamed that she was ready to bite. "You're the only symbol this country has. After it's all done, aye, they'll build a new identity. They won't need you. But right now—"

"Right now, they need to see that symbol," Luca growled.

"If the enemy doesn't see you," Aranen said, putting a hand on Luca's arm, "they may leave when they realize this is a hospital. Help me here." She held Jaghotai's eyes for a moment, something silent passing between them. "Go. Bring back the wounded as you can."

Jaghotai turned to her makeshift squad. "Let's go save your runny shit of a city!"

Miraculously, that stirring speech bolstered them, and they ran out, yelling their own battle cries.

Then only Aranen, Aliez, Luca, and the civilians who were too ill or too injured or too frightened remained. Luca counted herself among the latter. If she weren't, it wouldn't matter what Jaghotai said. She would be *out there*. She laughed disparagingly.

"Your Majesty?" Aranen said archly.

"Don't call me that."

"Luca din. What's so funny?"

"Nothing. It's only—the last queen of Balladaire, and she's a sky-falling coward." She gestured down at herself with her borrowed crutch. Her civilian clothing, her noble's braid cut off. It all felt unfortunately prescient.

"Yes. You have done some truly cowardly things in the brief time I've known you."

"I do so prize your honesty, Aranen din." Luca raised an invisible glass in salute. "You don't get that often as a royal."

"It shows. More's the pity. There's always time to change."

"Unless you're dead."

Outside the tent and closer than Luca had ever hoped to hear again in her life, she heard the roar of a great animal, followed by the Jackal's furious shouting in Shālan.

Touraine would kill Luca if she let something happen to her mother—

Before she knew it, she was running out of the tent at a limping sprint, Aranen beside her.

Perhaps Luca had built the world she'd meant to. If she died today—and it was looking more and more likely that she would—she would die fighting beside Qazāli rebels she had turned into allies; Balladairan revolutionaries who trusted her just enough; Shālan immigrants fighting for their new home; priests of two faiths, bringing the gods' magic to bear against a third. This was a world her father would never have conceived of. A world her uncle could never have built.

She would die today, but she would die defending a stupid dream she'd had, that had turned out not to be quite so stupid after all.

She wouldn't die alone.

Luca emerged from the tent as a gigantic brown bear flung the Jackal into Balladaire's Heart, the famous statue of a Balladairan farmer. It had been modeled off a great-great-grandfather or the like, and she doubted he'd known how to use a tool that wasn't a sword or his cock. And yet, here it was, breaking the fall of a woman he surely would have counted among his enemies.

Jaghotai fell to the statue's pedestal and was still.

"Jak!"

Aranen was faster than Luca, dashing toward the Jackal on light feet, holding her robes from her ankles as they streamed behind her. Graceful as a leaf on the wind. She caught the bear's attention.

No.

Luca scooped the nearest weapon she could find from the ground. A rusty officer's sword from the hand of a dead woman in rough-hemmed trousers and a patched shirt. Luca focused on the too-heavy sword and its worn leather grip.

"Leave them alone!" Luca limped toward the bear. She recognized that pelt, the shape of that maw. She'd seen it on the high priest's back often enough. "Your business is with me, Albric!"

He ignored her.

Aranen kept running.

When Albric caught Aranen on his claws, Luca saw blood darken the back of Aranen's robes immediately. He flung her to the side like a piece of refuse.

Somewhere, someone shouted, "No!" Probably the last of the good sense in Luca's head as she faced Albric down. She swallowed hard and fought the terror folding her belly in two.

The Jackal was right. Luca was no hero.

CHAPTER 69

THEN CAME ANOTHER BEAST

Touraine chased Albric back through the breach and through the streets of La Chaise. Her legs were so sky-falling heavy. Every thrust and slice of a sword that she dodged was a miracle; every shot that missed her, pinging into dirt or stone or some other body, was sheer luck. Her own knife found its mark in the backs and throats and tendons of Taargens who didn't expect the enemy behind them.

The air was full of screaming. Her city was fully under attack.

The Taargens were already at the Parc du Coeur. Soldiers in green coats and fur mantles cut down the desperate Balladairans like weeds in every corner as Moyenne's soldiers caught up and a few remnants of Valmorin's cavalry rode the Taargens down. Where there was grass, it was slick with blood. The pitted ruts between the cobbles, where wagons carrying the dead had passed every day for months, had been churned to red mud. Frightened physicians stood outside of their tents, holding their tools and their buckets as makeshift weapons, ready to protect their patients.

Touraine's attention was across the square. The Jackal, with her sweep of dreadlocks, her amputated arm, was unmistakable. She roared defiantly at the bear that was Albric, and he swiped at her with paws the size of her head and claws as long as the knife that was her only weapon.

Touraine tried to ignore the burning in her legs, tried to pick them up off the ground faster, but she had nothing left to give. Any harder and she'd collapse right here. She should never have wasted her strength on Kiras.

It wasn't enough.

Albric caught the Jackal across the ribs with a backhand of his paw. She flew into the statue of the farmer, shattering his stone hoe and falling in a lump at its base. The Jackal didn't get up. Of course she didn't. The statue was marble—beautifully carved, a soulful rendition of Balladaire, the folds of the coat and the baggy trousers made to look like the soft fall of fabric. Like so much of Balladaire, that was only an illusion. Stone was not as generous as flesh. Not so quick to give. Not so quick to break.

"Jak!" The voice could have come from her own throat, but it hadn't. It was Aranen, racing toward her friend, a streak of bright robes.

"What are you doing?" Touraine whispered. Aranen couldn't fight, she couldn't use Shāl's magic. *Not both of them.* She yelled her throat raw with the last of her breath. "Aranen!"

"Your business is with me, Albric!" Luca's voice, clear, cold, hard. She approached Albric as Aranen ran past him. She readied a heavy cavalry sword that didn't fit her, struggling to hold it up.

Please, Touraine begged. Her legs, the gods, her lungs, anyone who would listen. She trudged over the grass, desperation lending her new reserves.

Albric ignored Luca. As Aranen ran past him, he lashed out with his claws. For a moment, the priestess hung there, speared like meat on a fork. Touraine stuttered to a stop. She watched Aranen slide from his claws to the ground.

"No!"

Albric sauntered toward Luca.

Go, go. Help Aranen. Luca can wait. Luca probably could not wait, but Aranen certainly couldn't. Touraine forced her legs moving again, pleading with them, one more step, just one more, until she knelt at Aranen's side.

"Aranen din, it's me."

Aranen blinked up at her in pain and confusion. Then her face cleared.

"Use me, Touraine," she said, closing her bloody hands over Touraine's. Her words bubbled with blood.

"No, Aranen din. I can't. I—I can heal you."

A hundred paces away, Luca stumbled out of Albric's reach, each attack coming closer to home. Albric was toying with her. He paused to swat down the Balladairans who strayed too close, crushing them beneath his paws, making them scream.

"Too—hurt. You heal me, you're done. He takes her."

"I don't want— I can't—" Touraine's stomach turned. She thought of Kiras and her advice. *Go for the liver.* She couldn't reconcile it with her mentor on the ground in front of her.

"Become what you must, my girl."

"You priests and your fucking wisdom." Touraine tried to smile at her. Aranen's eyes were half-closed.

"Then fucking listen to it." Aranen grasped limply for Touraine's wrist, her fingers sticking with blood as she reached for the blade. Her eyes opened once more, golden and bright and lucid. "Do it now."

The command in Aranen's tone and the pain in her eyes did more to raise the knife than Touraine's own muscles could manage. When the blade hit home, all the tension in Aranen's body went out. Her eyelids fluttered half-shut again, a peek of gold glimmering beneath them and a half smile on her lips.

Another snarling, snapping growl and Touraine jerked her head up, expecting to see Albric's muzzle snapped around Luca's neck. *Not yet, not yet.* But close. Another soldier stepping between his queen and the great bear, now a mangled carcass on the ground. Luca wasn't even dodging now, just limping as fast as she could, away from Albric, toward another of the statues. She wasn't going to make it.

Fighting back her tears and the urge to be sick, Touraine cut through Aranen's tunic and the soft skin of her stomach. Everything glistened so pink and white and red and gray and so, so wet. She identified the liver, dark red, almost purple. Touraine cut a chunk of it off and put it to her lips, gagging.

"We thank the dead for the gift of their strength. We thank Shāl for the gift of the body, that we might better know what it is to live and to die." She lurched to her feet.

She chewed through the gamey, iron-tasting flesh until it was small enough to swallow without choking. Heat moved through her gut, and at first, she thought she really was going to be sick. Then the heat flowed from her gut and through her limbs, and the bone-dragging weight of exhaustion lifted. Her wounded shoulder itched as the flesh stitched itself back together.

New energy in her legs, new force in her lungs as Touraine surged forward. She came alongside Albric and stabbed her knife into his side. "Luca, run!"

Albric roared in pain and swatted Touraine like a fly. She skidded across the ground, groaning. She tasted blood in her mouth, but it was hard now to say if it was hers or Aranen's. She'd also lost the knife. From between Albric's legs, she could see Luca on her side, dragging herself along the ground.

The heat of Shāl's magic flowed through her. She didn't know how long it would last.

The greater the sacrifice, the greater the power, Kiras had said.

Touraine drew her sword and ran him down. It wasn't the kind of swordsmanship Durfort had taught her. In fact, Durfort would have been horrified by everything about it, but she hadn't taught Touraine how to fight a sky-falling bear. She didn't have to win. She just had to win Luca time.

Touraine darted in low, trying to score a cut on the bear's forelegs. If she could get around to the side, into the softness of the belly, without the teeth or the claws—

Albric reared onto his hind legs and Touraine rushed in, but he slammed down, long claws raking at her face. She ducked under them, coming in close. She was surrounded by heat like a furnace and the musky stink of sweaty fur. She grabbed him, ready to pull him apart, and—Shāl's magic wasn't there.

Why not? She'd already taken Aranen's life. Eaten of her. She'd done the hard part. Shāl's heat flowed through her and yet—she was scared, she was disgusted with herself, she resented everything that had led her to this moment.

The hot, meaty stink of Albric's breath closed around her.

Touraine jumped away from the snapping teeth, rolling over the grass. She was near the statue of the lovers, another corner of the octagonal park. Two robed figures, their genders indeterminate, locked in an embrace.

Touraine cursed herself. The only chance she was likely to get, wasted. Back on her feet, sword in hand, she circled him.

"Again," she taunted. "Don't you want to test your god against mine?"

Albric roared again, standing to his full height, near as tall as the fucking East Gate doors. He made a fair point. Touraine steadied the fear in her knees, holding her sword in the boar guard.

Become what you need to become.

Albric slammed all his paws on the ground and charged her.

Somewhere beyond Albric, Luca screamed.

Like a fool, Touraine let her eyes shift away from the speeding hulk coming toward her and saw Luca wrestling desperately with a soldier in a dark green coat and a woven belt.

Right before Albric slammed into her with his lowered head and heaving shoulders, Touraine dropped to the ground and rolled to the side. She leapt up in a sprint, making her own charge into the Taargen who held Luca pinned to the ground, both hands around a knife as he tried to push it into her throat.

With a roar, Touraine looped her forearm around his throat and dragged him off her.

"Get out of here!" Touraine shouted as Luca gaped at her, breathing heavily, each exhale a whimper.

The soldier in her arms was jabbing desperately into her ribs, into her stomach with his elbows. The adrenaline in his blood radiated at her. Touraine could practically smell it. So full of life. The desire to survive. A hot hunger. It called to Touraine. She could feel it in her fingertips where her hand brushed his jaw, the angry pulse of his throat. She unhooked her forearm to hold him by the throat with her bare hand, pressed her head close to his, his back firm against her chest. She shared his panicked breath. They could have been the lovers in the statue.

Touraine reached into him and thought, *Unknit.* From the channels carrying his blood to the heart that pumped it, the muscles that made him tense and jerk in her arms to the bones that held him rigid.

This was what it meant. This was what it was to have *power.* To be able to make and unmake at a whim. Who was this man to come between her and what she wanted? Who was anyone to tell her what she could and could not do, what was uncivilized?

Tears of blood dripped down his cheeks, and he gurgled in protest. As Luca crawled back in horror, Touraine crushed his throat like parchment and threw his body to the ground.

Touraine turned as the ground trembled beneath her feet. Albric rushed at her again and Touraine grinned with bloody teeth. She picked up her sword where she had dropped it. His jaws opened and she waited. One raised paw, ready to take her head off in a single swipe.

She ducked beneath it to his outside as the blow came down. His momentum carried him forward, and all Touraine had to do was hold her sword out to let his own weight make the cut. But Touraine had never fought a bear. Never even hunted one. She underestimated the thickness of fur and fat and muscle beneath, and the sheer size of Albric's holy form, stretching above her.

His claws left deep, dark furrows in the bright grass. He turned faster than Touraine could reckon, and as she twisted round to meet him, a crushing force hit her in the chest.

For a moment, she was weightless. Then she crunched against stone. She lost time. When she blinked her eyes open again, Albric was walking toward her, stately and unhurried. Touraine fumbled for her sword. Not there. She was slumped against the statue of the vigneron, a bundle of grapes in one hand. The other hand, with the stone chalice carved with intricate stone jewels, was on the ground now, digging into Touraine's ribs. She tried to move her legs and almost wept with relief when her knees bent. Shāl's magic still burned in her. It held the pain at bay and knit the smaller wounds.

Get up.

Her body didn't obey. She flicked her eyes around the square, looking for Luca. Maybe that blond-topped pile of rags at the edge of the park. Or—no, there she was, arm draped over the shoulder of a Balladairan who was leading her away. Not far enough, though. Not fast enough. If Touraine died here, Albric would get Luca next and it would all be a waste.

Who is he, to take what's mine? I have a god in my veins. I can destroy him with a touch.

Albric pulled his foreleg back, and Touraine followed the arc of the yellowed claws, ready to grab him when they come close, even if close meant claw-deep into her rib cage. She had taken a man to death with her before.

He growled and she yelled back in defiance and a gunshot sounded through the air, crisp and clear. It shocked them both, but Touraine had already been reaching forward, reaching for his leg. He swiped at her again, but a second shot hit him, breaking his momentum and giving Touraine an opening. She lunged through it, both hands stretched to the girth of his stomach. She calmed herself and pressed into him, digging her fingers into his fur. She sank into the connection of their bodies.

A distant part of her marveled. She hadn't been sure it would work. Animals were different than humans. Maybe there was something to what the Taargens and the Many-Legged believed, and all the creatures of the world *were* some kind of kin. Whatever the truth was, Touraine didn't stop to think about where a bear's heart rested and how to stop a bear's lungs. She only *felt*. The thudding beat against her ears. The swell of the massive rib cage. The coil of tons of muscle, ready to tear her in two if she lost concentration for a second. If she didn't tear him, first.

Touraine closed her eyes and *pulled*. Everything her senses could reach, she unknit. From very far away, her ears registered a roar of pain that became a shriek of agony. His. Hers. Beneath her hands, the shape of the body changed, but the body she was destroying did not. Heart, lungs, intestines, muscles. Bone was too hard, too many dense layers, so she flowed around it. She shredded as much as she could until, gasping, she fell away.

She lay curled on the ground, tangled with Albric the man. Blood leaked from his slack mouth and blank eyes, from his ears. She stared at him, unblinking. Her own hands were bloody, yes, but it was already dried. Aranen's blood. Kiras's blood. Nothing about her showed what she had done to Albric.

Boots crunched on the cobblestones behind her. Touraine spun, trying to clamber to her feet, and collapsed again, head almost pillowed by Albric's body. Instead of Albric's Taargens, Pruett jogged over, holding the rifle slung on her back with one hand.

"You?" Touraine croaked. Her mouth was sticky and cloying.

"Who else is going to pull your ass out of the fire?"

"Anyone ever tell you, you've got the best eye in three empires?"

"They don't need to." Pruett sniffed. "And it's four. If we're still calling ourselves that."

After a second that lasted an eternity, Pruett held out her hand. "El-Atyidi?"

"Safe. Your queen?"

Touraine looked, but couldn't find her. Touraine's dismay must have showed in her face because Pruett looked around, too, lip curled. "There she is." Pruett pointed her spent pistol at the broken statue where Jaghotai had crashed. Luca walked toward them, using the broken stone tool as a walking staff. The Balladairan who'd been helping her knelt beside the Jackal. Aliez.

"Thank the sky above." Touraine practically crawled up Pruett to stand upright.

She held on to Pruett as Luca ran a hand along her face, her gaze snagging on what must have been Touraine's bloody lips and chin.

"Aranen?" Luca whispered.

Touraine closed her eyes and looked away, pulling away from Luca's tenderness.

Pruett cleared her throat.

"Is he dead?" Luca turned quickly to Albric. A pistol dangled from one hand. She clutched her broken crown in the other, with her staff. She looked coolly at Pruett.

"Looks dead to me," Pruett said.

"Then I'll take your surrender now."

Pruett looked Luca up and down, lingering on the broken stone staff and the gun. "You think you're going to hit me with that thing? Or shoot—I mean, *miss* me?"

"Stop it," Touraine croaked. "Jak. Is she—"

Luca's face softened again. "She's alive. Broken leg, broken ribs, but alive. She said, and I quote, 'Don't ask Qazāl for another Shāl-damned thing.'" She looked toward Aranen's body, though, her jaw tightening and throat working hard.

Hot spit flooded Touraine's mouth. "This isn't over until the army knows Albric's gone. If you have to give the order, Pruett, go—"

"I shot him. Every Taargen who was in this fucking square ran when they saw Albric fall, and they know I helped. Throw his head over the wall like you did with Roric and be done with it. Whoever's left will take the hint."

"We didn't—" Luca started, but stopped when Touraine shook her head wearily.

She needed to lie down and never wake again. The magic had all but fled her, leaving her with high debts to her body.

First, we finish this.

She knelt on one leg by Albric and took his hair in her fist.

"Don't you need a—"

Touraine touched the skin at his neck with her other hand and bid it to unknit, down through the layers of muscle and the joints of his spine.

"—knife."

Luca and Pruett both turned to be sick. Touraine almost followed suit, but the magic had hollowed everything out of her, down to the bile. She looked in the direction of her mother and raised a hand in salute. The Jackal raised her own hand back.

"Let's go throw them a hint," Touraine said.

CHAPTER 70

THE THORN

Luca limped through the city with Touraine at her side, the grisly trophy of Albric's head dangling by his hair, his beard dragging along the cobbles. She wished it—he—had stayed in his bear form.

The Taargens and Masridāni who had broken into the city surrendered when they saw their leaders dead or bound.

Pruett, the Masridāni qā'id, walked warily at Luca's other side, her hands behind her back and the rope binding her in Luca's hand. Pruett had sworn she wouldn't do anything, but Luca had a tender spot in her belly and a handful of scars that prevented her from trusting so easily.

The fighting at the East Gate was still so thick that no one noticed them.

"Use that pistol of yours," Pruett told Luca. "That'll get their attention."

Luca sincerely doubted it. The fighting was so loud. She reloaded it anylight and did as Pruett said. It didn't stop the noise but it made a lull long enough for Pruett to shout into it.

"Ceasefire!" she barked in Taargen, then in Shālan. "By order of the qā'id of Masridān, by order of Her Majesty the Bear Queen, hold your fucking fire!"

Touraine echoed the order in Balladairan, and slowly, people turned to see the gruesome tableau.

The high priest's head, held by Touraine El-Qazāli. The qā'id, with her hands bound by the queen of Balladaire, wearing her bent and broken crown of leaves and thorns.

One by one, the Taargens and Masridāni lowered their weapons and fell to their knees, raising their hands behind their heads. The few who continued to fight fell quickly without the support of their comrades. Luca saw no Taargen priests—in their beast forms or their cloaks—in the melee. Only the great hulking form of a wolf, unmoving upon the cobbles. A relief. She did not think they could survive another creature like Albric.

The city was hers again. Balladaire was hers. For a little longer, at least.

After that, Luca went to the West Gate, where the battlefield was far beyond what Ghadin's report had led her to imagine. *Field* wasn't an adequate word. *Forest*, more like. The trees had grown almost as tall as Luca. Though some fighting had been done at the edges of the field of adolescent thorntrees, many, many more bodies were snarled among the young trunks themselves.

Despite all she'd witnessed, Luca still gasped and fell back when she saw the first body trapped within them. A man hung suspended, pierced through the chest and abdomen, hanging by thorns in his arms and legs. His face was a rictus of pain, and the thorns had taken advantage of that, too, growing through his cheek. Like a giant shrike had picked him up and thrown him there.

He was not the only one. Soldiers in all coats and no coats at all, horses and even some beasts that she suspected were Taargen priests had been caught within that deadly forest.

She shivered. She had asked for this, and Fili had given it to her. This was what their blood had bought.

No wonder Ghadin couldn't speak of it.

Sabine was supposed to be here, but few figures moved among the bodies at the fringes and within the wood itself—Luca pitied any who yet moved. Crows had already landed to peck and search. She scattered them away.

She made her way along the edge, peering through the thorns even as she wanted to burn the hedge away and the miserable victims within. She walked halfway down, leg aching, pointing out wounded from both armies who could be easily extracted from the thorns and ordering them carried to the hospital tents, which would be growing more and more crowded.

And no Aranen to take care of them.

No Aranen, and still no Sabine.

"It's all right," Deniaud said softly, in mollifying tones. It wasn't the first time she'd stumbled upon one of Luca's lovers, dead.

Luca turned to her guard only to remember—Deniaud was dead. This was a different woman with the same blunt haircut and the same quiet voice. Her red Travers coat was littered with rips, and tiny scratches covered her face and her hands. Luca's chest hitched with gasping breaths. "We have to find her."

"We will." It was comfort freely given, a moment of generosity amid the bleakness.

It would be an insult to the other Balladairans for her to yell for Sabine, when they had all fought for her, maybe even died for her. It would cause a scene. It would be an undignified last act for the last queen of Balladaire. But they had never cradled her head in their laps.

"Sabine!" she yelled anylight. "Sabine!"

Luca screamed until her throat was raw and she was short of breath. She sagged under the heaviness in her chest, and the gentle Travers soldier put a hand beneath Luca's arm to support her.

"You're looking for the marquise?" the woman said dubiously.

"Yes, sky above, I'm looking for the marquise!" Luca said sharply. "Where is she?"

"I— Your Majesty. Forgive me. I didn't know." The woman led Luca farther around the edge of the thorntree forest to a point where others in Travers clothing and people Luca vaguely recognized from La Flottille were hacking through the thorntrees with swords and knives to get to the center, where the thorns and the bodies were thickest.

They had carved a path about thirty paces deep, barely wide enough for two people to walk through without snagging their clothes. They labored together, some chopping, holding the branches delicately in leather-gloved hands, others carrying the cuttings gingerly back out to keep the path clear. Others carried bodies as they were freed from the thorns.

And there, still locked in the thicket, was a humongous black bear, bigger even than Albric's holy form. Its muzzle was scarred and gray-furred, and its maw dripped red with blood and shreds of flesh. Thorns the size of Luca's forearm bit deep into its shaggy fur. Open, unseeing eyes glared at its opponent in death.

Luca's legs shuddered beneath her, threatening to spill her to the ground. She clutched at a branch, forgetting the thorns until one grazed her palm. She barely felt the sting.

Sabine's mouth was frozen in a snarl, her sword angled up through the bear's rib cage bigger than three wine casks together. Blood coated her hands and clotted on the blade. Thorns pierced all the way through her chest and back, their points thrusting the air, and through her thighs, holding her in place. Blood spread in patches over her shirt. One thorn had gone clean through her left eye.

Luca's legs gave out.

"Your Majesty!" The Travers woman rushed to help Luca to her feet, and Luca shoved her away.

"Get her down! Get her out of there." Luca rolled onto her knees, but a wave of nausea took her and she collapsed, face buried in her arms. The earth smelled metal rich.

"We're trying, Your Majesty—"

"Try faster," Luca growled, clawing the earth beneath her. "We need to get her to the prince for healing."

"Your Majesty, she's—" The soldier knelt beside Luca and spoke to Luca as if she were a child, confused over a broken toy. "The marquise is dead."

No platitudes for the grieving queen.

Luca turned a cold eye on the woman. "Get her out and get her on a horse."

Something in Luca's look or her voice stopped the soldier from arguing again. The work went faster. When Sabine was extricated, the Travers woman, who identified herself as Captain Domrémy, placed Sabine across her saddle. Luca took another horse and led Domrémy to the Parc du Coeur to find Touraine.

Leaving Valmorin in charge of the Taargen surrender, Touraine returned to the Parc du Coeur. She dropped Albric's head at his body. It was one thing to know it was necessary, and something fucking else to have to dangle it between your fingers and feel it bump against your leg.

She dragged herself the few steps farther to where Jaghotai had crawled over the rubble-strewn carnage of the park to pull Aranen's body into her arms. Ghadin sat there, too, staring down at the priestess with wet cheeks, sniffling. Aranen's eyes were closed and her lips were still quirked in that same almost-smile. Someone had pulled closed the slit Touraine had made in her robes, to better hide the slits Touraine and Albric had made in her belly.

Touraine went to both knees. Grabbed a fistful of Aranen's robe. She closed her eyes tight and hid her face in the other hand, as if it could stop the noise that ripped out of her. As if it could keep everyone from seeing her. From blaming her for it.

Neither Ghadin nor Jaghotai said anything.

She felt the weight of someone new kneeling beside her and was surprised to see not Luca but Pruett. Pruett, solemn as the rest of them, misty eyed as she tried to blink back her own tears.

Touraine lashed out with her elbow, catching Pruett on the chin. "Fuck off!"

Instead of letting Pruett obey, Touraine leapt on her, pounding her with her fists. She couldn't fight back, but Touraine didn't stop, even when Pruett's lip split or her nose cracked.

"This is your fault," Touraine growled. "This is your fucking fault. If I'd gotten here sooner, I could have saved her."

"I know," Pruett hissed, spitting blood, words distorted. She was crying, too. "I'm sorry."

Touraine let her fist fall uselessly against Pruett's chest. She collapsed on top of her.

"She never wanted this." Touraine wept into Pruett's filthy shirt. "She was better than this."

"No," Jaghotai said thickly. "She was human. But she was the best of us."

"Touraine!" Luca, riding up to them on a horse, next to a familiar woman Touraine couldn't quite place.

Luca slid out of the saddle clumsily, almost falling, grabbing the reins for balance and jerking the horse's head. It shied and jerked back, almost knocking her over. Touraine jumped up to help, but Luca was already tugging at something in front of the other rider's saddle.

"Touraine, please, you have to help her." Luca's voice was frantic, and Touraine knew with disastrous clarity who was lying in the other rider's lap.

Touraine helped Luca pull Durfort down. The other woman's name suddenly came to her—Captain Domrémy, the sister of one of Durfort's heartbroken conquests. They'd met on the road to Carleis. A different world. Now, the captain did her best to ease Durfort into Touraine's arms.

It was too late. Touraine could see that even as she laid Durfort down next to Aranen. Her stitches stood stark against her too-pale skin, and her left eye was a bloody gouge. Puncture wounds all over her body had turned her clothes crimson, but the blood had stopped flowing. Her handsome face was slack, no trace of the ready smirk that had been certain as the sky.

She started to shake her head, but Luca knelt beside her, stroking Durfort's dark hair with one hand, and clutching Durfort's bloody shirt with the other. Luca pressed her lips to Durfort's forehead.

"Please, Touraine," Luca whispered. "Please, try."

So Touraine did. She reached her hands beneath Durfort's shirt to the cold skin beneath, and she delved within. She hunted for the heart, to restart that all-important muscle. It had been pierced, as if by a spear. When Touraine tried to seal the wound, to pull the fibers of flesh back together, nothing happened. The spark that moved it all—*the soul*, Pruett had called it once—was gone.

All her power was nothing against this. She was no god after all. She was simply their plaything.

She pulled Luca to her chest.

"She's gone. They're gone."

Luca's wail echoed across the ruined park.

CHAPTER 71

THE TRIAL

Luca lay in her bed again, staring at the ceiling. Dawn had broken some time ago; the sky outside was bright, but all the world was quiet. Too quiet to match the upheaval that had struck her city. La Chaise was a wretched beast, hunkered in its cave, licking its wounds.

So was Luca. Numb, she had returned automatically to her rooms with no intention to leave them ever again. When she was not staring at her ceiling, she was upright, staring at her walls. When she was not staring listlessly at her blue-and-gold wallpaper, she was weeping, and the only time she slept was when she sobbed herself unconscious.

Touraine hovered at the edges. She had tried to comfort Luca once, and Luca had flinched away so violently that she'd strained herself. She was sorry for the pain that passed over Touraine's face, but Luca had not forgotten the way Touraine had looked as she yanked the Taargen soldier off her. Her chin stained red, her teeth bloody as she snarled with the man's throat in her hands. Her bloody, bloody hands. Some sort of madness gleamed in her eyes as the man jerked and gasped until his eyes and nose, mouth and ears leaked fluid.

Still, Touraine had not left Luca's side. She made a pallet for herself at the foot of the bed; she kept her clothes on and her weapons close. She slept perhaps even less than Luca did.

They did not know yet where they stood in this new order of the world. Pounding on the outer door of her chambers made Luca bolt upright. At the foot of the bed, Touraine was already on a knee, her long knife drawn. Another knock, steady but insistent.

"I suppose if they wanted to kill me, they wouldn't bother knocking," Luca grumbled.

Touraine gave her a flat look, but she moved with a warrior's ready tension as she answered the door. Luca pulled a robe over her dressing gown and followed.

A handful of the Fingers stood outside Luca's chambers, four of them large men and women, two of them with shabby swords at their belts. Velte stood in front of them, the point of the arrow. She scowled up at Luca, her arms crossed over her chest. Her eyes were red, too. The last few days had been kind to no one.

"What do you want?" Luca asked tartly.

"It's time for you to face judgment." Velte tried to sound haughty, but she hadn't spent a lifetime in the royal court.

Luca chuckled softly, but Touraine wedged herself between Luca and the Fingers.

"If you want to take her, you'll have to get through me, first." As Touraine's golden-eyed glare passed over the bruisers, they took a step back, hands going to their weapons. Luca was not the only one who'd seen Touraine fighting Albric in the Parc du Coeur. Rumors of the bear-slaying cannibal witch had spread wide, never mind the bare blade in her hand.

Luca's first instinct was to back away, to barricade herself back in her bedroom while Touraine defended her. What were a few more dead on their joint conscience?

"Stand down, Touraine." Luca squeezed Touraine's shoulder. "Thank you," she murmured, stepping forward in Touraine's place. "Who will judge me?"

"We will."

It was not clarifying, nor did it fill Luca with hope. If the Fingers were her jury, an execution would follow.

"Very well. Wait here. If I'm to submit, I'll not do it in my nightgown." Luca closed the door in their faces.

"Are you sure?" Touraine hissed as they returned to the bedroom.

"It's the least that I deserve." Luca pulled out her clothing. A pair of pale trousers. A dark blue coat embroidered with green and gold, and a cream chemise.

"For what? You gave them what they wanted. You fought with us, you helped us save the city—"

"And before that?" Luca pulled her nightgown over her head and stared at Touraine, waiting for a response. Goose bumps stippled her body and she reached for her bandeau and her chemise.

Touraine looked away.

"Exactly." Somehow, Luca's fingers were quick and steady on her buttons.

"They're no judges. They hate you. It's an excuse to string you up in Traitor's Corner—"

"A place that is no stranger to injustice."

"I won't let them kill you," Touraine muttered as she knelt to help Luca put on her boots. "I didn't damn myself just for that. But fine. If you say so, fine."

Luca bent over and tilted Touraine's chin up to meet her eyes. Touraine was afraid.

You may have to, she opened her mouth to say. She couldn't make the words come out.

"How can you be so calm?" Touraine whispered.

"Calm? I'm terrified." In the churning of her stomach and the rapid thump of her heart, she felt it. "Touraine, if...if they do hang me, bury Sabine beneath the oak. No more burning. Bury me with her, if they let you."

Touraine hid her face in Luca's palm. "Please don't talk like this. I can't—"

Luca made Touraine look at her again. She stroked her cheek.

"What if this is justice?"

The Fingers escorted Luca to the throne room, and Luca took in every corridor, every carpet, sealing it all in her mind for the last time. Her home. The place she had loved and hated, won and lost everything she held dear. Tapestries and vases and gold fittings had been stolen, shredded, or shattered. Faint patches of reddish pink stained the pale marble floors, and the stone pillars that flanked the door to the Grand Hall were pitted and cracked where bullets had hit them. The bodies were gone. Her throne, the chair itself, had not escaped unscathed. Someone had taken a blade to it, hacking great chunks out of the wood, and wadding tufted from the cushion. Its legs had been broken, leaving jagged splinters.

The seat of the first Ancier, no more than firewood.

In front of the throne, in a rough semicircle, sat the people Luca suspected would judge and sentence her:

Fili, of course, but also Ghadin and Jaghotai. An empty seat that Velte took, and a few others Luca didn't know. Civilians. No nobles.

Nor was Luca the only prisoner brought in today. To her right, Pruett and Kiras the ākilah were under similar escort. Though she was likely about to be sentenced to death and was weak enough that she needed to be supported by Pruett, the ākilah's golden eyes took in her surroundings with curiosity. They alighted on Luca and Touraine briefly before flicking over the audience that had come to watch them.

People filled the edges of the hall, but there were no chairs, so there was plenty of pushing to get the better view. And the noise of them! It quieted, for a moment, as Luca was ushered in and the ones in front recognized her, then the chatter rose louder than before.

"We're here to—" Fili started, but her voice was swallowed up by the jeering that had started. The girl looked uncertain, but she was at the center of the semicircle, so she had claimed some sort of primacy.

"Quiet!" the Jackal shouted. "Or we'll kick you out, ass first!"

In the silence that fell, Fili began again. "For your crimes against Balladaire, you will all be tried. Touraine El-Qazāli. For betraying Balladaire and fighting with the enemy."

Touraine glanced around, startled. Then her betrayed look fell on Jaghotai. "Jak, you know that's not what—"

The thick-shouldered escorts clamped their hands around Touraine's arms and held her still.

Fili rose from her chair and came to stand in front of Touraine. She was shorter than Touraine, and soft where Touraine was sharp angles. Despite that, Touraine was the one who looked trapped.

"Your actions have been explained, yes," Fili said. "And you've advocated for us to the former queen more than once. You convinced her to abdicate for the sake of the nation and its people, for a better rule. You led our people against the invaders you brought to our gates and killed their leader." Then, quietly, Fili added, "And you spared me when you didn't have to."

Touraine stilled in her captors' arms.

What did Fili mean?

Fili turned to the rest of the room. Her fists fidgeted nervously at her sides, as if she wanted to be using them.

"Because of her service, we pardon the crimes of the former prince consort." The formality sounded stilted on Fili's tongue, but Luca saw how rapt the civilians were.

They were as much there for Fili's sake as they were for Luca's public humiliation. An audience was a witness. Transparency of the law. Proof of Fili's authority. Accountability. Binding.

Fili moved on to Pruett. "You, however, are the last living commander of the enemy army."

"Aye, I am," Pruett growled. "And you haven't gotten half what you deserve for everything you did to us." She spat at Fili's feet, spattering the marble floor.

An angry gasp rose from the sides of the room, but Fili looked back toward her half circle. Young Ghadin nodded, encouraging.

"You wanted justice. We understand." Fili returned to her seat. "Luca Ancier, step forward."

Luca did not think she had ever been commanded before, outside of the bedroom. She did not like it.

One of the escorts shoved her forward, and Luca lurched as her leg went out. Only her cane kept her from hitting the ground. Titters and snickering. Her face flushed hot, but she ignored them all and stood before the half circle of Balladaire's new order. A whole line of people who despised her, ready to condemn her life.

"Luca Ancier, you're accused of murdering your citizens in the Traitor's Corner. Of false justice."

Despite what she'd said to Touraine in their chambers, a part of Luca was furious now, and it took everything in her not to sneer down at them, at their sky-falling audacity—! To have all that she had done for Balladaire reduced like this and misunderstood was too much. It wasn't fair.

"There are also the crimes of Balladaire against Qazāl," said Ghadin, "including theft and exploitation, kidnapping and killing." The girl was even younger than Fili, and her voice was high and piping in comparison.

A farce. A farce that Luca had agreed to. A farce that she needed. She *needed this*. Balladaire needed this.

"Do you have anything to say for yourself, princess?" Jaghotai cocked her head to the side. Her arms were folded in her lap, her hand holding her stump in a poised dignity Luca had never seen in the woman. *This* was the head of the Qazāli Council. This was where Touraine got that unfortunate streak of integrity.

For once, all Luca's excuses fled her. Everything she'd thought to say in her anger, every justification she'd planned as she walked from her room to this spot, the points she'd made when she woke up in La Flottille, the reparations she'd given, the financial plans she'd put in effect—vanished, all of them. What testimony could she give here that mattered?

She held her chin up and let her court mask fall—she wouldn't need it anymore—as she looked around the room, meeting the eye of everyone she could in that audience of her people—*her people*.

On the edge of the half circle, Velte sat back righteously in her chair, her lip curled.

"No."

"No?"

"No. My actions speak for themselves. For good and ill."

You see, buzzed the crowd, *you see, yes, they do speak for you, give her death, death, you killed them, you killed us, you sacrificed us, you stole, you took, you took, you took.*

The Jackal stomped her foot again, and the hum of accusations sank to a whisper.

Behind Luca, Touraine grunted, trying to yank herself free, but it was Ghadin's voice that rang out as the girl rose to her feet.

"I do not love the former queen, but she saved me once." Despite her pitch, there was a grim maturity to her young features, or perhaps a sullenness. Her eyes were not a child's eyes. She sat down abruptly.

"Luca isn't—" Touraine fought to speak, but when Luca looked back, she saw an escort had clamped a hand over her mouth.

In the semicircle, the Jackal stood now. "She's been a pain in my ass, and I lost good people in the Rain Rebellion." The lines of Jaghotai's face were deep, deepened as she held Luca's eyes. "But she did what no other Balladairan did. She left Qazāl and started to make up for the occupation. I know she offered to pull her soldiers out of Masridān." Her dark look shifted to Pruett, who only sucked her teeth.

When Jaghotai sat, Fili started to stand again. There was a yelp of pain, though, and a moment later, Touraine was standing beside Luca.

"Luca isn't perfect. Neither am I. Neither are any of you—she's lied, yes, and her orders have killed any number—"

"Touraine, this is not helping—" Luca hissed through her teeth.

"—but she loves Balladaire. Everything she has done has been for this country, even when it was wrong. It was for you." Touraine jabbed her finger at Fili. "Even when you didn't see it. It was for all of you! And if you let her, she'll help you get Balladaire on its feet again. You can remake it better than it was before."

Silence except for Touraine's shaky breathing. Luca took her hand and squeezed it.

Fili stood fully. "Despite her crimes, witnesses have spoken for her. And the things they've said—all of them—are true. With the former queen's help, we beat back the army at the West Gate. She also agreed to abdicate to save our city."

The girl stepped forward and stopped in front of Luca. Her eyes were the same green as the moss on the stone bridges arcing over the Nervure. Luca was beginning to suspect that this trial was a performance in more ways than one. Now, though, Fili was secure in her role.

"Still," Fili said, without taking her eyes from Luca, "there is no room for a former royal of Balladaire in this new state, whatever it may become."

Luca felt as if she'd been punched, for all that she'd expected it. She closed her eyes, tears prickling.

"You can't!" Touraine shouted. One of the Fingers grabbed her again, and Touraine punched her in the jaw. The woman fell, out cold. Touraine stepped between Fili and Luca, but the Jackal stood beside Fili.

Touraine stared her mother down, anguish writ over her face.

"You will be sentenced to death," Fili said, "or you will accept exile."

Luca's mouth hung open. Touraine looked back at her, just as stunned.

But Luca could think only of all she'd lose.

The palace, with its rooms and its gardens, yes, her luxuries, but the parks? The tree where Gil was buried? The royal libraries, all her books, the art, the food, the wine, the *land*, its seasons, the—the people. *Her* people. The chance to rebuild. To further shape what the nation would become. Her legacy. She had not expected to be queen, but she had expected—something.

A ragged sound tore free of her.

Everything she had fought for, truly beyond her grasp—to live like that for the rest of her days? Impossible.

To have no home.

To belong nowhere.

It was worse than death.

And yet.

It would be good for Balladaire. To grow without the shadow of the nobility. Of royalty. Yverte would recommend it. (Yverte would not offer her mercy at all.) They would struggle without Luca, but then, it would not be easy even if she were permitted to midwife this new era.

And she would get to rest.

That thought alone uncoiled some of the tension in her shoulders, and she raised her head.

"Exile."

Perhaps a hero would have chosen death rather than abandon everything dear to her, but Luca was no hero.

"Exile."

Touraine almost sagged with relief.

Fili walked back to Pruett. "You wanted justice against the queen. Do you accept her sentence? Will you take your Masridāni away and ask no more reparations from Balladaire for *any* state of the Shālan Empire?"

Many of the Masridāni had died on the field, smashed between the East Gate and Moyenne's army. Those who hadn't had been captured and locked in Le Fontinard and the palace dungeons.

Pruett tongued her teeth again, looking from Fili to the Jackal, then stopping on Luca and Touraine with a sneer.

"Aye, we'll go and good fucking riddance."

"Then we're done here. You have a week's grace to prepare for travel." Fili's look included both Pruett and Luca.

Two pairs of escorts led them back to their respective prisons, Touraine and Luca, and Pruett and Kiras. As they were taken away, the raucous noise of the audience reverberated off the walls of the Grand Hall again.

Beneath the noise, Pruett said, "That's better than you deserve."

Luca whirled around.

"Luca," Touraine warned.

"What? You going to stab me, Your *Majesty*? Oh, excuse me, I'm being impolitic." Pruett got in Luca's face and snarled, "You may have them fooled in there, with your wounded nobility, but I know you. You don't give a shit about anyone or anything unless it gets you what you want. You are Balladaire, and Balladaire isn't changing. If they're smart, they'll change their minds and put you on the fucking pyre."

Touraine heard the telltale click of Luca's cane, the twist before the sword was drawn. She slammed her hand on Luca's, trapping the sword in its sheath, and slid between the two women. Her chest was pressed against Luca's.

"Luca, stop." Touraine could feel the furious beat of Luca's heart, her angry breathlessness. "She is mine, like you are mine. Please."

"I am not," Pruett growled behind her.

Touraine almost laughed. It was funny how similar these two women were. Infuriating, both of them. And yet...

"You are, too. Like it or not," Touraine said over her shoulder. "I'm not going to let her hurt you."

"I don't need your help." Some of the vitriol had leaked from Pruett's words, though, and she stepped away.

"You have your verdict," Luca said. "Take your soldiers and go. If you ever show your face here—"

"Still giving orders?" Pruett clicked her tongue, smiling wickedly. "We'll be right behind you, Your Majesty."

Luca's face twisted in pain and hatred, and Touraine held one finger up against Luca's chest.

"Pruett, please." It was too soon for forgiveness, and maybe it would always be, but she was so exhausted.

"Sky above, Touraine. You are a fucking fool. If either of you show your face in Masridān, I'll do what they should have done to you here."

Luca was still silent; her face had gone blank, as if the words exchanged in the Grand Hall moments before had only now caught up to her. Touraine caught her as her knees gave.

"Pruett, wait!" Touraine growled in frustration.

Pruett was already walking down the corridor, supporting Kiras at her side. She didn't look back as she called, "We've settled all our scores, Touraine."

Touraine considered running after them. If she didn't do it right now, there might never be another chance. She still didn't know if she wanted another chance. But Luca was heavy in her arms.

Kiras did look over her shoulder—she locked eyes with Touraine and nodded once, slowly.

The next day, they were gone.

A HOMECOMING
(REPRISE)

Sweet sky above, what have I done?

Luca and Touraine knelt beside a patch of freshly turned earth in front of the Royal Oak. The warm summer night was cloudless, and the stars stretched endlessly above, but the oak's branches blotted them all out.

Not the Royal Oak anymore, Luca supposed, but the god's oak again. Sabine was in there now. The Fingers had given her that much. And soon, Luca would leave Sabine behind, and Gil, and this tree, and her mother's garden.

"I won't have time to have a ring made before I go." Luca twisted her fingers around one of the few empty knuckles remaining. Not only had Luca utterly failed, but she had let down everyone who had loved her. She'd killed them all for . . . this.

"And . . . Nicolas?"

Luca stilled her hands. Focused on the gold band with its little blue stone.

"No. I will not wear one for him."

After a long silence, Touraine said, "Gold. With a wine-red stone."

Luca nodded, the lump in her throat making it difficult to speak. She imagined the gold band etched with grape vines. She imagined it with thorns.

"I'm going to miss our sword lessons." Touraine smiled ruefully at a memory as she, too, stared into the dirt.

"I'm going to miss beating her at échecs."

"I'm going to miss riding with her. Horses."

"I'm going to miss the jokes she made at the courtiers' expense."

"I'm going to miss her cock."

That startled a laugh out of Luca, the first laugh since—maybe since the war began. She blinked up at the sky to stop new tears from starting, but it was hopeless. She laughed through them. "Sky above, me too."

"You hear that, Durfort? The whole world has fallen apart and we're still talking about how good you fuck."

They giggled and cried some more until they heard a light footfall behind them. Luca turned, half expecting to see Deniaud or Mareau shifting their feet.

It was Fili Guérin, the Rose, the Miracle, the savior of Balladaire. Yes, there were new broadsides. If a few were of Touraine and Luca holding a severed head and wolf-woman on a leash, most of them were of Fili. Fili before a wall of thorntrees, hands outstretched, either in benevolent mercy or in terrifying power—Luca wasn't sure which it was supposed to be. A veritable cult had sprung up around her, with people dancing barefoot in the grass and digging their fingers into the earth. The truly devoted made small cuts in the shapes of vines on their forearms or pricked themselves with thorns, bleeding into dirt as they prayed.

The girl before her, however, was neither benevolent and merciful nor terrifying with power. She was just a girl.

Luca wanted to hate her. She wanted to hate her more than anything. Truthfully, she did hate her more than many things. Luca was only human, after all.

She was only human, and Luca liked to think she could be honest about her human faults, aware of the mistakes she'd made in her past and able to look at them with a critical eye. Luca hadn't been able to do what she needed to do to beat the girl. Fili hadn't outmaneuvered her. Luca *had* been able to beat her. She had *chosen* not to. Was still choosing not to.

If only dear Uncle Nicolas could see her now.

"Oh, I didn't know—you were out here." Fili spoke stiffly, changing her voice mid-sentence, trying to make herself sound older, surer.

Luca laughed. *We all have to learn our court voices sometime.*

It would be so easy to be rid of her right now. To take her own boot knife and slide it up beneath the girl's chin—she had done worse with that little knife before, hadn't she? Right here. Fili had more than earned it, and she was young and new to the dangers of power. She trusted too easily. Or perhaps she could call thorned vines to strangle Luca in her death throes.

To kill Fili would also strangle the hope of magic for Balladaire. Luca had searched for so long. Would she take that away, all because she was not the one to wield it?

"It's no bother," Luca lied. "Touraine, would you please give Fili and me a moment?"

Touraine rose, wary. She had no weapons; she wasn't allowed to carry them in the palace. They couldn't take away the weapon that was her body, though.

"Are you sure?" Touraine looked between the two of them, lingering on Luca, searching.

That was another thing. Luca felt more terrified of Touraine than she ever had been before. She wanted to ask her what *she* wanted, if Touraine still wanted—but if Touraine said no, and Luca lost that, too, she didn't know how she would survive it.

"I'll be fine." Luca gave her boot a subtle tap. A hint of a smile curled Touraine's lips and she left.

Fili sat in the dirt beside Luca.

"I felt like the garden was calling me," she said. "Ever since that battle, everything's been—" Fili jumped as if someone had jabbed her in the ribs, and rolled onto her knees. She pressed her hand against the dirt and then looked at Luca, eyes wide in wonderment. "It's you. You watered this tree with your blood?"

Luca drew her eyebrows together, frowning. "You could say that. Why? Is something...different?"

She had been trying to buy time when she asked Touraine to kill her here, but there was a chance it would change something. Her research had shaped a negative space. She'd hoped she fit in its place.

"I don't know if it's different. I don't know how it was before. It's different from other plants, though. I mean, maybe it's not the tree, just the blood, because it feels like it did when I was outside the wall. It's like it's...alive? And maybe hungry? Or, no—it was hungry, but it's satisfied."

An unpleasant shiver ran down Luca's spine. She imagined the earth opening up like a maw, jagged roots and teeth of stone, swallowing her down. Ghislaine and Nicolas had told her she didn't know what she was meddling with. That there was a reason her ancestors had decided Balladaire was better off without a god.

"And this is your...god?"

"I don't know."

"How long will it stay sated?"

Fili shook her head. Misgiving lined her young face. "The earth needs watering. Food, too. Like the way animals die and rot? All of it goes back into the dirt and feeds the plants and so on. I can feel it in the wood I work with." She drew a circle with her hand.

"We didn't use to burn our dead. That started with the plagues. We used to bury them." Luca pointed to Sabine's grave at the oak's foot. "If we start that again, perhaps we can..." *Sate the god's hunger* felt too ominous. Too uncivilized. She was beyond such thoughts, though. She needed to know more.

Or, whoever wanted to govern Balladaire did. Luca wasn't responsible for it anymore. She stood.

"Good night, Fili." *Good luck.*

The ship creaked and swayed on the river. They docked on the Queen's Bank, not La Gouttière, on a formerly royal ship bound for Qazāl. The dock men were loading barrels of grain and jewels and other tribute and recompense back to El-Wast for the Qazāli Council to spread as it saw fit.

Whatever that council would look like now, with Aranen gone and the other half turned traitor to follow Pruett.

Touraine hoisted her pack higher on her shoulder and looked for Jaghotai, but her mother was out of sight. Probably hawk-eyeing the goods to make sure no Balladairan decided to shortchange her of decades' worth of grievances. Ghadin, however, leaned against the ship railing, staring down the river. At first glance, Touraine thought it was her usual sullen posture: the furrowed brow, the tight mouth, the cocked hip.

Ghadin turned at the sound of Touraine's boots on the deck. It was a blow to the chest how much lurked behind the surly mask. She reminded Touraine of Pruett, and that frightened her. Touraine smoothed the hitch in her step and settled in beside the girl.

"Ready to go home?" Touraine said in Shālan.

"I guess."

"Don't tell me you're going to miss it here."

"I don't know what was scarier—the rebellion in Qazāl or the palace." Ghadin jerked her head toward her arm. "Know which one hurt worse, though."

She didn't mention the other things she had seen, though Touraine knew she woke screaming every night unless she drank a sleeping draught from one of the physicians.

"I'm sorry. I wish...I wish I'd taken better care of you. And I'm sorry I wasn't what you thought I was."

Ghadin gazed back toward the river, intensely focused on the smaller craft in the water.

"I brought you something. To take back to Qazāl." Touraine dropped the pack off her shoulder and dug through it until she found the small book inside. She handed it to Ghadin, who propped it on the rail and flipped through it with her hand. The title on the first page read *The Mulāzim and the Emir.*

"What's this?"

"A new chevalier tale. It's not a Balladairan story, but it's not a Qazāli one, either." Touraine rubbed the back of her head, her face warming. "I wrote it. It's not that good, but if you show it to Saïd, I think he can fix it. But it's for you. Maybe you'll like that ending better."

"Oh."

It wasn't the reaction Touraine had hoped for. She sighed and let her own gaze track out toward the water, too. A couple unloaded the morning's catch from their boat on La Gouttière. A dockworker hawked a gob of snot into the water, and it vanished before Touraine could see where it landed, swallowed up by the murky rush of dark green.

"When you go back, you get to help rebuild Qazāl," Touraine started. "That's why the council agreed to let you come. So there'd be someone to lead as we got old. I know it's a lot and there's a lot of time until then, but..." She trailed off. Saying it out loud felt like placing a crushing weight on the girl's shoulders. Touraine turned back to the river.

"I just want everything to be back like it was before," Ghadin murmured without looking at Touraine.

She was too young to be a part of this.

No younger than you when Balladaire trained you for war.

Touraine had fought so that would never happen again.

"You can't look backward. You assume it was always better then and you'll never be able to live today. You wallow in it. Aranen din once told me..." Touraine swallowed around the rising lump in her throat, the welling in her eyes. "She told me that the things that touch us, that change us, we can change them, too. Not back, never back. We can't change back, either. But we keep touching things and changing things and becoming different things ourselves. The world is something we can touch. You get to choose how it changes you. You get to touch it however you want."

Ghadin gave Touraine a quizzical look. Touraine sighed and tried to tease her meaning out better.

"It's not just who we were then. I mean, you and me, we don't really know what Qazāl was like before Balladaire came, so what we do now can't be about that. It's who we are now and how we face the rest of the world, as sovereign people. People who fought for something. That's part of our story now, too. Part of your story." Touraine tapped the book in Ghadin's hand. "You can't undo that, either, no matter what you do when you go back home. Whether you ever come back here or not. You fought. You survived."

They both turned at Jaghotai's familiar heavy tread.

"Where'd you come up with that?" The Jackal eyed Touraine curiously. "One of your wife's books?"

Touraine's cheeks grew uncomfortably warm. "Not exactly. Why? Did it work on you, too?"

Jaghotai shrugged, but her face was thoughtful as she joined them at the rail. Her eyes lingered on the scarf draped loose around Touraine's neck. Her gift.

"I'm going to put this away," Ghadin murmured.

Touraine watched her retreat helplessly. When the girl vanished belowdecks, Touraine sighed, sagging into her shoulders.

Jaghotai raised an eyebrow. "What's up with the kid?"

"I wanted to try to make things at least a little right before you left." Touraine opened her hands plaintively over the water.

Jaghotai grunted.

"You sure about going back?" Touraine asked. "Didn't the rest of the council try to have you killed?"

Jaghotai tapped her fingers with a studied nonchalance. "I don't know how the rest of the council will feel, but you should know..." She shifted against the railing and worked her mouth.

Now Touraine knew how she had appeared to Ghadin, and braced herself.

"You did good work here." The Jackal extended her hand, and Touraine clasped it. They stood like that, awkward in this intimacy. Then, without warning, Jaghotai pulled Touraine close and wrapped both her arms around her.

Touraine froze and all the breath left her body, and not because of Jaghotai's fearsome grip. Jaghotai didn't let her go, though, and there was a dampness on Touraine's cheeks that didn't belong to her. It was enough for her own eyes to spill over.

"Jak." Touraine reached her own arms around the Jackal's broad back.

"I mean it. Come within the year. They don't deserve all of you."

"Aye."

Jaghotai gave her a rough pat on the back and released her. Touraine blinked her eyes clear in time to see Luca stepping up the gangplank. Touraine hailed her with a raised hand.

"I came to say my farewells." Luca squinted around the ship, making the same tallies as Jaghotai. Her cheeks were flushed with the heat, her golden hair loose and windblown.

"I don't think you'll get anything out of Ghadin. She's..." Touraine shook her head.

"I didn't think she'd welcome me, anylight." Luca bowed to

Jaghotai. "Your Excellency, I meant what I said when we spoke before. I'm in your debt. This"—Luca gestured wide with one arm at their surroundings—"this is only a small part of what you're owed as far as I'm concerned. Not that I'll have any more say in it. But I owe you. More than I can say."

"Careful, princess. I'll hold you to that."

"Please do. And call me Luca."

Jaghotai snorted and muttered something in Shālan too quick and too low for Touraine to catch. Still, she gave Luca a less-than-grudging nod before she left to find her own cabin.

"So. Exile." Touraine leaned her back against the railing, propping herself up on her elbows as they watched the sailors finish the last touches before setting sail.

Luca stood close beside her, their sides touching. She gave Touraine such a flat side-on look that Touraine laughed out loud. Luca's lip twitched into an almost-smile, and Touraine felt herself go soft.

Instead of asking what she really wanted to, Touraine blurted, "When do you leave?"

"Soon." Soberly, Luca said, "I think I might be making the worst mistake of my life, and I've made quite a few. However, someone whose advice I apparently took to heart made a very convincing argument. I am not a throne, they said."

"And you trust them?"

Touraine wasn't sure she trusted her heated words now. On the outside of the war with the Taargens, stealing the crown from Duke Ancier, throwing the Balladairans out of Qazāl—she just wanted something to be settled. She wanted to know how things worked instead of worrying which end of the knife would hit. Luca as queen was clear, maybe even easy. In time, she might have been a good one.

"They brought me back to life. Would be a shame not to."

Touraine smirked. "Once or twice."

"Oh, far more than that. Far more." Luca met and held Touraine's gaze. Before Touraine could fall into her, Luca cleared her throat and looked away. "As I said, it was a convincing argument. Besides, there are some philosophers who don't believe in monarchies. They call them *uncivilized*." She crooked a smile that showed a few teeth. "You can imagine, I didn't enjoy them very much at the time, but perhaps there's more to the theory."

Luca drifted off, biting her bottom lip and staring out at the Nervure, watching it flow beneath the bridge and onward.

"And...where will you go?" Touraine wondered if Luca's *where* would have a place for her. If hers had a place for Luca.

"Perhaps I'll found a public library. Guérin once told me that literacy among the civilians hadn't been...well attended to. I could try that." Belatedly, she added, "Somewhere." She didn't sound convinced. She sounded lost.

"Ah." The idea itself sounded nice. She could almost see Luca doing that. Reading the books, writing her own histories or treatises like her favorite philosophers. It wasn't the power Luca had once commanded, though. It sounded boring, if Touraine was honest. Was that what happiness was? A pleasant dullness?

"And without the queen, what happens to the prince consort?"

Luca fumbled. "I dare say—well—that is—the Jackal invited me to Qazāl—for a little while—"

Touraine shook her head, looking down at her folded hands. Her newest grief ring flared, a simple band on her middle finger, the same color as Aranen's eyes. Neither of them had one for Sabine, yet.

"Oh. I suppose Balladaire will still need an ambassador. Of course." For once, Luca was awful at hiding her emotions. Her voice fell, her shoulders drooped subtly. She looked with new intensity at the pack at Touraine's feet.

Touraine smiled. "I have so much learning to do still. It'll be hard, but I want to do it where I can be myself."

Luca was blinking a lot, but then a brisk wind had picked up. "I understand. Truly, I do. If you'll meet me on occasion? I think I shall miss you terribly, and I know I may not be completely welcome in El-Wast, or perhaps anywhere across the Triaume, but I would like to. See you. And would you keep a good distance between Jaghotai and Balladaire? I don't think any government they devise here could handle it if *she*—"

"Luca."

Luca pressed her lips tight and shut her eyes. "I'm sorry, I only—"

Touraine took her hand, their clasped fingers dangling. Luca opened her eyes again. They were wide and uncertain.

"Luca, I want to leave—"

"Oh. Of course. I'm sorry, I shouldn't have assumed—"

"With you. I want to leave with you."

Luca's lips parted. "With…me?"

"Mm. If you'll have me. They asked me to be general, but…" Touraine bit her lip. "If I could stop fighting for a while, it would be nice. Probably not forever. Hard to find a peace that lasts forever. But I could do healing work."

"Where?"

"Wherever you wanted to be. "

"I'm sure we could find somewhere." Luca tightened her grip on Touraine's hand. Her smile opened up, the real smile, not the court smile.

It made Touraine's mouth go dry, that smile. Made it hard for her to think the words she needed to say next, let alone say them.

"About one other thing. The…consort thing. I know that was technically a political arrangement and…"

Luca waited warily.

Touraine dug back into her pack. "You gave me a wedding gift, and I never got to give you one. What I wanted—"

"It's all right, Touraine. You don't have to. We don't have to be married. You married a queen, for the stars' sake." She gestured dismissively and her eyes shadowed. "I'm no one now. Things have changed."

Touraine stilled, hand in the open mouth of the bag. "You're not no one, Luca. You never could be."

"That's unfortunate. I need to try very hard to be, or I'll end up back in Traitor's Corner, or worse, rotting in Le Fontinard."

"Luca. The last time we did this, you brought me up to your level. You made me a royal. Now we're just…people. Not everything has changed. You're not your crown. You never have been. Not just that. Not to me." She pulled the bow of a violoncelle out of the case and held it out to Luca. "Maybe…we could try again? Without every country watching our every move?"

Luca took the bow gingerly, open-mouthed. She examined it from the tip, across the heavy ironwood to what the luthier had called the frog, which was inlaid with pearl, and the ivory button at the end. She ran the nail of her thumb delicately across the pale, silken horse hairs.

"Touraine," she whispered.

"There is, um, a violoncelle as well. I know your mother's—"

Luca's mouth stole the rest of the words from her lips. Her hand on the back of Touraine's head pulled her close, fierce and perfect. She was wearing her rose eau de parfum again, and Touraine felt a crushing need to be close. To see what new ways they could fit.

"Luca? Let's go home."

"I don't have a home anymore." Disbelief, the words half sob, half baffled laughter.

"So we'll make a new one." Touraine smudged away the kohl-stained tears below Luca's eyes and kissed her. "Again and again if we have to."

As they crossed the bridge, Touraine gave the sky one last glance, watching the gulls and the pigeons and even the sparrows flitting above the ships, from crow's nest to crow's nest. If there was a falcon among them, she did not see it.

ACKNOWLEDGMENTS

The end of a trilogy is no small feat, and so I'd like to acknowledge everyone who made this conclusion possible. My thanks to the publishing professionals: my agent, Mary C. Moore; my editors Brit Hvide and Tiana Coven, whose feedback told me where I was pulling my punches; Jenni Hill and Nick Burnham for the assistance; my marketing and publicity teams, Angela Man, Nazia Khatun, Ellen Wright, and Maddy Hall; my copyeditor, Vivian Kirklin; and the artists, including Lauren Panepinto on design, Tommy Arnold on the cover, and Tim Paul on the map.

Thank you to all my writer friends online and off, who kept me on course during the writing of this book (and several others). Especial thanks to Chris Ruz and K. A. Doore, who read an earlier draft, and also to Grace Curtis, Ben Schroder, Tasha Suri, Alix E. Harrow, Lee Mandelo, Shelley Parker-Chan, Kate Dylan, Hannah Kaner, Saara El-Arifi, and Jess Barber. You saved me from myself.

And of course, thank you to all the readers—whether you've been here since 2021 when this all started, or if you've just arrived; whether you're a fan turned friend, or a friend turned fan; whether you've ever shared this series with someone else or drawn art or written fics, or just held it close and quiet to your own beloved chest: thank you, thank you, thank you. This could not have happened without you.

Finally, S, thanks for always betting on me.

MEET THE AUTHOR

Meg White

C. L. CLARK is the author of the Magic of the Lost trilogy (including *The Unbroken* and *The Faithless*), *Ambessa: Chosen of the Wolf* (an Arcane novel), and *Fate's Bane*. When she's not writing or working, she's swinging swords or chasing trails. Her short stories and essays have appeared in *The Best American Science Fiction and Fantasy*, *Reactor* (formerly Tor.com), *Beneath Ceaseless Skies*, and more. Stay in touch at clclarkwrites.com/newsletter.

Find out more about C. L. Clark and other Orbit authors by registering for the free monthly newsletter at orbitbooks.net.

orbit

Follow us:

/orbitbooksUS

/orbitbooks

/orbitbooks

Join our mailing list
to receive alerts on our
latest releases and deals.

orbitbooks.net

Enter our monthly
giveaway for the chance
to win some epic prizes.

orbitloot.com